Rob

The Life of Major General James Wolfe

SALZWASSER
VERLAG

Robert Wright

The Life of Major General James Wolfe

Reprint of the original, first published in 1864.

1st Edition 2022 | ISBN: 978-3-75259-154-5

Verlag (Publisher): Salzwasser Verlag GmbH, Zeilweg 44, 60439 Frankfurt, Deutschland
Vertretungsberechtigt (Authorized to represent): E. Roepke, Zeilweg 44, 60439 Frankfurt, Deutschland
Druck (Print): Books on Demand GmbH, In de Tarpen 42, 22848 Norderstedt, Deutschland

THE LIFE

OF

MAJOR-GENERAL JAMES WOLFE.

THE LIFE

OF

MAJOR-GENERAL JAMES WOLFE

Founded on Original Documents

AND

ILLUSTRATED BY HIS CORRESPONDENCE,

BY

ROBERT WRIGHT.

"A man but young,
Yet old in judgment; theoric and practic
In all humanity, and, to increase the wonder,
Religious, yet a soldier."—*Massinger*.

LONDON

1864.

Jam: Wolfe.

From an original picture in the possession of Admiral Warde. K.H

PREFACE.

THE military reputation of England has never been so debased as it was at the beginning of the Seven Years' War. With the bravest soldiers in the world, excellent regimental officers, and a large staff of veterans who drew the pay of Generals, Great Britain had not one commander capable of leading her armies to victory. Since the time of Marlborough she had produced no military genius but Clive. No other man exhibited that comprehensiveness which is the most indispensable qualification of a successful General. The Duke of Cumberland was indeed brave, but, at best, rarely fortunate; Lord Stair was no master of strategy, and Marshal Wade's talent lay in engineering. The incapacity of Braddock, Loudoun, and Abercrombie, brought disaster after disaster upon our arms in America; while nearer home the failures which arose from the same cause were more alarming and disgraceful, if not so bloody.

"I know," said Pitt, "that if any man can save England, I can," but the Great Minister's very first warlike undertaking was foiled through the inefficiency of the commanders to whom he had entrusted it. He, however, noted the exceptional conduct of a young officer, whom he raised to the rank of Brigadier-General. Nor was he mistaken, for to the zeal and ability of Wolfe the capture of Cape Breton was mainly attributable. Hitherto known only as a superior disciplinarian, Wolfe was now marked out as a leader of men, and all eyes turned hopefully towards the "Hero of Louisbourg" as to the promised restorer of England's military renown. Mr. Pitt was thus encouraged to give the command of the grandest and most perilous of his schemes to a man whose age was but two-and-thirty years,—a case without parallel in the annals of our army. When the extreme rarity of the highest degree of military talent, the youth of the hero, and the importance of the achievement in which he fell are considered, it is not surprising that by his contemporaries Wolfe's death should have been regarded as little short of an apotheosis. Like a meteor he had suddenly burst from obscurity, and while his compatriots were rapt with wonder that England had brought forth a General, he vanished "in the blaze of his fame."

But there were further grounds for the applause given to Wolfe. The peace had brought avarice, idleness, and debauchery into the army. That care for the wants, and that guardianship of the rights of the common soldier and sailor, which is now the rule in the United Services, was then the rare exception. Officers received bribes from commissaries for the privilege of pillaging their men and defrauding the Government. In short, self-aggrandisement was so prevalent amongst the servants of the public, that the Statesman or the Commander who was above corruption, was necessarily an object of wonder and admiration. Pitt and Wolfe, therefore, were considered as characters above ordinary humanity, not so much on account of the power and eloquence of the Minister or the prowess of the General, as because they made the honour and welfare of their country their sole aim. "They dared," as Sir Walter Scott says, "to contemn wealth; the statesman and soldier of the present day would, on the contrary, not dare to propose it to himself."* Besides, instead of an honourable rivalry, there had béen a long existing jealousy between the army and navy,—a jealousy which frustrated the design of many a conjoint expedition. Military officers detested the sea-service, and were unwilling to acknowledge the ability of naval commanders. But Wolfe was eager to serve by land or by sea, and while he deplored the incapacity and indifference of his own chiefs, he openly admitted the merits of sea officers. To him is due no small share of the harmony—as novel as it was beneficial—which subsisted between the naval and military branches of the expeditions to Louisbourg and Quebec, for—

> "Wolfe, where'er he fought,
> Put so much of his heart into his act,
> That his example had a magnet's force,
> And all were swift to follow whom all loved."

With this attractive power over the hearts, Wolfe's intensity of will gave him a like influence over the minds of others. These innate qualities were displayed a few months after his entrance into the army, in that talent for command which enabled a boy of sixteen years to act as adjutant in a great battle,—an instance of military

* Miscellanies: Life of Charles Johnstone.

precocity probably unique. Wolfe has been deservedly styled "the officers' friend and the soldiers' father." His integrity and intelligence caused him to be respected by his superiors; his disinterestedness and the warmth of his attachments endeared him to his equals; and his generosity and condescension won the hearts and minds of his inferiors. Withal, he was not faultless.

It would not always be advisable, if it were possible, to withdraw the veil which obscures the everyday lives of many men whose names have become celebrated; but there is no reason why the halo of Wolfe's fame should blind his fellow-mortals to the lessons that may be learned from his "battle of life" ere he acquired greatness; nor is there any risk that the knowledge of his private history will lessen his public renown, for—

> "There is in him, so much man, so much goodness,
> So much of honour, and of all things else
> Which make our being excellent, that from his store
> He can enough lend others."

The story of his life ought, therefore, to be as well calculated to point a moral as that of his death is to adorn a tale. Few, very few men have accomplished so much within so short a term of life, or have given such promise of further service to his country. Had he been spared, how different might have been the history of the late United States!

The only so-called "Life" of Wolfe was published in the year 1760, under the following title:—"The Life of General James Wolfe, the Conqueror of Canada; or the Eulogium of that renowned Hero, attempted according to the Rules of Eloquence, with a Monumental Inscription, Latin and English, to perpetuate his Memory. By J—— P——, A.M." This curious production occupies twenty-four quarto pages, and was published at the moderate price of one shilling. In his "Epistle Dedicatory to the Men of Kent," the modest author declares,—"I willingly undertook the task, unbiassed and unasked, presuming, though my abilities were far unequal to it (for an Achilles should be described by a Homer, and an Alexander painted by an Apelles), that it would meet with a favourable reception, from the novelty of the composition, rarely attempted among us, and the excellence of the object it celebrates."

One contemporary reviewer, more sparing of his paper than of J. P.'s feelings, briefly condemns the work as "a very florid, not to call it fustian eulogium;"* while another, less caustic critic, damns it with faint praise, in these terms:—"The good design of this piece, not its eloquence, must, we think, reprieve it from too harsh a censure. There is no circumstance mentioned of the hero but what is well known, and the whole may be styled a preachment rather than an ornament. The author, who writes himself A.M., is not very correct in his phrase, and though he may understand the rules of eloquence, does not seem to be the most able hand at the exercise of them."†

Numerous notices and characters of Wolfe appeared immediately after his death; but they are all restricted to his historical achievements and disclose no incidents of his everyday life as a man. The most remarkable of

* 'The British Magazine,' February, 1760.

† 'London Magazine,' December, 1759.

these panegyrics—for they are all eulogistic—are Burke's in the 'Annual Register,' Smollett's in his 'History of England,' and Walpole's in the 'Memoirs of the Reign of George II.' and in his 'Letters.' The only approach to a Memoir of Wolfe that has hitherto appeared, is the sketch by the Rev. G. R. Gleig, in his 'Lives of British Military Commanders.' Mr. Gleig's original materials were very scanty, consisting of extracts from about a dozen of Wolfe's letters to his parents. It is but just to bear in mind, that the reverend author professes to treat more especially of the hero's career as a soldier; but as Mr. Gleig has been accepted as an authority, and as numerous errors into which he has fallen have been followed by subsequent writers, it becomes necessary, at the risk of appearing invidious, to point out a few of his mistakes.

In spite of indisputable evidence to the contrary, he asserts that James Wolfe was born on the 6th of November, 1726. Mr. Gleig was doubtless deceived by imagining that he had the testimony of Wolfe's own words in a letter supposed to have been written on the 6th of November, 1751. The letter begins thus:—"The winter wears away, so do our years; . . . this day am I five-and-twenty years of age." Unfortunately Mr. Gleig having been furnished with extracts only, it was not in his power to ascertain the true date of the letter in which these words occur; nor does it seem to have struck him that winter could not be said to wear away when it had but just begun. Wolfe's letters frequently fill two or three sheets of paper, and almost invariably they are dated at the end. In course of time the detached sheets got intermixed, and when they came to be re-arranged—

or, more correctly, mis-arranged—the first sheet of a letter written on the 22nd–25th of December, 1751 (2nd–5th January, 1752, N.S.), was connected with the last sheet of another bearing date the 6th of November. The latter date consequently was prefixed, by the transcriber, to the extract which led Mr. Gleig astray. Next, we are told that young Wolfe embarked with his father, in 1740, for *Flanders*. As Flanders cannot be a misprint for *Carthagena*, it must have been a slip of the pen; for surely the biographer was well aware that the British troops were not sent to the Continent until 1742. Again, it is stated that Wolfe fought at Fontenoy, and in 1746 served with Ligonier at Liers.

The author of 'The Conquest of Canada,' enlarging on a mistake of Mr. Gleig's, says that in April, 1742, Wolfe "appears to have been on leave, travelling probably for health; in this month he writes to his mother, dating *Rome*, a grateful and affectionate letter."* Now, in the first place, instead of being on leave of absence in April, 1742, it was in that very month that Ensign Wolfe embarked with his regiment for Flanders: consequently he could not have written from Rome. Secondly, the only letter in the domestic series dated as above was, as internal evidence proves, really not written until 1743, although it is headed, "*Bonn*, April 7, N.S., 1742." According to the Old Style, the year 1743 had but just commenced, and we know that most people are prone to use the more familiar number until they become accustomed to the new one. The said letter, as the reader will find, was written upon the march previous to the

* 'The Conquest of Canada,' vol. ii. p. 494.

battle of Dettingen;* nor was it James Wolfe's, but his brother's. It is enough to add, that Wolfe never was in Rome.

Amongst the numerous articles of which our hero is the subject, in Encyclopædias, Biographical Dictionaries, and Magazines, there is scarcely one, be it ever so brief, that does not abound with errors. Probably there never has been a man concerning whom so few facts have been published, whose name has been exposed to a greater number of false statements, misconceptions, and wrong inferences, on the part of his biographers.

It is a much more agreeable duty to relate the vicissitudes of Wolfe's letters to his parents. Mrs. Wolfe carefully preserved and treasured every letter that she and her husband received from their celebrated son. After her death they came into the possession of her principal executor, the Right Honourable General George Warde, from whom they descended to his nephew, another General George Warde. In the year 1822, the Reverend Thomas Streatfeild, of Chart's Edge, near Westerham, who was then collecting materials for a History of Kent, obtained from General Warde thirteen of these letters, from which he extracted such passages as he considered adapted to his purpose, and then returned the originals.† Mr. Streatfeild not having carried out his design, these extracts were, at Earl Stanhope's (then Lord Mahon) request, communicated to the Rev. Mr. Gleig when writing his 'Lives of British Military Commanders.'‡

* See page 33 of this volume.

† Original Correspondence between General Warde and Mr. Streatfeild.

‡ See History of England, etc., by Lord Mahon, vol. iv. p. 225.

In the meantime—about 1827—Charles Hampden Turner, Esq., of Rook's Nest, near Godstone, borrowed such of the Wolfe papers as were then in the possession of the Warde family, with the intention of lending them to Mr. Southey, who contemplated contributing a 'Life of Wolfe' to Murray's 'Family Library.' Southey, being unable to procure sufficient materials, abandoned his purpose.* It is believed that he returned the letters to Mr. Turner; but, after several inquiries and diligent search, they could not be found, and their owner lost all trace of them for years. At length, in 1858, when the manuscript collection and other literary effects of the late Dawson Turner, Esq., of Yarmouth, were advertised for sale by Messrs. Puttick and Simpson, the military commissions of Lieut.-General Edward Wolfe, and those of his son Major-General James Wolfe, together with the letters of the latter, formed lots 531 and 532 in the auctioneers' catalogue. Admiral Warde, to whom, after the death of his father, the property belonged, immediately wrote to Mr. Turner's executor, and in consequence of his claim all the Wolfe papers were withdrawn from sale.

After a friendly investigation into the circumstances of the case, the commissions and letters were eventually restored to their proprietor. Mr. Dawson Turner had likewise collected several additional letters and other manuscripts illustrative of Wolfe's life. These he had

* See 'Life and Letters of Robert Southey,' vol. v. p. 307. Southey's proposed work has been more than once spoken of as if it were published; and an anticipatory review of it, by Christopher North, appeared in 'Blackwood's Magazine,' November, 1826.

bound up into a folio, entitled 'Wolfiana.' This volume and another consisting of transcripts were generously presented to Admiral Warde by Mr. Turner's representatives, who considered that the whole collection ought not to be separated. Through the friendly intervention of Mr. Hawkins, Admiral Warde gave me access to all of these manuscripts during my first visit to Westerham, and afterwards allowed me to carry them to London, and keep them long enough to copy, or otherwise use, at my own discretion, those papers which form the foundation of this biography. Considering the previous mischances of the highly prized family treasure, this mark of the Admiral's confidence calls for my special acknowledgment.

The domestic series of Wolfe's letters—about 240 in number—having been bound together in a thick quarto volume, without regard to their correct arrangement, the task of determining their true consecutive order was much more tedious and laborious than can readily be conceived. The difficulty arising from the circumstance of several letters occupying two or three detached sheets, dated only upon the last, has been already alluded to; it may be added, however, that Wolfe generally wound up a paragraph at the end of each sheet, and started on a fresh topic with the next, so as not to leave what actors call a "cue." It was therefore necessary to make abstracts of the contents—no matter how trifling—of each sheet, and compare them one with another. For instance, in the sheet which was supposed to be the first of the letter written on the 6th of November, 1751 Wolfe says:—"I have writ to my father by the *last post*, to rectify my friend Charles's mistake." Now, as the correction of the mistake is contained in a letter of the 13th of December, it became evident that the sheet in which the foregoing passage occurs must belong to a letter posterior to the latter date; and upon further investigation it was conclusively found to have been written on the 22nd of December, 1751. This will suffice for an example of numerous similar cases.

But more serious obstacles, arising out of the alteration of the Style, still remained to be encountered. Although every one is aware that previous to 1752 the new year did not legally begin until the 25th of March, it does not follow that when one meets with an old paper dated, suppose, the 1st of May, 1750, it would be recollected that the said paper was written ten months *before* another document bearing date the 1st of March, 1750. It is remarkable that the fact thus exemplified escaped even the penetration of Southey. This assertion is corroborated by a letter to Robert Chambers, Esq., wherein Southey says that Wolfe's "earliest letter from Scotland is dated January, 1749;"* whereas, in fact, he had had at least a dozen of Wolfe's letters in his possession, written from Glasgow several months before the one he speaks of. It might be supposed that once aware of the change in the style, the rest would be plain sailing; but then the question had to be considered which style—old or new—was followed, for although the latter did not become the law of the land until September, 1752, it had been to some extent practically anticipated; and, on the other hand, so habituated were

* See 'The Book of Days,' vol. i. p. 38. (January 2.)

many persons to the old custom, that they could not forget it for years.* Thus Wolfe dates a letter "January 21, 1757," which could not possibly have been written before January, 1758.

Wolfe's letters to his father and mother, however valuable as elucidatory of his private character and of his conduct as a subordinate officer, do not, as Southey found, supply materials for a complete memoir. They become less frequent as the interest of his career increases, and throw no light upon the last and most eventful epoch of his life. But happily I have been favoured with other letters and papers which countervail their deficiency. The discovery also, in the year 1849, of a packet of Wolfe's letters to his early companion in arms and intimate friend, Colonel Rickson, has materially added to the biography of the hero. The late Thomas Ferguson, Esq., of Glasgow, who was related to Rickson, possessed for about forty years an old military chest formerly the property of the Colonel. As it was supposed to contain only useless papers, it remained uncared for; but the key having been broken in the rusty lock, the contents fortunately were preserved from dispersion and loss. After the death of this gentleman, the old chest came into the possession of the late William Robertson, Esq., of Rosebank, Partick, whose widow is the niece of Mrs. Rickson. On breaking it open, it was found to be filled with army reports and other like documents, and in a corner, carefully tied up by themselves was discovered a packet of letters bearing the signature

* To increase the confusion, sometimes the day of the month is in one Style, and the year in another, without any notification.

"James Wolfe." Mr. Robertson lent the letters thus disclosed to his friend John Buchanan, Esq., of Glasgow, who first published them, with a biographical sketch, in 'Tait's Magazine' for 1849, and reprinted them in a work of much local interest, but not intended for general circulation, entitled 'Glasgow, Past and Present.' (1856.) The originals were, in 1862, presented by Mrs. Robertson, through Mr. Buchanan, to the Antiquarian Society of Scotland, in whose museum at Edinburgh they are deposited. These letters exhibit the tone and bent of Wolfe's mind even more fully than do those to his parents. Written as they were without premeditation or reserve, to a brother-officer in whom he confided, and of whose character and abilities he entertained the highest opinion, they afford access to their writer's inmost thoughts on matters of public as well as of private interest, and at the same time show the sincerity and warmth of his friendship.

The hitherto unpublished correspondence between General Amherst and Wolfe during the siege of Louisbourg, the originals of which were kindly entrusted to me by the Right Hon. Earl Amherst, together with letters written by General Murray, Lieutenant-Colonel Alexander Murray, and other officers, still further add to the knowledge of events in which Wolfe was concerned towards the end of his life. The collection of 'Wolfiana' made by Mr. Dawson Turner, likewise abundantly illustrates the same and a subsequent period. The publication of the Chatham and Bedford Correspondences disclosed some important particulars; and the inquiries of Mr. Buchanan and other correspondents of

'Notes and Queries,' drew forth additional items of information.

It is perhaps but right to mention the circumstances that led me to undertake the "labour of love" of which this book is the issue. During a residence in Canada, some years ago, I became acquainted with a citizen of Quebec who, with much general as well as local knowledge, felt interested in everything appertaining to the Conqueror of Canada; and after several excursions in the neighbourhood I became familiar with the scene "where breathed the gale that caught Wolfe's happiest sigh." Subsequently, in America and at home, I noted whatever fell in my way connected with the subject, and my notes having accumulated, I was induced to seek for further information in old magazines, newspapers, gazettes, military records, etc. At length I found that I had collected materials for a fuller and more accurate account of Wolfe's career than any that had appeared, and the idea of compiling a memoir suggested itself. But thinking it probable that much original matter still remained to be discovered, I began to trace it, and followed the pursuit until, as I fancy, the field was quite gleaned.

I have been careful not to write beyond my knowledge, and the few inferences I have drawn, are given as such, to be accepted or rejected at the reader's option. As to the manner in which I have arranged the abundant materials at my command it is not for me to speak further than to observe, that I have thought it advisable as far as possible to allow the hero to tell his own story. It may not, however, be amiss to warn those who peruse the following pages that a biography so narrated should be read in a very different spirit from that which ought to guide the reader of an autobiography or a diary, for as these are written with deliberation and reserve, we seldom find the whole truth stated; whereas private letters demand allowance for the impulsive expression of thoughts and opinions which the writer's matured reflection would not always support. Let it then be remembered that, the official dispatches excepted, not a single letter in this volume was penned with the remotest idea of publicity. It may not be needless to explain that in the Index, where, under Wolfe's name, I have grouped together various references, as, for instance, "On Contentment," and such-like subjects, it is not with the idea of setting him up as a philosopher, but merely to show the scope and tendency of his mind. I would likewise hint that Wolfe ought not to be judged by isolated expressions, but by the general tenor and spirit of his correspondence.

It remains only for me gratefully to acknowledge the kindness and consideration with which those noblemen and gentlemen from whom I sought information have responded to my applications. It is impossible to particularize all the channels through which I have received contributions; I must therefore content myself by expressing my great obligations, and returning my sincere thanks to:—the Right Hon. Earl Amherst; the Right Hon. Lord Elibank; the Right Hon. T. Sotheron-Estcourt, M.P.; the Hon. Richard Carleton; the Venerable Archdeacon Wilkins; Sir Frederic Madden; Admiral Warde, K.H.; Mrs. Murray, Roseanna, Athlone;

Lady O'Donnell; James Wolfe Murray, Esq.; Edward Hawkins, jun., Esq.; W. C. Streatfeild, Esq., Chart's Edge; Thomas Board, Esq., Westerham; John Buchanan, Esq., Glasgow; Robert Carruthers, Esq., Inverness; Thomas Keightley, Esq., Lesness Heath; Robert Cole, Esq., F.S.A.; G. Moffatt, Esq., M.P.; J. H. Anderdon, Esq,; and John Young, Esq., Blackheath.

R. W.

March 28, 1864.

CONTENTS.

CHAPTER I.

WESTERHAM.—GREENWICH.

1727–1742.

CHAPTER II.

GHENT.—ASCHAFFENBURG.

1742–1743.

CHAPTER III.

CAMPAIGNS.

1743–1745.

CHAPTER IV.

NEWCASTLE.—FALKIRK.—CULLODEN.—LONDON.

1745–1746.

CHAPTER V.

CONTINENTAL CAMPAIGNS.—LONDON.

1747–1748.

CHAPTER VI.

STIRLING.—GLASGOW.

February—October, 1749.

CHAPTER VII.

PERTH.

NOVEMBER, 1749—SEPTEMBER, 1750.

CHAPTER VIII.

DUNDEE.—LONDON.—BANFF.

OCTOBER, 1750—SEPTEMBER, 1751.

CHAPTER IX.

INVERNESS.

OCTOBER, 1751—MAY, 1752.

CHAPTER X.

FORT AUGUSTUS.—DUBLIN.—BLACKHEATH.

MAY—SEPTEMBER, 1752.

CHAPTER XI.

PARIS.

OCTOBER, 1752—MARCH, 1753.

CHAPTER XII.

GLASGOW.—READING.

APRIL—NOVEMBER, 1753.

CHAPTER XIII.

DOVER.—EXETER.

NOVEMBER, 1753—MARCH, 1755.

CHAPTER XIV.

WINCHESTER.—SOUTHAMPTON.—CANTERBURY.

MARCH, 1755—MAY, 1756.

CHAPTER XV.

DEVIZES.—STROUD.—CIRENCESTER.

JUNE, 1756—MARCH, 1757.

CHAPTER XVI.

CAMP.—ISLE OF WIGHT.—COAST OF FRANCE.

April—September, 1757.

CHAPTER XVII.

BLACKHEATH.—LONDON.—BATH.

October—December, 1757.

CHAPTER XVIII.

LONDON.—PORTSMOUTH.—HALIFAX, N.S.

January—February, 1758.

CHAPTER XIX.

THE CONQUEST OF CAPE BRETON.

JUNE—OCTOBER, 1758.

CHAPTER XX.

SALISBURY.—BATH.—LONDON.

NOVEMBER, 1758—FEBRUARY, 1759.

CHAPTER XXI.

EXPEDITION TO THE ST. LAWRENCE.

FEBRUARY—JUNE, 1759.

CHAPTER XXII.

BANKS OF THE ST. LAWRENCE.

JULY—AUGUST, 1759.

CHAPTER XXIII.

ABOVE QUEBEC.—HEIGHTS OF ABRAHAM.

SEPTEMBER 1–13, 1759.

CONCLUSION.

THE LIFE

OF

GENERAL WOLFE.

CHAPTER I.

WESTERHAM.—GREENWICH.

1727–1742.

IRELAND as the scene of agrarian outrages, faction fights, and political agitations, is familiar enough to us; but it is not so commonly known that Ireland a few centuries ago was the asylum of many a good old English family, whose scions there retrieved their fallen fortunes. Besides Spenser, Raleigh, and other men of mark to whom large tracts of land were assigned by Elizabeth and the first James, not a few forsook their ancestral homes with hopes of bettering their condition in the Emerald Isle. Amongst these adventurers were some of the Goldsmiths, the Seymours, and the Wolfes, all of whom settled in the western counties of Limerick and Clare. Of the Seymours, who were no less remarkable for their sudden fall than for the splendour they had attained, the three grandsons of Sir Henry Seymour of

Wolfe Hall, who was knighted at the coronation of his nephew King Edward VI., alienated their paternal property, and, attracted possibly by their affinity to the Wolfes,* established themselves in the same neighbourhood.

The precise time when a branch of the Wolfes—who seem to have been of Welsh extraction—migrated to Ireland does not appear. During the sixteenth century, however, they acquired landed estates and considerable influence. In 1605, a James Woulfe was one of the bailiffs of Limerick, and in 1613 a sheriff named George Woulfe, together with his colleague and the mayor, were deposed for refusing to take the oath of supremacy. This George Woulfe is said to have been the grandfather of his namesake the proscribed captain, of whom we shall presently speak.† Like all English settlers beyond "the pale," the Woulfes became in time "more Irish than the Irish." Consequently, it is not surprising to find that during the wars of the Commonwealth, when the Duke of Ormond was anxious to defend the city of Limerick against the assault of Cromwell's army, he was thwarted by one Francis Woulfe, head of the order of Franciscan friars. The Duke, on his arrival in February, 1650, urged upon the citizens the necessity of their receiving a garrison from his forces, as well for their own security

* Sir Henry Seymour married Barbara, daughter of Morgan Wolfe, Esq., who is not to be confounded with the goldsmith to Henry VIII., whose name was Phelppe, *alias* Wolfe. (Collectanea Topographica et Genealogica, vol. v. p. 22; Burke's 'Landed Gentry,' ed. 1850, p. 1218.)

† See article by "J. R.," of Cork, who gives the late Lord Chief Baron Wolfe as his authority for the consanguinity, in 'Notes and Queries,' vol. v. (1852), p. 280. The Chief Baron, Lord Kilwarden, and the Rev. Charles Wolfe, author of the poem on the "Burial of Sir John Moore," have distinguished the stock that remained in Ireland.

as for the preservation of the kingdom; but they rejected his proposal,—a course which Ormond attributed to the intrigues of the priests, who exulted in his misfortune. The bishops and nobles at length persuaded the lower ranks of clergy and laity to permit a garrison to be quartered outside the walls; but when the Duke of Ormond himself would have entered the city, it was found that Friar Woulfe with his faction, having forced the keys from the sheriff, had seized the gates and guarded them against him. When eventually some degree of order had been restored, the Duke was invited into the city, but he refused to venture into a place where the power of a Franciscan friar was above both ecclesiastical and civic authority. He therefore left the city to its fate, and retired to France.

In the following year Limerick was besieged by Ireton, and obliged to capitulate, when, by the terms of capitulation, the lives and properties of the citizens were secured, with the exception of twenty individuals "who had opposed and restrained the deluded people from accepting the conditions so often offered to them." Amongst the proscribed were the Friar and his brother Captain George Woulfe.* The garrison, after laying down their arms, evacuated the city, and, according to Ludlow, who was one of Ireton's officers, many on their way out dropped dead of the plague. The chief delinquents were immediately executed, one of the sufferers being Friar Francis; but his more fortunate brother succeeded in making a timely escape.

* It is curious to find the reputed great-grandfathers of Wolfe and Burke acting in the same scene. See Macknight's 'Life and Times of Edmund Burke,' vol. i. p. 5.

Captain George Woulfe, some years later, married and settled in the North of England, at the same time adopting the reformed faith and erasing the *u* from his name.* We have no further account of the Captain's career, but the authority upon which the above details are founded assures us that Edward Wolfe—the father of the subject of this memoir—was his grandson.†

Edward Wolfe was born in 1685. In his sixteenth year—the first of Queen Anne's reign—he entered her Majesty's service as second lieutenant of Marines, under the command of Viscount Shannon.‡ Three years afterwards he became a captain in Sir Richard Temple's regiment of foot, and in the year 1708 was brigade-major of the army in the Low Countries commanded by Marlborough. He was engaged in active service on the Continent until the peace of Utrecht, in 1713, and during the rebellion of 1715 served under Wade in Scotland. His commission as Lieutenant-Colonel bears date July 10th, 1717, and is distinguished from the others in being counter-signed "J. Addison." Edward Wolfe's merit

* In like manner the Gouldsmiths and other families discarded the superfluous letter from their names.

† 'The History of Limerick,' by J. Ferrar, Limerick, 1787. It would certainly have been more satisfactory had the local historian given the connecting link between Captain Woulfe and his grandson. No trace of the latter's father can now, probably, ever be discovered. I do not hesitate, however, to adopt Ferrar's account of Wolfe's ancestry, as it has never been disputed, though there were many persons living who were well acquainted with the family when it was published; and, as will appear further on, James Wolfe had first cousins by his father's side who resided in the same locality.

‡ The original commission, signed by Queen Anne, and dated St. James's, 10th March, 170½, and fourteen others of Lieut.-General Edward Wolfe's, together with eleven of his son's, are in the possession of Admiral Warde, at Squerries.

as an officer must have been great, for it is rare to find so rapid a rise in the profession of arms in those days, when family influence and political interest were the chief levers; and he possessed neither one nor the other.

As the peaceful policy of Cardinal Fleury and of Sir Robert Walpole caused almost a total cessation of warfare during the reign of George I., there was little scope for the exercise of military ability. Lieut.-Colonel Wolfe therefore thought it was time to settle down for life, and accordingly married Henrietta, daughter of Edward Thompson, Esq., of Marsden, in Yorkshire.* Mrs. Wolfe was descended on her mother's side from the ancient family of Tindal, at Brotherton, in that county.† Some time after their marriage the Lieutenant-Colonel and his wife established themselves in Westerham, Kent, where, at the Vicarage, on January 2, 1727 (N.S.), their son *James* was born; ‡ and on the 11th of the same month, as the parish register records, was baptized.

The city of York long disputed with the Kentish village for the honour of being the birthplace of James Wolfe; but all trustworthy evidence is, we may see, in favour of the latter.§ Besides the church register, there exists in Westerham a tradition in support of the highly-prized local right. The Rev. Richard Board, who died in 1859, aged ninety-six, and who had been for sixty-seven years Vicar of Westerham, has frequently been heard to say that he knew several inhabitants who perfectly

* Burke's 'Landed Gentry,' ed. 1850, p. 1389.

† See Nichols's 'Literary Anecdotes,' vol. ix. p. 304.

‡ Or, according to the Old Style, December 22nd, 1726.

§ See 'Public Advertiser,' October 27, 1759; 'Scots' Magazine,' 1759, p. 554, etc.

remembered the event, and "stated positively that the General's father and mother were living at the Vicarage at the time of his birth."* The room may still be seen, and the bed was preserved by the late General Warde.† At the time of their celebrated son's birth, the Lieutenant-Colonel was in the forty-third year of his age, and Mrs. Wolfe in her twenty-fourth. Soon afterwards they quitted the Vicarage, which had been rented from the Rev. George Lewis, and removed to a larger house still standing,—a low square mansion situated in a hollow at the foot of the hill down which winds the eastern outlet of Westerham, leading to Brastead and Sevenoaks. Quebec House,‡ as it is now called, was evidently a picturesque, if not comfortable abode, before modern alterations disfigured its exterior. Viewing it from the height upon which stands the venerable church, it is seen to most advantage, as the original gables of the rear are preserved, while those of the front facing the road have been converted into an unsightly parapeted wall.

Here, under the watchful eye and careful training of their mother, passed the childhood of James and his younger brother, Edward Wolfe.§ There was not more

* From a MS. statement of 'Facts connected with General Wolfe,' by John Board, Esq., of Westerham, as related to him by his father, the late Rev. Richard Board.

† "Among many things I have, originally his [Wolfe's], I sleep constantly on the bed in which he was born." (From a letter of General George Warde's, dated "Woodland Castle, November 15, 1822," to the Rev. Thomas Streatfeild, of Chart's Edge, Kent.)

‡ This name is said to have been given to the house by a lady who rented it some years ago for a boarding-school.

§ The entries of their baptisms in the parish register are as follows:—

"James, son of Collonel Edward Wolfe, bapt. January 11th, 1726." [o. s.]

"Edward, son of Collonel Edward Wolfe, bapt. January 10th, 1727." [o. s.]

than a year's difference between their ages, and their mutual attachment was closer than is common between brothers. They were both delicate, sensitive children, whose precarious health caused their mother many an anxious hour; but they grew up into ardent and fearless, though not robust boys. They received their first instructions in book-learning at a small school kept by a Mr. Lawrence, in a house still standing, near Westfield Grange, Westerham.* Nothing, beyond his name, is known of the village pedagogue; nor has tradition conveyed to us a single incident illustrative of the conduct or abilities of his celebrated pupil, the subject of this memoir. The young Wolfes, however, were but a short time under Mr. Lawrence's ferula, for their father removed to Greenwich while the brothers were still children.

Before he left his native village James had formed a friendship that was to endure for life, with a lad about two years his senior—George, youngest son of John Warde, Esq., of Squerries.† Their tastes and aspirations were similar; for young Warde, like young Wolfe, was an embryo soldier. Squerries Court was the favourite resort of James, where he was ever a welcome guest; and with his companion he wandered through the woods, climbed the steep hills, and strolled along the banks of

"Silent Darent stained with Danish blood."

* John Board, Esq., as above.

† Squerries Court, a manor which gave both surname and seat to a family resident as early as the reign of King Henry III. The family bore for their arms a squirrel browsing on a hazel nut; which coat was formerly painted in the window of Westerham Church. At the opening of the eighteenth century the estate was in the possession of the Earl of Jersey, who sold it to John Warde, Esq. (Hasted's 'History of Kent,' vol. i. p. 384.)

There are few more delightful neighbourhoods even in "the Garden of England" than the country around Westerham. Its natural beauty is well seconded by a high state of culture, so that hill and vale are alike fruitful. In the month of May the numerous orchards are masses of apple blossom; while the lilac, laburnum, and hawthorn, each adding to the other's charms, bloom simultaneously in many a garden by the roadside. On approaching the village from the west, the fine old red brick mansion of Squerries is seen upon an eminence, at the foot of which is a small lake; and behind the house, the ground, rising still higher, is studded with majestic trees. At the other side of this hill several springs uniting in a stream form the tributary Darent, which, after a winding course of about thirty miles, enters the Thames near Dartford.*

From the valuation of Westerham, in Domesday Book, it appears to have been a place of some importance as early as the reign of Edward the Confessor, when it was held of the Crown by Godwin, Earl of Kent.† The parish church, dedicated to St. Mary, is a fine specimen of the architecture of the fifteenth century; and the interior must have been very imposing before churchwardens began to mar it by their preposterous repairs. Some recent restorations are in better taste; and it is

* According to Leland, the term *Darent* signifies "clear water;" and Spenser, describing the rivers attending on the Thames, notices the translucency of—

> "The still Darent, in whose waters cleane
> Ten thousand fishes play, and deck his pleasant streame."
>
> *Faerie Queen*, bk. iv. c. xi. s. 29.

† George's 'Westerham Journal,' 1844.

to be hoped that the old oak roof will be again exposed to view, by the removal of the lath-and-plaster ceiling that now hides it. The aisles are crowded with mural monuments, and some sepulchral brasses remain, though many were barbarously removed more than half a century ago.*

James Wolfe enjoyed little of his father's society during his boyhood, for the Lieutenant-Colonel was obliged to be constantly with his regiment; but, when occasionally he visited his family, he had many a tale to tell of Marlborough and Prince Eugene, that kindled the latent ambition of the boy.

Young Edward Wolfe, notwithstanding the courage he exhibited during his short military career, had not so strong a passion for arms as his elder brother. His constitution being even more delicate than James's, he was not intended for the service. But docile and tractable as he was, he looked up to his more enthusiastic and impulsive brother as his leader; and it is evident that he entered the army—some months later than James—solely with the view of being with him whom he fondly loved, and pined after. But these remarks anticipate the order of events.

The death of Queen Caroline, in 1737, may be said to have ended the era of peace; for the Queen had exercised her influence over George II. to support the power of Sir Robert Walpole, for whom the King had little personal regard. Consequently, after her Majesty's death, the minister could no longer restrain the monarch from

* A correspondent of the 'Gentleman's Magazine,' 1807, writing upon this subject, declares that he discovered one of these brasses doing duty as a fender before a fireplace in the house of the parish clerk.

following his own inclination towards a more fiery foreign policy than that which had hitherto been pursued. So the peace which England had enjoyed for a comparatively long while was now near its close, and stormy times were at hand.

It was about this time that Lieut.-Colonel Wolfe removed his family to Greenwich, when his two sons attended the school of the Rev. Samuel F. Swinden, a gentleman for whom they continued to have the highest respect, and whose name is often mentioned in their letters.

But rumours of war soon disturbed James's studies. The outcry of the English merchants against Spain, backed by the Parliamentary opposition, could no longer be resisted, and Walpole, rather than lose his place, yielded to the popular will by entering into an imprudent and fruitless, if not an unjustifiable war. On October 30th, 1739, Garter and Norroy, accompanied by Knights-Marshal, and escorted by a troop of Horse Guards with drums and trumpets, proceeded to Charing-Cross and the Royal Exchange, where they proclaimed his Majesty's declaration of war against Spain, amidst a vast crowd that signified the popular assent by loud acclamations.*

Amongst other preparations, orders were issued for raising six additional regiments of Marines,† and, on November 27th, Lieut.-Colonel Wolfe received his commission as Colonel of the first of these regiments. A great military encampment also was formed upon Blackheath,‡ which had no slight attractions for one at least of the

* Wade's British Chronology. † Salmon's Chronology. ‡ *Ibid.*

Greenwich schoolboys, who ever delighted in military and naval spectacles, and who now began to long for the day, not far distant, when he should be no longer a mere spectator, but an active performer in a similar display.

Great was the joy of England when, in March, 1740, the news arrived of Vernon's victory at Porto Bello. Hero-worship has seldom enthralled more abject votaries than those who bowed down before the idol of the hour. Innumerable were the medals struck to perpetuate "the British glory revived in Admiral Vernon."* When the hero's birthday came round, it was celebrated throughout the land with bonfires and illuminations, marrow-bones and cleavers, etc.; and the inhabitants of a parish in Cornwall, who could bestow no higher honour, elected him their churchwarden.† This patriotic frenzy was stimulated by the timely appearance of Glover's beautiful ballad,‡ alluding to which a wit of the day said, "The patriots cry it up, the courtiers cry it down, and the hawkers cry it up and down."§

The English public, although not easily excited, when once roused knows how, not only to express its sentiments, but also how to see them carried into action. Notwithstanding great distress amongst the working-

* One of these medals was recently dug up in a garden. See 'Notes and Queries,' July 26, 1862 (p. 70). "The medal," says the editor, "is of abominable workmanship; but such was the demand for it, that upwards of one hundred varieties of it are in the British Museum."

† 'Athenæum,' June 15, 1861.

‡ "Admiral Hosier's Ghost. To the tune of 'Come and listen to my Ditty.' London: printed for Mr. Webb, near St. Paul's, 1740 (price sixpence)."

§ The Hon. Henry Seymour Conway. See Walpole's Letters (Cunningham's ed.), vol. i. p. 62.

classes, and the unusual severity of the winter of 1739–40, when the Thames was one mass of ice, a general enthusiasm prevailed, which nothing short of the total destruction of Spanish power in America would gratify. An expedition, therefore, was fitted out under Commodore Anson, with the view of ravaging the western coast of Spanish America; and a large fleet, commanded by Sir Chaloner Ogle, assembled at Spithead to reinforce the West Indian fleet, of which Admiral Vernon was continued in the command. Meanwhile an army of 10,000 men was collected in the Isle of Wight, under Lord Cathcart, an experienced officer, of high honour and integrity.

These were busy times with Colonel Wolfe, who was appointed Adjutant-General to Lord Cathcart's forces in July, 1740. James was now but thirteen years and six months old, a tender age for the hardships inevitable to so distant a service, even under the most favourable circumstances. But the boy's strong will could not be subdued by his mother's remonstrance, and the Colonel was induced to take the young volunteer along with him to the camp. Mrs. Wolfe could not possibly have used more effective means in endeavouring to dissuade her son from his purpose than in doubting his love, but even this was of no avail; for dearly as he loved both her and his brother, who remained at home, there was more powerful attraction for him elsewhere. His parting grief was soon dissipated by the view of the fleet at Portsmouth, or, in his own words upon a future occasion, "the dreadful though pleasing sight of our mighty navy." He had not been long with the army, and had therefore acquired little experience of a soldier's life, when he wrote his first letter to his mother, as follows:—

Newport, Isle of Wight,
August 6th, 1740.

Dear Madam,

I received my dearest Mamma's letter on Monday last, but could not answer it then, by reason I was at camp to see the regiments off to go on board, and was too late for the post; but am very sorry, dear Mamma, that you doubt my love, which I'm sure is as sincere as ever any son's was to his mother.

Papa and I are just now going on board, but I believe shall not sail this fortnight; in which time, if I can get ashore at Portsmouth or any other town, I will certainly write to you, and when we are gone by every ship I meet, because I know it is my duty. Besides, if it was not, I would do it out of love, with pleasure.

I am sorry to hear that your head is so bad, which, I fear, is caused by your being so melancholy; but pray, dear Mamma, if you love me, don't give yourself up to fears for us. I hope, if it please God, we shall soon see one another, which will be the happiest day that ever I shall see. I will, as sure as I live, if it is possible for me, let you know everything that has happened, by every ship; therefore pray, dearest Mamma, don't doubt about it. I am in a very good state of health, and am likely to continue so. Pray my love to my brother, and accept of my duty. Papa desires his love to you, and blessing to my brother. Pray my service to Mr. Streton and his family, to Mr. and Mrs. Weston, and to George Warde when you see him; and pray believe me to be, my dearest Mamma,

Your most dutiful, loving, and affectionate Son,

J. Wolfe.

P.S.—Harry gives his love to Margaret, and is very careful of me. Pray my service to Will and the rest.

To Mrs. Wolfe, at her house in Greenwich, Kent.

This boyish effusion, in no way remarkable perhaps, beyond its passionate outbursts of affection, was carefully preserved by Mrs. Wolfe; and every letter of her son's to either his father or to herself was, one by one, added to her store, until, nineteen years after the date of the above, his last letter to her from the banks of the St. Lawrence completed the collection.

The fleet had not departed at the expiration of the fortnight, nor did it sail until November; neither was young Wolfe destined to go with it. His assertion that he was in a good state of health, and likely to continue so, was not well founded, for ere long he fell seriously ill, and it became necessary to put him ashore at Portsmouth on his way homewards. His father was not so fortunate, but lived to look back with horror upon the sufferings he was now about to undergo; and years afterwards he recalled his Carthagena experiences, in order to warn his son against embarking in a conjoint expedition.

Although the purport of this book is to narrate the story of James Wolfe's life, not his father's, yet, in order to gain some insight into the way great national undertakings were managed when our hero was about entering upon his active career, it may be excusable slightly to trace the fortunes of the fleet with which the Colonel sailed. The opening prospect was bright enough, insomuch that Lord Cathcart wrote to Vernon,—"In the troops I bring you there is spirit, there is goodwill, which, when properly conducted, will produce, I hope, what the nation expects from us—will make us the glorious instruments of finishing the war with all the advantages to the public that its happy beginning promises, and with this distinguishing circumstance, that those happy effects have been owing to a perfect harmony between the sea and land forces." But unfortunately, Cathcart died soon after his arrival in the West Indies, when the command of the army devolved upon Brigadier Wentworth, an officer who had neither experience, resolution, nor authority. One quality, however, he possessed in common with Vernon,—obstinacy; and his contempt for the navy was as great as the Admiral's contempt for the army:*

The minutest and best account of this ever-memorable expedition is that given in 'The Adventures of Roderick Random,' wherein the author relates his own hard-bought experience as a surgeon's mate on board a man-of-war belonging to the fleet. After describing the effects of the storm that overtook them outside the Channel, with other trying incidents of the outward voyage, and the unnecessary delay at Jamaica, Smollett says:—"At length we set sail, and arrived in a bay to the windward of Carthagena, where we came to an anchor and lay at our ease ten days longer. Here, again, certain malicious people took occasion to blame the conduct of their superiors, by saying that in so doing they not only unprofitably wasted time, which was very precious considering the approach of the rainy season, but also allowed the Spaniards time to recollect themselves from the terror occasioned by the approach of an English fleet at least three times as numerous as ever appeared in that part of the world before. But if I might be allowed to give my opinion

* Russell's 'Modern Europe.'

of the matter, I would ascribe this delay to the generosity of our chiefs, who scorned to take any advantage that fortune might give them, even over an enemy." *

As it does not come within our province to enter into details of the attack upon Bocca Chica, the castle of St. Lazar, and other warlike proceedings of this ill-starred expedition, one or two more passages from our author will suffice to show the total disregard of the commanders for the health or comfort of their men,—a state of things compared with which the care of military and naval chiefs in our day presents a happy contrast.

In the same ironical tone, Smollett goes on to say:—"How simply do those people argue who ascribe the great mortality among us to our bad provision and want of water; . . . seeing, it is to be hoped, that those who died went to a better place, and those who survived were the more easily maintained. After all, a sufficient number remained to fall before the walls of St. Lazar, where they behaved like their own country mastiffs, who shut their eyes, run into the jaws of a bear, and have their heads crushed for their valour."†

The description of the so-called hospital-ships is too disgusting for quotation. It will be enough to say that the inhuman neglect of the sick and wounded was imputed to the scarcity of surgeons. "Though," continues the surgeon's mate, "it is well known that every great ship in the fleet could have spared one at least for this duty,—an expedient which would have been more than sufficient to remove this shocking inconvenience. But

* 'The Adventures of Roderick Random,' vol. i. ch. xxxi.

† *Ibid.*, ch. xxxiii.

perhaps the General was too much of a gentleman to ask a favour of this kind from his fellow-chief, who, on the other hand, would not derogate so much from his own dignity as to offer such assistance unasked; for I may venture to affirm, that by this time the demon of discord, with her sooty wings, had breathed her influence upon our councils; and it might be said of these great men (I hope they will pardon the comparison) as of Cæsar and Pompey, the one could brook no superior, and the other was impatient of an equal."*

With such ill-associated commanders there could possibly be but one result—the total failure of the expedition, after a most wanton sacrifice of human life. To complete the ruin, the rainy season set in with its attendant pestilence, against which the dejected survivors were badly fitted to cope; so the few forts that had been taken from the enemy were relinquished, and the wreck of the armament retired to Jamaica.

The evil had been enough, if the jealous feeling that existed in one service towards the other had been confined to the superior officers; but unhappily, the example of the chiefs was followed through all grades. Nor was this contemptuous spirit exhibited only between

* Although it is well known that in this instance Smollett has not exaggerated the facts, but has only, by his bitter irony, made them appear more glaring, some apology may be necessary for quoting a work of fiction as historical authority. I shall not, by way of excuse, offer Fielding's witticism, that the only difference between the historian and him was, that with the historian everything was false but the names and dates, while with himself nothing was false but these, but will adduce Mr. Thackeray's opinion:—"I take a volume of Dr. Smollett, or a volume of the 'Spectator,' and say the fiction carries a greater amount of *truth in solution* than the volume that purports to be all true." ('English Humourists of the Eighteenth Century.')

the land and sea forces; for in those days naval officers, as a rule, treated with scorn men of other professions necessarily associated with them, clerical as well as medical. The chaplain, however, if a jovial companion and a good hand at mixing *bumbo,* might sometimes be honoured with an invitation to the wardroom.*

Colonel Wolfe was sent to Cuba in charge of the sick and wounded, and did not return home from the West Indies until the autumn of 1742. James had in the meanwhile recovered his health, and again joined his brother at the worthy Mr. Swinden's school in Greenwich. They were very companionable boys, forming many friendships amongst their schoolfellows and neighbours, the Allens, Bretts, Cades, Hookers, Masons, Strettons, and others, whose names may still be seen upon stately monuments in St. Alphage's and elsewhere; and some of them are conspicuous in the rolls of our Admirals and Generals.

It could have been only towards the end of his education under Mr. Swinden that Wolfe had a schoolfellow in little John Jervis, for "Master Jackey" was six years younger than James. He was nevertheless a hardy youngster, with considerable thirst for salt water, though his father, the Treasurer of Greenwich Hospital, designed him for the law.†

"What are you to be, Master Jackey?" asked the old coachman of the boy who sat beside him on the box, one day while the family was driving out. "A lawyer, I believe," was the answer. "Oh, don't, Master Jackey,

* See "The Chaplain's Petition," in 'The Gentleman's Magazine,' for September, 1796.

† 'Memoir of John Jervis, Earl St. Vincent,' by J. S. Tucker.

dear," rejoined the blunt driver, "for lawyers are always rogues!" Whether the hint had any influence or not, young Jack ere long ran away to sea, to begin, through great trials and hardships, the career that was to end in the renown of the admiral, Earl St. Vincent.* In their after years Wolfe and Jervis saw little of one another, until the last days of Wolfe's life, when he reposed in his friend a sacred trust, the story of which will appear in due course.

There were also visits to Westerham at this time. Towards the end of the year 1741, when James was at Squerries, the post arrived one day while he and his companions, John and George Warde, were amusing themselves in the pleasure-grounds near the house. Mr. Warde soon afterwards approached and handed his visitor a large letter, "On his Majesty's service," which, on being opened, was found to contain the young soldier's first commission, dated "St. James's, November 3rd, 1741," duly signed by King George II. and countersigned by Lord Harrington, appointing him Second Lieutenant in his father's regiment of Marines. The incident was not forgotten; for the inheritor of the estate, who had been by, after victory had crowned the hero, erected a testimonial to perpetuate the event on the spot where it had occurred.† This memorial, embowered by lofty trees, still stands upon the terrace at the south side of Squerries House, and consists of a pedestal surmounted by an ornamental urn. The base is covered with inscriptions, amongst which are the following lines:—

* 'Life of Earl St. Vincent,' by Captain Brenton. London: 1838.
† Communicated by Admiral Warde, K.H.

> "Here first was Wolfe with martial ardour fired,
> Here first with glory's brightest flame inspired;
> This spot so sacred will for ever claim
> A proud alliance with its hero's name."

The corps of which young Wolfe was now a commissioned officer, originated in the reign of Charles II., when it was known as "The Maritime Regiment of the Lord High Admiral of England,"—his Royal Highness the Duke of York and Albany. After the Revolution, William III. disbanded them, but raised a similar body under his own warrant; and Queen Anne added to the number by converting three infantry regiments into Marines.* It was in one of these regiments that Colonel Wolfe had seen his first service, and it was chiefly owing to their daring gallantry that Gibraltar became a British possession.†

But there is no evidence to prove that James Wolfe ever actually served as a Marine; nor is it probable, as his father's regiment had not as yet returned to England. It was a service, too, for which he was ill suited physically, for he never could overcome the torture which he invariably suffered at sea; and it may possibly have been a short experience of this that determined his exchange, within a few months, into the Line.

The British army has never been at a lower ebb than when Wolfe entered it. It was the heartless policy of those "good old times" when war was at an end, to disband suddenly the greater part of the forces, and thus a treaty that brought peace and prosperity to the

* Stocqueler's 'British Soldier.'

† The Marines were honoured with the prefix "Royal" by George III., in 1802, in consideration of their services during the war with revolutionary France. (*Ibid.*)

nation at large, was followed by distress, if not ruin, to those whose swords had been the means of effecting it. The Peace of Utrecht terminated the Continental warfare in which England had been engaged, and the army came home to be turned adrift upon the world,—officers, who had no political interest, to support their families upon half-pay, or to enter upon other avocations for which they were unfitted, and privates, to recruit the ranks of the highway.

During the reign of George I. and the earlier part of his successor's, there was little call for the services of soldiers, and consequently only foppish officers, attracted by love of scarlet and gold-lace, with a few companies of regiments billeted here and there, for barracks were not yet in vogue, constituted what was called the British army. But now, after thirty years' peace, the recruiting sergeant had to be set at work to allure rustics from the plough, for the pay of sixpence a day, to contend against the ably-officered and well-trained troops of France.

"In the beginning of each war," says a great military historian, "England has to seek in blood the knowledge necessary to ensure success; and like the fiend's progress towards Eden, her conquering course is through chaos followed by death!"* It may be safely asserted that to no period of England's history do these unquestionable words more fitly apply than to that when Wolfe became an ensign of the Twelfth, or Colonel Duroure's regiment of foot.

* Napier's 'History of the Peninsular War.'

CHAPTER II.

GHENT.—ASCHAFFENBURG.

1742–1743.

In the beginning of the year 1742, when England had once more embarked in European warfare, the British army was comprised of fifteen cavalry regiments, in addition to the Horse Guards, fifty infantry regiments, besides the Foot Guards, and four companies of Royal Artillery. Sixteen thousand men had been set apart for Continental service; and of these, such corps as were ready for embarkation in the spring were collected upon Blackheath.

Accordingly, on Tuesday the 27th of April—one month exactly after the date of Ensign Wolfe's commission—King George II., accompanied by his sons, their Royal Highnesses the Prince of Wales and the Duke of Cumberland, and attended by Field Marshal the Earl of Stair, with a large staff of Generals, proceeded to the Heath, in order to review the flower of his Majesty's army. There were three troops of the Horse Guards, and the whole of the "Blues," with five regiments of Dragoons; and of foot, there were thirteen regiments, one of which was Colonel Duroure's.*

As such a sight was not often to be seen, no small

* 'Gentleman's Magazine.'

number of citizens turned out to view the show. It was a busy time upon the Thames, for the "silent highway" was preferred before the Greenwich road, long ere steamboats upset the vested rights of the "jolly young waterman."

Of little significance, amidst the brilliant array whose manœuvres were criticized by the crowd upon this April day, was the blue-eyed boy that carried the colours of Duroure's. Some few friends and neighbours there were, indeed, who felt more interested in him than in either Field Marshal, Prince, or King. Although his father had not yet returned from the West Indies, Mrs. Wolfe and young Edward had not far to come; Mr. Swinden was probably there with some of his scholars; and George Warde was certainly there,—a cornet of dragoons.

Judging by the manly air and lofty stature of the young ensign, those who did not know him would have supposed his age to have been much more than fifteen years and three months; nor was this premature appearance of age lessened by the powdered wig, which, according to the fashion of the time, concealed his own naturally red hair. Although the most partial admirer could not have considered him by any means a handsome youth, yet his countenance was so expressive of an ingenuous, hopeful spirit as to make it remarkably attractive. The most striking lineament, however, was the singular form of his profile, which might be nearly represented by two lines of an obtuse angle meeting at the tip of the nose.* When in repose, his face had little colour, but when excited—owing to that transparency of the skin which com-

* Wolfe's profile bears a remarkable resemblance to that of the younger Pitt, as may be perceived by comparing his portrait by High-

monly accompanies a sanguine complexion—it blushed all over; and the somewhat high and prominent cheek-bones betrayed the share of Celtic blood he inherited. The mouth denoted great decision and firmness, while the leading expression of the sparkling azure eyes might be most truly qualified as inquiring.

The military costume of the day, though not so smart perhaps as that of the modern soldier, was much more picturesque, as well as more comfortable. The scarlet frock, instead of being buttoned up in front, was merely closed by two or three loops above the waist, while from the chest it was folded back in broad lapels, exposing the bosom of the shirt. The skirts descended to the knees, where the corners were turned up, displaying, as at the breast, the white or yellow lining of the coat. Breeches and gaiters covered the legs, and the head was surmounted by a cocked hat,* edged with gold lace. Without noticing minuter points, if to the above are added the belt and sword, a sufficiently accurate conception may be formed of Wolfe's appearance at his first review.

more with the bust of the statesman in the National Portrait Gallery. The likeness has been noticed by Neale, in his 'Westminster Abbey.'

* "The cockade was simply the knot of the ribbon that served to cock the broad flapped hat worn by military men in the eighteenth century, and which in fine weather, or going into action, etc., they used to cock, by means of hooks, laces, and ribbons. We still see in the cocked hats of coachmen and beadles the traces of these old ligaments. . . . Coats were of the shape we now call frocks, and lined throughout, generally, with a different colour from the outside. When a person in one of these coats was going about any active work, and particularly into fight, he doubled back his sleeves, and folded back the collar, which being of a different colour came to be what we now call the *facings* of military uniforms. The French, truer to their origin, still call them the *revers*." (Notes and Queries.)

The spectacle over, there was but little time left for parting scenes. Two regiments at least—Howard's and Duroure's—marched immediately from the ground, the first for Woolwich, the other for Deptford, where they embarked in the transports ready to convey them to the Austrian dominions in Flanders.* After being for several days wind-bound at the Nore, they at length reached Ostend, whither they were convoyed by the 'Argyle,' of 50 guns, on the 10th of May; and next day they proceeded to Bruges. It appears that their arrival was anticipated by another body from England:—"By our last advices from Ostend," says one of the newspapers, "we learn that on the 2nd instant a large body of British troops arrived there for the service of her Hungarian Majesty; but that as they were all of the fair sex, and no provision having been made by Brigadier Bland for quartering them, it occasioned a great confusion in the town; however, it is said they will soon be reinforced by their husbands and sweethearts, who are now confined at the Nore by contrary winds."†

Nothing further is to be learned of our young soldier's proceedings until after his arrival at Ghent, in which garrison Duroure's was quartered, but where the troops of their sovereign's ally were by no means welcome to the inhabitants. The Ghentois were composed of a mixture of French and Dutch, not well incorporated, and, therefore, not the most loyal of Maria Theresa's subjects. "They hate the English, and *we* hate them," writes one of the British officers, in a letter home; "and

* 'The Country Journal; or, the Craftsman.'

† *Ibid.*, Saturday, May 8, 1742.

the Queen of Hungary holds them like a wolf by the ears."*

It is no wonder, then, to hear of frequent collisions between the people and their garrison. The most trifling circumstance excited a tumult; for instance, we learn from a contemporaneous letter:—"On the 3rd instant (July), at night, some English soldiers being in the market-place, one of them, as the butchers say, stole a piece of meat, but, as the soldiers say, that he only took it up to smell if it was sweet; upon which the butcher cut him across the face with a knife, and one of the soldiers ran the butcher through the body. Immediately the fray became general; the butchers with knives and cleavers, and the burghers with old rusty swords and spits, killed some of the soldiers; but twelve dragoons coming to the relief of the Foot, cut down all before them, and put the mob to flight. The rest of the soldiers were, by direction of the officers, locked up in the barracks. The tumult continued above two hours, and several were killed on both sides. On this occasion the magistrates assembled, and ordered an edict to be issued, that whoever should offer the least affront to the subjects of the King of Great Britain, should be *whipped, burnt in the back, and turned out of the town.*"†

Ghent, since known as the "Belgian Manchester," had then no manufactures, and but little trade. The priest-ridden population, if report be true, kept at least two, and sometimes three or four holidays in each week. Their dress was somewhat after the Spanish mode; but,

* 'Gentleman's Magazine,' 1743, p. 528.
† *Ibid.*, July, 1742, p. 390.

"seeing the gay appearance of the English gentlemen, they grew ashamed of their wooden shoes, and old greasy, ragged cloaks, which served for coat, waistcoat, and, I believe breeches, but I am not sure of stockings, and began to spruce themselves up in leather shoes, etc."* Bating the satire, after making a little allowance for national prejudice, the above representation of the towns-people, and their condition at the time when Wolfe was first stationed amongst them, will help us to form as correct notions of them as can now probably be arrived at.

The earliest of the ensign's letters from Ghent, that has been preserved, is evidently not the first he wrote there. The novelty of his situation seems to have worn off by the time the following was penned, consequently we gain little insight from him into the state of public affairs. Yet, although the contents are not of much general interest, there are, adopting a favourite phrase of his own, some "strokes" so indicative of character therein, as to make it, unimportant though its details are, worthy of being read.

His father had, ere now, come back from the West Indies, and been appointed Inspector of Marines; but upon this occasion Wolfe writes to his mother:—

Ghent, August 27th, 1742.

Dear Madam,

I just got your kind letter by Captain Merrydan; I'm very much obliged to you for it, and am heartily glad to hear you are all well.

I pity my uncle Tim much.† I think, by what I have

* 'Gentleman's Magazine,' 1743, p. 528.

† "Uncle Tim" was probably Mrs. Wolfe's eldest brother, Edward Tindal Thompson.

heard you say of him, he does not deserve such ill luck. I saw my friend George Warde yesterday for the first time, though the Horse have been here these two days, for I happened to be on guard when they came; nor have I as yet seen Captain Merrydan, for my Captain brought me the letters from him. I intend waiting on him this afternoon.

I am vastly obliged to you for your good advice, and will follow it as much as lies in my power, I assure you. I got a letter from my father two days ago, by Captain Stanhope, which I intend thanking him for next post; and then, perhaps, I shall write to him from camp, for our colonel has desired us to have everything ready against Monday next. I have just now done packing up, and can be ready to march in two hours.

I wish my uncle Brad may be coming home as you heard, for I know it would give you great pleasure to see him.* I am very sorry my brother Ned complains of my not answering his letters; I think I have never missed any, nor ever will. Pray be so good to give my kind love to him. My shirts are in very good order, and, I hope, will last me a great while; but I fancy (by what people say) not so long as we are in Flanders.

Pray, my duty to my father, and love to cousin Goldsmith;† and with best compliments to my good friends at Greenwich, and hearty wishes for your healths, I must beg to . . . .

Dear Madam,

Your dutiful and affectionate Son,

JAMES WOLFE.

N.B.—Cope's Dragoons are expected here to-night. I often play on my flute, and am going to it now.

* Bradwardine Thompson, Mrs. Wolfe's brother, a lieutenant-colonel.

† *Edward* Goldsmith of Limerick, it would appear, was Wolfe's father's sister's son; Oliver Goldsmith, therefore, had reason for claiming relationship to the hero. Prior, in his 'Life of Goldsmith,' states that Oliver "was accustomed to say that by the female side he was remotely connected with the family of the Protector, Oliver Cromwell, from whom his Christian name was derived; and by the father's side

In spite of his readiness for the road, Wolfe was destined to spend the ensuing winter in Ghent, which furnished no less dear than damp and dreary quarters; for, although provisions were said to be abundant and cheap, the numerous garrison of foreigners soon made living much more expensive than it then was in London. The fortified town, with its network of canals splitting the triangular area within the walls into six-and-twenty islands, with its numerous bridges and narrow, dirty, irregular streets, antique houses bedizened with paint and whiting outside, and overtopped by fantastic gables, however picturesque, was not the most cheerful of places for a winter residence. Dismal enough must have been the sound of the young ensign's flute,—of which, by the way, we never hear again,—within some large, dark, low room of one of these old Ghentish habitations.

Although it might appear from his next letter home that he was not just now overburdened with work, yet it is certain that at this time he devoted many hours in preparing himself for a more onerous office than carrying colours. The practical illustrations also which Ghent afforded for the study of fortification were not neglected; for, though not indifferent to the beauties of architecture, the citadel, walls, and gates of the place had more attraction for him than had the cathedral of St. Bavon, or the Hôtel de Ville. So, between business and amusement, his time was fully occupied; and it is evident that his spirits were good from the following letter to his mother:—

he claimed affinity with General Wolfe, the conqueror of Quebec." (Vol. i. p. 6.) It is not probable, however, that the poet and the soldier were personally acquainted.

Ghent, September 12th, 1742.

Dear Madam,

I got yours two days ago by Captain Guy. I'm heartily sorry to hear that the pleasure of hearing from you is now at an end. I fancy the expense is not so great as you imagine. I'm told by several gentlemen that 'tis no more than sixpence, and that, once a month, wouldn't hurt your pocket. I answered the packet you was so good to send me by Captain Merrydan; I dined with him yesterday, and think he seems to be a very good sort of man.

I'm glad you've got a house. Long may you live to enjoy the blessings of a good and warm one!—a thing not easily found in this town, but that we young ones don't mind.

You desire to know how I live. I assure you, as to eating, rather too well, considering what we may come to. For drink I don't much care; but there is very good rum and brandy in this place, and cheap, if we have a mind to take a little sneaker now and then at night just to warm us. The weather begins now to grow coldish: we have had rain for the last two weeks, and the people say 'tis likely to continue till the frost comes in. I have not begun with fire yet, neither do I intend till I know where we shall encamp.

This place is full of officers, and we never want company. I go to the play* once or twice a week, and talk a little with the ladies, who are very civil, and talk French.

I'm glad to hear with all my heart that my brother is better. He says he goes to the cold bath, and that does him good. Pray my love to him. I hope my father is well, and keeps his health; be so good as to give my duty to him, and to my Aunt Allanson if she is with you, and believe me,

Dear Madam,

Your dutiful and affectionate Son,

J. Wolfe.

I see my friend George often; he has just left me, and desires his compliments.

* In 1737 a fine opera-house was built in Ghent. (Seally's Geog. Dict., 1787.)

One more letter from the old place requires no introduction:—

Ghent, December 17th, 1742.

Dear Madam,

I should have answered your letter when I wrote last to my father, had not the business I was forced to write about prevented me. I was heartily sorry you got into your new house with a cold. I hope it has left you, and you enjoy perfect health, without which there can be no happiness to you, nor consequently to me. My brother is much to be commended for the pains he takes to improve himself. I hope to see him soon in Flanders, when, in all probability, before next year is over, we may know something of our trade. Some people imagine we shall return to England in the spring, but I think that's not much to be relied on; however, I'm no judge of these things.

There is a talk of some of the regiments of Foot will march to garrison two or three towns (the Austrians have quitted to go and join the army in Bohemia*);—they are about fourscore or a hundred miles from hence. Their names are Mons, Charleroy, and another I don't know; but it is not certain.

We have had extreme hard frost for about a fortnight, so that all the rivers and canals, whereof there are great plenty about the town, are frozen, so that no boats can go, nor any commerce be carried on by water. There was a little thaw last night, so that we are in some hopes of its going away.

I shall not miss writing to you every fortnight as you desire. Be so good to give my duty to my father, uncles and aunts, and love to my brother.

I am, dearest Madam,

Your dutiful and affectionate Son,

J. Wolfe.

Mr. Warde desires his compliments; mine to that family, if you please. I hope Miss is well.†

* "The Austrians in Flanders have separated from our troops, a little out of humour, because it was impracticable for them to march without any preparatory provision for their reception." (Walpole to Mann, December 9, 1742.)

† Miss Warde, sister to George, afterwards Mrs. Clayton.

We learn from the above that young Edward Wolfe was about to join his brother in Flanders, and from a former letter it appears also that his health was delicate. He longed nevertheless to be with James, but probably was prevented until his father's return to England, when a further delay may have arisen from the difficulty of obtaining an ensigncy in the same regiment. Duroure's quitted Ghent, on the march towards Germany, early in February, 1743, by which time, as there is no message to him in James's next letter, it may be concluded that Edward had left home for the army upon the Continent.

Many columns of the newspapers and magazines of the time are filled with detailed accounts of the hardships suffered by the British forces upon their march into Germany; but it will not be necessary to add to the story of a few days' experience of the road as plainly but hopefully told by Wolfe in the letter which follows:—

St. Tron, in the Bishopric of Liége,
February 12th, 1743.

Dear Madam,

I got your letter of the 23rd of last month, at Ghent, and should have answered it as I told my father I intended, at Brussels, but was very much fatigued and out of order, so deferred it till now.

This is our fifth day's march; we have had very bad weather all the way. I have found out by experience that my strength is not so great as I imagined; but, however, I have held out pretty well as yet. To-morrow is a very bad road to Tongres, so if I can I will hire a horse at this place, and march afoot one day and ride the other, all the rest of the journey.

I never come into quarters without aching hips and knees;

and I assure you the wisest part of the officers got horses at Ghent, though some would have done it if their circumstances would have allowed it.

We have lived pretty well all the way, but I have already been glad to take a little water out of a soldier's flask, and eat some ammunition bread. I am now quartered at the head man of the town's house, one of the civilest men I ever met with in my life. The people where I was billeted refused to let me in, so I went to the townhouse and complained, and this gentleman took me and another officer that was with me to his house.

I shall write to my father when we get to the end of our march; I'm glad to hear, with all my heart, that he is well. I'm in the greatest spirits in the world; I have my health pretty well, and I believe I shall be very well able to hold it out with a little help of a horse. Pray be so good to give my duty to my father. This is the best paper St. Tron affords; I have got a sergeant's pen and ink, which are commonly very bad; so I hope you'll excuse everything that is bad in this letter.

I am, dear Madam,

Your dutiful and affectionate Son,

J. Wolfe.

To Mrs. Wolfe, at Burlington Street,
near Burlington Gardens, London.

Only four letters written by Wolfe's brother are extant; the first of these—following the chronological sequence of our narrative—finds place here.

Bonn,* April 7th, 1743.

Dearest Sir,

I am sent here with another gentleman to buy provisions, for we can get none upon our march but eggs and bacon and sour bread; but I have lived upon a soldier's ammunition

* The original is dated "Bonn, April 7, N. S., 1742." However, that it was written in the year 1743 is self-evident. The new year had but just begun. This probably is the letter which Mr. Gleig was led to suppose was written in *Rome*.

bread, which is far preferable to what we find upon the road. We are within two leagues of the Rhine, which, it is most people's opinion, we shall pass the 14th, and then encamp. I have no bedding, nor can get it anywhere; not so much at this place, where the Elector's Court is, which I think a little extraordinary. We had a sad march last Monday in the morning. I was obliged to walk up to my knees in snow, though my brother and I have a horse between us, and at the same time I had it with me. I seldom see him, and had I had the least thoughts of coming to this place, I am sure he would have wrote to you. This is the first opportunity I have had since I wrote to you from Aix-la-Chapelle, which letter I hope you have received.

I do not expect a letter from you, if it does not come by my captain, this great while. I have often lain upon straw, and should oftener had not I known some French, which I find very useful; though I was the other day obliged to speak *Latin* for a good dinner, which if I had not done, I should have gone without it. Most people talk that language here. We send for everything we want to the priest, and if he does not send what he has, we frighten him pretty much. The people are very malicious here and very poor, except the priest and burgermaster, who live upon the republic; but I have had the good luck to be billeted at their houses, where there is everything good but their bread.

We are here at the worst time, for they kill no meat because it is Lent. They say there are many wolves and wild boars in the woods; but I never saw any yet, neither do I desire. Now I think I may end troubling you with my nonsense; but I flatter myself that you have a pleasure in hearing from,

Dear Sir,
Your dutiful and affectionate Son,
EDWARD WOLFE.

Pray my duty to my mother, and I may venture very safely the same from my brother to you both.

Young Edward Wolfe had had more time and opportunity for literary acquirements than his brother had enjoyed; and it is evident that he had availed himself of his advantages. More fortunate than the unlucky surgeon's-mate of the Carthagena expedition, whose knowledge of Greek brought him to grief,* Edward's familiarity with Latin proved of substantial service. A passage in the preceding letter cannot fail to remind the readers of Fielding, of the conversation between Dr. Harrison and the noble lord; and shows how truly the great historical novelist portrayed his own times:—

"'I am persuaded,' says the doctor, 'there is scarce a foot-soldier in the army who is more illiterate than the colonel.'

"'Why, as to Latin and Greek, you know,' replied the lord, 'they are not much required in the army.'"†

Had all the officers' dinners depended upon a Latin speech, it is likely that most of them would have fared worse than the new ensign.‡

Nearly a month later than the last, another letter of Edward's turns up, from which it appears they are drawing near the enemy; he has no misgivings however about the consequences.

On this occasion he writes to his mother:—

Frankfort, May 4th, N. S., 1743.

Dearest Madam,

I don't doubt but you will think me very neglectful

* 'Roderick Random,' ch. xxx.

† 'Amelia,' book xi. ch. ii.

‡ See "The adventure of a company of officers," in 'Tom Jones' (book vii. ch. xii.). "'Grecians and Trojans!' says one of the ensigns, 'who the devil are they? I have heard of all the troops in Europe, but never of any such as these.'"

Fielding, whose father it will be recollected was a General, knew the condition of the army well.

in not writing to you, but I assure you 'tis no fault of mine, for whenever I had an opportunity of sending a letter to you I did it with a great deal of pleasure. I don't expect to hear from you till we have beaten the French, and return to Flanders, which time is very uncertain. We are now within a day's march of the French army, which it is reported we shall soon engage, but there is no credit to be given to half is said here. It is likewise said in case the French should go into Bavaria we shall follow them, which is about two months' march; so I reckon this summer will be spent in that agreeable manner, though I feel no more of it that anybody else, so I am as well contented as if we were marching in England.

I have at last bought my bedding at Frankfort, which place I think has a little the resemblance of London, though not half so large. I reckon you think I have forgot Mrs. Cade, but I assure you I have not, though I must confess there's not a woman in Frankfort, nor indeed in all Germany, that that has half beauty enough to put me in mind of her. Pray be so good to remember me to all our neighbours at Greenwich, and if Mr. Swinden or any one else should ask after me, you will be pleased to mention that was I in a settled place they should have no room to complain of my not writing to them, but now as I am always hurried about in mounting pickets, etc., I am not able to write to any one but where my duty forces me.

I keep my health very well; live merrily, and if it please God that you and my dearest father do yours, nothing else will make me do otherwise. I hope and pray when you write to uncle Brad you will be so good as to make my compliments to them both; and my duty to my father concludes me, dearest Madam,

Your dutiful and affectionate Son,

EDWARD WOLFE.

Nigh as the hostile armies now were to each other, no engagement took place till some weeks later. News from the seat of war was anxiously looked for in London, where it was reported that a battle had been already fought. But it was a false alarm. It appears, however, that on the 9th of June, Lord Stair having heard that the French under the Duc de Noailles were in full march towards the confederate armies, gave orders to the several corps under his command to advance that night to a plain between the forest of Darmstadt and the Maine. At daybreak next morning they were drawn up in line of battle, and so remained until the afternoon, when, the enemy not appearing, they returned to their camps.*

The next of the brothers' letters was written by James. The longest, and by far the most business-like of his productions as yet, it brings matters down to within a few days of the battle of Dettingen.

Camp near Aschaffenburg,
June 21st, 1743, N. S.

Dear Sir,

Captain Rainsford joined the regiment yesterday; he brought us your letter, and made us both very happy with the good news of yours and my mother's health. We also got a letter from you by the post. Your kindness is greater than our best behaviour can deserve, and we are infinitely happy in having so good parents.

My brother is at present very much fatigued with the hard duty he has had for some days past. He was on a party last night, and saw shot fired in earnest, but was in no great danger, because separated from the enemy by the river Mayne.

* 'London Gazette,' no. 8230. Walpole, writing to Sir H. Mann about this time, says:—"The post is come: no battle! Just as they were marching against the French they received orders from Hanover not to engage, for the Queen's Generals thought they were inferior, and were positive against fighting. Lord Stair, with only the English, proceeded, and drew out in order, but though the French were then so vastly superior they did not attack him." (Letters, vol. i. p. 251.)

The French are on the other side that river, about a mile from us. We have now and then small skirmishes with those people. They attacked the other night a party of our men, but were repulsed with the loss of an officer and four or five men killed, and some made prisoners. They desert prodigiously; there were yesterday no less than forty deserters in the camp, that came over in the middle of the day, and brought with them great numbers of horses, for the river is fordable. 'Tis said there are 2000 Austrian hussars come to us; I fancy they will harass them a little. The Hessians, Pulteney's and Bligh's regiments have not yet joined us, as likewise some Hanoverian horse. I believe we only wait for them to attack our enemy. We shall soon know what we are to do now that our King is come. His Majesty came two days ago. The Duke of Cumberland is declared Major-General.

The Earl of Stair had like to have been hurt by an escort of two squadrons of English and Hanoverian cavalry (when he was reconnoitring the enemy), who retreated with a little too much haste before some squadrons of French hussars, who, upon their retreat, fired upon them, and killed a trooper and a dragoon of ours. The reason of the retreat, as I heard, was this,—the word being given to a sergeant and twelve men, who were an advanced guard, to go to the right about, the whole did it, thinking they were ordered, and, I fancy, at the odd and unexpected appearance of the hussars out of a wood. However, they were rallied by General Cope, and would have charged the hussars had they been permitted.

Colonel Duroure, who acts as Adjutant-General, was thrown from his horse yesterday by a Hanoverian discharging his pistol just by him, and was much bruised. We are all sorry for it. He has been very good to his ensigns this march; we have had the use of his canteens whenever he thought we had occasion for them. We are now near forty miles from Frankfort, which we marched in two days and two nights, with about nine or ten hours' halt, in order to gain a pass that is here, and now in our possession. The men were almost starved in that march. They nor the officers had little more than bread and water to live on, and that very scarce, because they had not the ammunition bread the day it was due. But I believe it could not be helped.

We have left a very fine country to come to the worst I ever saw. I believe it is in the Prince of Hesse's dominions. The King is in a little palace in such a town as I believe he never lived in before. It was ruined by the Hanoverians, and everything almost that was in it carried off by them, some time before he came. They and our men now live by marauding. I hope we shall not stay here long; if we do, I don't know how it will be possible to get provisions. The French are burning all the villages on the other side of the Mayne, and we ravaging the country on this side.

I am now doing, and have done ever since we encamped, the duty of an adjutant. I was afraid when I first undertook it that the fatigue would be too much for me, but now I'm used to it, I think it will agree very well with me, at least I hope so. Brigadier Huske inquires often if I have heard from you lately, and desires his compliments to you. He is extremely civil to me, and I am much obliged to him. He has desired his Brigade-Major, Mr. Blakeney, who is a very good man, to instruct me all he can. My brother intends writing very soon. We both join in love and duty to you and my mother, and I am, dear Sir,

Your dutiful and affectionate Son,

J. Wolfe.

CHAPTER III.

CAMPAIGNS.

1743–1745.

When King George II., accompanied by his son the Duke of Cumberland, and his Minister Lord Carteret, arrived at the camp of the allies, he found the army most critically situated. The Earl of Stair, who commanded the British and Hanoverian troops, numbering about 40,000 men, having been joined by some Austrian regiments under the Duke d'Aremberg, the two commanders, instead of concerting for the general welfare, were not only divided in their counsels, but at actual enmity one with the other. The confederates were cooped up in a valley, bounded on one hand by impassable mountains, and on the other by the river Maine, the opposite bank of which was occupied by a French army of 60,000 men, under the most skilful general of the time, the Duc de Noailles. Their reinforcements intercepted and their supplies cut off, the men, already almost starved upon the march, were reduced to half rations, while the horses were dying from want of forage.

Under such circumstances, there remained but "a choice of difficulties" The allies must either surrender to the French army, or, hopeless though the project appeared, attempt a retreat upon Hanau, where their magazines were situated, and where a Hessian and Hanoverian reinforcement of 12,000 men was detained.

The brave old King determined upon the latter alternative. Accordingly, on the evening of Wednesday, the 26th, the troops were ordered to strike their tents, and lie on their arms all night. At daybreak next morning, without beat of drum or sound of trumpet, but "with great secrecy and silence," as they fancied, they began to move. But Noailles no sooner perceived them in motion than he altered his position, and then sent a large detachment of his army, commanded by his nephew, the Duc de Grammont, across the river to the village of Dettingen, there to await the approach of the retiring foe. When the English King saw the French pouring over the bridge, he halted his columns, and immediately drew up his army in order for battle. Meanwhile the French batteries, on the other side of the Maine, opened a deadly fire, and the position which the allies had occupied at Aschaffenburg was already in the enemy's possession.

Had Grammont been prudent enough to wait for the arrival of the retreating army at the defile near Dettingen, no human power could have saved it from destruction; but, fortunately for the allies, the impetuous Frenchman, forsaking his advantageous position, passed the ravine, and advanced upon his opponents, now ready to receive him upon an equal footing. Noailles, certain as he was of his prey, when informed of his lieutenant's fatal error, was struck with dismay; and after ordering his batteries, to which his own men were now exposed, to cease their fire, he advanced with the remainder of his army to the assistance of Grammont's division. But too late!

This preliminary sketch will serve to introduce the simple account of the battle which young Edward Wolfe sent home to his mother.

June 19th, O. S. [30th, N. S.], 1743.

Dearest Madam,

I take the very first opportunity I can to acquaint you that my brother and self escaped in the engagement we had with the French, the 16th June last [O. S.], and, thank God, are as well as ever we were in our lives, after not only being cannonaded two hours and three-quarters, and fighting with small arms two hours and one-quarter, but lay the two following nights upon our arms, whilst it rained for about twenty hours in the same time; yet are ready and as capable to do the same again. We lost one captain and a lieutenant. Captain Rainsford is very well, and not wounded; he desires you will send his wife word of this as soon as you hear it. Our colonel had a horse shot under him, but escaped himself. The King was present in the field. The Duke of Cumberland behaved charmingly.* . . . .
Duke d'Aremberg is dangerously wounded. We took two or three general officers, and two princes of the blood, and wounded Marshal Noailles.

Our regiment has got a great deal of honour, for we were in the middle of the first line, and in the greatest danger.†

* "Le roi Georges, qui, au sortir de l'enfance, avait combattu à Oudenarde, haïssait les Français comme un élève d'Eugène et de Marlborough. Le second de ses fils, le duc de Cumberland, depuis guerrier distingué, quoique rarement heureux, l'accompagnait, et c'était comme un autre *Prince Noir* marchant à côté d'un autre Édouard." (Lacretelle, tome ii. 257.)

† According to the official returns, "Duroure's" had twenty-nine officers and soldiers killed, and sixty-eight wounded; more than any other regiment.

. . . .

My brother has wrote to my father, and I believe has given him a small account of the battle, so I hope you will excuse it me. The Emperor is come to Frankfort, and we are encamped about two leagues from it; and it is said that the King is to meet him there, and that there's a peace to be made between the Queen of Hungary and the Emperor.

I hope I shall see you some time or another, and then tell you more; but think now that I have given you joy and concern enough. Pray, my duty to my dearest father, who I hope is well.

I am, dearest Madam,

Your dutiful and affectionate Son,

E. WOLFE.

Pray be so good to excuse my writing for this time, I am in such a hurry to send you this news.*

The substance of the paragraphs struck out from the above are repeated by James in his more detailed and masterly report to his father.

Höchst, July 4th, N. S., 1743.

Dear Sir,

This is the first time that I have been able or have had the least time to write, otherwise I should have done it when my brother did. The fatigue I had the day we fought and the day after made me very much out of order, and I was obliged to keep my tent for two days. Bleeding was of great service to me, and I am now as well as ever.

The army was drawn out this day se'nnight between a wood and the river Maine, near a little village, called Dettingen, in five lines—two of foot and three of horse. The cannon on both sides began to play about nine o'clock in the morning, and we were exposed to the fire of theirs (said to

* The writing, penned though the letter was in the confusion of a camp tent, probably on the end of a trunk, is very creditable; the spelling, too, with one exception, is correct. Many a competitor for a Government appointment now does far worse.

be above fifty pieces) for near three hours, a great part of which flanked us terribly from the other side the water. The French were all the while drawn up in sight of us on this side. About twelve o'clock we marched towards them; they advanced likewise, and, as near as I can guess, the fight began about one. The *Gens d'Armes,** or *Mousquetaires Gris*, attacked the first line, composed of nine regiments of English foot, and four or five of Austrians, and some Hanoverians. They broke through the Scotch Fusileers, who they began the attack upon; but before they got to the second line, out of two hundred there were not forty living, so they wheeled, and came between the first and second line (except an officer with a standard, and four or five men, who broke through the second line and were taken by some of Hawley's regiment of Dragoons), and about twenty of them escaped to their army, riding through an interval that was made for our Horse to advance. These unhappy men were of the first families in France. Nothing, I believe, could be more rash than their undertaking.

The second attack was made on the left by their Horse against ours, which advanced for the first time. Neither side did much, for they both retreated; and our Horse had like to have broke our first line in the confusion. The Horse† fired their pistols, which, if they had let alone, and attacked the

* "An Officer of Foot," describing the attack, writes:—"The *Gens d'Armes* behaved most charmingly; they rode up to us on a full trot, with a broad-sword slung on their wrists, and a pistol in each hand, which, as soon as they had fired, they flung at our heads, and fell on sword in hand." ('British Glory Revived,' London, 1743, p. 39.)

† The conduct of the "Blues" is severely censured in the periodicals of the day. But an officer of the corps ascribes their error to impetuosity, and, though he admits that they may have shown want of experience, stoutly repels the charge of cowardice. "I can't help observing," concludes the advocate, "that this repulse was lucky in its consequences, and not a little instrumental in gaining the victory; for the French household troops, flushed with their success, ran in directly upon the line of our infantry, who flanked them, gave them their whole fire, and almost tore them to pieces." See Gentleman's Mag., vol. xiii. p. 381.

French with their swords, being so much stronger and heavier, they would certainly have beat them. Their excuse for retreating—they could not make their horses stand the fire!

The third and last attack was made by the Foot on both sides. We advanced towards one another; our men in high spirits, and very impatient for fighting, being elated with beating the French Horse, part of which advanced towards us; while the rest attacked our Horse, but were soon driven back by the great fire we gave them. The Major and I (for we had neither Colonel nor Lieutenant-Colonel), before they came near, were employed in begging and ordering the men not to fire at too great a distance, but to keep it till the enemy should come near us; but to little purpose. The whole fired when they thought they could reach them, which had like to have ruined us. We did very little execution with it. So soon as the French saw we presented they all fell down, and when we had fired they got up, and marched close to us in tolerable good order, and gave us a brisk fire, which put us into some disorder and made us give way a little, particularly ours and two or three more regiments, who were in the hottest of it. However, we soon rallied again, and attacked them with great fury, which gained us a complete victory, and forced the enemy to retire in great haste. 'Twas luck that we did give way a little, for our men were loading all the while, and it gave room for an Austrian regiment to move into an interval, rather too little before, who charged the enemy with great bravery and resolution. So soon as the French retreated, the line halted, and we got the sad news of the death of as good and brave a man as any amongst us, General Clayton, who was killed by a musquet ball in the last attack.* His death gave us all sorrow, so great was the opinion we had of him, and was the hindrance of anything further being done that day.† He had, 'tis said, orders for pursuing the

* The General's body was found stripped on the field. The Gazette notices the death of this distinguished officer without a single remark of panegyric or regret.

† The Gazette attributes the non-pursuit of the enemy to caution on the part of Lord Stair, who, "not thinking it prudent to venture the

enemy, and if we had followed them, as was expected, it is the opinion of most people, that of 27,000 men they brought over the Maine, they would not have repassed with half that number. When they retreated, several pieces of our artillery played upon them, and made terrible havoc; at last we followed them, but too late; they had almost all passed the river.* One of the bridges broke, and in the hurry abundance were drowned. A great number of their officers and men were taken prisoners. Their loss is computed to be between six and seven thousand men, and ours three thousand.

His Majesty was in the midst of the fight; and the Duke behaved as bravely as a man could do. He had a musquet-shot through the calf of his leg. I had several times the honour of speaking with him just as the battle began, and was often afraid of his being dash'd to pieces by the cannon-balls. He gave his orders with a great deal of calmness, and seemed quite unconcerned.† The soldiers were in high delight to have him so near them. Captain Rainsford behaved with the greatest conduct and bravery in the world. I sometimes thought I had lost poor Ned, when I saw arms, legs, and heads beat off close by him. He is called "The Old

Horse into the wood till the Foot could come up, ordered the former to halt; but most of the enemy had by this time repassed the river, either over the bridges or fords, where in the hurry many of them were drowned."

* "La retraite précipitée des Gardes-Françaises devint un sujet de plaisanterie parmi les autres corps de l'armée. On les nomma les *Canards du Mein*, et ce sobriquet fit, pendant cinquante ans, répandre beaucoup de sang dans des duels." (Lacretelle, tome ii. 260.)

† So much has been written upon the cruelty of the Royal Duke's disposition, that it is no more than fair to show it in a more favourable light. Earl Russell relates the following anecdote, after Voltaire ('Histoire de mon Temps'):—"The Duke of Cumberland gave a proof of his courage and humanity. He was wounded in the leg, and a surgeon was about to extract the ball, when the Duke perceived a French mousquetaire of the name of Girardau, on the ground. 'Begin,' he said, 'with the French officer; he is more wounded than I am, and I shall be certain of assistance, which he is not.'" (Memoirs of the Affairs of Europe, etc., London, 1829, vol. ii. p. 179.)

Soldier," and very deservedly. A horse I rid of the Colonel's at the first attack was shot in one of his hinder legs, and threw me; so I was obliged to do the duty of an adjutant all that and the next day on foot, in a pair of heavy boots. I lost with the horse, furniture and pistols which cost me ten ducats; but three days after the battle got the horse again, with the ball in him,—and he is now almost well again,—but without furniture and pistols.

A brigade of English and another of Hanoverians are in garrison in this town, which we are fortifying daily. We are detached from the grand army, which is encamped between Frankfort and Hanau, about twelve miles off.

They talk of a second battle soon. Count Khevenhüller* and Marshal Broglie are expected to join the two armies in a few days. We are very well situated at present, and in a plentiful country. Had we stayed a few days longer at Aschaffenburg we had been all starved, for the French would have cut off our communication with Frankfort. Poor Captain Merrydan is killed. Pray, mine and my brother's duty to my mother. We hope you are both perfectly well.

I am, dear Sir,

Your dutiful and affectionate Son,

J. Wolfe.

It has already been stated that the ensign, when quartered in Ghent, was preparing himself for a wider sphere of action than carrying colours. Yet one cannot but be astonished to find a boy under seventeen years of age, who had had little more than a year's military experience, adequate to the post of adjutant, and that, too, in the field. The duties of this office do not much

* Field-Marshal Andrew, Count of Khevenhüller-Frankenburg. There is no name more renowned in Austria than that of Khevenhüller, or one that can boast of having rendered more signal services to the sovereign. An interesting account of the family castle on the shore of the Attar See, and a letter of the Empress Maria Theresa's to the Count, may be found in the 'Parthenon,' December 27, 1862.

differ now from what they were in Wolfe's time; and in these "Volunteer" days it would be supererogatory to explain them.* "To be able to command men properly," says an old military writer, "we should first know them, to have seen them in different stations, to watch the most minute movements of their souls, to distinguish their talents, to form and employ them *à propos*. There is no profession in which all this is so absolutely necessary as that of arms; it is impossible for a man who fails in these respects to command a discipline, that is to say, to form soldiers for the most laborious and fatiguing exercises, to wean them from any kind of will or opinion, to reduce them to an obedience the most exact and implicit, and from stubborn clowns to form machines only animated by the voice of their officers, beats of drum, or sounds of fife. Every one certainly has not these talents; a man may be alert in his business and expert in conducting a march, commanding a company, or even a regiment, but yet very far from being able to make a perfect adjutant. It is therefore evident that the discipline should not be trusted but to sensible and experienced officers."†

From the fact of a mere youth's filling so onerous a post, two inferences may be drawn; first, the incapacity of older officers, and secondly, the extraordinary vigour and ability of the young soldier. We also have good proof that he performed the trying duties he had volunteered with applause; for within five days after the battle he was appointed adjutant of his regiment, by

* See Grose's 'Military Antiquities.'

† 'The Military Guide,' by Thomas Simes, Esq.

royal commission,* and a few days later was promoted to a lieutenancy.† But,

"Not once or twice in our rough island story,
The path of duty was the way to glory."

Yet it would be wrong to conclude that mere merit, or the strictest attention to the routine business of a company officer, would have been sufficient to gain promotion in those corrupt times, when hundreds of meritorious men remained subalterns all their lives. For, as the "noble lord," in continuation of the dialogue before quoted from, exclaims, "My dear, dear Sir, what is the merit of a subaltern officer?" It is therefore to the rare talent for command exhibited by Wolfe so early in his career, that his rapid advancement must be attributed.

The discomfiture of the French army opened a passage for the allies to Hanau, whither they marched the morning after the battle, leaving the wounded to the care of the enemy, who treated them with great humanity, and buried the dead. At Hanau, the allied army being joined by reinforcements, it was proposed by Lord Stair that they should follow up their victory; but owing to the rivalry of the generals nothing was done, and his lordship resigned his command in disgust.‡

In the meantime the expectations of the people in England were at the highest pitch. Even an invasion

* Dated, "Head Quarters at Hanau, July 2 (o. s.), 1743." Signed, "George." Countersigned, "Carteret."

† July 14 (o. s.), as above.

‡ The Earl of Stair being asked by a French officer what he thought of the battle of Dettingen, is said to have replied, "You committed one mistake and we committed two; yours was, passing the hollow way and not having patience to wait; ours were, exposing ourselves to destruction, and then not making a proper use of our victory."

of France was anticipated. "I flatter myself," writes Walpole to Sir Horace Mann, "they will tempt no more battles. Another such, and we might march from one end of France to the other." But the King crossed the Rhine at Mayence, and fixed his head-quarters at Worms, whence the adjutant and lieutenant of Duroure's writes to his father:—

Camp near Worms, Sept. 1, N. S., 1743.

Dear Sir,

By a letter I received from you some days ago, I had the happiness and satisfaction to hear that you and my mother are well; but it being my brother's turn to write (which we intend to do by turns every Saturday), I put off answering it until to-day.

The army passed the Rhine the 23rd, N. S., a little below Mentz, and came to this ground yesterday. It was possessed by the French before the action of Dettingen. The fortifications of the Swiss camp (who would not pass the Rhine) are just by, and those where the bridge was that the French went over upon is close to it. The boats that made our bridge below Mentz are expected here to-morrow for the Dutch troops to come over, who, we hear, will be with us in six or seven days. There are numbers of reports relating to Prince Charles's army, so that I won't pretend to send you any account of it, only that most people think he has not passed the Rhine. The French are now encamped between Landau and Wissemberg. Captain Rainsford says if they have any spirit they will attack us here before we are joined by the Dutch, and so I believe our commanders think, for they have just given orders to have all encumbrances removed from before the front of each regiment, in order to turn out at a minute's warning, and a chain of sentries are to be immediately placed in front of the camp. Our camp is tolerable strong; we are open in the front, with hills, from which cannon cannot do us much harm. At the bottom of these hills is a little rivulet; in our rear is the Rhine. The left is secured by the town of Worms, and the right is open; but neither the front nor right have greater openings than we have troops to fill them up; so I believe we are pretty safe. I am just now told that a party of our hussars have taken a French grand guard; they have killed the captain and thirteen men, and have brought sixty-four to Worms. I'm convinced of the truth, because some gentlemen of our regiment saw them go along the line, and are going to buy some of the horses. I cannot tell if the Duke of Cumberland knows what you mentioned in your letter; I have never had any opportunity of inquiring. It is but a few days that he is come abroad: he has marched, since we crossed the Rhine, at the head of his second line of English, which is his post. He is very brisk, and quite cured of his wound. His presence encourages the troops, and makes them ready to undertake anything, having so brave a man at the head of them. I hope some day or other to have the honour of knowing him better than I do now; 'tis what I wish as much as anything in the world (except the pleasure which I hope to enjoy when it shall please God), that of seeing my dear friends at Greenwich. Poor Colonel Duroure is, I am afraid, in great danger; we left him on the other side of the Rhine very ill with a bloody flux. Our major is at the same place likewise, very much out of order. Our colonel was never more wanted to command us than now.

I shall say nothing now of the behaviour of the Blue Guards; I wish they may do better next time, and I don't doubt but they will. It would give me a great deal of sorrow if they did not.

We have a great deal of sickness amongst us, so I believe the sooner we engage (if it is to be) the better. I hope you, Sir, and my mother are perfectly well. I heartily wish it, and that you may continue so. My brother joins with me in duty and love to both.

I am, dear Sir,

Your dutiful and affectionate Son,

J. Wolfe.

The French made no attack upon the camp at Worms. Prince Charles of Lorraine having driven De Broglie across the Rhine, near Manheim, Maréchal de Noailles, finding himself placed between two great hostile armies, destroyed his own magazines and withdrew to the French frontier on the Lauter, leaving all Germany unoccupied by an enemy. The King of England returned to London, and the campaign of 1743 was at an end.

Although the result of the year's warfare was by no means commensurate to the popular expectations, his Majesty was heartily welcomed home by his people. Handel had set to work immediately after the news of the victory arrived, once more to compose music for the sublime hymn attributed to St. Ambrose, and produced upon this occasion the last and grandest of his *Te Deums*. Five times within the space of thirty years the great composer set the same words, and "always with new beauties, always with a fresh colour;"* for although, as is asserted by an excellent authority, he borrowed ten movements of the *Dettingen Te Deum*, without acknowledgment, from an old Italian master, yet he "picked up a pebble and changed it to a diamond."† After two rehearsals in Whitehall Chapel, the *Te Deum* and Anthem were solemnly sung before the King on the 27th of November in the Royal Chapel of St. James's.

It seems to bring those old times nearer to us when we read in Mrs. Delany's letter:—"Mrs. Percival came to invite us to dine with her yesterday, and to go in the

* Schœlcher's 'Life of Handel,' p. 283.

† Vincent Novello, in the preface to his edition of Purcell's Sacred Music, quoted from Schœlcher, p. 284.

morning to Whitehall Chapel to hear Mr. Handel's new *Te Deum* rehearsed, and an anthem. It is excessively fine. I was all rapture, and so was your friend D. D., as you may imagine. Everybody says it is the finest of his compositions. I am not well enough acquainted with it to pronounce that of it; but it is heavenly."*

The excitement of the populace in consequence of the battle of Dettingen was excessive. That incomparable letter-writer who "scoffed at Courts and kept a chronicle of their most trifling scandal," but who, nevertheless, depicts the passing events of his day most vividly, tells his friend Mr. Chute:—"I expect to be drunk with hogsheads of Maine-water, and with odes to his Majesty and the Duke, and *Te Deums*. . . . We are all mad—drums, trumpets, bumpers, bonfires! The mob are wild, and cry, "Long live King George, and the Duke of Cumberland, and Lord Stair, and Lord Carteret, and General Clayton, that's dead!"†

While such was the prevailing delirium at home, the camp at Worms was broken up, and the regiments repaired to their old stations for the winter. Duroure's formed part of the fifth division, under Major-General the Earl of Rothes, and reached Brussels on the 22nd of November, whence the regiment marched to Ostend, where the Adjutant remained until the opening of the ensuing campaign.‡

The fatigue and excitement of the late campaign were too trying for the delicate constitution and gentle dispo-

* Autobiography, vol. ii. p. 222.

† Walpole's Letters (Cunningham), vol. i. p. 255.

‡ Records of the British Army (Cannon), Twelfth regiment.

sition of young Edward Wolfe, and as his regiment was now stationed so near England, he embraced the opportunity to visit home and enjoy for a short time the quiet and comfort of the paternal roof. Although James likewise was by no means a strong or hardy youth, yet his military enthusiasm and invincible spirit, apparently at least, counteracted for the present any detriment which his health may have suffered by the hardships he had undergone. "Don't tell me of constitution," said he, years afterwards, when it was remarked that a certain officer, who had been ill, was a poor puny creature; "he has good spirits, and good spirits will carry a man through everything." These words arose from his personal experience. It is evident that his own spirits were good at this time, from the following letter, the only one that exists of the correspondence between the brothers:—

Ostend, March 21st, O. S., Wednesday, 1744.

Dear Ned,

I got yours of yesterday from Dover by a gentleman who was so good to take it up and bring it to me from thence. I expected to have had my box at the same time, for I thought our going to England (or rather the appearance of it) was entirely laid aside. I shall be obliged to you if you'll take the first opportunity of sending it. I want it very much. I have not a pair of boots I can wear. The regiment will be out soon for exercise. You and I are to be tented together next campaign. The marquee is making, and will cost us about £4. I shall send to Ghent very soon to bespeak a cart, which, with harness for two horses, I'm told will come to £10 or thereabouts. I shall get everything I find necessary for us; so you need not be in any pain about your equipage.

I think Rainsford is not so brutal as to send you from England, who have done all his duty, these three or four months. Sure he knows better. I have a better opinion of his understanding.

I hear of no promotion in the regiment, except Thickhead* has got his father's company. Stephens is certainly going out. He is to be surgeon to the second troop of Horse Guards, and sell his employment with us; so you'll get a step by that. Ryder, I believe, will get the surgeonship.

I'm glad you find the mantua-maker pretty; I thought so, I assure you. I give up all pretensions. Pray use her kindly. Doubtless you love the company of the fair sex. If you should happen to go where Miss Seabourg is, pray don't fall in love with her. I can't give her up tamely. Remember I'm your rival. I'm also in some pain about Miss W——. Admire anywhere else and welcome (except the widow Bright). Miss Patterson is yours if you like her, and so is the little staring girl in the chapel, with £20,000. Pray give my duty to my mother. I hope she is well. The plum-cake she gave me was very good, and of singular service to me.† I don't believe the box would hold any. They say it is particularly wholesome at Ostend.

I am, dear Ned,
Sincerely yours,
J. Wolfe.

N'oubliez point mes complimens à ces adorables femmes, que je viens de nommer.

To Captain‡ Wolfe, at Brigadier Wolfe's, in
Old Burlington Street, Burlington Gardens, London.

Fortune favoured the Wolfe family in the first half of the year 1744. In February the Colonel had been promoted to the rank of Brigadier-General, and on the 3rd of June James obtained his commission as Captain in the

* "Thickhead," Lieutenant Romer, whom Edward Wolfe succeeded.

† Two large volumes, containing Mrs. Wolfe's receipts, carefully written by various female hands, are still extant.

‡ The title of "Captain" was merely complimentary. Edward was still an Ensign.

Fourth, or King's Regiment of Foot, commanded by Lieutenant-General Barrell. Edward also, on his return to the Continent, rejoined his old corps as Lieutenant; and both Barrell's and Duroure's joined the army under the command of Field-Marshal Wade, at the camp near the banks of the Scheldt, where the allies lay for some time inactive.

Cardinal Fleury having died in 1743, the French Government abandoning all care for economy, determined to use every means in order, if possible, to render the reign of Louis XV. as glorious as his predecessor's. *Le Bien-aimé*, now in the fortieth year of his age, and in person, at least, every inch a king, took the field early in May, 1744, with an army of 120,000 men under the immediate command of Maréchal Saxe. On the 15th of the month Louis arrived at Lisle, and on the 18th Courtrai surrendered to him,—a loss to the allies that was speedily followed by the fall of Menin and of Ypres. Menin, situated about ten miles south-east of Ypres, though but a small town, was remarkable for the strength of its fortifications, which were considered a masterpiece,* and the city of Ypres, one of the barriers of the Austrian Low Countries, though esteemed impregnable, was shamefully delivered up by the Dutch garrison almost as soon as the French came before it, together with the whole chartelary.† Some account of affairs at this juncture

* "The French battering cannon were of the first order and their engineers of the highest reputation. These advantages depend more upon schools of science and regular magazines than any other of the means of warfare, and in these the superiority of the French was undisputed." (Lord Russell's 'Memoirs of the Affairs of Europe,' etc., vol. ii. p. 184.)

† Simes's Military Guide.

will be found in a letter from Edward Wolfe to his father:—

Camp near Berlingham, June 17th, o. s., 1744.

Dear Sir,

I am sorry to inform you of so disagreeable a piece of news as Ypres being surrendered after a siege of eight days. No doubt but it gives great spirits to our enemy, who, 'tis said, have lost very few men; but I have not yet heard their loss.

We have some expectations of their visiting us next. They have a party of men very near our advanced guard, on the other side of the Scheldt. However, we are prepared for them; so they won't find it very easy to pass that river. We suspect the designs of Duke d'Harcourt, with his army, between thirty and forty thousand men, who, 'tis said, are encamped between Mons and Mauberge. Our last motion, I'm told, retarded the siege of Ypres two days. They, expecting we were coming towards them, were under arms a quarter of an hour after we left our ground.

I have a list of our army, which I would willingly send you, but Major Rainsford gave it me, and desired I would be cautious of showing it, and advised me not to venture sending it over. We are in hopes of the six English regiments coming to join us with 6000 Dutch. The wind has been fair for bringing them to Ostend; but we don't hear they are landed.

Duke de Chartres was killed at the siege of Ypres. He was one of their chiefs, and a very experienced officer. The French had a hundred pieces of cannon and five or six batteries of small mortars. The taking of the town is really no great feat, if we consider the strength of the garrison, which was said to be but four weak battalions.

I wrote to my dear mother by Sergeant Somerset, who I suppose will be with you before you receive this. I don't doubt but she is in some apprehensions of our being in danger; but I hope she'll not fright herself while we continue in health, as we are both now. We have had no fatigue yet in comparison of that we had in Germany; but nobody knows what we may have. We are here a defensive army, and fewer in numbers than we were last campaign; still we never despair of coming off with laurels whenever we meet our enemy. Our men keep up their spirits. The taking of these two towns and the number of men they imagine the French have does not in the least deject them, but makes them only wish for a meeting. My brother desires his duty to you and my dearest mother.

I am, dearest Sir,

Your dutiful and affectionate Son,

EDW. WOLFE.

I return you many thanks for my Lieutenancy.

The day after the above letter was written Fort Knocque surrendered to the Duc de Boufflers, and on the 11th of July Count de Clermont fixed the French colours on the walls of Furness.* But the further progress of the arms of France in Flanders was at length arrested by the news that Prince Charles of Lorraine, at the head of an Austrian army of 60,000 men, had passed the Rhine, and driven the French before him to the ramparts of Strasburg. Consequently Louis, to avert the impending danger, withdrew with half of his forces, leaving Saxe with the remainder to maintain their conquests. The allies had now a favourable opportunity of effecting some important operations, but the jealousy of D'Aremberg, the Austrian general, and the tardiness of the Dutch, under Count Maurice of Nassau, frustrated Wade's designs, and the campaign ended ingloriously.

* Dr. Challice, 'Secret History of the Court of France under Louis XV.'

The year which had opened so prosperously was destined not to close without bringing a great affliction to the Wolfes. In October young Edward fell, but not by war. Although we are not informed of what disease he died, there can be but little doubt that it was consumption, accelerated by the hardships of campaigning, against which his frail frame was ill adapted to struggle. The mortal blow was all the heavier, in that the amiable "old soldier" departed amongst strangers in a foreign land. Even his brother, though not far distant,—ignorant of, or perhaps, in the hopefulness of youth, unwilling to realize the near approach of death,—was not by to comfort his last moments; for, unaware how imminent was the danger, James was restrained by a sense of duty from quitting his post. It is satisfactory, however, to be assured that the dying lad was attended by a faithful servant; and though his death-bed was unwatched by any member of his own family, it is reasonable to conclude that among his brother-officers he found the sympathy and attention of a friend; for all the family—father, mother, and sons—were endowed with the power of winning the friendship of those, either of higher, equal, or lower rank, with whom they came in contact.

The loss of their younger son was keenly felt by the Brigadier and Mrs. Wolfe, and the sorrow of the bereaved brother is pathetically expressed in a letter to his mother soon after the sad occurrence.

Ghent, 29th October, 1744, O. S.

Dear Madam,

I received your letter this morning with a great deal of

pleasure, and have with this wrote to my father about coming to England. I hope he will be able to get the better of some obstacles, and I shall be sincerely happy.

Poor Ned wanted nothing but the satisfaction of seeing his dearest friends to leave the world with the greatest tranquillity. He often called on us. It gives me many uneasy hours when I reflect on the possibility there was of my being with him some time before he died. God knows it was being too exact, and not apprehending the danger the poor fellow was in; and even that would not have hindered it had I received the physician's first letter. I know you won't be able to read this paragraph without shedding tears, as I do writing it; but there is a satisfaction even in giving way to grief now and then. 'Tis what we owe the memory of a dear friend.

Though it is the custom of the army to sell the deceased's effects, I could not suffer it. We none of us want, and I thought the best way would be to bestow them on the deserving whom he had an esteem for in his lifetime. To his servant—the most honest and faithful man I ever knew—I gave all his clothes. . . . I gave his horse to his friend Parry, with the furniture. I know he loved Parry, and I know for that reason the horse will be taken care of. His other horse I keep myself. I have his watch, sash, gorget, books, and maps, which I shall preserve to his memory. Everything else that I have not mentioned shall be taken care of, and given to proper persons.

He was an honest and a good lad, had lived very well, and always discharged his duty with the cheerfulness becoming a good officer. He lived and died as a son of you two should, which, I think, is saying all I can. I have the melancholy satisfaction to find him regretted by his friends and acquaintances. His Colonel is particularly concerned for him, and desired I would assure you of it. There was in him the prospect (when ripened with experience) of good understanding and judgment, and an excellent soldier. You'll excuse my dwelling so long on this cruel subject, but in relating this to you, vanity and partiality are banished. A strong desire to do justice to his memory occasions it.

There was no part of his life that makes him dearer to me than that where you have often mentioned—*he pined after me.* It often makes me angry that any hour of my life should pass without thinking of him; and when I do think of him, that though all the reasons I have to lament his loss are now as forcible as at the moment of his departure, I don't find my heart swell with the same sorrow as it did at that time. Nature is ever too good in blotting out the violence of affliction. For all tempers (as mine is) too much given to mirth, it is often necessary to revive grief in one's memory. I must once more beg you will excuse my tiresome length and manner of writing, but I know your indulgence. I'm just now going to write to my uncle Wolfe.

I am, dearest Madam,
Your dutiful and affectionate Son,
J. Wolfe.

The character of his brother is so clearly and touchingly drawn by Wolfe, that even if it came within our scope it would be unnecessary to dilate upon the brief earthly career of one who may be classed with those who "come like shadows, so depart." We have done with the Old Soldier. "He shall return no more to his house, neither shall his place know him any more."

It is not surprising that our young Captain should have looked forward with aversion to the prospect of passing another winter in Ghent, and that in the loneliness of his heart he longed for the society of his home. But, unfortunately, the obstacles he anticipated proved to be insurmountable. In fact, it may safely be concluded that he was too useful an officer to be spared; and consequently, upon this, as well as upon many future occasions, he was denied the indulgence granted to others less worthy of it. He was very sensitive to such denials; but whatever momentary resentment he may have felt, he did not neglect his duty. Indeed, mere duty did not reach his standard, and his sorrow was ere long dissipated in strenuous action; for, as during his former abode in the old Flemish capital he had mastered the qualifications of an adjutant, so now, during the winter of 1744–5, he prepared himself for the higher position of Brigade-Major—an office he was soon called upon to fill. Thus early did he court responsibility, and, as it were, try his wings, in order to soar in due time to the lofty goal which he ever kept in view.

A few years ago, the fragment of a letter in Wolfe's handwriting was discovered in Glasgow. Though written subsequently, it depicts his own youthful behaviour, as well as exhibits his regard for the dignity of his profession. The cover being lost, the name of the young officer to whom the letter was written cannot be told; it only appears that he had recently joined Lord Charles Hay's regiment, and he is addressed as "Dear Huty."* Omitting the practical details, a brief quotation will answer our purpose:—"The field you are now going into is quite new to you, but may be trod very safely if you only get into it by the proper entrance. I make

* This interesting fragment was found in the old military chest belonging to Colonel Rickson, along with Wolfe's letters to him. It appears to have been written in the year 1756 or 1757, and probably was addressed to Mr. *Hugh* Lort, a nephew of Rickson's. The handwriting is undoubtedly Wolfe's, and, by a curious coincidence, the water-mark of the paper, *Pro Patria*, resembles his family motto, *Pro Patriæ amore*. See 'Notes and Queries,' vol. v. (1852), p. 249.

no doubt but you have entirely laid aside the boy and all boyish amusements, and have considered yourself a young man going into a manly profession, where you must be answerable for your conduct. Your character in life must be that of a soldier and a gentleman; the first is to be acquired by application and attendance upon your duty, the second by adhering most strictly to the dictates of honour and the rules of good breeding."

Although enough has been preserved to enable us to judge of Wolfe's early conduct, it is to be regretted that we have not that portion of the letter wherein he dilated upon honour and good breeding, as, from his counsel upon these points, we should probably have learned the secret by means of which, in spite of his fiery temperament, he won and retained for life the friendship of his brother-officers.

In April, 1745, another campaign opened in Flanders. There had been a change in the English Government in November, 1744, in consequence of the resignation of Lord Carteret. But the new Ministry, notwithstanding their outcry against the Hanoverian policy while in Opposition, continued to pursue the same course as their predecessors. Parliament had voted half a million sterling for the Queen of Hungary, besides large subsidies to the petty princes; and an alliance was concluded between England, Austria, Holland, and Saxony.

The Duke of Cumberland was nominated Commander-in-chief of the allied forces, though subject to the control of the Austrian General, Marshal Königsegg; and altogether, the confederates numbered but 50,000 men, while France sent 80,000 into the field under Maréchal Saxe. The French began the campaign by besieging Tournay, to the relief of which city the allies immediately advanced. Saxe therefore, leaving a detachment to cover the blockade, drew up his army behind the town of Fontenoy, where was fought the fatal battle, a brief account of which is contained in the following letter.

Ghent, 4th May, o. s., 1745.

Dear Sir,

I'm concerned I must send you so melancholy an account of a great but unsuccessful attempt to raise the siege of Tournay.* I shall just tell you what a letter before me from Captain Field, who commanded Colonel Duroure's regiment, says of it:—

"We attacked a numerous army, entrenched with a multiplicity of batteries, well placed both in front and flank. The action began the 30th of April [o. s.], about five o'clock in the morning, and lasted till two in the afternoon. There has been a great deal of slaughter, particularly amongst the infantry, officers more in proportion than soldiers. The enemy's army were supposed to be 70,000, and ours about 50,000. The soldiery behaved with the utmost bravery and courage during the whole affair, but rather rash and impetuous. Notwithstanding the bravest attempts were made to conquer, it was not possible for us to surmount the difficulties we met with."†

* Tournay, a strong and beautiful city, divided into two parts by that river, over which are several bridges, thirty miles south of Ghent, and thirteen miles south-east of Menin. Henry VIII. besieged and took it in 1513 and built a citadel; but it was delivered to the French again, upon a treaty of marriage between the Dauphin and the Princess Mary. The Spaniards took it in 1581, but the French surprised it again in 1667. Whilst in their hands, its fortifications were brought to great perfection. Vauban built a citadel, which he called his masterpiece. All the works were undermined, and in that consisted its chief strength, as the allies found by dear-bought experience, when they besieged it in 1709.

† "The soldiers have spirit enough to undertake anything, and say

Thus the gentleman speaks of the affair. The army made a fine retreat, in such order that the French did not think proper to pursue them. The Duke, I hear, has shown in this action most unparalleled bravery, but was very sensibly touched when he found himself obliged to give over the attack.* The Hanoverians have shown themselves good troops, and the Blues have regained their reputation, having been several times broken by two battalions, as often rallied, and returned with fresh vigour to the charge. The French go on with the siege of Tournay, and will have it very soon. We expect every hour to be ordered into the field, and replaced by a weak battalion. Our army is encamped at Ath, and I'm afraid will make but an indifferent defensive figure the rest of the campaign. I shall write to-day to Major Rainsford, for an exact return of the loss our troops sustained. In the meanwhile, I will give you an account of some unfortunate men that have fallen, and some others that are wounded, down to the majors, though we are not yet exactly sure. I will be particular in your regiment (of which I wish you much joy), because I imagine you will be glad to know how it goes with them, as I had it this morning from the Paymaster.† No officers killed, but several wounded, and them you'll find hereafter to be very good ones:—Colonel Keightley; Major Grey; Captains Dallow, Loftus, Hill, Ekins. Subs, Rickson, etc. . . . I don't hear that any of their wounds are mortal.

. . . .

The old regiment [Duroure's] has suffered very much; 18 officers and 300 men, killed and wounded; amongst the latter is Major Rainsford. I believe this account will shock you not

they don't doubt of 'winning the rubber;' that Dettingen and Fontenoy are 'only game and game.'" (Lady Sarah Cowper to Mrs. Dewes.) See Mrs. Delany's Autobiography, vol. ii. p. 354.

* See Mrs. Delany, as above.

† The Eighth, or King's Own regiment of Foot, of which Brigadier-General Wolfe had been appointed Colonel on the 25th of April, in room of Major-General Onslow.

a little; but 'tis surprising the number of officers of lower rank that are gone.* Pray, my duty to my mother.

I am, dear Sir,
Your dutiful and affectionate Son,
J. Wolfe.

As it has turned out, we may thank Providence we were not there.

Wolfe was as lucky in quitting Ghent in good time, as in not having been present at Fontenoy. After the battle, his regiment was ordered to relieve one of those that had suffered in the engagement; and, on the 21st of May, joined the army encamped upon the plains of Lessines.† Having taken Tournay, the French, on the 30th June, surprised Ghent; and a reinforcement sent by the allies, under the Hanoverian General, Molke, having been routed in a skirmish at Mêlle after five days' siege, the citadel surrendered. Ostend fell next.

Such was the situation of affairs on the Continent, when the Government was obliged to withdraw the British forces from Flanders, to assist in suppressing the Jacobite rebellion in Scotland. In London, no *Te Deum* was sung this year. The French Marshal, "Bully Belle-isle," who had been for some time in England a prisoner, declared "that he saw we were so little capable of making any defence, that he would engage, with 5000 scullions of the French army, to conquer England."‡ When told of the capture of Cape Breton by Pepperel's 4000 New

* "'Tis said the French king, looking upon the English that were killed, said, 'Ma foy, ces gens méritoient de vivre.' And Marshal Saxe said, 'Cette poignée de gens m'a fait plus de peine que tout le reste.'" (Lady S. Cowper, as above.)

† 'Records of British Army,' Fourth regiment of Foot.

‡ Walpole's Letters, vol i. p. 379, Cunningham's ed. The marshal and his brother had been sent, in 1744, by Louis XV.

England Volunteers, "I can believe that," said he, "because the Ministry had no hand in it."* Perhaps he was not far wrong; for all was gloom and confusion when, on the 31st of August, the King arrived from Hanover, and "men's hearts failed them for fear."

on a mission to the King of Prussia; while changing horses at Elbengerode, they were taken and conveyed to England, where, as they refused to give their parole, they were confined in Windsor Castle. In 1745 they were liberated, and left England on the 13th of August. See *Ib.*, pp. 337 and 379, notes.

* After forty-nine days' siege, Louisburg and the whole island surrendered on the 15th of June, 1745. Belleisle was not quite correct, however, for the Ministry had had some hand in the undertaking. The colonists were assisted by a body of Marines, and supported by a squadron of ten ships of war, commanded by Admiral Warren. See Lord Mahon's History of England, vol. iii. p. 299.

CHAPTER IV.

NEWCASTLE.—FALKIRK.—CULLODEN.—LONDON.

1745-1746.

Prince Charles Edward, notwithstanding the failure of his attempt to invade England in 1744, when backed by the power of France, re-encouraged by the result of the battle of Fontenoy, landed with half-a-dozen followers in Moidart, on the 25th of July, 1745.* So imperfect were the means of communication in those days, that three weeks had elapsed before tidings of the event reached the Commander-in-chief at Edinburgh.

On the 19th of August—the very day on which the Stuart standard was raised in Glenfillan by the Marquis of Tullibardine—Sir John Cope, after having collected his troops at Stirling, set out from the capital with about 1500 men. He directed his march towards Fort Augustus,—the most central point of the Highlands,—but finding the pass of Corryarrack defended by the rebels, he altered his course and made for Inverness.† Mean-

* Moidart, a district in the south-west corner of Inverness-shire, lying between Loch Shiel and the west coast. It is indented by Loch Moidart, a bay rendered interesting by its singular and deceptive intricacy. (Chambers's Gazetteer of Scotland.)

† See 'Waverley,' ch. xxxii.

while, the Young Chevalier had begun his descent upon the Lowlands, and arrived in Perth, where he was joined by the Duke of that ilk, and Lord George Murray. Continuing his progress, each day bringing new adherents, he entered Stirling on the 14th of September, and three days later took possession of the palace of his ancestors in Edinburgh.

Cope, too late to hinder the advance of the insurgents, yet still hoping to save the capital, marched from Inverness to Aberdeen, where he embarked his troops, but did not land at Dunbar until the 18th. Pursuing his course towards Edinburgh, on the 20th he came in view of the rebels, and immediately drew up his men near the village of Prestonpans. That night both armies lay upon their ground; and at daybreak next morning, the battle began which, ending in the defeat of the Royalists, left the Pretender master of all Scotland, save the castles of Edinburgh and Stirling, with a few Highland forts.*

Previous to the return of George II. from Hanover, the regency had slighted every information concerning the enterprise of the Stuarts. The Government remained supine, until the whole kingdom was struck with consternation at the progress of the rebellion. The presence of the King, however, restored some degree of public confidence, and addresses, expressing the strongest attachment to the reigning House, were presented to his Majesty. Merchants and traders bound themselves to take the notes of the Bank of England in payment for all sums due to them; means were adopted to secure the loyalty of those who were wavering, while, in order

* Lord Mahon's History of England.

to strike terror into the disloyal, the Habeas Corpus Act was suspended, and many persons suspected of treasonable designs were taken up.* Six thousand Dutch auxiliaries arrived at Newcastle-on-Tyne, and a portion of the British troops, recalled from the Continent, landed at the same place, with the Earl of Albemarle as their leader. The militia of each county assembled; several corps of volunteers were raised by nobility and gentry, to whom arms were liberally distributed, and the southern counties were put in a state of defence. The adventurer, after playing at royalty for six weeks in Holyrood, notwithstanding these formidable preparations, descended upon England by the western border, with some 6000 followers. The city of Carlisle was immediately invested, and after a feeble show of resistance, surrendered within a few days.

In the meantime, Marshal Wade had collected an army of 10,000 men at Newcastle. Amongst his forces were Wolfe's and Barrell's regiments, the former commanded by Lieut.-Colonel Martin, the latter by Lieut.-Colonel Rich. The elder Wolfe, though now rather infirm, took the field as a General of Division,† and his son as a Major of Brigade, to which office he had been commissioned while abroad.‡ An order, which is still in existence, was issued by the Marshal on the 2nd of November, 1745, directing "Major James Wolfe to be paid £930, for allowance of 93 baggage horses to the seven battalions lately come from Flanders." It would

* Russell's 'Modern Europe,' part ii. letter 29.

† Major-General, 4th June, o. s., 1745.

‡ Commission, dated "Lessines, June 12th, 1745," signed "William."

appear from this, that the Brigade-Major had also, for a time, assumed the functions of a Deputy Quarter-Master-General.

A short letter to his mother turns up at this period:—

Newcastle, November 14th, 1745.

Dear Madam,

I received yours the day the last post went out, but as my father was then writing to you I thought it needless. I was under some apprehension for him on the road to Berwick, and was even told he was made prisoner, but not with foundation to give much credit to, as it has fallen out. I really believe you need not concern yourself about my father's safety, for 'tis the opinion of most men that these rebels won't stand the King's troops; and as to marching north and south with the army in his post-chaise, it does him so much service that I never saw him look better.

It is said the Pretender's people made an attack on Carlisle, but have been repulsed with loss; this, however, is not to be depended upon.

You can't doubt the sincerity of my intentions, but to convince you I must beg you will think no more of what you have mentioned in your letter. I wrote to you in a style of complaint, just as the accident happened, but I have now got the better of that, and am in a condition to repair the loss. I know very well the many good uses you have of putting your money to; pray don't let me be the instrument of preventing it. Besides, you give it to a person that ought to give you, by the difference of income. I desire you won't imagine I am so unreasonable a dog as to think of it.

There is one thing that I must beg leave to assure you, that though I don't take it I am not the less obliged to you, and shall always own a proper acknowledgment for this and the innumerable kindnesses I have always received from you. I heartily wish you your health, and am,

Dear Madam,

Your dutiful and affectionate Son,

J. Wolfe.

A few days before the above was written, Major-General Wolfe had marched northwards along the eastern coast, with a detachment commanded by General Bland; while James remained with the main army under Marshal Wade. From this date there is a considerable gap, owing, no doubt, to the ruthless zeal of autograph-hunters, in our hero's home communications; consequently we can trace his steps only through such military records as exist, helped out by a few "fractions snatched from the circumambient paper vortex," as the biographer of the Great Frederick sympathetically styles those scraps laboriously gleaned from contemporary publications.

Wade was so perplexed by contradictory reports of the route of the rebels, that he seems not to have known how to act. Having encamped his troops upon the moor near Newcastle, winter had set in, and the snow lay thick upon the ground, when news arrived that the Highlanders were approaching Carlisle; upon which he determined to advance towards Hexham, with the hope of intercepting them. Amidst a storm of hail and snow the Royal army began to march westward, on the morning of Saturday, November 16.* Besides the severity of the weather, the progress of the troops was retarded by the badness of the road. In order to make a passage for the artillery and baggage, the pioneers were obliged to cut away hills, fill up ditches, and remove obstructions, so that they did not arrive at Ovington—a distance of about ten miles—until ten o'clock at night, after fifteen hours' march. The ground was frozen so

* 'History of Newcastle,' by E. Makenzie, p. 55.

hard that it was found impossible to pitch their tents, and the wearied men "lay one upon another" covered with straw. Next morning the march was continued. In the biography of a remarkable volunteer attached to Wade's army, an incident of this Sunday morning is related. It was customary to burn the straw the men had slept upon, to warm them before they set out, so the versatile volunteer, who was not only a soldier, engineer, and many other things besides, but a musician also, "took out his fiddle, notwithstanding the day, and played to the men whilst they danced round the fire; which made the rest of the army observe them, though they did not follow the example."* A picture of this curious scene would form a suitable pendant to another, of the French soldiers' dance described by Smollett.† The army halted at Hexham in the afternoon, where the General decided upon resting his men until the arrival of further intelligence. On Monday, the 18th, however, upon hearing of the surrender of Carlisle, it became unnecessary to advance further in that direction, and accordingly he marched his troops back to Newcastle. On account of the inclemency of the season, the magistrates and loyal inhabitants lodged the men in the public halls, glass-houses, malt-houses, and other available buildings of the town, in which they remained until it was determined by a council of war to march southward in pursuit of the enemy.‡

But we need not follow; for as several detachments

* 'Life of John Metcalfe,' Leeds, 1801.

† See 'Roderick Random,' chap. xliii.

‡ 'Gentleman's Magazine,' vol. xv. p. 613.

were sent off from the main army, it becomes impossible in the maze of marches and counter-marches to trace the footsteps of Wolfe until after the Young Pretender's retreat from Derby and return to Scotland, late in December.

By this time "hangman Hawley" had superseded Marshal Wade in the command of the army to which our Brigade-Major was attached. But before resuming our sketch of the proceedings in which he was personally engaged, it may be well to take a glance at the state of the public mind at this period in London. We cannot do so more briefly than by availing ourselves of an extract from a letter written by Mr. John Forbes to the famous Lord President, on the 9th of January, 1746. "We flatter ourselves here," says the writer, "that the Duke will go to Scotland himself; but that seems now to be no longer believed, and the whole burden is left upon Hawley, and your friend Hugh, his aide-de-camp. No mortal disputes Mr. Hawley's genius for the management of a squadron, or prosecuting with rigour any mortal to the gallows; although, at the same time, they wish that he had the lenity to make converts, or the absolute force to make them fly before him. . . . It may appear odd to you that this kingdom is by trifles either raised to a prosperity that exceeds impertinence, or falls, from the smallest adversity, below compassion. . . . We at present begin to breathe, as the rebels have retired to Scotland, which to the generality here is the same as Norway; and that they are no longer in terror of invasion, and now indeed countermand (as we are told) the Hessians and our own eighteen squadrons, and are become so brave as to think of sending troops to Flanders by May next to invade France."*

But the rebellion was not so near an end as was imagined. Prince Charles, after spending a week in Glasgow, proceeded towards Stirling, and on the 5th of January summoned the town and castle to surrender. The town was taken three days after, but the castle was bravely defended by General Blakeney. Hawley marched from Edinburgh in order to raise the siege, and Charles advanced to meet him. The details of the battle of Falkirk have however been so often told, that it is needless to repeat them here. Suffice it to say, the rebels claimed a victory upon the grounds of the Royalists abandoning their camp and cannon.†

Wolfe's view of the matter is shown by the following passage extracted from a letter to his uncle Sotheron:—"If you have not seen the Gazette, you will have heard of our late encounter (for 'twas not a battle, as neither side would fight); and possibly it will be told you in a much worse light than it really is. Though we can't have been said to have totally routed the enemy, we yet re-

* 'Culloden Papers,' p. 468.

† "The abandoning the camp and the loss of the cannon, looks so like a defeat that it gave the Jacobites a handle to vaunt, as if the rebels had got the victory, whereas they were indeed beat by a handful of men, and fled shamefully. The facts are true, the camp was abandoned and the cannon lost; but the first was done with judgment, and preserved the men, who must have lain upon their arms all night, which was so rainy and stormy that they were wet to the skin, had no provisions, and would have been subject to continual alarms all night; and the last was occasioned by the misbehaviour of the officer who had the charge of the train, who, finding that he was to be tried by a court-martial, cut an artery in his arm, and made his escape by going out of the world." ('A Compleat History of the Rebellion,' by James Ray, of Whitehaven, Volunteer; York, 1749, pp. 265–6.)

mained a long time masters of the field of battle, and of our cannon, not one of which would have been lost if the drivers had not left their carriages and run off with the horses. We left Falkirk and part of our camp, because the ammunition of the army—on which we can only depend—was all wet and spoiled; but our retreat was in no ways molested by the enemy, as affecting our superiority. The loss of either side is inconsiderable, and we are now making all necessary preparations to try once more to put an end to this rebellion, which the weather has hitherto prevented, and in my opinion can at any time be the only objection."

Barrell's and Wolfe's regiments were conspicuous in the fight, and all the Royal troops, though badly commanded, fought well. Hawley retreated to Edinburgh, and the insurgents entered the town of Falkirk that night, January 17th.

Prince Charles returned to the siege of Stirling Castle; while fruitlessly engaged there, the army in Scotland was reinforced, and the Duke of Cumberland appointed Commander-in-chief. Although his Royal Highness was no master of military art, and had been unsuccessful on the Continent, yet he was beloved by the soldiery, and it was hoped that the presence of a Prince of the blood would intimidate the rebels as well as inspirit the King's troops. The Duke arrived at Edinburgh on the 30th January, where he was received with the warmest expressions of joy. After collecting his forces he advanced towards the enemy, who thought it prudent to retreat northwards.

Charles took possession of Inverness without opposition, the Earl of Loudon and his men having on his approach crossed the Moray Frith to Cromarty. The old citadel was speedily reduced, and Fort Augustus, after a short siege, was taken and destroyed by a party of the rebels. In the meanwhile Cumberland, having been further reinforced by 6000 Hessians, left a few battalions at Stirling and proceeded to Aberdeen. During his stay in Aberdeen, where he was detained awaiting supplies, and by the severity of the weather, the Duke was indefatigable in training his men. He also sent parties through the surrounding districts to search for arms, and make prisoners of suspected persons. Having heard that the Earl of Airlie was raising his clan to join the rebels, a detachment took possession of his lordship's house, and confined him therein until all his people had delivered up their arms. His Royal Highness likewise ordered Major Lafausille, with 300 men, to go to Glen Esk, one of the most disaffected parts, to attack all whom he found armed, and burn the houses of those persons who had left them to join the enemy.* Lafausille's raid, as will appear, was long remembered in the district.

In the city of Aberdeen two non-juring churches were burnt by the soldiers, "but with good husbandry and frugality," says the Whitehaven volunteer, "not consuming the pile at once, as was often the case; the wood being industriously reserved for our bakers' ovens." Besides such cruel events as these, there were others of a more harmless description during the Duke's stay in Aberdeen. One was a ball given by his Royal Highness to the ladies, at which—as there were no bands with any of the regiments, except the Old Buffs, whose performers, being Germans, were unaccustomed to country-dances—

* Ray, p. 330.

the blind musician of Captain Thornton's corps played the fiddle. Five-and-twenty couples, we are told, danced eight hours, and his Royal Highness made one of the set, and as he passed Metcalfe, who stood on a chair, shouted, "Thornton, play up."*

While in Aberdeen, the Duke occupied the house of Mr. Alexander Thomson, Advocate; and General Hawley took possession of Hallhead, the residence of a Mrs. Gordon. Mr. Thomson, it appears, was a Whig, and firmly attached to the established Government; nevertheless, according to report, he received no recompence for the use of his house and furniture. In other respects he fared much better than his neighbour, for after the departure of the unwelcome visitors, he had only occasion to complain that his bed and table-linen had been abused and spoiled, and that "they broke open a press in which Mrs. Thomson had lodged a considerable quantity of sugars, whereof they took every grain weight." Hawley's entertainer was not so fortunate. The lady's statements, however, are so conflicting as to render it difficult to state the case, and to do so will take up more space than the matter is worth; but as Wolfe's name is mixed up with it, for reasons that will be obvious it must not be passed over without notice. Perhaps the best course will be to quote one of Mrs. Gordon's own accounts, of which the following is the most definitely related:—

"The Duke came to my house, attended by General Hawley and several others. The General lay in my bed, and, very early on Friday morning, sent a messenger to the house where I was, demanding all my keys. . . . That evening, one Major Wolfe came to me, and after

* Life of Metcalfe, p. 41.

asking me if I was Mrs. Gordon, and desiring a gentleman who was with me to go out of the room, he said that he was come to tell me, that by the Duke of Cumberland's and General Hawley's orders, I was deprived of everything I had, except the clothes on my back. After delivering this message, he said that General Hawley, having inquired into my character of several persons, who had all spoke very well of me, and had told him I had no hand in the Rebellion, and that I was a stranger there, without any relatives in that country, he the General, therefore, would make interest with the Duke, that I might have any particular thing that I had a mind to, and *could say was my own*. I then desired to have my tea, but the Major told me it was very good, and that tea was scarce in the army; so he did not believe I could have it. The same answer was made when I asked for my chocolate. I mentioned several other things, particularly my china. That he told me was, *a great deal of it*, very pretty, and that they were very fond of china themselves; but, as they had no ladies travelled with them, I might perhaps have *some of it*. I then desired to have my pictures. He said he supposed I could not wish to have *them all*. I replied that I did not pretend to name any, except my son's. He asked me if I had a son, where was he? I said I had sent him into the country, to make room for them. To what place? said he. I answered, to Sir Arthur Forbes's. He asked, how old my son was. I said, about fourteen. Said he, then he is not a child, and you will have to produce him; and thus we parted. This Major Wolfe was aide-de-camp to General Hawley." The next day the poor lady petitioned the Duke, and goes on to say, "Major Wolfe came to me again and told me, that the Duke had sent him to let me know that my petition had been read to him, and that he would take care that everything should be restored to me. Notwithstanding this, when I sent to the house to ask for anything, as, in particular, I did for a pair of breeches for my son, for a little tea for myself, for a bottle of ale, for some flour to make bread, because there was none to be bought in the town, all was refused me." After some irrelevant matter, the narrator continues:—"I should have mentioned above that Major Wolfe did one day bring me my son's picture, but without the frame; and he then told me that General Hawley did with his own hands take it out of the frame, which was a gilt one, and very handsome. This frame the General left behind him, and I afterwards found it in the house."*

More than one of the many who have formed a high estimate of Wolfe's character, either believe, or wish to believe, that he was not the Major who figures in the above narrative. For instance, a Scotch friend writes to me:—"Our hero had too much kindness of heart to act so meanly and cruelly as the Bishop records; at least I hope so, for I should be sorry to see even the least shade on his noble character." The able editor of the 'Jacobite Memoirs' likewise, in introducing the papers connected with this subject, says in a note:—"It is proper to mention that the Major Wolfe here alluded to could hardly be the same person with the amiable hero

* Bishop Forbes's 'Jacobite Memoirs,' edited by Robert Chambers, 1834.

of Quebec. Of this the editor has been satisfied by the polite attention of Mr. Southey, who it is well known has made collections for a Life of General Wolfe." By what means Southey arrived at his conjecture cannot be ascertained, but most probably the wish was father to the thought.

For my own part, I am persuaded that our hero was the man; and I cannot see any reason why his most ardent admirers should hesitate to identify him in association with the affair. He, a staff-officer, was ordered by his superiors to perform a certain service—neither a pleasant nor an honourable one, it is true,—and knowing that a soldier's first duty is obedience, he did perform it with, as it appears to me, exceeding tact and discernment for a young man of nineteen. Mrs. Gordon, it is evident, was a lady of some substance, yet what she could want with so large a store of salt beef, pickled pork, brandy, rum, tea, chocolate, etc., as is included in her inventory, it is not easy to imagine. In the said inventory there is an item moreover which looks rather suspicious, viz. "One set of blue and white, ten dishes, forty plates, and three dozen plates. Note. These were not my own, but *were sent to my house* to see if I would buy them." If the reader will now turn back to the words I have italicized in the lady's statement, I think it will strike him as highly probable that Mrs. Gordon had concealed the property of some of her proscribed friends. If this be so, the drift of Wolfe's shrewd replies to her demands is apparent. In restoring the portrait, his own feelings may have prompted him to go beyond his duty.

According to the records of the regiment, Barrell's

formed part of the advance-guard under Major-General Bland, which proceeded to Inverury on the 12th of March, and on the 17th advanced to Strathsbogie to attack a rebel force, which fled at their approach. It does not follow, however, that Wolfe was with this division, for, being a staff-officer, he may have remained with the grand army.

On the 6th of April the Duke issued orders to march next day; but before the troops were in motion intelligence arrived that the 'Sheerness,' man-of-war, after having chased the 'Hazard' sloop, about fifty leagues, had driven her ashore and obliged the French and Spaniards aboard to land. It therefore became necessary to send a detachment against these men, who were soon subdued, and a large supply of arms, etc., with £12,000 in money, destined for the Chevalier's use, were seized.

The day following, Tuesday the 8th, his Royal Highness quitted Aberdeen, and the weather being now calm the transports at the same time sailed along shore with a favourable wind. Having forded the Spey without opposition, the army entered Nairn on the 14th. As the Duke's birthday fell upon the 15th of April, his men were allowed to rest and enjoy themselves. The rebels, therefore, expecting to find them "merry," marched that night with the intention of attacking the Royal camp; but when they had advanced seven or eight miles it became apparent that they could not arrive at Nairn before dawn, and consequently they returned to Culloden Moor.

At break of day on the 16th, the Royal forces began their march in the direction of Inverness. The enemy, on first sight of their advance, formed in two lines with a reserve, while Prince Charles took his position upon an eminence behind the right of his second line.

The Duke perceiving the insurgents in order of battle, broke his columns into two lines flanked by cavalry, with a strong reserve of horse and foot.* Two field-pieces being disposed in each interval of the first line, the Royalists remained in this position, having Culloden House on their right and a park wall on their left, while their Commander-in-chief addressed them in a short but politic speech. After the cannon of both sides had opened fire, there was a change made in the disposition of the armies by bringing troops from the rear to the front, each endeavouring to outflank the other. The Highlanders were so galled by the Royal cannon that they grew impatient and called out for the attack, for which orders were immediately given.† Rushing upon the right wing of the army, where Barrell's and Monro's were stationed, the rebels after firing their pistols flung them at their adversaries' heads, and then with their broadswords cut at the two Royal regiments, who received them upon their espotoons and bayonets. The Dragoons coming to the relief of the infantry, who had already made dire havoc, completely broke the Chevalier's left, and the total rout of the rebels ensued.

A more detailed report of the battle is contained in a letter from Wolfe to his uncle William Sotheron, Esq., of Pomfret.‡

* 'Home's History of the Rebellion.'

† 'A Particular Account of the Battle of Culloden,' by an officer of the Highland Army. London, 1749.

‡ "The Sotherons," says Burke, "have been most respectably settled in their own estates at Holm, Spaldingmore, in the East Riding, and

Inverness, April 17, 1746.

Dear Sir,

I have the pleasure to tell you that yesterday, about one in the afternoon, the Duke engaged with the rebel army, and in about an hour drove them from the field of battle, where they left near 1500 dead; the rest, except prisoners, escaped by the neighbourhood of the hills. The action was three miles short of this place, on Lord President Forbes's land, from whence it takes its name, the battle of Coloden.

The rebels had posted themselves on a high boggy moor, where they imagined our cannon and cavalry would be useless; but both did essential service. The cannon in particular made them very uneasy, and after firing a quarter of an hour, obliged them to change their situation and move forward some hundred yards to attack our front line of Foot, which they did with more fury than prudence, throwing down their firearms, and advancing with their drawn swords. They were however repulsed, and ran off with the greatest precipitation, and the Dragoons falling in amongst them completed the victory with much slaughter. We have taken about twenty pieces of cannon in the field, and near it a number of colours, and I believe seven hundred prisoners, amongst which are all the Irish piquets, most of the remainder of Fitz-James's horse, and some of Drummond's regiment; great quantity of powder, ball, muskets, bayonets, broadswords, etc. Plaids innumerable.

The troops behaved themselves as they ought to do, and no regiment was wanting in their duty. The enemy by their own order of battle had 8300 men in the field, and the utmost of our number was 7200, of which we had about twenty officers and three hundred men killed and wounded. Barrell's regiment suffered particularly, having out of three hundred and fifty had one hundred and twenty officers and men killed and wounded, fighting in a most obstinate manner against the

Hook in the West Riding of the county of York, for more than two centuries." William Sotheron, Esq., of Pontefract, married Mrs. Wolfe's sister, Lucy, co-heiress of her brother Tyndal Thompson. Their son and heir, William, married Sarah, daughter of Samuel Saville, Esq., of Terrybridge, and was succeeded in the family estates by the late Admiral Sotheron. ('Commoners,' ed. 1838.)

Camerons, the best clan in the Highlands. Orders were publicly given in the rebel army, the day before the action, that no quarter should be given to our troops.* We had an opportunity of avenging ourselves, and I assure you as few prisoners were taken of the Highlanders as possible.

You must observe that it blew and rained very hard almost from the time we marched from our camp at Nairn, till just the battle began, when it became fair and continued so the remainder of the day. Another thing you must take notice of, that the rebels were the night before the action within three miles of our camp, intending to surprise and attack us in the dark; but some unforeseen accident, together with a great deal of superstition, turned them back. These circumstances, with many others I could name, will make every discerning man observe from whence only our success can proceed. I heartily wish you joy of the happy end of so horrid an undertaking. And may they ever be punished in the same manner who attempt the like!

I am, dear Sir, etc.,
J. Wolfe.

Subsequently, after he had gained more than five years' further experience, Wolfe reviewed the field of Culloden. His criticism upon the conduct of the battle will appear in its proper place;† it is therefore unnecessary to dwell upon the subject. An anecdote with which probably every reader is familiar cannot be passed over without remark. Mr. Robert Chambers, in his account of the proceedings after the engagement, says: "In the

* A copy of the Orders issued by Lord George Murray to the rebel army, previous to the battle, was found in the pocket of one of the prisoners. It begins thus:—

"Parole. Roy Jaques.

"It is his Royal Highness's positive orders that every person attach himself to some corps of the army, and remain with the corps night and day until the battle and pursuit be finally over, and to give no quarter to the Elector's troops on any account whatsoever." (Ray, p. 366.)

† See Letter, "Inverness, October 17th, 1751."

sycophant publications of the time it is stated that after the Duke had refreshed himself, he took a 'serious walk' over the field, followed by some of his attendants, who observed him to be in deep meditation. He laid his hand upon his breast, and with eyes lifted up to heaven, was heard to say, 'Lord, what am I, that I should be spared, when so many brave men lie dead upon the spot?' —an expression of such deep humility towards God and compassion towards his fellow-creatures as is truly worthy a Christian hero.' "* Every rational man will coincide with Mr. Chambers in rejecting the fulsome, time-serving adulations of which the above is a comparatively moderate specimen. As a counterpoise, however, to the discarded story, he repeats a "better authenticated" anecdote, illustrative not only of Cumberland's cruelty, but also of Wolfe's magnanimity. Instead of borrowing Mr. Chambers's paraphrase, I shall quote from the 'Anti-Jacobin Review' the passage wherein it was, I believe, first printed:—" When the celebrated General Wolfe, at this period a Lieutenant-Colonel [?] in the army, was riding over the field of battle with the D— of C–m–b–l–d, they observed a Highlander, who, although severely wounded, was yet able to sit up, and, leaning on his arm, seemed to smile defiance of them. 'Wolfe,' said the D—, 'shoot me that Highland scoundrel, who thus dares to look on us with such contempt and insolence!' 'My commission,' replied the manly officer, 'is at your Royal Highness's disposal, but I never can consent to become an *executioner*.' The Highlander, it is probable, was soon knocked on the head by some ruffian less scrupulous than the future conqueror of Quebec. But it was

* History of the Rebellion of 1745.

remarked by those who heard the story, that Colonel Wolfe from that day visibly declined in the favour and confidence of the Commander-in-chief. We believe that some officers are still alive who are not unacquainted with this anecdote."*

It is a pity Sir Henry Stuart Allanton, to whom is attributed the essay from which the above extract is taken, did not in some degree confirm the truth of the story, by naming at least one of those officers who were acquainted with it; yet even had he done so, it would not have followed that either his own or his referee's familiarity with the *anecdote* should be taken as a proof of the *facts* which it purports to embody. It is not improbable that some incident did occur upon that day which formed a foundation for the tradition.† But traditions, as in other instances relating to Wolfe, are subject to strange twists, even in so short a space of time as fifty years. My evident desire to uphold the character of my hero, as far as truth allows, will perhaps be sufficient to show that I would not gratuitously deprive him of a magnanimous reply, in order to "whitewash" his commander's reputation; yet I cannot accept this story as it stands. It is hardly credible that the Duke of Cumberland, stern and relentless though he was when the kingdom was at stake, would have been beloved by the British soldiery had he been so bloodthirsty a monster as to be capable of a deed base enough for Hawley, a man whom they abhorred.

* See article upon Home's History of the Rebellion in 'Anti-Jacobin Review,' vol. xiii. (1802), p. 125, note.

† Bishop Forbes relates what is doubtless the same story, but much less circumstantially, and does not mention Wolfe's name in association with it. See 'Jacobite Memoirs,' p. 255.

Neither is it probable that Wolfe would have continued to respect him if the facts were as stated. But casting aside all doubts grounded upon the improbability of the story, one portion of it at least is unquestionably erroneous; for, as the reader will learn by-and-by from Wolfe's own words, he did *not* decline from that day in the favour and confidence of the Commander-in-chief. I shall put an end to this subject by recalling an anecdote related by Sir Walter Scott (no admirer of his Royal Highness), which presents at once a parallel and a contrast to the foregoing. It is, briefly, to this effect:—Colonel Whiteford having pleaded unsuccessfully for the protection of the family and property of the rebel chief, Stewart of Invernahyle, resigned his commission, upon which the Duke was so affected, that he immediately granted the request.*

Never was victory more complete, and few battles have been more important in their results than that of Culloden. It is said of both parties that orders were issued to give no quarter. The unfortunate adventurer, who had played his last stake, fled to Aird, Lord Lovat's house, where he remained that night; and then ensued those romantic wanderings so graphically described by Earl Stanhope. The Duke found quarters at Culloden House, where his rival had passed the previous night, and immediately dispatched his aide-de-camp, Lord Bury, to London with the news of the victory.† But the wel-

* See Introduction to Waverley.

† "My friend Lord Bury," writes Walpole, on the 25th, to Sir H. Mann, "arrived this morning from the Duke, though the news was got here before him, for with all our victory it was not thought safe to send him through the heart of Scotland; so he was shipped at Inverness

come intelligence arrived before his lordship. "I was in the coffee-house with Smollett," says Dr. Carlyle, "when the news of the battle of Culloden arrived, and when London all over was in a perfect uproar of joy. . . . About nine o'clock I wished to go home to Lyon's, in New Bond Street, as I had promised to sup with him. . . . I asked Smollett if he was ready to go, as he lived at Mayfair; he said he was, and would conduct me. The mob were so riotous and the squibs so incessant that we were glad to go into a narrow entry to put our wigs into our pockets, and to take our swords from our belts and walk with them in our hands, as everybody then wore swords; and after cautioning me against speaking a word, lest the mob should discover my country and become insolent, 'for John Bull,' says he, 'is as haughty and valiant to-night as he was abject and cowardly on Black Wednesday, when the Highlanders were at Derby.'"*

After the battle the infantry were encamped near Inverness, and the cavalry quartered in the town and adjacent villages, which were found to be but ill provided, the rebel army having been there so long. Before the end of May the Duke, with Barrell's, Wolfe's, and some other regiments, marched from Inverness to Fort Augustus, where the barracks having been destroyed by the insurgents, his Royal Highness lay in a tent until "a neat

within an hour after the Duke entered the town, kept beating about at sea five days, and then put on shore at North Berwick, from whence he came post in less than three days to London, but with a fever upon him. The King has immediately ordered him £1000, and I hear will make him his own aide-de-camp." (Letters, vol. ii. p. 18.)

* Autobiography, p. 190.

bower" was built for his accommodation near the ruins. Parties of troops were sent out through the Highlands, who burned houses and carried off the cattle. According to a Scotch periodical of the time, the Duke began with the disaffected "in a gentle and paternal way," promising pardon and protection to those who brought in their arms and submitted. Such as complied were dismissed with protections; but the majority, after having promised to surrender within a certain time, either failed to do so or concealed their arms and brought in only old swords and useless guns. The Duke was therefore obliged "to lay the rod more heavy upon them," by carrying fire and sword through the surrounding country and driving off the cattle.* The deluded people were reduced to the most deplorable condition, and many of the soldiers grew rich upon their spoil. In order to diversify the scene, and keep up the spirits of his men amidst their fatigues and hardships, the Duke patronized races and other amusements. In a letter from "Fort Augustus, June 17th," we read:—"Last Wednesday the Duke gave two prizes to the soldiers to run heats for, on bare-backed galloways taken from the rebels. . . . These galloways are little larger than a good tup, and there was excellent sport. Yesterday H.R.H. gave a fine holland smock to the soldiers' wives to be run for on these galloways, also bare-backed, and riding with their limbs on each side of the horse, like men. Eight started, and there were three of the finest heats ever seen. The prize was won, with great difficulty, by one of the Old Buffs' ladies. In the evening, General Hawley and Co-

* 'Scots Magazine,' 1846, p. 287.

lonel Howard ran a match for twenty guineas on two of the above shalties, which General Hawley won by about four inches."* Most of the soldiers had horses, which they bought and sold amongst themselves at low prices. One of these cavaliers being met by a comrade who asked him, "Tom, what has thou given for the galloway?" answered, "Half-a-crown." On which the other replied, with an oath, "He is too dear; I saw a better bought for eighteen-pence." As the men rode about the country and neglected their duty, an order was at length published that they should dispose of their steeds, or the animals would be shot. A fair or market was held, which was attended by jockeys and farmers from Yorkshire and the Lowlands, who purchased the horses, oxen, sheep, goats, etc., taken from the rebels; and notwithstanding the low prices, a large sum of money was obtained and divided amongst the army.†

On the 18th July, the Duke, whose presence afforded pleasure to every soldier, left the army in Scotland, of which the Earl of Albemarle was appointed Commander-in-chief. In London, his Royal Highness was hailed as the deliverer of his country, and rewarded for his services with a pension of £25,000 a year. The victory of Culloden was also celebrated by the performance of the great historical, as well as the greatest of sacred, composer's new Oratorio of 'Judas Maccabæus.'

Soon after the Duke's departure the forces in Scotland were dispersed. Wolfe's, Pulteney's, and other regiments were ordered to Flanders; while Barrell's and Conway's were quartered in Stirling and various outposts. It is

* 'Scots Magazine,' 1846, p. 288. † Ray, p. 392.

stated in local guide-books, that Wolfe, about this time, commanded the small fort of Inversnaid, situated between the Lochs Lomond and Katrine. But the fort, having been taken by Rob Roy's nephew, Ghlune-Dhu, previous to or during the Rebellion, was now in ruins; and the tradition must have arisen from the fact that our hero was in command there at a later period. Yet, even at this time, it is not improbable that an outpost from Stirling was established in the locality; and Wolfe may have superintended the reconstruction of the little keep at Inversnaid.*

Although nothing can be positively asserted of his doings for a few months, it is certain that he was actively engaged during the remainder of his stay in the Highlands, and that he now acquired an intimate knowledge of the condition of the people, as well as of the physical features of the country. Wolfe quitted Scotland before winter set in, and passed the short time until his return to the Continent, early in the following spring, in London. So here may be closed the chapter which relates all the information that has come down to us concerning the humble but efficient part played by our young hero—

> "In a rebellion,
> When what's not meet, but what must be, was law."

* See Introduction to 'Rob Roy' for an account of this Highland fort. Sir Walter Scott adds:—"When we find the celebrated General Wolfe commanding in it, the imagination is strongly affected by the variety of time and events which the circumstance brings simultaneously to recollection." Towards the north-eastern end of Loch Lomond a little stream, called the Snaid, falls into it. The Snaid runs from Loch Arklet through a wild gorge, and gives the name of *Inversnaid*, the mouth or outlet of the Snaid, to the district. The little fort built in 1713 to keep the Macgregors in awe, stood in the heart of this gorge.

CHAPTER V.

CONTINENTAL CAMPAIGNS.—LONDON.

1747–1748.

THE winter season of 1746 was inaugurated in London on the 9th of October by a public thanksgiving for the total reduction of the rebels, which we are told was observed by a great resort to the places of worship, and extraordinary illuminations at night. The seven alarm guns that had been placed in St. James's Park were now removed; and patriotic parish clerks no longer thought it necessary to excite a sanguinary spirit in their congregations by singing, "to the praise and glory of God," the most vindictive verses of the 59th, 83rd, and 137th Psalms.*

Although human heads were exposed to view on Temple Bar, where people made a trade of letting spying-glasses at a halfpenny a look,† and notwithstanding the Special Commission still sitting at St. Margaret's Hill, Southwark, and the hanging, drawing, and quartering of condemned traitors upon Kennington Common, the town was as gay and heartless as if there never had been a Black Derby Day.

* 'Gentleman's Magazine,' 1846, p. 422 *et seq.*

† Walpole's Letters, Cunningham's ed., vol. ii. p. 50.

Only those who have had occasion to explore old magazines and newspapers know how comparatively small a space is filled by the matter, from which is formed the so-called history of any period. The rare, or, so to speak, episodical events embalmed for the edification of future generations, are, in fact, mere by-plays in the grand drama of human life; and, oblivious of them, the world goes on after the old fashion, marrying and giving in marriage, every individual feeling much more interested in his own ephemeral affairs than in those remarkable occurrences, the memory of which only survives.* We need not wonder, then, to find contemporaneous accounts of the Rebellion, and its sequel, interspersed with articles "On marrying a brother's widow," "On the efficacy of tar-water," "On a method for exercise within-doors," and even upon less momentous subjects than these. A plate in the 'Gentleman's Magazine' affords us a curious illustration.† On the same page are represented a machine for cutting away mole and ant hills; bullets found upon the field of Edgehill; a section of a machine for rubbing, cleaning, and winnowing corn all at once; a candlestick, with apparatus to preserve the eye from the light, and obtain a stronger light from a small candle than a large; an hour-glass, found in a coffin in Clerkenwell churchyard;

* For instance, D'Israeli says:—"In the journal of a Yorkshire squire, who lived in the immediate neighbourhood of Marston Moor, it appears that he went out hunting on the very day of that memorable engagement; but our sportsman, in the details of his chase, has not even made an allusion to the battle, though the roar of the cannon must have echoed to his 'Tally-ho!'" (Commentaries, etc., vol. v. p. 49.)

† Plate viii., December, 1846, p. 640.

and the portrait of Lord Lovat, "curiously engraved." In like manner Justice, engaged though she was in State trials, had leisure to look after barbers, one and fifty of whom were mulcted in the sum of £20 each, "for having in their custody hair-powder not made from starch, contrary to Act of Parliament."* The King's birthday was celebrated with more than the ordinary display of loyalty; and, at the ball in St. James's Palace, H.R.H. the Duke danced minuets with the Princess of Wales. A few days afterwards the Duke set out for the Hague, in order to confer with the States-General, and to arrange with the Austrian and Dutch commanders the operations for the ensuing campaign. During his Royal Highness's stay there he was much caressed, and there was a great assemblage of people of distinction who made court to him. Their High Mightinesses, animated by his presence, and the resolutions of the British Parliament, determined upon fitting out a fleet, and to have an army of 40,000 men early in the field. Having finished his business, the Duke returned to England.

The most remarkable of the state prisoners whose doom was as yet unpronounced still lingered in the Tower when the eventful year drew to an end. At Court the new year was opened with the routine festivities; but the 7th of January, being a solemn fast, was religiously observed throughout London and Westminster; consequently, the ceremonies of Twelfth Night were not observed at St. James's until the 9th, when his Majesty and the Royal Family, with several of the nobility, played at "hazard" for the benefit of the groom-porter.

* 'Gentleman's Magazine,' 1846, p. 611.

The General and Mrs. Wolfe were residing at their town house in Old Burlington Street when their son visited them, apparently for the first time since his entrance into the army, upon his return from Scotland, late in the year 1746. His stay in London was of short duration, barely sufficient to lay in his outfit, and make other necessary preparations for his Continental campaign. Mrs. Wolfe busied herself about the minor matters, and paid many a little bill for her son out of her own private purse. The General also was wont to come forward on such occasions with a round sum; and if he did not do so now, he had a very good excuse, for there were three years' arrears of pay, upwards of £1600, due to him for his services as Inspector of Marines. Some months previously he had memorialized the Lords Commissioners of the Admiralty, under whose direction he held his office, whereupon their lordships referred him to Mr. Pelham, First Lord of the Treasury; Mr. Pelham referred him to the Secretary at War, when that Minister referred him back again to Mr. Pelham. But the only effect of all this "circumlocution" was to make the memorialist fear that he was looked upon as a dun, for the Pay Office would not give him one shilling of the money due to him, neither would the King allow him to resign his appointment; so the Major-General, in consequence of his Inspectorship of Marines, "was in a worse position than any man who had the honour of having a regiment in his Majesty's service."*

* Bedford Correspondence, vol. i. p. 123; and an unpublished letter from Major-General Wolfe to his Grace the Duke of Bedford, dated, "Burlington Street, February ye 16th, 1746–7."

Brigade-Major Wolfe accompanied the British reinforcement, which sailed for the Netherlands early in January, 1747. In February the confederates began to assemble in the neighbourhood of Maestricht, where great preparations were made for opening the campaign.

While the English troops had been withdrawn during the progress of the Rebellion, the French had become masters of nearly the whole of the Austrian Netherlands. Prince Charles of Lorraine had been worsted at Roucoux, and as the congress which had met at Breda could not agree upon terms of peace, it was resolved on all sides to pursue the war with vigour. Maria Theresa hoped, by the co-operation of England and Holland, to recover Flanders; King George vowed vengeance against the King of France for supporting the Pretender; and the States-General had become sensible of their danger, and of the necessity of a closer alliance with England and Austria. The confederate armies, numbering about 120,000 men, took the field early in March. The Duke of Cumberland had been appointed generalissimo; the Austrians were commanded by Marshal Bathiani, and the Dutch by the Prince of Waldeck. Owing, however, to the negligence of the Austrian and Dutch commissaries they lay inactive for six weeks, almost destitute of provisions and forage, and exposed to the inclemency of the weather; while the French army of 150,000 men, under the command of Saxe, who appreciated the value of his soldiers' health, was well supplied and carefully sheltered.* Unfortunately also for

* "Count Saxe having been pleased to say that he thought the Duke of Cumberland the greatest General of the age, for that he had main-

the allies, the Prince of Orange, who had been declared Stadtholder of the United Provinces, arrived to take the command of his troops, and his inexperience of war, together with his jealousy of his brother-in-law, produced a want of harmony that augured unfavourably for their success.

At length Louis XV. arrived at Brussels, when it was resolved to besiege Maestricht.* Saxe immediately advanced towards the Maese, and Cumberland, perceiving his design, in order to place himself between the enemy and the threatened town, endeavoured by forced marches to get possession of the heights of Herdeeren. But the enemy had occupied this advantageous post before his arrival, on the 1st of July. The allies remained under arms during the night, and anxiously awaited the approach of day. Early on the 2nd the French infantry, moving down into the plain in one vast column of ten battalions in front and as many deep, directed their whole force towards the village of Val, or Laffeldt, three miles west of Maestricht, occupied by the British Foot. As the French approached, they were assailed by a deadly fire of musketry that soon broke their front; but, gaining ground, they brought their batteries to bear upon the village, and attacked with their first brigades, which were repulsed. Three times the attack was inef-

tained 100,000 men on a spot of ground where *he* should not have thought of feeding so many rabbits, the Duke, hearing it, replied that his men were well enough fed to fight the French on any ground." ('Gentleman's Magazine,' 1748, p. 250.)

* Maestricht, or *the passage of the Maese*, a city on the borders of the Duchy of Limburg, about four miles in circumference, whose fortifications, in the then "modern way," were reckoned amongst the strongest in Europe.

fectually renewed by division after division, until fresh forces advancing, the English infantry in Val, overpowered in numbers and exhausted with fatigue, were at length forced to give way. They quickly rallied however, regained the village, and drove back the enemy with great slaughter; but the battalions ordered to sustain them not all arriving in time, and the French still crowding upon them, they were obliged to evacuate Val and form upon the plain. The action now became general, and by mid-day victory appeared to declare for the allies, when the Dutch in the centre fell into disorder, and in their flight overthrew some Austrian battalions, who were slowly advancing to reinforce the line. At this crisis the Duke of Cumberland, as he was animating his troops to renew the fight, was almost surrounded by the enemy, when Sir John Ligonier, fearing his capture, advanced rapidly to his relief at the head of the British cavalry, and charged so furiously that he bore down all before him, until, proceeding too far, his horse was killed, and Sir John taken prisoner by a French carbineer.* The Duke, who now perceived that further efforts to repulse the enemy were impracticable, was enabled by Ligonier's chivalrous charge to collect his scattered forces, and retire to Maestricht without molestation. Thus, although the French won the battle,

* General Ligonier presented his purse and ring to his captor, who refused them, saying, he would only have his sword. Sir John was afterwards presented to the French king, and treated with great consideration. On his Majesty's inquiring whether he had been respectfully treated, he represented the heroic generosity of the carbineer, whom the king rewarded immediately, and promised to make him an officer. ('Gentleman's Magazine.')

the allies succeeded in reinforcing the city, which they continued masters of during the campaign. The confederates are said to have lost, in killed, wounded, and prisoners, from 5000 to 7000, and the enemy not less than 10,000 men.* It is generally admitted that if the English had been properly supported by the Austrians and Dutch, their victory would have been decisive. The valour and endurance of both infantry and cavalry was never more conspicuous; they bore the brunt of the battle, so as to justify the remark of Louis XV., "The English not only paid all, but fought all!" †

Of Brigade-Major Wolfe's conduct on this occasion we have few particulars. From the Gazette we learn that he was wounded; and it is stated that he was publicly thanked by the Commander-in-chief for his distinguished services. No account of the conflict from his own pen has come down to us, but by anticipating a paragraph from a letter which he wrote four years afterwards, we obtain a faint glimpse of him at Laffeldt, as well as of his ordinary camp life. Giving a character of his faithful servant, Old Roland, Wolfe says: "He came to me at the hazard of his life in the last action with offers of his service, took off my cloak, and brought a fresh horse, and would have continued close by me had I not ordered him to retire. I believe he was slightly

* "The French bought their victory dear. Their least loss is 12,000 men, ours at least 5000. His Royal Highness's valour shone extremely, but at the expense of his judgment." (Walpole to Montagu, July 2nd, 1747.)

† "The Dutch are deficient in vigour, and the Austrians in men. They each of them amuse and trifle with Great Britain, while she, good-natured lady, lavishes her blood and treasure to defend their territories." ('Westminster Journal,' July 11, 1747.)

wounded just at that time, and the horse he held was shot likewise. . . . Many a time has he pitched my tent, and made the bed ready to receive me, half-dead with fatigue; and this I owe to his diligence."

After reinforcing the garrison of Maestricht, Cumberland crossed the river, and extended his army towards Vist, a small fortified town seven miles north of Liége. Saxe remained in the neighbourhood of the city he so ardently coveted, and where, he said, the peace lay, until, thinking its reduction hopeless for the present, towards the end of August he burned his magazines and marched off.

Count Lowendahl had, in the meantime, invested the hitherto impregnable fortress of Bergen-op-Zoom, which, after two months' siege, he reduced and possessed himself of. On account of this great achievement Louis XV. rewarded him with the rank of a Maréchal of France. Having appointed Saxe governor of the vanquished Netherlands, the king returned in triumph to Paris, leaving the reduction of Maestricht for the next campaign; and before the end of October all parties had retired to their winter quarters.

On the 13th of November the Duke arrived from Holland at St. James's; General Ligonier, having been liberated, also reached London on the same day; and on the 16th twenty transports landed five regiments of infantry at Gravesend.

Wolfe returned home probably about the same time, for it is certain that he spent three or four winter months of 1747–8 in London. Yet it is only from future correspondence that we get an inkling of one or two incidents of his life at this period. Amongst his brother-officers in London at the same time was one whose name has already appeared in the list of wounded in Major-General Wolfe's regiment at Fontenoy, Lieutenant William Rickson. The corps had returned to the Continent soon after the battle of Culloden, and fought under Prince Charles of Lorraine—then Commander-in-chief—in the engagement on the 12th of October, 1746, at Roucoux, where Rickson was again wounded. He and the young Brigade-Major were on the most confidential terms, and it is in a letter to this friend that we find the earliest mention of Wolfe's first love. But as it appears that he met the lady only occasionally during this winter, and had not as yet been deeply smitten, it is unnecessary to enter into the tender affair until there will be occasion to do so when we come to speak of his next visit to London. The 22nd of December, 1747 (o. s.), or, as it would now be called, the 2nd of January, 1748, was, as may be imagined, a high festival in Old Burlington Street. It must have gratified Mrs. Wolfe and the General to have their brave son with them when he became of age. They had good cause to be proud of him, for few have ever distinguished themselves more remarkably before entering manhood.

Both France and England now considered that they had suffered enough from the war that had been raging for the last six years; and the captivity of Sir John Ligonier gave Louis XV. an opportunity of discussing the subject of peace with the English General, whom he treated with the greatest consideration. "Would it not be better," said the French king, "to think seriously of peace, than to occasion the death of so many brave men?" Plenipotentiaries were therefore appointed by the several Powers, and assembled in congress at Aix-la-Chapelle, the beginning of 1748. Nevertheless all parties prepared for another campaign, and Maréchal Saxe struck the first blow by investing Maestricht. Wolfe sailed from Harwich for Holland in March, and joined a detachment of English troops, stationed with the Austrian army, which was encamped in the neighbourhood of Breda. Some particulars of this period, personal as well as historical, are related in the following letter to his father:—

Osterhout, April 12, N. S., 1748.

Dear Sir,

General Fowkes is left here with four regiments of Foot, and eight pieces of cannon, to assist in defending this part of Holland. The troops are cantoned in the village, two leagues from Breda and one from Gertruidenberg, and wait the orders of him who is appointed to lead the army here; 'tis at present the Prince of Wolfenbüttel, but we are apprehensive of losing him.

As a Major of Brigade, and the first of that rank, I am here, though I took some pains to avoid it. The corps that I hear is intended to assemble in this quarter will be of thirty-five or forty battalions and some squadrons, unless the enemy's present undertaking should require them upon the Maese. I hear Maestricht is invested. Marshal Lowendahl passed the Maese with some troops at Namur, was joined by those that wintered in Louvain, marched through a country that is almost impassable in the finest seasons, seized Limbourg, and is, we are told, on the other side the river, where our army lay the greatest part of last campaign; while M. de Saxe moves with the larger part of the French army, and invests Maestricht on this side. If so, the body of Austrians there will be inferior to either of these corps, and will certainly retire, or rather has retired, and leave the unhappy fortress to its garrison and a Dutch commander. I am much at a loss to know whether that place is thought of such worth as to risk a battle with disadvantage, especially in numbers; though the situation is such that a fortunate stroke might be the total ruin of the besieging army, from the extreme breadth of the Maese, and difficulty of retiring with a beaten army over a bridge or two. But if in two or three days these regiments should move, I shall think the attempt a thing determined, and be out of doubt as to our destination.

The Prince of Orange is expected here soon. Marshal Bathiany is laid up with the gout (and in an evil hour) at Bois-le-Duc.* H.R.H. has been ill again at Venlo,† but is something better, and perhaps gone to Roremonde; the greatest part of the army is in full march to that place. Neither the English regiments from the north, nor that expected from the river, are yet arrived, though never so much wanted as at this unlucky time.

I am preparing to tell you the purport of a conversation with Colonel Yorke, the then Adjutant-General, to whom I addressed myself on being ordered to remain here. He said some civil things in relation to having a person with these people that was acquainted with this country, and the customs of the army; and proceeded to tell me that the Duke, in discourse with him, had expressed great concern at not having it in his power to serve me, but that his intention was just, and he would take an opportunity soon of making it appear. And Yorke, as a secret, told me H.R.H. intended that Field should succeed Cossley, and that he would give me the Major's commission of Bragg's regiment for nothing, and (as he was pleased to say) in order to my being Lieutenant-Colonel to it, for Jocelyn is dying. Cossley, you know, is to go out with a government, and the sale of his company only. If this be

* Bois-le-Duc, situated at the confluence of the rivers Aa and Dommel, twenty miles east of Breda, and forty-three miles north-east of Antwerp.

† Venlo, a strong town of Guelderland, situated upon the Maese.

true, you will make the proper reflections on it, and think me not much hurt. I'm sure the thing is yet far off, possibly may fail as heretofore; but with sincerity I assure you, I am out of the reach of disappointment. I heartily wish you both well. I writ to my uncle Wat from Harwich, and foretold the siege of Maestricht. He will be astonished at their early proceeding, and equally displeased with us. My duty to my mother.

I am, dear Sir,
Your most obedient and affectionate Son,
J. Wolfe.

It is evident, from Wolfe's situation at this period, that he had not lost the confidence of the Commander-in-chief on account of the imputed rebuff upon the field of Culloden. If he had, the Duke would not have stationed him with the foreign troops, as an officer of proved experience and sagacity, nor have authorized Colonel Yorke to go even so far as to say "civil things," and express his Royal Highness's interest in the Brigade-Major's advancement. Although Wolfe's promotion did not immediately follow, the delay may with great probability be partly attributed to his extreme usefulness in his present capacity. He appears to have done all kinds of work, and, in addition to the strict business of his office, to have had control over the commissariat; as, from documents still extant, it is shown that he corresponded with bread contractors, and issued orders for forage, etc.*

A letter without date, but which must have been written soon after the last, supplies the following extract:—"The Duke of Newcastle and Lord Sandwich

* A letter from Wolfe to M. de Prado, contractor for bread, dated "July 10, 1748," was lately in the possession of Robert Cole, Esq.

are expected at the army in a few days; they will see the sight, and go off. . . . The Imperialists march to-morrow towards Roremonde. The neighbourhood of Bois-le-Duc cannot furnish to an army without money. These troops must receive great assistance from the country about them. The conferences at Aix are rather languid; the warlike spirit conceives favourably, from the interest or intrigue perhaps of some mischievous particular, who may retard the general good, and keep the world in arms. Sincerely I believe you'll think I'm crazy in the brain. In one letter I tell you all is at an end, and in the next that things have a fairer face. I'm sorry to say that my writings are greatly influenced by the state of my body or mind at the time of writing; and I'm either happy or ruined by my last night's rest, or from sunshine, or light and sickly air: such infirmity is the mortal frame subject to.* I thank you for the part you are so ready to act in my behalf. Your officers are all well, and free from complaint, as from any cause."

While the congress was deliberating at Aix, Saxe and Lowendahl continued the siege of Maestricht. By the 17th of April they had brought their approaches to the covered way, which they attacked and carried that night with the loss of nine hundred grenadiers; when the governor of the city, Baron D'Aylva, made a sally, and drove them back with much slaughter. Thus they continued to keep each other at bay, and the result was doubtful, when it was notified that the preliminaries of

* "The greatest hero is nothing under a certain state of the nerves. . . . His mind is like a fine ring of bells jangled out of tune." (Lord Bolingbroke. Spence's Anecdotes, p. 76.)

peace had been signed, with orders for the cessation of hostilities. Pursuant to the articles, the Duke of Cumberland, who was preparing for the relief of the besieged, sent an officer to the governor ordering him to deliver up the fortress to the French. The garrison, therefore, marched out with all the honours of war, and Maréchal Saxe entered Maestricht on the 3rd of May, to keep possession until the ratification of the treaty between the belligerent Powers.

Although the war may be said to have now ended, the armies remained encamped until the approach of winter. Wolfe did not like a comparatively idle life, and as he agreed with the King of Prussia in thinking that having seen some service, and been in several engagements, did not suffice to constitute a real officer,* he soon began to agitate a matter, to which he was encouraged, if not prompted, by his uncle Major Walter Wolfe. Having left school so early, and been ever since associated only amongst soldiers, with little opportunity for study, he felt the deficiency of his education, and therefore was anxious to obtain leave of absence for some time, in order to travel and improve himself in the science of his profession, as well as, by intercourse with the politer world, to acquire those accomplishments which he considered indispensable to a gentleman. These remarks will explain the opening of the following heterogeneous epistle to his mother:—

* "Frederick the Great, on being told, by way of remonstrance, by one of his Generals, that he had seen many campaigns, replied, 'So has the jackass that carries my pack!'" (James's Military Dictionary, pref. xiii.)

Dear Madam,

When you have anything to grant, or a good-natured thing to say, you don't lose time. I got your letter much sooner than I expected, but upon opening it easily perceived the reason.

There will be difficulties in everything that contradicts a principle or settled opinion, entertained amongst us, that an officer [neither] can, nor ought ever to be otherwise employed than his particular military functions. If they could beat men's capacities down, or confine their genius to that rule (to be observed with the expected nicety so as to exclude all other attachments), no man would ever be fitted for a higher employment than he is in. 'Tis unaccountable that who wishes to see a good army can oppose men's enlarging their notions, or acquiring that knowledge with a little absence which they can't possibly meet with at home, especially when they are supposed masters of their present employment and really acquainted with it. In all other stations in life, that method is usually pursued which best conduces to the knowledge every one naturally wishes to have of his own profession.

Whether my request will be consented to or not I sha'n't pretend to say; it depends on them whether even I shall ask it. Pray tell my father that I thank him much for his approbation, but I can't help differing both from him and you in your objection, that I must lay aside all thoughts of preferment; because, if we may judge of what has happened, attendance, or the frequent offer of one's person to their observation, has had hitherto little effect, and I know myself secure of your voices and endeavours whether absent or not; and more particularly that, if I rise at all, it will most probably be by the means of my father's pocket. But, not to be tiresome upon this subject, I'm told that my intended journey will really be put off. I spoke to my uncle Wat in my last letter to him to this purpose. Perhaps he may mention it to you with his

such undertaking.

* "The

. . . .

. . . His m.

Bolingbroke.ı in question puts me into the very state you wish

s truly wish myself, I mean that of independency;

and though I dare not pray for money, £10,000 is worth asking for fair purposes, and might be prettily disposed of. None but earthly gods and goddesses . . . for or with the precious bane.*

Though I don't think the troops will any of them embark till the end of October, I would not have you lose time in fixing upon what you would have brought over; and if you know of anything that would be agreeable to my father, pray mention it. I know nothing that can justly excuse my putting you to an extraordinary expense. My inclination to much talk can never be a good reason. A man should shorten his discourse, or learn to write close. Everything that seems to prevent any scheme of economy I am a bitter enemy to. In the notions I entertain at present, spare diet and small beer have a strong place. Nothing but an unlucky knowledge of the immediate necessity of living well and drinking claret could, sure, persuade me to such a practice in opposition to good, close, parsimonious maxims. But what is there one may not be forced to do, where the health is concerned, however averse to inclination? To repel the vapours (as my friend justly terms them), Jemmy Donnellan and I are obliged to have recourse to a couple or three good things every day, and some Bordeaux: the management of all which he has solely undertaken, and calls for my weekly partition.

If Mr. Fox† knew how well we feed, and that sometimes the table for four is crowded, he would be jealous of our emoluments and censure our extravagance, refuse perhaps our arrears, and cut off the non-effectives. My duty to my father. I always wish you both well, and am,

Dear Madam,

Your most obedient and affectionate Son,

J. Wolfe.

Although the definitive treaty was signed in October, the English troops did not decamp until December;

* Two or three words are illegible. The allusion is doubtless to some matrimonial speculation of his mother's for his behoof.

† The Right Hon. Henry Fox, Paymaster-General.

and Wolfe, disappointed of leave of absence, impatiently awaited a change. The last of his Continental letters runs thus:—

Camp, Nesselroy, 10th November, 1748.

Dear Madam,

You have given me the greatest pleasure imaginable in your account of my father's situation. He not only can walk well, but I hope does, or at least takes such exercise as fits his inclination and contributes to his health. I would recommend the like to you, if I did not know how sensible you are of the necessity of it, and how ready to give a good example. I have been prodigiously careful of my own thin person, and I think have used all the remedies, . . . unguents, etc., that were not only useful, but even thought so, in complaisance to your opinion; and I am thoroughly reinstated. Your green oil in particular was of singular service to me, for a hurt I received by the falling of my horse (not *from* my horse), and that's well likewise.

Captain Thornton is the only one of our countrymen that thinks our army worth looking at; he was present at a review of six Wolfenbüttel battalions, and expressed both satisfaction and astonishment. He is gone away very well pleased with his reception and entertainment. It is really surprising that in the multitude of the idle and curious, it does not enter into any of their heads to be for once spectators at a military show, and amuse themselves some little time with a view of the variety of troops that compose the three separate bodies in this country. The English should accustom themselves to such sights, that they may be less at a loss, and act like men when anything new or extravagant presents itself, and that a plaid, whiskers, or a ruff cap may not be esteemed by them altogether terrible and invincible.

I received a letter yesterday from my father, and one from Rickson. The little man seems to entertain but a very indifferent opinion of widows, and threatens to be much better acquainted before he engages a second time; he even carries it so far as to suspect some of them of coquetry and deceit, and with great earnestness advises his friends to avoid that species.

My father's good designs are seen by me in the very light he means them; but 'tis too late. Other views and interests succeed at the end of a war, and favours are thrown into quite a different channel. For my particular, I wish nothing so much as the means of escaping from noise and idleness. I never till now knew our army otherwise than as I could have desired it (I don't mean as to the successful part); but then I never knew what it was to wait, in smoke and subjection, the signing articles of peace, and till now have always had, or imagined I had, a prospect of better times. I'm even flattered with the distant view of a happy arrival at Gibraltar or Minorca,—a very desirable retreat, and well adapted to my years and inclination!

I have sold my poor little grey mare; I lamed her by accident, and thought it better to dismiss her the service immediately, than wait a long while for her recovery, as has been sometimes the custom. I grieved at parting with so faithful a servant, and have the comfort to know she is in good hands, will be very well fed and taken care of in her latter days. Such another good animal I shall hardly meet with. Mrs. Inwood may give herself what airs she pleases, and boast all her ability; but I shall return, perhaps, more than her match. I have taken care by practice, and a well-regulated attention to the game, to prepare myself for the greatest trials; and so I think she should be informed, to put her the more upon her guard, and make my attacks (as they say at chess) less formidable. I heartily wish you both your health, and am,

Dear Madam,

Most dutifully and affectionately your Son,

J. Wolfe.

I believe we shall remain at least six weeks in this camp.

Although both England and France had entered into the war of the Austrian Succession merely as allies of the contending sovereigns of Austria and Prussia, before its termination, from being seconds they had become the principals. The end brought no benefit to either. Indeed the very treaty of peace was a satire on their strife; for by one of the chief articles all conquests were to be restored. The House of Hanover, it is true, had saved the much-loved Electorate, and bound down Louis no longer to harbour the Pretender,—scarcely an adequate recompence to England for all the blood and treasure she had spent, not to speak of the indignity of sending two noble hostages to Paris, until the restoration of Cape Breton should be effected. The pretended peace was nothing more than a truce, to which France was compelled by political necessity; for her resources were drained, and her people impoverished, while her navy had been annihilated by Anson, Warren, and Hawke. Bent, as she still was, upon extending her settlements in America and India, the object of France was to gain time for the purpose of recruiting her resources and renewing her navy. So the proclamation of peace was received in Paris with even greater demonstrations of joy than in London. *Te Deum* was sung in the metropolitan church on the 13th of February, 1749; and the same evening there was a grand display of fireworks in the Place de Grève. The crowd was so dense upon the memorable occasion, that fifteen persons were crushed to death, and to crown the calamity, the Seine having overflowed and inundated the *Place* during the exhibition, many more were drowned. Alluding to the treaty of Aix-la-Chapelle, Maréchal Belleisle is said to have observed to Madame de Pompadour, "It leaves affairs in America as they are, and we have twenty savage nations in Canada to take our revenge." With equal truth, Pompadour some years afterwards remarked, "Revenge cost us that country!"

When Wolfe once more returned home after his seven active campaigns, he may be said to have served his apprenticeship to the art of war, and as Mars was dethroned, our hero immediately enlisted under the banner of Cupid. The young lady who had "pleased" him the previous winter, and who fascinated him now, was Miss Lawson, one of the maids of honour to the Princess of Wales, and eldest daughter of the late Sir Wilfrid Lawson and Elizabeth Lucy Mordaunt, niece of Charles, third Earl of Peterborough.* But as Wolfe was gazetted on the 5th of January, 1749, as Major, with a view to the Lieutenant-Colonelcy of the 20th regiment, then serving in Scotland, his present stay in town lasted only three weeks. In this short space of time, Miss Lawson made rapid progress in his affections. Let us leave it, however, for himself to describe the fair charmer, his rivals, and other attending circumstances.

* Sir Wilfrid Lawson, of Isell, was one of the grooms of the bedchamber to George I., and M.P. for Cumberland. He died in 1737, leaving two sons, Wilfrid and Mordaunt, and *two* daughters, *Elizabeth* and Charlotte. (Burke's 'Extinct Baronetage.')

CHAPTER VI.

STIRLING.—GLASGOW.

FEBRUARY—OCTOBER, 1749.

SIR WALTER SCOTT, writing in 1815, said that the people of Scotland were as different from their grandfathers as the people of England from those of the reign of Elizabeth.* Certainly no other country—in the Old World, at least—exhibits within a like space of time so marked a contrast in its condition as Scotland in 1750 and Scotland to-day. This unparalleled progress may be attributed to several causes; we need name but one—the sagacious, energetic, and "self-contained" character of the people, who, as soon as ever the barriers to their advance were removed, began to overtake their competitors in the march of civilization. Few of the London tourists who "do" the Highlands in two or three weeks reflect that it would have occupied about as many days to reach the *terra incognita* of one hundred years ago, as it does hours to enter the same well-mapped districts in the present time, and that the adventure would have been much more hazardous and laborious than an excursion to the backwoods of Canada is now. The world-

* Waverley, chap. 72.

wide readers of 'Waverley,' etc., are generally so enchained by the genius of the great Wizard of the North, that instead of being instructed by the truths contained in his descriptions, they retain only the romance, and lose sight of the ugly facts which it envelopes. Rob Roy is remembered as a dashing, generous freebooter, but not as a vulgar thief; MacIvor, as a martyr to misplaced loyalty, but not as an oppressive feudal lord; and the Highland tribes, as hardy mountaineers, ever faithful to their chiefs, but not as idle, half-starved, superstitious serfs.

Until about the year of Wolfe's birth the Highlands may be said to have been almost undiscovered, and even of the more accessible parts of Scotland the greatest ignorance prevailed.* "The edge of the ancient animosity between the people of the northern and the southern divisions of this island, now happily broken and removed, was still keen. The Scottish mind was filled with distrust; it rankled with the remembrance of the treachery which forced on Scotland the then hated Union. The Hanoverian succession was by no means popular in the north, and men's minds fluctuated between the old and

* Captain Burt, writing about the year 1730, says:—"The Highlands are little known even to the inhabitants of the low country of Scotland, for they have ever dreaded the difficulties and dangers of travelling amongst the mountains; and when some extraordinary occasion has obliged any one of them to make such a progress, he has, generally speaking, made his testament before he set out, as though he were entering upon a long and dangerous voyage, wherein it was very doubtful if he should ever return. But to the people of England, excepting some few, and those chiefly soldiery, the Highlands are hardly known at all; for there has been less, that I know of, written upon the subject than of either of the Indies." (Letters from the North of Scotland, vol. i. p. 6.)

the new race of kings."* The prominent part played by the Highland clans in the Rebellion of 1715 had indeed alarmed the Government, and instigated an official survey of those mountain regions of which nothing was known except that their dreary recesses swarmed with wild warriors, who regarded with disdain the avocations of civilized life, and who, at the signal of their chiefs, were ready to descend with fury upon their comparatively peaceful neighbours of the Lowlands. After Mar's rebellion had been quashed, General Wade was ordered to reconnoitre the Highlands, with instructions to observe their strength and resources, to take a rough census of the population, and suggest such measures as he considered best calculated to promote the internal improvement of the country. In his Report, which was not delivered until 1725, Wade estimated the number of men capable of bearing arms at about 22,000, fully one-half of whom were disaffected; and, after describing their mode of life and their thieving propensities, he showed the necessity of disarming the clans, and recommended the construction of forts, with military roads to render them easily accessible to the army.† The Government determined upon carrying out the recommendations of the General, and assigned to him the duty of disarming

* Tait's Magazine, December, 1849.

† Speaking of the Highland inhabitants, the General says in his Report:—"Their notions of virtue and vice are very different from the more civilized part of mankind. They think it the most sublime virtue to pay servile and abject obedience to the commands of their chieftains, although in opposition to their Sovereign and the laws of the kingdom; and to encourage this their fidelity, they are treated by their chiefs with great familiarity; they partake with them in their diversions, and [illegible]m by the hand wherever they meet them."

the clans, and making the roads. The first he only partially effected; but his abilities as an engineer are still evinced by the excellent highways, "smooth as a college green at Oxford,"* that penetrate to the very centre of the mountain wilds.

Like all possessors of vested interests, the Highland Chiefs did not approve of Wade's work, and he encountered opposition from many of them; neither did the turbulent clans wish that their gloomy glens should be too curiously inspected. Nevertheless Wade completed his design. There still existed, however, no sufficiently powerful check upon the lawless proceedings that kept the rest of Scotland in a state of perpetual alarm. The old systems of blackmail and cattle-lifting were still carried on, and, in spite of the weakly-garrisoned forts, rebellion was fostered in the Highlands. It was not, therefore, until the hopes of the Stuarts had been finally extinguished at Culloden, that, to put an end to so grievous a state of things, the Ministry of George II. resolved to enforce the power of the law. Accordingly, a series of very stringent Acts of Parliament were passed in the autumn of 1746 and in the year following. By the Rebellion Statutes, military tenures, or in Scottish legal parlance "wardholdings," were abolished; the hereditary jurisdictions heretofore wielded by great families were transferred to the Crown; the clans were to be more effectually disarmed; the tartan and all party-coloured dress were strictly forbidden;† the Scottish Episcopalian clergy (mostly

* Carruthers's 'Highland Note-book.'

† The Disarming Act came into operation in June, 1748. The term for the total abolition of the national garb was enlarged until the 1st

Jacobites) were required to abjure their allegiance to the Stuarts, to acknowledge the Hanoverian succession, and to pray for King George and his House. These enactments were enforced with severe penalties. If arms were found in a Highlander's possession, or if he wore a philabeg; if a priest officiated contrary to the Act, or if either refused to take the oaths prescribed, he was liable to six months' imprisonment for the first offence, and transportation to the American Plantations for the second.*

While the war on the Continent lasted, few troops could be spared for Scotland; but after peace had been declared, several battalions were sent thither to serve as a kind of military police. One of these regiments was Lord George Sackville's, or the 20th Foot, which was quartered in Stirling when Wolfe was appointed Major of it, in the beginning of the year 1749.† As more than once before it had been his lot to act in a higher capacity than his commission warranted, the Major, immediately after he had joined his corps, was called upon to undertake the duties of commanding officer; the Lieutenant-Colonel, the Hon. Edward Cornwallis, having been appointed Captain-General and Governor of the new settlement of Acadia, or Nova Scotia. Under the most favourable circumstances the position must be a trying one to so young a man; but when the social and political condition

of August, 1749; but "such parts thereof as are called the plaid, philabeg, or little kilt," were prohibited after the 25th of December, 1748.

* 'Glasgow Past and Present,' vol. iii.

† His commission is dated "January 5th," but from the following passage in a letter from John Warde, Esq., to his brother George who was then in Scotland, it appears that he did not join the corps before the end of the month:—"Conduit Street, 24th January, 1748/9. . . . I saw Major Wolfe the other day, who is going northward and tells me he shall see you."

of the country, together with the predominance of the military power, are considered, it is evident that the actual commander of a regiment in Scotland had occasion for no small degree of self-control and prudence, in order to combine conciliation with the necessary firmness of purpose,—so as to act, in short, with tact.* Wolfe's early official acts as local commander of a corps are traceable through his regimental minutes, which are still preserved. It is enough to say that they show his zeal for the welfare of the service as well as his fatherly care of his men. The first is dated "Stirling, February 12, 1749." He desires to be acquainted in writing with the men and the companies they belong to, and as soon as possible with their characters, that he may know the proper objects to encourage, and those over whom it will be necessary to keep a strict hand. The officers are enjoined to visit the soldiers' quarters frequently; now and then to go round between nine and eleven o'clock at night, and not trust to sergeants' reports. They are also requested to watch the looks of the privates and observe whether any of them were paler than usual, that the reason might be inquired into, and proper means used to restore them to their former vigour. And subalterns are told that "a young officer should not think he does too much."

It appears that the soldiers were billeted about the town, which would seem to have been neither the cleanest nor soberest in Scotland. At a later period, when the population of Stirling was under 5000, there were seventy licensed dram-shops, with many more whose owners did

* The "General Orders" issued in 1748, to the commanders of regiments serving in Scotland, show that their strictly military duties formed but a very slight portion of their work.

not trouble themselves with a license. The tourist who visits Stirling now, and views with admiration from the castle-crowned rock, the highly cultivated valley through which the Forth winds its tortuous course betwixt peninsulas and islands, carries away very different impressions from those which a survey of the same district would have caused a century ago. We have it from excellent authority that Stirling was nearly stationary in extent, population, and general condition, from the time of the Reformation down to the middle of the last century.* Consequently a brief extract from a local history will afford a picture of some of the features of the town when Wolfe was quartered there. "The shops used formerly to be only long narrow arches, or *pends*, frequently without a fireplace in them. In these the old *Binorabia* sat from morning to night, mopping [*sic*] like an owl, waiting for his customers."† The burgesses were so conservative, that none but a freeman of some of their guilds could enter into any business; and their restrictions were such that no one dare so much as sew a button on his "breeks," or put a patch upon his brogues, unless he was free of the craft of tailors or shoemakers. "And had the barbers been a corporation," says the same authority, "no one durst shave himself or employ a ser-

* 'New Statistical Account of Scotland,' vol. viii.

† 'A General History of Stirling' (Stirling, 1794), p. 161. The name of the town is attributed to the perpetual *striving*, during the Pictish wars, for the possession of it, owing to its position between the two empires. The Gaelic word is *Struilla*, "a place of strife;" and the name by which the ancient Britons distinguished it was *Binobara*, having the same signification. (*Ibid.* p. 30.)

Dumbarton has been called the lock of the Highlands, of which Stirling Castle keeps the key. (De Foe's Tour, edited by Richardson.)

vant to do it for him, without being entered a freeman of that trade." As an instance of the frugality of the townsfolk, it may be added that so late as the year 1794, when many of them possessed handsome fortunes, there were only four male servants in the town. There cannot have been much agreeable society for the officers in Stirling, probably therefore they did not regret being ordered to Glasgow. Wolfe's first letter from Glasgow bears date the 25th of March, 1749, and is addressed to his mother. An extract, to show the state of his finances as well as of his feelings, will be enough for transcription.

Colonel Cornwallis does certainly go to Nova Scotia; he is to be absent for two years; all his share of duty will then fall upon me. Six or seven campaigns, and an age in Scotland; I shall be sick of my office. The very bloom of life nipped in this northern climate. I'm determined to make some use of my stay here at least. Two hours every day are given up to application: in the morning I have a man to instruct me in the mathematics, and in the afternoon another comes to assist me in regaining my almost lost Latin. The college furnishes almost all parts of learning to the inquisitive. My horses will be here in a day or two; they have cost me forty-five guineas. I'm half undone with these expenses. The common demand for my horses, servants, washing, lodging, and diet is no less than £3. 10*s*. a week. Judge, then, what there is over for many things not less requisite at £15 a month. I reckon myself to have one shilling and a penny a day for what they call pocket-money.

The next letter from the Major is addressed to his old companion William Rickson, who, from a lieutenancy in General Wolfe's regiment, was promoted to a captaincy in Colonel Peregrine Lascelles' (47th Foot) in February, 1748.

Glasgow, 2nd April, 1749.

Dear Rickson,

When I saw your writing upon the back of a letter I concluded it was in consequence of the mandate I sent to you by Lieut. Herries, of this regiment. That letter he carried upon your account and mine, not his own, as you will easily discover; but I find myself more in your debt than I expected. 'Twas your desire to please, and to express the part you take in your friend's good fortune. These were the motives that persuaded you to do what you knew would be agreeable. You'll believe me when I tell you that, in my esteem, few of what we call advantages in life would be worth acceptance if none were to partake them with us. What a wretch is he who lives for himself alone—his only aim! It is the first degree of happiness here below, that the honest, the brave, and estimable part of mankind, or, at least, some amongst them, share our success.

There were several reasons concurring to have sent me into Italy if this had not happened to prevent my intentions. One was, to avoid the mortifying circumstance of going a Captain to Inverness.* Disappointed of my sanguine hopes, humbled to an excess, I could not remain in the army and refuse to do the duty of my office while I stayed in Britain. Many things I thought were, and still are, wanting to my education. Certain never to reap any advantages that way with the regiment; on the contrary, your barren battalion conversation rather blunts the faculties than improves; my youth and vigour bestowed idly in Scotland; my temper daily changed with discontent; and from a man may become a martin or a monster.

Here follows a paragraph respecting a courtship of Rickson's.

You shall hear, in justice, and in return for your confi-

* As he had previously held but brevet rank as a Major, his promotion to the majority of the Twentieth was the success to which Wolfe alludes. His commission as Brigade-Major ended with the war.

dence, that I am not less smitten than yourself. The winter we were in London together I sometimes saw Miss Lawson, the maid of honour, G. Mordaunt's niece. She pleased me then; but the campaign in view, battledore and dangerous, left little thought for love. The last time I was in town, only three weeks, I was several times with her,—sometimes in public, sometimes at her uncle's, and two or three times at her own house. She made a surprising progress in that short time, and won all my affections. Some people reckon her handsome; but I, that am her lover, don't think her a beauty. She has much sweetness of temper, sense enough, and is very civil and engaging in her behaviour. She refused a clergyman with £1300 a year, and is at present addressed to by a very rich knight; but to your antagonist's misfortune, he has that of being mad added, so that I hold him cheap. In point of fortune, she has no more than I have a right to expect, viz. £12,000. The maid is tall and thin, about my own age, and that's the only objection. I endeavoured, with the assistance of all the art I was master of, to find out how any serious proposal would be received by Mordaunt and her mother. It did not appear that they would be very averse to such a scheme; but as I am but twenty-two and three months it is rather early for that sort of project; and if I don't attempt her, somebody else will. The General and Mrs. Wolfe are rather against it, from other more interested views, as they imagine. They have their eye upon one of £30,000. If a company in the Guards is bought for me, or I should be happy enough to purchase any lieutenant-colonel's commission within this twelvemonth, I shall certainly ask the question; but if I'm kept long here, the fire will be extinguished. Young flames must be constantly fed, or they'll evaporate. I have done with this subject, and do you be silent upon it.

Cornwallis is preparing all things for Nova Scotia; his absence will overbother me. My stay must be everlasting; and thou know'st, Hal, how I hate compulsion. I'd rather be a Major upon half-pay, by my soul! These are all new men to me, and many of them but of low mettle. Besides, I am by no means ambitious of command, when that command obliges me to reside far from my own, surrounded either by flatterers or spies, and in a country not at all to my taste. Would to God you had a company in this regiment, that I might at least find some comfort in your conversation. Cornwallis asked to have Loftus with him. The Duke laughed at the request, and refused him.

You know I am but an indifferent scholar. When a man leaves his studies at fifteen he will never be justly called a man of letters. I am endeavouring to repair the damages of my education, and have a person to teach me Latin and the mathematics, two hours a day, for four or five months: this may help me a little.

If I were to judge of a country by those just come out of it, Ireland will never be agreeable to me. You are in the midst, and see the brightest and most shining in other than a soldier's character. I wish it more pleasing to you than you mention, because probably you will stay there some time. The men here are civil, designing, and treacherous, with their immediate interest always in view; they pursue trade with warmth and a necessary mercantile spirit, arising from the baseness of their other qualifications. The women, coarse, cold, and cunning, for ever inquiring after men's circumstances; they make that the standard of their good breeding. You may imagine it would not be difficult for me to be pretty well received here, if I took pains, having some of the advantages necessary to recommend me to their favour; but . . .

My dear Rickson,

Your affectionate friend,

J. Wolfe.

To Captain Rickson, of Colonel Lascelles' Regiment.
To be left at Lucas's Coffee House, Dublin.

From the concluding paragraph of the above, it appears that Wolfe was not favourably impressed by Glasgow society. But the town at that period was very different from the fine city of the present day. In extent it stretched no further along its great arterial street than the head of Stockwell on the west, to the old Gallowgate port, on the east; and the population did not exceed twenty thousand.* The houses of the main street were lofty stone structures, the heavy fronts of which gave an exceedingly sombre aspect to the town. Probably there had been little change in either the place or its inhabitants from the days of Bailie Nicol Jarvie; but Dr. Carlyle gives a sketch of Glasgow society, in 1743, which proves that Wolfe's strictures were little, if at all, exaggerated.† The people improved, however, in his estimation on further acquaintance, and, on the whole, he seems to have liked his residence in Glasgow better than any other of his Scotch quarters.

The General, thinking thirteenpence a day's pocket-money hardly enough for the Major, needed only the hint to replenish his son's empty purse. In reply to his father's letter, in which the veteran advanced some remarks upon the advantages of a military life, James writes as follows:—

Glasgow, 7th April, 1749.

Dear Sir,

That variety incident to a military life gives our profession some advantages over those of a more even and constant nature. We have all our passions and affections roused and exercised, many of which must have wanted their proper employment had not suitable occasions obliged us to exert them. Few men are acquainted with the degrees of their own courage till dangers prove them, and are seldom justly informed how far the love of honour or dread of shame are superior to the love of life. This is a knowledge to be best acquired in an

* John Buchanan, Esq., in 'Glasgow Past and Present.'

† See Autobiography, pp. 74–5.

army; our actions are there in presence of the world, to be freely censured or approved. Constancy of temper, patience, and all the virtues necessary to make us suffer with a good grace, are likewise parts of our character, and, as you know, frequently called in to carry us through unusual difficulties.

What moderation and humility must he be possessed of that bears the good fortune of a successful war with tolerable modesty and humility, and he is very excellent in his nature who triumphs without insolence. A battle gained is, I believe, the highest joy mankind is capable of receiving, to him who commands; and his merit must be equal to his success if it works no change to his disadvantage. Lastly, a defeat is a trial of human resolution, and to labour under the mortification of being surpassed, and live to see the fatal consequences that may follow to one's country, is a situation next to damnable. But I make my introduction a little too long; however, as you started the subject, and gave me the first hints, you won't be displeased.

Your letter and several others mention Cornwallis's new officers. He will certainly get the regiment in America, and I shall as certainly have a Lieutenant-Colonel put in. In this great demand for employment, Lord George's interest, or even the Duke's own, will hardly be sufficient to keep out a new man. The Ministry must manage their people, and secure them by obligations. Let it be as it will, the sooner 'tis determined the greater share I shall have of freedom, and be more at liberty to visit you in the south.

I have this morning received a letter from my mother, by which it appears how great your consideration is for your poor Major, and how much I'm obliged to you for your ready assistance. I promise you these sums are not employed but in a manner that you yourself might approve; and I should be ashamed ever to ask, but to such purposes as becomes your son; and that I should be somewhat cramped in a sort of generous notions that are part of my inheritance, you should not hear from me on this subject; for, though I had rather be indebted to you for any kind of aid than to any man alive, yet the name of a debt is more than enough to make it disagreeable in the affair of money only. My duty to my mother.

I am, dear Sir, etc.,

J. Wolfe.

A week later, the Major, writing to his mother, after thanking her and the General for sending him relief as soon as they knew of his distress, continues:—

At the same time I can't help saying that the fruits of my own labour are perhaps the most proper supplies, and if I should go any length beyond the usual bounds, 'tis just I should pay for it. If ever my opinion differs from my father's, 'tis certain to be in my own favour. I don't believe he ever thought better of me than I do of myself. The same reasoning may serve for the greater part of mankind, so that it does not say that I am right when opposed to his sentiments. I can produce a ready excuse for not attending to the miseries of those that might look up to me for relief when I declare an inability to help them, and that the common expenses of my office at least require the revenue. But this is enough, and more than I intended, since for twenty-two, a Major's pay is pretty well; however, without any extravagance, I could easily find use for more.

. . . .

Mrs. Inwood's care of you during your illness was very obliging; she deserves everything of me for her love to the House. I wish the boxes ten times more beautiful upon her account. She shall beat me at chess, scream in a coach unreproved, or do anything she pleases when I am with her. Don't send any money by the sergeant, you'll find employment for it.

They prosecute the wearers of cambric* with great severity

* "John Miller, merchant in Hamilton, has offered a reward of one guinea, over and above what is promised by Parliament and by the trustees, to each of the first five persons who shall inform against wearers or sellers of French cambrics or lawns in Lanark." (Scots Mag., May, 1749.)

The Act 18 Geo. II., which came into effect in June, 1748, declared in this place, so that I stand in need of some change of stocks (not Bank Stocks nor South Sea). If you can get me a dozen made of whatever sort you please, I shall thank you. This place is very far from being so disagreeable as it appeared at first. The ladies are very civil and in great numbers, and they are not so desperately afraid of a soldier as formerly. The inhabitants still retain all the religion they ever had, I dare say, with rather less outward ostentation and mockery of devotion, for which they are justly remarkable.

My uncle Wat has sent a drummer to the regiment; he is not a beauty. I wish Lord George don't dismiss him. The Major writ to me about him; I consented, provided his figure was tolerable.

I do several things in my character of commanding officer which I should never think of in any other; for instance, I'm every Sunday at the Kirk, an example justly to be admired.* I would not lose two hours of a day if it did not answer some end. When I say "lose two hours," I must explain to you that the generality of Scotch preachers are excessive blockheads, so truly and obstinately dull, that they seem to shut out knowledge at every entrance. They are not like our good folks. Ours are priests, and though friends to *venaison,* they are friends to sense.

As there were no barracks in Glasgow, Wolfe, desirous of retirement in order to pursue his plan of self-improvement, lodged in the eastern suburb of Camlachie. His

that "it shall not be lawful for any person to wear in Great Britain, in any garment or apparel whatever, any cambric or French lawn, under a penalty of £5 for every offence." The same applied to venders and milliners. Owing to the prohibition of foreign manufacture, the fine Scotch linens called *Carolines* came into general use. (Scots Mag., vol. x. (1748) p. 260 *et seq.*)

* The officers not being particularly attentive to this branch of their duty, there is a Regimental Minute of July 1, 1749:—"Lord George Sackville hopes that decency, and a proper sense of duty, will for the future prevail upon the officers to attend Divine Service, and that the commanding officer of the regiment may not be obliged to order them to church with their respective companies."

abode, which is still standing, is a quaint-looking, two-story house, built in 1720 by Mr. Walkinshaw, the father of Prince Charles's mistress.* In this quiet retreat he sat down to his self-imposed tasks under the guidance of the College tutors. At the same time he did not shun society, but frequently visited at Shawfield, the residence of Colonel Macdowall, Mr. Barclay's, of Capelrig, and other houses of the neighbouring gentry. The presence also of his friend and Colonel, Lord George Sackville, who visited his regiment in the course of the summer, while it relieved the Major of the responsibility of command, added to his pleasures an agreeable companionship.

On the 28th of April, Wolfe informs his father:—

I am within this hour returned from Edinburgh, where I was a necessary person in a most disagreeable office. I went there to bury a Captain of the regiment who died of a spotted fever at his return from Shetland; that same Milbourne whose fortitude and good understanding preserved our four companies, lived to see them safe, and then left them for ever.† The regiment has lost an excellent officer, and can little spare a Captain of his abilities at a time like this, as may be imagined. He was our Paymaster. His long absence from the corps has thrown the accounts into confusion, and there are few men like him capabie of setting them to rights.

I saw several letters from London y^t spoke of our affairs. It gives me some concern y^t my old master [Colonel Rich]

* The Celtic name *Camlachie* signifies, "the miry bend of the burn," a winding stream running through the village. The house was sold after Mr. Walkinshaw's death, in 1730, and at the time of Wolfe's residence was the property of Mr. Orr, of Burrowfield. (John Buchanan, Esq., Glasgow.)

† Notwithstanding much inquiry, it has been found impossible to explain the manner in which the Paymaster preserved the companies; nor is his death noticed in the obituary of 'Scots Magazine.'

has had ill-natured things said of him. He is strong to bear up against those sort of attacks, and if they put him upon the staff will laugh at their rage.

About fifteen hundred men will be ordered this summer to the roads; our battalion furnishes their proportion.* Would you think that they intend to strike off a little extraordinary pay hitherto allowed the subaltern officers upon that duty? Such scandalous, ill-timed parsimony was never practised in any army before, and never can be without creating uneasiness and dislike.† These poor gentlemen are slaves to the service, and hardly get bread from it; and should they be cut off from this little seasonable advantage?

A few noticeable events in the annals of Glasgow occurred about this time. One of them was a tremendous fire that devastated the Gorbals, on the south side of the Clyde, by which one hundred and fifty families were rendered homeless. There being no Glasgow police in those days, the regiment exerted itself upon the occasion, and the officers afterwards subscribed liberally towards the fund for the relief of the sufferers, Lord George heading the list with fifty pounds.‡

* "April 25, 1749.—By the Duke's orders, two captains, six subalterns, six corporals, and three hundred men of the regiment, to work on the road from the Pass of Leny to the head of Loch Earn. All paviors, carpenters, smiths, miners, and bricklayers, to be sent on this service; no recruits nor awkward men, unless they happen to be of these trades."

The privates were to be furnished with coarse shirts for working in; but *check* ones were on no account to be bought. (Wolfe's Regimental Orders.) Perhaps the pattern of check was considered to verge upon *plaid* (?).

† The extra pay of the military road-makers was, to lieutenants 2*s.* 6*d.*, sergeants 1*s.*, corporals 8*d.*, and privates 6*d.* a day.

‡ "Major Wolfe and the other officers of Lord George Sackville's regiment were present all the time, and were of singular service, by placing guards upon the bridge and at all the avenues, to keep off the crowd and prevent their stealing the effects belonging to the poor

Another incident, which caused no little stir in the town, is alluded to in a letter from Wolfe to his mother, on the 21st of May:—"We expected a great tumult and some mischief at the punishment of the two men concerned in the mob; but they have prevented all that by escaping from prison. The timorous behaviour of the magistrates will not fail to create suspicions to their prejudice."* The riot, which had occurred in March, arose from a corpse having been raised by a party of resurrectionists. The body was supposed to have been carried to the College, upon which the mob attacked the building, smashed the windows, and perpetrated other depredations. Several of the rioters were tried, but only two were found guilty, and sentenced to be whipped through the town, and banished for life; but, during the time of divine service on the Sunday before the day appointed for their punishment, they made their escape. Three surgeon-apprentices also were indicted for the grave robbery, who were "fugitated for non-compearance."†

A more important event, though probably it caused less sensation amongst the populace, was the starting of a stage-coach between Glasgow and Edinburgh on the 24th of April. A vehicle was advertised to set out twice

sufferers. Many of the soldiers exerted themselves in quenching the flames and saving people's lives." (Glasgow Courant.)

* It was probably some indiscretion arising out of this affair which caused the following minute:—"June 1st. The Major desires that none of the officers will oblige him to put out any orders that may relate particularly to them, and hopes they will avoid all quarrels with the inhabitants, which must necessarily tend to their discredit and mischief, as may clearly be perceived from what already has happened."

† Scots Magazine.

a week from either place; the passengers, who were allowed a stone weight of luggage each, were to be conveyed the entire distance of forty-four miles for nine shillings a head; and the journey was to be performed in two days.* Grave burgesses, who had heard of the failure of former attempts of the same kind, shook their heads at so rash an undertaking; for wise men were not wont to run to and fro over the earth, when a fortnight was spent in the journey from Glasgow to London, and when the arrival of the English mail in the north was signalized by firing a gun.†

Neither business, study, nor pleasure prevented Wolfe from keeping up his correspondence with home. In a letter to his mother (July the 19th), there is a portrait of himself after illness, with some mention of Miss Lawson, and of his old schoolmaster, which are worth extracting:—

It is not easy to describe myself in my present state. If I say I'm thinner, you'll imagine me a shadow or a skeleton in motion. In short I'm everything but what the surgeons call a subject for anatomy; as far as muscles, bones, and the larger vessels can serve their purpose, they have a clear view of them in me, distinct from fat or fleshy impediment.

. . . .

My Maid of Honour (for I think she should, somehow or other, be distinguished,) you say was not of the party you

* 'Scots Magazine.' In the year 1768, a contract was entered into between the magistrates of Glasgow and one Wm. Hoom, of Edinburgh, by the terms of which a stage-coach, drawn by six horses, was to travel from one town to the other, once or twice a week, "as encouragement offered." As a consideration for their patronage, the contractor was bound to provide seats for the burgesses of Glasgow in preference to all others. ('The Picture of Glasgow,' Glasgow, 1812.)

† Smiles's 'Lives of Engineers,' vol. i.

met; nor do I believe, had she been there, that you would have thought ill of her companions; such superiority has virtue and good sense over their opposites. It is the greatest mistake to place a young woman of any condition in that office; 'tis but the genteeler way to wickedness; and, in truth, with submission to General Mordaunt's notions, his niece need not be for ever in public to be taken notice of, admired, and married.

. . . .

If Mr. Swinden desires it, I will write to him; but he often hears by you, and cannot doubt of my esteem for him. Writing to men of business about trifles is stealing so much necessary time from them.

The climate had already affected the Major's health. The summer of 1749 was unusually wet, and so cold that he could not sit in his room without a fire. Lord George proposed that he should have leave of absence for three months in the winter, and mentioned the necessity of his keeping up acquaintance "with the heads of our trade." It appears, however, from Wolfe's next communication to his father that he was likely soon to lose his friendly Colonel. On the 2nd of August, he writes:—

If Lord George Sackville's father is again Lord Lieutenant of Ireland, you'll see our Colonel a very considerable man in that country.* We are to lose him without hopes of finding his equal. It is almost sure that he will have Hamilton's Dragoons; and unless Colonel Conway falls to our share, among the many that solicit, none will be found that can, in any measure, make amends for the loss of him.† For my particular, I may expect his assistance, whether he is in the

* Lord George Sackville was the youngest son of Lionel Cranfield, Duke of Dorset, who, at three different periods was Lord Lieutenant of Ireland.

† The Hon. Henry Seymour Conway.

regiment or not; he has given such strong marks of his esteem that there can be little doubt.

I am almost out of conceit with Scotland; the season has been so unusually bad that it has been a summer lost to us: such rains and winds as we might expect in the month of November. I had very near relapsed for want of sun; and as it is more or less clouded every day, I am better or worse in health.

On the 13th of the same month, the Major tells his mother:—

The elements seem to have conspired against the face of the earth, first by the destruction of every kind of fruit, and now by endangering the harvest. There is not in the country a field of any sort of corn cut down. If the hand of the Lord be not upon them, they are in a terrible latitude.

This is Sunday, and we are just come from church. I have observed your instructions so religiously, that rather than avoid the word, I got the reputation of a very good Presbyterian, by frequenting the Kirk of Scotland till our chaplain appeared. I'm now come back to the old faith, and stick close to our communion. The example is so necessary, that I think it a duty to comply were that the only reason, as, in truth, it is not.

To-morrow Lord George Sackville goes away, and I take upon me the difficult and troublesome employment of a Commander. You can't conceive how difficult a thing it is to keep the passions within bounds, when authority and immaturity go together; to endeavour at a character that has every opposition from within, and that the very condition of the blood is a sufficient obstacle to. Fancy you see me, that must do justice to good and bad; reward and punish with an equal unbiassed hand; one that is to reconcile the severity of discipline with the dictates of humanity; one that must study the tempers and dispositions of many men, in order to make their situation easy and agreeable to them, and should endeavour to oblige all without partiality, a mark set up for everybody to observe and judge of; and last of all, suppose me employed in discouraging vice and recommending the reverse at the turbulent age of twenty-three, when it is possible I may have as great a propensity that way as any of the men that I converse with.

As Wolfe was a human barometer, an improvement in the weather may have helped to give a more cheerful tone to the following:—

Glasgow, 8th September, 1749.

Dear Madam,

I don't know how the mathematics may assist the judgment, but they have a great tendency to make men dull. I, who am far from being sprightly even in my gaiety, am the very reverse of it at this time. I'm heavier in discourse, longer at a letter, less quick of apprehension, and carry all the appearances of stupidity to so great a height, that in a little time they won't be known from the reality; and all this to find out the use and property of a crooked line, which, when discovered, serves me no more than a straight one, does not make me a jot more useful or more entertaining, but, on the contrary, adds to the weight that nature has laid upon the brain, and blunts the organs.

I have been writing congratulatory letters to General Mordaunt and Colonel Rich; they are both quick-sighted men; I wish they don't pass censure upon my labours, and criticize my style of *writ* (as 'tis termed here); but I could not deny myself the pleasure of assuring the General how glad I was of his success, and the Colonel that he had the fairest title to the gift, large as it is.*

I have got a gun from Mr. Barbar; now I propose to amuse myself a little in that way, and in a few weeks I shall hunt. The regiment keeps hounds, and my horses are pretty good.

* Sir John Mordaunt had been placed on the Staff as one of the Reviewing Generals; and Robert, second son of Sir Robert Rich, Bart., who as Lieutenant-Colonel commanded the Fourth, or King's Own regiment of Foot at Culloden, succeeded to the Colonelcy on the death of General Barrell, in August, 1749.

I forgot in my last to speak of Captain Flight; I know him quite well, and can assure those that inquire after him that there is nowhere a man of a better disposition. He is greatly esteemed among us, and by all his acquaintance; 'twas the highest injustice of me not to mention him before, as I could not in truth say anything that was not to his advantage. My duty to my father. I am,

My dear Madam, etc.,

J. Wolfe.

The Major's promotion to the Lieutenant-Colonelcy was now in agitation, for it had been determined that Cornwallis was not to return to the corps. On the 18th of September, Wolfe writes to his father:—

Lord Tyrawley said humorously, being asked if the King spoke to him, and how he received his lordship, that "few words are best among friends."* The Duke has not kept you in suspense, from whence we may conclude—according to Lord Tyrawley—that our affairs are well there. I hope his Royal Highness will make such a choice as must oblige us to own his justice. If he is an older officer, it is to be supposed he is a better, and then there can be no complaints on our side. I have attained to such a height of indifference and diffidence together, that a denial sits very easy upon me. Frequent refusals might in time alienate my affections from the service, especially if many years are wasted in exile, with no very entertaining objects to employ the thoughts upon.

* "Lord Tyrawley," says Walpole, "had a thorough knowledge of the world, though less of his own country than of others. He had long been minister in Portugal, where he grew into such favour, that the late King, to keep him there, would have appointed him a General. He had a great deal of humour, and occasional good-breeding; but not to the prejudice of his natural temper, which was imperiously blunt, haughty, and contemptuous, with an undaunted portion of spirit. Accustomed to the despotism of Portugal, Muscovy, and the army, he had little reverence for parliaments, and always spoke of them as the French do of the long robe." (Memoirs of George II., vol. ii. p. 291. See also, 'Chatham Correspondence,' and Walpole's Letters.)

Mrs. Wolfe was desirous that her son should pass the winter months at home; and he writes to inform her that it cannot be so, in the following terms:—

Glasgow, 2nd October, 1749.

Dear Madam,

It will not be possible in my circumstances to get leave of absence for four months; we can expect no such indulgence. A less time is not worth asking for, and therefore I'll pass the winter at Perth. I must hunt and shoot for exercise, and read for entertainment. After Christmas, when the company comes into Edinburgh, and the place is in all its perfection of dirt and gaiety, I'll repair thither, and stay a fortnight or three weeks. It will help to dispel melancholy, and I have been told that a certain smell is a remedy for the vapours; there I can't fail to meet the cure.

This day fortnight we leave this town, and till we return to it cannot hope to find so good quarters. According to the rotation of the troops in Scotland, the sixth year brings us back; but 'tis a dreadful interval, a little life to a military man; and for my particular, so far from being in love with the country, that I'd go to the Rhine, or Italy, nay, serve a campaign against the Turks, rather than continue in it the time I have mentioned, and that too in the very blooming season of our days. It is my misfortune to miss the improving hour, and to degenerate instead of brightening.

Few of my companions surpass me in common knowledge, but most of them in vice. This is a truth that I should blush to relate to one that had not all my confidence, lest it be thought to proceed either from insolence or vanity; but I think you don't understand it so. I dread their habits and behaviour, and am forced to an eternal watch upon myself, that I may avoid the very manner which I most condemn in them. Young men should have some object constantly in their aim, some shining character to direct them. 'Tis a disadvantage to be first at an imperfect age; either we become enamoured with ourselves, seeing nothing superior, or fall in the degree of our associates.

I'll stop here, that you may not think me very uneasy. As I now am, it is possible that I might be better pleased, but my duty and a natural indolence of temper make it less irksome; and then a pretty constant employment helps to get me through, and secures me from excess or debauch. That, too, is enough prevented by the office of a commander. My duty to my father.

I am, dear Madam,

Your obedient and affectionate Son,

J. Wolfe.

CHAPTER VII.

PERTH.

November, 1749—September, 1750.

The regiment under the command of Major Wolfe enjoyed favourable weather on the march, of one-and-sixty miles, from Glasgow to Perth, for the autumn turned out as fine as the summer had been unseasonable.

It is scarcely necessary to remind the reader that the Royal Burgh of 1749 bore little resemblance to the "Fair City" of our day. The leading thoroughfares were but narrow lanes, seldom swept except by an opportune overflow of the Tay; and the town, composed of wood-fronted houses, had neither trade nor manufacture, while the building of most note was John Knox's Kirk. The environs, though then, as now, naturally beautiful, presented a very different degree of culture; for the vale through which the broad river winds was little better than a marsh. It may, therefore, be within the truth to say, that all the centuries from the time when Agricola is said to have exclaimed, "*Ecce Tiber! Ecce Campus Martius!*" down to the middle of the eighteenth, left fewer marks of man's industry than the single century which followed.

The Twentieth regiment had not been long stationed in Perth when Lord Bury was appointed Colonel; and as the Major was obliged to correspond frequently with his new commander, probably he had little leisure to write home. At all events no letter of his from Perth has reached us prior to one of the 15th of December. A short extract from his communication to his mother on that day furnishes a picture of the times:—"The women in this country partake very much of society with men, and by that means gain a certain freedom of behaviour uncommon in England. 'Tis a usual thing for the matrons to sit at table with the men till very late, and concur in everything but the actual debauchery; and as the men warm with wine, they speak openly enough to give offence with us."

This might appear to be somewhat overdrawn, had not recent representations by native writers on Scottish manners, at even a later period, more than borne it out. It was a time when gaudy ostentation and disgusting slovenliness were common to both sexes: when elderly ladies wore worsted gowns with aprons, and huge linen caps, called *toys*, and gentlemen lounged away the morning in greasy nightcaps and dirty dressing-gowns; drunkenness, instead of being considered a vice, was looked upon as a sign of manhood, and clergymen felt no shame in being regarded as jovial companions. Domestic comfort was as yet unthought of. The rap of a poker, or the heel of a shoe, served all the purposes of a bell, and was answered by a lassie without shoes or stockings. Earthenware and glasses were represented by less brittle wooden platters and pewter pots; and guests commonly came provided with their own knives and forks. As to cookery, the less said of it the better. The bedchambers seldom had fire-places, and half-a-dozen pairs of Scotch blankets were not too many for winter nights in the North. As windows were not made to open, the low-ceiled apartments of ordinary houses were never thoroughly ventilated; and soap and water being deemed superfluous, the natural consequences were frequent infectious disorders.*

But to return to the Major's correspondence. He opens the new year, as we would call it, with the following unusually short letter to his mother:—

Perth, 16th January, 1750.

Dear Madam,

Since Lord George Sackville left the regiment I have changed my way of life. When we were at Glasgow together I had taken that opportunity to acquire a few things that I was before ignorant of, and in which I might expect assistance from some of the people of the College. I was even so far engaged that I did not give up such a share of time and attention as was due to his lordship. Now all this is vanished, and I am entirely at leisure to prosecute such entertainments as I find of use to my health and agreeable to my taste. As the latter is generally subservient to the first, I have improved and strengthened my constitution beyond what I have hitherto known.

Your letter confirmed some unsteady thoughts I have had of providing a little coarse linen, and I made the purchase the day after I received it. Seven shirts at three shillings a yard will be durable wear. Yes, I shall be very rich whenever we meet! I have the talent for heaping up wealth, and the temptation must be very great when I am persuaded to part with it!

* Dr. Somerville's Life and Times.

My Lieutenant (Partridge) came by here a few days since, and delivered Miss Hoskins's compliments. He is her neighbour at Croydon. He tells me he thinks her a complete woman, and advises me, as a friend, to make up to her. This is his counsel, and the manner in which he offered it. But he did not know Miss Lawson; he confessed that. I thank you for remembering my birthday; I had almost forgot it myself, and was in dispute about my own age—whether twenty-three or twenty-four. My duty to my father, etc.

J. WOLFE.

It will be recollected that in his letter to Captain Rickson the Major represented that his parents discouraged his attachment to Miss Lawson, whose fortune they deemed inadequate, and that they had "an eye upon one of thirty thousand pounds." The lady they approved of as a suitable match for their son was the above-mentioned Miss Hoskins, of Croydon, whose compliments were delivered by Lieutenant Partridge. It would also appear from a passage in the letter preceding the last, either that the General and Mrs. Wolfe had positively forbidden the banns, or that Miss Lawson had rejected his suit, for he had written:—"This last disappointment in love has changed my natural disposition to such a degree, that I believe it is now possible I might prevail upon myself not to refuse twenty or thirty thousand pounds, if properly offered. Rage and despair do not commonly produce such reasonable effects; nor are they the instruments to make a man's fortune by but in particular cases."

But neither his duty to his parents,—which, by the way, he carried to an extent unknown to grown-up children in these our days,—nor the prospect of a larger fortune, nor the fair one's coldness, could abate the fervour of Wolfe's love. His next letter, being addressed to his father, turns chiefly upon professional affairs. On the 31st January he writes:—

My Colonel (Lord Bury) and I have very exact correspondence. He is extremely bent upon procuring all the knowledge of regimental affairs that the distance between us will allow of, in order, I suppose, to make such alterations and amendments as seem requisite, and to be the better prepared against he comes amongst us. I answer his letters very punctually, and endeavour all in my power to satisfy him in such particulars as are properly within my sphere; confining, however my judgment of men and things to what is purely military and belonging to my office. He can give you weekly intelligence as far as the assurance of a letter can go, whenever you are so good to make inquiry after me.

I have heard very lately from Gibraltar, and both my friends Loftus and Donnellan seem to detest their situation, and are a little displeased with their Governor. They complain of being too strictly confined, and of too much duty. These are real grievances at the end of seven campaigns, when men very naturally desire some respite from the fatigue of a soldier's life, especially as they see almost all their brethren in quiet and ease. I am afraid General Bland is not quite so well bred and polite as might be wished; he has a roughness about him that breaks out sometimes into ill manners, when he is in authority.

. . . .

I'm glad that my cousin Goldsmith has at last got a company.* I suppose it is so. I dare say he is obliged to you for some assistance; or, if you have not done him some service, I'm sure there was no want of inclination in you to do it. All your relations will, I am persuaded, agree that if they have deserved well of you they have not found you backward.

* "January, 1750. Edward Goldsmith, Esq., appointed Captain in Otway's (35th) regiment of Foot." (Scots Magazine, from Gazette.)

From a subsequent letter to Mrs. Wolfe a couple of passages are selected :—

Your opinion of Miss Lawson has inflamed me anew, and you have exactly hit upon that part of her perfection (her behaviour) that worked the strongest upon me; for I have seen a hundred handsome women before, and never was in love with one. How could you tell me that you liked her, and at the same time say her illness prevents her wedding? I don't think you believe she ever touched me at all, or you could never speak with so much indifference of her ill-health and marriage,—the only things in relation to that lady that could give me the least uneasiness, except that I thought you were averse to her; and even that you have taken care to clear up by your approbation of her manners and person, and by that means have left me absolutely destitute of relief.

. . . .

I think I told you in one of my letters that Roland was ill. He has been in so terrible a condition for four months that I have had hardly any service from him. At length we thought it would be best to get him into Chelsea, which I have endeavoured to do to the utmost of my power. I did not mention it to my father, as I knew he does not love to be troubled with these sort of things; nor did I tell Roland to wait upon you, concluding he would do that of course. But I perceive the poor fellow's modesty is greater than . . . Captain Wilson has undertaken to do his business . . . where the honest old servant is to be found. 'Twas death to me to part with him. It has made me vast . . . though accidentally I hired a tolerable English . . . * pretty well.

In his next letter to his father, in reply to some observations on "obstinacy and perseverance in error," the Major declares his complete submission to paternal authority. A few days later he complains that his mother does not answer his letters, and hopes that "the

* The seal of the letter has obliterated the missing words.

penalty will not exceed his crime." The nature of the crime will be readily inferred. These little domestic jars were, however, soon happily dissipated by his promotion, on the 20th of March, to the Lieutenant-Colonelcy of the regiment. He expresses his feelings upon the occasion as follows:—

Perth, March 29th, 1750.

Dear Madam,

'Tis a vast accession to my successes in life that it never fails to give my father and you as much satisfaction as I myself am capable of receiving. That I have the happiness to be so far in your esteem and opinion as firmly to unite our interests I cannot doubt, especially as every day I see both in greater anxiety for what regards me alone, than for the highest of your own concerns. This is what increases and improves my good fortune, by making you partakers of it. The post to-morrow will bring me some positive account. As yet, Lord Bury has only said that the King has consented to the Duke's recommendation. Former examples have taught me not to think the business done till I'm sure of it. The Duke himself has been sometimes disappointed when he has thought every obstacle removed.

If the causes of the earthquakes are natural (which I suppose they are), and to be accounted for, they are in the right who remove at a distance from the danger. There may be more moisture in some parts of the island than in others, and consequently less to be feared in those parts. Though these shocks are very unusual in England, and of course very terrible, I don't hear of much mischief following. It is to be hoped it will have a good effect. Most people imagine these tremblings supernatural, and such consciences as are under the heaviest loads of iniquity will tremble in proportion to that weight, and to the convulsions of the earth.*

* On Thursday, 8th February, 1750, an earthquake was felt throughout London and its environs, which set furniture a-shaking, threw down several chimneys, and greatly alarmed the lawyers in the Courts

I left my letter open till the post came in. Everything is confirmed without possibility of repeal. I'm very sensible of the greatness of the favour done me, and receive it with tolerable humility. This you would have a further proof of had you been by when the first advice came. I try to prevent its working too strongly upon me, that I may not disappoint the givers and those that rejoice.

I am, dear Madam, etc.,

J. WOLFE.

The foregoing was followed by a letter to the old General, containing the loyal and grateful acknowledgments of the new Lieutenant-Colonel, who on the 6th of April writes:—

The Duke's behaviour to you in the business of my promotion was right noble. As he made you very happy in the main point, your concession to my mother, by satisfying the desire she had of sending me the earliest intelligence, was in imitation of the example given us by that Prince,—that we are not only to enjoy the good that has fallen to us, but make other people partakers of it.

The Duke has employed his power and influence upon this occasion where, at least, it is sure to be remembered. There are not many opportunities in life, and the prospect, as things stand at present, very distant; but if ever he commands the

at Westminster Hall. There was a violent and continuous shock on the 8th of March, at half-past five A.M., which caused many folks to turn out of their beds earlier than usual, and run into the streets "almost naked." Church bells were set a-ringing, and vast quantities of china were broken. Dogs howled in an uncommon manner; and fish jumped out of the water. A crazy Life Guardsman having prophesied a more fatal repetition on the 4th of April, incredible numbers of people left their homes, and walked in the fields, or lay in boats all night. People of fashion drove out of town and sat in their coaches till daybreak, and the roads were never more thronged with fugitives. "So far, and even to their wits' end had their superstitious fears or guilty conscience driven them." See 'Gentleman's Magazine,' vol. xx. pp. 89, 137, and 184.

army of this nation in its defence, I shall wish to be with him, and glad to contribute something to his success. This is the only return that can be justly made from me to him, and all, I believe, he would expect. I think myself much obliged to Lord George Sackville, and have writ him the strongest assurances of it. What he said some time ago to his Royal Highness left, no doubt, a favourable impression, and forwarded this succession. I did not forget to tell Colonel Napier that some thanks are certainly due to him. The last three years of the war I was immediately about his person, and without his friendship and approbation things could not have gone on so smoothly.*

From a great deal of little trifling business I have fallen into a state of inactivity. If it were possible, while I am capable of improvement, and young enough to apply, I could wish to be allowed an interval to be bestowed upon myself; a year and a half or two years would wear off the rough, unpolished coat, and give a gloss to all my future actions. It may be reasonably said that I have not for seven years past been at liberty to acquire the common accomplishments, much less to embellish or refine. I'm persuaded you would have thought it necessary, had not the war prevented your intentions, to have sent me from England to some place proper for the purpose. I hope you still think it not too late, and this the fairest opportunity. Turin seems the best calculated to answer my ends. I shall be glad to have your opinion, and to know whether you approve my choice and inclination, and what steps should be taken for effecting it.

On the 27th of April the Lieutenant-Colonel again writes to his father, stating that Lord Bury did not wish

* Lieut.-Colonel (Robert) Napier became Deputy Quartermaster-General in 1745. The following year he was promoted to the rank of Colonel, and appointed Adjutant-General. George II. gave him the colonelcy of a new regiment (51st Foot) in 1755. He rose to the rank of Lieutenant-General in 1759, and died in November, 1766. ('Records of the British Army.')

him to be absent for any length of time from the regiment. "I am nevertheless," he continues, "still determined to employ some years of my life in the real business of an officer; and not sacrifice all my time to idleness, or our trifling soldiership. Some of the nations of Europe will soon give me an opportunity to put this resolution into practice. I have this day received a letter from my uncle Wolfe. He says he has writ to you about my going to Turin; he certainly means well, but I know it to be unnecessary and superfluous. What is to be done for my advantage you were never backward to comply with; nor need you any second application when the first appears reasonable, of which nobody will dispute your right of judging."

In the next letter Mrs. Wolfe is told that her son cannot visit her until some months later, and he expresses great concern at not being able to spend part of the summer at Greenwich; for nothing would do him so much good, or agree so well with his constitution, as the air of Kent; and that "it blows nowhere clearer or purer than upon Shuter's Hill, or in the Park." Then, commending his mother's tenderness, and her desire to make the old General's life easy and happy, the writer adds:—"I have only one thing to say, which is that as my father has already made as complete a provision for us both as is necessary to our well-being, no future views for you or me can any longer be looked upon as sufficient reasons to debar him any enjoyment that it is possible to procure him in this life; so don't wait for me to take such resolutions as you think most agreeable to his inclination."

From the same letter, out of much irrelevant matter, we may pick a passing remark upon the Greenwich schoolmaster:—"It gives me vast pleasure that Mr. Swinden is in so fair a way of obtaining the character of a father; his understanding and good temper fit him for the education of children."

There is also a touch of satire in reference to his aunt's, Mrs. F. Thompson's, marriage, which that lady's nephew speaks of as a "pleasant thing," and hopes that the happy man, whom he supposes to be a philosopher, "as a grammarian does not depend upon his rhetoric to keep her in good humour." *

In order to enjoy a little recreation and recruit his health, our young Lieutenant-Colonel, in the beginning of June, retired into the country, where goats' whey and bathing did him much service; but after two or three weeks' absence from Perth he was obliged to return thither to meet Lord Bury, who then paid the regiment his first visit, ran through the Highlands, looked at the forts, and returned, all in three weeks. As his lordship expected his lieutenant to see to the men's clothing, and to make the necessary arrangements for change of quarters in October, Wolfe's leave of absence was further postponed. Meanwhile, the home correspondence is not neglected. There is no letter, however, of general interest until we come to one of the 15th July to his father, wherein the condition of the Highlands is the chief topic,

* Mrs. Wolfe's sister, *Frances*, married Stephen Abthorpe, D.D., Fellow of Eton College, step-brother of William Cole, who speaks of his nieces Frances and Anne Abthorpe as first cousins to Wolfe. (Additional MSS., B. M. 4832; Nichols' 'Literary Anecdotes.') Mrs. Abthorpe died in 1755.

and to which a long postscript is appended, containing, lady-like, the matter of most importance to the writer, who was as pertinacious upon this point as he was constant to his first love.

Everything in Scotland is in the most perfect calm and quiet. But late discoveries have made it very apparent that the tranquillity of this country is no-how so well secured as by a considerable armed body; and such a body is now so disposed throughout the whole Highlands that any attempt must be crushed in the beginning. The Highlanders are so narrowly watched that they are even forced to abandon the favourite practice of stealing cattle, and are either reduced to live honestly and industriously, or starve through excess of idleness.

Since I writ my last letter to you, I have been in a country where Colonel Lafausille's name is still dreadful in their ears, and where we have a detachment chiefly intended to prevent the officers of the Scotch regiments in the French service from recruiting. I went three days successively a-shooting in the hills from five in the morning till night. I never knew such fatigue. Some amends were made us by the quantity of game and elegance of the sport; but I, who am a very bad shot, had an equal share of the labour and less of the entertainment.

P.S.—I have some thoughts of going this winter into Lorraine, to Metz, or Thionville, if you approve the notion. If I am to be absent from the regiment, I suppose it is the same thing to the Duke where I am, but to myself of vast importance. I want to be perfect in the French language. There is a fine academy of artillery and the business of an engineer at Metz. I shall be glad of your opinion, by which I shall always be regulated. A winter idly spent in London (and 'tis difficult not to spend it idly) would, at this time, be of sensible prejudice; perhaps infuse such notions and inclinations as are not to be got the better of.

On the 13th of August Wolfe replies to a letter of his

mother's, relative to domestic losses, and consoles her in a manner not less philosophical than affectionate.

Though your letter has in it some unpleasant particulars, the weak condition of your health is by far the more so. It is easy for us all to bear up against attacks of a lesser kind, but to be disabled and cut off by distemper from the enjoyment of life and common tranquillity is the heaviest of all calamities. For some years past we have begun a course of good fortune, preserved and protected where was most need, and, my brother's death excepted, free from affliction. We may make some allowance now, and, for my part, who am likely to be the greatest sufferer by any diminution of the stock, I can easily console myself for losses that way. All I desire is, that you two may meet with no disturbance to your own persons, but pass your days in health and peace. I heartily wish that these lighter accidents may not interrupt your felicity, which I would have fixed upon the firmest foundation.

. . . .

I have but just returned from Lord Glenorchy's, where I stayed a week. Lady Glenorchy is your acquaintance, and expresses a great regard for you. She says you have surprising luck at quadrille, and bid me tell you she wishes it may continue. The poor woman is in a state of banishment; she hates the country and dislikes the inhabitants. Her love to her husband, and immoderate fondness for her young son, are just enough to make her stay tolerable.* They invited and entertained me with all imaginable civility.

George Warde made me a visit of four days. I could not help being astonished at the strength of his understanding,

* John, Viscount Glenorchy, was the only son of the third Earl of Breadalbane. He married Willielma, daughter of William Maxwell, Esq., of Preston, and died (before his father) in 1771, without surviving issue. (Burke's 'Peerage.') As Taymouth Castle did not exist in Wolfe's time, most probably the place visited by him was Balloch Castle, the ancient seat of the Breadalbane family, only a few miles from Perth.

which I never discovered so fully before. To that he has added a just and upright way of thinking very uncommon, and the strictest morals of any young man amongst my acquaintance; this last won't surprise you, because he was never reckoned vicious. He is extremely indifferent as to preferment and high employment in the army, partly from his defect of speech, but principally from an easiness, or rather indolence, of temper that make him unfit to bear a heavy part in life.

The following letter to his father shows how far in advance of the day Wolfe's ideas were upon the proper qualification of a military officer:—

Perth, 1st September, 1750.

Dear Sir,

I am glad to have your approbation in whatever I undertake, especially in those things that are most worth your consideration, and are of importance to myself. The assurances you give me of your assistance are kind and friendly. If the request be properly examined, there can be no objection to it; for I ask no more than an opportunity to be better acquainted with the duty of an officer, and to have it in my power to speak the French language correctly,—a language that is now in such general use. For idleness or amusement I need not go out of London, or at least not further than Paris; but as the business I am going upon will require all my labour and attention, I chuse to be at a distance from any temptation. If the Duke consents, it will be with regret; for the perfection of military knowledge, in his Royal Highness's eye, is the command of a regiment to men of our rank, and his notion of care and diligence centres entirely in sticking eternally at the same point, viz. the Battalion; though I could undertake to make it appear that nothing is more necessary towards doing one's part well than a little respite at convenient seasons.

Lord Bury, too, will with difficulty be brought to hearken to such a proposal. I intend to try him in a post or two, and ask ten months' leave at once. Though I have all the reasons in the world to be satisfied with his behaviour to me, yet there are many circumstances that foretell his opposition; but the manner in which he will express himself will leave me no room to be displeased even with a denial as to his part, or rather he'll endeavour to satisfy me of his good intentions, and fix the refusal somewhere else.

I shall be cruelly disappointed if this fails, for my time of application will soon be over, and the sooner by the discouragement and mortification that follow the disappointment. If General Mordaunt is in town, I can write to him. He may say something upon the occasion that might be serviceable.

Donnellan complains bitterly of Gibraltar; he desires me to speak to you in favour of him, but as it is a regimental business, I shall be tender, though I heartily wish he could be indulged.

. . . .

I beg my duty to my mother,

And am, dear Sir, etc.,

J. Wolfe.

After the date of the above, some more time was passed by the Lieutenant-Colonel visiting the neighbouring gentry. His health was now comparatively strong, and as he still entertained the hope of being permitted to pursue his scheme of improvement on the Continent, his spirits also were good.

The last filial missive from Perth is an amusing medley. It exhibits, however, some characteristic traits; a few passages from it may therefore interest the reader.

23rd September, 1750.

Dear Madam,

I am a little later in answering your letter than I ought to be. The truth is, I have been at a gentleman's house in the country, where they would not allow me leisure even to do the most pleasing parts of my duty, and hindered me from writing to you. I'm sorry to hear that knavery has crept into your town, and to your very doors. These are interruptions and inconveniences in life that we are in England very much troubled with, and yet much more to be desired than the murdering bloody genius of the other nations. The mildness of our laws does not enough discourage the practice of robbing, but in a great measure prevents the terrible effects of despair.

. . . .

I hope Lady Vanbrugh will accept your offer, or, if she does not, I hope you'll come up to her price. A good and healthy situation can't be purchased at too high a rate, and the Castle you speak of, if I remember right, is so situated.* I want to have you well fixed in a comfortable house in a wholesome air, and when you procure that for yourselves, you'll help me to a great share of tranquillity that I am unacquainted with, while there remains anything to be done that can furnish you with the means of happiness. I give you my word that though I have in myself a wandering and unsettled turn of mind, regardless of any fixed condition, and indifferent as to many of the great concerns of life, yet I am perfectly steady when I consider of your well-being, and earnestly bent upon seeing you in quiet possession of the few things that are necessary to satisfy your moderate desires. I am delighted to hear you say my father has been so well this summer. Am I never to eat figs with him in his own garden? How readily would I resign my military authority, and lay down my command, for the pleasure of walking with him upon the dry ground, and gathering his fruit!

There's no fish in this part of the world but salmon; in the

* The Castle built upon Maize Hill by that "wit full of mirth in his comedies, and architect full of gravity in his buildings," Sir John Vanbrugh, was not purchased by General Wolfe, but by Lord Tyrawley, who afterwards sold it to Charles Brett, Esq. A neighbouring structure of Sir John's is said to have been modelled after the Bastille. Leigh Hunt says that Vanbrugh was the son of a Dutchman by a French mother. He died in 1726. Lady Vanbrugh survived him fifty years.

Orkneys and Shetland there are various kinds, and well cured. I don't believe it will be difficult to get what you want, though I have not the best talents for those sort of things. In this I resemble a friend of yours most exactly. I wish there was as strong a resemblance in many other respects. I never give anything away that I intend for you, but I think the hood is hardly worth your acceptance. I believe my father did not get the skins I brought from Holland. I have sent to Norway for most elegant furs; enough for linings of all sorts.

My journey to London will be very short, if the Duke gives me leave to go abroad; if not, I move but slowly, and visit my uncle Tim and the rest. It matters little what season of the year I travel in, for I am absolutely as hard as flint, and can bear all the excesses of heat and cold that are known in these climates with great ease.

My duty, etc.,

J. Wolfe.

CHAPTER VIII.

DUNDEE.—LONDON.—BANFF.

OCTOBER, 1750—SEPTEMBER, 1751.

ON the 1st of October the last division of Lord Bury's arrived at Dundee, where the regiment assembled to be clothed and quartered. The superintendence of this business, with the preparation of the companies for detachments, devolved upon the Lieutenant-Colonel; for Colonels-in-chief in those days contented themselves with their profits accruing from the "off-reckonings," "vacant pay," and other perquisites, without interfering in the more laborious details of the work.* So Wolfe had enough to do just now, yet he did not fail to keep up his correspondence with absent friends. Although the date of the letter which follows has been obliterated by

* "One of the perquisites of Colonels mentioned, arises from *vacant pay*, *i. e.* the pay of such officers and men as happen to die or be killed, till they are either respited at the musters, or filled up; which in the late wars was pretty considerable, as King William and the Duke of Marlborough seldom filled up vacancies which happened in action till the beginning of the next campaign; but the Duke of Cumberland generally fills them up immediately, so that there are seldom any, but if there are, they go to the Colonel." The profit derived by the Colonel of a Foot regiment out of the clothing fund, or *off-reckonings*, was upwards of £200 a year. (Abstract of Inquiry into the State of the Army, 'Gentleman's Magazine,' 1746.)

time, internal evidence shows that it was written at this period. Captain Rickson was now serving with his regiment in Nova Scotia, whither he had sailed from Dublin in June. It will be seen that Wolfe felt no little interest in the settlement of the colony under the government of his late superior officer, the Hon. Edward Cornwallis:—

Dear Rickson,

You were embarked long before I thought you ready for your expedition, and sailed before I could imagine you on board. I intended to have bid you farewell, and sent my good wishes to attend you; indeed, I was not without hopes of hearing from my friend before he went off, for upon such changes he seldom forgot to make me acquainted with his destination. I am not entirely indifferent as to what befalls you, and should have been glad to know how such an undertaking as this is agreed with your way of thinking, and whether, after a good deal of service, you would not rather have sat down in peace and rest; or if your active spirit prompts you to enterprise and pushes you on to pursuits new and uncommon, whether this [expedition], certainly great in its nature, suits your inclination.

Since I cannot be clearly informed of these matters till I hear from you, I shall content myself with entertaining some conjectures that are favourable to your interest. You are happy in a governor, and he'll be happy to have one near him that can be so serviceable to him as you have it in your power to be. I dare say you are on good terms together, and mutual aid will confirm your former friendships. He will require from you industry and assiduity, and, in return, you may expect his confidence and trust. I look upon his situation as requiring one of his very way of thinking, before all things else; for to settle a new colony, justice, humanity, and disinterestedness are the high requisites; the rest follows from the excellent nature of our Government, which extends itself in full force to its remotest dependency.

. . . . . .

In what a state of felicity are our American colonies, compared to those of other nations, and how blessed are the Americans that are in our neighbourhood above those that border upon the French and Spaniards! A free people cannot oppress, but despotism and bigotry find enemies among the most innocent. It is to the eternal honour of the English nation that we have helped to heal the wound given by the Spaniards to mankind by their cruelty, pride, and covetousness. Within the influence of our happy Government all nations are in security.

The barrier you are to form will, if it takes place, strengthen ourselves, protect and support our adherents; and, as I pretend to have some concern for the general good and a vast desire to see the propagation of freedom and truth, I am very anxious about the success of this undertaking, and do most sincerely wish that it may have a prosperous issue. I think it is vastly worth your while to apply yourself to business, you that are so well acquainted with it; and, without any compliment, I may venture to assert that Cornwallis has few more capable to do him and the public considerable service than yourself.

I beg you will tell me at large the condition of your affairs, and what kind of order there is in your community; the notions that prevail; the methods of administering justice; the distribution of lands, and their cultivation; the nations that compose the colony, and who are the most numerous; if under military government, how long that is to continue; and what sect in religious affairs is the most prevailing. If ever you advise upon this last subject, *remember to be moderate.* I suppose the Governor has some sort of council, and should be glad to know what it is composed of. The southern colonies will be concerned in this settlement, and have probably sent some able men to assist you with their advice, and with a proper plan of administration. Tell me likewise what climate you live in, and what soil you have to do with; whether the country is mountainous and woody, or plain; if well watered.

I see by a map (now before me) that you are between . . . . . of latitude; in most part of Europe the air is . . . degrees, because we are sheltered by the prodigious . . . . of Norway and Lapland from the north winds. I am afraid you are more exposed; your great cold continent to the north may . . . some severe effects upon you. Direct to me at your agent's . . . if you think I can serve you, or be of any use, I . . . . I will send you anything you have a mind for, when . . . directions to have it sent, for I expect . . . to go abroad for eight or ten months; do not let the . . . prevent you from writing. I set out for London next . . . . if it is allowed; shall be in less than forty days . . . Metz, in Lorraine, where I propose to pass the winter; you will easily guess my aim in that. I intend to ramble in the summer along the Rhine into Switzerland, and back through France and the Netherlands, and perhaps more.

I hope you have a good provision of books. Rutherford has published his; and there is a Frenchman has told me many excellent truths, in two volumes, entitled 'L'Esprit des Lois.'* It is a piece of writing that would be of great use where you are. Will you have him?

Tell Cornwallis that I thank him for making me a Lieutenant-Colonel (which, by the bye, you did not take the least notice of); if I was to rise by his merit, as upon this occasion, I should soon be at the top of the list. He promised to write to some of us, but has not; they are not the less ardent for his prosperity; and the whole corps unites in one common wish for his welfare and success. Pray tell him so, as you may do it safely.

Your old corps comes back from Gibraltar next summer. I will correspond constantly with you in whatever part of the world we happen to be thrown, provided you do not force me,

* "I want to know Dr. Cocchi's and your opinion of two new French books. One is Montesquieu's 'Esprit des Lois,' which I think the best book that ever was written,—at least I never learned half so much from all I ever read. There is as much wit as useful knowledge." (H. Walpole to Sir H. Mann, "January 10, 1750." See also Gray to Dr. Wharton, "March 9, 1749.") The original edition was printed, anonymously, at Geneva, in 1748, 2 vols. 4to. It was reprinted in London, in 1749, 2 vols. 8vo, and in Edinburgh, in 1750. (Brunet, 'Manuel du Libraire.')

by neglect, to leave off writing. We have but this one way left to preserve the remembrance of each other as lively as I could wish, and as I hope you do. The old General, your friend, preserves his health, and is . . . he has often wished to have you again in his regiment. Farewell! I am, most affectionately, my dear Rickson,

Your faithful friend,

J. WOLFE.

Soon after the foregoing was penned, Wolfe got a few months' leave of absence, but was informed by Lord Bury, that the Commander-in-chief objected to his going abroad. On receipt of the unwelcome intelligence the disappointed officer in a letter to his father, observed:—"I must submit, though my inclinations lead me a different way." In the same letter, written on the 7th of October, he gives vent to his feelings in these indignant terms:—"How much does the Duke mistake my sentiments, or how greatly does he oppose the only method that can be fallen upon to preserve any knowledge of military affairs in the army, I sha'n't say to introduce it, for infinite pains have been taken to make us acquainted with some particular branches, which, yet, do not amount to all that may be required from an officer. I believe you would be very glad to see your son from amongst the ignorant, and wish to have a representative something worthy of yourself; from which I conclude, that your concern at this disappointment will not be less than mine."

His regimental business completed, the Lieutenant-Colonel at last started for Edinburgh, whence he set out on the 4th of November, for York, where he arrived on the morning of the 6th; a rapid journey in those days. After visiting his relations, the Thompsons and Sotherons, at Soterington, Pomfret, and Terrybridge, he proceeded on his way homewards, and on the 14th reached London; but too late to have the pleasure of walking with his father upon the dry gravel of the Greenwich garden and gathering the fruit, for the old General and Mrs. Wolfe had already removed for the winter to their house in Old Burlington Street.

Wolfe was warned by the delicacy of his constitution that his life naturally could not be a very long one. He seems also to have had a foreshadowing of the future in a presentiment that ere long he was destined to accomplish some great work; hence his anxiety to prepare himself for his country's call. A winter idly spent in London ill accorded with his ideas, anxious as he was to turn every moment to profitable account. Yet it was not in his nature to submit tamely to restraint, and, crossed in love, as well as thwarted in his designs, he gave himself up for the moment to pleasures which afforded him no permanent delight; for habitually he neither drank, gambled, swore, nor scoffed at religion and morality, as was then the vogue in the best society.

It was, emphatically, a frivolous, sensual age,—perhaps at the core quite as immoral as that of Charles II.; an age with all the depravity, but without the fictitious lustre of the Merrie Monarch's. Gambling assumed a variety of forms, but in polite society cards were the only panacea for *ennui;* cards, it was said, were better than scandal, as if no other alternative were possible.* Consequently, young ladies were not qualified to "come out"

* Mrs. Trench. 'Leadbeater Papers.'

until they had been duly instructed in whist by Professor Hoyle, whose moderate fee was one guinea a lesson. Large fortunes were "flirted away," as Walpole says, in a single night at hazard. "What a curse to nations," writes Mrs. Delany to her sister, "is such a pit of destruction as White's. It is a sad thing that in a Christian country it should continue undemolished." But the good lady may not have known that there were at the same time in the metropolis scores of much viler dens, to suppress which taxed all the energies of Mr. Justice Fielding. The vice was not confined to the higher ranks, but prevailed amongst all alike; "for while luxury produces want, idleness forbids honest labour to supply it."* Therefore Hogarth painted his "Idle Apprentice" gambling on a tombstone, as well as lords and ladies at play in gilded saloons.

Betting was another fashionable form of the pervading passion. One noble lord, to win a wager, spits into another noble lord's hat; but never perhaps in the annals of folly, was anything more absurd related than the race between geese and turkeys, upon whose relative speed a Marquis and an Earl staked £500.†

Drinking may not have been carried to such gross excess by well-bred gentlemen as by country squires; but amongst the lower classes in London, intemperance must have been general, from the incredible number of private gin-shops within the Bills of Mortality, in February, 1751.‡ The frightful condition of society may be

* Fielding's charge to the Grand Jury of the Middlesex Sessions, June, 1749.

† Mrs. Delany's Autobiography and Walpole's Letters.

‡ See 'Gentleman's Magazine,' vol. xxi.

exemplified by an extract from the King's speech on the opening of Parliament, in 1751:—"I cannot conclude without recommending to you, in the most earnest manner, to consider seriously of some effectual provisions to suppress those audacious crimes of robbery and violence which are now so frequent, especially about this great capital; and which have proceeded in a great measure from that profligate spirit of irreligion, idleness, gaming, and extravagance, which has of late extended itself in an uncommon degree to the dishonour of the nation, and to the great offence and prejudice of the sober and industrious part of my people." A better example from Majesty itself would have produced more good than all the power of the legislature. The criminal law of England was, forsooth, already sufficiently stringent; for although Wolfe compares its leniency with the severity of other nations, on the last day of the year 1750 fifteen malefactors were executed at Tyburn, and a few days later about as many more, three of whom were boys. The reduction of the army at the end of the late war had something to do with the amount of crime amongst the poor at this period; but the patterns of profligacy and idleness set by the majority of the wealthy and high-born, were still more pernicious. Alluding to the latter, no mean observer of his times remarked:—"So immoderate are the desires of many, so hungry is the appetite for pleasure, that they may be said to have a fury after it; and diversion is no longer the recreation or amusement, but the whole business of their lives."*

To return to our hero. The report which his mother

* Fielding, as above.

had repeated to him, that Miss Lawson was about to be married to a rival, was unfounded; but whether Wolfe renewed his suit personally while in town, there exists no evidence to show. The General and Mrs. Wolfe were strongly averse to the connection, and besides the inadequacy—as they considered—of the lady's fortune, it would seem that they had some other objection. Mrs. Wolfe, indeed, tried every means to dissuade her son from his "senseless passion," and appears to have insinuated a blemish upon the fair fame of his charmer's mother, for in one of his letters after his return to Scotland, the lover writes:—"Old Lady Lawson, if she had stumbled in her youth,—as Charles Brett has been told, —I would join with Falstaff and say there was no virtue extant." It will be remembered that there had been another young lady in the case, whose hand and fortune Mrs. Wolfe wished her son to obtain,—Miss Hoskins, of Croydon; but the mother's project was frustrated by the marriage of that lady to John Warde, Esq., of Squerries, in February, 1751.

The dissipations of London life wrought their wonted effects upon Wolfe's delicate frame; for during the latter part of his visit he was confined by a serious illness. He was still weak in bodily health and much chagrined in mind, when he returned to Scotland in April, 1751. The head-quarters of the regiment were then at Banff, 165 miles north-east of Edinburgh. His letters home are for some time filled chiefly with apologies for his past misconduct, impatience of temper, and restlessness of disposition, with forcible assurances of sincere contrition. In one, written early in June, he says:—

The warm expressions that fell from me, upon the Duke's refusing to let me go abroad, savoured much of ingratitude, and the words, it must be confessed, were arrogant and vain. Passion and disappointment produced them. Certainly his Royal Highness could not have so truly convinced me of his kindness as by consenting to a reasonable and salutary request; for if eternal imprisonment and exile are to follow preferment, few will be thankful for the favour. . . .

My mother might safely have ventured to send me her blessing, though she should build it upon the strength of a return from me. I do sometimes leave out of my letters what I least intended, and when I omit expressing my affection for either of you, there remains little else that is valuable.

Few places were worse calculated than Banff to "pluck from the memory a rooted sorrow." Exposed to the storms of the North Sea, it was one of the coldest and dreariest spots in Great Britain, without society or commerce, and approachable only by a ford across the wide river.* In this cheerless situation, Wolfe reverted to the consolations afforded by his books and correspondence. His letters consequently are unusually long, frequently covering three or four sheets of paper. Not the least interesting of them is the following to Captain Rickson:—

Banff, 9th June, 1751.

My dear Friend,

I am prepared to assist you in your apology whenever you think it requisite; but I desire you will never assign that as a reason for not writing, which, in my opinion, should prompt you for it. Attachments between men of certain characters do generally arise from something alike in their natures, and should never fall from a certain degree of firmness, that

* There was no bridge over the Deveron before 1772, when a fine one was built by Smeaton, near the town of Banff. (Smiles's 'Lives of the Engineers,' vol. ii. p. 61.)

makes them the same all the world over, and incapable of any diminution. I have, as you justly acknowledge, a perseverance in friendship, that time, nor distance, nor circumstances, can defeat—nay, even neglect can hardly conquer it; and you are just as warm and as near me, in North America, as you would be upon the spot.

I writ to you lately from London, and sent my letter by one that I recommended for your countenance.* I hope what has befallen him will be a shield against accidents of that sort for the future. When I writ that letter, your poor friend was in the utmost distress, otherwise you should have had more of me. It is not an hour since I received your letter. I shall answer all the parts of it as they stand in their order; and you see I lose no time, because in a remote and solitary part of the globe.

I often experience the infinite satisfaction there is in the only one way that is open to communicate our thoughts, and express that truly unalterable serenity of affection that is found among friends, and nowhere else. I conceive it no less comfortable to you. I believe that no man can have a sincerer regard for you than myself, nor can any man wish to serve and assist you with more ardour, and the disappointment you speak of affects me greatly, and the more, as I have been told that you lived with Cornwallis, and, consequently, had some employment near him that must be creditable and profitable, which I imagined you filled with all the integrity, diligence, and skill that I know you possessed of. I cannot otherwise account for the preference given to Mr. Cotterell, than that there has been an early promise, or some prevailing recommendations from England that Cornwallis could not resist. However, if I was governor, methinks I should choose about my person some experience and military ability, as requisite in the affairs of a new colony, situated as yours is, as any branch of knowledge whatever.

* A short letter, written by Wolfe from "Old Burlington Street, March 19, 1751," was carried to Rickson by Lieutenant Porter, whom "want of precaution, and not want of honesty," obliged to leave the regiment.

This disappointment is followed by a resolution in you that I approve of greatly, because it will release you from a life that cannot but be disagreeable, and place you where you will be well received. But I take it to be a thing much easier conceived than effected; for though I grant that ——— is a beast, and fit only to hunt the wildest of all wild Indians, yet his consent to the change, I doubt, would be very difficult to obtain, though everything else went smoothly on, and you know without it the matter rests. You have done well to write to my father. He is extremely disposed to do you any good office, and I shall take care to put him in mind, and excite him by all the motives that will touch him nearest, to assist you.

I thank you for partaking with me in the satisfaction of a promotion. You found your expectations, from my future fortune, upon the best grounds—my love and thorough sense of your worth; but I would not wish you should wait for my power. I should blush to see myself in the capacity. Take my inclinations and good wishes in the meantime, and believe that whatever falls to my share you will have a demand upon. If you look round and see my powerful rivals and competitors, examine who and what they are; we must both think that a little moderation in our views is very becoming, and very consistent with my situation. I believe you are of opinion with me, that a great deal of good fortune has fallen to my share already.

You have given me a very satisfactory account of the settlement, as far as you have observed or have had an opportunity to inquire. Till your letter came I understood that we were lords and proprietors of the north coast of Fundy Bay, for there's a vast tract of country between that and the river St. Lawrence. It appears to me that Acadia is near an island, and the spot where you are, a very narrow space between the Gulf and Bay. If so, I conclude your post will be greatly improved; and instead of the shallow works that you describe, something substantial will be erected, capable of containing a large garrison, with inhabitants trained to arms, in expectation of future wars with France, when I foresee great attempts to be made in your neighbourhood. When I say thus, I mean in North America. I hope it is true what is mentioned in the newspapers, that a strong naval armament is preparing for your assistance. I wish they would increase your regiment with drafts from the troops here. I could send you some very good little soldiers. If our proposal is a good one, I will shorten the work and lessen the expense. The present schemes of economy are destructive to great undertakings, narrow in the views and ruinous in the consequence.

I was in the House of Commons this winter, when great sums of money were proposed for you, and granted readily enough, but nothing said of any increase of troops. Mr. Pelham spoke very faintly upon the subject; wished gentlemen would well weigh the importance of these undertakings before they offered them for public approbation, and seemed to intimate that it might probably produce a quarrel with our everlasting and irreconcilable adversary. This I took to be a bad prognostic; a minister cool in so great an affair, it is enough to freeze up the whole! but perhaps there might be a concealed manœuvre under these appearances, as, in case of accidents, "I am not to blame," "I was forced to carry it on," and so forth; in the meantime I hope they are vigorous in supporting our claims. The country is in all shapes better than we imagined it, and the climate less severe; the extent of our territory, perhaps, won't take a vast deal of time to clear; the woods you speak of are, I suppose, to the west of Sheganecto, and within the limits that the French ascribe for themselves and usurp.

Yours is now the dirtiest as well as the most insignificant and unpleasant branch of military operations; no room for courage and skill to exert itself, no hope of ending it by a decisive blow, and a perpetual danger of assassination; these circumstances discourage the firmest minds. Brave men, when they see the least room for conquest, think it easy, and generally make it so; but they grow impatient with perpetual disadvantages. I should imagine that two or three independent Highland companies might be of use; they are hardy, intrepid, accustomed to a rough country, and no great mischief if they fall. How can you better employ a secret enemy than by making his end conducive to the common good? If this sentiment should take wind, what an execrable and bloody being should I be considered here in the midst of Popery and Jacobitism!

I don't understand what is meant by the wooden forts at Halifax. I have a poor conceit of wooden fortifications, and would wish to have them changed for ramparts of earth, the rest in time; it is probable that the great attention that must be given at first to building the habitations and clearing the ground about the town, left no interval for other work; but I hope to hear in your next letter, that our principal city (Halifax) is considerably improved in strength. You gentlemen, too, with your parapet three or four feet thick, that a heavy shower would dissolve, you ought to increase it, and put yourselves into a state of security. You appear to be the barrier and bulwark of our settlements on the land, and should be lodged in a sufficient fortress, and with an eye to enterprise. I understand by your account that the post you occupy is at a very small distance from the end of the bay; and should be glad to know how far that is from the nearest part of the Gulf of St. Lawrence, or from what in the map appears to be a lake, or harbour communicating with that gulf.

I rejoice much that you commanded that detachment with which your Lieutenant-Colonel marched; the Indians might have had courage, in that case you would have overcome them in battle under the eye of your chief; as it was, he saw you well disposed to fight. Perhaps I am talking at random, but it is conformable to the idea I have of this Colonel Lawrence,* whose name we often see in the papers. I suppose him to be amongst the first officers of the expedition, high-minded himself, and a judge of it in others; his ready march to the enemy marks the first, and his being the head of your undertaking gives one an opinion of his judgment. If 'tis to his advantage, I desire you to let me have his character at full length;

* Afterwards Brigadier-General Lawrence, with whom Wolfe served before Louisburg.

perhaps there's a strong mixture, as it generally happens in ardent men: in that case let's have the best fully, and the other slightly touched.

I am sorry that you are not so linked in with some of your brethren as to form an intimacy and confidence; without it the world is a solitude, and what must your part of it be? I pity you very heartily, for I am sure you are very ready to mingle with a good disposition. 'Tis doubly a misfortune to be banished without the relief of books, or possibility of reading; the only amends that can be made to us that are sequestered in the lonely and melancholy spots, is that we can fill up our time with study. When I am in Scotland I look upon myself as an exile: with respect to the inhabitants I am so, for I dislike 'em much; 'tis then I pick up my best store, and try to help an indifferent education, and slow faculties; and I can say that I have really acquired more knowledge that way, than in all my former life.

I would by all means have you get home before the next winter, but I don't approve in the least of the resolution you seem to have taken rather than continue in that service. Do everything in your power to change, but don't leave the army, as you must when you go upon half-pay. If there is any female in the case, any reasonable scheme for marriage, I have nothing to say; that knocks down all arguments; they have other sorts of passions to support them. In reality, the most I can offer (were you unbiassed) would not amount to weighty matter, for I see no early appearance whereon to mould a bait for your ambition; yet I cannot consent to your leaving us entirely, in the hopes of fairer days. If I did not love you personally, and wish your happiness very heartily, I should advise you to stay where you are, and would say you ought to be kept there; and give, as a reason for saying so, that I do think the infancy of a colony has need of able hands, civil and military, to sustain it, and I should be for sacrificing you and all the men of worth to the general good. You speak of a Mr. Brewse, the engineer;* pray say a word or two of his

* Probably the same Major Brewse of the Engineers whom Dr.

capacity, and tell me if there are among you any connoisseurs in that business.

Is the Island of St. John in the possession of the French, or do we occupy it? It would be unpardonable in me if I omitted to send you intelligence of what is stirring amongst us; I mean, if I kept from you anything that comes to my knowledge; but in truth we are here almost as much in the dark as to public transactions as can be conceived; however, I picked up some account of the Act for settling the Regency, and as, perhaps, you have not seen it, it will be worth your perusal; it is a subject of no small importance.*

[Here follows an analysis of the statute.]

Three large ships of war (guard ships) are sailed with the Scotch Fusiliers and Conway's regiments to relieve the King's and Skelton's, and they, as we hear, are to march directly into Scotland, which, by the bye, is a little out of the way, to carry them from the hottest to the coldest part of the King's dominions; if they come, our regiment goes to Inverness, where I shall remain all the winter; if one only comes, or neither, I go to Aberdeen. Loftus and Donnellan are both in England; the former had been dangerously ill, is a little recovered. Donnellan, too, has been out of order, and is gone to Bristol for health.

I am not sure whether I mentioned it or not in my last letter, but as it is a great grief to me, I will hazard the repetition to tell it you. I got powerful people to ask the Duke no less than three times, for leave to go abroad, and he absolutely refused me that necessary indulgence: this I consider as a very unlucky incident, and very discouraging; moreover,

Johnson met at Fort George, in 1773, and who said that he had dined at a house in London where there were three Bruces, one of the Irish line, one of the Scottish, and himself of the English line; and that in the Heralds' office, he was shown the name spelt in fourteen different ways. See Boswell's Tour, first edit. p. cxxxii.

* Frederick, Prince of Wales, died on the 20th of March, 1751. He expired suddenly, in the arms of Desnoyers, the celebrated dancing-master, who was near his bedside, engaged in playing on the violin for his amusement. (Wade's 'British Chronology.')

he accompanied his denial with a speech that leaves no hope, —that a Lieutenant-Colonel was an officer of too high a rank to be allowed to leave his regiment for any considerable time. This is a dreadful mistake, and if obstinately pursued, will disgust a number of good intentions, and preserve that prevailing ignorance of military affairs that has been so fatal to us in all our undertakings, and will be for ever so, unless other measures are pursued. We fall every day lower and lower from our real characters, and are so totally engaged in everything that is minute and trifling, that one would almost imagine the idea of war was extinguished amongst us; they will hardly allow us to recollect the little service we have seen: that is to say, the merit of things seem to return into their old channel, and he is the brightest in his profession that is the most impertinent, talks loudest, and knows least.

I repeat it again to you that poor Porter left this regiment with the approbation of all his brethren, and with the reputation of honesty and upright behaviour. It will be a charitable thing to do him any good office.

I went to London in November, and came back in the middle of April. In that short time I committed more imprudent acts than in all my life before. I lived in the idlest, dissolute, abandoned manner that could be conceived, and that not out of vice, which is the most extraordinary part of it. I have escaped at length, and am once again master of my reason, and hereafter it shall rule my conduct, at least I hope so. My father has offered money for the prettiest-situated house in England, and I believe he will have it for about £3000.* It is a great sum to be so employed; but as it procures him the pleasure he likes, and a fine air, it is well laid out. It looks as if he intended to sell or let his house [in Greenwich],

* The house eventually purchased by the General is situated on the west side, and within the wall of Greenwich Park, near the Ranger's Lodge, then Chesterfield House. It is at the top of Croom's Hill, and faces Blackheath. He had previously occupied a house in the town of Greenwich, passing the winter months at his house in Great Burlington Street. The latter was disposed of after the removal of the family to Blackheath.

since the other is upon Black Heath; the new bridge* . . . his way easily to St. James's.

I will write to Loftus to send you some porter and the books. [I cannot bear to] hear you making excuses for imaginary trouble. I will . . . hogshead of claret from Ireland to Gibraltar. You cannot do me a greater pleasure than by pointing out to me a way to relieve you, though ever so inconsiderable. Write to me by the first opportunity, and believe me, dear Rickson,

Ever your affectionate friend,

J. W.

. . . .

Our Lieutenant-Colonel passed two or three weeks of July in Peterhead, six-and-thirty miles to the south-east of Banff, and tried the mineral waters for which the place was famed, but the effects they produced upon him were injurious rather than beneficial. He was diverted, however, by the company; for writing to his mother after his return to Banff, he says:—"I am obliged to your sex for many cheerful hours. In general there were women of good understanding, some of great vivacity, and others very handsome; so that a man could not fail to be pleased with such variety. I always think a pretty maid has all the beauties, or does not want them." He then begs a jar of honey, such as he devoured in London, and adds:—"That I may not fall away with spare diet, and diminish to a very skeleton, I propose to nourish

* Westminster Bridge was opened at midnight, on Saturday, November 17, 1750, "with a grand procession, preceded by trumpets, kettle-drums," etc. The architect of the bridge, which cost £389,500, was Charles Labeyle, a Swiss, patronized by the Earl of Pembroke. Labeyle asserted that three of the arches were wider than Westminster Hall, and that the bridge contained twice as many cubic feet of stone as St. Paul's Cathedral. See Walpole's 'Anecdotes of Painting,' vol. iii.

myself with chocolate and milk, and therefore desire six or eight pounds may be sent from London. Our winter is begun already. I am writing now by a great fire; dreadful season, that lasts from the beginning of August to the middle of May." His last letter from this cold region, omitting a few paragraphs the substance of which is repeated elsewhere, is as follows.—

Banff, September 17, 1751.

Dear Madam,

. . . .

It would be a kind of miracle for one of my age and complexion to get through life without stumbling. Friendly aid and counsel are great and timely supports, and reproof is most effectual when it carries with it a concern for the person to whom it is addressed. This is the way I understand it both from my father and you, because I am sure nothing but a base and villainous action could entirely remove your affections; and that I don't find myself capable of.

I am sometimes in the character of a military parent, and am obliged to lay great restraint upon myself that others may profit by it, and I never find my advice so well attended to, as when there goes along with it a mixture of care for the good and reputation of the youth that errs. You'll be apt to think that a man so subject to weakness as I may be supposed to be, can work very little upon the minds of others, or give them a strength and firmness that I do not possess. But a man might for a time conceal, though not conquer his infirmities, and may direct where he can't execute. The sense of duty, too, in the way of one's profession, may operate strongly in some things, though quite useless and impotent in others.

. . . .

By the description you give me of your new house, most people will be as well pleased with it as you seem to be. It is the work of your own hands, and you'll be much to blame if anything is wanting to make it every way convenient and to your taste. It has a thousand natural advantages that you may improve till it becomes delightful. All I ask is that in the little detached apartment, where Charles [Brett] may laugh at leisure, there may be a very hard bed, upon which I hope to extend my long limbs in twelve or fourteen months, and take a little rest from care.

Old Roland lived five or six years with me, and laid the obligations of faithful service upon me. He bore pretty well the warmth and uncertainty of my temper, though at length, tired of that and eternal wandering, he begged to be released. I can safely say that I have known him very honest, and think he must still be so. He has a wonderful calmness and quietness of disposition, that I sometimes thought degenerated into stupidity. I hardly ever knew him to give offence to any but myself, and then perhaps I was as much to blame as he.*

. . . .

Thus much for his valour and honesty; I think myself in his debt. I never intended to abandon him. I propose to take his son when old enough to serve me. . . .

I hope to hear from you now and then; you shall always be as short or as long as you please. Only remember that one side is very agreeable, but four sides, four times as agreeable, and so on in proportion.

I am, dear Madam, etc.,

J. Wolfe.

* The succeeding passage has been anticipated. See Chap. V. p. 100.

CHAPTER IX.

INVERNESS.

OCTOBER, 1751—MAY, 1752.

IN a calm at sea, when the watery plain is as still and smooth as its cloudless azure dome, it is not easy to form in one's mind a picture of the same element when lashed into fury by a storm. Quite as difficult is it to identify the Inverness of the eighteenth century, politically or otherwise, with the present flourishing capital of the Highlands. Now, when every Scot is a loyal subject, when Highland forts are garrisoned by Highland regiments, and our beloved Queen retires from State cares to her Highland home, it is almost impossible to imagine how different was the state of things in the reign of George II., when English soldiers were sent into Scotland to keep a large proportion of the people in subjection. Therefore, as juries are directed by judges to found their verdict exclusively upon the evidence of the trial, the reader should endeavour, for the nonce, to forget the sympathy which now happily exists between north and south, and remember that in the year 1751, when Wolfe was stationed at Inverness, that town was the head-quarters of Jacobitism, and consequently that an officer of the Royal Army could scarcely regard it under any other aspect than as the central point of an enemy's country. It is only necessary to bear this fact in mind to palliate some expressions in Wolfe's letters, which otherwise might make him appear in a false light; for, notwithstanding his occasional flings at Scotland, he numbered more than one Scotchman amongst his trustiest friends.

The Lieutenant-Colonel was no sooner settled in his new quarters than he wrote as follows to his father:—

Inverness, October 3rd, 1751.

Dear Sir,

The preparations and march of the regiment have taken up the time that would have been employed in writing to you and to others that have a title to expect it from me. The post goes hence but once a week, which makes my letter something later than I could wish, as I have been several days in town.* A little while serves to discover the villanous nature of the inhabitants, and brutality of the people in its neighbourhood. Those too who pretend the greatest attachment to the government, and who every day feed upon the public purse, seem to distinguish themselves for greater rudeness and incivility than the open and professed Jacobites. With these disadvantages there are many others that concern us as officers, not worth relating to you; and yet, I believe we shall find means to get through the long winter tolerably well.

A gentleman came from Perth the other day and told me he saw Mrs. Wilkinson very disconsolate and unhappy at the bad accommodation she meets with there. I can't wonder at it, as little, dirty, stinking lodgings must be quite new to one that comes directly from London, and was never out of it till now. But I would advise her to prepare for worse

* It was not until after the Union that a regular post was established between Inverness and the South; and for more than fifty years letters were carried by foot-runners once a week. (Carruthers' 'Highland Note-Book,' p. 121.)

places than Perth. By degrees I hope she'll be inured to it, and then become familiar. Mrs. Lafausille, who has served several campaigns, is an older and better soldier than the other, will put up with any inconveniences for the sake of doing her duty with applause, and to the satisfaction of her Lieutenant-Colonel and commanding officer, to whose pleasure she always wishes to contribute; and I dare say never refuses her assistance to make him perfectly happy. I had a long letter from Rickson some days ago. He gives me no great opinion of the settlement, from the want of a more considerable armed force, the present being insufficient for its defence. He seems to apprehend some attempts from the French, who injure and insult us. He laments his own melancholy condition, and wishes it were possible to come again amongst his old friends and companions. I imagine your regiment must be in Scotland by this time. In the spring they are to take those parts in the Highlands that we have occupied this summer.

I turned aside to look at the new Fort of Ardersier, or Fort George, and find a vast quantity of earth thrown up for ramparts, and the counterscarp and glacis finished.* But I believe there's still work for six or seven years to do. When it is finished one may venture to say (without saying much) that it will be the most considerable fortress, and the best situated, in Great Britain. I fancy your neighbour, Mr. Skinner, the architect, thinks it a very good fortification. I dare say he finds it so. I beg my duty, etc.

JAMES WOLFE.

A fortnight later the Highland postboy carried another

* Fort George, twelve miles from Inverness, is situated on the low sandy point of Ardersier, which projects far out into the Moray Firth. It was commenced immediately after the rebellion, and cost £160,000. "Fort George," says Anderson, "is considered a model of a fortified place; yet it is only secure against attacks from the sea. . . . The few officers who are obliged to reside in it during 'the piping time of peace' find it exceedingly dull." (Guide to the Highlands.) The barracks are capable of accommodating 3000 men, and the works cover about fifteen acres.

letter for General Wolfe, in which, after complaining of paucity of "furniture," his son says:—

I have surveyed the field of battle of Culloden with great exactness, and find room for a military criticism as well as place for a little ridicule upon some famous transactions of that memorable day. The actors shine in the world too high and bright to be eclipsed; but it is plain they don't borrow much of their glory from their performance upon that occasion, however they may have distinguished themselves in later events. The defects were not so visible there as in the lower agents. I dare say you don't think I strike at the Head. One may safely pronounce that he had a very good title to the command; there was no rival in rank nor in abilities. If you were upon the spot, perhaps you might be tempted to say that this *risk* should not have been adventured, nor this *advantage* neglected. You would not have left those ruffians the only possible means of conquest, nor suffer multitudes to go off unhurt with the power to destroy. One must examine the field of battle to judge of the merit of Colonel's Rich's great resistance, or, which is the same thing, the behaviour of the battalion under his command. But why this censure when the affair is so happily decided? To exercise one's ill-nature? No; to exercise the faculty of judging,—since I mention this to you, but not to the world. The more a soldier thinks of the false steps of those that are gone before, the more likely he is to avoid them. On the other hand, the examples worthiest of imitation should never be lost sight of, as they will be the best and truest guides in every undertaking.

Besides the multitude of evils that this town contains, we have the additional mortification that the country about us affords very little relief; no hunting or shooting,—both healthy and manly diversions that I take great delight in. Instead of these, I ride about for the fresh air and motion; but when the snow falls, we shall have little else to do but to eat and sleep. I wonder how long a man moderately inclined that way would require, in a place like this, to wear out his love for arms, and soften his martial spirit. I believe the passion would be something diminished in less than ten years, and the gentleman be contented to be a little lower than Cæsar in the list, to get clear of the incumbrances of greatness.

Loftus wrote to me, giving intimation of his arrival in Scotland, and desiring that I would go directly to Perth to see him: it is about a hundred miles through the Highlands. One would think my friend Arthur did not know the *carte de pays*, by his invitation. Wilkinson writes me word that your clothing is come; that is, he tells me that the present you were so kind to send is safe, and in the same ship. Ours is as yet at sea, to my sorrow, for we want a great many men, and I can't send off the recruiting-parties till they are clothed. I shall be broke for not completing the regiment; they sent me a reprimand for not doing it last year, though I was all the winter in London. The reprimand was due to my neglect in general, but not at all as it was applied; unless it could be supposed that I had any extraordinary influence over Lord Bury and acted for him, whereas it is notorious that he always acts for himself.

The population of Inverness in 1751 was about five thousand, and in the town there were but four principal streets, which diverged from the market-cross. The houses were so variously modelled that no general description would embrace their several styles, the only resemblance between one house and another being in height, which rarely exceeded a single story.* This common characteristic showed the prudence of the builders in not exposing loftier structures to the tempestuous winds from the adjacent mountain gorges. The gable end of each house faced the street, from which it was separated by a court, leading alike to the shop on the

* "They call a floor a *house;* the whole building is called a *land;* an alley is a *wynde;* a little court or turnagain alley is a *close;* a round staircase a *turnpike;* and a square one goes by the name of a *skalestair*." (Captain Burt's Letters, vol. i. p. 63.)

ground-floor, and to an exterior staircase that ascended to the story above; and the walls were built with loose, unhewn stones, filled in with pebbles, and finished off with a coat of *harling*. The rooms were generally unceiled, and each plank of the flooring retained the large round hole bored for the rope by which it had been dragged from the sawyers.* Sashes being unusual, the upper half only of each window was glazed, while the lower portion had wooden shutters, and as these were closed in cold weather, nothing outside the room was visible.†

Such were the leading features of the domestic architecture bordering the main streets; but the poorer quarters of the town consisted, for the most part, of wretched turf hovels, surmounted, by way of chimneys, with bottomless baskets or superannuated tubs. The streets, at the period of which we speak, were possibly not so foul as they were before 1746, when, as appears from the town records, they were first swept at the common expense, by order of the Duke of Cumberland.‡ Besides two or three unornamental churches, the only public build-

* Richardson's 'Defoe's Tour,' vol. iv.

† "Asking the reason of this, I was informed that these people still continue those shutters as an old custom, which was at first occasioned by danger; for that formerly, in their clan-quarrels, several had been shot from the opposite side of the way, when they were in their chambers, and by these shutters they were concealed and in safety. But I believe the true reason is the saving the expense of glass, for it is the same in the outparts of all the towns and cities in the Low country." (Captain Burt's Letters, vol. i. p. 70.)

‡ "I asked the magistrates one day, when the dirt was almost above one's shoes, why they suffered the town to be so excessively dirty, and did not employ people to cleanse the streets. The answer was, 'It will not be long before we have a shower.'" (Burt's Letters, vol. i. p. 73.)

ing was the rubble townhouse, erected in 1708; and no other noteworthy objects remain to be mentioned except the ruins of the fort built by Oliver Cromwell, and the stone bridge across the Ness. This uncoloured sketch will perhaps be sufficient to convey some idea of Inverness as it was.

Wolfe's next letter, to his mother, is an exceedingly long one, taking up, in close writing, three large sheets of paper. It contains no small portion of gossip concerning their friends in Greenwich and elsewhere, with further extraneous matter, which we omit. Other passages have been retained, which, though of no great moment, help to give an insight into the writer's character.

Inverness, 6th November, 1751.

Dear Madam,

You must not be surprised if this letter does not reach you till a long time after the date of it, for 'tis very possible that the snows will retard the march of our Highland post-boy, who, in the finest seasons, cannot pride himself on much expedition. The winds sometimes drive the snows with such violence that the roads are utterly impassable; and again, when it thaws, the rivers swell so prodigiously that there is no less danger and difficulty on that side. I have not been, from the severity of the weather, able to get on horseback for many days, and can have no manner of diversion out of my own room, unless to shoot woodcocks at the risk of rheumatism. It would be unmanly and very unbecoming a soldier to complain of little evils, such as bad food, bad lodging, bad fire. Whoever finds these inconveniences too hard to put up with will never be a match for a multitude of others that he is likely to meet with in his travel through life, especially if he has taken the trade of war. With these sort of reflections I reconcile myself to Inverness, and to other melancholy spots that we are thrown upon, and find (all things considered and thoroughly examined) there is in reality, to a contented mind, very little difference between one place and another, and that if a man possesses a certain degree of firmness and serenity, he is equal to almost every calamity. Besides, in aid of this disposition, I like a military life, and endeavour to make my actions correspond in some measure with that liking. Not that you are to understand your son captivated with the glare and blaze of our employment. No, there is an object much beyond it that attracts my eye; and it is with some concern that I see those that direct us often miss the proper mark, and set us, their servants, upon wrong pursuits. This is not, I believe, from ill intention, but from other causes. I expect you'll think this sort of discourse a little unnatural, and perhaps may think it discourse only; but you may judge by my former letters and my general manner of acting that I oftenest speak as I am, and that it would not be in this style if I did not sleep sound. The death of the Stadtholder, and the Princess of Orange's ill state of health, I suppose alarm people a little.* Two minorities, perhaps, together may give the common enemy some advantage over us. I hope the Duke will do his part steadily and with honour. He has a great task, and I dare say will perform it as becomes a prince.

. . . .

If I were to advise, as you now live altogether in the country, you should call some that you like to dine and sup with you often; and above all things, claret for the General. He is never better than when he uses it freely, but without excess. It is vast pleasure to me that your new mansion is now put into good condition, and the garden planted. I know no-

* Walpole writes to Sir H. Mann (October 14th, 1751):—"The Prince of Orange is dead; killed by the waters of Aix-la-Chapelle. The Princess Royal was established Regent some time ago; but as her husband's authority seemed extremely tottering, it is not likely that she will be able to maintain hers. Her health is extremely bad, and her temper neither ingratiating nor bending." The Princess Anne, eldest daughter of George II., married the Prince of Orange in 1734, and died in 1759. (See Lord Hervey's Memoirs, and Walpole's Memoirs of the Reign of George II.)

thing more agreeable than to see our own little improvements flourish in our view, and increase every year in strength and beauty. For my part, while I am young and in health all the world is my garden and my dwelling; and when I begin to decline, I hope my services by that time may fairly ask some little retreat, and a provision so moderate that I may possess it unenvied. I demand no more; but while I have vigour, if the country wants a man of good intentions, they'll always find me ready,—devoted, I may say,—to their service. Though not of the most melting compassion, I am sometimes touched with other people's distresses and participate their grief. Men whose tenderness is not often called upon, obtain by degrees,—as you may particularly observe in old bachelors,—a ferocity of nature, or insensibility about the misfortunes that befall others. There's no more tender-hearted person than a father or mother that has, or has had, many children.

I don't know Dr. Squire at all, and very little of Miss Hooker;* but must say that matches purely of interest (as I suppose it is on her side), and made up in a hurry, though with everybody's consent, are purchases too high and hazardous to have my approbation. And then again, at sober times, I have no very high opinion of love affairs except they are built upon the judgment. So you'll say, "Where then would you choose?" Why nowhere, to men of whimsical disposition; but otherwise the choice reason directs is the best: moderate fortunes and sense enough on both sides to give aid in ticklish times. If the maid only seeks preferment in the Church or anywhere else, she cuts out her own misery, unless

* The match between the Rev. Dr. Squire and Miss Hooker, of Greenwich, was broken off. The lady afterwards married Wolfe's friend, Charles Brett, R.N., and the Doctor wedded Miss Ardesolf, of Soho Square. Dr. Squire, who was rector of St. Anne's, Soho, and Vicar of Greenwich, became Dean of Bristol, and the 107th Bishop of St. David's. (Gentleman's Magazine; Beatson's 'Political Index.') Bishop Warburton, being asked by Ralph Allen what sort of men Dr. Squire and Dr. Tucker were, is said to have replied that "the one made religion his trade, and the other made trade his religion." (Watson's Life of Warburton.)

indeed all her passions and affections give way to ambition, and then, no doubt, a doctor, a dean, or a bishop have power to please.*

. . . .

I have a certain turn of mind that favours matrimony prodigiously, though every way else extremely averse to it at present, and you shall know it. I love children, and think them necessary to us in our latter days; they are fit objects for the mind to rest upon, and give it great entertainment when amusements of other kinds have lost their value. Sure, next to being an honest man and good citizen, it is meritorious to produce such characters amongst men. Our endeavours here seldom fail of success; for young people are as capable of receiving good impressions and good sentiments as bad ones, and if their natures incline to evil, custom and education correct them. Two or three manly, courageous, upright sons are a present to the world of the highest estimation, and the father that offers them sees with satisfaction that he is to live in his successors, and that his good qualities will contribute to adorn and illustrate manhood when he is no longer amongst them. Is not this a pleasing sort of reflection? If I don't speak much of the females, 'tis not that they are of less concern to us, or ought to be less prized; but as the management of them belongs chiefly to you ladies, methinks I would not seem to infringe upon your prerogatives.

. . . .

Lord Bury professes fairly, and means nothing; in that he resembles his father, and a million of other showy men that are seen in palaces and in the courts of kings. He desires never to see his regiment, and wishes that no officer

* Had not the above passage been written some years before the publication of the dedication to Warburton of Churchill's Sermons, it would look like a plagiarism.

> "Doctor, dean, bishop, Gloster, and my lord,
> If haply these high titles may accord
> With thy meek spirit, if the barren sound
> Of pride delights thee, to the topmost round
> Of Fortune's ladder got."

would ever leave it. This is selfish and unjust. They have a way of trifling with us poor soldiery that gives many very honest brave men high disgust. I am sensible it is my duty to be here, and that silences me; otherwise, the care of a regiment of Foot is very heavy, exceeding troublesome, and not at all the thing I delight in, though, as I told you before, the occupation in general is a good one, and hits my genius. My duty to my father. I wish you both much health, and am, dear Madam,

Your most obedient and affectionate Son,

JAMES WOLFE.

In a letter of the 6th of December, to Mrs. Wolfe, we light upon a paragraph describing the character of Lieutenant Brett, of the Royal Navy.*

I learn that my good friend Charles is near his departure. His friends and neighbours will feel the want of him, for there's no more valuable person amongst men than one of his character,—active to serve and assist, honest and fair in his dealings, and incomparably merry and sweet-tempered; equally disposed for business or society. I reckon his sister will be in great grief, for she loves him very sincerely. If he's gone before this letter gets to you, I must beg you to let it follow him with a frank, if you have one to spare, because it is double. I shall lose a good correspondent as to public affairs, and an agent and advocate to be depended on in private concerns. I

* Charles Brett became one of the Lords Commissioners of the Admiralty when Lord Howe was at the head of the Board, and represented Sandwich in two parliaments. He married the granddaughter of Sir William Hooker, of Croom's Hill, and died, far advanced in years, at his house in Spring Gardens, February 10th, 1799. His brother, Captain John Brett, who was one of Anson's lieutenants in his voyage round the world, lost much tranquillity, as well as money, by being involved in a lawsuit with an itinerant quack, whom he, as a magistrate, endeavoured to prevent from deluding the unwary. The mountebank, however, having a diploma of some sort, obtained damages against the benevolent Captain. Another brother, Timothy, is mentioned by Wolfe on a future occasion.

owe him £1. 3*s*. for the eleventh portion of a lottery-ticket* with the young ladies, Mr. Swinden, and others, which, if you'll be so kind to pay him or his brother, shall be returned to you whenever I have the good fortune to find myself in a condition to pay my debts; and that may be soon, since they are not very considerable.

Wolfe was as uneasy in his cold prison as Sterne's starling in its cage, and if not in words, in thought at least, he reiterated the cry, "I can't get out!" He felt that he was losing irrecoverable time. But his hopes of seeing more of the world were not quenched by previous discouragements, for on the 13th of December he tells his father :—

I dropped a hint to Charles Brett some time since as if I had thoughts of going into Ireland. You may be sure if the thing had been serious I should have mentioned it to you, with my reasons for so doing, and should have asked your opinion and taken it as a guide. I did not imagine that it would have been looked upon by Charles as a matter of easy execution, but only an object of the fancy to play with till some new shadowy project as light as that takes place.

. . . .

I did not tell you that we have an assembly of female rebels every fortnight, entirely composed of Macdonalds, Frazers, and M'Intoshes. I had the honour to dance with the daughter of a chieftain who was killed at Culloden, the Laird of Kippock.† They are perfectly wild as the hills that breed them;

* *Monday, November* 11, 1751.—" The drawing of the State lottery began, when, notwithstanding the united efforts of several societies and public-spirited men to check the exorbitancy of the ticket-mongers, the price rose to sixteen guineas just before the drawing. It was also demonstrated that to have an even chance for any prize a person must have seven tickets," etc. ('Gentleman's Magazine,' vol. xxi. p. 520.)

† The Macdonalds, who claimed the privilege of taking the right of the line of battle, were so mortified at being placed on the left at Culloden, that when ordered to attack, in spite of the urgent appeals of

but they lay aside their principles for the sake of sound and movement. They make no converts, which I chiefly attribute to a strong dialect of the Erse that destroys the natural softness of their notes.

Sooner or later there happens an interval in the life of every thoughtful man, when he is prompted to pause and review his past career; when he asks himself:—What have I been?—What might I have been? What have I done?—What should I have done? What am I?—What ought I to be? Who can respond to such questionings with self-approval? St. Paul's answer,—"the saddest of all human confessions, made by one of the greatest men,"* was, "That which I do, I approve not; for what I would, that I do not; but what I hate, that I do." There was but One

"——the best of men
That e'er wore earth about him," . . .

who could reply without a qualm.

In his Highland chamber, at midnight, on the twenty-fifth anniversary of his birth, Wolfe thus communed with his own heart. His ingenuous confession of human weakness, though never meant for strangers' eyes, surely cannot tend to degrade him in the esteem of his fellow-mortals. We may imagine his tall, attenuated figure, as, in mental conflict, he paces the room, and then sits down,

the Duke of Perth, they stood motionless, and beheld their clansman of Kippock struck down whilst exclaiming, "My God! have the children of my tribe forsaken me?" The chieftains of Kippock were distinguished for their bravery, and their followers were amongst the hardiest of the mountaineers. One of the Lairds of Kippock is said to have outshone an English owner of silver candlesticks by producing several Highlanders bearing pine torches,—an incident which Sir Walter Scott adapted to his 'Legend of Montrose.'

* 'Friends in Council.'

with his writing-case spread before him, to pen the reflections contained in the following letter to his mother :—

Inverness, 22nd–25th December (o. s.), 1751.
[2nd–5th January, 1752, n. s.]

Dear Madam,

The winter wears away, so do our years, and so does life itself; and it matters little where a man passes his days and what station he fills, or whether he be great or considerable; but it imports him something to look to his manner of life. This day am I five-and-twenty years of age, and all that time is as nothing. When I am fifty (if it so happens) and look back, it will be the same; and so on to the last hour.* But it is worth a moment's consideration that one may be called away on a sudden, unguarded and unprepared; and the oftener these thoughts are entertained, the less will be the dread or fear of death. You will judge by this sort of discourse that it is the dead of night, when all is quiet and at rest, and one of those intervals wherein men think of what they really are, and what they really should be; how much is expected, and how little performed. Our short duration here, and the doubts of hereafter, should awe and deter the most flagitious, if they reflected on them. The little time taken in for meditation is the best employed in all their lives; for if the uncertainty of our state and being is then brought before us, and that compared with our course of conduct, who is there that won't immediately discover the inconsistency of all his behaviour and the vanity of all his pursuits? And yet, we are so mixed and compounded that though I think seriously this minute, and lie down with good intentions, it is likely I may rise with my old nature, or perhaps with the addition of some new impertinence, and be the same wandering lump of idle errors that I have ever been.†

* "Ah! what shall I be at fifty,
Should nature keep me alive,
If I find the world so bitter
When I am but twenty-five?"—'Maud.'

† "God gives me good resolves sometimes, and I lead a better life; they last for a time or so, sometimes more and sometimes less, and

You certainly advise me well. You have pointed out the only one way where there can be no disappointment, and comfort that will never fail us,—carrying men steadily and cheerfully in their journey, and a place of rest at the end. Nobody can be more persuaded of it than I am; but situation, example, the current of things, and our natural weakness draw me away with the herd, and only leave me just strength enough to resist the worst degree of our iniquities. There are times when men fret at trifles, and quarrel with their toothpicks. In one of these ill habits I exclaim against the present condition, and think it is the worst of all; but coolly and temperately it is plainly the best. Where there is most employment and least vice, there one should wish to be. There is a meanness and a baseness not to endure with patience the little inconveniences we are subject to; and to know no happiness but in one spot, and that in ease, in luxury, in idleness, seems to deserve our contempt. There are young men amongst us that have great revenues and high military stations, that repine at three months' service with their regiments if they go fifty miles from home. Soup and *venaison* and turtle are their supreme delight and joy,—an effeminate race of coxcombs, the future leaders of our armies, defenders and protectors of our great and free nation!

You bid me avoid Fort William, because you believe it still worse than this place.* That will not be my reason for wishing to avoid it; but the change of conversation, the fear of becoming a mere ruffian, and of imbibing the tyrannical principles of an absolute commander, or giving way insensibly to the temptations of power, till I become proud, insolent, and intolerable;—these considerations will make me wish to leave

then, through the fickleness of my temper and too great confidence in myself, I fall into my old courses—ay, often far worse." (Edmund Burke (1744). 'Leadbeater Papers,' vol. ii. p. 32.)

* Fort William, at the foot of Ben Nevis, in Lochaber, Inverness-shire, so named after King William III., in whose reign it was built, stands on the site of a larger fort erected by General Monk. It is an irregular work, defended by fosse, glacis, and ravelins; and in 1745 successfully stood a siege of five weeks. The adjacent town of Mary-

the regiment before the next winter, and always (if it could be so) after eight months' duty; that by frequenting men above myself I may know my true condition, and by discoursing with the other sex may learn some civility and mildness of carriage, but never pay the price of the last improvement with the loss of reason. Better be a savage of some use than a gentle, amorous puppy, obnoxious to all the world. One of the wildest of wild clans is a worthier being than a perfect Philander.

. . . .

I have had a mind to burn this letter. You'll think it too grave, unreasonably so; or you may suspect I play the hypocrite, with design to lead you into an opinion of our reformation. Charles has bought me a French translation of Thucydides, and has not been paid. I wish you would desire my father to lay down the money for me till we meet. It is a most incomparable book. I wish I may get £20, to pay these little incumbrances; anything more would be unreasonable to expect.

It is said that Lafausille is preparing to publish a new treatise of Discipline and Reflections upon the Government of Armies. I hope Loftus will add his Notes and Remarks, for the amusement of the public and great diversion of all his acquaintance. There is already so much nonsense upon this subject, and it is in itself so barren and dry (in the manner it is commonly treated), that I wonder at any attempt of the kind. Lord Molesworth and General Kane—two very accurate writers—have expressed their thoughts in a very pretty, concise discourse, to the great advantage and improvement of those persons for whom they were intended.* These are the

burgh, intended as a suttlery to the garrison, was built of wood and turf, so that it might be easily destroyed when there was danger of its becoming a lodgment for an enemy. One face of the fort is bordered by a navigable arm of the sea, and on the land side there are rapid streams. Owing to the great height of the neighbouring mountains there is almost perpetual rain. (Richardson's 'De Foe's Tour,' Chambers's Gazetteer, etc.)

* Robert, Viscount Molesworth, translated 'Franco Gallia; or, an

patterns for my brother lieutenant-colonel to imitate. Perhaps you'll imagine that this is all ill-nature in me, and that I envy him the reputation which must follow his labours. Upon my word, I do not; but I could wish that he could be contented with his share of fame. To speak fairly, I don't believe what I have heard, from my opinion of my friend's moderation.*

Mrs. Inwood's great vivacity and great good-nature make her an excellent winter companion. She is very well in all seasons, but particularly in cold weather; her lively discourse in December makes some amends for her inactivity in May. One thing grieves me, that you must necessarily keep house while she stays; for I think I have heard you say that her wind won't last her a hundred yards, and that her action soon fails. If you will do me the favour to present my compliments to her, and assure her that I do not *rowll* about the room now, nor am I in that desperate condition that she has seen, and known, and laughed at! I was shamefully beat at chess by a Scotch laird about five months ago; this has put me out of conceit of my own play. I must again become a scholar under Mrs. Inwood, to make me attentive to the game and teach me to think.† I beg my duty to my father, and am,

Dear Madam, etc.,

JAMES WOLFE.

Account of the Free State of Ancient France, originally written in Latin by the famous civilian Francis Hotoman.' Brigadier-General Richard Kane, Governor of Minorca, was the author of 'Campaigns of King William and the Duke of Marlborough,' and of 'A New System of Military Discipline.'

* Whether Wolfe himself ever published a similar work is questionable, notwithstanding the fact that one, entitled 'Wolfe's Instructions to Young Officers' (12mo, 2*s*. 6*d*.), was advertised in a catalogue of military books printed for T. and J. Egerton, Whitehall, 1781.

† Mrs. Inwood was Annabella, second daughter of the Hon. and Rev. Henry Brydges, D.D., Archdeacon of Rochester, and brother to the first Duke of Chandos. She married Thomas Inwood, Esq., of Stanmore, Middlesex, and died at Chelsea, January 26, 1781. (Collins, ed. 1812, vol. vi. p. 728; and obit., 'Gentleman's Mag.')

The reader will have observed that the foregoing letter was not completed at one sitting; and it requires little discrimination to perceive where the "night thoughts" end. The sarcasm and humour of the latter part are, in their way, quite as characteristic as the gravity of the opening. In the message to Mrs. Inwood the writer unwittingly reveals his habitual restlessness within-doors; and the desperate condition which the lady had laughed at exhibits him while suffering under the vexations of arbitrary restraint and the pangs of unrequited love.

Wherever Wolfe was stationed he availed himself of whatever facility the place afforded towards the prosecution of his favourite studies. There being a mathematician of local celebrity in Inverness, it appears the Lieutenant-Colonel profited by his instructions; and it may be hoped that Mr. Barber* survived to boast of having been the tutor of the conqueror of Quebec. Although he is not named in his pupil's next letter, it is probable that he would have disapproved of the jocular manner in which the science is treated in the following, to the General:—

Inverness, 12th January, 1752.

Dear Sir,

I have read the mathematics till I am grown perfectly stupid, and have algebraically worked away the little portion of understanding that was allowed to me. They have not even left me the qualities of a coxcomb; for I can neither laugh nor sing, nor talk an hour upon nothing. The latter of these is a sensible loss, for it excludes a gentleman from all good company, and makes him entirely unfit for the conversation of the polite world. However, a man may make a

* Chambers's 'Picture of Scotland,' vol. ii. p. 303.

neighbourlike appearance in this cold region with a moderate competency of knowledge, and with a degree of gravity that may supply the deficiency. And whoever goes to kirk (as I do) once a week, and there comports himself with more reverence to the priest than consideration for the nature of the business—herein I sometimes fail—will most assuredly and deservedly obtain the reputation of great wisdom and discretion. We are allowed to be the most religious foot officers that have been seen in the North for many a day, and some words are thrown away every Sunday in prayers for our amendment and exemplary life and conversation. See the variety and constant change of things: in most of our quarters we have been looked upon no better than as the sons of darkness, and given up unto Satan; here we are white as the snow that covers all the hills about,—not from want of temptation to sin, you may believe, but from sudden conversion and power to resist.

. . . .

My uncle Wat has given over corresponding with me,—at least, I imagine so. I believe we don't agree in our system of military affairs, and therefore he drops me, as an innovator in discipline. I hear he is very well. Mr. Fisher* is empowered to do prodigious things with my prize in the lottery; amongst the rest, he will pay for my French Thucydides—our historian—I speak as a soldier. I am thinking what a noble balance there will be on my side when our accounts are settled! I beg my duty to my mother, and am,

Dear Sir, etc.,

JAM. WOLFE.

The next post carries a communication to Mrs. Wolfe from her son, who complains that an "easy stupidity" has crept over him, which, however, "acts the part of reason in keeping the vessel steady," and is preferable to a violent chase after nothing.

* Mr. Fisher was the General's agent.

He has received a letter from "little Rickson," who languishes and pines for his native land, though the affairs of the province have improved, and who never forgets to inquire after her and the General. He hopes she gives parties, to enliven the winter evenings; and adds,—"Mrs. Wilmot is one of the oldest of my old friends; I love to hear her name mentioned. Is she as merry as ever? Does she still laugh her life away? I hope her good humour will never forsake her." With suchlike familiar pen-chat he fills four ample pages, never touching upon general matters except in a passing remark that his naval friend, Charles Brett, has told him there are thirty sail in Plymouth Harbour.

From a letter to the General on the 1st of February, it appears that Sir John Mordaunt had unsuccessfully applied to Lord George Sackville, on Wolfe's behalf, for an appointment as aide-de-camp; whereupon the Lieutenant-Colonel observes:—

It is, no doubt, a ready road to recommendation and preferment, if a man acquits himself as he ought; but to speak truly, I am by no means calculated for an office of that kind, upon several accounts, and therefore don't grieve much at the refusal, though not the less obliged to Sir John for proposing it. While I do serve I do not wish to be out of my character, nor receive my pay in idleness.

. . . .

The snow begins to melt, so that the roads and rivers will be for a while impassable. There are some rapid rivers in this country that have neither bridge nor boat, upon the highway from Inverness to Edinburgh, so that when a quantity of water falls from the mountains, the post and passengers are retarded till it runs off. We had no other way of distinguishing Christmas than that we found it, as it commonly is, the coldest time of the year, and made a larger fire than usual, and ate exceeding bad mince-pies that our suttler, who is a very religious woman, begged we might taste. . . . The spring, that gives a new face to the whole creation, will enliven us all."

Out of another of those gossiping letters to Mrs. Wolfe one or two illustrative grains may be gleaned. Mr. Swinden has reminded him of standing for a boy; and the little godson is recommended to the maternal care.* The lottery prize, of which Fisher informed him, will not recompense him for a horse he has lost through the negligence of a groom. And Major Loftus, who, it seems, would dress the General's regiment according to his own taste, is designated as an "old-fashioned coxcomb,—a tawdry kind of beau, who thinks there can't be too much finery." Concerning the oft-recurring subject of matrimony, he says:—"I should hardly engage in an affair of that nature purely for money; nor do I believe that any infatuation will ever be strong enough to persuade me that people can live without it. Unless there be violence done to my inclinations by the power of some gentle nymph, I had much rather listen to the drum and trumpet than to any softer music whatever." Finally,—but what a fall from martial sounds to—— well! that species of inner armour which all warriors, perhaps, if we except Falstaff's, have worn since the days of the ancient Britons,—"My washerwoman thinks

* This godson did not survive. Mrs. Wolfe bequeathed £500 to Susannah, daughter of the Rev. S. F. Swinden; but no son of his is mentioned in her will. Wolfe was godfather to many other boys, amongst whom was the late Lord Cringletie, son of Lieut.-Colonel Murray, and father of James Wolfe Murray, Esq., who has three sons, all of whom bear the name of "Wolfe."

my linen will last till autumn." The letter which comes next is better worthy of notice :—

Inverness, 6th March, 1752.

Dear Madam,

The greatest pleasure your letters can give me is to know that you are both in good health, and, consequently, in the enjoyment of every good that follows it. If I could be always well assured of that, I should not insist any further, but leave it to any moment of your leisure to treat of lighter matters. An empty house is a very burdensome possession, and you are happy that you have got rid of yours, if there was no other reason than that it eases your mind of an encumbrance otherwise not easily shaken off; for as we accustom ourselves from infancy to measure our real good by the condition of our little affairs, and do often place our happiness or misery in opinion, and the comparing our situation with that of other people, we are apt to torment ourselves with crosses and accidents much more than their nature deserves. This leads one to a conclusion that perhaps there is a possibility of going through the business of the world without any strong connection or attachment to anything that is in it, and with a kind of indifference as to what happens. The danger of this indifference is, that in time it may turn to dislike, and, unless reasonably curbed, may influence our conduct, and make us fall out with ourselves, which of all quarrels is the most dangerous, and the most difficult to reconcile. But, sure, every man of common sense will discover beauty and virtue enough to keep him in good temper; and if not, he will try to possess himself of magnanimity to resist evil, and a certain portion of benevolence that shall incline him to think charitably of what is due to the crowd.

I have lately fallen into the acquaintance (by mere chance) of two young Scotch ladies, with whose conversation I am infinitely delighted. They are birds of a fine feather, and very rare in this country. One of them is a wife, the other a maid. The former has the strongest understanding, the other has the prettiest face; but as I am not disposed to become the slave of either, the matron stands first. I mention this circumstance to clear up all doubt that might rise from the subject; and I speak of these ladies to show that we should not despair, and that some satisfaction may be found even where it is least expected.

Lord Bury comes down in April; he'll stay six weeks, and then swear there's no enduring it any longer, and beg leave to return. "Wolfe, you'll stay in the Highlands; you can't, with any face, ask to quit the regiment so dispersed; and when you have clothed and sent them to their different quarters, towards the end of November you shall come to London, my dear friend, for three months." This will be his discourse, and I must say, "My Lord, you are very kind!" Here are people that remember to have seen my father at Fort William. I never heard him mention that. Perhaps he has been silent because there is a circumstance attending it that does him honour. Of all men upon earth, I believe he speaks the least in his own praise, and that's the reason why I never expect to see his name in the Gazette.

. . . .

I am, etc. etc.,

JAM. WOLFE.

There is good reason to conclude that the "matron" alluded to above was Mrs. Forbes, wife of John, only son of the famous Lord President. It will be seen that Wolfe entertained a high regard for that lady, concerning whose health he frequently inquires after he left Scotland. It is much more pleasing to look upon the old historic house as the scene of Mrs. Forbes's genial hospitality towards the as yet comparatively undistinguished officer, than as the temporary abode of the young Chevalier and of his successful rival before and after the bloody battle that terminated the rebellion.

The entertainment of Culloden House under Mrs. Forbes's *régime* suited her guest much better than that of his host's uncle and namesake "Bumper-John." An officer who visited about the year 1730, thus describes the manner of life followed by the latter worthy:—"There lives in our neighbourhood, at a house or castle called Culloden,* a gentleman whose hospitality is almost without bounds. It is the custom of that house at the first visit or introduction to take out your freedom by cracking his nut (as he calls it), that is, a cocoa-shell which holds a pint, filled with champagne, or such other sort of liquor as you shall choose. You may guess by the introduction at the contents of the volume. Few go away sober at any time; and for the greatest part of his guests, in the conclusion, they can't go at all."†

Wolfe's host, who had inherited the impoverished estate on the death of his father in 1747, was another sort of man. Although in his youth he exhibited a tendency towards his uncle's excessive conviviality, with maturer years he acquired moderation, and displayed characteristics more worthy of the son of Duncan Forbes. After quitting the army, in which he had served some years, Mr. John Forbes sought retirement in Suffolk, where he remained until he had paid off the debts which had been incurred by the Lord President in behalf of the

* "The Castle of Culloden was, if we may judge of it from some old pictures of the battle of Culloden, where it is represented in the distance, a huge, tall, strong pile of buildings, with little ornament. It was considered a fortification of considerable political importance, and being attacked by the rebels (in 1715), was held out by Duncan until the return of his brother with a very important ally had the effect of raising the siege."—(Burton's 'Life of Duncan Forbes,' p. 284.)

† Captain Burt's 'Letters from the Highlands.'

Government; and eventually, as a recompense for his father's losses, he was awarded a paltry pension of £400 a year.

A glimpse of the military morals which then obtained is afforded by Wolfe's next letter to his father.

Inverness, 20th March, 1752.

Dear Sir,

The meeting of the whole regiment and Lord Bury's presence will put me to the necessity of changing my manner of living, and if I don't acquire more knowledge I shall certainly get more health by the change. I have already mentioned what kind of weather and how severe a winter we have had, and when I add the impossibility of stirring out of the town and the difficulty of finding a conversible fit companion in it, you may believe that my long confinement has perhaps been more from necessity than choice. I can't drink nor play without the fear of destroying the officers, and some of them are already but too much inclined to that ruinous and disastrous vice.

It will be the middle of May before we are reviewed, and near the latter end when we send out our Highland detachments. June is everywhere a pleasant month, and in July we may begin to shoot. Lord Bury likes this diversion, and so do I. He'll keep me to carry his powder-horn and flints; we shall ramble from post to post till he's tired and goes off, and then I shall retreat into Fort William and remain there until further orders. Years roll on in this way, and are (unluckily for us) never to be recalled. Our friends forget us; we grow rustic, hard-tempered and severe, and insensibly fall into a course of thought and action that is more readily observed than corrected. We use a very dangerous freedom and looseness of speech amongst ourselves; this by degrees makes wickedness and debauchery less odious than it should be, if not familiar, and sets truth, religion, and virtue at a great distance. I hear things every day said that would shock your ears, and often say things myself that are not fit to be repeated, perhaps without any ill intention, but merely by the force of custom. The best that can be offered in our defence is, that some of us see the evil and wish to avoid it.

I have shut my books and am every fair day on horseback. I am sorry you have entirely given up that sort of exercise, because it is, beyond all dispute, the best. I hope you are persuaded that motion of some kind or other is necessary to your health. I take the freedom to put you in mind of it, because you seem sometimes less solicitous about it than it really deserves. My mother suffers when you do, so that I am doubly interested in your welfare.* I beg my duty to my mother, and am, etc.,

JAM. WOLFE.

A few extracts will suffice to represent a letter to Mrs. Wolfe, on the 10th of April, when, it would appear, the Lieutenant-Colonel was very discontented. After complaining that his projects were controlled by the arbitrary power of his Colonel, he writes :—

However I may be disposed of, you may be secure and satisfied that I shall in all things consider my condition; shall bear any ill-treatment with patience and fortitude, and must always think that he who has lost his liberty, or was never free, has nothing worth contending for. If it was left to my choice, I should run away to the Austrian camp at Luxembourg, or to the French army in Lorraine; for I don't think myself quite secure in England, and my course of thought leads me to shun danger and seek improvement.

. . . .

The Lieutenant-Colonel you speak of (I suppose you mean Aldercron) is near the top of our list; he has been strongly

* This sentence is an amplification of one which Wolfe wrote upon another occasion. "I pray you," he says to his mother, "take care of yourself, if you would take care of me." The manner of expression in the latter instance, though not the sentiment itself, may have been prompted by Ovid:—"Si tibi cura mei, sit tibi cura tui." (Heroides, Epistola xiii. 166.)

recommended from Ireland, with the title of long service to support the recommendation.* My success in that way depends upon events not to be wished or hoped for. I can only rise in war, by my willingness to engage in it. In these cooler times the parliamentary interest and weight of particular families annihilates all other pretensions; then I am amongst the youngest of my own rank, and have had as great favour shown me as I could modestly expect. Don't believe that I am insensible of your affectionate concern and my father's in the matter; I know well from whence it flows, and that knowledge will help me to bear little afflictions without wavering or repining; for I know no better reason to be contented than that you wish it, and when I'm not truly satisfied I'll endeavour to appear so. I must send off my books and recommend them to your care; the weight grows too considerable for long journeys, and a few well chosen is a great library for a soldier.

His long-expected Lordship at length joined his regiment, on the 13th of April; and thereby hangs a tale. On his arrival in Inverness, the magistrates of the town invited him to an entertainment on the Duke of Cumberland's birthday. Lord Bury graciously thanked the deputation, and assured them that he would not fail to represent their loyalty to his Royal Highness; but added, that he thought it would be still more complimentary to the Duke if they would postpone the celebration until the day following,—the anniversary of Culloden. The astonished officials said they could not take upon themselves to alter the day, but would consult their brethren.

* Lieut.-Colonel John Aldercron, of the 7th Foot, succeeded to the colonelcy of *Richbell's* — 39th (East Middlesex), in March, 1752. Early in 1754 he embarked for Madras with his regiment,—"*Primus in Indis,*"—and was nominated Commander-in-Chief in India. He became a Lieut.-General in 1760, and died in July, 1766.

On their return, they told his Lordship they regretted his request could not be complied with; whereupon Lord Bury replied, he was sorry they had not given a negative at once, for he had already mentioned the matter to his soldiers, and that he could not answer for their conduct under the disappointment, which, he feared, would provoke them to some outrage upon the town. The threat had the desired effect, for, under compulsion, the battle of Culloden was celebrated in Inverness.* Such an impolitic proceeding bespoke as little wisdom as generosity. It was a bad balm for a closing wound. Wolfe does not allude to the incident; but writing to his father on the 23rd of April, says:—

This is the first letter that I have penned since Lord Bury came here. His Lordship pays my attendance upon him with fair words and promises; and he thinks it highly reasonable that my long confinement should have an end, though he is far from being sure of the Duke's consent. I tell him the matter of fact, that when I feel any extraordinary restraint, and am kept longer with the regiment than is equitable, I hate the sight of a soldier; have, nevertheless, too much niceness to neglect the service, and too much indifference, as to reputation and applause, to exert myself in any high degree. Some of these young men have borrowed their notions of arms, and the people that compose them, from neighbouring nations, and seem of opinion that a stupid kind of obedience and conformity to their will supplies the want of military virtue and ability."

Wolfe, as has been shown, carried his own circulating library; otherwise, he would have found little mental food in Inverness, for there was no 'Courier' nor other local publication so far north in those days. A stray

* Walpole's Letters (June 6th, 1752), vol. ii. p. 288.

pedlar, or travelling tailor, satisfied all demands for foreign intelligence. An odd London or Edinburgh newspaper may indeed occasionally have reached the Coffee House, if that establishment still existed in 1752; for although there had been a coffee-house some twenty years before, kept by a *gentleman* merely to gratify his own social inclinations, without any view to pecuniary profit, it is a question whether the proprietor himself survived, or found a successor equally disinterested.*

But our Lieutenant-Colonel has now got rid of his superfluous books and other encumbrances in anticipation of his proposed journey, for, at last, he has not only the hope of speedy liberty, but has already partly mapped out his route. The more cheerful tone of his mind is apparent in his next letter home,—another of those filial effusions which may seem trivial to a few stern readers, who fancy that a soldier should be always a soldier, and nothing more, but will be seen by others in a different light. "I don't know," writes Walpole, portraying the Duke and Duchess of Hamilton, "whether you will not think all these very trifling histories; but for myself, I love anything that marks a character strongly."

Inverness, 16th May, 1752.

Dear Madam,

The best return I can make for your kind inquiry and care about my health is to inform you, as quick as possible, that I am extremely well, much better than I have been ever since I came last to Scotland. I wish you would always en-

* According to Burt, every petty trader called himself a *merchant*; a messenger received his *commission*, and brought back a *report*; lodging-house bills were *placards*; doors, *ports*; a few acres constituted a *park*; a laird's wife was, *Your ladyship*, etc.

tertain yourself with cheerful thoughts, believe your friends as you desire they should be, and put off your concern till you are convinced of the contrary. Though I would not willingly be forgot, nor even remembered with indifference, yet, rather than disturb your peace and felicity, I should be content not to be much thought of. Half of our misery arises from self-tormenting imaginations. The apprehension and dread of evil is the greatest of our misfortunes in this life. Take away the mischiefs that the fancy suggests, and it will considerably lighten our burthen.

Lord Bury at first advised me not to ask leave of absence, but afterwards he changed his opinion. I have reason to think that it will not be refused. My curiosity and the necessity of riding about will put me upon undertaking a very long journey. I find that a sedentary life is a very dangerous one, and therefore propose this new plan by way of trial, and to refresh and amuse myself. At the end of this tour I shall have the pleasure of seeing my father and you, and if I find you in health I shall find what I most wish for.

Teeth are valuable from their great use; the other day I broke a fine large one all to pieces. At Paris they put in artificial teeth that are every way as serviceable as the natural ones, and perhaps they may do the same in London. I see no harm in repairing any loss of this kind, as we really can't eat nor speak properly without them. Don't let accidents of this kind disturb you a moment; there are looks for all seasons of our life. You may stand by any lady of your age in Christendom, and have through your whole time been a match for all the beauties your contemporaries.* We have this

* Mrs. Wolfe, judging from her portrait by Hudson,—probably about the time of her marriage,—was a very beautiful woman. She had black hair and dark brown eyes, with a clear, delicate complexion, pretty mouth, and straight, well-shaped nose. The picture represents her in a pale yellow satin dress, with pearl necklace and pearls in her hair, and holding a rose in her right hand. It is strange that her son, who inherited her delicacy of constitution and some of her mental qualities, did not partake of her beauty. Yet, though every feature of their faces differed, there was an evident resemblance in general expression.

comfort, that a leg, an eye, or a tooth lost, does not necessarily carry away with it any one good quality. We can be as charitable, as liberal, and as honest, wanting any of these members, as with them. There is an old General mentioned in history that had but one left of what everybody else has commonly two; and yet, with one leg, one arm, one eye, and one ear, he was, for a drunken man, the best officer of his day.*

You cannot but pass your time agreeably. What addition of happiness could you desire? A pleasant house and garden, fine air, beautiful walks, plenty of good food, books, a sweet-tempered young lady to read to you and help to divert you. You have a great deal of company, you owe nobody a sixpence, and your friends and acquaintances love and esteem you. For my part, I think this a situation to be envied, and that all these fair appearances would be nothing without a conscience free from pangs and an universal benevolence to mankind. With these supports we enjoy the present hours, but are not therefore unmindful of our natural end. You say your trees are in bloom, and you wish not to kill them with too much fruit. The remedy is very easy; pluck off the superfluity, and only leave as much as they can afford to nourish, and that will be but very little. Let other gardens find you fruit

* Josias, Compte de Rantzau, of the distinguished family of that name in Holstein. In his boyhood he entered the Swedish service; but visiting France in the year 1635, he was induced by Louis XIII. to join the French army. At the siege of Dole he lost an eye, and at Arras, in 1640, he was deprived of a leg, an arm, and an ear. In 1645 he took Gravelines, of which he was named Governor, and in the same year received the bâton of Maréchal de France. Cardinal Mazarin suspecting him of favouring the malcontents, he was imprisoned in the Bastille, where he lay for eleven months, and the confinement brought on a dropsy, of which he died soon after his release, on the 4th of September, 1650. Rantzau possessed every quality of a great general; his chief defect was an excessive love of wine. A portrait of this redoubted warrior is to be seen in the Museum at Versailles, and a specimen of his handwriting (1648) may be found in Sims's 'Handbook of Autographs.' (See 'Biographie Universelle;' and 'Notes and Queries,' 3rd series, vol. iii. p. 469, and vol. iv. p. 36.)

this year and the next, and then your own will supply you.

. . . .

Mr. Skinner * has brought my shirts, and they please me much. Are not the ruffles a small matter too long? I have wore my old linen to shivers, and do really thank you for this seasonable relief.† I sent a trunk to London with books and two pieces of Irish cloth, under the care of an old sergeant of the regiment. You may open it if you please. I beg my compliments to Miss Brydges.‡ My duty to my father, etc.

Jam. Wolfe.

After a residence of nearly nine months, Wolfe left Inverness, early in May, not without carrying away a kindly feeling towards many of the inhabitants. Everything considered, he had found endurable quarters; for he did not cease to remember with gratitude the care and attention he had received from his landlady, Mrs. Grant. It speaks favourably for his conduct as the commanding-officer of a regiment, and shows his policy to have been conciliatory, that the people, who were amongst the most disaffected, had, towards the end of his command, so far changed their political sentiments in favour of the House of Hanover as to propose the celebration of the Duke of Cumberland's birthday,—an advance so ungenerously and injudiciously slighted by Lord Bury's practical joke.

* Mr. Skinner, of Greenwich, it would appear, was the architect or builder of Fort George.

† From the constant demand for *coarse* shirts, it is evident that Wolfe did not wear them all to shivers himself. It appears also that the surgeon of the regiment was never at a loss for lint.

‡ Catherine, fourth daughter of the Hon. and Rev. Henry Brydges, and sister to Mrs. Inwood. She afterwards married Lindley Simpson, Esq., of Babworth, Notts. Mrs. Wolfe bequeathed her the sum of £200, "together with my picture of her sister, and my painted dressing-glass and boxes, in my house at Bath."

The rebellion checked the traffic of the Highland capital, small though it previously had been; for the impulse which Cromwell's soldiers had given to trade and general improvement died away after the withdrawal of the garrison, and at the period of the Union commerce was at a very low ebb. It was not until many years afterwards that any kind of grain was sown, or potatoes planted, so far north. In the year 1740 the magistrates were obliged to advertise for a saddler to come and settle in the town; and still later there was but one (*bad*) baker in Inverness. But the measures taken by the British Government after the rebellion proved a wholesome, though rough remedy. The arbitrary power of the Highland chiefs was broken, and the general acknowledgment of the laws of the realm spread a feeling for justice. "With peace came liberty and order, and their attendant, public prosperity. Parliament, out of the funds of the confiscated estates, opened up the country by the formation of excellent roads, and as few towns in the kingdom were so backward as Inverness, so few have made more rapid progress."*

* Carruthers' 'Highland Note-Book,' p. 121.

CHAPTER X.

FORT AUGUSTUS.—DUBLIN.—BLACKHEATH.

MAY—SEPTEMBER, 1752.

IT was a long summer day's march through grandly wild scenery from Inverness to Fort Augustus. The journey, though agreeable and exhilarating for those who rode and could appreciate nature in her sternest mood, was toilsome enough to subalterns and soldiers who travelled afoot. For a distance of ten or twelve miles the road runs along the south-eastern side of Loch Ness, skirting the mountain range which here walls in the waters of the great Caledonian vale. As a highway could only have been made by cutting off so much from the base of the rocky barrier, the artificial pass, while washed on one hand by the lake, on the other is overhung by huge cliffs, which appear as if ever threatening to fall. Ere the morning mists had "gathered up their fleecy wings," those companies of Lord Bury's regiment bound for Fort Augustus were on their march by the loch-side. The secluded road they travelled was in itself an enduring memorial of their fellow-soldiers' labour as well as of the ability of the military engineer. By noon they had reached the "General's hut," so called from having been

Wade's headquarters while superintending the operations of his "highwaymen,"—as he facetiously termed the working soldiers; about a mile beyond which,—

> "Among the heathy hills and ragged woods,
> The roaring Fyers pours his mossy floods."

A little further on, the road, leaving the verge of the loch, begins to ascend the mountains, and as it winds from ridge to ridge the barren summits of the everlasting hills rise tier beyond tier. A sharpe curve now opens on a bleak moor with its sullen tarn, and anon, another bend discloses some little glen through which a foamy burn bounds over its rocky bed, set in banks of luxuriant ferns, juniper, and fragrant birch.* Having at length gained the highest level, soon after the road begins to descend, Fort Augustus is suddenly seen in the middle of a vast hollow, close by the end of Loch Ness. Of the three great strongholds connected by the chain of military roads which crosses the Highlands from the Moray Firth to Loch Eil, Fort Augustus is central between Fort George on the north-east, and Fort William to the south-west. It was built after the first rebellion, and having been taken by the insurgents in 1745, was afterwards more strongly reconstructed. The fortress had now become Wolfe's headquarters, while his regiment was dispersed among the several outposts of the surrounding district. Shortly after his arrival he wrote to his father as follows :—

Fort Augustus, May 28, 1752.

Dear Sir,

We have been here about ten days, and the garrison at

* 'Highland Note-Book.'

present consists of two field-officers, five or six other officers, and fourscore recruits. Lord Bury was soon tired and went off to Fort William; from thence he goes to Lord Breadalbaine's, and in a little while after to England. I can't find work enough to employ me here, and as the weather is tolerably fair, will visit some of our posts, and perhaps accept of an invitation from the Laird of Macleod, who offers to show me a very extraordinary old castle in the Isle of Skye.* Mr. Collingwood, our Lieutenant-Governor, is an old acquaintance of yours; he expresses great esteem for you, and desires me to tell you so. He is very agreeable to us all in his character of Governor, and if he can't make the place quite pleasant, he endeavours to make it easy.

You have heard of the strange murder that was committed about a fortnight since by two Highlanders, at the instigation, it is believed, of a lady, the wife of a banished rebel. The gentleman was an Argyleshire man, and factor upon some of the forfeited estates. Several men are apprehended upon suspicion, but I'm sure it will be very difficult to discover the actors of this bloody deed. The factor intended to remove the old tenants and to plant others in their room, and this is supposed to be their reason for killing him.

One of our officers has sent me a roebuck. It is a curious kind of deer, less than our fallow-deer, but seldom fit to eat. I intend to have it tamed and carried to England, as a present to my mother. It will be three weeks or a month before we shall be told whether we may go or must stay. They are more exact and ready in warning us of the expiration of our

* Dunvegan Castle, the family-seat of the Macleods, though a very ancient structure is still in perfect repair. It stands upon a rock projecting into the water, at the head of a bay formed by two low promontories, between the points of which the distant mountains of Long Island are visible. The castle forms three sides of an oblong figure enclosing an area facing the sea, and fenced by a low wall pierced with embrasures. A fine view of Dunvegan forms one of the illustrations of Pennant's 'Tour in Scotland.' See also Anderson's 'Guide to the Highlands,' where will be found an account of the fairy flag, the horn of Rorie More, and other relics of the Macleods.

leave than in granting it. I wish you much health, beg my duty to my mother, and am,

Dear Sir, etc.,

J. WOLFE.

The murder of Colin Campbell, of Glenure, caused a great sensation for some time. He had been appointed by the court of Exchequer, factor of the forfeited estate of Charles Stewart, of Ardshiel. Having been directed by the court to eject the tenants of the late proprietor, Campbell, on his way to execute his orders, whilst passing through a wood, was shot dead from behind a tree. One Allan Breck Stewart, a French cadet, was strongly suspected to be the assassin; but although a large reward was offered for his apprehension, he effected his escape.* James Stewart, natural brother of the late owner of the estate, was convicted of participation in the murder, and sentenced to be hung on a conspicuous eminence near the place where the foul deed had been perpetrated. Tied upon a horse, and guarded by a large body of soldiers, he was carried from Inverary to Fort William, whence he was conveyed to Ballachelish, under a guard of 100 men of Bockland's regiment. On their arrival at the ferry the weather was so boisterous that the river could not be crossed until the next morning, and it was midday when they reached the place of execution. "The storm was so great all the time," wrote the correspondent of the 'Edinburgh Courant,' "that it was with the greatest difficulty one could stand upon the hill, and it was near five o'clock before the body was hung in

* Some interesting incidents of the future career of Allan Breck Stewart are related by Sir Walter Scott in the introduction to 'Rob Roy.'

chains." It does not appear from the report of the trial, which is continued month after month in the 'Scots Magazine,' that the murder was instigated by the wife of the banished rebel, as was rumoured; but his sister, it was shown, had sheltered and facilitated the escape of the fugitive. This was neither the first nor the last of such outrages, for the lives of factors were then held as cheap in the Highlands as those of agents have more recently been in Ireland.

But, returning to our hero; he was not kept quite so long in suspense as he had anticipated, for it is evident, from his subsequent proceedings, that he set out on his travels about a fortnight after the date of the last letter. On his way to Perth he visited some of the posts occupied by his regiment. One of these, the first *en route*, was at Ruthven, in the district of Badenoch, six or seven miles from the fort. The small barrack here was built in 1718, on a mount by the Spey-side, from the ruins of an old castle which previously occupied the site. It was stoutly defended in 1746, by Sergeant Molloy and twelve men, against 300 of the rebels. It was in this neighbourhood also that the Highland chiefs re-assembled after the battle of Culloden, in hopes the Chevalier would try another engagement. The adjacent village of Ruthven is only remarkable as the birthplace, in 1738, of (Ossian) M'Pherson.

We trace Wolfe at Ruthven by means of a report forwarded to the Commander-in-Chief at Edinburgh, on the 4th of July, by Lieutenant Hartley, who, speaking of the capture of two notorious thieves, says:—"M'Pherson and William M'Donald, *alias* Gilbrandick, are confined in the gaol here, though your orders are not come for that purpose. It is owing to orders from Colonel Wolfe, to whom I showed the information when here, and also to the informers petitioning the justices of the peace." In addition to the three strong forts which commanded the great artery of the Highlands, there were twelve military posts established throughout the shires of Aberdeen, Banff, Forfar, Perth, Sterling, and Inverness, including a large sweep of the Hebrides, thus embracing the greater portion of the territories of the rebellious clans. Each of these stations, situated at a commanding point of a given district, was garrisoned by a captain's or a lieutenant's guard, and threw out a series of sub-posts, occupied by a sergeant or a corporal with a few men. The intervening distances were under the surveillance of patrols, while special parties were frequently sent to scour the mountains.

The first duty of every officer commanding a detachment was to send out the several small parties to the minor stations; and the Sunday after his arrival he was to cause the minister of each parish within the district to read and explain to his congregation an advertisement setting forth the objects which Government had in view, viz. the protection of the persons and properties of peaceable and honest subjects, and the suppression of the lawless depredations to which they were exposed. Each officer was likewise provided with a copy of exceedingly minute instructions for his own guidance in the irksome and onerous duties required of him. The sergeant or corporal of each sub-post was obliged to send a written return, weekly, to the captain of the parent post, detailing all breaches of the law, captures, etc., within his watch; and the superior officer was bound to forward these returns, together with his own report of whatever had happened within the limits of his command, the condition of his men, prices of provisions, and other particulars, to the Commander-in-Chief. The severity of the rebellion statutes, though justifiable only on the plea that milder measures had already been ineffective, tended eventually to benefit the country. The energy of the people was turned towards honest industry, while the martial character of the Highlanders became properly developed by enlistment in the royal army. Wolfe lived long enough to lead many of them to victory, and bitterly did the breechless braves revenge his death.

The duties of military officers in the posts above-mentioned were as unpleasant as the execution of them was vexatious. It is unnecessary, however, to enter into dry details of the system, for happily it can be illustrated, in a more interesting manner, by means of a few extracts from reports by others of Wolfe's officers, concerning whom the reader may probably desire to know something.* Captain Walter Johnson, who had marched from Inverness on the 18th of May, arrived at Invercomrie on the 21st. This post, situated on the banks of Loch Rannoch, in a very wild district of Perthshire, commanded the memorable pass of Glencoe leading to the sea-arm, called Loch Linnhe. In his first report, on the 7th June, the captain writes:—"In this country we

* The original reports were transcribed by Colonel Rickson in a folio volume, which was found amongst his effects, and is now in the possession of John Buchanan, Esq., of Glasgow, to whom I am indebted for much local information.

have great scarcity of provisions. A great many cattle have died, and what are alive are scarcely able to crawl, so that the men get very little to buy, unless milk and eggs." On the 13th of July the same officer says:—"When the sergeant was passing through Appinadow, he took a fellow wearing a blanket in form of a philabeg. He carried him to Perth, but the Sheriff-substitute did not commit him, because the blanket was not a tartan. On his return, he met another of the same kind; so, as he found it needless to carry him before a magistrate, he took the blanket philabeg and cut it to pieces."

Captain Alexander Trapand, who was stationed at Laggan Achadrom, an important position between Lochs Lochy and Oich, commanding several gorges towards the sea, in his return of the 12th of Junes, writes:—"Provisions are yet scarce, but plenty soon expected, as the people are coming from their sheilings." After describing the hardships of married soldiers with young children, owing to the scarcity of meal and of fuel, the captain quotes the prices of such provisions as the country afforded:—"Sheep, *when to be had*, three or four shillings; goat, the same; lamb, sixteen to eighteen pence; butter, fourpence per pound; eggs, three halfpence a dozen." The same officer's report of the 30th October supplies a more exciting passage:—

"The sergeant stationed at Knockfin apprehended, on Sunday the 15th instant, one John Farquharson, a Popish priest, dressed in all his sacerdotal vestments, as he was preaching to above three hundred persons in a great barn at the bridge of Cannich, in Strathglass. He was brought to me, and I sent him with a party and the witnesses, together with his vestments and all the altar furniture, to the Sheriff of Inverness-shire, who committed him to gaol. The next day he was bailed out. The sergeant ran a great hazard of his life in taking the above priest, as he was disguised, by a small sword and two soldiers with their bayonets, the people making an attempt to rescue the priest."

Captain Charles Desclouseaux,* reporting from Braemar Castle, in the district of Mar, Aberdeenshire, on the 15th June, writes to General Churchill in these terms:—

"Sir,—In obedience to your commands, I send you a report of my detachment, with several letters in regard to M'Pherson, taken up for wearing the Highland dress. I beg you would please to let me know your commands on that head. I have got the plaid. When my corporal was going to take the prisoner before a justice of the peace by my order, the mob rose; on which my corporal secured Allan Coats, and brought him to me at Braemar; on which I sent Ensign Butler with him to Mr. Gordon, who, I was informed, was a justice of the peace; but he refused acting, as not being qualified. One Shaw, a half laird, who came with my corporal and party to Braemar, has given his note for Coats's appearance. He pretends to say the soldiers were in fault; but, by all accounts I can receive, this Shaw was the occasion of the riot, calling to his men in Irish to secure the soldiers, and I now find that this Coats is his servant. I long to know your commands. We want magistrates that will or dare exert themselves. This is a nest of rogues and rebels. You may rest assured that neither pains nor cost shall be wanting in me to bring any of these vile miscreants to a due obedience of the laws."

Captain Desclouseaux again reports, on the 15th of August:—

* Captain Desclouseaux was an officer of General Wolfe's regiment, which succeeded Lord Bury's in their several Scotch stations. He acted as adjutant at Fontenoy, where he was wounded, and, in the year 1755, was made Fort-Major of Berwick. Wolfe speaks of him as "an officer of skill and capacity."

"Mr. Small, of late Lord Loudoun's regiment of Highlanders, paid me a visit, the purport of which was to inform me that Sergeant Moore, *alias* Cameron, was on a thieving party with seven of his companions, and to advise me to take care of the passes between Dee and Sands, which I accordingly did. At his return to Spittle he sent for my sergeant, and, as we had concerted, advised him to patrol as usual, but to go out afterwards in dead of night; and my patrol was ordered to meet them at the foot of a cairn, which being done, both patrols, with proper guides, proceeded to the place suspected. When they came to the cairn they crouched in, and found eight persons asleep. Recovering from their surprise, they attempted to seize their arms and defend themselves; but my people bound them all prisoners, and brought them to the castle. They had arms and plaids, which were secured. It seems they are all great rogues, and the first (Mackenzie) is strongly suspected of some murders. As my patrols since my last report have been so irregular, you will, I hope, dispense with the usual form of the return; it being impossible for me or the sergeant and men to tell what glens or passes they went over, it being in the dead of night, and trusting to the guides appointed."

Captain John Beckwith, who was stationed at the head of Loch Arkaig, entering into the humour of the subject, informs the Commander-in-Chief:—"On the 24th of last month (August), one of my men brought me a man to all appearance in a philabeg; but on close examination I found it to be a woman's petticoat (which answers every end of that part of the Highland dress). I sent him to the sheriff-substitute, who dismissed him."

It was a hard task to hunt down the philabeg, for the poor Highlanders clung to it as fondly as do ladies now to their crinolines. In their endeavours to evade the law, various dodges were resorted to, but the simplest mode was by means of a few stitches in the garment to convert it into a rude sort of *knickerbocker.** Now to pursue our traveller.

On the 20th of June Wolfe reached Perth, where he enjoyed for a few days the society of the officers of his father's regiment. His host upon this occasion was the old friend at whose expense he so frequently vents a sarcasm, Major Loftus, who is now represented to Mrs. Wolfe as being "more humorous and pleasant than he used to be; at least, he appears so to me, who am almost grave." Another passage in the same letter from Perth (June 24) affords an instance of the tyranny of fashion:—"If you know of a good servant that can or will learn to dress a wig, and save me that prodigious expense in London, it will be a favour done to me to engage him. John is dirty and grows impertinent; the other I have turned away for killing one horse and for spoiling the rest." As some degree of skill in arts such as that of the *friseur* was required of valets in those days, these accomplished gentlemen entertained high notions of their personal importance; and as the Lieutenant-Colonel was somewhat hasty in his temper and abhorred a "coxcomb,"—his strongest term of contempt,—there happened occasional collisions between master and man. Wolfe also, though ever grateful for

* In the year 1755, a captain of Lord George Beauclerk's regiment wrote with his return from Loch Arkaig:—"I have a report from the officer commanding in North and South Morer that the inhabitants begin to wear, instead of breeches, stuff trousers, much after the fashion of those that seamen use, but not longer than the kilt, or philabeg. I am at a loss to know whether to look upon that as part of the Highland dress, and to take notice of such people as offenders against the law."

faithful services, looked upon a mere servant as very inferior to a private soldier. An anecdote is related of him in a military compilation, so characteristic, that it may be adopted as an illustration.* It is said that one day, when taking a ride, he dismounted, and left his horse for his servant to hold. On his return, finding a Grenadier holding both horses and the servant gone, he immediately took hold of the bridles, thanked the Grenadier, and told him to remain. When the groom came back, "Sirrah!" cried Wolfe, "what do you mean by deserting your service, and taking up the time of this soldier? Had I employed him as you have, it would have been proper enough; but can you be such a fool as to think that a man who has the honour to wear the King's uniform, and is engaged in the service of his country, ought to supply the place of an idle servant? Know that it is your duty, and my command, that you wait upon the soldiers, and not the soldiers upon you!"

After this picture of our hero, the contrast presented by a paragraph in the letter already quoted from appears ludicrous enough:—"I have another favour to beg of you, and you will think it an odd one. It is, to order some currant-jelly, to be made in a crock for my use. It is the custom in Scotland to eat it in the morning with bread; and I find it not only a very pleasant custom, but a very wholesome one. You know what a whimsical sort of person I am, and how variable and unsteady; nothing pleases me now but the rougher kind of entertainments,—such as hunting, shooting, and fishing. There's none of that kind near London, and I

* 'The Soldier's Companion; or, Martial Recorder.' London, 1824.

have distant notions of taking a little, very little house, remote, upon the edge of a forest or waste, mostly for sport, and keep it until we go to Minorca."

Wolfe was accompanied by the Major as far as Glasgow, where he added, by way of postscript to the same quaint missive:—"I wrote the above at Perth, and close it at Glasgow. Loftus is by, and makes such a noise that I must finish as quick as possible." Our traveller, with the intention of crossing to Ireland and visiting his father's brother, Major Wolfe, at length started for Portpatrick. So wonderful has been the transformation within the last century of everything connected with Portpatrick, that it is with difficulty we, who are "to the manner born" of railroads, steamers, piers, and lighthouses, can form any conception of the condition of the town and its inhabitants in 1752. As there was no artificial harbour, the only shelter for the craft which entered the port was that provided by nature in the narrow inlet between two long ridges of rocks projecting into the sea. Whenever the wind blew towards the shore, the weight of water thrown in between these barriers was so great as to render it necessary to run the vessels aground, to facilitate which operation they were built with flat bottoms. The chief occupation of the townsfolk—women and children as well as men—was dragging boats by main force up the beach, out of the reach of the waves, which otherwise would have dashed them to pieces. "The inhabitants," says Sir John Sinclair, "were the happiest of mortals. Their continual exertions, in launching and dragging up the vessels, excited wonderful spirits, which they knew how to recruit when exhausted. Every day that a vessel sailed or arrived was a festival." These happy mortals were equally ready, whenever the opportunity offered, to plunder vessels wrecked upon the coast, when the division of the spoil usually ended in a riot. Magisterial authority was so inefficient, that the lawlessness of the place became proverbial on the other side of the Channel; insomuch, that when any of the people in Donaghadee fell out, it was a common threat,—"I'll not meddle with you now; but wait till I get you at Portpatrick, where there is no law."

The earliest postal communication between Scotland and Ireland was established in 1662, by the Earl of Newburg.* The mode of conveying the mail has undergone many changes. For a time there were regularly appointed packet-boats, but before a quay was built they were very uncertain; for as, work or play, the pay of the sailors was running on, they were frequently not forthcoming when wanted. A rule was then adopted, that the boat which sailed first should have the mail, and a certain sum for carrying it. This operated as a premium for a good while, until the increase of trade rendered the government allowance no longer a primary object, and the post had to wait until some vessel completed her cargo of merchandise.

After being detained probably for days in Portpatrick, passengers, before they embarked, were subjected to the annoyance of a ruffianly band of porters, whose extortions were so notorious that they were known by the significant name of the *Robbery*. The short, and fre-

* Chalmers's 'Caledonia,' vol. iii.

quently rough, voyage of one-and-twenty miles was rarely made in less than eight hours; and the accommodation aboard the *Flats** was not such as to render a longer time at sea, as occasionally happened, desirable. The harbour of Donaghadee was comparatively safe and commodious, and the town was chiefly remarkable as the resort of runaway lovers about to cross to Portpatrick—the Gretna Green for Ireland,—where they were wedded *more Scotico.*†

Wolfe has left no record of his journey in the north of Ireland; but as he did not arrive at Dublin until the 12th of July, he must have gone out of the direct route and visited many places. From a description of the mode of travelling at a much later time, it appears to have been well calculated to agitate both body and mind. The horses, though presenting a very inferior appearance to those in England, got along tolerably well, and the post-boys, though ragged, were generally civil; but the chaises are represented as being in a very wretched state, many of them having broken windows, besides great holes in the panels, stuffed with wisps of straw; some were without cushions or linings, while in others, these appendages were so filthy and tattered, as to make the occupant wish there were none. "In the yard of a principal inn," says an English traveller, "I saw five chaises, and only one of them had any step, and that but a bad one, a kitchen-chair supplying the place

* "It was but lately that two of these large *Flats*, which had formerly been Government packets, were to be seen on our shore, as monuments of ancient barbarity." (Sinclair's 'Statistical Account of Scotland' (1791), vol. i. p. 38.)

† Lawson's 'Gazetteer of Ireland.'

of a step when the chaises were brought to the door; and, absurd as it may appear, it may be relied upon, that in heavy rain an umbrella has often been found to be a great convenience *in the inside* of an Irish post-chaise." *

As the weather was wet on Wolfe's journey, an umbrella might have been serviceable; but umbrellas were then unknown in Ireland, and he, as yet, had never seen one. It is probable, however, that he had the advantage of better conditioned machines than the traveller's some sixty years after him, for in 1752 postchaises had been but very recently introduced. But not to linger on the road: after his arrival in the capital the Lieutenant-Colonel wrote the following to his father:—

Dublin, 13th July, 1752.

Dear Sir,

This is the first day of rest since I left Glasgow. I came here last night not a little fatigued, you may believe, with such continued hard exercise, but otherwise in better condition than I have known for fourteen months past, leaner than can be described, and burnt to a chip. I have seen your letter to my uncle, and am greatly concerned that your health is not so perfect as I always wish it to be. If the season has been of the same sort that they have had in this country,—very wet and cold,—it may be accounted for, and a drier air and more sun will, I hope, relieve you. My uncle has complaints in his back and limbs, and is obliged to put on flannels: whether it be the rheumatism or gout flying about him, his physicians cannot determine. He is otherwise cheerful and well. I stay here four or five days, and then set

* 'An Englishman's Descriptive Account of Dublin,' etc., by Nathaniel Jefferys (1810). Miss Edgeworth also, in her tale of 'Ennui,' gives an amusing description of Irish posting.

out for Cork, where I shall embark in one of the Bristol ships; and if I find myself strong in health and in circumstances shall continue my journey from Bristol through the West, and so home.

I came yesterday from Drogheda, but not till I had seen that ground and that river so remarkable in our history.* The Protestants have erected a monument in memorial of their deliverance, very near the ford where the King crossed the Boyne. The inscriptions take notice of the happy consequences of that battle, and on one side of the pillar they do honour to the memory of Duke Schomberg.† I had more satisfaction in looking at this spot than in all the variety that I have met with; and perhaps there is not another piece of ground in the world that I could take so much pleasure to observe.

The north of Ireland and the neighbourhood of this city are very little inferior for beauty and fertility to any parts of England that I have seen, and others they exceed in both. And there is yet great room for different improvements, particularly in planting and draining the boggy grounds. They have fine clear streams as can be seen, and very large timber where it is encouraged; but I am told that the best estates

* "Mr. Wilde, in his account of the battle of the Boyne, says: "Grander battle-fields, more extensive plains, as that of Waterloo,—or with the mountains looking upon the sea, as at Marathon,—may easily be found; but for inland, sylvan beauty, the diversity of hill and dale, with wooded banks and a shining river, this scene of action may well challenge competition." ('The Boyne and the Blackwater,' p. 242.)

† The Boyne monument is founded upon a rock on the southern brink of the river, two miles above Drogheda. The base is 80 feet in circumference, and the obelisk rises to a height of 170 feet. According to the inscription,—"This memorial of our deliverance was erected in the ninth year of the reign of King George II., the first stone being laid by Lionel Sackville, Duke of Dorset, Lord Lieutenant of the kingdom of Ireland, 1736." The monument, designated by Twiss "the grandest modern one in all Europe," was designed by La Cordi, and engraved by Vivares; it also forms the frontispiece to Wright's 'Louthiana.'

are involved deeply in debt, the tenants racked and plundered, and consequently industry and good husbandry disappointed or destroyed.

This appears to be a prodigious city, and they continue to build; the streets are crowded with people of a large size and well limbed, and the women very handsome. They have clearer skins and fairer complexions than the women in England or Scotland, and are exceedingly straight and well made. You'll be surprised that I should know this so soon, but I have seen a multitude already, for they take some pains to show themselves. My uncle seems to have preserved his cheerfulness and vivacity. He joins with me in wishing you both all manner of good.

I am, dear Sir, etc.,

JAM. WOLFE.

The interest felt by Wolfe in the place where the last of the Stuart kings lost the chance of recovering his crown was heightened by the recollection of Culloden, where the hopes of that dynasty were completely destroyed. But the survey of the field in a military aspect interested him more than political associations or the beauty of the surrounding scenery. He observed the ground on the north bank of the river occupied by William's army the night before the battle, and the position of the Irish camp upon the opposite side. Here, on the morning of the 1st of July,—two-and-sixty years ago,—the right forced the passage at Slane ford; here, leading on the centre, fell the brave old warrior Meinhardt, Duke Schomberg; and here it was that the monarch of "immortal memory" himself, at the head of his cavalry, crossed the Boyne, drove the enemy before him, and forced James to flee. The battle of the Boyne furnished an admirable topic for conversation between "Uncle Wat" and his favourite nephew. The veteran, who, it would seem, regarded James as an adopted son, whether a bachelor or not, had no children; for Wolfe, who frequently speaks of his cousins Whetham, Thompson, Goldsmith, Sotheron, and Burcher, never mentions a cousin of his own name. Letters already given and others further on show the fatherly feeling of the old Major, who was not only ready to supply funds for travel, but was so anxious for the young man's improvement that he considered four masters a day not enough for him. They, nevertheless, differed in their opinions about military matters. The old soldier of Marlborough's time was so conservative as to think the young officer's notions of discipline to be innovations. But, notwithstanding, their mutual friendship never abated; and it is gratifying to know that Major Wolfe survived to see his high expectations of his nephew realized.

It cannot now be ascertained in what part of Dublin the old Major resided; for Wolfe's letters to him are directed to Lucas's Coffee-house. This place of military resort was situated on Cork Hill, near the Castle, occupying part of a mansion erected by Richard Boyle, first Earl of Cork, and consequently called Cork House. The building existed until the year 1768, when it was demolished under an Act of Parliament for improving the approaches to the Castle. Before the "Fifteen Acres" became notorious as a duelling site, the ground where so-called affairs of honour were settled was the yard behind Lucas's Coffee-house. Upon occasion of such rencounters, it was usual for the company to watch the combat from the windows, and lay wagers on the issue.*

With the exception of London, the Irish capital was by far the most considerable city Wolfe had yet seen. At the time of his visit Dublin was apparently at the summit of prosperity. As the seat of the Irish Parliament, and of a Viceregal Court, at that time more than a mere pageant, peers and commoners resided in the city, where many splendid mansions, now converted into public offices and merchants' warehouses, dispensed lavish hospitality as well as adorned the principal streets. The "Liberty" was inhabited by wealthy silk and poplin weavers; and many other manufactures flourished in different quarters of the town. The linen trade with the north also added to the wealth of the capital. Wolfe's representation of the "prodigious city" may therefore be accepted as within the facts. Nor is it less true that the tenants on many of the estates which supplied the wealth dissipated in the capital were "racked and plundered;" for absentees existed before the Union. Those political troubles, however, which ended in the Rebellion of 1798, had not yet been agitated, and Ireland generally was in that state of calm which usually precedes a storm. That storm, and subsequent ones, have tended to the removal of religious and political grievances; and there is now also an equitable balance between the capital and the provinces. Dublin possesses much more real wealth at the present day than when she could boast of a local parliament; but, being more equally distributed, it is not so ostentatious. The city is now more

* Gilbert's 'History of Dublin.'

beautiful than ever. Streets have been widened, paved, and lighted; the old bridges over the Liffey, with their houses and booths, have been replaced by new ones without obstructions, and many sanitary improvements have been effected.

As the Lieutenant-Colonel spent about a week in Dublin, and, like the hero of the Boyne, "had not come to let the grass grow under his feet," he had time enough to see all the sights. There were the University and the Castle, but no Lord-Lieutenant inhabited the latter just then. There was also Strongbow's tomb in the nave of Christ Church, and another tomb in the choir of St. Patrick's, which he regarded with greater interest,—Schomberg's.* In his perambulations he passed through "Hell;" for such was the unsavoury name given to the arched passage which led into the area on the south side of Christ Church, and east of the law courts. A representation of the Devil, carved in oak, stood above the entrance. The name and uncouth effigy, however, were the only objectionable features of the place; for it was nothing worse than what would now be called an arcade, occupied by retailers of nick-nacks and children's toys. Furnished apartments, too,—usually advertised as "well suited to lawyers,"—were to be had therein.† The fame of the region was not confined to Ireland, for Burns says in 'Death and Dr. Hornbook,'—

* "Schomberg's body was immediately carried across the river to the English camp. His skull is still shown in the cathedral of St. Patrick's, where Dean Swift caused a monument to be erected to him. The family vault of the Schombergs is in the Cathedral of Mayence." ('The Boyne and the Blackwater,' p. 251.)

† Gilbert's 'History of Dublin.'

> "But this that I am gaun to tell,
> Which lately on a night befell,
> Is just as true as the Deil's in Hell,
> Or Dublin city."

Wolfe had occasion to call at the Royal Barracks, then the only barrack in Dublin; and here he was not far from the Park, wherein his father's neighbour at Blackheath,—the Earl of Chesterfield,—when Lord-Lieutenant of Ireland, erected the column surmounted by a phœnix, from which it has been erroneously supposed the Park derives its name.* The only other military institution then existing in the neighbourhood of the city was the Royal Hospital at Kilmainham—the Chelsea of Ireland; and there is reason to believe that the Lieutenant-Colonel paid a visit to the "old fogies," as they are locally called, who inhabited here.†

It is not probable that Wolfe again saw his uncle Walter after he took leave of him towards the latter end of July. The old officer, who, though cheerful and vivacious, was now infirm, had been Major of the 39th Foot (Richbell's). His last service was on board the fleet, in which the regiment was employed during the years 1745 and 1746 as a marine corps; and he appears to have left the army in 1747; at least, his name does not occur in any return or list of a later date.‡

* The term "Phœnix" is said, by competent authorities, to be a corruption of two Irish words, signifying a "clear spring," from the *spa* which rises in the little dell near the Military Hospital.

† The hospital at Kilmainham for superannuated soldiers was founded by Royal proclamation, at an expense of £23,559, in the year 1679.

‡ These few particulars concerning the Major are gleaned from 'Quarters of the Army in Ireland,' published at Dublin. Haydn, in his 'Book of Dignities,' says: "The earliest Army List our research

Of our hero's travels in the south of Ireland, his voyage to Bristol, and tour in the west of England, no record is extant.* We only know that he arrived at Blackheath about the time when those who went to bed on the night of Wednesday, 2nd of September, did not get up until the morning of the 14th, and found themselves no more refreshed than after an ordinary night's rest. This was the period when, as not a few wise folks imagined, eleven days were curtailed from their lives by Act of Parliament.† The Bill, which had become a law (26 Geo. II.) in September, 1752, was introduced into the House of Lords, in February, 1751, by the Earl of Chesterfield. It did not pass without opposition from Peers who, like the Duke of Newcastle, hated newfangled notions, and considered it dangerous to meddle with long-established customs. The scientific details were managed by Lord Macclesfield, assisted by Dr. Bradley and other eminent men; and the abstruse sub-

has enabled us to discover is one in the Military Library at Charing Cross for the year 1744. The earliest in the British Museum is for the year 1754, from which time the series of Army Lists at the War Office also commences." (Note, p. 317.)

* "A writer in the 'Gentleman's Magazine,' in 1752, says that a Londoner at that time would no more think of travelling into the west of England for pleasure than of going to Nubia." (Smiles, 'Lives of Engineers,' vol. i. p. 196.)

† "I shall never forget an itinerant orator of that his day, who was mounted on a joint-stool near the Royal Exchange, and whom, as I passed by, I heard declaiming in an impassioned style, and with the true oratorical flourish, against the measures of Administration. 'They rob us of our money,' said the fellow, 'and they rob us of our *time* too. What d'ye think they did with the eleven days they took from us in last September? Why, they sent them to Hanover; d—e, they sent them all, every one of them, to Hanover!'" (Gentleman's Magazine, March, 1800.)

ject was popularized by the energetic Earl. In one of the celebrated letters to Philip Stanhope—with whom, by the way, Wolfe was soon to become acquainted—Chesterfield writes: "I have of late been a sort of an *astronome malgré moi,* by bringing into the House of Lords a Bill for the reforming of our present calendar, and taking the New Style." In a subsequent letter (March 18, o. s., 1751) he gives the following account of the method by which he carried this important measure:—"It was absolutely necessary to make the House of Lords think that I knew something of the matter, and also make them believe that they knew something of it themselves, which they did not. For my own part, I could just as soon have talked Celtic or Sclavonian to them as astronomy, and they would have understood me full as well; so I resolved to do better than speak to the purpose, and to please instead of informing them. I gave them, therefore, only an historical account of calendars, from the Egyptian down to the Gregorian, amusing them now and then with little episodes; but I was particularly attentive to the choice of my words, to the harmony and roundness of my periods, to my elocution, to my action. This succeeded, and will ever succeed: they thought me informed because I pleased them; and many of them said that I had made the whole very clear to them, when I had not even attempted it."

Another provision of the Act, that of making each year begin on the 1st of January instead of the 25th of March, was not so unpopular as the loss of the eleven days, for it had, to some extent, been practically anticipated by writing additional figures to the number of the year, from the beginning of January until Lady Day; thus 1750–51, or $17\frac{51}{52}$. In not a few instances, however, where this rule has not been invariably adopted, —the originals of Wolfe's own letters, to wit,—the uncertainty of the year frequently causes no little trouble and loss of time to those who are called upon to investigate old documents.*

The Lieutenant-Colonel did not obtain permission from the Commander-in-chief to go abroad until after his arrival in London. The Duke, who was too short-sighted to perceive the necessity or propriety of an English officer learning anything beyond what was required for his regimental duties, was not easily persuaded to sanction the step. But Lord Bury, remembering Wolfe's wrath upon the previous refusal, now interposed in his behalf. His lordship also rendered his lieutenant another essential service, by recommending him to the notice of his father, the Earl of Albemarle, British ambassador at the French Court. Provided with this and many other introductions, Wolfe departed from Blackheath for Paris.

* Sir Harris Nicolas has pointed out remarkable instances of the confusion of historical events, owing to some writers using the *Civil and Legal*, and others the *Historical* year. See "Chronology of History," Cabinet Cyclopædia. In Chamberlayne's 'Present State of Great Britain' (1741), we likewise read: "The year beginning the 25th of March, according to the computation of the Church of England, two Easters may happen in the year; as in 1667 the first Easter fell out the 25th of April, and the second the 22nd of March following, and not one Easter in the ensuing twelve months."

CHAPTER XI.

PARIS.

OCTOBER, 1752—MARCH, 1753.

THE times rendered remarkable by those great events, of which historians, in stage phrase, make "points," are by no means the most influential in the annals of a country. Battles, rebellions, revolutions, in short, all national crises, are but the strikings of the clock whose monotonous ticks attract little attention. Though there happened no extraordinary incident in the history of France during Wolfe's residence in Paris, there were foreshadowings of coming calamities, for even then the storm was gathering which was to burst in the French Revolution. Beneath the superficial splendour of the capital were an arbitrary government, a profligate court, a discontented people, and an ambitious priesthood. While Paris was in all its gaiety, the provinces groaned under intolerable burdens; but the *noblesse* were too deeply absorbed in the festivities of the day to be anxious about the morrow. Intellect was perverted, industry discouraged, and the true welfare of the kingdom sacrificed for the dream of foreign domination.

The peace which existed between England and France

was no more than a suspension of hostilities, affording time to prepare for another war. There was no desire on the part of either nation for permanent amity, and the representative of each court appears to have been chosen, not for his ability, but for such personal qualities as were calculated to render his residence endurable for a while. Thus, when the Duc de Mirepoix was sent as ambassador to St. James's, Marshal Saxe observed, "It is an excellent appointment, for he has a good leg, and can teach the English to dance;" while of the British ambassador in Paris, Madame de Pompadour remarked, "Milord Albemarle passes his time agreeably here. The King of England, who loves him, though I know not why, sends him his lesson all ready, and he comes to repeat it, like a schoolboy, to the Minister of Foreign Affairs."

Wolfe's first letter from Paris is dated the 9th of October. After the warmest expression of gratitude to his father for enabling him to accomplish his long cherished desire, he gives the following account of his journey:—

I think it was the 2nd of October that I left Blackheath. I lay that night at Canterbury; an old friend, a captain of Dragoons, supped with me, and helped to deliver me from my own thoughts. The 3rd I went to Dover, and as my old Lady Grey's house was in the way I called upon her, and was very graciously received. She pressed me to dine, but that could not be, as the time of the packet's sailing was uncertain. At her house I met a Miss Scott, whom my mother has heard of. The good old lady diverted herself with us two, told each that the other was not married, offered her mediation, and thought it a very lucky rencounter, for the young lady and I got to the house exactly at the same time. However, I escaped untouched, and left my old friend to make up matters as she pleased. The packet did not sail that night, but we embarked at half an hour after six on Wednesday morning, and got into Calais at ten. I never suffered so much in so short a time at sea. There were two English gentlemen of condition in the ship travelling my way; we agreed to come together, and on Saturday, the 7th, in the morning, arrived at Paris without any sort of difficulty or inconvenience.

The people seem (as their character is) to be very sprightly, and to deal largely in the exterior; for a man can hardly commit a greater crime than to be *mal mise, ou mal coiffé.*

The buildings are very magnificent, far surpassing any we have in London. I mean the houses of the higher nobility and peers of France. The Gardens des Tuilleries, that you have heard so much of, is as disagreeable a sandy walk as one would wish. They are indeed near the Seine and the Louvre, but have little else to recommend them. The Mall, or your park at Greenwich, are infinitely superior. There are no fortified towns between Calais and Paris; the country is very beautiful in most places, entirely in corn, and quite open where the woods allow it to be so; that is, there are few or no enclosures.

Mr. Selwin* has recommended a French master to me, and in a few days I begin to ride in the Academy, but must dance and fence in my own lodgings, for fear of a discovery. A letter would miscarry that had any strokes of politics in it, so I shall never touch that matter; besides, it is neither your taste nor mine. The Dauphin is perfectly recovered, and I believe the people are very hearty and sincere in the satisfaction and pleasure they profess upon that occasion. The Duke of Orleans, to signify his particular joy, has given an entertainment at St. Cloud, in the highest taste and magnificence, and at a prodigious expense.†

* An English banker in Paris.

† The recovery of the Dauphin from the small-pox gave rise to numerous *fêtes*, the most remarkable of which was an allegorical display of fireworks exhibited at Bellevue by Madame de Pompadour. The royal

On the 26th of October, Wolfe wrote as follows to his mother:—

Dear Madam,

Having discovered that I understood but little of the French language, and that I speak it very incorrectly (notwithstanding Mr. Haren's honourable approbation),* I am disposed to fall upon some method that may lead me to a better knowledge of that useful tongue. The first necessary step is to leave off speaking English, and to write it as little as possible. This resolution of mine shall not, however, extend so far as to cut off all communication between us, for I had rather lose this or a much greater advantage than be denied the satisfaction of expressing my regard for you in the plainest and dearest manner; and I will borrow neither the language nor meaning of these airy people when I speak of that.

Lord Albemarle is come from Fontainebleau to his country house within two miles of Paris, and will soon be fixed for the cold season. I went to Fontainebleau to pay my respects to him, and have very good reason to be pleased with the reception I met with. The best amusement for strangers in Paris is the opera, and the next to that is the playhouse. There are some fine voices in the first, and several good actors in the last.† The theatre is a school to acquire the French language, for which reason I frequent it more than the other. Besides, it is a cheaper diversion. You'll be glad to hear that

heir was represented as a luminous dolphin in the centre of a lake, surrounded by grottoes occupied by monsters, who disgorged flames against him. But his tutelary deity, Apollo, darting thunder and lightning from the clouds, the enemy with their habitations were totally destroyed. The scene then changed into a gorgeous palace of the Sun, wherein the dolphin reappeared amidst illuminations, which lasted till morning. (See 'Annual Register,' 1766.)

* Wolfe had letters of introduction from Mr. Haren, with whose family Mrs. Wolfe was on intimate terms.

† Besides the Opera, in the Palais Royal, there were at this time two theatres in Paris,—La Comédie Française, in the Faubourg St. Germain, and La Comédie Italienne, rue Mauconseil. Operas were introduced into Paris in 1669 by the Abbé Pierre Perrin. The Comédie Française, doubtless the theatre frequented by Wolfe, is thus described in a con-

your nephew Whetham* is in very good hands; his governor, or companion, is a gentleman of Switzerland, who was formerly in the army, and is very well spoken of. My cousin is expected here in three weeks or a month, and he stays all the winter in Paris. Madame Pompadour is a very agreeable woman. I had the good fortune to be placed near her for a considerable time. I beg my duty to my father, and wish you both health and all the good you deserve.

Madame de Pompadour was at this time at the height of her glory. Endowed with great talents as well as beauty, she, in fact, governed the kingdom. Her position was not considered anomalous, for the condition of society amongst the *bourgeoisie* was no less immoral than amongst the aristocracy, and all classes overlooked the irregularity of the monarch. She supported the military power of the state, and greatly encouraged the re-establishment of the navy. In her desire to advance the arts and to provide employment for the people, she founded a manufactory to rival that of Dresden, and with her originated the beautiful ware of Sèvres, for which her own pencil frequently furnished designs. In supporting the authority of the Parliaments she incurred

temporaneous account of Paris:—"Toute la troupe est composée de trente comédiens et comédiennes; tous sont très-richement habillez, et mieux que dans aucun autre pays. C'est dommage que le théâtre et les décorations ne répondent pas à la magnificence des habits, et à la bonté des pièces qu'on y joue; comme les tragédies de Corneille et de Racine, et les comédies de Molière." ('Mémorial de Paris,' par M. l'Abbé Antonini.)

* John Whetham, Esq., of Kirklington Hall, Nottinghamshire, was the only son of Lieut.-General Thomas Whetham, and *Mary*, daughter of Edward Thompson, Esq., of Marston, Yorkshire (Mrs. Wolfe's sister). He was born in 1731; married Elizabeth, daughter of Evelyn Chadwick, Esq., of West Leak; was sheriff of the county of York; and died without surviving issue in 1781. (Burke's 'Landed Gentry,' ed. 1850, *Supplement*.)

the hatred of the priesthood, who used every endeavour to win over the Dauphin, whose regular life cast reproach upon his father's; but he was neither permitted nor inclined to assume power; while the Queen tacitly bore with the insults of her husband, and soothed her sorrows by asceticism. In January 1753, *la Marquise*, being raised to the *tabouret*, with the rank and prerogatives of *Duchesse*, became qualified to be seated in the Queen's presence, to be called "cousin," and receive the royal kiss. But when, according to etiquette, the *parvenu* was presented to the Dauphin to be kissed, he turned away with scorn, for which spark of manliness his father dismissed him from Court, and did not restore him to favour until he had begged the royal mistress's pardon in the presence of witnesses. The favourite's fall was, however, drawing nigh. After the banishment of the Parliament of Paris in the same year, she, who had all through supported their interests, was ordered to retire from the Court. The Jesuits, through the royal confessor, tried every artifice to alarm the King's feeble sense of religion and morality; but these means failing, the Pompadour was supplanted in his affections by the daughter of an Irish officer in the pay of France. Thus she, who at one time might have exclaimed with Louis XIV., "*L'état c'est moi!*" became as much contemned as she had been caressed. Whether or not it was she who uttered the words, "After me the Deluge," no one could have spoken them with more truth.

In compliance with Mrs. Wolfe's desire that James should write alternately to her and to his father, on the 2nd November he informs the latter:—

Lord Albemarle has behaved to me in a manner that I could not presume to expect from him. Whenever he comes to Paris he immediately sends for me to his house, and puts me upon so easy and genteel a footing there that I have not language enough to return him proper thanks. If you should see Lord Bury, I beg you'll be so good to take notice of it. I have writ to his Lordship to acknowledge the effect of his letter, and to signify my grateful sense of his and his father's excessive politeness. There's but little company in town at present. In ten days, however, it will be crowded. Mr. Stanhope, Lord Chesterfield's son, is here; he came to visit me the other day, after his arrival, but we have made no acquaintance yet, so that I cannot give you any judgment upon the offspring of so great a man; but I fancy, not without some grounds, he is infinitely inferior to his father. Lord Brudenell is at one of the academies, and is the direct reverse of the Earl. One could hardly believe that a creature of his stamp could have any relation or connection with a man of Lord Cardigan's sweetness of temper.* We have had the finest autumn that has been known for many years. The dry air and constant exercise have restored me to a condition to be envied.

Philip Stanhope, who was now in his twenty-first year, became, about this time, an attaché to the British Embassy. The Earl of Chesterfield had spared neither pains nor expense upon his education. His travelling tutor was the Rev. Walter Harte, afterwards a canon of Windsor, and author of the 'Life of Gustavus Adolphus." Stanhope, although well informed, and possessed of a good understanding, was most deficient in

* John, Lord Brudenell, only son of George, fourth Earl of Cardigan and Lady Mary, daughter of John, Duke of Montagu. He was born in 1735, raised to the peerage as Lord Montagu of Boughton, in 1762, and died unmarried in 1770. The Earl of Cardigan, afterwards created Duke of Montagu, dying in 1790, the dukedom became extinct. (Collins; ed. 1812.)

the very points in which it was his father's ardent wish that he should shine,—*les grâces:* he was careless in his dress, muttered in his speech, and became a great eater! Lord Chesterfield's educational philosophy is summed up in his counsel to this youth:—"Study the characters of the people you have to do with, and know what they are, instead of thinking them what they should be; address yourself generally to the senses, to the heart, and to the weaknesses of mankind, but rarely to their reason." In addition to his precepts, he pointed out several examples of men who had achieved greatness by means of their address; one of his instances may be appropriately quoted here:—

"Between you and me, what do you think made our friend Lord Albemarle Colonel of a regiment of Guards, Governor of Virginia, Groom of the Stole, and Ambassador to Paris; amounting in all to sixteen or seventeen thousand pounds a year? Was it birth? No, a Dutch gentleman only. Was it his estate? No, he had none. Was it his learning, his parts, his political abilities and application? You can answer these questions as easily and as soon as I can ask them. What was it then? Many people wondered, but I do not; for I know, and will tell you. It was his air, his address, his manners, and his graces. He pleased, and by pleasing became a favourite, and becoming a favourite, became all that he has been since. Show me one instance where intrinsic worth and merit, unassisted by exterior accomplishments, have raised any man so high."*

* Arnold-Joost Van Keppel, who came to England with King William in 1688, is said, by Noble, to have been employed in copying papers, and other trivial services, until instigated by Lord Sunderland to supplant the favourite, Bentinck, when he was created Baron of Ashford, Viscount Bury, and Earl of Albemarle. His son, William-Anne, the second Earl, who is spoken of above, entered the army in 1717; served on the Continent during the war of the Austrian succes-

How different was the schooling of Wolfe and of Stanhope! What a contrast between the men!

The Lieutenant-Colonel, in his next letter to his mother, relates his manner of life:—

I am up every morning at, or before seven o'clock, and fully employed till twelve; then I dress and visit, and dine at two. At five, most people (I mean strangers) go to the public entertainments, which keep you till nine, and at eleven I am always in bed. This way of living is directly opposite to the practice of the place; but I find it impossible to pursue the business I came upon and to comply with the customs and manners of the inhabitants at the same time. No constitution, however robust, could go through all. My cousin Whetham is near me, and lives much in the same way that I do. We are a good deal together, and as far as I can perceive he has an exceeding sweet temper. He has been strangely managed in his education, not in point of learning, but in other respects. However, his principles are right, and I hope unalterable.

There is another letter on the 25th of November, full of what the writer calls "chit-chat nonsense," concerning domestic rather than French affairs; for, as if seeking relief from the distractions of the foreign capital, his "heart untravelled" turns homewards. He wishes he could send home some of the finest grapes he had ever seen, gathered for him fresh every day from the garden of a convent,—"the same the King eats, and a great curiosity at this season;" and says he has been intro-

sion, and commanded a division at Culloden, after which he was appointed Commander of the Forces in Scotland. He married Lady Anne Lennox, daughter of Charles, Duke of Richmond, by whom he had eight sons and seven daughters. After the peace, in 1748, he was appointed British Ambassador to the French Court, and died at Paris on the 22nd of December, 1754. See Walpole's Letters, Grenville Correspondence, Mémoires de Marmontel, etc.

duced to the well-known Lady Archibald Hamilton. But he is not totally indifferent to what is passing under his eye; for towards the end of his roundabout missive, he remarks:—"The poor people of this land are going into confusion upon religious matters, and at a critical time, when they might free themselves from an intolerable burden. I hate to see misery or the prospect of misery, even amongst those likely to become our enemies. This is all that can be said upon the subject."

The religious dissensions to which Wolfe alludes arose out of the dispute, in the previous reign, between the Jesuits and the Jansenists upon various theological questions. The Jesuits, with the King's consent, having referred the disputed points to the decision of Rome, the Pope issued the Bull known as "Unigenitus," from the word with which it begins. But instead of composing the differences of theologians, the Bull condemning the doctrines of the Jansenists spread disturbance throughout the country. The people, the parliaments, many of the inferior clergy, and a few bishops would not obey a decree which they considered infringed the laws of the realm as well as the privileges of the Gallican Church. After the death of Louis XIV., the Regent, Orleans, put a stop to the persecutions inflicted by the Papal partisans, and for a time there was at least outward peace. In the year 1750, however, it was ordained by the clergy that Extreme Unction should not be administered to dying persons without confessional notes signed by priests who adhered to the Bull, and all recusants were denied the last rites of the Church. This cruel ordinance was enforced by the Archbishop of Paris, but being opposed by the Parliament of Paris and the provincial Chambers, such priests as refused to administer the sacrament were, by their orders, imprisoned. The Church thereupon appealed to the King, who forbade the parliaments to interfere in religious matters; they replied that their duty compelled them to do justice between all parties, and regardless of the royal prohibition continued to exercise their functions.* Matters had arrived at this juncture when Wolfe wrote as above; in the following year Louis XV., at the instigation of the predominant party, banished the members of the several parliaments, when fresh troubles and difficulties ensued. To resume the correspondence; on the 4th of December Wolfe writes to his father:—

Dear Sir,—The post comes in almost as regularly as if there was no water-carriage, so that when you do me the honour to write I get your letter very soon. That of the 27th November came to me on the 2nd instant.

It is, as you say, Sir, some sort of advantage to me to have admittance to the Ambassador, and an honour to be under his protection; but it does not include all the advantages that one would be apt to imagine. His Lordship does not see so much company as Ambassadors commonly do; and though he is vastly liked and generally esteemed in France, his way of living and that of the people of the country is something different.†

* Lord Chesterfield, in a letter to his son, on April the 13th, O. S., 1752, writes prophetically:—"I do not know what the Lord's anointed, his vicegerent on earth, divinely appointed by him, and accountable to none but him for his actions, will either think or do, upon these symptoms of reason and good sense which seem to be breaking out all over France; but this I foresee, that before the end of this century, the trade of both king and priest will not be half so good a one as it has been."

† Walpole writes to Mann (May 19, 1750):—"Lord Albemarle keeps

The Duke of Richmond is in Paris. I have met him sometimes at Lord Albemarle's, and by that means have the honour to know him. As far as my discernment goes, he promises to make a considerable figure in our way, to which his genius seems to lead him, and what is uncommon at eighteen he is not entirely taken up with the outward appearances and gildings of soldiership, but aims at the higher and more solid branches of military knowledge.*

Mr. Haren's nephew is lately returned from his country-house. He and a very civil old lady, his mother, have endeavoured to convince me that a recommendation from Mr. Haren has all imaginable regard paid to it. They have received me in a very polite manner, and sufficiently proved their affection for their relation and deference for strangers by that reception. Lady Archibald Hamilton died last night of a fever, after an illness of a few days. She has left her little family in the utmost grief and distress. Lord Archibald is extremely old and infirm; his son and daughter are both

an immense table there, with sixteen people in the kitchen; his aides-de-camp invite everybody, but he seldom graces the banquet himself, living retired out of the town with his old Columbine [Mademoiselle Gaucher]. What an extraordinary man! with no fortune at all, and with slight parts, he has £17,000 a year from the Government, which he squanders away, though he has great debts." George II. aptly said that the Earl was a "sieve."

* Charles, third Duke of Richmond, of the Lennox family, was born in 1735, and succeeded to the dukedom on the death of his father in 1750. Although he never distinguished himself as a military commander, his future career did not belie Wolfe's expectations. Having received the thanks of Prince Ferdinand for his conduct at Minden, he was made Colonel of the 72nd Foot. In 1763, he may be said to have begun his political life, and two years later, under the Rockingham administration, was principal Secretary of State. In 1782, he was appointed Master-General of the Ordnance; on resigning which post, in 1795, he received the command of a regiment of Horse Guards, and was created a Field-Marshal. He was much given to literary pursuits, a princely patron of the arts and of all useful and charitable institutions, and his private life was unimpeachable. He died without issue, in 1806, leaving, in the words of Sir E. Brydges, "a character for persevering talents and an assiduous love of business."

very young, and nobody to direct or assist them,—I mean no relation, for I believe Lord Albemarle will do everything that is right and proper. The son is an Ensign in the Third Regiment, and my friend and companion. You may believe that if I can be of the least use to him I sha'n't neglect the opportunity.*

I have inquired after the Pretender, and can't hear where he hides himself. There are people that believe him to be secreted in Poland with some of his mother's relations. My friend Colonel D—— has got a regiment of Dragoons. There is a sort of interest that man has crept into, better and of more efficacy than service, worth, or honour. It would almost make one forswear open, fair behaviour as lumber, and the impediment to success and a marischal's staff; but, on the other hand, a man sleeps well that uses moderate exercise, and never dabbles in a dirty pool. There are multitudes of extravagant customs that divert, but there is one that makes me laugh every day. The coachmen here drive with enormous black bear-skin muffs, tied round their waists, and that, when their horses go on, are turned behind. The people here use umbrellas in hot weather to defend them from the sun, and something of the same kind to secure them from snow and rain. I wonder a practice so useful is not introduced into England, where there are such frequent showers, and especially in the country, where they can be expanded without any inconveniency.†

* Lady Jane, daughter of James, sixth Earl of Abercorn, was the second wife of Lord Archibald, youngest son of William, third Duke of Hamilton. Lord Archibald Hamilton, who was Governor of Jamaica and of Greenwich Hospital, died about a year after his wife, aged eighty-two. They had three sons, of whom the youngest was William, who became one of the King's equerries, and M.P. for Midhurst. He is better known as Sir William Hamilton, the British envoy at the court of Naples, whose wife was Nelson's Lady Hamilton.

† A few years later, Jonas Hanway, in spite of the jeers and missiles of the mob, walked through London with an umbrella. "When it rained," says his biographer, "a small *parapluie* defended his face and wig." Yet it was not until after Hanway had used one for thirty years that umbrellas were generally carried by gentlefolks. An old

The Lieutenant-Colonel's next letter, which is addressed to his mother, is as follows:—

Paris, 12th December, 1752.

Dear Madam,

I sit down to write a letter to you which, if it does not entertain you, will convince you, at least, that I think of you, and remember your kindness. If I should imitate the practice of this country, I should study how to talk, how to persuade you that I am the thing I am not; but my experience tells me that I shall succeed better by doing what is right than by a handsome speech of empty consequence. There are men that only desire to shine, and that had rather say a smart thing than do a great one; there are others—rare birds—that had rather be than seem to be. Of the first kind this country is a well-stored magazine; of the second, our own has some few examples. A Frenchman that makes his mistress laugh has no favour to ask of her; he is at the top of his ambition. Our countrymen are too grave, too sanguine, too intent, to be satisfied with such success.

I hear a piece of news from England that gives me, and all of us, great concern. We are told that Lord Harcourt and the Bishop of Norwich have resigned. Could Mr. Stone over-

lady, now in her ninety-fourth year, informs me that in her youth an umbrella was a great novelty in Dublin, and that one was capacious enough to shelter half-a-dozen persons. It appears also from 'Notes and Queries' that the first umbrella seen in Bristol—a huge red one—was imported from Leghorn in 1780. Before they were made portable enough for pedestrians, umbrellas were kept in halls, to be held over ladies while stepping in or out of their sedans or coaches. As early as 1710, however, "the tucked up sempstress" and "good housewives" carried "oiled umbrellas." (Swift's 'City Shower;' Gay's 'Trivia,' 1712.) The umbrella, in the literal sense of the word, *i. e.* the *parasol*, or "sun-shade," as Americans call it, was noticed in Italy, a century before, by Fynes Moryson; and Corryat, in his 'Crudities,' speaks of leathern *umbrellaes* as "things that minister shadow against the scorching heat of the sun;" while the poet Drayton alludes to umbrellas which—

"Sheeld you in all sorts of weathers."

throw two such men? Could he, or anybody else, behave to them so as to oblige them to give up the most important charge in the kingdom?* Somebody more subservient, perhaps, is to be placed; somebody that will lead the pupils to proper purposes, and bring them to think that only one set of men are fit to govern the kingdom. *J'enrage*, as the French say when they are provoked, that my trusty Lord Harcourt is deposed. He had the general voice of the people for him, and nobody was thought so proper for that high office.†

I told my uncle Wat that I had four masters every day, which he does not think sufficient. His concern for me goes so far as to make him wish that I had not time to eat or sleep. I have been forced to pacify his rage for improvement with assuring him that I can't bear above so much at a time. I'll charge you with an office of great trust. I'll give you power to speak to Mr. Fisher, or anybody else you can think of, to renew my credit, as far as it will go, about the middle of next month. It would be almost as ungracious to want credit in an enemy's country as it would be disagreeable to want money in a friend's. I never think upon this subject without recollecting of my good friend Fitz.,‡ and the cries of poor Arthur [Loftus], who is afraid he shall starve in my country-house if I stay long at Paris. Your nephew Whetham is the best-tempered youth that I know. He offers his respects to you.

* Earl Harcourt was the Governor, and Dr. Hayter, Bishop of Norwich, the tutor to the Prince of Wales and Prince Edward. Walpole thus accounts for the dispute between their lordships and their deputies, Stone and Scott:—"The Princess says the Bishop taught the boys nothing; he says he was never suffered to teach them anything. The first occasion of uneasiness was the Bishop's finding the Prince of Wales reading the 'Revolutions of England,' written by Père D'Orléans to vindicate James II." (Letter to Sir H. Mann, December 11, 1752.)

† Lord Harcourt was afterwards sent as ambassador to demand the hand of the Princess Charlotte of Mecklenburg-Strelitz in marriage for George III. He was some time Lord-Lieutenant of Ireland, and was accidentally drowned in a well in his own park at Nuneham in 1777.

‡ Probably Lord Fitzmaurice.

On the 22nd December, Wolfe writes to his father:—

I wish I could send a piece of tapestry from the Gobelins, or a picture from the Palais Royal, instead of a letter; either would be a present worthy your reception, as either would be matchless in their kind. I had the good fortune to see the manufacture of tapestry at a time when they showed it to an ambassador. Then it is that they produce all that invention and industry can contrive and execute. I was a good deal surprised to find that the principal director of that ingenious workmanship is a Scotchman.*

My friend Carleton sends me conjectures about a successor to Lord Harcourt. I am sorry any such person is necessary, because I think that high office was in fit hands before. It is melancholy that in an affair of such trust and importance there should be men so placed and so confided in that the leaders are in a manner subordinate to their inferiors. The French have their domestic trouble too, as well as ourselves; but theirs are still of a more serious kind. The clergy and people are in opposite sentiments for the present, and it will require the exertion of very great authority to reconcile them to each other. The ecclesiastics have unluckily been the authors of almost all the mischief that has been done in Europe and in America since the first introduction of Christianity, and they do in some places continue their evil practices. It is surprising that there are so few potentates in Europe that are able to keep them in any order, and the more surprising that the example of these few has no effect upon the rest, notwithstanding the visible difference between a well-governed body of clergy and the reverse.

Paris is full of people; that is, all the company is come

* The name of the Gobelins is derived from one Goblei, a dyer of Rheims, who settled here in the reign of Francis I. In 1667, M. Colbert converted the establishment into a Royal manufactory, wherein about eight hundred artificers—painters, sculptors, goldsmiths, embroiderers, etc.—were engaged, and enjoyed certain valuable privileges. The celebrated Le Brun was at one time the Director; but I have not been able to find out the name of the person of whom Wolfe speaks.

in from the country, and an abundance of genteel persons of both sexes are every day exposed to public view. The natives in general are not handsome either in face or figure; but then, they improve what they have. They adorn themselves to more advantage, and appear with more outside lustre, than any other people, at least that I have seen or heard of.

On January 2, 1753, Wolfe tells his mother:—

I was yesterday at Versailles, a cold spectator of what we commonly call splendour and magnificence. A multitude of men and women were assembled to bow and pay their compliments in the most submissive manner to a creature of their own species. I went through the different apartments with our Ambassador, who did me the honour to allow me to wait upon him, and saw him do his part very gracefully, well received by the Queen, the Dauphin, the Dauphiness, the Infanta, the Mesdames, the Secretary of State, and lastly by the Marquise de Pompadour, who seemed to distinguish him from the rest by her civilities and courtesy.* All the courtiers, as in England, go to court upon the New Year's Day, and as they are more numerous here than there it makes a very fine show. The Duke of Richmond offered me a place in his coach, an honour that I could not refuse, especially as Lord Albemarle was so kind as to give me a room at his house, with invitation to sup with him. Lord Albemarle has proposed to present my cousin Whetham and me to the King, which I have no objection to but the fear of the expense of a new coat. However, as it comes from his lordship in so handsome a manner, I don't think it is to be rejected. This is the first time that I have been at Versailles, and luckily there was an installation of a Knight of the Order of the Holy Ghost, and we were placed in such a manner in the King's Chapel by the master of the ceremonies that no part of

* The Queen, Marie Lescinska, and the Dauphiness were daughters of the rival kings of Poland—Stanislaus and Augustus. The Infanta was the favourite daughter of Louis XV., who married Don Philip, son of Elizabeth Farinese.

the ceremony escaped us. The weather was so severe that it was impossible to see the gardens, or to examine the buildings.

. . . .

Sir John Mordaunt did me the honour to write to me from Bath, where he is, or has been for his old rheumatic complaint. He touches lightly upon a *certain subject* in his comic style, and, with a jest upon the sex, wonders at my perseverance. I have answered his letter, and have given him to understand that as I did not mean to conceal anything from him, I had mentioned that affair to him, but that I was extremely well pleased with my situation, and did not intend to be troublesome. The Duke of Richmond is to have a company in Lord Bury's regiment; he wants some skilful man to travel with him through the fortified towns of the Low Countries and into Lorraine. I have proposed my friend Carleton,* whom Lord Albemarle approves of; but as things may take another turn, it must not be mentioned. It is reported at Paris that the Pretender has changed his religion. We are too well governed in England to apprehend that or any other change. I believe he might as well keep his confessor.† An acquaintance of mine goes to England in a few days, and takes with him two black laced hoods for you, and a *vestale* for the neck, such as the Queen of France wears.

The following paragraphs are extracted from a letter to the General on the 10th of January:—

The Duke has consented to Carleton's coming abroad to attend the Duke of Richmond as a military preceptor in his

* Captain Guy Carleton, afterwards the celebrated Lord Dorchester.

† "The Young Pretender having changed his religion is again mentioned in a letter from Amsterdam, dated November 20, in the following terms :—'Some people here tell, but with what view is not known, that several private accounts from Silesia make it suspected that the eldest son of the Pretender is there *incognito;* and some of them insinuate that he has abjured the Romish religion, of which, however, there is but little probability, unless he has a dispensation for so doing, as it would show him to be as bad a politician as his father, his grandfather, or the uncle of his father.'" ('Scots Magazine,' November, 1752.)

tour through the fortified towns of the Low Countries. It will be of singular use to the young man, and I hope of great service to my friend. Lord Falkland,* Mr. Dawney,† Whetham, and myself were introduced yesterday to the King and the Royal family, and lastly to Madame Pompadour and Monsieur de St. Coutest, the minister. They were all very gracious as far as courtesies, bows, and smiles go, for the Bourbons seldom speak to anybody. Madame la Marquise entertained us at her toilette.‡ We found her curling her hair. She is extremely handsome, and, by her conversation with the Ambassador and others that were present, I judge she must have a great deal of wit and understanding.

Exclusive of Lord Albemarle's being the English ambassador, I observe that at Versailles they pay a particular respect and deference to his person, which is a proof that he is extremely in the King's good graces; and I should wonder if it was not so, considering how accomplished a man he is for Courts, and how particularly calculated he seems to be for the French nation. I wish you both health, and a happy New Year.

Mrs. Wolfe was displeased that her son had not offered himself for the military tutorship of the Duke of Richmond. In a letter written on the 19th January, he acquits himself thus :—

You have known me long enough to discover that I don't always prefer my own interest to that of my friends. I was

* Lucius Charles, sixth Viscount Falkland, who had recently married the relict of the Earl of Suffolk. He afterwards commanded the British forces in Tobago, where he died in 1780.

† The Hon. John Dawney, second son of Henry, Viscount Downe. His brother, Henry Pleydell Dawney, third Viscount Downe, dying of a wound received in the battle of Campen (1760), he succeeded to the title, and died in December, 1780.

‡ Pompadour received visitors in her dressing-room, in which there was no seat except her own. It was only when the King entered that she ordered a chair for his Majesty. See 'Annual Register,' 1765.

asked if I knew a military man fit to accompany the young Duke, and immediately named Carleton, who is appointed to attend him. It would have been as easy for me to hesitate about the question, and afterwards to have offered my services; but, exclusive of my liking to Carleton, I don't think myself quite equal to the task, and as for the pension that might follow, it is very certain that it would not become me to accept it. I can't take money from any one but the King, my master, or from some of his blood. The Duke of Richmond's friendship will be an honour to me, provided he turns out well, and serves his country with reputation, which I think is very likely to happen. If he miscarries from bad principles, I shall be the first to fly from his intimacy.

Turning to a more tender topic, he continues:—

Though I suppose myself recovered in a great measure from the disorder that my extravagant love for Miss Lawson threw me into, yet I never hear her name mentioned without a twitch, or hardly ever think of her with indifference. Every good account of her helps to justify me, and the better you know her, the easier you'll find excuses for me. Pray tell Miss Haren that I'm obliged to her for helping to convince you that at least my choice was a good one. A man may be greatly prepossessed in favour of a lady without bringing many people to be of his opinion. My amour has not been without its use. It has defended me against other women, introduced a great deal of philosophy and tranquillity as to all objects of our strongest affections, and something softened the disposition to severity and rigour that I had contracted in the camp, trained up as I was from my infancy to the conclusion of the peace, in war and tumult.

. . . .

My exercises go on extremely well. Monsieur Fesian, the dancing-master, assures me that I make a surprising progress, but that my time will be too short to *possess* (as he calls it) the minuet to any great perfection; however, he pretends to say that I shall dance not to be laughed at. I am on horseback every morning at break of day, and do presume that, with the advantage of long legs and thighs, I shall be able to sit a horse at a hand-gallop. Lastly, the fencing-master declares me to have a very quick wrist, and no inconsiderable lunge, from the reasons aforesaid. The General will explain the word *longe*, or lunge.

I pronounce the French tongue, and consequently read it, better than when I came; but in the capital of this great kingdom, I speak more English than French, and therefore don't do so well as I ought. Thus I have made my report to you concerning the reasons of my coming here, and shall conclude my letter with very hearty wishes for both your welfares.

From a long preface to a letter of the 29th of January, it appears that the old General had replenished his son's purse, and, at the same time, administered a lecture upon extravagance, which calls forth the remark :—"I believe there are few young men that live in the manner I do, and though the objects of my attention are not in themselves the most essential, they are still such as have their uses in life, and may help to advance me in the army."

After speaking of the prodigious expense of the best masters Paris produced, together with coach-hire, lodgings, and servants, he assures his parents that notwithstanding the strongest temptations, he had not spent upon play, and all other avoidable charges, the sum of twenty louis-d'or, and that his tailor's bill, including liveries, did not exceed £70. He then goes on to say :—

The fortune of a military man seems to depend almost as much upon his exteriors as upon things that are in reality more estimable and praiseworthy. You may be assured I have no more demands to make upon you, already too well convinced of your kindness and generosity to abuse either.

The good Bishop is at last released from the misery and pain that he so long laboured under, oppressed by a disease at his time of life incurable. His death is not to be lamented otherwise than as concerns his family. If there's any place for good men hereafter, I believe he is at rest, and entirely free from all complaints.* By what you have said about matrimony, I judge you are averse to it. However, there's a fit time, and it's commonly later with us soldiers than with other men, for two reasons: the first is, that, in our younger days, we are generally moving from place to place, and have hardly leisure to fix; the other has prudence and necessity to support it. We are not able to feed our wives and children till we begin to decline. It must be a solitary kind of latter life to have no relations nor objects to take up our thoughts and affections,—to be, as it were, alone in the world, without any connection with mankind but the tie of common friendships, which are at best, as you have experienced, but loose and precarious. Our tastes for pleasures and debauchery have an end, or should have, when the excuse or pretext of youth and warm blood is no longer allowed us; and one terrible, frequent, and almost natural consequence of not marrying is an attachment to some woman or other that leads to a thousand inconveniences. Marshal Saxe died in the arms of a little w—— that plays upon the Italian stage,—an ignominious end for a conqueror!†

I hope the severity of the weather is confined to the Continent. It has not been known to freeze so hard since the

* The celebrated Bishop of Cloyne, whom Pope eulogizes in the well-known line,—"To Berkeley, every virtue under heaven." He died at Oxford on Sunday, January 14th, 1753."

† Marshal Saxe was the natural son of Augustus II., King of Poland, but a Frenchman at heart as well as by naturalization. He died "by Venus, not by Mars," says Walpole, in 1750. In religion he was a Lutheran, which occasioned the *bon-mot* of the Queen, "Il est bien triste de ne pouvoir dire un seul *De Profundis* pour un guerrier qui a fait chanter tant de *Te Deum!*" When the King was told of the Marshal's death, he cried, "Alas! I have lost my General, and have only Captains left." Saxe desired his body to be burned, that nothing of him but his glory should remain; but Louis XV. ordered that his remains should be interred in the Lutheran Church of St. Thomas, at Strasburg, where a magnificent monument was erected to his memory.

Great Frost. The poor people suffer excessively, not only from the want of fire, but, as the navigation of the river has been stopped, provisions of all kinds are dearer upon that account. I am a sufferer in particular, for as I commonly go out at break of day, till lately that it has been impossible, the cold seizes my nose and fingers, and distresses me considerably. I desire you to accept of my thanks and acknowledgments for the last mark of your favour, and I wish to convince you that my greatest ambitition is to deserve your esteem.

An unusually brief letter, for a communication to his mother, follows the above. It is remarkable, however, as containing the *finale* to the story of the constant lover's pursuit of the frozen fair one :—

Paris, 13th February, 1753.

Dear Madam,

I shall make but one step from this place to the foot of the mountains, and I shall hardly give you time to observe how many fine airs and accomplishments I have picked up at Paris. The north-east wind that blows in that country will disperse all my foppery, and ribbons and feathers, and snuff and essence in the air, and disorder my whole person, so that when I return you will hardly discover me to be a coxcomb; at least, if it is so, I shall try to conceal it from you.

I had a letter from my friend Gage,* last post, in answer to one that I writ him by Lord Albemarle's directions. He says the little Maid of Honour is as amiable and alas! (as he expresses it, poor gentleman!) as cold as ever. What can that lady mean by such obstinate self-denial? or is she as much mistress of her own as of the hearts of all her acquaintances? Is she the extraordinary woman that has no weakness? or happily constructed without passions? or, lastly, and most likely, does she bid her reason chuse? She may push that matter too far, for common sense demonstrates that one should

* The Hon. Thomas, afterwards Viscount Gage, Commander-in-chief in North America.

not be a maid—of honour too long. I writ a long letter to her uncle this post, and send him some books that he desired. I touched upon the tender string some time ago, as I told you; his answer was, that he was sorry to find me so serious upon that old story; and there the matter *rests for ever*.

It was happy for our hero that his desires were not exclusively absorbed by love, and that his passion for arms was fully as seductive as the more tender one. An opportunity which now offered for the acquirement of unwonted professional experience is therefore eagerly jumped at. The progress and sequel of the matter will appear from the few remaining letters written in the French capital. On the 22nd of February the General is told:—

Lord Albemarle was saying a few days ago that the French king proposes to encamp a great part of his army early in the summer. His lordship judged that it would be agreeable to the Duke to have an officer of our troops sent to see what they were doing in their camps, and he did me the honour to say that he thought it would be right in me to propose myself, not asking it as a favour, but ready to obey the Duke's command. The proposal agreed too well with my disposition to be neglected, and I writ immediately to Lord Bury to offer myself for the service, and told my Lord Albemarle that the least hint from him would have more weight than all that I should be able to say. Whether the project takes place or not, it may not be amiss to be mentioned upon such an occasion by the Ambassador at Paris. The French are to have three or four different camps; the Austrians and Prussians will probably assemble some corps, so that I may, before the end of the summer, have seen half the armies in Europe at least, and that, I believe, at a very little expense. Lord Albemarle must give me letters to the commanders if the Duke accepts my offer, but, to tell the truth, I suspect his Royal Highness will not.

To his mother, he writes on the 1st of March:—

If the air of Blackheath has been as sharp as that of Paris, I don't wonder at your complaints, nor that you give it as a reason for not writing. We had a little interval of mild weather, and now the cold is returned more dangerously, though less severe. They have little spring in this country; from cold and very wet it suddenly changes to excessive heat. What a melancholy account you give of Mrs. A——, her unhappy fanaticism preying upon weak nerves. A conscience at rest and free from guilt, with a tolerable portion of health, and moderate circumstances, are the utmost bounds of our felicity. If we would be happy here below, these are the objects, and no further; refinements in religion, or any pursuit of exquisite pleasures, throw us quite out of the road of peace.

Whetham has gone into Flanders; from thence he goes into Holland, back to Calais, and so home. What he will do with himself till he is thirty years of age, or till he marries, I am at a loss to guess. It is a misfortune not to have an employment or profession of some kind or other to fill up the intervals of our time. To live merely for the sake of eating, drinking, etc., without the prospect of any business, or of being useful, is, in my mind, a heavy condition. I was invited to a ball last night, where I saw some of the best company in Paris, and some of the handsomest women. At this season of the year the people of the first condition give balls by turns, and do it in a very genteel manner. Instead of tea and coffee they give ice, *orgeat*, lemonade, oranges, and sweetmeats, and in the morning (commonly by daylight) they have all sorts of cold meats. I never stay to see them eat, though, I believe, it would not be the least diverting part of the entertainment, for the ladies are well bred, delicate, and genteel. They are, nevertheless, a little inclined to gluttony, and are troubled with frequent indigestions. The women at these balls wear a sort of domino, or rather gown made of that kind of light silk, slightly trimmed, with sleeves of a very particular make, falling near a yard behind them from the elbows. Their hair is either combed behind, with little curls before, or their heads are all over curls, and abundance of diamonds about their heads and necks. They dance genteelly, and I think their country-dances preferable to ours; first, because there is a greater variety of figure and step, more easy dancing, and they are not so tedious. They dance four couples at a time and succeed each other, then partners change every dance. Some of the men are prettily-turned, and move easily and gracefully. They have in general good faces and fine hair, but they have generally bad limbs, and are ill-shaped. I speak of the nobility and those that are born or commonly live in Paris, for in the provinces remote from the capital men are of a better figure.

The Lent that succeeds the Carnival puts an end to all these pleasures, the delight and occupation of the younger people of Paris. Their thoughts are entirely employed upon the figure they are to make in public, their equipages and dress; and their entertainments within consist of luxurious suppers and deep play. Some of them are elegant enough to be pleased with music, and they all sing well. A few there are—a very small number—that read and think. I begin to be tired of Paris. The English are not favourites here; they can't help looking upon us as enemies, and I believe they are right. The best and ablest men amongst them respect the nation, admire the Government, and think we are the only men in Europe that act like men. This party must be very inconsiderable, and very secret. I forgot to tell you formerly that the laced handkerchief that I bought did not go with the hoods, but you'll have it.

Notwithstanding the ambassador's interest, Wolfe was denied permission to visit the Continental camps. The scheme evidently was opposed by Lord Bury, who did not wish him to remain away longer from his regiment. It seems also to have been discountenanced by the General and Mrs. Wolfe, on the score of expense. He writes to his father on the 9th of March:—

Lord Bury surprised me a few days ago with H.R.H. the Duke's orders to return to England even before my leave of absence expires. I think I told you that I asked and begged to continue here until the 20th of April; this is refused, and I am to hasten home. I dare not disobey openly, but I will venture as far as a slight reprimand. There's an inconceivable obstinacy in this way of proceeding, a minute exactness that is quite unnecessary and excessively disagreeable. Everybody knows how difficult it is to get out of England, and yet they won't allow us to make use of the opportunity that offers, and that perhaps can never come again. Twenty days or a month to me at this time is inestimable, the season and situation of my affairs considered. A Major and an Adjutant (if the Colonel is to be indulged himself) are not to be considered as equal to the great task of exercising, in our frivolous way, a battalion or two of soldiers!—men whose duty and business it is, and who must know that. "His Royal Highness expects and orders me to tell you to be with the regiment by the time they assemble." These are the terms of his lordship's letter, and he goes on to inform me that he believes the companies will be collected towards the latter end of this month. Notwithstanding these hints, I sha'n't be in England before the 7th or 8th of April, and the only one thing that gives me any satisfaction or reconciles it to me is, that I shall have the pleasure of paying my duty to you and to my mother; and though the time that I shall be with you will be very short, those few days will make me some amends for the many disagreeable ones that are to follow.

Wolfe writes again, on the 13th, stating that he has had a second letter from Lord Bury, which made it plain that he must immediately return to Scotland, as the Major has had a fit of apoplexy. Had he known that before, he would not have asked for additional leave of absence, nor proposed visiting the foreign camps. He therefore prepares for his journey, and hopes to call at

Blackheath in ten or twelve days. But before he starts, a letter from his mother calls forth a reply, on the 22nd of March :—

Dear Madam,

I beg you to remember how the undertaking I spoke of was proposed, and by whom; whether it was in my power to refuse it as it was offered, supposing that I had not liked the project. I mentioned to you that the ambassador was to have given me letters for the commanders to our ministers in Germany, and my business was only to see if there was anything new amongst them, and therefore there was no risk. You may believe I should never undertake anything of this kind if there was reason to apprehend what my father seems to think,* nor would I throw away my time if it could be of no manner of use. As to the article of expense, I proposed to do it upon my pay, because I could not in reason require more than has been already done for me.

I should have been oftener at Madame Haren's if her grand-daughter's illness had not shut her door. She is the most agreeable lady of fourscore that I have ever met. It is very polite of her to speak handsomely of me, because it is almost impossible to be less known to her than I am. But you know how little it costs the French to be civil. My letters from Scotland came to me. The extraordinary direction covered a petition from a very good woman, who desires me to write to a friend in her favour. The women of the regiment take it into their heads to write to me sometimes, and their letters are really curious. I have a collection of them somewhere that would make you laugh.

* It would appear that the General feared Wolfe might be induced to enter the Prussian service.

CHAPTER XII.

GLASGOW.—READING.

APRIL—NOVEMBER, 1753.

WOLFE, although he had not added to his professional knowledge by his six months' residence in Paris, by friendly intercourse with foreigners gained more enlarged views, and obtained that familiarity with the French language which he afterwards turned to good account. Long ere any military school was established in England, at a time, too, when bulldog courage in the field, expertness in a few evolutions at a review, and the slavish observance of regimental duties, were the highest qualifications of a British officer in the eyes of the Commander-in-chief, he aspired to the science as well as the practice of his profession. It is no wonder, then, that being disappointed in his expectation of visiting the Continental encampments, he should not be in the best of humours when, after spending three or four days at Blackheath, he had returned to Glasgow, where his regiment was again quartered; and the strange condition in which he found the corps, together with the tortures of his journey, were not calculated to allay his vexation. He writes to his father on the 22nd of April:—

It is almost impossible to suffer more than I have done upon the road, and quite impossible to find a regiment in more melancholy circumstances than we are. Officers ruined, impoverished, desperate, and without hopes of preferment; the widow of our late Major and her daughter in tears; his situation before his death, and the effects it had upon the corps, with the tragical end of the unhappy man in everybody's mouth; an ensign struck speechless with the palsy, and another that falls down in the most violent convulsions. He was seized with one the first night I came to the regiment (after supper), that so astonished and affected all that were present, that it is not to be described. I should have fallen upon the floor and fainted, had not one of the officers supported me, and called for immediate relief; and this, as well as I can remember, for the first time in my life. Some of our people spit blood, and others are begging to sell before they are quite undone; and my friend Ben will probably be in jail in a fortnight. In this situation we are, with a martinet and parade major to teach us the manual exercise with the time of the First Regiment.

To leave this unpleasant subject for one that concerns me much less. I must tell you that I was beat to pieces in the new close post-chaises; machines that are purposely constructed to torture the unhappy carcases that are placed in them.* I was at length forced to have recourse to post-horses; and as they had been accustomed to wear harness, and to be supported by stronger powers than my arms, I was every minute in danger, and fell twice, at the hazard of my neck. Add to this that the movements of these brutes were so rude, that I bled to the saddle. In short, it is not possible to travel more disagreeably, nor enter into a more unpleasing task than the present; and this, as you may believe, not at all at my ease, without horses, or other means to dissipate or divert.

* Doctor Carlyle, describing a journey to London in 1758, says:—"It is to be noted that we could get no four-wheeled chaise till we came to Durham, those conveyances being then only in their infancy; the two-wheeled *close* chaise, which had been used for some time, and was called an Italian chaise, having been found very inconvenient." (Autobiography, p. 331.)

I saw my uncle Brad. in Yorkshire; he tells me he writ to my mother, but never received an answer from her. He was far from being well when I saw him. I forgot to ask for franks of the senators of my acquaintance, so that you must pay more for my letters, by far, than they are worth. We march out of this dark and dismal country early in August. By that time I imagine that ambition, and the desire to please, will be utterly extinguished and lost from amongst us. I did not know, till I came here, that his Majesty sent his thanks in particular to Lord Bury's regiment for their behaviour in the Highlands; and immediately, I mean a month or two, or three perhaps, Major Wilkinson steps in!

On the 13th of May he tells his mother :—

We are all sick, officers and soldiers. I am amongst the best, and not quite well. In two days we lost the skin off our faces, and the third were shivering in great coats. Such are the bounties that Heaven has bestowed upon this people, and such the blessings of a northern latitude. My cousin Goldsmith has sent me the finest young pointer that ever was seen; he eclipses Workie, and outdoes all. He sent me a fishing-rod and wheel at the same time, of his own workmanship, that are inestimable. This, with a salmon-rod from my uncle Wat, your flies, and my own guns, puts me in a condition to undertake the Highland sport in June, and to adventure myself amongst mountains, lakes, and wildest wastes.

It would take time to relate the variety of our amusements here; but my share of the entertainments might be shortly told. We have plays; we have concerts; we have balls, public and private; with dinners and suppers of the most execrable food upon earth, and wine that approaches to poison.* The men drink till they are excessively drunk. The ladies are cold to everything but a bagpipe;—I wrong them, there is not one that does not melt away at the sound of an estate; there's the weak side of this soft sex. I have bought a horse for £7, a horse that was never meant to move under the dig-

* See Dr. Somerville's 'Life and Times,' p. 364.

nity of a commander of an old legion; but there are times when our greatness lets itself down a little,—it was very near walking afoot, and can yet hardly be said to rise above the ground.*

I see by the papers that General Guise has got the government of Berwick. My father had better pretensions than that extraordinary person.† I wish he would try; there might be some advantages even from being refused. I told Lord Bury that my observation pointed out to me that to do one's duty well, and not to talk of it, was the roundabout way to preferment, and that I did not believe that a man could serve into favour; to which one might have added, that 'tis better to tell a story than fight; better bow than be honest! This is as it always has been in courts, and ever will be. The men that are forward to ask are supposed to have titles, and military men, of all others, should be the oftenest

* This charger is doubtless the animal mentioned in the following anecdote, related by Mr. Buchanan:—"A Glasgow lady, who died at a great age about twenty-five years ago [*circa* 1830], recollected quite well having seen Wolfe on one occasion at Capelrig [Mr. Barclay's, ten miles from Glasgow], where she was staying when a girl. He rode up the avenue, to pay a visit, on a very spirited grey charger, which plunged violently, and the inmates were afraid he would be thrown. He was an excellent horseman, however, and maintained himself well in the saddle; then dismounting gracefully, he entered the mansion, and conversed for some time with great politeness. He remounted his charger and rode off to Glasgow. These circumstances, and Wolfe's subsequent fame, fixed his appearance firmly in the lady's memory, and my informant often heard her relate these particulars." ('Glasgow, Past and Present,' vol. iii. p. 759.)

† Walpole relates some curious stories of this "extraordinary person":—"Your relation, Guise," he writes to Mann (July 7, 1742), "is arrived from Carthagena madder than ever. As he was marching up to one of the forts, all his men deserted him; his lieutenant advised him to retire; he replied, he had never turned his back yet, and would not now, and stood all the fire. When the pelicans were flying over his head, he cried out, 'What would Chloe [the Duke of Newcastle's cook] give for some of these to make a pelican pie!' When he is brave enough to perform such actions as are really almost incredible, what a pity it is that he should for ever persist in saying things that are totally so!" Again (Oct. 6, 1754),—"I have heard Guise affirm that the colliers at Newcastle feed their children with fire-shovels!"

in the path of promotion. I wish you both health, which is better than riches; but one may almost as well be sick as poor.

To his father he writes, on the 24th of May:—

I begin to have an inconceivable aversion to writing, and to all business that I am not absolutely forced upon, and yet now and then a spark breaks out through the surrounding obstacles, but is almost smothered in the birth. I have hardly passion enough of any kind to find present pleasure or feed future hope, and scarce activity to preserve my health. The love of a quiet life, I believe, is an inheritance which is likely to strengthen with my years; that, and the prospect your example gives me,—that a man may serve long and well to very little purpose, and make a sacrifice of all his days to a shadow,—seems to help my indifference, and to incline me to get off quietly and betimes to the edge of the forest. If a man tries on to forty and something more, I think he does very handsomely; and then, not finding it to answer, he may make his bow and retire. Our sickly infirm General could not proceed to review the corps in the north. He came back to Edinburgh from Perth, and he has since been in extreme danger. People that see him think he is always a-dying, and yet the good-natured old man struggles with all and still holds out; but this mortal combat can't be for long. Your regiment is, I hear, upon its march to Fort George. That duty has some inconvenience, particularly to the officers, but it is of great use to the men, and keeps them healthy.

I dined a few days ago with the famous Duchess of Hamilton. They live about ten miles from Glasgow, and the Duke is civil to us. The lady has lost nothing of her bloom and beauty, is very well behaved, supports her dignity with tolerable ease to herself, and seems to be justly sensible of her good fortune.* After our detachments are sent out, I pro-

* Elizabeth, daughter of John Gunning, Esq., of Castle Coote, Ireland, and sister to the Countess of Coventry. She married the Duke of Hamilton on the 14th of February, 1752, and at the time of Wolfe's

pose to go for a month to the Highlands. Our people work upon the side of Loch Lomond, in Argyleshire, where the country is beautifully rough and wild. There's plenty of game, and the rivers are full of fish. I intend to establish myself at the upper end of the lake, and live upon milk and butter, as the inhabitants do.

In a letter to Mrs. Wolfe, on the 1st of June, her son writes:—

Your house and your garden and your park (I call it yours, as you have the possession of it) must be vastly pleasant at this time of the year. Nature puts on her best appearance at this season, and every production of the earth is now in the highest beauty. The beasts have their new coats, and the birds their fine feathers; and even our species, for whose pleasure all these seem to have been intended, are properly disposed for the enjoyment of them. Without doubt you walk a good deal in the fresh air, and taste the blessings that a bounteous Maker has bestowed. Happy those that have justice and piety enough to acknowledge and to thank the liberal hand that gives them! I have had frequent occasion to mention to you the many changes of weather we are subject to in this country, because I have frequently suffered by them. At present I don't complain; I amassed such a store

visit was in the twentieth year of her age. Walpole, in a letter to Sir H. Mann (May 13, 1752), says: "The Gunnings are gone to their several castles, and one hears no more of them, except that such crowds flock to see the Duchess of Hamilton pass, that 700 people sat up all night in and about an inn in Yorkshire to see her get into her postchaise next morning." It is a pity Wolfe does not describe his entertainment at Hamilton Palace. Walpole, whose descriptions of characters are generally exaggerated, writes again to Mann (October 28, 1752):—"Duke Hamilton is the abstract of Scotch pride; he and the Duchess at their own house walk in to dinner before their company, sit together at the upper end of the table, eat off the same plate, and drink to nobody beneath the rank of earl." The old palace close to the town of Hamilton still stands, but a fine modern structure was added to it about forty years ago. It was not an hour's ride for Wolfe from Glasgow.

of health in France that I hope it will last during our stay here, though I am persuaded the consumption will be very considerable.

On the 25th, the Lieutenant-Colonel writes from the "Camp of Inverdouglas:" *—

We are encamped with five companies of the regiment that are working on the roads. It will be late in August before they return to Glasgow, and consequently we can't begin our march until September. Though we are not much above twenty miles from the Low Countries, yet I think this part of the Highlands is as wild as any that I have seen. We are upon the side of a great lake, bordered round with exceeding high mountains, whose tops are, for the most part, barren,—either bog or rock; but at the first of these hills there is a good deal of wood, some grass, and very little corn. A man in health might find a good deal of entertainment in fair weather, provided he has strength to climb up the mountains, and has keenness to pursue the game they produce.

It has been said that the road, as well as the legion, made the Romans masters of the world;* and it is equally true that military roads opened the way for the civilization of the Highlands. After the last rebellion, Government saw the propriety of enlarging upon General Wade's scheme, and with this object in view an encampment was formed near Fort Augustus in 1747.

* Inverdouglas is situated on the west side of Loch Lomond, in Dumbartonshire, nearly in the centre of the line of the Loch. A small gorge, called *Glen*douglas, opens upon the western shore of Loch Lomond, at nearly right angles, and through this glen runs a little stream, the "water of Douglas," which, like the Snaid, where it enters the Loch, gives the name *Inverd*ouglas to a district. The word is usually pronounced, and the place known, as Inveruglas, the consonant *d* being silent. Inveruglas is nearly opposite Ben Lomond, and the aspect of the lofty mountain across the Loch is very grand.

† Smiles's 'Lives of the Engineers.'

Lieutenant-General Watson, who was appointed to superintend the works, having conceived the idea of a map of Scotland, General Roy was ordered to make the preliminary survey; and under these officers parties of soldiers, drafted from the several corps, continued to work upon the roads and bridges for many years. It was usual, when they had completed their summer's task, for the men to have a jollification in the English fashion,—eating, drinking, racing, wrestling, etc.,—and a tablet was erected by the wayside recording the date and name of the regiment. One of these tablets, supposed to have been put up by the men under Wolfe, in 1753, was pulled down years ago by a farmer at Ardvoirlich, and transformed into a hearthstone. Another, on the road near Tynaclach, Arrochar, bore the mark of the 20th Regiment, but neither the year nor the name of the commanding officer can be ascertained.*

Four days later, in reply to a lecture of his mother's upon his warmth of temper, Wolfe writes from Glasgow:—

I think I am not positively blind to my own infirmities,

* Mr. Buchanan, through the 'Glasgow Herald,' has inquired whether any tablet set up by the men under Wolfe is still preserved, and has also, through Mr. Irving, the historian of Dumbartonshire, communicated with the present road surveyors, but, notwithstanding numerous replies, without satisfactory result. A tablet of comparatively recent date bears the inscription,—"Rest and be thankful. Military road repaired by the 47th Regt. 1768. Transferred to Commrs. for H. R. & B. in the year 1814." After the Highland roads and bridges were completed, they were placed under the charge of commissioners, who have been superseded by a recent Act of Parliament; and many of the roads will soon be superseded by railways, for the last of the mail-coaches departed from Inverness in September, 1863.

but that I oftener perceive my defects than I have power to correct or even to disguise them; and there are times and particular situations in which people are apter to lose that power than at others. I believe we are so compounded of good and bad that accidents easily incline the balance on either side, and I am sure that none of us, even the most virtuous, are entirely free from faults, though some have the art to hide them. That warmth of temper, which you so justly censure when it breaks out improperly, is what I depend upon to support me against the little attacks of my brethren and cotemporaries, and that will find the way to a glorious, or at least a firm and manly end when I am of no further use to my friends or country, or when I can be serviceable by offering my life for either.

Nobody has perhaps more reason to be satisfied with his station and success in the world than myself, nobody can have better parents, and I have hitherto never wanted friends; but happiness, or ease, which is all we can pretend to, lies in the mind or nowhere. A man must think himself so or imagine it, or it cannot be; it is not circumstances, advancement, fortune, or good relations and faithful friends that create it, 'tis the temper, or truly the force of overcoming one or more of the leading passions that otherwise must disturb us. These passions seem to be in our first composition or in nature, and the remedy, as you observe, in reason. But this often fails, at least in our younger days. Those tempers are very ticklish that may undergo a considerable change by any alteration of air, diet, or exercise, and this I often experience. It is most true that no one has a better claim to my care and esteem than yourself, and no person is more truly the object of it; but as you have been indulgent and kind hitherto in everything that you believed for my advantage, so now your indulgence must extend to overlook, or forgive at least, those defects that are visibly in the blood, and hard at this time of life to overcome. And if you think I have any good qualities, they may be set in opposition to the bad ones, and that is what our feeble condition here seems in justice to require.

On the 7th of August, Wolfe writes to his father from the "north-west side of Loch Lomond:"—

Though there have been great pains taken to put the regiment into order, yet for two reasons we shall make but a very indifferent appearance when his Royal Highness reviews us. The first is, that our clothes are vastly damaged by the work here and by long wear; and the other, that Lord Bury would have changed our exercise from very quick to very slow, so that at present, in attempting to conform to his lordship's directions, we are between the two, and can neither do one nor the other as they ought to be done. All the soldiers know that it is not very material, but some of those that will be present at our review may have other notions. These are matters that give me as little concern as anybody. If a man does his duty to the best of his judgment and ability, the thoughts and reflections that arise from so doing are, in my opinion, sufficient satisfaction. I have been confined ever since my coming to this place to within the last few days, and now that I am able to go about the bad weather keeps me close. It is strange that neither temperance nor exercise can preserve me in any tolerable health in this unfriendly climate. The moisture of this air overmatches all the precautions that I can take to resist its bad effects, and yet we have had a finer season in Scotland than has been known for many years.

The Lieutenant-Colonel returned to Glasgow on the 24th of August, and two days later wrote as follows to his mother:—

I deferred answering your letter till my return from the Highlands,—that is, till I got out of a dirty smoky hut, and free from the noise of a camp. My stay upon the side of Loch Lomond would have been extremely agreeable and pleasant but for two or three interfering accidents. This mixture of good and evil waits upon us from our introduction into life to the latest hour; the easiest are those who have no violent pursuits, for they are seldom disappointed. The loss of my poor facetious friend Loftus grieves me; he was preparing to make me a visit just before he went off.* Since I came here I learned the death of our good General.† Lord Cathcart has made a judicious choice, and Miss Hamilton has a fair prospect of happiness with a man of his worth and honour.‡ There are very few young ladies that I have met with who, in my opinion, deserve better than she does. If I had not seen Miss Lawson, I would have probably been in love with Miss Hamilton. I can't say the lady would have had a great conquest to boast of, but speak of it as a proof of my good taste.

. . . .

'Tis an unpleasant thing to be surrounded, as you are, by such numbers of villains; whatever they do without-doors, it is to be hoped they respect the insides of houses. There must be some strange neglect in the magistrates and officers of justice in the county, or these robbers would not range through it in this manner with impunity. I am surprised that in the counties near London they don't establish a company of light horse to guard the public roads or pursue these vermin. They need not be military, but people hired for that purpose, with good pay, and entirely under the sheriff's directions.

* Arthur Loftus, the late Major of General Wolfe's regiment, second son of Dudley Loftus, Esq., of Killyan, co. Meath, died of fever on the 31st of July, at Fort Augustus.

† Lieutenant-General George Churchill, Commander of the Forces in Scotland, died at Smeiton House, near Dalkeith, on the 19th of August.

‡ Charles, ninth Lord Cathcart, who succeeded to the title on the death of his father, at Dominica, in 1740, married (July, 1753) Jane, eldest daughter of Lord Archibald Hamilton, and soon after was elected one of the Representative Peers of Scotland. He rose to the rank of Major-General, was sometime Adjutant-General of North Britain, and died in 1770. Lord Grey de Ruthyn, second Earl of Sussex, and Lord Cathcart, were the two noble hostages who, agreeably to one of the terms of the treaty of Aix-la-Chapelle, resided in Paris until the restoration of Cape Breton to France.

There are abundance of officers that would be glad of such employment, and proper men, if they pay 'em well, might easily be found.* They have what they call *maréchaussée* in France to protect travellers, and people travel there in great security.†

Elections are the great business all over the island, and the competitors are struggling, not, I am afraid, for the public good, but for their private interest and advantage. The Parliament House is now the seat of profit, and people generally seek a place there as they would an income. We have everything to fear from these general self-interested views, but one must hope that these very men who are so sanguine for themselves will pay some regard to their posterity, and leave things at least in as good a condition as they find them.

In his last letter from Scotland, dated the 8th of September, Wolfe informs his father:—

The first division of our regiment marched out of town this morning, and I stay behind it one day to finish my business and to write letters. I have got myself tolerably well mounted upon a horse of poor Loftus's. Donnellan had bought him at the auction, but resigned him to me, knowing my necessity. I am glad to find that the promotion is gone in your regi-

* This is not the only measure for the public good anticipated by Wolfe. It was not until some years afterwards that the germ of a metropolitan police was established by Sir John Fielding. In 1819, one hundred foot patrols perambulated the environs for a distance of two or three miles, and forty horsemen went from ten to fifteen miles on the roads leading from London. Both of these bodies were under the jurisdiction of the chief magistrate of Bow Street. (Rees's Cycl.) The horse patrol, then numbering seventy-six men, were placed under commissioners by Act 6 & 7 Will. IV. cap. 50. ('Encyclopædia Britannica,' 1842.)

† "Maillart dit: 'Qu'en Lyonnois et dans les pays circonvoisins, les terres sont chargées d'une certaine redevance, en espèce ou en argent, nommée *maréchaussée*, laquelle étoit originairement payée aux maréchaux des princes, en considération de ce que ces officiers défendoient les peuples, tant en guerre qu'en paix.'" ('Encyclopédie Méthodique,' Paris, 1785.)

ment, and that Mr. Secretary-of-War has consented to be civil to you upon this occasion. Your demands upon them are so just and moderate, that you may very well expect good manners, at least; a person that does not ask favours has a right to fair speech.*

I am sorry that Lord Cathcart's affairs require so much attention that he must necessarily quit; he is an officer of such reputation that the army loses considerably by his resignation. I hope, however, that he will preserve his rank amongst us, and that I shall, some day or other, have the honour to serve under him. We are so long absent, and removed to so great a distance, that I am almost surprised to hear that anybody is at the least trouble to inquire about me, especially a Paris acquaintance. I am particularly obliged to Stanhope, because his acquaintance is so extensive that I might expect to be lost in the crowd. He is a lively, civil little man, and has a great store of learning and knowledge. I beg my compliments to him. From time to time you shall hear of our progress.

With the expiration of his service in Scotland, Wolfe may be said to have finished the second phase of his military career. Although not yet seven-and-twenty, he had been engaged in the field during seven years of war, and had commanded a regiment for five years in a country recovering out of a state of anarchy, so as to call forth the King's approbation, and win the grateful remembrance of the people.

English soldiers have done some good for Scotland

* Captain Nehemiah Donnellan succeeded to the majority of the General's regiment, *vice* Loftus, deceased. When promotion went in the same regiment, the "difference" was one of the perquisites of the colonel; and although he could not be said to sell a commission, when the King accepted of his recommendation, the colonel was understood to have disposed of such commission. ('Gentleman's Magazine,' vol. xvi. p. 481.)

besides making roads. It is generally admitted that the Highlands were greatly benefited by Cromwell's troops, and though the moral and religious state of the army in the middle of the eighteenth century was much below that of the Protector's time, we have at least one instance to show that a few soldiers, even in 1753, could enlighten the people amongst whom they were thrown. It is related that when General Wolfe's regiment was quartered in Aberdeen, some of the privates were heard practising sacred music; and Thomas Channon, having been found capable of giving instructions, was engaged to lead the psalmody in one of the churches. His success and good conduct induced a number of ministers to apply to Lieut.-General Bland for his discharge from the army, and his Excellency having granted the request, the soldier settled in Aberdeen, where he continued to teach singing in the "reformed way."*

The Lieutenant-Colonel's first report of the march southward is from—

Carlisle, 17th September, 1753.

Dear Madam,

The last division of our regiment passes the Eske to-morrow, and salutes the land of England once more. We begin our march from Carlisle on the 20th, and shall be at Reading the 16th of October, which is a day sooner than my former calculation. The weather has been fair and favourable as possible hitherto, and so warm, that we have more the look of troops that came from Spain or Africa than from the north. We are really a good deal browner and more tanned than the battalion from Minorca that relieve us. We are come thus far in our military rotation, and a good way in the revolution of our lives. The regiment has undergone as great

* 'Scots Magazine,' vol. xvii. p. 412.

change as was perhaps ever known in time of peace and in so short a while. There are come fifteen new officers to the corps, besides myself, since the beginning of the year 1749, and there are several alterations to make that may soon take place.

A mile on this side the river that divides England from Scotland one begins to perceive the difference that labour and industry can make upon the face of a country. The soil is much the same for some space either north or south, but the fences, enclosures, and agriculture are not at all alike. The English are clean and laborious, and the Scotch excessively dirty and lazy, though far short, indeed, of what we found at a greater distance from the borders. Colonel Stanwix is Governor of this place, and I believe you are acquainted; at least, he inquired much after my father's health and yours. He has been extremely civil to our people.* The castle of Carlisle is a fortress that ought by no means to have been given up to the rebels in the manner it was.† The present Governor would not, nor, I dare say, ever will surrender it into such hands. Our second division is just now marching in, and that obliges me to stop here.

The next report of the regiment's progress is from Warrington, on the 30th of September:—

Dear Sir,

The greatest good-fortune that can happen to people that travel slow is to have fair weather, and we have been particu-

* Afterwards Lieut.-General Stanwix. In 1764 he succeeded the Hon. John Barrington as Colonel of the 8th Foot (General Wolfe's regiment), and was drowned on his passage from Dublin in 1766.

† Wolfe's father, then a major-general, was a member of the general court-martial held at the Horse Guards in September, 1746, to examine into the conduct of Lieut.-Colonel James Durand, from the time he took the command of the city and castle of Carlisle till they were surrendered to the rebels on the 15th of November, 1745. Durand was unanimously acquitted. ('The Occupation of Carlisle in 1745,' ed. by George G. Mounsey, 1846.)

larly lucky hitherto. There has been but one rainy day since we set out. As the season advances we must expect a change; and indeed it has begun this day, with appearances that are much against us. Men harden in the air with marching, as they harden in iniquity by practice. We are to halt at Warwick, where Lord Bury meets and reviews the regiment. The men are healthy, and so active, that they have worn their clothes threadbare.* We are no politicians, or we should have done as our predecessors the Fusileers did, that is, clothe four months later than usual, to appear clean. I do believe we shall be the most dirty, ragged regiment that the Duke has seen for some years.

In Cumberland, Westmoreland, and the north of Lancashire, part of the country is almost as rough and barren as the Highlands of Scotland; but there is variety of well cultivated, beautiful spots intermixed. Every day as we move more south the country appears richer and more delightful; and the women hereabouts, and in this place in particular, are surprisingly handsome. They astonish us that have been accustomed to look at the hard-favoured Scotch lasses. They have very pretty faces (I mean the Lancashire women), but they are not, in the towns, of such stature as I expected. The peasants are straight, well made, tall, good-looking men. There's a great quantity of cattle bred in Lancashire, and some horses. The gentlemen seem fond of hunting (by the quantity of hounds I judge), though the country is not best for that sort of sport, as the enclosures and fences are vastly strong, and the corn-ground very deep. Our march is something more than half over, and I heartily wish it was at an end, because these slow movements are not agreeable to my disposition of mind.

* By the warrant of George II., dated July 1, 1751, for establishing uniformity in the clothing and colours of the several regiments, the facings of the *Twentieth* were ordered to be of pale yellow; the coat of scarlet to be turned up with yellow, and ornamented with white lace; scarlet waistcoat and breeches, with white gaiters reaching above the knee, and cocked hat bound with white lace. (Cannon's 'Records of the British Army.')

There is a letter, on the 16th of October, from Warwick, which is described as "one of the prettiest little towns in England. Lord Brooke's castle, for the situation and antiquity of it, is as great a rarity as any in the kingdom.* The country about us is extremely beautiful. We hunted yesterday upon a delightful plain, and had exceeding fine sport." By the 22nd, the regiment had reached Reading, whence the Lieutenant-Colonel writes to his father :—

I have received a very kind letter from my mother, inviting me to her house, and to a warm room that she promises to provide for me; but I am not able to say when I can have the pleasure of paying my duty to you both. If our route leads through Deptford and Greenwich, I shall wait upon you; if not, my visit will be deferred till my return from Dover. The Major seems disposed to leave the regiment, in which case I shall be confined to it, because I can't, in conscience, assert that I have any weighty business to call me away. And yet, the prospect of passing a winter in the castle of Dover ought to quicken a man's invention for means to get free. The Duke reviews the regiment on Saturday, in their old clothes; so that if his Royal Highness piques himself upon finery of that kind, we shall inevitably be disgraced. It is true that we have numbers, for there's but five men wanting to complete; but I can't say much for their beauty or fine performance; for many of them have been separated from the regiment, and others ought to be severed from it for ever. If we had any religion or piety, or were at all sensible of favours from above, we should be thankful for the finest season that ever was. And though we are not, I am sure, the objects or peculiar care of Heaven, yet, as we have profited by the good things bestowed upon mankind in general, we

* Francis, eighth Lord Brooke, was afterwards created Earl Brooke and Earl of Warwick. He married Elizabeth, daughter of Lord Archibald Hamilton.

should join with them in acknowledgments. If I stay much longer with the regiment, I shall be perfectly corrupt; the officers are loose and profligate, and soldiers are very devils.

Wolfe's picture of the state of military morals would appear over-coloured if we had not, in the periodicals of the time, numerous instances of the vice and ignorance which then prevailed in the army amongst officers as well as soldiers. The subject, however, is too repulsive to be dwelt upon. The expected review did not take place, owing to the Duke's illness; nor was the Lieutenant-Colonel ill-pleased at being spared the exhibition. Writing from Reading on the 4th November, he says they were at exercise for four or five hours every day, and adds:—"The men of these times have not iron enough in their constitutions for this work. Our ancestors would have done twice as much in colder weather without coughing; but our debaucheries enervate and unman us." Shortly afterwards they marched into Kent, in which county they were stationed for the winter,—Wolfe, with six companies in the castle of Dover, and the remainder at Maidstone.

CHAPTER XIII.

DOVER.—EXETER.

NOVEMBER, 1753—MARCH, 1755.

THE Castle of Dover, like the Tower of London, is said to have been founded by Julius Cæsar. "In memory of whom," says Lambarde, "they of the castle keep till this day certain vessels of old wine and salt, which they affirm to be the remains of such provisions as he brought into it. As touching the which, if they be natural, and not sophisticate, I suppose them more likely to have been of that store which Hubert de Burgh laid in there." The old topographer did not believe that the fortress originated with Cæsar, and thought that report more credible which ascribed the foundation to the British King Arviragus, who married the daughter of the Emperor Claudius. "But whosoever," he says, "were the author of the castle, Matthew Paris writeth, that it was accounted in his time (which was under the reign of King Henry III.) *Clavis et Repagulum totius Regni,*—the very lock and key of the whole realm of England." *

Several alterations were made in the fortifications from

* 'A Perambulation of Kent, etc., written in the year 1570, by William Lambarde, of Lincoln's Inn, Gent.'

time to time, and different sovereigns added apartments to the castle until the breaking out of the Civil War, after which period the buildings were suffered to moulder into ruin; and although barracks were erected in 1745, to accommodate a regiment of infantry, they had not been kept in repair,* so that in 1753, when the castle became the head-quarters of Lord Bury's regiment, it was scarcely habitable.

Wolfe, on his way from Reading, stopped for a day or two at Blackheath, and after arriving at his destination, wrote to his mother as follows:—

Dover Castle, 19th November, 1753.

Dear Madam,

As soon as ever I could get my green cloth spread upon the barrack table, and pen, ink, and paper out of my baggage, I sit down to write to you, to inform you that the remainder of our march was as fortunate in point of weather as the former part had been; and here our labours end, I can't say comfortably or warmly, but in a soldier-like starving condition. The winds rattle pretty loud, and the air is sharp, but I suppose healthy, for it causes great keenness of appetite. I lodge at the foot of a tower supposed to be built by the Romans, and cannot help wishing sometimes that they had chosen a snugger situation to erect their fortress upon; or that the moderns, who demolished a good part of the works of antiquity, had been so kind to us, their military posterity, as not to leave one stone upon another.

The strength of our fortification is removed by discord and by time; but caissons are raised upon the ruins as prisons, and a proper mode of punishment for those wild imaginations that prefer the empty sound of drum and trumpet to sober knock of hammer in shop mechanic. Here's a ready deliverance down the perpendicular cliff to such as are tired of their existence. They need not run very far to get out of

* 'Beauties of England and Wales.' (Kent.)

this world; one bold step frees them from thought. I'm afraid I shall lose my interest at Court by this distant recluse life, and shall never be *notticed* (as the Scotch say) but to be reprimanded for some dispute with a cobbler who has a vote in such a dirty borough as Dover. Sincerely, I beg you'll make my best compliments to the General, and desire him to convince the King and Duke that he is not displeased with them, for otherwise I shall be involved with him in the resentment that must follow this seeming contempt of majesty and dignity.

On the 6th of December the Lieutenant-Colonel informs his father that he seldom stirred outside the gates of the castle, was stupefied with smoke and sulphur, and goes on to say:—

The best and most agreeable service that you can possibly do me (since you are so good to offer your service) is to amuse and divert yourself with such change and variety as the neighbourhood of London, or inconsiderable distance from Bath, or other places of public resort, put within your reach. I know by myself how necessary it is to refresh the mind with new objects to prevent its sinking, and how very useful a fresh collection of thoughts are in supporting the spirits. Let me alone six or seven days in my room, and I lose all sort of sensation, either of pain or pleasure, and am in species little better than an oyster.

A missive from the haunted castle, on Christmas Eve, will interest the antiquarian as well as the cursory reader:—

Dear Madam,

I find our afternoons hang so heavy that expedients are wanted to divert the time. Our conversation from dinner till five o'clock is kept up with some difficulty, as none of us have any correspondence with the capital, nor communication with coffee houses or public papers, so that we are entirely in the dark as to exterior things. From five till eight is a tedious interval hardly to be worked through. I have inquired for good green tea in Dover, as an aid, and can find none;* it will be some relief and an act of charity if you will send me a pound of the best. I put off my demand until I knew your rents were due, although I should rather wish you could persuade the General to pay for it, as I take his purse to be in better order than either yours or mine.

This castle is haunted with the spirits of some of our restless forefathers, the old Saxons, and some of their wives, for here are ghosts of both sexes. Whether these shadowy beings are restless, or our consciences weak and our imaginations strong, you may easily conjecture. But here are people that believe there are spirits to be seen, and others that are ready to swear to the sight; or, in other words, there are minds unable to bear the darkness of the night without trembling. We know that Christmas is at hand, by the sutlers' mince-pies. I hope you have all the gaiety and good-fellowship that these times generally produce, to enliven the otherwise cold and dreary season.

The sprightly tone of our Lieutenant-Colonel's letters from Dover indicates a considerable improvement in his health and spirits. The milder climate of his native county seems, notwithstanding the discomforts of the ruinous fortress, to have acted like a charm in restoring his natural good-humour. His duties, too, were now much less burdensome and vexatious than they had been in the north. He was no longer subjected to those

* *Green* tea was not used in England until the year 1715. Its price about 1753 was from 15*s*. to 30*s*. per pound, and that of black tea from 13*s*. to 20*s*. The first duty imposed was eightpence per gallon upon made tea; but the leaf was first taxed in 1689, at the rate of 5*s*. per pound and five per cent. on the value. In 1745 the duty was altered to 1*s*. per pound and twenty-five per cent. on the value.

inevitable collisions with the civil power and with the people, such as the peculiar position of a commanding officer in Scotland necessarily incurred. His men also, instead of being billeted here and there, were under his own close inspection within the walls of the Castle, therefore Wolfe had leisure to read, while his officers passed their time playing at piquet; and in favourable weather he enjoyed himself riding upon the downs, or shooting. So, upon the whole, though Maidstone would have been preferable, he considered the Castle had some advantages. "It would be a prison," he writes, "to a man of pleasure, but an officer may put up with it."

The ladies of Dover, feeling aggrieved at the defective gallantry of the garrison officers, who, it appears, were not the liveliest of the regiment, complained, through Miss Brett, to Mrs. Wolfe. The rumour reaching the Lieutenant-Colonel, on the last day of the year he encounters the charge:—

If Nanny Brett's ladies lived as loftily and as much in the clouds as we do, their appetites for dancing, or anything else, would not be quite so keen. If we dress, the wind disorders our curls; if we walk, we are in danger of our legs; if we ride, of our necks. And how can the tender-hearted sex expect we should go down unto them at such a risk and disadvantage? But there's a truth which my flame must not know,—some of our finest performers are at present disabled, and the rest disheartened from attempting it by the terrible example of the sufferers. There are but two that can be reckoned to be whole and entire,—both very tall and thin; and we can't undertake to please all these ladies alone. The task is more difficult than Mrs. Anne seems to be aware of. If it was not for fear of offending you, I should almost confess that I think we are grown old; whether constitutionally so, or philosophically resigned, or sequestered from the world by being almost always deprived and cut off from the common enjoyments of it,—habit by degrees creating tastes agreeable to our condition, and different from those that are most in vogue. Part, or all joined perhaps together, and years really creeping on, with notions conformable, cooling the blood and spring of action till dancing and all its light train of amusements appear vain or contemptible.

Notwithstanding this, I always encourage our young people to frequent balls and assemblies. It softens their manners and makes them civil; and commonly I go along with them, to see how they conduct themselves. I am only afraid they shall fall in love and marry. Whenever I perceive the symptoms, or anybody else makes the discovery, we fall upon the delinquent without mercy till he grows out of conceit with his new passion. By this method we have broke through many an amorous alliance, and dissolved many ties of *eternal* love and affection. My experience in these matters helps me to find out my neighbour's weakness, and furnishes me with arms to oppose his folly. I am not, however, always so successful as could be wished. Two or three of the most simple and insensible in other respects have triumphed over my endeavours, but are seated upon the stool of repentance for the rest of their days.

I believe my cousin Goldsmith is already persuaded that we are a set of the worst correspondents in Europe. I have been six months in his debt without rime or reason. I owe him a thousand thanks for a pointer that is my happiness and my very existence here, and I acquit myself towards him this very night, and mention your commands. He's the most unreasonable man alive; his requests seldom go beyond the desire that he has to know that we are all well. He never asks any other favour than to be satisfied in this particular. I am a pair or two of spectacles behindhand with him, and I long to send him that little promised token of my esteem.

I find Mr. Conolly is in a lingering way; his liver is affected, and 'tis impossible that he can recover.* This is a deadly blow to my poor friend [Carleton], and will touch him deeply; but I hope the Duke of Richmond's protection, which I am sure he will deserve, may make him some amends. Your present is arrived, and is extremely valuable, both on account of the person sending it and its goodness. You have my best thanks. To-morrow the new year begins. I salute you upon it, and wish you both all pleasure and peace.

The foregoing was followed by a letter of a more professional character to the General:—

Dover Castle, 6th January, 1754.

Dear Sir,

I am very glad to find you in a resolution conformable to the rest of your character. If you have ever omitted the performance of that duty which is due from an officer of your rank, and from a man of your attachment and way of thinking to the King, it has proceeded from reasons rather commendable and praiseworthy than blameable. You knew he was environed with a hungry, greedy set. As you had no favour to ask or expect beyond a good reputation, you would not seem (however free from the thought) to augment the number of petitioners that surround the throne. But his Majesty will now be convinced that no motives of interest direct you to him; he may easily distinguish you from the rest, because I am fully persuaded that you are the only one, however fair soever your title and pretensions may be, that has not asked something. Such persons are so rare in courts that kings may look upon them as miracles; and our good

* The Right Hon. Wm. Conolly, of Stratton Hall, Staffordshire, M.P. He was the nephew and heir of the Right Hon. Wm. Conolly, Speaker of the Irish House of Commons, and died at Castletown, Celbridge, on the 3rd of January, 1754. (Lodge's 'Peerage of Ireland' (1789), vol. vii.) Wolfe speaks of him in a letter written a few days before the above as the protector of his friend Carleton and his brother. Mr. Conolly's only son, Thomas, married a daughter of the second Duke of Richmond, well known as Lady Louisa Conolly, who was aunt to the unfortunate Lord Edward Fitzgerald, and likewise to the Generals Sir Charles and Sir William Napier.

old monarch would find out and reward the modesty of some of his subjects if the impudence of others did not prevent it. I am highly pleased that your going to St. James's was graciously received, and that you yourself were satisfied.

I have sent you some birds of my own killing; few indeed they are in number and small in kind, but quails are a rarity at this season. I had a pheasant and some partridges, but these I durst not send, as we are not authorized by law to kill them; and as they examine strictly upon the great roads I should be unwilling to be reputed a smuggler. It is a misfortune for a man that likes this sort of sport preferable to any other to be liable to law and fine, or to be obstructed in the pursuit of a very innocent and wholesome diversion. Over the water 'tis death to shoot without license; here 'tis prosecution, damages, and costs.* I suppose you have heard that the French have been working at Dunkirk a kind of reservoir which, with a communication with the neighbouring canals, will be a backwater sufficient to cleanse their harbour. Sir Peircy Brett and an engineer have been there to examine these late dangerous operations.† Their report is not yet made public, or, at least, it has not reached the top of our hill. But I think our neighbour's meaning is pretty plain, and I hope we sha'n't misunderstand him.

In the middle of January Wolfe was ordered to prepare his men for cantonment upon the Kentish coast, to

* "Any officer or soldier in or near quarters, without leave of the lord of the manor, killing any hare, coney, pheasant, partridge, pigeon, or any other sort of fowls, poultry, or fish, or his Majesty's game, within the kingdom of Great Britain, if an officer he forfeits £5. The commanding officer to pay 20*s*. for every such offence committed by a soldier under his command. Officers refusing or neglecting to pay the above penalties within two days after conviction before a justice, and demand made by a constable or overseer of the poor, shall forfeit, and are hereby declared to have forfeited their commissions." ('The Military Guide for Young Officers,' 3rd ed., 1781, page 321.)

† Admiral Brett, who was one of Anson's officers in the voyage round the world, was knighted in 1753, and became one of the Lords of the Admiralty in 1766.

prevent suspicious vessels from approaching the shore,—a proceeding which he considered would prove ineffectual, "as the villainy of the smugglers would overcome all precautions." A hard frost setting in, the order was rescinded. In February he presided at a court-martial for the trial of a deserter,—the first time of acting in that "grave office,"—and thinks that "such courts of justice should not be held too often, lest the troops should lose the veneration they ought to possess." *

The Lieutenant-Colonel was kept long in suspense as to the ultimate destination of the corps, the orders received from the authorities one day being countermanded the next. At length we find them, more than a fortnight later than the date of the last letter, on the halt, in the pleasant little rural town of Sittingbourne, well pleased to get out of the old castle. In pre-railway-days Sittingbourne was enlivened by the coach-guard's bugle and the rattle of wheels; and its venerable hostelries—many of them built before the reign of Henry VIII.—enjoyed great traffic. In Wolfe's time, however, it was not so bustling a place as it afterwards became, but its ancient church, containing several remarkable monuments, was unimpaired,† and the environs were enriched by gardens and orchards.

* It appears that recruits for the French service were shipped at Dover, and deserters escaped by the same means. In one of the regimental orders Wolfe wishes certain men who had been in the service of France, or desire to be there, to know that he sets no value upon them, and had much rather they were in the Irish Brigade than in the army of Great Britain; but if any one of them hereafter should threaten to desert, he shall be immediately whipped out of the regiment as a fit recruit for the rebel battalions hired by the French to serve against their country.

† Among the monuments "was that of Sir Richard Lovelace, marshal

On Sunday, the 24th of March, the commanding officer of the marching regiment writes from "Sittinburne" to his mother:—

Although this is not the most agreeable weather to march in, yet we are glad to get out of our old castle upon any terms. It was to no purpose to complain of our condition or quarters, nor becoming the character of a soldier to do it; but since the bad part is over, and we have borne it with patience, a man may be allowed to rejoice at the escape. I am sure there is not in the King's dominions a more melancholy dreadful winter-station than that we have just left; and the neglect of the Board of Ordnance adds considerably to the natural horror that the situation and buildings raise in men's minds, and even makes it dangerous to reside in it in cold weather. So much for the vile dungeon!*

Our orders of march have been changed two or three several times, but at last it is resolved that we shall bend directly towards Guildford, where five of our companies are to assemble to be reviewed by Lord Bury; the rest are to proceed to Bristol with expedition, being strongly solicited thereto by the magistrates of that place, who, I suppose, are in some dread of the colliers and other riotous persons in their neighbourhood. I told my father the reason why I

of Calais in the reign of Henry VIII., richly inlaid with brass; but this, with many others, have been injured by a fire that burned the inside roof of the church in the year 1763. It is said that there was an organ in it about the time of Queen Elizabeth. Philipot says, that in the year 1420 King Henry V., with his retinue, was entertained in Sittingbourne by John Norwood, Esq., when the bill for wine amounted to 9*s.* 9*d.*, it being one penny per pint." ('The Kentish Traveller's Companion,' 2nd ed. (1779), p. 130.)

* Until its recent restoration under the direction of Mr. Scott, the chapel of St. Mary's in the castle was in a miserable and disgraceful condition. "Roofless, shattered, and exposed to the damaging effects of rain, frost, and mischief, it was used as a coal cellar; while the Roman Pharos at the west end, one of the most interesting landmarks of history in the kingdom, was applied to a purpose even more degrading and disreputable." ('The Builder,' September 7, 1862.)

could not hope to have the pleasure of seeing you before I am dismissed by authority; but it may happen that the cross road from Dartford to Croydon is so bad that we shall be obliged to march over the Heath and by Lewisham,* in which case I'll do myself the honour (in the polite phrase) of waiting upon you for an hour, and I wish I may find you triumphing over the inclemency of the season.

After the review Wolfe got leave of absence for some months, and passed the greater part of the time at Blackheath. In July we find him on a visit with his old friend General Mordaunt, from whose house at Freefolk† he writes to his mother on the 14th:—

Sir J. Mordaunt's civility, good-breeding, and good-humour make his house easy and pleasant to his guests, and the country round about has a variety of charms, especially to those that love sport. As far as my disposition will permit, I live everywhere as they live with whom I am, and put off the fixing upon a way of life, or preferring one method to another till I can do it at home,—in all simplicity following nature without control.‡ My mistress's picture hangs up in the room where we dine. It took away my stomach for two or three days, and made me grave; but time, the never-failing aid to distressed lovers, has made the semblance of her a pleasing, but not a dangerous object. However, I find it

* "When Mr. Rennie, the engineer, was engaged in surveying the Weald, with a view to the cutting a canal through it, in 1802, he found the country almost destitute of practicable roads, although so near the metropolis on the one hand and to the seacoast on the other. The interior of the country was then comparatively untraversed, except by bands of smugglers, who kept the inhabitants in a state of constant terror." (Smiles, 'Lives of Engineers,' vol. i. p. 232.)

† At Freefolk, a small hamlet east of Whitchurch, are the paper-mills and seat of John Portal Bridges, Esq. (1805), where the paper for bank notes has been manufactured ever since the reign of George I. ('Beauties of England and Wales:' Hampshire, p. 236.)

‡ "The tyrant Custom had not shackled man,
But free to follow Nature was the mode."
Thomson's 'Autumn.'

best not to trust myself to the lady's eyes, or put confidence in any resolutions of my own.

The above is the last allusion to Miss Lawson, who had finally rejected Wolfe's suit more than a year before. A love so ardent and so constant could not soon abate, and it was long until another lady again engaged his affections. He did not submit to his fate without a struggle, but when all his hopes were blighted he bore the disappointment with resolution, if not with resignation. Instead of sinking under the sorrow, or endeavouring to smother it in the dissipations of the world, in singleness of soul he devoted himself to the service of his country. How far matrimony might have influenced his remaining years it would be futile to surmise. His military ambition was so nearly counterpoised by his desire for domestic life as to make it doubtful whether the one would have prevailed over the other. As we shall hear no more about the "old story" of Wolfe's first love, it may here be stated that Miss Lawson died unmarried, in March, 1759.*

On the 21st, Wolfe writes again from Freefolk to his father:—

I have rambled over several places in this neighbourhood. The Duke of Bolton's park and gardens at Hackwood† are

* Obituary, 'Gentleman's Magazine.'

† *Hackwood*, a corrupt abbreviation of Hawking-wood. The pleasure-grounds and adjoining park formerly composed one wood, connected with Basing House by long avenues of chestnuts. The mansion, originally a lodge, built in the reign of Queen Elizabeth, was used as a place of meeting for company who assembled for hawking, and as a banqueting-room after the sport. See 'Beauties of England and Wales' (Hampshire). In 1754 Harry Paulet, fourth Duke of Bolton, and Marquis of Winchester, succeeded his brother Charles, who married Miss Fenton.

well worth a journey to see them. I was there and at Basingstoke races the same day, and had the pleasure to see the Duke win a plate. If I had understood matters of that sort, or had been a more refined politician and better courtier than I really am, I should have carried off my pockets full of money, for there were great odds offered against the Duke's horse, and some of the country gentlemen seemed to propose wagers with more passion than judgment. The Duke was not present. Boscawen managed his interest upon the course, and except him there was not a soul that I had the least acquaintance with.*

For more than two months we have nothing from Wolfe's pen, whence we may infer that he was at Blackheath; but on the 29th of September, we find him at Bristol, where he remained a week. After wandering about and visiting his friends during the summer months, his leisure came to an end early in October, when he took up his winter quarters in the city of Exeter, and settled down to business.

"The emporium and principal ornament of the west," as Exeter has been called, has undergone many changes since the time when the Lieutenant-Colonel crossed the Exe by its old bridge with houses on both sides, and entered the city by one of the six gates. The walls, which had borne the brunt of many a siege, still remained, though the ancient Castle of Rougemont had been demolished by Fairfax after it had held out for some time against the Parliamentary army. There were but four streets, meeting in the centre of the town, hence called "Carfox, from the old Norman word *quatre-voix*,

* The Hon. John Boscawen, fifth son of the Earl of Falmouth, and brother to the Admiral.

i. e. the four ways."* An extensive trade was carried on in "serges, *perpetuanas*,† long-ells, and other woollen goods;" but besides traders and manufacturers there were many resident gentry, who adhering to the city motto, "Semper fidelis," sympathized with the Stuarts, or, in other words, were Jacobites. "Time works wonders," insomuch that probably nothing now appertaining to the city, except the cathedral, would identify it with Exeter a hundred years ago.

On the 17th of October, Wolfe wrote to his mother, saying that he was very busy, though nothing prevented him from writing to her. He had to draft 100 of his men to Colonel Dunbar's regiment for the Virginian expedition, and would be employed all the winter in recruiting, as it was no easy matter to replace so many men where industry was well paid. "My honest friend Gage," he adds, "is to be of the Ohio party. I hope his health will enable him to stand it, but fear it will not."‡ After wishing her and the General a pleasant journey to Bath, he concludes, "the men are going out to exercise, so I must shut up and follow." The General's regiment having been reviewed at Reading, Wolfe congratulates him in these terms:—

Exeter, 25th October, 1754.

Dear Sir,

I have just received a letter from Lord Bury, concluding

* Seally's 'Geographical Dictionary' (1787).

† Perpetuana,—"A sort of stuff; by its name it should be something like *everlasting*." (Nares.)

‡ Dunbar's and Sir Peter Halket's regiments sailed from Ireland for America, in January, 1755. The Hon. Thomas Gage was Lieutenant-Colonel of the latter, and commanded the advanced guard of Braddock's fatal expedition.

with this short paragraph, "I am just returned from the review of your father's regiment; they did well, and the Duke was very well pleased with him." Lord Bury never carries his complaisance to his inferiors further than the truth. I wish people would stick to that above as well as below,—to be honest if possible at both ends; but that's foreign to the present purpose. I am extremely pleased that this business has passed over so much to the Duke's satisfaction and to yours. It is a pity you are not better acquainted; for his Royal Highness only begins to know you,—he has but just found out that nobody means better than General Wolfe.

. . . .

I begin to flatter myself that we shall soften the rigorous proceedings of our adversaries here, and live with them on better terms than hitherto. It is not our interest to quarrel with any but the French; and they must be devilish minds that take a pleasure in disputing. I hope my good mother will tell me what's doing at Bath, and I hope I shall hear from her that she is sensible of the good effects of its waters and of its cheerful variety and company. Tim. Brett passed through here some days ago, in his way home; he had company with him, and could not even dine with me.*

As the continuation of the following fragment has been lost, neither time nor place is attached to it, but internal testimony proves its proper position to be hereabouts.†

Dear Madam,

My father said very little upon the subject of his review; just as much as helped me to conjecture that he was not ill pleased; but he did not mention a syllable of the Duke's

* Timothy, brother to Charles Brett, is described as a man of "a most mild, benignant, and amiable character;" he was sometime Clerk of the Cheque at Portsmouth, and died at Greenwich in 1790, unmarried, and much respected. ('Gentleman's Magazine,' March, 1799.)

† The originals being generally dated at the end, near the signature, the terminations of some of the letters have been cut off for the sake of the autograph.

civility to him, which I am very glad to learn from you; and I was much rejoiced to perceive that you had been present at this military show and had been diverted with it. If I did not profess the business myself, I should follow all the Reviewing Generals for the sake of seeing the troops. I know nothing more entertaining than a collection of well-looking men uniformly clad, and performing their exercise with grace and order. I should go further,—my curiosity would carry me to all parts of the world to be a spectator at these martial sights, and to see the various produce of different climates and the regulations of different armies. Fleets and fortifications too are objects that would attract me as strongly as architecture, painting, and the gentler arts. Have you seen any of our people at Bath? They go over now and then from Bristol for a day to dance, and then return; the poor devils can't stay long, they can't bear the expense. We have one very extraordinary person gone from hence,—a lieutenant that you have heard me speak of, his name is H——; we call him Bardolph! If his figure does not frighten you it will certainly make you laugh. He'll be at some gaming-table. That poor, infatuated old fool, Will, deserves compassion; he may now be considered as the most helpless, abandoned wretch upon the earth. Blind folly! to prefer the momentary satisfaction that ale can give to the solid certainty of care and good usage in your easy service. These creatures are insensible of present advantages or prospect of future misery.*

Would you believe it that no Devonshire squire dances more than I do? What no consideration of pleasure or complaisance for the sex could effect, the love of peace and harmony has brought about. I have danced the officers into the good graces of the Jacobite women hereabouts, who were prejudiced against them. It falls hard upon me, because of my indolence and indifference about it.†

* Will had been more than fourteen years in the General's service. See postscript to letter, "August 6, 1740," p. 13.

† A literary lady who appears to have known Wolfe personally, in a letter, "On the Grace and Propriety of Dancing," portrays his per-

We are upon such terms with the people in general that I have been forced to put on all my address, and employ my best skill to conciliate matters. It begins to work a little favourably, but not certainly, because the perverseness of these folks, built upon their disaffection, makes the task very difficult. We had a little ball last night, to celebrate his Majesty's birthday,—purely military; that is, the men were all officers except one. The female branches of the Tory families came readily enough, but not one man would accept the invitation, because it was the King's birthday.* If it had not fallen in my way to see such an instance of folly I should not readily be brought to conceive it.

Wolfe's letters now, though not less frequent, become shorter; he is so busy that he is obliged to contract them. Long ones take up time. "I have seen," he says, "ladies' letters a mile long, but they have an ease in writing that men want." Towards the close of the year he seems to have had more leisure, for his correspondence regains it wonted length, and improves in vivacity. Including passages which have been cancelled to avoid repetition, the following amusing fragment covers four pages of ample, old-fashioned letter-paper, of dimensions such as may be remembered by

formance thus:—"I remember the great General Wolfe to have been much admired for his talent in this science likewise; but he was generally ambitious to gain a tall, graceful woman to be his partner, as well as a good dancer; and when he was honoured with the hand of such a lady, the fierceness of the soldier was absorbed in the politeness of the gentleman. When thus innocently animated, the General seemed emulous to display every kind of virtue and gallantry that would render him amiable in a private character. Such a serene joy was diffused over his whole manners, mien, and deportment, that it gave the most agreeable turn to the features of that hero, who died for his country." ('Miscellanies in Prose and Verse,' by Mrs. M. Deverell, Gloucester, 1781, vol. i. p. 74.)

* The 30th of October.

some of us, though seldom used in these days of envelopes, notes, penny postage, steel pens, and telegraphs. Old Lady Grey, at whose house Wolfe called when on his way to Paris, was now at Bath. Her ladyship appears to have had a talent for match-making, and to have been very anxious to provide a suitable partner for her favoured client.

Dear Madam,

Lady Grey knows so well how to value a constant temper, that she must necessarily encourage such a lover, and keep his hopes alive. For my part, I don't feel the least disposition to change; but if ever I do, it shall be upon the plan prescribed by her. I will look where she points, but I must warn her that there are little wandering stars of very bright aspect at first, whose beauty and light are soon obscured, and will hardly bear a close inspection; there are others of a nobler nature,—fixed and permanent,—upon whose friendly aid and guidance a traveller may depend. Now, to distinguish between these heavenly bodies requires a pretty good telescope and strong sight. But, to descend a little from things celestial to things that are material, I must acknowledge her ladyship's great goodness in offering such security to the General as she is possessed of.

The Right Worshipful the Mayor of Exeter and myself are hand and glove. We drink Church and King together upon extraordinary occasions at the Guildhall; but when he does me the honour to dine, we leave out the divine part of the toast, which makes him suspect my religion, and he cannot help thinking that the officers of the army are no better than they should be. The people seem to be tolerably well disposed towards us at present. How long they will continue in such good humour it is quite uncertain. I hope it will last our time, for as the town has nothing in it either inviting or entertaining, the circumstances of a civil war would make it intolerable. I am in a perfect solitude with a crowd of people around, for all our conversable officers are sent off upon different duties, and the inhabitants are of a species not to be frequented. There are some sensible, well-bred men amongst the clergy that are seldom seen. The Bishop was very civil, but he is gone to Parliament.*

The night of dreadful thunder which affected you did not in the least disturb my rest. Nothing wakes me, which I reckon a misfortune, and I draw an inference from it to the disadvantage of my future affairs. Sound sleep is the mark of an inactive mind, and such are never great or useful; but, to balance it, quiet rest and a clear conscience are constant companions.

As a correspondent, Mrs. Wolfe was very sensitive and hard to please. Occasionally indulging herself in a quiet game, she has taken offence at some remarks of her son's upon card-playing. Having deprecated the maternal wrath in his letter of the 5th of December, Wolfe explains his meaning:—

We that are young have a thousand different ways of employing ourselves, and of getting through our time. It is not so with people more advanced in years, and though I am not particularly fond of cards myself, yet I think they are reasonable and innocent instruments of diversion, and I am always sorry when I suffer myself to censure any entertainment that is quite harmless because it is not to my taste. My meaning is, that young folks should be careful of engaging in any pursuit that may sacrifice the hours of their improvement, and that they who have the warmest tempers are most likely

* Dr. George Lavington, an eminent scholar, strongly attached to the Protestant succession, was born in 1683. In 1746 he was raised to the See of Exeter, where he resided among his clergy, a faithful and vigilant pastor, and died in 1762. He published several works, one of which, on 'The Enthusiasm of the Methodists and Papists compared,' involved him in a controversy with Whitfield and Wesley. See Chalmers's Biographical Dictionary, vol. xx. p. 71.

to push into excesses that way, as in all things else that they are bent upon.

Then come a few characteristic sketches of his subordinate officers:—"Maxwell dances remarkably well for a man of his uncommon size. I suppose he's liked at Bath, for I dare say he's much known. He's the best-humoured man alive.* Poor H—— (*alias* Bardolph) had such a cold while he was at Bath, that he could not go out of his lodgings, and so escaped being seen." Having told his mother that he will try and run over to see her next month, he concludes:—"I have so many letters to send to poor subalterns and recruiting-officers, that I cannot spare you a frank, and have so much to do before the post goes out that I must make an end."†

Wolfe passed the Christmas holidays with his father and mother at Bath, and returned to Exeter on the 3rd of January. Next day he informs the latter that he expects to be put on board the fleet, and fears he will be sent to Bristol to try men by court-martial for their

* Maxwell was the senior captain of the corps, and became Major in 1758. He was probably the Lieut.-Colonel Hamilton Maxwell of the 71st regiment, who distinguished himself at Gibraltar under General Elliott, and afterwards in India.

† The privilege which Members of Parliament enjoyed of franking letters by writing their names on covers is well known to have given rise to various evasions. Wolfe, being above resorting to such devices, considerably preferred that his mother should incur the expense of postage to inflicting the tax upon poor subalterns. It is evident that "Lord Bury's" was not the favoured corps alluded to by Sir Walter Scott. "One noble lord, to express his regard for a particular regiment, franked a letter for every rank and file. It was customary also to save the covers and return them, in order that the correspondence might be carried on as long as the envelopes could hold together." ('Redgauntlet,' Letter 1, n.)

lives. Hopes Uncle Brad. offers his services to Government. Wants shoes; Rymer, of Charing Cross, has his measure. Will be troublesome to her for other matters he requires, but father will pay the bills.

His next letter is dated "Bristol, 19th January." The solemn duty he has been engaged in has cast a gloom over his sensitive mind, and the severity of the weather affecting his equally sensitive frame, a sombre tinge pervades the whole production. One paragraph will suffice. After hoping that the General and Mrs. Wolfe,—who have returned to their "little house at Blackheath,"—have been benefited by the Bath, he goes on to say:—

> Folks are surprised to see the meagre, consumptive, decaying figure of the son, when the father and mother preserve such good looks; and people are not easily persuaded that I am one of the family. The campaigns of 1743, '4, '5, '6, and '7 stripped me of my bloom, and the winters in Scotland and at Dover have brought me almost to old age and infirmity, and this without any remarkable intemperance. A few years, more or less, are of very little consequence to the common run of men, and therefore I need not lament that I am perhaps somewhat nearer my end than others of my time. I think and write upon these points without being at all moved. It is not the vapours, but a desire I have to be familiar with those ideas which frighten and terrify the half of mankind that makes me speak upon the subject of my dissolution.

Wolfe's foreshadows, however, did not make him indifferent about his advancement in the army; but contrariwise, perhaps, prompted his desire of promotion. General Mordaunt interested himself as much to forward that object as Lady Grey to provide him with a wife. Sir John devised various schemes, one of which was that General Wolfe should resign the colonelcy of his regiment in favour of James, who was to settle an annuity upon his father. The son, having turned the matter in his mind, writes as follows:—

Exeter, 7th February, 1755.

Dear Sir,

I have writ to Sir John Mordaunt by this post to decline his obliging offers of service with thankfulness and gratitude. A soldier's life in war is too great an uncertainty for you to hazard a necessary part of your income upon. I should be afraid to die, more than is natural, if it left my parents unprovided of a subsistence depending upon my life. Besides, how far an expensive war may affect the funds I know not. Your better judgment upon this point may furnish you with reasons for or against any alteration of your affairs. Some security there should be for my mother if she should outlive you, and me, and the public credit,—a thing, in my mind, not altogether impossible.

As I said in my last letter, we expect to go on board the fleet, and 'tis a service that we all like, from the importance of a success at sea, to which we should be happy to contribute ever so little. I know, if your health and time of day would allow, you would offer your services to the good old King. He will, however, be pleased to see what remains of his faithful old soldiers, and I hope you now and then appear with the rest, to give those proofs of your attachment. Excuse the freedom I take to say that you can't better exert your strength in the spring than by going a few days to your regiment, to look at them with a cheerful, friendly face, and to see if there be anything wanting which is in your power to supply. Such an attention pleases the troops, and must be acceptable to his Royal Highness the Duke.

He remains still in suspense as to his probable destination; when four days after the above, a letter, from which the following passages are extracted, was written to his mother:—

We are in expectation of sudden orders for some service; what it is we know not. If we are ordered on board the fleet either to cruise, or to Virginia, it will be absolutely necessary that I get myself furnished with a quantity of coarse shirts; and how to do it I really am at a loss to know, and if we were to take the field I should be wholly ruined. This is the state of my affairs,—I am eight-and-twenty years of age, a Lieutenant-colonel of Foot, and I cannot say that I am master of fifty pounds. My preparations for Minorca have run me aground, and, in short, I am so distressed that I feel myself a little uneasy, and am surrounded with miserable devils in the same circumstances, to whom a battle would be a happy event. Don't trouble yourself about my room or my bedclothes; too much care and delicacy at this time would enervate me, and complete the destruction of a tottering constitution. Such as it is, it must serve me now, and I'll make the best of it, and the fittest use while it holds.

My uncle Wat's scheme is either very extravagant or a very prudent one. If my uncle means to mend his health by a soft climate, he can't take a better method than what you say he proposes. If his intentions were to be useful to me, I can't but think myself highly obliged to him; although I could well wish that he would not put himself out of his way upon my account, as it will not answer the end that I know he proposes. The case, as it appears to me, is this,—that the uncle has much more ambition than the nephew, and that he has a better opinion of me than I have of myself, and far better than I deserve. He wants that I should make a considerable figure in our profession; and as he is a skilful man himself he would willingly contribute to it. His letters are all calculated to answer that end, but he never mentioned a syllable to me of his late project. If he had, I should certainly have opposed it.*

* What the Major's project was does not apppear.

On the 18th of February Wolfe acknowledges his father's promised aid in these terms :—

By my mother's letter, which came to me this morning, I find that your bounty and liberality keep pace (as they usually do) with my necessities. I shall not abuse your kindness, nor receive it unthankfully, and what use I make of it shall be for your honour and the King's service,—an employment worthy the hand that gives it. I cannot bear the thoughts of asking these sort of supplies from any foreign purse, and therefore should have been more distressed without your assistance than can well be described. I would not wish that anything should take off my attention from the most important parts of my duty; nor feel myself cramped and tied down by the narrowness of my circumstances at the time when the thoughts should be free and at large. If a man be ill served, or ill armed in the field, he is deprived of the necessary aids to his well-doing; and that spirit will guide others but indifferently which bends under its own wants. I shall husband your gifts with discretion, and be gratefully mindful of your goodness.

To his mother he writes on the same occasion :—

I put both your letters under one cover; the thanks that are due to one are due to the other, for your intentions and kindness to your son are alike. I am now able to come to you, and may have leave for eight or ten days perhaps. Before, I could not undertake the journey without dreading the expense.

Concerning two of his schoolfellows, the Stretons, he remarks :—

Jemmy's conduct astonishes me. He should blush to be anywhere but at his colours at this time. A young lieutenant loitering up and down Greenwich Park! If he belonged to us I would soon bring him to quarters, and find him full employment. What is my old friend about? If this comes to be known, Jemmy's reputation must suffer; the monthly returns of his regiment will publish his idleness. Jack is of other mettle, and has good need of it. It has fallen hard upon that poor lad; I wish the other had his share. Where does Jack go next? He will have visited all the remote corners of the earth. I beg you'll tell him that I wish him well, that I regret his hard lot, and that I should have been much pleased to have seen my old friend and schoolfellow.*

Although the General's and Mrs. Wolfe's letters to their son have not been preserved, we can occasionally detect some of their topics from the answers they call forth. The old General, it would appear, mindful of his own experience, endeavoured to dissuade James from being too forward to offer his services on board the fleet. But our hero, feeling that his duty to his country was a higher call than the obedience due to his parents, expresses his sentiments in the following chivalrous letter to his mother:—

Exeter, 19th February, 1755.

Dear Madam,

May I be permitted to say that my father's apprehensions, and consequently yours, are not well grounded? He was on board the fleet in the beginning of the war preceded by a peace of thirty years, in which the sea officers as well as ours had almost forgot their trade. Matters are not now so circumstanced, and there are many commanders in the fleet who are men of high courage and spirit. Let me add that things were inconveniences, and disagreeable ones at his time of life which are not so at mine. I please myself that we are likely to do our country good service by going on board the fleet. The sickness that we feel at first will soon be over, and I flatter myself, if occasion be, that we shall spur them on to their duty. The success of our fleet in the beginning of the

* Wolfe's schoolfellow was probably General John Streton, who died in the year 1803.

war is of the utmost importance, and we shall have great merit in contributing ever so little towards it.

It is no time to think of what is convenient or agreeable; that service is certainly the best in which we are the most useful. For my part, I am determined never to give myself a moment's concern about the nature of the duty which his Majesty is pleased to order us upon; and whether it be by sea or by land that we are to act in obedience to his commands, I hope that we shall conduct ourselves so as to deserve his approbation. It will be sufficient comfort to you two, as far as my person is concerned, at least it will be a reasonable consolation, to reflect that the Power which has hitherto preserved me may, if it be His pleasure, continue to do so; if not, that it is but a few days or a few years more or less, and that those who perish in their duty, and in the service of their country, die honourably. I hope I shall have resolution and firmness enough to meet every appearance of danger without great concern, and not be over-solicitous about the event.

. . . .

The dogs are to be disposed of as follows,—you are to have Flurry instead of Romp, and Romp is to be given to Sergeant Goodman whenever he calls for her. The two puppies I must desire you to keep a little longer, till I can dispose of them so as not to be troublesome to you. I can't part with either of them, but must find good and secure quarters for them as well as my friend Cæsar, who has great merit and much good, humour. I have given Sancho to Lord Howe, so that I am now reduced to two spaniels and one pointer, all of excellent kinds.* Beckwith is just come into the room.† He always puts a stop to my writing; I must therefore present my duty to my Father.

In many points there is a remarkable resemblance between Wolfe and Nelson; in other points they as widely

* Trivial though the matter is, the termination of the letter has been thought too characteristic to be withheld.

† Beckwith was the Major of the regiment.

differ. Both had delicate constitutions, suffered much from ill-health, and were subject to periodical fits of despondency. Nelson is said to have often repeated, that when recovering from a state of mental depression, "a radiant orb was suspended in his mind's eye which urged him onward to renown." * The reaction of Wolfe's spirit likewise bore him aloft, and sustained him. Both heroes were beloved by their men and respected by their officers; and though Wolfe had not so many opportunities of exhibiting his genius for command, he was Nelson's compeer in zeal for the public good, untiring energy, intuitive judgment, and prompt decision. But Nelson, it must be admitted, was vain-glorious; his race was for "a peerage or Westminster Abbey." † Herein he was inferior to Wolfe, whose highest ambition was to prove his disinterested patriotism, "and not be over-solicitous about the event."

The Lieutenant-Colonel writes to his father, on the 26th of February, that, as things had taken a more pacific turn, he would not, for the present, require any pecuniary assistance; and some days later he says, that whenever he calls for aid, "it shall be to serve the King as you yourself would serve him. If there is a war, I must either rise or fall; in either case I am provided for; but as I would willingly enjoy the society of my friends without being troublesome to them, I should rather prefer the former as the means of doing it, and having, as yet, some little relish of life." Then, commenting on the promotion of officers of his own and

* Southey's 'Life of Nelson,' chap. i.

† *Ibid.*, chap. v.

his father's regiments, he adds: "It is a sound piece of policy to put troops in good humour before a war, and to keep them so afterwards by repeated acts of justice and kindness. The affections of military men are easily won, and as easily kept; they only ask regular preferment, and to be treated with common humanity." In conclusion, he observes that musketry will be wanted on board the fleet, and until marines are raised they must have Infantry; and a letter is enclosed for young Allen, to be forwarded to him by his mother.*

The letter which follows is to Wolfe's old friend Rickson, who, having returned from Nova Scotia, was now at Fort Augustus. It exhibits the fervour of his friendship as well as his zeal and vigilance, and shows that, like Nelson, Wolfe could not bear tame and slow measures. Qualities so opposite,—such gentleness and such fierceness,—are seldom united, and it is still rarer to find them so vividly expressed by the same pen.

My dear Friend,

Just as I received your letter the drum beat to arms, and we have been in a bustle ever since. Now that it has become a little calm again I will gather up my wits together, and collect my friendly sentiments (a little dispersed by the sound of war) to answer it. Be so good, for the time to come, to presume with yourself that you have a right to correspond with me whenever you please, and as often; and be persuaded that you cannot do me a greater pleasure than by writing to me. I want to persuade you that neither time nor

* The Allens were connected with Greenwich Hospital, and the youth for whom the letter was written was Richard Allen, who had recently been appointed an ensign of Otway's, then serving in Ireland. The subject, doubtless, was similar to that of the letter to "Dear Huty," and to another be noticed.

distance, nor different fortune, either has, or ever will, make the least alteration in my affection towards your little person, and that, in all probability, I shall die as much your friend as I have lived, whether at the end of one or twenty years, of which disposition in me, if I had opportunity to convince you, you should have sufficient proof. Though I know how reasonable and philosophic a man you are, yet I shall not allow you quite as much merit as I should to another in your situation. The remembrance of Nova Scotia makes Fort Augustus a paradise; your sufferings there will be no small aid to your contentment, for nothing can well happen of greater trial than what you have already overcome.

Since I began my letter to you yesterday, there's a fresh and a loud report of war. More ships are ordered to be fitted out, and we must expect further preparations suited to the greatness of the occasion. You in the north will be now and then alarmed. Such a succession of errors, and such a train of ill-behaviour as the last Scotch war did produce, can hardly, I believe, be matched in history. Our future annals will, I hope, be filled with more stirring events. What if the garrisons of the forts had been under the orders of a prudent, resolute man (yourself, for instance), would not they have found means to stifle the rebellion in its birth? and might not they have acted more like soldiers and good subjects than it appears they did? What would have been the effect of a sudden march into the middle of that clan who were the first to move? What might have been done by means of hostages of wives and children, or the chiefs themselves? How easy a small body, united, prevents the junction of distant corps and how favourable the country where you are for such a manœuvre! If, notwithstanding all precautions, they get together, a body of troops may make a diversion, by laying waste a country that the male inhabitants have left to prosecute rebellious schemes. How soon must they return to the defence of their property (such as it is), their wives, their children, their houses, and their cattle!

But, above all, the secret, sudden night-march into the midst of them; great patrols of fifty, sixty, or one hundred men each, to terrify them; letters to the chiefs, threatening fire and sword and certain destruction if they dare to stir; movements that seem mysterious, to keep the enemy's attention upon you, and their fears awake; these, and the like, which your experience, reading, and good sense would point out, are the means to prevent mischief. If one was to ask what preparations were made for the defence of the forts, I believe they would be found insufficient. There are some things that are absolutely necessary for an obstinate resistance,—and such there always should be against rebels,—as tools, fascines, turf or sods, arms for the breach (long spontoons or halberds), palisades innumerable; whole trees, converted into that use, stuck in the ditch, to hinder an assault. No one of these articles was thought of, either at Fort Augustus or Fort George; and, in short, nothing was thought of but how to escape from an enemy most worthy of contempt. One vigorous sortie would have raised the siege of Fort Augustus; one huudred men would have nailed up the battery, or carried the artillery into the castle.

I wish you may be besieged in the same manner; you will put a speedy end to the rebellion, and foil their arms in the first attempt: *les Messieurs de Guise se sont très-mal comporté!* If there's war, I hope the General in the north will not disperse the troops by small parties, as has been practised hitherto, but rather make choice of certain good stations for bodies that can defend themselves, or force their way home to the forts, if occasion require it. At Laggan Achadrom, for example, they should build a strong redoubt, surrounded by rows of palisades and trees, capable to contain two hundred men at least. This is a post of great importance, and should be maintained in a most determined manner, and the Mac Donalds might knock their heads against it to very little purpose. Old doting Humphrey,* who is newly married I

* Lieut.-General (Humphrey) Bland, who succeeded General Churchill as Commander-in-chief in Scotland, was married to Miss Betty Dalrymple, niece to the late Earl of Stair, on the 13th January, 1755. (Gentleman's Magazine.)

find, will be a good deal occupied at home, and fondly, no doubt; so you must not expect much aid from that quarter; there's our weak side.

Mr. M'Pherson should have a couple of hundred men in his neighbourhood, with orders to massacre the whole clan, if they show the least symptom of rebellion. They are a war-like tribe, and he is a cunning, resolute fellow himself. They should be narrowly watched; and the party there should be well commanded. Trapaud will have told you that I tried to take hold of that famous man with a very small detachment. I gave the sergeant orders—in case he should succeed, and was attacked by the clan, with a view to rescue their chief—to kill him instantly, which I concluded would draw on the destruction of the detachment, and furnish me with a sufficient pretext (without waiting for any instructions) to march into their country, *où j'aurais fait main basse, sans miséricorde.* Would you believe that I am so bloody? It was my real intention; and I hope such execution will be done upon the first that revolt, to teach them their duty, and keep the Highlands in awe.* They are a people better governed by fear than favour.

My little governor talked to me, some time ago, of a parcel of musket-balls that belonged to us, which he offered to send us. We fire bullets continually, and have great need of them; but, as I foresee much difficulty and expense in the removal, I wish he would bestow them, or a part, upon you; and let me recommend the practice, you'll soon find the advantage of

* Evan M'Pherson, of Cluny, Lord Lovat's son-in-law, had been a captain in one of the Independent Highland companies appointed by Government previous to the rebellion of 1745. He was made a willing prisoner by a party of the rebels, and joining the Pretender's cause, became an outlaw. Notwithstanding the vigilance of the military, he contrived to conceal himself for years after the battle of Culloden, and occasionally ventured to join his family in his own castle. On one of these occasions—possibly the same that Wolfe speaks of—a detachment repaired to his house, in hopes of securing him. One of the clan, however, perceiving the soldiers, gave warning of their approach, when, Cluny being intoxicated, his servants wrapped him up in a plaid, carried him out, and concealed him in the brushwood that skirted the river until the party had passed. (See Anderson's 'Guide to the Highlands.')

it. Marksmen are nowhere so necessary as in a mountainous country; besides, firing balls at objects teaches the soldiers to level incomparably, makes the recruits steady, and removes the foolish apprehension that seizes young soldiers when they first load their arms with bullets. We fire, first singly, then by files, one, two, three, or more, then by ranks, and lastly by platoons; and the soldiers see the effects of their shots, especially at a mark or upon water. We shoot obliquely, and in different situations of ground, from heights downwards, and contrariwise. I use the freedom to mention this to you, not as one prescribing to another, but to a friend who may accept or reject; and because, possibly, it may not have been thought of by your commander, and I have experience of its great utility.

I have not been in London all this winter. If the state of our affairs had permitted it, I should certainly have waited upon your sister. You could not propose a thing more agreeable to me; for I think I must necessarily love all your kindred, at least all that love you. Pray ask Trap if he knows anything of Lady Culloden*—how she is as to health; for I have a particular esteem for her, am obliged to her for civilities shown me, and interest myself in her welfare. She seemed, poor lady, to be in a very ill state of health when I was in that country. I could pass my time very pleasantly at Fort Augustus upon your plan, and with your assistance. There is no solitude with a friend. I hope to hear from you now and then, as your inclination prompts, or your leisure allows; the oftener the better. I wish you all manner of good, and am truly, my dear friend,

Your faithful and affectionate servant,

J. W.

Exeter, 7th March, 1755.

My compliments to Mrs. Trapaud and the governor.

I was interrupted in the beginning of the letter, and the post came in from London before I began afresh."†

* Mrs. Forbes, of Culloden.

† A tradition exists, in Exeter, of a disturbance in the town from

It will be recollected that Captain Alexander Trapaud, whom Wolfe familiarly calls "Trap," had been one of his own officers when at Fort Augustus in 1752. In June, 1753, he became Lieutenant-Governor of the fort; and so content was he with his Highland home, that he remained there until his death, in December, 1796, in the eighty-fourth year of his age. As there were no inns for the accommodation of tourists in this remote region during the three-and-forty years of Trapaud's residence, he occasionally had the opportunity of extending his hospitality to strangers. Thus, in 1773, when Dr. Johnson and Boswell were on their way to the Hebrides, they were entertained at Fort Augustus on the night of the 30th of August. "Mr. Trapaud, the Governor," says the Doctor, in his own stately style, "treated us with that courtesy which is so closely connected with the military character. He came out to meet us beyond the gates, and apologized that, at so late an hour, the rules of a garrison suffered him to give us entrance only at the postern."*

Boswell tells us that the Governor was delighted with the Doctor's talk :—" I like to hear him (said he), it is so majestick ; " and gives us a peep into the interior of the fort :—" It was comfortable to find ourselves in a well-built little square, and a neatly-furnished house, in

the circumstance of a soldier being struck on parade by, it is said, Wolfe himself. "This," as the editor of a professional periodical remarks, "is most likely incorrect, and may have been done by the Adjutant, or some other officer, as Wolfe had a great dislike to anything of the kind, and would not permit it on any account." ('Naval and Military Gazette,' Saturday, July 13th, 1850.)

* 'Journey to the Hebrides,' Johnson's Works, Oxford ed. vol. ix. p. 30.

good company, and with a good supper before us; in short, with all the conveniences of civilized life in the midst of rude mountains. Mrs. Trapaud, and the Governor's daughter, and her husband, Captain Newmarsh, were all most obliging and polite. The Governor had excellent animal spirits, the conversation of a soldier, and somewhat of a Frenchman,* to which his extraction entitles him."†

* The Captain and his brother, General (Cyrus) Trapaud, who died in 1801, the oldest officer in the service, are said to have been descended from Marshal Turenne. See Haydn's 'Book of Dignities,' p. 319.

† Boswell's 'Journal of Tour,' etc.; London, 1785, p. 147.

CHAPTER XIV.

WINCHESTER.—SOUTHAMPTON.—CANTERBURY.

MARCH, 1755—MAY, 1756.

THE Earl of Albemarle having died, at Paris, in December, 1754, his eldest son, George, Lord Bury, succeeded to the peerage, and was soon afterwards appointed to a cavalry regiment. The colonelcy of the Twentieth being therefore vacant, Wolfe very justly considered that, after having efficiently commanded the corps for six years, he had a right to the promotion, or, at least, that none but a General officer would be put over him. The appointment was in abeyance when he quitted Exeter, and he remained in suspense for some days after his arrival at his new quarters in Winchester on the 25th of March. In a letter home on the following day, he expresses his impatience to know whether it will be peace or war. "All my hopes of success," he writes, "must be grounded upon right and just pretensions. I must serve, and serve well, or I can't get forward; for who will be at the trouble to solicit for me out of pure friendship?" Writing to his father on the 12th of April, he observes that Honeywood's having been appointed to succeed Lord Bury was no compliment to *him*, and that he was resolved not to serve one moment longer than he could with honour, if he should starve.* After desiring the General not to speak about his vexation, he adds: "I am going to Portsmouth to see how the fleet hold their anchors in a storm, for the wind rages most violently."

A few days after, Mrs. Wolfe is told—"It is difficult to say whether there will be a war or not; the French will determine that as they please, as it suits their interest or conveniency. If you arm yourself with philosophy, you are mistress of all events. I have a natural indolence of temper that helps me in some cases, but I have too much impatience for much sharp pain." Reverting to his dogs, about whom he would not trouble her did he not know that she loved them, he says: "Little Romp is come up, and a pretty creature she is. If you would have me keep her in preference to Flurry, I can do it, and you may have her again when you get rid of the rest."†

In his next letter to his father, the Lieutenant-Colonel explains the cause of his discontent. Lord Albemarle had informed him that the regiment was to be given to General Fowke, and that he (Wolfe) was to be conti-

* Philip Honeywood was gazetted to the colonelcy of the Twentieth on the 8th of April, 1755, and removed in May the year following to the 9th Dragoons. He rose to the rank of General, was many years Governor of Hull, M.P. for Appleby, and died in 1785.

† Another time he writes: "I am afraid the cook gives the dogs too much meat; flesh is very dangerous for dogs, and spoils their noses. While Ball eats his dinner, the coachman might lock up the spaniels and give 'em a little pot-liquor, or bread and milk, or oatmeal and water. Servants think that a dog is never well fed unless he gets scraps of salt beef, pork, etc., whereas these strong victuals are certain destruction; and they should never want water." On another occasion, he orders any dog that refused water to be instantly shot.

nued in the command, when, three or four days afterwards, Honeywood was appointed. Although by no means pleased, he endeavoured to console himself by the consideration that it would save him additional pains and expense; and says: "I may jog on in the easiest position in the army, and sleep and grow fat." Admirals Boscawen and Moyston had sailed from Spithead with twelve sail of the line, and he feared that Boscawen would sweep away a detachment of his best men stationed at Plymouth.

On the 1st of May, Wolfe was on a visit at Freefolk, only fourteen miles from Winchester. Colonel Honeywood had consented to his absence for two or three weeks, and he purposed running home to see his father and mother. Winchester was very dull, but five- or six-and-twenty young military men would enliven it. The people in general were civil and obliging. On his return from Blackheath to quarters, towards the end of May, his first business was to look out for a horse for his mother, but the horse he had been recommended turned out to be a broken-winded mare. He would try again, however, and won't rest till he sees her properly mounted. His restlessness is very apparent; one day he is at Southampton, regulating the affairs of the detachment there; another at Freefolk, whence he returns to Winchester, where they are going to execute a deserter, "which, though necessary, is a very dismal sight."

On the 20th of June, Mrs. Wolfe is informed that the fleet is more formidable than any England had ever fitted out, and that the army was getting more and more complete. The cost was the worst feature. He urges the propriety of the General's investing some capital in a little landed estate for *her* security,—two or three hundred a year. There must be some secure provision for her; his father has his regiment, and he himself has his "trade." He dances incessantly, and mends upon it; his success will encourage him to be more the servant of the ladies. And finally, reverting to public matters, he is going to Portsmouth, to see "the dreadful, though pleasing sight of our mighty navy."

He tells his father, on the 29th, that seven- or eight-and-twenty great ships, fully manned with able seamen, lie off Spithead, waiting for news from America. "In the meanwhile the naval officers eat and drink very comfortably, and entertain their friends in a sumptuous manner." He is going to Portsmouth again; his Royal Highness the Duke is expected; such a military scene is not to be neglected. Has heard favourable reports of Braddock, and the good behaviour of the people under him. There are hopes of success if Baron Dieskau does not arrive in time with succours to stop his progress.* "Our affairs in the East Indies," he adds, "are upon the decline. At the expiration of the truce for three months, it is supposed that hostilities will be resumed with as much violence as ever. Our military concerns are under the guidance of a very poor, insignificant officer, and the death of Scott is an irreparable damage to the Indian Army."†

* The French General, Baron de Dieskau, had recently been sent to Canada with 3000 men. In an unsuccessful attack upon General Johnson's camp, near Lake George, on the 8th of September, 1755, he was taken prisoner, mortally wounded.

† A suspension of hostilities for three months was agreed upon by

On the Lieutenant-Colonel's return to Winchester after his second visit to Portsmouth, the General is informed that the scene was splendid. The Duke, who was well received, had been remarkably kind to him. He had dined with Lord Anson on board the 'Prince,' and Governor Hawley, as vivacious and spirited as ever, was at his post to receive his Royal Highness.* Wolfe then states that he is going back to Southampton, and, while in the neighbourhood of his Aunt Burcher, he would wait upon her if he knew her direction.

Amidst his professional distractions, the dangerous illness of his mother calls forth an admirable token of filial piety:—

Lymington, 19th July, 1755.

Dear Madam,

I wish I could say anything that could comfort you or advise anything that would do you good. By gentle exercise and care of yourself I hope your strength will return, and with that your spirits. I have gratitude and tenderness enough to be greatly affected at your distress, and though grief is not to be sought after, yet I would not for the world but partake of all your misfortunes. Would to God that the little moment that is allowed us in this life had some ease and peace in it,

M. Godheu and Mr. Saunders, on the 11th of October, 1754, and on the 26th of December a provisional treaty was signed. The insignificant officer to whom Wolfe alludes was Colonel Aldercron, who, after the death of Colonel Scott, had superior rank in the Royal Army in India, and consequently took precedence of Clive. See Keightley's 'History of India,' pp. 69, 72.

* The 'Gentleman's Magazine' gives a vivid account of the Duke's reception at Portsmouth:—"His Royal Highness was met by the rope-makers of the dockyard, three miles from the town, in white shirts and black caps, carrying streamers in their hands. They ran before his landau into the town. . . . The bells rang, colours were displayed, and everything to demonstrate the pleasure of the inhabitants in seeing his Royal Highness amongst them." (July, 1755.)

or that we had firmness enough to overcome our ills. I know you would be content with a little share of health, and for my part, I have nothing to ask but just as much resolution as fits a soldier. For riches, honours, possessions, and the dazzling advantages of this world, I disregard them; my utmost desire and ambition is to look steadily upon danger, and the greatest happiness that I wish for here is to see you happy. Resignation to the will and disposition of Heaven is so consistent with piety, charity, and a good mind, that I doubt not your thorough resignation. Don't let a thought about me disturb you. You have done more than I am afraid I deserve. I lament that ever I gave you a moment of uneasiness, though, I think, I did not mean it, and of that I hope you will be convinced. I wish you better health with great sincerity, and beg my duty to my father.

Such is the affectionate consolation of the son. On the very same day he wrote to his old companion Rickson, who was, at this time, Aide-de-camp to Major-General Lord George Beauclerk, at Inverness. The contrast presented by the two letters shows how forcibly the writer could express the opposite phases of his mind:—

My dear Friend,

If I had not been well convinced by your letter that you needed not my counsel to guide you, and that the steps you were taking were prudent and sensible beyond what I could advise, you should have heard from me something sooner; for the public service, and your honour and well-doing, are matters of high concern to me. I am sorry that I cannot take to myself the merit of having served you upon this occasion. I would have done it if it had been in my power; but I knew nothing of your new employment till Calcraft mentioned it to me.* You are, I believe, so well in the Duke's

* John Calcraft, originally a clerk in the War Office, was the most influential army agent of the time. After enriching himself under the

opinion, that Mr. Fox had no difficulty to place you where you are, and where, I am fully persuaded, you will acquit yourself handsomely. To study the character of your General, to conform to it, and by that means to gain his esteem and confidence, are such judicious measures that they cannot fail of good effects. If I am not mistaken, Lord George is a very even-tempered man, and one that will hearken to a reasonable proposal.*

If the French resent the affront put upon them by Mr. Boscawen,† the war will come on hot and sudden; and they will certainly have an eye to the Highlands. Their friends and allies in that country were of great use to them in the last war. That famous diversion cost us great sums of money and many lives, and left the *Pais-Bas* to Saxe's mercy. I am much of your opinion, that, without a considerable aid of foreign troops, the Highlanders will never stir. I believe their resentments are strong, and the spirit of revenge prevalent amongst them; but the risk is too great without help: however, we ought to be cautious and vigilant. We ought to have good store of meal in the forts to feed the troops in the winter, in case they be wanted; plenty of intrenching tools and hatchets, for making redoubts and cutting palisades, etc.; and we should be cautious not to expose the troops in small parties, dispersed through the Highlands, where there is the

patronage of Henry Fox (Lord Holland), he deserted to Pitt, whose confidence he possessed for many years, as appears from the 'Chatham Correspondence.' Calcraft is supposed to have been in the secret of "Junius;" yet that writer accuses him of rioting in the plunder of the army, and becoming a patriot because he could not be a peer (Letter 59). He died at Ingress Abbey, Kent, in 1772, worth upwards of a quarter of a million sterling; and bequeathed £1000 to Sir Philip Francis, and to Lady Francis an annuity of £200.

* Lord George Beauclerk, sixth son of Charles, first Duke of St. Albans, was Colonel of the 19th Regiment, and a Major-General. He was Commander-in-chief in Scotland for some time, Member of Parliament for Windsor, and died in 1768.

† The capture of the 'Alcide' and the 'Lys,' off Cape Breton, when the Governor of Louisbourg, with four French officers of note, were made prisoners, and £30,000 sterling taken.

least apprehension of a commotion. A few well-chosen posts in the middle of those clans that are the likeliest to rebel, with a force sufficient to entrench and defend themselves, and with positive orders never to surrender to the Highlanders (though never so numerous), but either to resist in their posts till relieved, or force their way through to the forts, would, I think, have lively effects. A hundred soldiers, in my mind, are an overmatch for five hundred of your Highland milice; and when they are told so in a proper way, they believe it themselves. It will be your business to know the exact strength of the rebel clans, and to inquire into the abilities of their leaders, especially of those that are abroad. There are people that can inform you. There ought to be an engineer at the forts to inform the General of what will be wanted for their defence, and to give directions for the construction of small redoubts, where the General pleases to order them.

Nobody can say what is to become of us yet. If troops are sent into Holland, we expect to be amongst the first. We are quartered at Winchester and Southampton, but turned out for the assizes. The fleet at Spithead expects orders to sail every hour. They are commanded by Sir E. Hawke, who has the Admirals Byng and West to assist him. There are about thirty great ships, and some frigates; the finest fleet, I believe, that this nation ever put to sea, and excellently well manned. The marines embarked yesterday, to the number, I suppose, of about 1000 men; others will be taken up at Plymouth, if they are wanted.

I lodged with a Mrs. Grant,* whom perhaps you know. She was very careful of me, and very obliging. If you see her, it will be doing me a pleasure if you will say that I remember it. Do you know Mrs. Forbes, of Culloden? I have a particular respect and esteem for that lady. She showed me a good deal of civility while I lay in the North. If you are acquainted, pray make my best compliments to her, and let me know how she is as to her health. *Au reste*, you must be so kind to write now and then, and I will be punc-

* When he was stationed at Inverness.

tual to answer, and give any intelligence of what is doing where I happen to be. A letter, directed to me at General Wolfe's, at Blackheath, Kent, will be forwarded to the remotest regions. I am, my dear friend,

Your affectionate and faithful servant,

JAMES WOLFE.

Lymington, 19th July, 1755.

Having paid the promised visit to his father's sister in the New Forest, the interview with his poor relation is described in the following to the General:—

Southampton, 14th August, 1755.

Dear Sir,

I paid my respects to Mrs. Burcher a few days since, and found a very surprising old gentlewoman. I was struck with the resemblance between my uncle Wat and her. She has not only all his features, but his manner and way of talking, and his gestures. She has a healthy florid look, though a little paralytic, and is full of grievous complaints. Mr. Burcher has the appearance of civility and good-breeding. They live in a lonely miserable mansion in the forest, and all about has the look of indigence and decay. The poor gentlewoman expressed herself in a very grateful manner for the kindness and support that she has received from you, and seemed a good deal affected at the sight of me. You may believe I did not stay long there; but I have promised to see her again before we leave this place, if our march is not too sudden.

I find that some of the troops in our neighbourhood are in motion towards the capital; whether we shall follow or march elsewhere is to us unknown, but my private sentiments are that we sha'n't long lie idle. You are nearer to the fountain of intelligence than we are, but I believe you take as little pains to be informed as your son. I don't think there are two men in the kingdom who are at less trouble upon that score. I hope my mother continues to mend. Mrs. Burcher sent you a buck last week, which she hopes you received in good order.

Although distant from the source of intelligence,—

and the morning newspaper did not reach Southampton before breakfast-time in those days,—it is not to be supposed that Wolfe was altogether so indifferent to passing events as his own words, if read literally, would lead one to imagine. He looked anxiously towards America, as if he foresaw that it was there the rivalry between England and France was eventually to be determined. Though the two nations had been nominally at peace since the hollow treaty of 1748, hostilities between their settlements in America and in India were continued with increased rancour year after year. In North America especially, the boundaries of the British and French colonies never having been definitely agreed upon, it followed, as a matter of course, that complaints of frequent encroachments were forwarded to the respective governments. Only one instance of these grievances, however, comes at present within our scope.

France, in order to connect Canada with Louisiana, had erected a chain of forts from the great lakes along the river Ohio to the Mississippi. The prospect of the French settling upon the Ohio, and their repeated incursions into the British territories, caused great alarm to the English colonists. At length, in 1753, the evil had grown so unbearable, that the Governor of Virginia determined to attack Fort Duquesne, the principal French post. He therefore sent Washington, then a major in the Colonial service, and about 500 men, with instructions, should remonstrance prove ineffectual, to reduce the fort; but ere they reached their destination they were attacked by a superior force, and obliged to surrender. Governor Dinwiddie having represented the critical state of affairs to the British Government, it was resolved, in 1754, to reinforce the Colonial army with 2000 Royal troops under General Braddock, who was appointed Commander-in-chief in America. Notwithstanding their desire for succour, the colonists were no less eager for pecuniary profit; so that, owing chiefly to the difficulty and delay of obtaining supplies and means of transport, Braddock's army did not set out from Alexandria, in Virginia, until the 10th of June, 1755, and it was the 8th of July before they arrived within a few miles of Fort Duquesne. The story of the massacre that ensued has been too often told to need repetition; the primary causes of the disaster, as traced by Wolfe in the following letter to his father, will have more novelty for the reader:—

Southampton, 4th September, 1755.

Dear Sir,

The accounts of Mr. Braddock's defeat are not yet clear enough to form a right judgment of the cause of it; but I do myself believe that the cowardice and ill-behaviour of the men far exceeded the ignorance of the chief, who, though not a master of the difficult art of war, was yet a man of sense and courage. I have but a very mean opinion of the Infantry in general. I know their discipline to be bad, and their valour precarious. They are easily put into disorder, and hard to recover out of it. They frequently kill their officers through fear, and murder one another in their confusion.* Their shameful behaviour in Scotland, at Port L'Orient, at Mêlle,†

* "It is said that the greatest slaughter among our officers was not made by the enemy; but that as they ran several fugitives through to intimidate the rest, when they attempted in vain to rally them, some others, who escaped the same fate, discharged their pieces at their officers." (Scots Magazine, 1755, p. 403.)

† An expedition sailed from Plymouth for Port L'Orient, on the

and upon many less important occasions, clearly denoted the extreme ignorance of the officers, and the disobedient and dastardly spirit of the men.*

Was there ever such a slaughter of officers as upon this expedition? and did ever the Geneva and p— of this country operate more shamefully and violently upon the dirty inhabitants of it under the denomination of soldiers? I am sorry to say that our method of training and instructing the troops is extremely defective, and tends to no good end. We are lazy in time of peace, and of course want vigilance and activity in war. Our military education is by far the worst in Europe, and all our concerns are treated with contempt or totally neglected. It will cost us very dear some time hence. I hope the day is at a distance, but I am afraid it will come.

On the 13th of September we find Wolfe once more at Freefolk, from which place he congratulates his mother upon the benefit she had derived from Mr. Warde's new medicine, and says, that if he had thought his being with her during the violence of her illness would have been any relief to her, he would have asked leave as a favour; but, being unaccustomed to sick people, he would only have been grieved to see her in a state he could not alleviate. A week later, he writes from Southampton to his father, and speaks of his aunt Abthorpe's death as a mercy, since she could hardly have

coast of Brittany, September 14th, 1746. The land forces, under General Sinclair, disembarked on the 18th, summoned the town to surrender, fired upon it, re-embarked without obstacle, and returned to England on the 14th of October. The men went marauding about the country, and upwards of 300 were killed by the French peasantry. The affair at Mêlle, in 1745, has been noticed.

* It is not improbable that these reflections prompted Wolfe, when soon afterwards stationed at Canterbury, to issue his "Instructions for the Twentieth Regiment in case the French should land." They were published in several periodicals after his death.

recovered her health, owing to her fanatical notions of religion.

The letter to his mother which follows, may be allowed to speak for itself:—

Southampton, 28th September, 1755.

Dear Madam,

I am delighted to hear that your sufferings are in some degree lessened; the presence of your friends will become every day more and more agreeable as you acquire strength and spirits for society. How happy I feel myself in your recovery, and with how much more satisfaction shall I see you than formerly, when I almost always found you overloaded with misery! I dare say you were always convinced of my affection for you, and of my gratitude. It was not this melancholy occasion that gave birth to it, though perhaps it brought it more to light. I am unfortunate in this respect, that my nature requires some extraordinary events to produce itself. I want that attention and those assiduous cares that commonly go along with good-nature and humanity. In the common occurrences of life, I own that I am not seen to advantage.

You must take care of cold this winter, as the medicine you have used is of very powerful operation, and leaves a weakness behind it that requires the utmost precautions. When you are below in the parlour, the hall-door should always be kept close shut, and you must sit upon carpets.*

* The general use of floor-carpets is of comparatively recent date. The first carpet made in England was manufactured (*circa* 1735) by one Anthony Duffosy, who was brought over from France by Lord Pembroke. A patent for the exclusive privilege of manufacturing carpets in England was soon afterwards obtained by a firm in Wilton. The patent specifying that the carpets were to be made with bobbin and anchor, some persons at Kidderminster procured looms on the same principle, and by using *bobbin and ball*, instead of *bobbin and anchor*, evaded the law. Such was the origin of Kidderminster carpets, the brilliancy and permanency of whose colours are said to be owing to the peculiar properties of the water of the river Stour for scouring

There are many fair days in October that will invite you out, and you should neglect none of them. Prefer that to all other affairs and concerns whatever. You must be extremely careful of what rooms you go to play at cards in, and where you sit; and beware of the Assembly. Have as many parties at your own house as possible, and go little abroad.

In the middle of winter, if you stay much at home, I will come and shut myself up with you for three weeks or a month, and play at piquet from morning till night, and you shall laugh at my short red hair as much as you please.* I'm sure you would smile now if you saw me as I am with the covering that nature has given me. I intend to devote myself this winter to my profession, and shall read without ceasing. If you would have me with you for a short while, it must be upon the condition that I never stir out of the house after dinner. With that indulgence, I shall engage to be at home whenever you are in the evening. My mornings are always, as you know, divided between exercise and study. I have been very idle all this summer,—if a man may venture to say so who has given up much of his time to the ladies. If there is to be a war, we should be prepared for it; if not, I am entirely at your service. I go back to-morrow to Sir J. Mordaunt's for a week; after that I shall take up my residence at Winchester.

After leaving Freefolk, on the 4th of October, the Lieutenant-Colonel met the regiment at Winchester, where the several detachments assembled to be reviewed, in the first instance by General Mordaunt, and afterwards

and striking. (Britton's 'Beauties of Wiltshire;' and 'Beauties of England and Wales,' Worcestershire.)

* The difficulty he frequently experienced in finding "a good honest groom that could dress a wig," may have induced him to anticipate the fashion of doffing the article. Officers were often nicknamed by the men from their wigs; thus, Lieut.-General Whiteford was known as *White-wig;* two Generals named Pattison were *Queue* and *Toupie;* and Mr. Wood, of the Artillery, was called *Wig-Wood*, to distinguish him from another officer of the same name. (Grose's 'Olio.')

by the Duke of Cumberland. "Our whole business," he writes, "seems to be confined to reviews."

A fortnight afterwards he remarks to his father:—"When the nations have armed themselves to the highest pitch of their strength, I suppose they will try which is the strongest. The French are getting their fleet into order, and threaten an invasion. Hostilities have begun in Europe and America." Under these circumstances, he again urges the necessity of providing a little landed security for his mother. "Should the war turn out to our disadvantage, she may be in danger of starving, if you keep all your money in the funds. You have your regiment, and my employment is always bread; but my mother may outlive the struggle, and then who will help the poor lady?" From the next and last letter from Winchester, written on the 24th of October, to Mrs. Wolfe, we learn that the troops are moving towards the coast. He is at a loss to conjecture whether this is a real or a political invasion, but hopes it will end well. Fisher, the General's agent, or Tim Brett, might assist in finding a little estate; but as it would be inconsistent with his father's honour to sell out his stock just then, it would be well to wait awhile. The letter concludes with these words:—

In case of an invasion, I imagine my father will think it his duty to be at the head of his regiment, at least as much as his strength will allow. Should matters be carried far, and money be wanted, he should be the first to offer his plate for the public service. He might buy a post-chaise, and hire horses to be in readiness; and if ever he is distressed for quarters, he may be sure of mine, or my field-bed in camp. The General should show himself at St. James's with a cheerful, willing countenance, that the King may see how good a servant he has, and how well his inclinations lead him to serve the good old monarch. If ever you happen to be distressed, you will find a certain support in your son. Be assured that you will know me best when you have most occasion for my assistance; but I desire no such proof of my disposition. May you both live long in ease and peace; but I fear there are ugly times at hand. Perhaps we may not see them.

It is not easy to bring home to ourselves now the panic throughout England at the period under notice, from the expected invasion by the French, when a wedding *cortége* so alarmed the inhabitants of the villages through which it passed, that they shut themselves up in their houses, and arming themselves with pitchforks, etc., cried out, "The invasion is come!"* Amongst the troops moved into Kent was Honeywood's regiment, which was quartered in Canterbury. On the 5th of November, the Lieutenant-Colonel wrote a short letter home, in which he says:—"We have two regiments of Foot and a regiment of Dragoons, a crowd of officers and soldiers. General Hawley is expected in a few days, to keep us all in order. If there is an invasion, they could not make use of a more unfit person; for the troops dread his severity, hate the man, and hold his military knowledge in contempt." The following letter to Mrs. Wolfe needs no abridgment:—

Canterbury, 8th November, 1755.

Dear Madam,

The officers of the army in general are persons of so little application to business, and have been so ill educated, that it must not surprise you to hear that a man of common industry

* See Mrs. Delany's Autobiography, vol. iii. p. 401.

is in reputation amongst them. I reckon it a very great misfortune to this country that I, your son, who have, I know, but a very moderate capacity, and some degree of diligence a little above the ordinary run, should be thought, as I generally am, one of the best officers of my rank in the service. I am not at all vain of the distinction. The comparison would do a man of genius very little honour, and does not illustrate* me by any means; and the consequence will be very fatal to me in the end, for as I rise in rank people will expect some considerable performances, and I shall be induced, in support of an ill-got reputation, to be lavish of my life, and shall probably meet that fate which is the ordinary effect of such conduct.

You have made yourself believe (perhaps it is to excuse your indolence) that you don't write well, but you sha'n't make me believe any such thing; or, if it was so, which is not really the case, you should remember that you are writing to your son, who is your friend, knows the many good qualities of your mind, and loves you. The Duke of Marlborough has been very civil to us all, and very particularly so to me; he goes to town to-morrow for a short stay.† I wish the French have not some mischief in their heads; but it can't reach you. If the General means to show himself, he should remember my former scheme for him. I have made some inquiry for a little purchase for you, but can't hear of anything fit for our purpose; and they are particularly high in their demands in this county, because of the extensive privi-

* "Illustrate."—Wolfe invariably uses this word in the sense of *to render illustrious.*

† Charles Spencer, fifth Earl of Sunderland, and second Duke of Marlborough, was grandson of the first and great Duke, who, leaving no male issue, his titles and honours were extended, by Act of Parliament, to the male issue of his daughters. On the death of Henrietta, Duchess of Marlborough, the above-mentioned Charles, as son and heir of Lady Anne Churchill, the second daughter, became Duke of Marlborough. Having entered the army, he fought at Dettingen, etc., and rose to the rank of Lieutenant-General. In 1758, he was the Commander-in-chief of the British forces on the Lower Rhine, and died of fever at Munster, on the 20th of October.

leges of a man of Kent who is a freeholder.* I wish it had been thought of two years ago. You may remember that I hinted it, and foretold that a war was not far off.

The letter you sent me came, as you guessed, from Goldsmith. I writ to him by the Duke's directions to inquire after an officer's widow in Ireland, who, he was told, had a son fit to serve, and his Royal Highness, who is for ever doing noble and generous actions, wanted to provide for that child. The father was killed at Fontenoy. If I don't keep a good watch on myself I must be a little vain, for the Duke has of late given me such particular marks of his esteem and confidence that I am ashamed not to deserve it better. We expect the Duke of Richmond next week, and Lord Albemarle. The Earl comes to introduce his cousin to the regiment,† and the Duke to do duty at quarters. That young man will make a considerable figure in our way, because he loves it, and has a strong understanding.

* The reason of the peculiar privileges enjoyed by the "Men of Kent" is said to be, "because the said county was not conquered with the rest of the kingdom, but surrendered itself up to the Conqueror by a peace made with him, saving to itself all liberties and free customs before that time had and used." As the story goes, some Kentish Malcolm improvised a moving wood, under cover of which his followers surrounded the Conqueror, when they threw away their "leafy screens," and with bow and arrow, spear and sword, demanded and obtained the confirmation of their customary laws. *Gavelkind* is the term applied to the privileges in general, the chief feature of which is the joint inheritance of all sons to the estate of their father; and lands are presumed to be subject to that usage till the contrary is proved. The first article of the Custumal of Kent declares "that all the bodies of Kentish men be free,"—a valuable boon under the feudal system. The men of Kent likewise claimed the right of being placed in the vanguard of the King's army; hence Drayton's eulogy on the county:—

"Of all the English shires be thou surnamed the free,
And foremost ever placed, when they shall reckoned be."

(See Hasted's 'Kent,' Lambarde's 'Perambulation,' etc.)

† The Duke of Richmond obtained a captaincy in the regiment under Wolfe, and his Grace's example was followed by the Marquis of Blandford.

In his next letter home, our hero puts in a plea for his father's Lieutenant-Colonel :—

Canterbury, 13th November, 1755.

Dear Sir,

I find that poor Lafausille has been extremely out of order. Nothing but the worst health in the world would, I am persuaded, have taken him away at this time. I mention this, because I remember that a sharp expression or two fell from me upon the score of my old acquaintance; and when one has done a man injustice, but in thought, the quickest and best reparation should be made.

I hear that the French are hard at work in cleaning the harbour of Dunkirk, and I hear they have got a good number of ships in that port. The English will never bear to have that harbour in its former condition; that alone is matter enough for a quarrel between the nations, already far advanced towards a war. We send a detachment to-morrow to escort our battalion guns (two for each regiment) from Rochester. Our camp necessaries will be with us in a few days. We are commanded to exercise as often as is convenient, that is, as often as the weather will permit. I am vastly distressed for a groom, or, rather, for a servant, who can take care of two horses for £7 or £8 a year, and seven shillings a week board wages. If my mother hears of any such person, I beg to have notice, and I beg she will employ somebody to inquire.

He writes to his mother, on the 2nd of December :—

I hear of you almost every day, which makes me some amends for the profound silence that reigns throughout the whole house. Donnellan tells you all the news of this place, and yet I believe his letters are short; however, better so than lists of the killed and wounded, or the progress of the French arms in Kent. They are extremely concerned that Admiral Smith is so posted as to make their attempts to land a little dangerous. They do not, I am sorry to say, discover the same degree of respect for us; on the contrary, they wish for nothing so much as to be quietly on shore, and then to make trial of our force. We have the name of the Duke of Marlborough to oppose to them, and some incomparable battalions, the like of which cannot, I'll venture to say, be found in any army. We are about as merry, as easy, and as indifferent as you may be supposed to be who sleep in security under our watch. Nobody seems to think that the French have either will, power, or inclination to resent the affronts put upon them; and some, I believe, doubt whether they are really out of humour with us or not. This melancholy destruction of the city of Lisbon is a great blow, though at a distance.* Long may such disasters be far off from us.

On the 27th of the same month the Lieutenant-Colonel tells his mother that they were so crowded together in Canterbury as to make him fear ill consequences, and the streets he describes as the dirtiest in the world. Speaking of the commission for the widow's son already alluded to, he says:—"The letter you sent me came from the widow of a poor officer who was killed at Fontenoy; she has a son fit to serve, and Lord Albemarle has undertaken to get him a pair of colours. I met with her by accident in my journey through Ireland, so, you see, I did not go there for nothing." As regarded himself, he had no prospect of preferment. If he knew how to secure his father £500 a year, in case he should give him his regiment, he might manage that; but would not enter into any arrangement without the Commander-in-chief's promise that it should be restored to the General should his son fall at the head of it; otherwise, the risk would be too great.

On the 8th of February, 1756, the Lieutenant-Colonel says:—"I believe the French would be pleased to invade

* The fatal earthquake on the 1st of November.

us, if they knew how to get over. My opinion is, that they will try what their fleet can do first, and if they beat ours, then we may expect a very formidable attack. We have been rather tardy in providing against their great power, but I still hope that it is not too late. The confidence, or rather stupidity, of the people of this country surpasses all belief. Secure in their ignorance and presumption, they set the whole force of France at defiance."

Mrs. Wolfe's brother, Captain Bradwardine Thompson, died about this time, after a lingering illness. Alluding to the circumstance, her son writes :—"I can't say I am sorry for my poor uncle's death, otherwise than as it is a matter of concern to you." The Duke's coming, he adds, must determine his going to town. From two short letters of the 12th of March, we learn that the regiment, which lay awhile at Dover, had suddenly marched for Portsmouth. All notions of peace were at an end; the most discerning people were of opinion that war must be the consequence of the steps taken by us in return for the attempts of the French. Embargo had been laid upon shipping, and there was a violent press for seamen: putting soldiers also on board the fleet showed that the maritime strength of the enemy was formidable. "However," the writer adds, "we must hope that fortune will favour us, since we will do our best to deserve her smiles." A few days afterwards Wolfe learned that his friend Amherst had got a regiment, and remarks to his father thereupon,—"Nobody deserves the King's favour better than that man."* In the same

* Jeffrey, afterwards Lord Amherst, was appointed to the colonelcy of the 15th Foot, May 22nd, 1756.

letter, he states that the Guards, who had been sent to Dover, comforted themselves with the hope of being soon recalled. On the 4th of April, he writes:—"The fine season will call us to business, and leave no excuse for the indolent. Many who call themselves soldiers, who, to excuse their shameful idleness, urge that there will be no war, act as if they were persuaded of the truth of it."

A fortnight later the Lieutenant-Colonel tells his father he has not been successful in the matter of young Adeane's commission, as the boy was too young, and wanted "a year more of the school."* He likewise alludes to the case of two unfortunate Ensigns, who were to be proceeded against in course of Common Law, one or both of whom were sure to be condemned; and, unless their youth and their condition when they committed the ill action should plead in their favour, forfeit their lives. The General being aware of the particulars, Wolfe does not narrate them; but contemporaneous periodicals furnish details of the painful story. A Mr. Brown and Mr. John Lauder, subalterns of Lord Charles Hay's regiment, were travelling in a post-chaise from Dartford to London. On reaching Shooter's Hill the post-boy naturally allowed his horses to slacken their pace, in spite of the drunken officers' threats. Brown at length jumped out of the chaise and knocked the boy down,

* James Whorwood, son of Simon Adeane, Esq., of Chalgrove, Oxfordshire, and Mary, third daughter of the Hon. and Rev. Henry Brydges (sister to Mrs. Inwood and Miss Brydges). In 1788 he was appointed to the colonelcy of the 45th Regiment, and became a lieutenant-general. He was a gentleman of the bedchamber to George III., M.P. for the county of Cambridge, and died in 1802.

and Lauder, following his companion, drew his sword, and ran it through the victim with such violence that the point stuck in the ground. They were tried at Rochester, when Lauder was found guilty of murder, and three days afterwards was executed on Penenden Heath.*

Towards the end of April Mrs. Wolfe is apprised that her son will visit her for three or four days; but, as he wishes to be retired, she must not mention it to any one, to save the trouble of visits. His last letter from Canterbury is dated the 20th of May, 1756, when the regiment had got the route, but as they would go no nearer to Blackheath than Westerham, he cannot wait upon his parents. "You can't imagine," he concludes, "how many heavy hearts there are; mine, although not altogether insensible, is the least oppressed of a score."

* In the same month a captain of Dragoons mortally stabbed the landlord of the Vine Tavern, in Bond Street, for not allowing him to sneak off without paying for his night's carouse; and another officer was killed by an infuriated corkcutter, whose wife he had seduced.

CHAPTER XV.

DEVIZES.—STROUD.—CIRENCESTER.

JUNE, 1756—MARCH, 1757.

ON the 1st of June the regiment arrived at Basingstoke, —about 120 miles from Canterbury,—after being eleven days on the road. The same evening Wolfe writes to his mother:—

In our march we have met with nothing extraordinary except the Hessian Grenadiers, whom we saw at exercise yesterday near Farnham. We have ruined half the publichouses upon the march, because they have quartered us in villages too poor to feed us without destruction to themselves. I saw Mr. and Mrs. Warde at Westerham; they asked much after you and the General, and presented their compliments. The Lisbon mail is arrived, so you may expect some account of the siege of Fort St. Philips, and of Admiral Byng's feats in the Mediterranean. If things take a bad turn, and by our management I don't know what other to expect, this war may rout the funds and destroy our public credit root and branch.*

* On the 16th of the same month, Pitt wrote from "Hayes" to Mr. Grenville:—"As to *quo sit Romana loco res*, I am almost as far from the hearing of it in our suburban village as you are in the midst of your quiet wide-spread lawn and deep embowering woods. I hear, however, from rumour that clouds gather on every side, and distress—infinite distress—seems to hem us in on all quarters. The same weak, infatuated conduct that begat this distress seems determined to increase and multiply it upon our heads. We are helpless and childish as ever,

The next letter (June 7) is from Bristol, whither Wolfe had come with the Duke of Richmond :—

As I believe that all the infantry of this nation is not sufficient to retake the Island of Minorca (by this time in the hands of the French), and as six or seven battalions may be thought enough for the defence of Gibraltar,—the Spaniards not interfering,—I conclude we shall lie quiet in our west-country camp or quarters till the enemy thinks to alarm us a second time with design to strike some fatal distant blow, either upon our islands or upon the continent of North America, or perhaps to complete the ruin of the East Indies. Are the measures taken for the relief of Minorca, or the proceedings of our Admiral, to be most admired? I shall be of your opinion hereafter, that we must have the odds of five to four to secure our success at sea. I flatter myself that the poor little abandoned garrison of St. Philip's will do courageously at least,—wisely and skilfully I do not expect; and that the troops in the course of the war will do nothing dishonourable, nor betray their country.

Minorca furnishes almost the sole topic of Wolfe's letters about this time; but it is needless to interrupt the personal narrative by any remarks upon a subject so generally familiar. Some time after his return to quarters, the following caustic note was dispatched to his father :—

Devizes, 27th June, 1756.

Dear Sir,

I wish you joy of Admiral Byng's escape, and of the safe arrival of our fleet at Gibraltar. General Blakeney has no great obligations to the Navy upon this occasion. They have

and worse still; if any among the ministry are disposed to be men, I hear they would be madmen, for the regret is that we have no Continent war. So much for those at the helm! The passengers, the city of all denominations are in alarm, and think the ship sinking." (Grenville Correspondence, vol. i. p. 167.)

left him in an ugly scrape, out of which, I am persuaded, he will only be delivered by a cannon-shot. The project of succouring Minorca, and the execution of the great design, went hand-in-hand successfully, and may probably end in a disgraceful peace. You are happy in your infirmity, for 'tis a disgrace to act in these dishonourable times. Our new colonel is expected to-day; his presence makes me a very idle man.*

The ancient town of Devizes, situated upon high ground in the middle of Wiltshire, was even then of considerable extent, with a large trade in broad-cloth. The houses, mostly of brick, having been built at various times and in different styles, their irregularity gave a quaint aspect to the narrow, crooked streets.† Although the duration of Wolfe's stay in Devizes was brief, there as elsewhere, tradition associates his name with the place,—an old house, once an inn, at the back of the Town Hall, being still pointed out as that in which he resided while enlisting soldiers into his regiment.‡ There is something so sacred about traditional associations, that, hazy and distorted though they commonly are, one should be cautious of disturbing them. But, as Wolfe loved quietness, and, when he could possibly do so, sought a retired locality for his abode, it looks improbable that he should lodge at an inn in the centre of the town. The local tradition, however, is sufficiently

* William Kingsley succeeded Honeywood in the colonelcy of the Twentieth on the 22nd May, 1756, and the regiment is better known as "Kingsley's" than by any other name. He commanded the corps at Minden, when the valour and discipline of the men whom Wolfe had trained contributed greatly to the victory. Colonel Kingsley was promoted to the rank of Lieutenant-General in 1760, and died in 1769.

† Britton's 'Wiltshire.'

‡ "Wiltoniensis." ('Notes and Queries,' first series, vol. v. (1852), p. 399.)

supported by the fact that business brought him occasionally to the inn, which served as a recruiting depôt.

Although confined to his room when he again writes home, he does not betray his illness in a playful letter to his mother on the 10th of July:—

Dear Madam,

The demand you make for my receipts looks as if you wanted them for your own use; I rather hope they are for your friends, knowing that you take as much care of them as of yourself. I have distinguished the receipts to do justice to both my old ladies. I have heard of my Lady Grey* very lately; she sent me her compliments, and, what was more (as she expressed it), her *love*. You see, I have the art of preserving the affections of my mistresses, and I may be vain of these conquests without offence, or danger to my reputation.

The King of Prussia (God bless him!) is our only ally, and we are solely obliged to the Duchy of Silesia for his friendship. I am sorry that they don't all unite against us, that our strength might be fully exerted and our force known. I myself believe that we are a match for the combined fleets of Europe, especially if our admirals and generals were all of the same spirit.

A week later he writes to his father as follows:—

Devizes, 17th July, 1756.

Dear Sir,

I am informed by a politician of this country that the loss of the Island of Minorca will not influence the Spanish court, nor engage them in a war against us. I wish my acquaintance may have good intelligence, and that the Spaniards may not be tempted by the cession of that island to

* There were three or four Ladies Grey at this period. Probably, however, the lady alluded to was Hannah, relict of Sir Henry Grey, of Howick, whose fourth son, Charles, afterwards Earl Grey de Howick, was then a captain of the *Twentieth*. It may therefore have been through him that Wolfe had heard of her ladyship.

become our enemies. But my own opinion is that they will, and the siege of Gibraltar by sea and land, with the combined fleets, will be the first consequence of that formidable union; in which, however, I am fully persuaded they will miscarry: provided always that the Lord Baron of Tyrawley, your neighbour,* takes care to have three months' provisions for eight or ten battalions, and 100 pieces of cannon towards the sea, and thirty or forty mortars with very large mouths, by way of sinking the 'Foudroyant'† and the 'Reâl' if they venture too near.

Mr. Byng has been a tedious time beating up to Minorca. These delays, either by wind or inclination, are fatal to us, because Sir Edward Hawke can hardly arrive in time to prevent the French admiral from taking away a part of the Duke of Richelieu's army, and escorting them safe to Toulon. So, upon summing up the whole of our conduct in this affair, both as to the project and execution, it does appear to me that we are the most egregious blunderers in war that ever took the hatchet in hand. But what makes me laugh is our extravagant fears of an invasion at a time when it is absolutely absurd and almost impossible, unless we are to suppose that the Danish fleet is coming out of the Baltic on purpose to escort ten or twelve French battalions to Edinburgh.

The high estimation in which Wolfe's opinion upon military matters was held has been already mentioned. His counsel was at this time sought by Mr. Townshend—afterwards Lord Sydney, son of the Right Hon. Thomas

* Lord Tyrawley, who had been the Governor of Minorca, succeeded General Fowke as Governor of Gibraltar. In a letter to the Right Hon. Henry Fox (August 27, 1756), he writes:—"That Gibraltar is the strongest town in the world, that one Englishman can beat three Frenchmen, and that London Bridge is one of the seven wonders of the world, are the natural prejudices of an English coffeehouse politician." (Chat. Corresp., vol. i. p. 202.)

† The 'Foudroyant,' of 84 guns and 950 men, was the largest of the French ships in the engagement between Admirals Byng and Galissonière off Minorca. She was taken by Admiral Osborne in 1757.

Townshend, Teller of his Majesty's Exchequer, for the guidance of his youngest brother, Henry, who had entered the army, and was now in the twentieth year of his age. It does not appear that the young officer ever served under Wolfe, but he evidently followed his advice.* The letter in which Wolfe recommends the course of study to be pursued by the military tyro runs thus:—

Devizes, Sunday, 18th July, 1756.

Dear Sir,

You cannot find me a more agreeable employment than to serve and oblige you, and I wish with all my heart that my inclinations and abilities were of equal force. I do not recollect what it was that I recommended to Mr. Cornwallis's nephew;† it might be the Comte de Turpin's book, which is certainly worth looking into, as it contains a good deal of plain practice.‡ Your brother, no doubt, is master of the Latin and French languages, and has some knowledge of the mathematics; without the last he can never become acquainted with one considerable branch of our business, the construction of fortification and the attack and defence of places; and I would advise him by all means to give up a year or two of his time now while he is young, if he has not already done it, to

* In the year 1760, Henry Townshend, then a captain of Foot-Guards, fought on the Continent, under Prince Ferdinand, and in the following year was wounded in the battle of Kirckdenckirk, on the 15th and 16th of July, when the allied army defeated the French under the Prince de Soubise. Having attained the rank of colonel, he was killed in June, 1762, in another Continental engagement. The young Colonel has been described as "being confessedly, for his heroic courage and his amiable manners, the favourite of the whole army, and of all who knew him" (Collins, ed. 1779, vol. vi. p. 47); and Walpole, seldom lavish of praise, calls him "a brave, spirited young fellow of parts." (Letter to Mann, July 1, 1762.)

† Charles, Viscount Broome, afterwards the celebrated Marquis Cornwallis, who entered the army in 1755.

‡ 'Essai sur l'Art de la Guerre,' Paris, 1754.

the study of the mathematics, because it will greatly facilitate his progress in military matters.

As to the books that are fittest for his purpose, he may begin with the 'King of Prussia's Regulations for his Horse and Foot,' where the economy and good order of an army in the lower branches are extremely well established. Then there are the Memoirs of the Marquis de Santa Cruz, Feuquières, and Montecucculi;* Folard's 'Commentaries upon Polybius;' the 'Projet de Tactique;' 'L'Attaque et la Défense des Places,' par le Maréchal de Vauban; 'Les Mémoires de Goulon;' 'L'Ingénieur de Campagne.' Le Sieur Renie for all that concerns artillery. Of the ancients, Vegetius, Cæsar, Thucydides, Xenophon's 'Life of Cyrus' and 'Retreat of the Ten Thousand Greeks.' I do not mention Polybius, because the Commentaries and the History naturally go together. Of later days, Davila, Guicciardini, Strada, and the 'Memoirs of the Duc de Sully.' There is an abundance of military knowledge to be picked out of the lives of Gustavus Adolphus, and Charles XII., King of Sweden, and of Zisca the Bohemian;† and if a tolerable account could be got of

* Don Alvar, Marquis of Santa Cruz, was a Spanish General and statesman of remarkable valour and ability, born in 1687. Having received a wound, and falling from his horse, he was taken by the Moors and massacred, in 1732.—Anthony de Pas, Marquis of Feuquières, performed such extraordinary services in Germany, during the campaign of 1688, at the head of 100 horse, that he was promoted to the rank of Maréchal-de-camp. He had great theoretical knowledge, but was so severe and censorious that it was said he was the boldest man in Europe, since he slept amidst 100,000 enemies,—meaning his own men. His 'Memoirs' have been esteemed among the best books on the art of war.—Raimonde, Count Montecucculi, one of the greatest captains of modern times, was born in Modena, in 1608, and served in the Imperial army. He obtained several victories over the Turks with very inferior forces. His last campaign he considered the most glorious of his life, not that he had been victorious, but that he had not been vanquished, having to contend against Turenne and Condé. He died at Lintz in 1681.

† John de Trocznow, whose military abilities are acknowledged by all historians of his times, rendered himself famous in the religious wars of Germany, in the fifteenth century. He received the sobri-

the exploits of Scanderbeg, it would be inestimable; for he excels all the officers, ancient and modern, in the conduct of a small defensive army. I met with him in the Turkish History, but nowhere else.* The 'Life of Suetonius,' too, contains many fine things in this way. There is a book lately published that I have heard commended, 'L'Art de la Guerre Pratique,'—I suppose it is collected from all the best authors that treat of war; and there is a little volume, entitled 'Traité de la Petite Guerre,' that your brother should take in his pocket when he goes upon out-duty and detachments. The Maréchal de Puységur's book, too, is in esteem.

I believe Mr. Townshend will think this catalogue long enough; and if he has patience to read, and desire to apply (as I am persuaded he has), the knowledge contained in them, there is also wherewithal to make him a considerable person in his profession, and of course very useful and serviceable to his country. In general, the lives of all great commanders, and all good histories of warlike nations, will be instructive, and lead him naturally to endeavour to imitate what he must necessarily approve of. In these days of scarcity,† and in these unlucky times, it is much to be wished that all our young soldiers of birth and education would follow your brother's steps, and, as they will have their turn to command, that they would try to make themselves fit for that important trust;

quet of *Zisca*, or "one-eyed," from having in his youth lost an eye in battle. He died of the plague in 1424. Zisca has been ranked amongst the Reformers, and a life of him, as such, by W. Gilpin, was published in 1765.

* George Castriot, son of an Albanian prince, was born in 1404, and sent as a hostage to the court of Sultan Amurath II., where he was educated in the Mahometan faith. Owing to his strength and courage, he was given the name of Alexander (in Turkish, *Scander*), which was accompanied with the title of *Bey*, or *Beg*. After distinguishing himself in numerous engagements, he died at Lissa, in 1467. His feats have been the subject of many poems and romances, and an account of his life was written in Latin by his contemporary, Barlesio. A Life of Scanderbeg, by Du Poncet, was also published at Paris in 1709. (See 'Biographie Universelle.')

† Scarcity of efficient commanders (?).

without it, we must sink under the superior abilities and indefatigable industry of our restless neighbours. You have drawn a longer letter upon yourself than perhaps you expected; but I could hardly make it shorter, without doing wrong to a good author. In what a strange manner have we conducted our affairs in the Mediterranean! Quelle belle occasion manquée!

I am, with perfect esteem, dear Sir,

Your most obedient and most humble servant,

JAM. WOLFE.*

The contrast presented by the foregoing and the opening of the next letter, to Mrs. Wolfe, is rather droll. Unfortunately, however, we are unable to gratify the inquisitive reader as to the nature of the transaction which caused the delinquent's threatened punishment.

Devizes, Monday, 26th July, 1756.

Dear Madam,

Looking over my papers, I found that rascal Mr. Philpot's two last receipts and the lawyer's receipt for what was due after the fugitive had evacuated those quarters. They will convince you of two points, that my landlord is a very great rogue, and that I am pretty exact. If ever I catch him I will break his bones. To-morrow we march towards our camp, and on Thursday morning we pitch our tents upon the Downs, within a mile and a half of Blandford. If there is an ounce of resolution left, we sha'n't lie long idle; but I'm afraid we have not spirit enough for an undertaking of any great moment. The Duke of Belleisle's name makes our pusillanimous tremble, and God knows there was never less cause.

I have been but once on horseback this month; however, I find myself well enough to march with the regiment, and shall probably recover apace. Our new Colonel is a sensible man, and very sociable and polite. Little Rickson is appointed

second

* From the 'Gentleman's Magazine,' March, 1791.

to act as Deputy Quartermaster-General in Scotland, a place of great trust, honour, and profit. The Duke recommended him to be Deputy Governor of Pennsylvania, which would have been worth £1500 a year to his Excellency, besides the glory of waging continual war with the wild men of America, but a more fortunate man stepped in with better support, and disappointed our friend.

Wish a great deal of joy to Mr. Aylmer in my name, and tell him if he will breed any soldiers I shall engage them as fast as they are able to serve.* I hear that Lafausille has been preparing for action, though I did not know with what design till you cleared it up. I'm tired of proposing anything to the officers that command our regiments; they are in general so lazy and so bigoted to old habits; though I must do him the justice to say that he differs from them in that respect, and is industrious beyond measure.†

If that Byng had been in haste to retrieve his own honour and the reputation of the British flag, he has had time and strength to do it. But I fear he is a dog, and therefore I hope the fleet did not sail from Gibraltar till after Sir Edward Hawke got there. It would have been of infinite concern to this nation that the castle of St. Philip's should hold out till the 2nd or 3rd of this month. If they had been all demolished by their obstinacy they could not die better. You see what haste the Duke of Richelieu made to get to the fort; he foresaw the danger of our fleet's returning with the Admirals that now command it, and therefore, under pretence of doing honour to the garrison for their brave defence, and to Blakeney in particular, he rejected no proposals that were made. His sole aim was to garrison the fort and get back to Toulon with the rest of his army before our squadron

* Brother to Lord Aylmer, Baron of Balrath, in the peerage of Ireland. Mrs. Wolfe bequeathed £100 to the second son of the Hon. Mr. Aylmer,—probably a godson of Wolfe's.

† John Lafausille, Lieutenant-Colonel of the 8th (General Wolfe's) regiment of Foot, was promoted to the colonelcy of the 66th in 1758. He was created Major-General in 1761, and died on his voyage home from the Havannah, in 1763.

could return from Gibraltar, and I am afraid he has succeeded in his wish. If Byng has lost one day at Gibraltar, he is the most damnable of traitors.

In the beginning of August a camp was formed at Shroton, near Blandford, in Dorsetshire,* whence Wolfe writes on the 4th, saying that six battalions of infantry, six squadrons and two troops of light Horse, with twelve pieces of artillery, were encamped upon a pleasant dry spot open to the wind, which scoured the camp and purified it. They had plenty of wood, straw, bread, and meat, and good care was taken of the men. This sort of life agreed well with himself, and his health was much better in the open air. His new colonel looked into and ordered everything for the best; and the vigilance of the commanders of the respective corps was to be praised.

In another letter from the camp, he informs his mother that the addition of a battalion to the infantry regiments† would make room for little Adeane; and, after recommending one of his father's lieutenants (Hamilton) to the General for promotion, he writes:—"There is a scheme set on foot to provide blankets for our men, and since the Government will not be at that expense, the officers contribute according to their abilities. Now that the General has had a battalion added to

* Blandford, situated between Salisbury and Dorchester. "This country," says De Foe, "is a fine variety of downs, woods, lawns, arable and pasture land, rich valleys, and an excellent air. The dry easterly winds, the cold northern, and the western moisture, are tempered by the warm southern saline breezes wafted hither from the ocean." ('Tour through Great Britain,' vol. i. p. 310.)

† On the 25th of August, 1756, it was determined to add second battalions, of 780 men each, to fifteen infantry regiments.

his regiment, he may afford to send them twenty guineas for that purpose; other colonels have done it, and I have answered for him."

On the 1st of September, the General himself is addressed as follows:—

Dear Sir,

I am afraid you will think me a little idle, and be still more convinced of it when you see my letter dated from Winchester. A lieutenant-colonel forty miles from his camp!—what carries him so far from his duty? The case is this:—The Prince of Nassau is going away, and the Duke of Richmond means to entertain him a day or two at Goodwood before his departure,* and we see the Hessians exercise as we go along. The Duke proposed this party to me, and undertook to get the General's leave. There was too much pleasure and too much honour in his Grace's offer to be refused. To-morrow morning four of the Hessian battalions and some artillery exhibit the Prussian discipline; after which we are to breakfast with Count d'Isembourg, their General, and dine at the Duke of Richmond's, which is five-and-twenty miles from hence.†

We had a general review and exercise of our forces yesterday upon Blandford Downs, to the great entertainment of the

* Mrs. Grenville wrote to her husband, on the 20th of April (1756):—"There is a Prince of Nassau, a sovereign, just arrived, who is much admired for his beauty, and a Morocco ambassador, as much admired for his great politeness. . . . The Duke of Richmond has put the Prince of Nassau in possession of his house at Whitehall during his stay in England; they went yesterday to Newmarket." (Grenville Correspondence, vol. i. p. 157.)

† Eight regiments of Hessian auxiliaries, commanded by Count d'Isembourg, landed at Southampton on the 15th of May. They are described as making "a fine appearance, being generally straight, tall, and slender. Their uniform is blue, turned up with red and laced with white; and their hair, plaited behind, hangs down to the waist. They are quartered in all the neighbouring towns, and observe the most exact discipline." (Scots Magazine, May, 1756.) Later in the year, the

ignorant spectators; though, according to my judgment, we do not deserve even their approbation. There are officers who had the presumption and vanity to applaud our operations, bad as they were; but I hope the General saw our defects, and will apply a speedy remedy, without which I think we are in imminent danger of being cut to pieces in our first encounter.

We have some suspicion of an enterprise in embryo, and we conclude that it will be in a warm climate.* If the least notice is given us, I shall send for all my thin clothes and linen. The Duke of Richmond talks of visiting the two camps in Kent, and he will, if I am with him, do us the honour to drink a dish of tea at your house. He has expressed a desire to see you; whence that curiosity arises I can't well imagine, but so it is. I send you both my best wishes.

On the 19th of October our Lieutenant-Colonel received orders to decamp, and march with six companies, —three of his own regiment and three of the Buffs,— into Gloucestershire, to assist the civil power in suppressing riots. He marched the next day, and notifies his progress as follows:—

Sodbury, Sunday, 24th October, 1756.

Dear Madam,

I write you this short letter to inform you that the Gloucestershire weavers and I are not yet come to blows, nor

innkeepers refusing to give them quarters, the Hessians built huts to contain sixty men each, and in the middle of every hut was a large fire, around which they sat. In December, however, they were again quartered in various parts of the country. ('Gentleman's Magazine' (1756), pp. 544, 592.)

* Mr. Potter writes to Mr. Grenville, on the 11th of September:— "There is much talk of an expedition; but the Ministers, I hear, deny there is anything in agitation. . . . Some think the Ministers mad enough to attempt retaking Minorca at this season; others suppose it is calculated merely to stop the current of clamour by pretending to do something." (Grenville Correspondence, vol. i. p. 172.)

do I believe we shall. The expedition carries me a little out of my road and a little in the dirt, but I believe there never was a more harmless piece of business, for I have men enough to beat the mob of all England collected. I hope it will turn out a good recruiting party, for the people are so oppressed, so poor, and so wretched, that they will perhaps hazard a knock on the pate for bread and clothes, and turn soldiers through sheer necessity. To-morrow I enter the enemy's country, and dispose my troops in their winter quarters; myself to a straggling, dirty village, over the ankles in mud. Bad accommodation and bad company are so familiar to me, that I am almost in danger of losing the taste of anything better. You'll be pleased to send my baggage to Plymouth as before desired, for I hope to get there time enough to look over it before we set sail to retake St. Philip's, or to seize the isle of Corsica for our use.

My nurse's sons were two of the finest soldiers in the camp at Shroton. Richard has behaved so well that he has hopes of preferment; the other is an exceedingly able fellow, and strong as ten common men. I furnished them for their march to Plymouth, and gave them hopes of many good things in the profession. You must direct for me at Stroud, in Gloucestershire,* and you must tell me how you are, and what is doing in your neighbourhood. London, I reckon, will soon be in an uproar. You are happy that you are out of the noise of the populace, and out of the smoke of the city. When is the unhappy Admiral to be judged? When does he offer an apology for the loss of St. Philip's, excuse himself, or pay the forfeit of his life for that inestimable fortress? I, who never read the news, never know what is doing, and my correspondents seem to have intelligence proportioned to my curiosity. Pray tell the General that I triumph in the King

* "West of Cirencester, upon the side of a hill, stands Stroud, a little market-town, distinguished by an extensive clothing trade carried on in the neighbourhood. By the town runs the river Stroudwater, which has the remarkable property of striking the scarlet dye with a fuller and deeper tint than any water yet discovered." (De Foe's 'Tour through Great Britain,' vol. ii. p. 222.)

of Prussia's success.* This was to have been a short letter, and if you knew what noise and what companions fill the room, you would wonder that it was otherwise.

Owing, no less to the spread of enlightenment amongst the lower classes than to the organization of police, happily it has not been necessary for some years past to call upon the military to assist the civil power in quelling riots. No duty is so galling to an officer, and in the execution of none other can he acquire less honour, unless by combining conciliation with decision he effects the desired object without bloodshed. Wolfe, having previously exhibited the necessary qualifications, was therefore selected to discharge the disagreeable duty in which we find him engaged. Upon his arrival at Stroud he wrote to his mother as follows, and in his haste neglected to date his letter:—

Dear Madam,

Very little society, and no amusement but walking or riding, forces me to be troublesome to you. The shortest of the two gun-cases contains a little gun for the woods; may I ask the favour of you to send that gun-case to the "George" upon Snow Hill, directed to me at Stroud, in Gloucestershire; the other I desired might go to Plymouth with my baggage. The obstinacy of the poor half-starved weavers of broad-cloth that inhabit this extraordinary country is very surprising. They beg about the country for food, because, they say, the masters have beat down their wages too low to live upon; and I believe it is a just complaint. Those who are most oppressed have seized the tools, and broke the looms of others that would work if they could. I am afraid they will proceed to some extravagancies, and force the magistrates to use our weapons against them, which would give me a great

* The defeat of the Austrians under Marshal Brown, at Lowositz, in Bohemia, on the 1st of October.

deal of concern. The face of this country is different from anything that I have seen in England. Numberless little hills, with rivulets running in all the bottoms; the lower parts of the hills are generally grass, the middle corn, and the upper part wood, and innumerable little white houses in all the vales, so that there is a vast variety; and every mile changes the scene, and gives you a new and pleasant prospect. The poor people in this neighbourhood are vastly well affected, further off they are as ill; but their chief, the Duke of Beaufort,* is, I hear, upon the point of death, which will probably disconcert the faction.

The public papers seem to have taken a turn in favour of our Admiral; but I, who am an eye-witness of the consequences of his fatal conduct, shall never be brought to soften towards him. If he did not personally engage through fear, or declined it through treachery; or if he went out with instructions not to be too forward in relieving Minorca, he deserves ten thousand deaths.† An English admiral who accepts of such instructions should lose his head; but, alas! our affairs are falling down apace. This country is going fast upon its ruin, by the paltry projects and more ridiculous execution of those who are entrusted. Remember how often I have pressed upon for your security, how I have warned my

* Charles Noel Somerset, fourth Duke of Beaufort, died on the 28th of October, 1756, aged forty-seven. Walpole speaks of him as "a most determined and unwavering Jacobite," who "openly set himself at the head of that party, and forced them to vote against the Court." (Letters, vol. i. p. 436.) He is elsewhere said to have "distinguished himself in the senate, both as a commoner and a peer, by a steady opposition to unconstitutional and corrupt measures, and endeared himself to mankind by his social virtues." ('Collins's Peerage' (1779), vol. i. p. 212.)

† John Wilkes writes to Mr. Grenville, on the 16th of October:— "The public indignation is rising very strong against Lord Anson, and Byng has everywhere some warm advocates, from an idea, I hope, of his innocence, at least a less degree of guilt; and not from the natural inconsistency of this, and, I believe, every other country. 'Poor Byng' is the phrase in every mouth, and then comes the simile of the *scapegoat*." (Grenville Correspondence, vol. i. p. 176).

father of the hazards and precarious state of our public funds. I have done my duty to you in that respect, and will do it in every other, if it should hereafter become necessary, and I live and have it in my power.

From the Lieutenant-Colonel's next letter to his mother, it appears that he has again offended her by a display of his vehement temper. Probably the good lady, who seems to have been rather testy, owing, it may be, to ill health, was at fault as well as her son.

Stroud, 13th November, 1756.

Dear Madam,

I should account myself little better than a barbarian if I wilfully and designedly added anything to the great misery that you are forced almost every day to undergo. My duty forbids me to increase your misfortunes, and I am not in my nature disposed to plague and torment people, more especially those I love. My temper is much too warm, and sudden resentment forces out expressions, and even actions, that are neither justifiable nor excusable; and, perhaps, I do not correct that natural heat so much as I ought to do. But you must have observed that people are apt to resent what they at first view, and often unadvisedly, take for injuries, with more than common quickness, when they come from an unsuspected quarter.

With regard to myself, you must leave to time and exerted reason for the correction of those errors and vices which may at present prevail most against sense and judgment, pointing them out in the gentlest and friendliest manner, and by that means help to weaken and destroy them. I have that cursed disposition of mind, that when I once know that people have entertained a very ill opinion, I imagine they never change. From whence one passes easily to an indifference about them, and then to dislike; and though I flatter myself that I have the seeds of justice strong enough to keep me from doing wrong, even to an enemy, yet there lurks a hidden poison in the heart that is difficult to root out. It is my misfortune to catch fire on a sudden, to answer letters the moment I receive them, when they touch me sensibly, and to suffer passion to dictate my expressions more than my reason. The next day, perhaps, would have changed this, and carried more moderation with it. Every ill turn of my life has had this haste and first impulse of the moment for its true cause, and it proceeds from pride.

It is remarkable that a man so impulsive and sensitive as Wolfe acknowledges himself to be, should have preserved so many enduring friendships; but his love for all that he deemed worthy of it was as fervid as his hatred of what was mean or treacherous. His heart was as warm as his temper, with this difference—the warmth of his heart was as permanent as that of his temper was transient. If he thought that those who entertained ill opinions seldom improved, he likewise believed that those in whom he had found good qualities were as little likely to lose them, hence he was wont to vindicate his friends when any of them was under a cloud. We need not go out of our way for an illustration, as one presents itself at the very time under review. His predecessor as Lieutenant-Colonel, the Hon. Edward Cornwallis, was now suffering under temporary disgrace; he had recently returned from Gibraltar, where, along with other superior officers of that garrison, he had signed the resolution of the council of war, on the strength of which the Governor, Lieut.-General Fowke, refused to reinforce Admiral Byng's fleet with a battalion. Fowke, as is well known, was tried by a court martial, of which Lieut.-General Wolfe was a member, sentenced to suspension for a year, and afterwards dismissed by the King from his service.* An investigation into the conduct of the officers who had acquiesced with Fowke was pending when, on the 27th of November, Wolfe wrote to his father. In reference to his friend, he says :—

I don't suppose there is a man living more to be pitied than poor Cornwallis. As he has more zeal, more merit, and more integrity than one commonly meets with among men, he will be proportionally mortified to find himself in disgrace, with the best intentions to deserve favour. I am heartily sorry to find him involved with the rest, of whose abilities or inclinations nobody has any very high notions; but Cornwallis is a man of approved courage and fidelity. He has, unhappily, been misled upon this occasion by people of not half his value.

The advocate ere long had the gratification of learning that his friend was restored to favour; in the February following he was created a major-general.

Wolfe having accomplished the object of his expedition, in putting an end to the disturbances which, he says, were never of any great consequence, sent the detachment of the Buffs he had commanded back to Plymouth, whence the main body of his own battalion marched into Gloucestershire. His last letter from Stroud is to his mother, on the 6th of December, when he shows cause for his wrath :—

* Alluding to this affair, Walpole tells his correspondent Chute :— "By all one learns, Byng, Fowke, and all the officers at Gibraltar were infatuated! They figured Port Mahon lost; and Gibraltar, a-going! a-going! Lord Effingham, Cornwallis, Lord Robert Bertie, all, all signed the council of war, and are in as bad odour as possible. The King says it will be his death, and that he neither eats nor sleeps,—all our trust is in the Hanoverians." (Letters, vol. iii. p. 17.)

I attribute it in some measure to the nature of my employment as well as to the condition of my blood, being everlastingly chagrined with the ill actions of the people about me, and in the constant exercise of power to punish and rebuke. I pass so much of my time at quarters, and am so intent upon having everything done in its proper way, that those aids which an equality of society, the conversation of women, and the wholesome advice of friends are known to give to minds of my cast, are totally cut off from me and denied; and if I was to serve two or three years in America, I make no doubt but that I should be distinguished by a peculiar fierceness of temper suited to the nature of that war. I don't know whether a man had better fall early into the hands of those savages, than be converted by degrees into their nature and forget humanity.

It may happen that a second battalion of those regiments may have colonels appointed to them without including your son in the number. A man who never asks a favour will hardly ever obtain it. I persuade myself they will put no inferior officer (unless a peer) over my head, in which case I can't complain, not being able to say that I have ever done more than my duty, and happy if I came up to that. If any soldier is preferred when my turn comes, I shall acquaint the Secretary at War that I am sensible of the injury that is done me, and will take the earliest opportunity to put it out of his or any man's power to repeat it. Not while the war lasts; for if 500 younger officers one after another werè to rise before me I should continue to serve with the utmost diligence, to acquit myself to the country, and to show the Ministers that they had acted unjustly. But I flatter myself that I shall never be forced to these disagreeable measures.

I don't believe that Mrs. Goldsmith is dead, but dying. They are still at Kinsale, because she is not able to move; for her desire was to be carried to die amongst her own relations. My cousin, whose good nature and gratitude are such that he can refuse nothing to a wife that he thinks deserves everything at his hands, had agreed to carry her to

Limerick; but she had not strength for the journey, and I expect to hear every day that she is at rest. I am afraid poor Goldsmith has been obliged to call in some expensive assistance, and therefore conclude that a present from the General would be acceptable. He has distinguished himself by a most considerable* regard for the poorer branches of his family, for which, I make no doubt but that he himself will be considered. All mankind are indeed our relations, and have nearly an equal claim to pity and assistance; but those of our own blood call most immediately upon us. One of the principal reasons that induces me to wish myself at the head of a regiment is, that I may execute my father's plan while there remains one indigent person of his race.

Soon after the date of the foregoing, Kingsley's regiment marched to Cirencester, where the head-quarters was established for some months. There is a letter from the Lieutenant-Colonel from that ancient town, dated the 26th of December. It commences with a receipt for the cure of rheumatism. Reverting to the Goldsmiths, he writes:—"The letter you enclosed was from my cousin; his wife declines apace: her illness gives him great concern, and I believe may have distressed him in his narrow circumstances. If my father would send him some assistance it might be a timely relief. I don't know what the poor man will do; when his wife dies he loses £40 a year of his income. I have no house to offer him for shelter, or I should be entirely at his service, because I think him to be an even-tempered, honest man."

From another paragraph it appears that Sir John Mordaunt, who had been "in with the King," took that opportunity to recommend Wolfe in the strongest terms

* "Considerable," *i. e. considerate* (?).

to his Majesty. "I did not ask this of Sir John," he says, "and therefore am the more obliged to him; but I don't expect it will produce much, because, by the King's rule, my turn is not yet come." The letter ends thus:—"The disagreement between Blakeney and Jeffery is unfortunate for both; it is an old quarrel revived, and will produce no good. We military men are not so much in love with the defence of St. Philip's as the mob of London. We think there appeared no great degree of skill, nor the most shining courage."*

The Duke of Bedford, an old friend of General Wolfe's, was at this period Lord-Lieutenant of Ireland. His Excellency having the patronage of the army on the Irish establishment, had now at his disposal a lucrative office, or rather two, those of Barrackmaster-General and Quartermaster-General of Ireland, which had become vacant by the death of Lord Forbes. On the 6th of February, 1757, Wolfe received a letter from Mr. Rigby, the Duke's Secretary, offering him these appointments, and giving him to understand that his Grace considered the King would make no difficulty of granting the rank of colonel which usually accompanied them. Informing his father of the circumstance, James says:—"I have writ to thank the Duke for the favour with which he is pleased to honour me; I have told him that although it is an office quite out of the course of my practice, nevertheless I

* "The King, of his own motion, has given a red riband and an Irish barony to old Blakeney, who has been at Court in a hackney-coach with a foot-soldier behind it. As he has not only lost his government, but as he was bed-rid while it was losing, these honours are a little ridiculed; we have too many governors that will expect titles, if losses are pretensions!" (Horace Walpole, Letter, 29th November, 1756.)

shall endeavour to execute it properly by a strict and exact obedience to his directions and commands. But I shall give it up immediately and come back to the battalion, if the rank of colonel is omitted; and I had rather see the King of Prussia's operations the next campaign than accept of this employment with all its advantages. As the matter is not yet completed, I believe 'tis better not to speak of it, lest his Majesty should think proper to refuse."

The Lieutenant-Colonel again writes to his father on the 19th:—

As I have no franks I am obliged to put you to the expense of a double letter, to enclose one that I received this morning from the Duke of Bedford, in so obliging and flattering a style that I should not be ready to show it to anybody else. But as the matter concerns what I formerly mentioned to you, it will be the best means of letting you see what steps have been taken, as well as what success has attended them. You'll observe that the Duke makes no mention of the employment of Barrackmaster-General, which I am not sorry for, wishing rather that they might be separated from each other upon this occasion. I won't trouble you with all that I have said to the Duke of Bedford and Lord Albemarle, but only in general that I have conformed to their sentiments in accepting the offer. I am far from being pleased with it otherwise than as a mark of the Duke's friendship and good opinion, being too much of a soldier to desire any but military employment, which this can hardly be reckoned.

The letter in which Wolfe expressed his obligations to the Duke of Bedford runs thus:—

Cirencester, February 19, 1757.

My Lord,

The honour your Grace has done me, and the particular obligations you have conferred upon me, leave me no choice how to act. That which is most agreeable to your Grace must determine me, and I should be extremely pleased to have it in my power to convince your Grace, by an exact obedience to your commands, that I wish to make myself more worthy of your protection. I am very sensible that there are many gentlemen upon the list whose pretensions are a check to mine, and some of such distinguished merit that I neither desire, nor could hope, to be preferred before them. The only circumstance that can at all lessen my satisfaction on this occasion is, to be in some measure distinguished from the officers who have held this employment before by a rank inferior to theirs, and which seemed to be annexed to the office. Such services as your Grace may expect from the best inclinations, I venture to assure you of; and, as I am ready to receive and follow your Grace's directions, they will be the best and surest rules for my conduct. The moment the officers of this country and of the regiments will permit, which I hope will be early in the next month, I shall pay my respects to your Grace in town. With all possible acknowledgments for these marks of your favourable opinion,

I have the honour to be, etc.,

JAMES WOLFE.*

Far from being absorbed in his own worldly welfare, our hero was deeply interested in everything that concerned the State. Instead of heaping up riches, as he now had the opportunity of doing, it seems to have been his highest ambition to spend and be spent in the service of his country.

On the 23rd of February he addresses his mother in these terms:—

I write to you upon a very particular subject. There is reason to think that the Spaniards will make war upon us, and of course that the public expenses will greatly increase as

* Bedford Correspondence, vol. ii. p. 239.

well as the danger. My desire therefore is, that you will interest yourself in behalf of the public as becomes a virtuous, good, disinterested lady, and that you will endeavour to persuade the General to contribute all he can possibly afford towards the defence of the island,—retrenching, if need be, his expenses, moderate as they are. I would have him engage in lotteries and all schemes for raising money, because I believe they are honestly intended; and though he should be considerably a loser, the motive of his actions will overbalance his losses. Let the General keep a little ready money by him for his own use and yours, and with the rest, if he has it, assist the State; nay, I should go so far as to advise him to lend three or four thousand pounds to the Government without any interest at all, or give it, since it is the savings of his salaries and the reward of his services. Excuse this freedom. I beg my duty to the General.

In March, Wolfe came to London, whence he wrote to his father on the 17th, saying that the Duke of Bedford had asked the King to grant him the rank of colonel, but his Majesty objected on the grounds of his short service. The Lord-Lieutenant, however, was determined to renew the charge. "There are rumours," he writes, "of a change of Ministry. In this fluctuating state of affairs military operations must be neglected in the contention of parties. I believe it is pretty certain (though not yet declared) that H.R.H. the Duke will command the army in Westphalia, and, as there is a greater probability of service there than here, I have desired my Lord Albemarle to get me leave to attend his Royal Highness, and I have some prospect of succeeding. This I am persuaded you will approve of, from the advantages to be reaped from an active campaign. There appears to be so general an opposition to sending any of our troops abroad, that I imagine they will have no share of the great war which is now carrying on upon the Continent. If my mother will let me know the hour she will take me up in her chariot at the bridge on Wednesday next, I shall be ready to wait upon her to Blackheath; and if she does not care to come herself, only signify your pleasure as to sending the chariot, and I shall be at my post." On the Monday before the appointed day the Lieutenant-Colonel wrote to countermand the carriage, as business would detain him in town; but unfortunately his note did not reach Blackheath in time to prevent Mrs. Wolfe from coming to Westminster Bridge, where she waited for two or three hours in the cold on a very severe day, greatly to her son's regret. On Sunday the 27th, he states that he has not yet kissed the King's hand on his appointment to the office of Quartermaster-General for Ireland. The ceremony, he says, is very tedious, but as soon as it is over he will have the pleasure of spending a few days at Blackheath.

CHAPTER XVI.

CAMP.—ISLE OF WIGHT.—COAST OF FRANCE.

APRIL—SEPTEMBER, 1757.

WE have traced Wolfe's personal narrative for thirty years, during one-half of which time he was actively engaged in the service of his country. We have seen how he endeavoured, by assiduous application in peaceful days, to turn to the highest purpose the practical experience he had previously acquired in the field. As yet, however, he had achieved nothing to make his name historical, for, though his genius was bursting for development, the occasion had not presented itself. We now enter upon a new phase of his short career, introductory to which let us briefly review the train of events that led to the Seven Years' War, in whose annals his name was to become the most glorious.

England and France were again the principal opponents; but their allies had changed sides. In the war which terminated in 1748, we found Austria allied with England; but now the Empress-Queen joined Louis XV. against her old friend King George, who had entered into a treaty with her mortal enemy, Frederic of Prussia. The King of England's first object was to preserve his

Electorate. Maria Theresa had set her heart upon the recovery of Silesia; and as an inducement for the assistance of France in regaining that province, she was willing to cede a large portion of her territories in Flanders. With this view "the proud Austrian Juno" did not scruple to flatter Madame de Pompadour, while her intriguing Minister, Kaunitz, aware of the hostility between England and France, amused the British Government with friendly assurances, while endeavouring to prevent the coalition of England and Prussia, until he succeeded in effecting an alliance with France. Notwithstanding her secret negotiations with the French Court, the Empress reproached her old ally for deserting her cause, and breaking up the friendship which had so long subsisted between the two nations.

On the 16th of January, 1756, a treaty was concluded between England and Prussia, to prevent the entrance of foreign troops into Germany. Mr. Keith, the British ambassador at Vienna, on delivering a copy of this treaty, justified it as calculated to preserve the peace of the empire, and relieve her Majesty from her apprehensions of Prussia. In reply, she expressed the utmost abhorrence of Frederic, exclaiming, "I and the King of Prussia are incompatible; and no condition on earth shall ever induce me to enter into any engagement of which he is a party." Mr. Keith then adverting to the treaty concluded at Versailles, she haughtily demanded, "Why should you be surprised, if, following your example in concluding a treaty with Prussia, I should enter into an engagement with France?"* The

* Coxe, 'History of the House of Austria.' The treaty of Versailles

Czarina, though she had been subsidized by England to furnish troops for the defence of Hanover, entered into the adverse league, which was likewise joined by Sweden and Saxony. Thus was the whole political system of Europe revolutionized, Spain alone remaining neutral; and England and Prussia were opposed by France, Austria, Russia, Sweden, Saxony, and the Germanic body.

Frederic's army, though small when compared with more than half a million of men whom his adversaries could bring into the field against him, was the best disciplined, and most efficiently officered, in the world; while, as a General, his foes had no one to compete with himself. He therefore lost not a moment's time; but was no sooner informed of the designs of the formidable confederacy arrayed against him than he invaded Saxony with an army of 60,000 men, took Dresden, invested the Saxon camp at Pirna, and hastening into Bohemia, encountered the Austrians under Marshal Brown, whom he defeated at Lowositz.

Meanwhile,—before any formal declaration of war, and while England was in daily dread of a Gallic invasion,—the French fleet appeared off Minorca, and, owing to the indecision or duplicity of the British Ministers as much as to the inefficiency of Admiral Byng, made an easy conquest of that island. England, in consequence of this act of hostility, together with the encroachments of the French in North America and the Indies, declared

was not, however, a necessary consequence of the alliance between Great Britain and Prussia; for, as Archdeacon Coxe explains, the plan of a union between France and Austria had been gradually matured during a long course of intrigue.

war against France on the 18th of May, 1756, from which day we may date the beginning of the strife which, in spite of its disastrous and humiliating opening, eventually proved "the most glorious war in which England had ever been engaged."*

As has been invariably the case, the British Government, regardless of long warning, was unprepared for the crisis. Instead of having an army ready, the work was now to organize one, and it was not until the end of August that an order was issued to raise fifteen new battalions, of 780 men each, in addition to the military force kept up during the peace. But still worse, England had no master-mind, either as a director of her councils or as a leader of her soldiers. In December, however, a new administration was formed under the Duke of Devonshire, when William Pitt became the principal Secretary of State; but the King's personal aversion to him and his colleague, Lord Temple, together with the apathy of the House of Commons, wherein nothing but corruption could ensure support, compelled him to resign in the following April; for, "constituted as Parliament then was, the favourite of the people could not depend on a majority in the people's own House."†

During the few months that Pitt had been in power, his influence was discernible in not a few energetic measures. The foreign mercenaries, who had been brought over while the late invasion panic prevailed, were dismissed, and a national militia established as a more efficient and constitutional defensive force. At the

* Lord Macaulay, Essay on William Pitt, Earl of Chatham.
† Lord Macaulay, *ib.*

same time two large corps were raised in Germany and Switzerland for service in America, and the regular land and sea forces were sufficiently increased to ensure the vigorous prosecution of the war. It was also during this brief ministerial reign that the hitherto disaffected Highland clans were organized into regiments of the line; by which "fine stroke of policy," as a recent historian remarks, "a nucleus of rebellion and civil war was eradicated once and for ever—a paralytic member was converted immediately into an arm of strength."*

On the 1st of January, 1757, it was ordered that 2000 men should be enlisted in the Highlands for the British service in America. Although the idea of this judicious proceeding did not originate with the great statesman who carried it into effect, its adoption not only exemplified his penetration and sagacity, but also showed the superiority of his mind to all local and vulgar prejudices. It appears that in May, 1756, a scheme for carrying on the war was submitted to the Duke of Cumberland, who, on Pitt's accession to power, ordered it to be transmitted to him. In this document it is suggested that two battalions, of 1000 men each, might be raised in the north of Scotland; and that, in order to induce the Highlanders to enlist for American service, they should be offered grants of land at the end of the war. Almon, who quotes the paper *in extenso*, does not name the author of it, but says that it was delivered to Mr. Pitt by the Earl of Albemarle.† Though it does not follow that the Earl devised the scheme, it is not impro-

* Massey, 'History of England,' vol. i. p. 28.
† 'Anecdotes of the Earl of Chatham,' vol. i.

bable that he was concerned in it. His information, however, respecting the Highlands must have been derived from some one of more local experience, for his lordship, when Lord Bury, paid his regiment but two flying visits during the time the corps was quartered in Scotland; and who was more likely to have discerned the feasibility of the project than his Lieutenant-Colonel, Wolfe? Without claiming for our hero the origination of the idea, the fact is palpable that he had entertained it so early as 1751, as the reader may perceive by turning back to his letter to Rickson on the 9th of June in that year, wherein he wrote:—"I should imagine that two or three independent Highland companies might be of use [in Nova Scotia]; they are hardy, intrepid, accustomed to a rough country."*

The public discontent which had subsided while Pitt presided over the national councils, upon his retirement again burst out with increased rancour. The most important constituencies directed their representatives to vote for an investigation of the miscarriages of the preceding year; the funds fell; and, in short, the country was in a state of chaos. Besides the loss of Minorca, in America the French had taken Oswego and Fort Ontario; and, to aggravate the general consternation, news arrived from India of the capture of Calcutta and the

* See *ante*, p. 168. It is at least a curious coincidence that Wolfe's words are equivalent to the final sentence of that portion of the abovementioned scheme which relates to the matter in hand:—"No men in this island are better qualified for the American war than the Scots Highlanders." The issue proved the truth of the assertion. If Wolfe did not incite this military measure, it is remarkable that he should have foreshadowed it, as well as the establishment of county constabulary upon a constitutional basis.

tragedy of the "black hole." The press teemed with bitter party pamphlets, while the pulpit proclaimed that the national calamities were the result of national sin, and foreboded evils to come. Thus, a popular preacher of the day, after reviewing recent events, arrived at the following conclusion:—"All these circumstances considered, the present appears to be a time of uncommon danger; affairs, look wherever we will, wear a lowering aspect. Judgments seem—more than seem—to be hovering all around us. How soon they may fall, God only knows!"* For three months the nation remained without a Ministry; at length, by the end of June, arrangements were completed, whereby the Duke of Newcastle took the Treasury, Pitt became principal Secretary of State, with the control of the war and of foreign affairs; Lord Holderness, Secretary for the Southern Department, Earl Temple, Privy Seal, the Duke of Marlborough, Master-General of the Ordnance, and Fox sank into the lucrative office of Paymaster. Such was the strange coalition that now began an Administration rendered powerful by the leadership of Pitt, in whose genius and patriotism the people were so confident, that they began to look hopefully towards the future.

Wolfe at this period had too much active work on hand to find leisure for letter-writing. The Twentieth regiment being one of those to which a second battalion had been added, he was obliged to attend to its formation and discipline, as well as to the ordinary business of his old corps. Consequently, his presence was required

* 'The Time of Danger;' sermon preached on the public fast-day, 1757, by the Rev. James Hervey.

in many different places. On the 13th of May he wrote from Gloucester, whither he had travelled from London with one of his captains, Lord Blandford, who, we are told, "goes very quick."* So it appears; for they got to Cirencester (by Oxford) the first night, stayed a day there, reached Gloucester the next, and on the following morning were to set out for Shrewsbury.

Ending his letter, Wolfe says:—

> Our second battalion is in very good condition, healthy, and forward in their exercises, and the soberest collection of young Englishmen that I ever saw. The Major [Beckwith] has been extremely lucky in recruiting. The loss of the Austrians is not so considerable as was expected, but it is for the reputation of the King of Prussia's arms to drive them before him.† I suppose we may soon expect to hear of a decisive action.

In June a large encampment was formed on Bradford Heath, near Dorchester, and Wolfe spent some time there with the two battalions of Kingsley's regiment.‡ Towards the middle of July he was summoned to Lon-

* George Spencer, Marquis of Blandford, who was then in his nineteenth year. He quitted the army on succeeding to the dukedom of Marlborough in 1758, married a daughter of John, fourth Duke of Bedford, and survived until 1817.

† The battle fought on the 6th of May, near Prague, in which the Austrian General, Marshal Brown, was mortally wounded, and 20,000 of the Imperialists killed.

‡ Hutchins, 'Hist. Dorset,' 2nd edition, vol. ii. p. 8. A correspondent of 'Notes and Queries' also says:—"That General Wolfe was in the above encampment, I had the information from a gentleman who knew him; and many years ago I accidentally met with a book with the autograph 'James Wolfe' written on the fly-leaf in a bold and gentlemanly style. The volume, being on a military subject, was not taken care of, and lost. It was left by the General in the hands of Messrs. Gould and Thorne, booksellers, in Dorchester, from whose successors I had it.—G. F. WEYMOUTH." (Vol. v. (1852), p. 186.)

don, whence he wrote as follows to his friend at Edinburgh, who was acting as Deputy Quartermaster-General for Scotland :—

My dear Rickson,

Though I have matter enough, and pleasure in writing a long letter, yet I must now be short. Your joy upon the occasion of my new employment, I am sure, is very sincere, as is that which I feel when any good thing falls to your share; but this new office does neither please nor flatter me, as you may believe when I tell you that it was offered with the rank of Colonel, which the King, guided by the Duke, afterwards refused. His Royal Highness's reasons were plausible; he told the Duke of Bedford (who applied with warmth) that I was so young a lieutenant-colonel that it could not be done immediately. But I should have known it in time, that I might have excused myself from a very troublesome business, which is quite out of my way. . . . .

We are about to undertake something or other at a distance, and I am one of the party. I can't flatter you with a lively picture of my hopes as to the success of it; the reasons are so strong against us (the English) in whatever we take in hand, that I never expect any great matter; the chiefs, the engineers, and our wretched discipline, are the great and insurmountable obstructions. I doubt yet if there be any fixed plan; we wait for American intelligence, from whence the best is not expected, and shall probably be put into motion by that intelligence. I myself take the chance of a profession little understood and less liked in this country. I may come off as we have done before; but I never expect to see either the poor woman my mother, or the old General again,—she is at present dangerously ill, he is infirm with age. Whether my going may hurry their departure, you are as good a judge as I am. Besides their loss, I have not a soul to take charge of my little affairs, and expect to find everything in the utmost confusion, robbed and plundered by all that can catch hold of them.

I heartily wish you were fixed in the employment you now exercise; but if David Watson is not misrepresented to me, you have everything to fear from his artifices and double-dealing.* I wish I was strong enough to carry you through, I'd take you upon my back; but my people are away. Calcraft could serve you—no man better. He is the second or third potentate in this realm. I may have an opportunity of speaking to Napier, but there Watson governs almost alone; and we are not sharp enough to dive into the hearts of men. The nephew goes with us. I must have succumbed under the weight of some characters of this sort if I had not stood out in open defiance of their wicked powers. A man will not be ill-used that will not bear it. Farewell, my honest little friend. I am ever your

Faithful and affectionate servant,
JAMES WOLFE.

London, 21st July, 1757.

No sooner was the great national minister firmly fixed at the head of the Government, than he began to exercise his power with vigour at least, if not with judgment. The Duke of Cumberland had a short time previously proceeded to Hanover, to take the command of the contingent forces provided for the defence of the Electorate; but Pitt did not approve of draining the strength of England by sending any large body of British troops to take part in the war upon the Continent. Daring and insolent as had been the conduct of France, he knew that her finances were disordered, that her navy was inconsiderable, and that the bulk of her army, to the number of 150,000 men, being engaged in Germany, but few remained for the protection of her shores. He therefore considered that Great Britain should no longer

* The Quartermaster-General of Scotland.

stand upon the defensive, and thinking the occasion opportune, resolved to dispel the invasion panic by inverting the order of things, in making a descent upon the French coast. If no other advantage were to result from the scheme, it was calculated to create a diversion in favour of the Duke of Cumberland and the King of Prussia, the latter of whom not only approved of the measure, but urged its speedy execution.*

The locality chosen for the project was determined upon in consequence of the representations of Captain Clarke, an English officer who had travelled through the west of France in the year 1754. A rupture between the two Powers being, even then, imminent, Clarke visited Rochefort, in Aunis, a considerable arsenal for naval stores, situated a few miles above the embouchure of the Charente, towards the centre of the deeply-curved coast which bounds the Bay of Biscay. Having observed the neglected condition of the fortress and noted the nature of the defences, with as much accuracy as was possible without exciting suspicion, he wrote to Sir John Ligonier, pointing out the facility of destroying the shipping in the harbour as well as the sea-stores. Sir John transmitted the letter to Mr. Pitt, with whose desires it so completely accorded, that, deeming every circumstance to concur in favour of a surprise,—advanced though was the season for the commencement of such an enterprise,—he immediately took the preliminary steps towards its execution. Pitt was not a man to be balked by difficulty. Lord Anson, who was at the

* Sir John Ligonier to General Mordaunt. See 'Scots Magazine,' 1757, p. 624.

head of the Admiralty, was ordered to have the fleet prepared to sail upon a given day; he replied, that it could not be equipped within so limited a time,—it was "impossible." Pitt's rejoinder was, that if the ships were not ready at the appointed period, he would lay the matter before the King, and impeach his Lordship in Parliament. This spirited menace aroused the First Lord to a sense of his duty, and, in spite of impossibility, the fleet was at the rendezvous upon the day named.*

It was the middle of July when the enterprise was determined upon. The speed and magnitude of the preparations were unprecedented, whilst the secrecy with which the destination of the armament was preserved, made it a subject of general speculation. The ships were ordered to take on board sufficient provisions for six months; and in order to man the fleet, sailors were impressed at every seaport,—2000 on the Thames alone. Scaling-ladders which could be instantly fixed, and were so constructed that thirty men might mount abreast, were prepared; and every transport was to have ten boats capable of holding thirty men each, so that the

* Almon, 'Anecdotes of the Earl of Chatham.' A similar anecdote possibly relates to the same occasion:—"During the administration of Lord Chatham, Sir Charles Frederick, Surveyor-General of the Ordnance, was ordered one day to attend him, at that time confined to his bed with a severe fit of the gout. Mr. Pitt said, 'The battering-train in the Tower must be at Portsmouth on the morning of the next day at seven o'clock.' Sir Charles attempted to show the impossibility of executing this order. Mr. Pitt, interrupting him, replied, 'At your peril, Sir, let it be done!' And it was done accordingly. Sir C. Frederick left him at seven o'clock in the evening. Mr. Pitt received an express from every stage the train reached in its passage to Portsmouth." (Seward's Anecdotes.)

entire force might land at once.* The fleet consisted of sixteen sail of the line, besides frigates, fire-ships, bomb-ketches, etc.; and the chief naval command was given to Sir Edward Hawke, under whom were Vice-Admiral Knowles and Rear-Admiral Broderick.

The leadership of the land forces, amounting to 10,000 men, was first offered to Lord George Sackville; but he declined the responsibility. Mr. Pitt then proposed Major-General Conway, to whom the King objected, as being too young an officer for so important an undertaking; and by his Majesty's desire, in an unlucky hour, Sir John Mordaunt was nominated Commander-in-chief.† Lieutenant-General Mordaunt, whose name is familiar to the reader, had seen considerable service. He was the son of the Hon. Harry Mordaunt, brother to the Earl of Peterborough, and entered the army in the year 1721. In 1745, he attained the rank of Brigadier, led a division at Culloden, and signalized himself by his intrepidity at Laffeldt. He was created Lieutenant-General in 1754; and though lacking the higher qualities of a military commander, had been remarkable for alertness and bravery, but was now infirm in both body and mind. He had had, as Walpole says, "a sort of alacrity in daring, but from ill-health was grown indifferent to it."

Conway, according to the same authority, could not help foreseeing that the conduct of the expedition would devolve upon him, and that he, though but nominally the second, must be regarded as the responsible com-

* 'Scots Magazine,' July, 1757.

† Walpole, 'Memoirs of the Reign of George II.'

mander. Walpole, who characterizes each of the leaders, describes Conway—the only person to whom he seems to have been sincerely attached—in these terms:—"Cold in his deportment, and with a dignity of soul that kept him too much above familiarity, he missed that affection from his brother-officers which his unsullied virtues and humanity deserved, for he wanted the extrinsic of merit. Added to these little failings, he had a natural indecision in his temper, weighing with too much minuteness, and too much fluctuation, whatever depended on his own judgment." Not a very flattering portrait of a soldier and future Field-Marshal! The third in command is thus sketched:—"Cornwallis was a man of a very different complexion: as cool as Conway, and as brave, he was indifferent to everything but to being in the right. He held fame cheap, and smiled at reproach."* Walpole continues:—"Under these was Wolfe, a young officer who had contracted reputation from his intelligence of discipline, and from the perfection to which he brought his own regiment. The world could not expect more from him than he thought himself capable of performing. He looked upon danger as the favourable moment that would call forth his talents." Wolfe's office upon this occasion was that of Quartermaster-General. Early in August, he repaired to the Isle of Wight, where the troops assembled; but, previous to his departure, he felt himself called upon, in consequence of his Irish appointment, to account for his absence. He therefore wrote to the Duke of Bedford as follows:—

* Wolfe, who was intimately acquainted with Cornwallis, would not have subscribed to the last sentence, for he speaks of him as being peculiarly sensitive to reproach.

My Lord,

The honour of holding an employment under your Grace, and my particular obligations to you upon that account, make it a point of duty, as well as of respect, to mention that a battalion of Colonel Kingsley's regiment is ordered to be ready to embark; and as Lieutenant-Colonel of that battalion, I embark with it, upon what service none of us pretend to guess; nor ought we to be very solicitous about it, rather desiring to serve well than to know where. If this business did not stand in the way, it would give me the highest satisfaction to endeavour to acquit myself so as to meet your Grace's approbation, being quite assured that you would take in good part whatever was well intended, and accept of industry to supply the want of skill. I beg to be allowed to wish your Grace most perfect health, and to add that I have the honour to be, etc.,

JAMES WOLFE.

By the 10th of August the army was collected and prepared to embark, but the transports were not ready. On the 22nd, Wolfe writes to his mother from Newport, Isle of Wight:—

I don't expect a letter from you,—I mean, that you will write till you have been a month at the Bath. Then, if ships come our way, whichever route we take, I shall be glad to have news from you. The winds do sharply oppose our enterprise, and so violently at this time, that we are well ashore, in my mind. We have much company, much exercise, a theatre, and all the camp amusements, besides balls and concerts. The General seemed to foresee my habitation. I am possessed of the farmhouse formerly General Wentworth's, which I find to be a dreary lodging;* however, it affects me as little as anybody, whose great concern in this life is neither food nor raiment, nor house to sleep in.

* A reminiscence of the year 1740.

In another letter from the same place, on the 3rd of September, the Quartermaster-General says to his mother:—

You know my history better than I could imagine. The ladies call that handsome (when they are well bred) which in reality is very moderate. My temper naturally leads me to that which my circumstances seldom admit of. Money would discover my turn to be rather liberal and social than otherwise. I was this day on board the 'Royal George,' when I inquired for Kit Mason, and saw him in perfect health. After the voyage he hopes to see his mother, and was mightily pleased to hear about her from me. He resembles Mrs. Mason; has beautiful eyes of her make, is grown tall, and in my opinion is a very fine boy. He was clean, and looked healthy. If we sail in the same fleet, I shall ask after him every now and then.* The wind is fair, and we expect the transports to-morrow.

The transports, however, had not all arrived until the 6th, when the troops immediately embarked. There were in all ten infantry regiments, with fifty light horse and a large train of artillery, besides draught horses, platforms for batteries, abundant stores, and, in brief, nothing was wanting to ensure success but a General! The whole got under sail on the 7th, and anchored for the night at St. Helen's, whence the expedition departed on the morning of the 8th. The 'Southampton,' man-of-war, spoke the fleet west of the Start, and brought a letter from an officer on board the 'Neptune,' which made it be believed that their destination was more distant than the coast of France. It was not until they

* Afterwards Vice-Admiral Christopher Mason, who died in 1802, aged fifty-seven. A monument to his memory may be seen in front of Greenwich Church.

had been a week at sea that the officers were informed of the real design, which, according to the General's instructions, was the destruction of Rochefort; but if that place should prove too strong, they were to seek an opening elsewhere, and spread alarm along the coast.

As soon as Wolfe was able to resume his pen, he wrote as follows to his mother:—

'Ramillies,' 17th September, 1757.

Dear Madam,

A man should always have a letter writ at sea, because the opportunities of dispatching them are seldom and sudden, and a sick, qualmish stomach is to consult the weather. He must write when he can; he may not be able to do it when he would. The progress of our arms has been greatly retarded by calms and fogs, and the formidable Gulf of Biscay, in which we are navigating, is just now as smooth as the river Thames in winter. Perhaps in twenty-four hours the waves may touch the clouds, and then the great machine will roll about like a tub, and we, the inhabitants of it, shall partake severely of the general perturbation. The troops are under good regulations and good care, and consequently are well and healthy. They feed well and lie well, and, being in their nature regardless of future events, their minds are in their usual state, roused a little, perhaps, by curiosity and the desire of something new.

For a man that does not feel the ship's motion, and whose nose is not too nice for the smells, this life for a little while is tolerable; it is then an easy, commodious conveyance to a distant place, and upon the quarter-deck of a ninety-gun ship a man may stretch and exercise his limbs. I have not myself been one hour well since we embarked, and have the mortification to find that I am the worst mariner in the whole ship. General, secretary, and aides-de-camp are all stouter, all better seamen than myself. If I make the same figure ashore, I shall acquire no great reputation by the voyage. The 'Royal George' is one of Sir Edward Hawke's seconds, is constantly on his larboard quarter, and very near, so that I have frequent opportunities of asking for little Mason, and always hear that he is well, which will be the most pleasing intelligence to his mother. Little Gusty is in the 'Burford,' and a hardy seaman.

In the following letter to his father, Wolfe relates the first proceedings of the expedition:—

Off the Isles of Rhé and Oleron,
21st September, 1757.

Dear Sir,

Yesterday morning the fleet made the land off the Isle of Rhé, and in the afternoon Vice-Admiral Knowles was detached with his division to go within the Pertuis d'Antioche,* and see what anchoring there was for the fleet; and I suppose he had orders to attack any fortifications or batteries of the enemy that might incommode us at an anchor, or prevent landing. While the Vice-Admiral was getting on to put these orders in execution, a large French man-of-war bore down into the middle of the fleet,—a ship supposed to be homeward bound from the East or West Indies,—upon which three ships of his division were directed to chase. They did so, and drove the French ship in with the shore above the river of Bordeaux, and there our great ships were obliged to leave her. This chase put an end to the operations of yesterday. As soon as the chasing ships returned this morning, it was resolved that the whole fleet should go down and anchor in the Basque Road, from whence we may attack either of these two islands [Rhé and Oleron], Rochelle, or Rochefort. A disposition was made, and the Vice-Admiral's division led in. Just as the whole fleet was getting within the Pertuis the wind took them short, and they were obliged to stand out again; and here we now are, beating on and off, waiting for a better day and a more favourable gale.

Since I writ my mother's letter we have had variety of

* The channel between the islands Rhé and Oleron.

winds, but in general moderate weather, and nothing remarkable but the circumstance of that ship's running in amongst us, and escaping by half an hour. It is believed that she would have been a very rich prize. The inhabitants are alarmed; they fired guns all along the coast last night, and we now see the smoke rising upon the sea-shore, as a signal, no doubt, of our appearance. These delays on our side, after notice given to the enemy, may have ill consequences; but they are such as, I suppose, were not easily to be avoided. We are come to an anchor in the Bay of Biscay (a thing uncommon), off the Isle of Rhé, in readiness to push in early in the morning. Sir Edward [Hawke] seems determined to do everything that can be done upon this occasion consistent with his orders and instructions, and the safety of the fleet.

22nd.—We are now at an anchor within the Pertuis d'Antioche, between the isles of Rhé and Oleron, waiting for a breeze of wind to go down upon the Isle d'Aix, which is in sight; but it is a perfect calm, and our whole force immovable.

23rd, in the morning.—All still at an anchor, the inhabitants of Rhé working hard at their entrenchments along the shore, to prevent our landing. The 'Medway,' 'Achilles,' and a fire-ship ordered to burn a French ship-of-war behind the Isle d'Aix as soon as Admiral Knowles's division begins the attack.

Isle d'Aix, 23rd, in the evening.—The fort of the Isle d'Aix taken by Captain Howe, in the 'Magnanime,' with a few distant shot from the 'Barfleur.' There were five great ships upon this business; but as Captain Howe led, he saved the rest the trouble of battering, and confounded the defendants to that degree with the vivacity of his fire that they deserted thirty pieces of cannon and eight mortars, and struck after thirty-five minutes of resistance. There were 500 men in the fort, of which very few were killed; and the 'Magnanime' lost but three killed, and eight or ten wounded. Mr. Howe's manner of going down upon the enemy, and his whole proceeding, have raised the opinion people had of his courage and abilities to a very high pitch.* The ship which Sir Edward ordered to be burned was further off than he imagined; and even now we perceive her to be within the mouth of the Charente.

We are preparing to land somewhere between Rochelle and Rochefort, for the sake of mischief more than any success we can propose to ourselves after such long preparations and notice to the enemy. I believe the expedition will end in our landing and fighting, and then returning to our ships; and we may bombard Rochelle, put the isles of Rhé and Oleron under contribution, blow up the fortress of the Isle d'Aix, and spread terror all along the coast. If we had set out upon this business in time, I believe we should have been thought very troublesome. This is a most pleasing climate, and the grapes upon the Isle d'Aix are exceedingly delicious, especially to a sick stomach. I have been told that General Conway, with three battalions, went down with Mr. Knowles's division to assist in the attack; but they were not wanted, only to take possession and guard the prisoners, who were used with all possible humanity by Captain Howe.

The latter part of the foregoing letter was written, as appears, in the captured island; but Wolfe does not explain the nature of his business there. Indeed, were we solely depending upon his own reports, we should know but little of those actions which reflect the most lustre upon his character; and it is singular that a man who was wont to lay bare the various and conflicting phases of his mind should have possessed the self-command not to allude to his conduct upon any occasion,

* Walpole describes Howe as being "undaunted as a rock, and as silent; the characteristics of his whole race. He and Wolfe soon contracted a friendship, like the union of a cannon and gunpowder." Upon which Sir J. Barrow observes:—"There is meaning in the metaphor. Howe, strong in mind, solid in judgment, firm of purpose, is the cannon; the gunpowder is Wolfe, quick in conception, prompt in execution, impetuous in action." ('Life of Richard, Earl Howe.')

when to mention it might savour of boast or vanity. Yet this reticence did not arise from that species of egotism which designedly refrains from speaking of one's self, but from that intuitive modesty, or self-unconsciousness, which ever accompanies genius. Wolfe's zealous endeavours, upon this 23rd day of September, to instil life and vigour into the expedition, fruitless though they were rendered through the pusillanimity of the chiefs, afterwards caused him to be singled out by Pitt as one likely to redeem the military reputation of England.

From his boyhood Wolfe had been on intimate terms with Sir John Mordaunt, whom he respected as an old friend who felt interested in his advancement; but friendship could not blind him to the failings of the General. His experience during their stay in the Isle of Wight, and on board the 'Ramillies,' made him fear that the nervous irritability and tremulous indecision of the Commander-in-chief, the cool caution or indifference of Conway, and the weakness of Cornwallis, foreboded the failure of the undertaking; for he knew that between such leaders—each of whom shrank from responsibility—there could not exist that unity which was essential to success. Wolfe could not but see that the welfare of their country was not the first object of any one of his superiors; nor could he recognize amongst them a particle of that self-denying patriotism which prompted his own zeal for the service.

Weary of inactivity, and unwilling that the navy should carry off all the honour, he broke through the trammels of official etiquette, and prevailed upon Sir John Mordaunt to allow him to reconnoitre the country whilst

Aix was being bombarded. At one o'clock he got into a boat, and, provided with a telescope, landed upon the island, which seemed to present the best position for his purpose, soon after its surrender. Instead of mixing with the crowd of victors and vanquished, he climbed the ramparts facing the mainland, and took a searching survey of it. Just opposite to him, and but a short distance off, he perceived the sandy promontory of Fouras, defended by a small fort, and he saw that this fort must be taken before Rochefort could be attacked. In the distance, towards the north, lay Rochelle, about midway between which place and Rochefort he descried the low point of Chattelaiellon, and noted it as the most favourable spot for landing the troops. These observations effected, he immediately returned to the 'Ramillies,' which lay anchored at a considerable distance from the island, and made his report to the Admiral and the Commander-in-chief.

After describing Fouras and its apparent strength, Wolfe told Sir Edward Hawke that a single man-of-war, provided the depth of water would allow her to approach near enough, would suffice to batter that fort; or, at least, so far attract the enemy's fire that the men might safely effect a landing. Sir Edward at once embraced the proposal, to which Mordaunt likewise assented, observing to the Admiral that he supposed Thierry, the pilot of the 'Magnanime,' could inform him of the depth of water. Wolfe then hinted that, in order to divide the enemy's attention, it might not be amiss to cause a diversion on the side of Rochelle, which he apprehended could be effected by means of bomb-ketches. Hawke accepted this suggestion also, and upon Wolfe expressing his opinion that not a moment was to be lost, he instantly sent for Thierry, and gave orders for the preparation of the ketches.

The pilot, on his arrival, seemed clearly to comprehend Wolfe's plans, and affirmed that there was no doubt about the possibility of taking the 'Magnanime' close enough to attack the fort, and enable a detachment of infantry to land upon both sides of it.* Meanwhile the Admiral, in order to be assured of a secure landing for the principal descent, dispatched Rear-Admiral Broderick, with three captains of the fleet, to sound and reconnoitre the shore of the mainland. It was the afternoon of the 24th before these officers returned, when, "after maturely considering their report," says Sir Edward, "I was of opinion that they might land; on which Sir John Mordaunt desired that a council of war might be assembled to consider of it." †

In this council, which occupied the whole of the following day, it was resolved that, having taken Admiral Broderick's report into consideration, and examined the pilots, it appeared that the troops could not be re-embarked in bad weather, the surf and swell being usually so great that no boats could approach the shore to take off the men. Also that, in case the troops were overpowered by superior numbers, they could have no protection from the cannon of the fleet, the shoal water preventing the ships coming within gun-shot. Owing to these

* Entick, 'History of the late War.'

† Letter to Mr. Pitt, dated "'Ramillies,' in Basque Road, September 30, 1757."

hindrances, together with the long detention in the Isle of Wight, the delay caused by contrary winds, fogs, and calms upon the passage, information of the French forces assembling in the neighbourhood, and the improbability of finding Rochefort unprepared, the court was unanimously of opinion that such an attempt was neither advisable nor practicable.*

Yet, notwithstanding this conclusion, and in spite of the impracticability, after two more days were lost in a second consultation, it was resolved, after "mature deliberation," to land the troops with all possible dispatch. Accordingly, at midnight on the 28th, the men debarked from the transports into boats; but, after being tossed about by the swell for three hours, a cutter arrived with orders that they were to return on shipboard. "I can hardly believe it," said the colonel in command; "show me your instructions." On being shown the written orders, the soldiers returned to their respective transports, but not without a general murmur of disapprobation.†

The reasons for the countermand assigned by the Admiral and by Sir John Mordaunt are strangely at variance. The former says:—"Part of the troops were actually in the boats when I received a letter from Mr. Broderick, viz.—'Sir, I have prepared all the boats, with proper officers, to land the troops agreeably to your orders, but am to acquaint you that the Generals are

* Admiral Hawke justified his assent to the resolution upon the grounds of his confidence in the judgment of the land officers, and their better knowledge of their own profession. (See letter as above, in 'Scots Magazine' (1757), p. 627.)

† Entick, vol. ii. p. 332.

come to a resolution not to land to-night, and to wait till daylight, when they can have a full view of the ground where they are to land.' " * On the other hand, Mordaunt writes:—"Unfortunately, such a high wind sprang up from the shore, that all the sea-officers gave their opinion that the landing should not be attempted; that the boats must be towed so very slowly that it would be daylight before the first embarkation could be landed, and it would be six hours before that body could be supported by a second." †

On the 29th, Admiral Hawke acquainted Mordaunt by letter, that if the general officers had no further military operations to propose, sufficient to authorize his detaining the fleet, he must return to England immediately. The General then desired that a third council of war should be held, but the Admiral declined to attend, saying, that seamen were not judges of operations to be performed by troops on shore.

Thus ended an expedition which cost the nation a million of money,—an expedition, whose design was pronounced by no mean judge, to be "wise, prudent, and well-timed." ‡ Had Wolfe and Howe had the conduct of it, instead of Mordaunt and Hawke, there is every reason to believe that it would have been crowned with success.

Wolfe informs his father of the failure in these words:—

* Letter as above.

† Letter to Mr. Pitt, dated "'Ramillies,' Rade de Basque, September 30." ('Scots Magazine,' p. 627.)

‡ Rodney to Mr. Grenville. See Grenville Correspondence, vol. i. p. 208.

Rade des Basques, 30th September, 1757.

Dear Sir,

By the 'Viper' sloop I have the displeasure to inform you that our operations here are at an end. We lost the lucky moment in war, and are not able to recover it. The whole of this expedition has not cost the nation ten men, nor has any man been able to distinguish himself in the service of his country, except Mr. Howe, who was a great example to us all. We shall follow close if the weather favours, and return to England with reproach and dishonour; though, in my mind, there never was in any troops, sea and land, a better disposition to serve.*

* "The judgment of all the great warriors whom all the nations of Western Europe had sent to the confluence of the Sambre and the Meuse, was that the English subaltern was inferior to no subaltern, and the English private soldier to no private soldier in Christendom. The English officers of higher rank were thought hardly worthy to command such an army. Cutts, indeed, had distinguished himself by his intrepidity; but those who most admired him acknowledged that he had neither the capacity nor the science necessary to a general." (Lord Macaulay, 'History of England,' vol. iv. p. 599.)

CHAPTER XVII.

BLACKHEATH.—LONDON.—BATH.

October—December, 1757.

Never was there a greater national disappointment than that caused by the failure of the expedition against Rochefort, for the people had counted on success. They could not believe that the first great war-measure of their Minister, whose energy had been displayed in the magnitude of the preparations, could possibly miscarry; but, like other men, Pitt had to purchase experience. Nor did this mortification come singly. The cause of England's only ally seemed to be rendered irremediable by the disastrous battle of Kolin; the Duke of Cumberland likewise had been defeated at Hastenbeck, and agreed to a convention whereby his army was disbanded, and France was at liberty to turn her arms against Prussia. The intelligence from America was also disheartening, while at home, owing chiefly to the dearness of provisions and the agitation consequent upon the Militia Bill, the lower orders were "dissatisfied, mutinous, and ripe for insurrection." No Minister but Pitt could have successfully struggled against such a state of things,—the natural result of the mismanagement of his predecessors.

On the opening of Parliament he reprehended with great warmth the indolence and caution of those entrusted with the execution of military operations. He declared his solemn belief that there was a determined resolution, in both naval and military commanders, against any vigorous exertion of the national power; and affirmed, that though the King was ready to embrace every measure proposed by his Ministers for the honour and interest of the country, yet scarcely a man could be found with whom the conduct of any design, in which there was the least appearance of danger, could with confidence be trusted. With a force much greater than the nation had ever maintained, and a Government ardently desirous of redeeming her glory and promoting her welfare, a shameful dislike to the service everywhere prevailed. Nor was it, he said, amongst the military officers alone that inactivity and neglect appeared; those who filled other departments were affected with a like indifference. Contractors, purveyors, victuallers were never to be found but upon occasions of their own personal advantage; in conversation they appeared totally ignorant of their business. The extent of their knowledge went no further than making of false accounts; in that science they were adepts.*

But Pitt, indefatigable and punctual in the fulfilment of his own official duties, by his example and authority soon awakened all those who were under him to a consciousness of their responsibility to a master whose keen penetration was not to be deceived. His detection and exposure of abuses in the several departments wherein

* Almon, vol. i. p. 332.

they had been long prevalent, eventually operated to the public advantage; and the superior officers of the army, as if electrified by the fire of the great Minister's mind, were aroused from their lethargy. The consequence was, that ere long order and promptitude were observed in the transaction of civil affairs, and the military renown of the nation was restored.

Returning to Wolfe, who had sought the retirement of Blackheath. On the 17th of October he writes to his mother:—

To save myself the trouble of answering questions, and for the sake of fresh air and exercise, I have taken up my quarters at your house, and, with Mrs. Eleanor's assistance, am like to do well.* By the bye, her husband was very useful to me on board the 'Ramillies.' I was glad you were gone to the Bath, though I lost the pleasure of seeing you for a time. It is a little melancholy to be left alone, especially to one who was a witness of our late miscarriage. By this trial I find that the cheerfullest temper requires the aid and prop of society. When Françoise comes to know what I would have for dinner, he distresses me with the question. Whenever I keep house somebody must direct, for I cannot.

As to the expedition, it has been conducted so ill that I am ashamed to have been of the party. The public could not do better than dismiss six or eight of us from the service. No zeal, no ardour, no care or concern for the good and honour of the country. I have begun to dismiss myself by surrendering up my office of Quartermaster-General for Ireland. They thought proper to put a younger lieutenant-colonel over me, and I thought it proper to resign. My Lord Barrington says he has nothing to do with Irish affairs, so refers me to Mr.

* Eleanor White, a domestic, to whom Mrs. Wolfe bequeathed an annuity of £20. To other servants, who had lived with her for two years and upwards, she left £20 each.

Secretary Rigby;* but his Lordship desired me to suspend my operations for a few days, which accordingly I do. I will certainly not go to Ireland without the rank of colonel, and am indifferent whether I get it or not. I can't part with my other employment, because I have nothing else to trust to; nor do I think it consistent with honour to sneak off in the middle of a war.

Next day, Wolfe writes the following epitome of the late proceedings to his uncle Walter:—

Blackheath, October 18th, 1757.

Dear Sir,

"Nous avons manqué un beau coup," as the French prisoners told us, after we had loitered away three or four days in consultations, deliberations, and councils of war. The season of the year and nature of the enterprise called for the quickest and most vigorous execution, whereas our proceedings were quite otherwise. We were in sight of the Isle of Rhé the 20th September, consequently were seen by the enemy (as their signals left us no room to doubt), and it was the 23rd before we fired a gun. That afternoon and night slipped through our hands,—the lucky moment of confusion and consternation among our enemies. The 24th,—Admirals and Generals consult together, and resolve upon nothing between them but to hold a council of war. The 25th,—this famous council sat from morning till late at night, and the result of the debates was unanimously not to attack the place they were ordered to attack, and for reasons that no soldier will allow to be sufficient. The 26th,—the Admiral sends a message to the General, intimating that if they did not determine to do something there he would go to another place. The 27th,—the Generals and Admirals view the land with glasses, and agree upon a

* William, second Viscount Barrington, was at this time Secretary-at-War. Richard Rigby, the son of a linendraper who had enriched himself as factor of the South Sea Company, was secretary to the Duke of Bedford, Lord-Lieutenant of Ireland. See Walpole's Letters, Junius, etc.

second council of war, having by this time discovered their mistake. The 28th,—they deliberate, and resolve to land that night. Orders are issued out accordingly, but the wind springing up after the troops had been two or three hours in the boats, the officers of the navy declare it difficult and dangerous to attempt the landing. The troops are commanded back to their transports, and so ended the expedition! The true state of the case is, that our sea-officers do not care to be engaged in any business of this sort, where little is to be had but blows and reputation; and the officers of the infantry are so profoundly ignorant, that an enterprise of any vigour astonishes them to that degree that they have not strength of mind nor confidence to carry it through.

I look upon this as the greatest design that the nation has engaged in for many years, and it must have done honour to us all if the execution had answered the intentions of the projector.* The Court of Versailles, and the whole French nation, were alarmed beyond measure. "Les Anglois ont attrapé notre foible," disent-ils. Alas! we have only discovered our own.† I see no remedy, for we have no officers from the Commander-in-chief down to Mr. Webb and Lord Howe; and the navy list is not much better. If they would even blunder on and fight a little, making some amends to the public by their courage for their want of skill; but this excessive degree of caution, or whatever name it deserves, leaves exceeding bad impressions among the troops, who, to do them justice, upon this occasion showed all the signs of spirit and goodwill. My health is a little injured by this summer's inactivity, as I have not been able to get ten times

* "Milord Holdernesse, long-tems ministre, avec qui j'en ai parlé depuis à Londres, m'a dit que de toutes les entreprises qui s'étoient faites sur nos côtes, c'étoit la seule qu'il eût approuvée, et qui dût réussir si elle eût été mieux conduite." (Duclos, 'Mémoires Secrets,' vol. ii. p. 456.)

† It was affirmed that Louis XV. said at a levée:—"By this time the English are in possession of Rochefort, and it will cost me more than thirty millions of livres to repair the injury they will do me." (Grenville Correspondence, vol. i. p. 217.)

on horseback; and I am here alone, partly to save myself the trouble of answering questions, and partly for air and exercise.

I am, dear Sir,
Your obedient Nephew,
JAMES WOLFE.*

On the 21st, the recluse transmits good news to his father:—

Mr. Fisher writes me word that the King has been pleased to give me the rank of colonel, which at this time is more to be prized than at any other, because it carries with it a favourable appearance as to my conduct upon this late expedition, and an acceptance of my good intentions. I am something indebted to Sir Edward Hawke for having spoken to Lord Anson, who took the trouble to repeat it to the King. I shall ask Sir John Ligonier's commands to-morrow whether I go to the regiment or to Ireland.† There is a storm gathering over the head of my unfortunate friend [Cornwallis], such a one as must necessarily crush him; though, in my mind, he acted in this affair but a second part. That, as far as I am able, I shall always be ready to assert, and will give him the best hints in my power for his defence. This must remain a secret between us, because I know he is ill-used and artfully ruined, after suffering himself to be misled by an over-fair opinion of his guide.‡

The Eighth regiment having formed part of the expedition, General Wolfe called upon his Lieutenant-Colonel

* The original letter is now in the possession of G. Moffatt, Esq., M.P., who has kindly sanctioned its publication.

† H.R.H. the Duke of Cumberland having resigned his military appointments after the Convention of Stade, Sir John Ligonier was appointed Commander-in-chief. Soon afterwards he was created Viscount Ligonier of Enniskillen, in the peerage of Ireland.

‡ Neither Conway nor Cornwallis, though for awhile in disfavour, were arraigned for their conduct upon this occasion. The Hon. Edward Cornwallis afterwards became a lieutenant-general, and died, Governor of Gibraltar, in 1776.

for a report of their proceedings. That officer, it appears, referred his Colonel to his son, who replied sarcastically as follows:—

Blackheath, 24th October, 1757.

Dear Sir,

'Tis an admirable circumstance for Lafausille to ask me about an expedition that he himself was engaged in. His lumbago left him very *à propos*; for just as he got to the Basque Road he revived. One's native air has surprising effects! All that I can tell about it is, that we blundered most egregiously on all sides—sea and land; that we lost three days without and three within, and consequently couldn't propose to march to Paris this season. I believe the country is not able to bear many jokes of this sort; nor have the fleets and arms of this nation reputation enough to excuse now and then a *faux pas*. However, let justice be done to the executive part; the seamen and soldiers in general were most desirous and most earnest for employment. These disappointments, I hope, won't affect their courage; nothing, I think, can hurt their discipline,—it is at its worst. They shall drink and swear, plunder and massacre, with any troops in Europe, the Cossacks and Calmucks themselves not excepted; with this difference, that they have not quite so violent an appetite for blood and bonfires.*

Sir John Ligonier's commission, appointing him Commander-in-chief of the armies of Britain, is come out, or to come out suddenly under the broad seal of England. I shall pay my duty to our new General, and inform myself whether I may set out for Ireland or not, taking the Bath in my way. I dine with Sir Gregory to-morrow; he and my Lady Page are very solicitous for your welfare.†

* Notwithstanding a stringent manifesto issued by General Mordaunt, the soldiers who took possession of the Isle of Aix got drunk, and cruelly insulted the inhabitants. Even the church was pillaged, the priest robbed of his library, and his vestments turned into masquerading habits by the drunken sailors. (See Scots Mag., p. 500.)

† The fate of Wricklesmarsh, near Blackheath, the magnificent seat of Sir Gregory Page, Bart., a wealthy India merchant, was similar to

To none of his correspondents was Wolfe wont to open his mind so unreservedly upon the conduct of military affairs as to Rickson. He now tells his friend the lesson he had learnt from the recent miscarriage,—a lesson which he did not fail, the following year, to turn to practical account. His letter is, therefore, rather a critique than a repetition of details:—

Dear Rickson,

I thank you very heartily for your welcome back. I am not sorry that I went, notwithstanding what has happened; one may always pick up something useful from amongst the most fatal errors. I have found out that an Admiral should endeavour to run into an enemy's port immediately after he appears before it; that he should anchor the transport ships and frigates as close as he can to the land; that he should reconnoitre and observe it as quick as possible, and lose no time in getting the troops on shore; that previous directions should be given in respect to landing the troops, and a proper disposition made for the boats of all sorts, appointing leaders and fit persons for conducting the different divisions. On the other hand, experience shows me that, in an affair depending upon vigour and dispatch, the Generals should settle their plan of operations, so that no time may be lost in idle debate and consultations when the sword should be drawn; that pushing on smartly is the road to success, and more particularly so in an affair of this nature; that nothing is to be reckoned an obstacle to your undertaking which is not found really so upon trial; that in war something must be allowed to chance and fortune, seeing it is in its nature hazardous,

that of Cannons, the palace of the Duke of Chandos, which arose and disappeared within half a century. Sir Gregory dying in 1775, Wricklesmarsh was inherited by his nephew, who sold the collection of pictures and sculpture by auction, and disposed of the estate. The mansion was afterwards pulled down, and the grounds let in building-lots. In a previous letter Wolfe spoke of Lady Page as "an estimable woman, one of the best of the children of Eve."

and an option of difficulties; that the greatness of an object should come under consideration, opposed to the impediments that lie in the way; that the honour of one's country is to have some weight; and that, in particular circumstances and times, the loss of a thousand men is rather an advantage to a nation than otherwise, seeing that gallant attempts raise its reputation and make it respectable; whereas the contrary appearances sink the credit of a country, ruin the troops, and create infinite uneasiness and discontent at home.

I know not what to say, my dear Rickson, or how to account for our proceedings, unless I own to you that there never was people collected together so unfit for the business they were sent upon—dilatory, ignorant, irresolute, and some grains of a very unmanly quality, and very unsoldier-like or unsailor-like. I have already been too imprudent; I have said too much, and people make me say ten times more than I ever uttered; therefore, repeat nothing out of my letter, nor name my name as author of any one thing. The whole affair turned upon the impracticability of escalading Rochefort; and the two evidences brought to prove that the ditch was wet (in opposition to the assertions of the chief engineer, who had been in the place), are persons to whom, in my mind, very little credit should be given;* without these evidences we should have landed, and must have marched to Rochefort, and it is my opinion that the place would have surrendered, or have been taken, in forty-eight hours. It is certain that there was nothing in all that country to oppose 9000 good Foot,—a million of Protestants, upon whom it is necessary to keep a strict eye, so that the garrison could not venture to assemble against us, and no troops, except the militia, within any moderate distance of these parts.

Little practice in war, ease and convenience at home, great incomes, and no wants, with no ambition to stir to action, are

* A portion of the evidence on the inquiry turned upon the question whether the ditch of Rochefort was wet or dry; M. Bonneville, a French volunteer, and another witness, asserting that it was wet, in contradiction to Colonel Clarke, who stated that it was dry.

not the instruments to work a successful war withal; I see no prospect of better deeds. I know not where to look for them, or from whom we may expect them. Many handsome things would have been done by the troops had they been permitted to act. As it is, Captain Howe carried off all the honour of this enterprise . . . . notwithstanding what that scribbling . . . been pleased to lie about that fort and the attack of it.*

This disaster in North America, unless the French have driven from their anchors in the harbour of Louisbourg, is of the most fatal kind; whatever diminishes our naval force tends to our ruin and destruction.† God forbid that any accident should befall our fleet in the bay! The Duke's resignation may be reckoned an addition to our misfortunes; he acted a right part, but the country will suffer by it.

Yours, my dear Rickson,
Very affectionately,
J. W.

Blackheath, 5th Nov., 1757.

In the beginning of November Wolfe was summoned to give evidence before the Board of General officers who had been appointed to inquire into the causes of the failure of the late expedition. Writing to Bath, on the 8th, he says:—"Better and more honourable for the country if the one-half of us had gone the great road of mortality together, than to be plagued with inquiries and censures, and the cry of the world."

The reports of inquisitions in those days are so very meagre that no satisfactory account of the proceedings

* The expedition was the subject of many party pamphlets, one of which was entitled, 'Reflections upon the Report,' etc. Being friendly to the Generals, the writer endeavoured to throw the blame of the failure upon the projectors, by showing the impracticability of the scheme. A masterly 'Reply' afterwards appeared, supposed by some to have been written by Pitt.

† The capture, by the French, of Fort William-Henry, and of the flotilla upon Lake George. (See Cooper's 'Last of the Mohicans.')

of the Board appointed to inquire into the conduct of Generals Mordaunt, Conway, and Cornwallis, could be given, were it necessary to enter fully into the subject. But the substance of Wolfe's evidence may be gleaned from contemporaneous periodicals. The officers appointed to investigate the matter—Lieutenant-General the Duke of Marlborough, Major-General Lord George Sackville, and Major-General Waldegrave—first assembled at the house of the Judge Advocate-General, on Tuesday the 8th of November, when they adjourned to Saturday the 12th. On that day the journals kept during the expedition, and the minutes of the councils of war were produced; but, not being properly authenticated, were disallowed. General Mordaunt having read his defence, the Board adjourned.

On the 14th, Wolfe was called in and examined. His evidence was to the effect that the men might have landed at *Chaitelaillon*,—a short distance north of Fouras,—the only defence there being a battery of six guns; but that, owing to the numerous sand-hills which the invaders would have been obliged to climb, their landing could have been prevented by 1000 foot and 400 horse. Fort Fouras, he considered, might have been carried by storm, as it had but one platform of twenty-four embrasures towards the water-side, and being situated upon a peninsula, it could have been attacked upon all sides while the men-of-war lay before it. One of the captains of the fleet, he said, had offered to batter the fort with his ship. Wolfe likewise stated that he himself had proposed a feint towards Rochelle and the Isle of Rhé during the landing and attack.*

* 'Gentleman's Magazine,' p. 491.

The General officers who presided at the inquiry delivered their Report on the 21st of November. They attributed the frustration of the design, in the first instance, to not attacking Fouras agreeably to Wolfe's plan; "which certainly," says the Report, "must have been of the greatest utility towards carrying your Majesty's instructions into execution." Another cause assigned was that, instead of taking active measures upon the return of Admiral Broderick, a council was held, in which it was resolved that an attempt upon Rochefort was impracticable, although it did not appear that there were either troops or batteries on shore to prevent a landing. They next justly remark upon the resolution of the council of war held on the 28th, that "no reason could have existed sufficient to prevent the attempt of landing *previous* to that day, as the council then unanimously resolved to land with all possible dispatch." The Report concludes thus:—"We cannot but look upon the expedition as having failed, from the time the great object of it was laid aside in the council of war of the 25th."*

On the 1st of December, Wolfe was at Blackheath, whence he writes to his mother as follows:—

I could not tell you what was to become of me when I left Portsmouth, because I did not know; but finding myself confined to the neighbourhood of London, and not being able to live there altogether, partly for health and partly to save trouble, I came here. Mrs. Scott assisted me with the few things that were wanting.† My demands are very moderate, and my way of life here is exemplary, and without vanity I

* 'Scots Magazine' (1757), p. 628.

† Mrs. Elizabeth, mother of Major Scott. Mrs. Wolfe bequeathed her an annuity of £30.

may say there is as good order, almost, preserved in your family, in every respect, as if you yourself presided. I lie in your chamber, dress myself in the General's little parlour, and dine where you did. The most perceptible difference and change of affairs (exclusive of the bad table I keep) is the number of dogs in the yard; but by coaxing Ball, and rubbing his back with my stick, I have reconciled him with the new ones, and put 'em in some measure under his protection. For this fortnight past I have lodgings in town, and live for the most part there; but am glad when a fine day invites me to get on horseback and come here. My servants, clothes, etc., are all in London. When I mean to dine here, Ambrose, who is my running footman, comes before upon his legs (for we have Criten's borrowed horse between us), and gets me something to eat. The next day he runs back with the same alacrity, and by that means preserves his own health and my money.

This Court of Inquiry has kept us close, and now they talk of a general court-martial to try Sir John Mordaunt, who is in such a miserable state of health that I don't believe he will go through with it.* Till that is over I'm still a prisoner, expecting, as before, to be called upon in evidence. When my family was here, Nelly made soup and Monsieur François made *bouilli*; so, between your maids and my men, I lived very elegantly and very cheap. To-morrow I dine *tête-à-tête*, in London, with my old friend Rich, who wants to know the short history of the expedition. At night I am to meet his guest, who is sent by the King of Prussia; Mr. Keith, our late envoy at Vienna; a son of Field-Marshal Count Lacy's; and Colonel Clarke, the engineer. These, with myself, make five very odd characters, and for the oddity of the mixture I mention it to you.†

* General Mordaunt was brought to trial soon afterwards, and acquitted. The King, after a week's consideration, approved of the verdict of the court martial.

† The first of the odd characters was Major Grant, aide-de-camp to Marshal Keith. On the 28th of November he arrived at the Court of

In December, Wolfe joined his father and mother at Bath, where, on the 29th, he wrote as follows to one of his captains who was recruiting at Wigan, in Lancashire:—

Dear Parr,

I must proceed in a regular way to answer your letters, but concisely, because, like other great men, I have many to answer, and much business upon my hands. I have always time enough to read a friend's letter, therefore pray no attempt hereafter to excuse yourself from writing upon the supposition that I have not leisure to read. I look upon the proceedings in the Bay of Biscay as flowing from natural causes, and could have told you in the Isle of Wight (what I actually did to some who were in the secret), either that we should attempt nothing, or execute ill what we did attempt. I will be open enough and vain enough to tell you that there

St. James's with intelligence of the victory gained by the King of Prussia, on the 5th, at Rosbach.

Mr. (Robert) Keith, of Craig, Kincardineshire, at first Secretary to the Forces under the Earl of Stair, was appointed Under-Secretary by Lord Sandwich while Minister for Foreign Affairs. On the conclusion of the peace he was sent as envoy to the Court of Vienna, where he resided until July, 1757, when he was recalled in consequence of the coalition between Austria and France. In 1758, he was made ambassador to the Court of St. Petersburg, and remained there until 1762, which he retired from public life, and died at Edinburgh, in 1774. He was a man of most amiable character, and was the father of Sir Robert Murray Keith, British representative at Copenhagen and Vienna.

Count Lacey, or Lascy, of Irish extraction, learned the art of war under the famous Russian General Marshal Münnich, and afterwards entered the Austrian service, in which he rose to the highest rank.

Colonel Clarke, whose report of the condition of Rochefort occasioned the attempt against it, was the son of an Edinburgh physician. Entick speaks of him as a worthy, intelligent, skilful officer; but Walpole, who owed him, as well as Wolfe, a grudge, because their evidences told against his friend Conway, portrays him "as a young Scot, by name Clarke; ill-favoured in his person, with a cast in his eye; of intellects not very sound, but quick, bold, and adventurous." (See 'Memoirs of the Reign of George II.,' vol. ii.)

might be a lucky moment to be seized for the public service, which I watched for; but it came too late, and there ended the reputation of three bad Generals. You must burn this insolent letter.

Your success gives me double satisfaction, for the regiment and for yourself, and I know full well that you will omit nothing that may tend to improve or to continue it. I thank God our officers, and those who have left us, profess a sense of duty and spirit that needs no quickening, no urging. I explained the nature of our discipline some days ago to the Prince of Wales, who is extremely desirous of being informed of these sort of things.* I told him that there was in the corps a necessary degree of obedience, joined with high spirit of service and love of duty, with which he appeared to be greatly pleased, knowing well that from good inclinations, joined with order and discipline, great military performances usually spring.

As I profess to introduce as many young gentlemen as I possibly can into the service, and to exclude *canaille* as much as in me lies, I am ready to give all possible assistance to the young man you speak of. I shall be glad to see him in London, and will put him in a way of succeeding as he desires; but his relations should beware of sending him too soon into the world, and more especially as he has not some steady friend in London, by whose advice he may be guided, and by whose authority he may be led. A good education is the first thing to be thought of; after that, a profession suited to the inclinations or abilities of the young man. In the army, as well as in other professions, learning is absolutely necessary, and a year or two of improvement is better than one with the insignificant duty of the capital. You did not name the tutor in your letter. As to the Roman Catholic, if he is young and expresses a great desire to serve, I would overlook his mistake in point of faith. Maybe, by our good doctrine, life, and example, we may work his conversion! One thing is cer-

* Of Wolfe's contemporaries, King George III. was perhaps one of the last survivors.

tain, that we shall shake his present belief, whether we give him better and sounder notions or not.

Yours affectionately,
J. WOLFE.

It was not in Europe only that the incompetency of the superior officers of the British army rendered the vast undertakings of the year 1757 futile. In America the campaign was no less inglorious, and far more disastrous. The Earl of Loudoun—of whom it was said "he is like St. George on the signs, always on horseback, but never rides on"*—had been sent thither as Commander-in-chief in 1756; but he arrived too late to effect anything that year, beyond strengthening some of the frontier forts. Meanwhile the French, encouraged by their successes under Montcalm, never abated their hostilities. Even during the severity of the Canadian winter, settlements within the borders of the British provinces were devastated, homesteads burnt, crops destroyed, cattle carried off, and the people scalped by the savage allies of France, and the hardly less savage *habitans;* while spies gained information of every movement of their adversaries.

In the summer of 1757, Montcalm marched towards Fort William-Henry, the advanced post of the New England States, when Webb, who commanded about 4000 men, hearing of his approach, fell back upon New York, leaving the gallant Monro, with a small garrison, to bear the brunt of the attack, and the butchery of Montcalm's bloodthirsty followers. But the grand scheme of the British government, for this campaign,

* Franklin's Autobiography (Sparks), vol. i. p. 219.

was the reduction of Louisbourg, where it was considered the naval power of England could be brought to bear. With this intent, Lord Loudoun was reinforced by several battalions and a detachment of artillery under General Hopson,—"a commander whom a child might outwit or terrify with a pop-gun;"* and a formidable fleet, commanded by Admiral Holborne, sailed for America at the same time. In July, an armament, such as had not previously been collected in the British colonies, assembled at Halifax; altogether, about 12,000 land forces and nineteen sail-of-the-line, besides smaller craft. Early in August the troops were embarked, with the intention of taking Louisbourg by surprise; but Lord Loudoun, on learning that the French were prepared to receive him, abandoned the idea of attacking the fortress, landed a portion of his men upon the coast of Nova Scotia, and returned with the remainder to New York. The fleet then sailed towards Cape Breton, but the sight of the French ships in the harbour of Louisbourg made Holborne return to Halifax. With the addition of four more men-of-war he again sailed for Louisbourg, but not finding the French Admiral inclined to quit the shelter of the batteries, he kept cruising along the coast until October, when a violent storm dispersed and almost ruined his fleet, the shattered remains of which returned to England towards the end of the year.

* Walpole to Mann, "February 13, 1757."

CHAPTER XVIII.

LONDON.—PORTSMOUTH.—HALIFAX, N.S.

JANUARY—FEBRUARY, 1758.

THE constant success of the French power in North America since the year 1755, rendered the condition of the British colonies almost hopeless. By the possession of Fort du Quesné, France retained command over the entire continent westward of the Alleghany mountains, and preserved unbroken communication with her southern settlements on the Mississippi. By the destruction of Oswego, in 1756, she acquired sole dominion over the great lakes of the St. Lawrence; and the acquisition of Fort William-Henry, in 1757, made her mistress of the smaller lakes Champlain and George. This transient predominance arose principally from the widely different positions, social as well as political, of the French and English colonists. The French, to a man, trained to arms, were united under a single governor; and as hunters, trappers, and voyageurs, intermixed with the aborigines, whose habits they adopted, and whose alliance they won. The English, on the other hand, though they had the advantage in numbers and in wealth, were farmers and traders unhabituated to adventure; and each of the provinces to which they belonged was as jealous of the rest as all were of the Home Government, from which they claimed protection, whilst they thwarted every measure taken for their defence.

It had by this time become evident that the French and English powers could not continue to co-exist in the West. Mr. Pitt therefore, undaunted by past miscarriages, resolved that America should be the field of more extensive operations than had previously been attempted. His first act was to recall the Earl of Loudoun; for which he assigned as a reason, that his Lordship had not troubled him with dispatches, and, consequently, he could not tell what was doing.* At the same time, he sent circulars to the several provincial governors, assuring them of support, urging them to renewed exertion, and promising the reimbursement of all extraordinary expenses. Mr. Pitt's scheme for the campaign of 1758 was threefold:—1st, the reduction of Fort du Quesne, which he entrusted to Brigadier Forbes; 2nd, an attack upon Ticonderoga and Crown Point, under General Abercrombie, who succeeded Lord Loudoun as Commander-in-chief; and 3rd, the reduction of Louisbourg, the key to the river St. Lawrence.

As the last undertaking must necessarily embrace a conjunct naval and military armament, and as expeditions of that nature had hitherto been invariably unsuccessful, the selection of proper commanders was of the first importance. An Admiral adequate to the duty was readily found in the Hon. Edward Boscawen; but where was the Minister to look for leaders of the land forces?

* Franklin's Autobiography.

There were scores of generals, lieutenant-generals, and major-generals on the Army List, it is true; but which of them was up to the mark? Who amongst them was desirous of responsible command? Conway, indeed, was anxious for employment; and it was represented to the King in his favour that he had proposed to do something at Rochefort. "Yes," said his Majesty, who, though no wit, could now and then make a caustic retort, "après dîné la moutarde." Pitt had had enough of the incapables; so, spurning the claims of seniority, and the pretensions of patrons, he looked lower down to see if he could find the men he wanted. Colonel Amherst, who had distinguished himself in Germany, he recalled, created him a major-general, and entrusted him with the control of the expeditionary army; and to Brevet-Colonel Wolfe he gave the command of a brigade. Two other brigadiers, whom he appointed for the service, Whitmore and Lawrence, were already in America.

Let us now revert to Wolfe's private history, as shown by his letters from the beginning of the year 1758 until the sailing of the expedition destined for Cape Breton. After spending a few days with his parents at Bath, he writes to his mother from Exeter on the 7th of January:—

Dear Madam,

Part in chaise and part on horseback, I got myself conveyed to this place yesterday by two o'clock, and this morning received a letter from London that hurries me back to town. I set out to-morrow at six o'clock, and shall hardly stop till I arrive at the great capital. Necessity obliged me to ride the same post-horses for three-and-thirty miles, till we were all heartily tired. However, with the help of cooling diachylon, I shall proceed with all dispatch, and give you the earliest notice of my journey's end. The taking of Breslau completes the ruin of the Austrian arms; and before the month of June, I conclude that the French will be driven over the Rhine.* I hope I did not disturb your pretty neighbours. You will be so good to make my excuses for any little annoyance of that sort, unavoidable; though I gave strict orders not to interrupt their sleep.

On Monday, the 8th, the rapid traveller writes from London to his father, giving an account of his remarkable journey:†—

You won't expect to hear from me so soon, though you will not be much surprised at the celerity of my movements. Yesterday, at five o'clock, I left Exeter, and was in town this day by *one*,—the distance 170 miles. I have seen nobody about business except Carleton, who informs me that things are going on. I met Amherst's regiment upon the march towards Portsmouth; the first division at Bagshot. It was pretty dark last night, and I was obliged to have lights all over Salisbury Plain. About midway our candle went out, and we seemed at a stand, when the provident François provided a tinder-box, struck a light, and we proceeded happily to our journey's end. He offers his services to go along with me, which I am glad to accept of, and so my equipage stands complete. I was hurried from Exeter by a letter, intimating the sudden departure of our forces for North America. To-morrow will fix my affairs, and in a few days my baggage will begin to move. Prince Ferdinand retires before the French, who have passed the Aller in force.

* Breslau surrendered to the King of Prussia on the 19th December, 1757, a fortnight after his great victory at Leuthen.

† If there be no error in the date of either letter, he must have started from Exeter on the afternoon of the 7th, instead of waiting until the following morning. In either case, considering the roads that were then, Wolfe's journey was wonderfully rapid. Mr. Smiles tells us that in the summer of 1774, after the Bath road had been improved, Burke travelled from London to Bristol in twenty-four hours; "but his biographer takes care to relate that he travelled with incredible speed." ('Lives of the Engineers.')

Busy though he was just now, Wolfe found time to take an active interest in the concerns of his old friend Rickson, who still performed the duties of the Deputy Quartermaster-General of Scotland, but was not yet officially confirmed in the post. In a letter from Blackheath, on the 12th of January, after explaining his efforts on behalf of his correspondent, Wolfe continues:—

My services in this matter, and my credit with the reigning powers, are not worth your acceptance; but such as they allow it to be, you are as welcome to as any living man. I can assure you that Davy [Watson] is double, and would shove you aside to make way for a tenth cousin: it becomes my Lord G. Beauclerk to confirm you in your office by asking and procuring a commission. If he is satisfied with your management, it is his duty to do it; these mealy chiefs give up their just rights, and with them their necessary authority. The Commander in Scotland is the fittest person to recommend, and the best judge of the merits of those that serve under him.

Though to all appearance I am in the very centre of business, yet nobody (from the indolent inattention of my temper) knows less of what is going on where I myself am not concerned. The proceedings in Parliament, intrigues of the parties, and the management of public affairs, are as much unknown to me as the business of a divan or seraglio. I live amongst men without desiring to be acquainted with their concerns; things have their ordinary course, and I pass on with the current unheeding. Being of the profession of arms, I would seek all occasions to serve, and therefore have thrown myself in the way of the American war; though I know that the very passage threatens my life, and that my constitution must be utterly ruined and undone, and this from no motive either of avarice or ambition.

On the 17th, he writes from London to his mother at Bath:—

Dear Madam,

I seldom have business enough to excuse my not writing to you, and now have as little as most men. The public affairs are pretty much fixed, and my private matters are so far advanced that I reckon to be ready at least as soon as the squadron, which will hardly be in a condition to put to sea till the latter end of the next week, or the beginning of the following one. The General's letter of credit has enabled me to proceed vigorously, and the more as my correspondent in Ireland affects some delay, which, without the timely interposition of Mr. Fisher, might prejudice or check my proceedings. The two gentlemen with whom I transact business in that kingdom do not, I think, use me quite kindly, as one who has not neglected their interests might well expect; but the members of a corrupt office are seldom free from the infection, and we are to look for such fruit as the soil and cultivation naturally produce.

I don't deserve so much consideration or concern as my father and you are so good as to express for me. He wishes rank for me; and you, my preservation. All I wish for myself is, that I may at all times be ready and firm to meet that fate we cannot shun, and to die gracefully and properly when the hour comes, now or hereafter. A small portion of the good things of this world will fully satisfy my utmost desire. I would not be tempted to set an unjust value upon life; nor would I wish to be thrown in the way of those trials which nature has not provided for. I mean that it would give me some concern to rise into a station that I knew myself unequal to. Upon recollection, it costs me dear to serve. £200 the last affair; £500 or £600 now; and an employment that I am about to resign, so that if we should miscarry, my condition will be desperate, and my finances exhausted. The ladies, too, will despise a beaten lover, so that every way I must be undone. And yet I run readily, heartily, and cheerfully into the road of ruin. If my thoughts could be greatly diverted from their present object, the youngest of your neighbours might rival my Lady Bath. My duty to the General. I wish you both all happiness.

In the various accounts of Wolfe which have hitherto appeared, his attachment to Miss Lowther has been mentioned. We should therefore expect to find that lady's name in some of his letters about this time, yet in none of them does it occur. It is not improbable, however, that she was the youngest of his mother's fair neighbours above alluded to, for disturbing whose rest on his departure from Bath he previously apologized. But, notwithstanding all that has been written to the contrary by historians, novelists, and biographers, it is evident from Wolfe's own declaration in a future letter that he and Miss Lowther were not "engaged" until after his return from America.

On the 21st, he writes from Blackheath to his uncle the Major in Dublin:—

Though I have no reason to love the seas, or to wish to be employed upon expeditions of any kind, since I do not enjoy one hour's health from the moment I go on board till my return, and am not only disabled from all kinds of business, but suffer pain that cannot be expressed; yet I readily engage in anything that is going on, for the sake of employment, flattering myself that in time I shall be able to overcome it, though hitherto I have found no relief. Another motive, too, pushes me on, which is, the desire of seeing some favourable change in our affairs, and the ambition of contributing something towards it. This far outweighs all considerations of advantage to myself, and gives me patience to bear my sufferings at sea.

The King has honoured me with the rank of Brigadier in America, which I cannot but consider as a peculiar mark of his Majesty's favour and confidence, and I intend to do my best to deserve it. The squadron is almost ready to sail; by the end of this month I reckon we shall get to sea. The reinforcements from England and Ireland consist of about five- or six-and-twenty hundred men, two very good battalions we have, and the rest is *la canaille* from the second battalions upon this establishment. The regular forces in America amount already to upwards of 20,000 men,—an army far overmatching the force of New France, and which undoubtedly should conquer Canada in two campaigns, if it was possible to subsist so great a corps together.

. . . .

You know in what a handsome manner the Duke of Bedford had offered me the employment of Quartermaster-General of Ireland. The handsomest thing I can do in return is to resign it, not being able to give that attention to it which the Duke had reason to expect, and had a right to expect from me. Accordingly, I shall resign that appointment into the hands from whence I had it, and trust to Fortune for future provision.* She is no great friend to the family, but has distinguished me at times by her smiles and favours; so encouraged, I put myself entirely in her power. I am totally ignorant of the state of our private concerns here, and have taken no precautions in case any accident should happen in my absence. I trust you will give the best advice to my mother, and such assistance, if it should be wanted, as the distance between you will permit. I mention this because the General seems to decline apace, and narrowly escaped being carried off in the spring; and that proceeding from a cause which still subsists and will in time work its natural effects,—I mean his excessive indolence and inactivity. On my mother's side there is no friendship or connection, nor do I know anybody to whom she can apply but yourself. She, poor woman, is in a bad state of health, and needs the care of some friendly hand to prop up the tottering fabric. She has long and painful fits of illness, which, by succession and inhe-

* He wrote to the Lord-Lieutenant on the 26th of January, resigning his Irish appointment, upon the grounds of not being able to give sufficient attention to the duties, and the King having been pleased to allow him to serve in America. In his letter to the Duke, he says:—"It is a mortification to have been so long in that office and so useless." (See Bedford Correspondence, vol. ii. p. 319.)

ritance, are likely to devolve on me, since I feel the early symptoms of them. I wish you health and peace.

Mrs. Wolfe being desirous that her son should use his influence on behalf of one of his cousins, on the 25th of January he replies as follows:—.

Dear Madam,

You cannot doubt my readiness to oblige you in anything that is of immediate concern to yourself; but you must not put me upon actions that I should blush to engage in, and that my uncle should blush to ask. I never can recommend any but a gentleman to serve with gentlemen. There is little prospect of a low dog's doing any shining act. When such a thing does happen, a reward is due to merit; so unexpected courage alone is no sort of recommendation to put a private soldier upon the footing of an officer. I don't apprehend that Mr. —— addresses himself to me, or that he has any just right to expect that I should interest myself in behalf of an idle vagabond; for such he must be, by the expression of his letter. I will write a civil letter to my uncle, which may serve as an apology for the General and myself.

I shall pay every shilling that I owe upon the whole earth, and shall leave all the receipts with Miss Brett, directed for you; so that the only running open account is Mr. Fisher's, and that, I believe, if my Irish remittances come in time, will not go very deep. Of late, no thought of matrimony; I have no objection to it, but differ much from the general opinion about it. The greatest consideration with me is the woman, her education and temper. Rank and fortune never come into any competition with the person. Any bargain on that affair is base and mean. I could not with any satisfaction consider my children as the produce of such an unnatural union. I shall set out for Portsmouth in four or five days. The King has refused Carleton leave to go, to my very great grief and disappointment, and with circumstances extremely unpleasant to him. Lord Fitzmaurice asked to serve the campaign in North America.* His Majesty did not absolutely refuse it, but spoke handsomely, and put it upon the footing of service nearer home.

Although neither of Wolfe's friends was permitted to accompany him to America upon this occasion, it will be seen that as regards one of them the King was compelled, at a future time, to give way. Colonel Carleton was sent to join the British troops commanded by Prince Ferdinand in Germany, and Lord Fitzmaurice served under General Bligh, as Adjutant-General, on a marauding expedition to the coast of France.

The Brigadier's business in London being completed, he set out on the 1st of February for Portsmouth, whence he writes next day to his mother:—

I take nothing ill from you, nor from anybody, that is not meant as ill. What I said upon my uncle Tim's letter arises from the frankness of my temper. When I have good reasons I don't conceal them. It is a public loss Carleton's not going. Prejudices against particular people often hurt the common cause. Misrepresentations, falsities, injustice, are too frequent to create any degree of surprise. Princes, of all people, see the least into the true characters of men. I came here this morning, two or three days sooner than was necessary; but a man in London, upon the point of his departure, leads a weary life, so I was glad to get out of town. The transports, with Amherst's regiment and those for Ireland, are supposed to have got out of the channel, and 'tis well, for the wind, as it blows here, would otherwise force them back again.

* William Petty, Viscount Fitzmaurice, who was now in his twenty-first year, entered the army when very young, On the death of his father, in 1761, he became Earl of Shelburne, and two years afterwards was appointed First Lord-Commissioner of Trade. In 1784 he was created Marquis of Lansdowne, and died in 1805, when he was the oldest General in the British army. The late venerable Marquis was his second son.

On the 7th of February, Wolfe writes to his old Colonel, Lord George Sackville, who was at this time Master-General of the Ordnance. In June following his Lordship served under the Duke of Marlborough, in the expedition against St. Malo; the result of which the old King truly foretold:—"That we should brag of having burned the French ships, and they would say they had driven us away." He was offered the command of a similar expedition later in the year, but declared "he was tired of buccaneering." To avoid such service he repaired to the Continent, and fell into disgrace the next year, in consequence of his unaccountable conduct at Minden. Although Lord George was exceedingly haughty, the familiar style of Wolfe's letter shows that they were on intimate terms:—

My Lord,

If I had any constitution to spare, I should certainly desire to succeed Monsieur de Vaudreuil in the government of Canada; but I can't trust to it. Your Lordship must let me put you in mind that one campaign in North America is as much as I can afford, though I hope to have mettle enough left for the siege of St. Philip's, or for a stroke in the bottom of the Bay of Biscay. Any long absence at this time would reduce me and my affairs to the lowest ebb. I can't help wishing that Louisbourg should be totally demolished, and all the inhabitants of those islands sent to Europe. It is said that the French were thirty years in putting that fortress into any tolerable condition of defence; we shall reduce them by other attacks to make peace with us, and to restore the Island of Minorca. I should think it possible to shelter the island at the entrance of the harbour in such a manner with mines, as to make it very difficult to raise any batteries there for the time to come. If indeed we think Louisbourg worth Minorca, and resolve to keep it,—that's another affair!

It is of consequence, my Lord, not to confine the Admirals and Generals too much as to the number of men to land with: five or six thousand men are sufficient for the preparations; it is of vast importance to get on shore before the fogs come on, and still more not to lose time. Amherst should inform himself of the rates established for works done at a siege. He will tell your Lordship his opinion of Carleton, by which you will probably be better convinced of our loss. I shall begin to write to your Lordship the day we sail, and continue writing until the end of the campaign. Whatever occurs worth your notice shall be transmitted to you; and when you have a leisure half-hour in the country, I shall beg the honour of a letter from your Lordship. If you seriously intend to attack the French in Europe, remember that boats should be procured to land at least 4000 men at a time, and sloops and cutters that may carry as many more close in shore, or upon occasion run aground to land them. Some small flat or round-bottomed vessels, carrying four or six heavy cannon, and boats fitted up with swivel guns or light field-pieces, will be found most useful in landing and bringing off the troops, and in all attacks upon small forts situated near the water. It is believed that the transports for Anstruther's regiment have got round to Cork.

There has been a most unaccountable delay in regard to the East India ships; they are like to be six months longer in India, or more, from those delays. Our squadron is all at Spithead, except the 'Lancaster,' and that ship is ready to go out of the harbour. The naval preparations at this port are pretty expeditious; but those great ships take more time to fit out than is commonly believed. The East India people here assure me that the loss of Chandernagore is a mortal blow to the French commerce, and that they will hardly be able to subsist at Pondicherry, because their provisions come chiefly from the Ganges. I hope Mons. Lally will not get in time to repair the damages done by our fleet before our own reinforcements arrive. Here is an officer of Amherst's with some sergeants and recruits, to the number of forty-three persons; three more officers are expected to-night. I shall apply to Mr. Boscawen for their passage. I am told that not one soldier of Amherst's regiment deserted upon this occasion; they want 160 men to complete. Mr. Boscawen gave directions to embark them in the most commodious manner.

The condition of the troops that compose this garrison (or rather, vagabonds that stroll about in dirty red clothes from one gin-shop to another) exceeds all belief. There is not the least shadow of discipline, care, or attention. Disorderly soldiers of different regiments are collected here; some from the ships, others from the hospital, some waiting to embark, —dirty, drunken, insolent rascals, improved by the hellish nature of the place, where every kind of corruption, immorality, and looseness is carried to excess; it is a sink of the lowest and most abominable of vices. Your Lordship could not do better than to get the company of Artillery moved out of this infernal den, where troops ought never to be quartered.

Give me leave to observe two or three things to your Lordship in relation to our last new exercise. The side-step has been introduced by mistake, I imagine, instead of the oblique step; one is as absurd as the other is useful. Wheeling by divisions to the right or left may be called a principle of motion; this excellent evolution is abolished, and the ridiculous wheel upon the centre introduced in its place. The ranks are opened to a very inconvenient distance for no reason that I can conceive, unless to double the ranks by the side-step with more ease. Here one absurdity has produced another. Practising the platoon firing with the ranks open, as front ranks, as centre ranks, etc., is all nonsense; every soldier should be trained to fire in each rank, and obliquely. A company or a battalion should as readily fire to the rear as to the front, and this they acquire in learning the platoon exercise,—that is, they should be so taught. When soldiers are masters of the use of their firearms and of their bayonets, the next great object is their marching in battalion, as your Lordship knows full well. For this, no good instructions have ever been given in my time, nor any principles laid down by which we might be guided. Hence the variety of steps in our infantry, and the feebleness and disorderly floating of our lines. General Dury, I think, has the merit of the late inventions; 'tis unlucky, however, that our great master in the art of war, Frederick of Prussia, was not preferred upon this occasion. He has made the exercise simple and useful; we cannot chuse so good a model.

I am credibly informed that at a council of war held at Calcutta, after the recovery of that settlement, Captain Speke was single for the attack of Chandernagore, declaring that nothing was done, nor could there be any security till that settlement was destroyed; and by persevering in his opinion, the rest were brought at length to agree to the enterprise. This, I believe, is a fact that may be depended upon.

Your Lordship has taken Beckwith, Maxwell, and the 20th regiment,—your old battalion,—under your immediate protection, and they cannot be better; but I have another friend to recommend to you as a very deserving and a very active officer,—Captain Rickson, who is doing duty as Deputy Quartermaster-General of Scotland. He wishes to be confirmed in his office by commission, as usual, and as it ought to have been long ago, if (as I believe) some bye-views and artifices had not prevented it. That employment has usually the rank of Lieutenant-Colonel annexed to it, which Rickson may pretend to in point of merit with almost any man in the service. Your Lordship, I think, is persuaded that I never did, nor ever will, undertake to establish any man in your good opinion but from a thorough conviction that he deserves your esteem.

We expect Mr. Boscawen every hour, and people think that he will not wait for a fair wind, but endeavour to beat down the Channel if the weather is moderate, so that we are likely to be soon under weigh. I wish your Lordship much health, and have the honour to be, with great respect, my Lord,

Your Lordship's most obedient and most humble servant,

J. Wolfe.

P.S. *Tuesday afternoon.*—Our Admiral is arrived, and is in haste to sail. I wish the voyage was over, and that we struck soundings upon the Banks. Take care to reinforce the fleet if it be necessary; don't let us be beat. Barré, who knows Whitmore better than anybody, assures me that he has no health nor constitution for such business as we are going upon; he never was a soldier, but otherwise, a very worthy gentleman. I pray you beware how you employ him near the top; this prevented, we may jog on tolerably. Here is a lieutenant of foot going with Draper* to the East Indies, who would be a most valuable man to Amherst. He seems to understand the war in America well, and speaks of it clearly and judiciously. Alas! there are but few such men, and those too often neglected. He has been at Montreal and Quebec, and has navigated down the river St. Lawrence. If I commanded in America, I would give him a company and £500 to go with me,—a modest, sensible, manly young officer. His name is Cheshire. I hope your Lordship will be the patron and protector of every deserving man of our profession.†

On the same day Wolfe dispatched the following letter to the friend on whose behalf he pleaded with Lord G. Sackville:—

Dear Rickson,

The title of Brigadier, which extends to America only,‡ has no other advantage than throwing me into service in an easy manner for myself, and such as my constitution really requires; our success alone will determine the more solid favours, for it is possible to deserve very well, and to be extremely ill received. The state of public affairs is such, that some measures must be pursued which prudence or military knowledge perhaps might not dictate. We shall have (if ac-

* Afterwards Sir William Draper, K.B., the captor of Manilla and the antagonist of Junius. He had recently been appointed Lieutenant-Colonel of the 79th Regiment, which he accompanied to India, where he acquired reputation as an officer.

† From original letter in the possession of John Young, Esq., Blackheath.

‡ Wolfe's commission as Brigadier-General is dated "St. James's, 23rd January, 1758," and countersigned, "W. Pitt."

cident don't prevent it) a great force this year in America, and the country has a right to expect some powerful efforts proportioned to the armaments. Success is in the hands of Providence; but it is in every man's own power to do his part handsomely.

I did not know that Barré was your friend, nor even your acquaintance. Now that I do know it, I shall value him the more upon that account; by accident I heard of his worth and good sense, and shall have, I trust, good reason to thank the man that mentioned him. Nay, I am already overpaid by the little I did, by drawing out of his obscurity so worthy a gentleman. I never knew his face till very lately, nor never spoke ten words to him before I ventured to propose him as a major of brigade. You may be sure that my information came from the best hands.*

I wish your success most heartily; it would be a lasting satisfaction to me if I had the power to forward it. You must give me leave to tell you, which indeed I should not do, that I have pressed it warmly to Lord G. Sackville, who has at present the power in his hands. I tried the Field-Marshal [Ligonier], but I have little weight there, and for your sake I wish I had more with Lord George. Write me, now and then, a letter, with all the Scotch news, and your own sentiments upon things as they fall out. Calcraft will forward your letters, and they will be received as so many marks of your affection and remembrance. We embark in three or four days. Barré and I have the great apartment of a three-decked ship to revel in; but with all this space, and this fresh air, I am sick to death. Time, I suppose, will deliver me from these sufferings; though, in former trials, I never could overcome it. I thank you for your kind wishes, and return them most sincerely. I am ever,

My dear friend,

Your faithful and affectionate servant,

James Wolfe.

Portsmouth, 7th February, 1758.

* The future celebrated political character, Colonel Isaac Barré.

Wolfe's concern for his mother, and the old General's increasing infirmity, caused him to write to the companion of his boyhood, George Warde, asking him to become one of his representatives during his stay in America. "Carleton," he told him on the 1st of February, "is so good as to say that he will give what help is in his power: may I ask the same favour of you, my oldest friend, in whose worth and integrity I put my entire confidence?" Major Warde having consented, Wolfe acknowledges the obligation thus:—

Portsmouth, February 11th, 1758.

Dear Major,

Though I thank you for the assurances contained in your letter, yet I needed not that proof to be secure of your kind offices to an absent friend. I don't even make you an apology for the trouble it may give you, because, from a consciousness of a readiness on my side to engage warmly in your interest, there is not a doubt of your inclinations to forward mine. If my father should die in my absence, I desire that you and Carleton will let my mother know that, jointly with her, you are empowered to transact my business, as the enclosed letter of attorney sets forth; and if you will assist her with your good counsel, I shall think of it with satisfaction, and acknowledge it with more gratitude than anything done to myself, though of every mark and testimony of your kindness not at all insensible. I knew you were in town, and that you had called, but not remembering where you lodged, I was obliged to come away without seeing you. We may live to meet; and to find you well and happy will be one very sincere pleasure at my return. I shall collect all the particulars of our campaign for your amusement. I wish you all manner of good, and am, my dear Major,

Your faithful and affectionate servant,

JAM. WOLFE.

To Major Warde, at the White Hart, Winton.

The same day, he takes leave of his parents :—

Portsmouth, February 11th, 1758.

Dear Madam,

When any matter of importance to a country is resolved on, the sooner it is carried into execution the better. Delays are not only productive of bad consequences, but are very tiresome and very inconvenient, as every unhappy person, whose lot it is to be confined for any length of time to this place, can certify. The want of company and of amusement can be supplied with books and exercise, but the necessity of living in the midst of the diabolical citizens of Portsmouth is a real and unavoidable calamity. It is a doubt to me if there is such another collection of demons upon the whole earth. Vice, however, wears so ugly a garb, that it disgusts rather than tempts.

The weather begins to be more moderate than it has been for some days past, and I fancy we shall go on board this afternoon, to be ready to get under sail with the first favourable turn of the wind. I should be glad if we were at sea, though I have no very agreeable prospect before me; however, I hope to overcome it, and if not, have a mind strong enough to endure that, and still severer trials, if there are any more severe. I heartily wish you all the benefit that you yourself can hope from the Bath. The General will be kind enough to put up with some inconvenience for your sake. I beg my duty to him, and am, dear Madam,

Your obedient and affectionate Son,

JAM. WOLFE.

P.S. You shall hear from me by all the opportunities that offer.

The Brigadier embarked on the 12th, and on the 18th dispatched the following note to his father :—

'Princess Amelia,' St. Helen's.

Dear Sir,

Our Captain sends me word that a boat is just going

ashore, and that I have time to write three or four lines. Mr. Boscawen, impatient to get out to sea, left Spithead the 15th, and brought his squadron here to be ready for the first favourable change of wind, which has blown for some days directly against us, and with great violence. The weather is now mild, and the moon old enough to light us in the night, but our mariners see no immediate prospect of sailing. We are extremely well in this ship, have great room, and much kindness and civility from the commanders, and hitherto the motion has not had any very great effect upon me.

The fleet sailed from St. Helen's on the 19th; but before getting out of the Channel, there is another note from Wolfe to his father, dated—

Plymouth Sound, 22nd February.

Dear Sir,

Some very bad weather, and the appearance of still worse, forced Mr. Boscawen to anchor in this place,—a berth that the mariners are not very fond of. The wind blew violently yesterday in the afternoon and good part of the night, so as to try our anchors and cables a little; but 'tis now calm, and promises to be fair. You may believe that I have passed my time disagreeably enough in this rough weather; at best, the life, you know, is not pleasant. We left the 'Invincible' upon a sand, and believe she is lost: the finest ship of that rate (74 guns) in the Navy, well manned and well commanded. By what fatal accident this happened we cannot guess.* The boat waits for my letter, so I will only add my best wishes for your health and my mother's

The 'Princess Amelia' did not reach Nova Scotia until the 8th of May, and after the long and boisterous voyage, Wolfe was not able to resume his pen for some days. On the 19th he wrote a short letter to his uncle

* The 'Invincible' was wrecked at St. Helen's on the 18th, but all her men and stores were saved.

Walter, which, however, contains nothing of importance that is not repeated in the following to his father :—

Halifax, 20th May, 1758.

Dear Sir,

General Hopson does me the favour to carry this letter. The King has thought proper to recall him, on account, I suppose, of his age, with which, and the assurance given him of a good reception at home, he is well pleased.* Our fleet and army have gathered together from many different places without any material accident. Sir Charles Hardy has been cruising off Louisbourg ever since the 2nd or 3rd of April, or thereabouts; but, notwithstanding Sir Charles's vigilance and activity, the French have contrived to get in three or four men-of-war, and as many small ships.† Others intended for that port, laden with stores and provisions, have been taken by our squadron. We shall be ready to sail in four or five days. Mr. Boscawen has been indefatigable on his side, and we have not been idle. Our army consists of fourteen regiments, and our fleet of about twenty sail of the line, and, I believe, as many frigates. Our General is not yet arrived, but we shall proceed without him. When the army is landed, the business is half done; and I hope it will be all done before you receive this letter. The troops are very healthy, and so are most of the ships; four or five are otherwise, and so will the French fleet be if they come upon this coast.

You will hear it said in England that Mr. Abercrombie has an army of 7000 regulars and 20,000 provincials. Of this last account you may deduct one-half, and depend upon it that the remaining 10,000 are not good for much. Lord

* General Hopson was afterwards given the command of the land forces in the expedition against the French Caribee Islands, and died in February, 1759, previous to the capture of Guadaloupe by Major-General Barrington and Commodore Moore.

† In his letter to his uncle, he added :—"If they had thrown in twice as much, we should not hesitate to attack them; and for my part, I have no doubt of our success. If the French fleet comes upon this coast, the campaign will, I hope, be decisive."

Howe is in high esteem with the troops in Albany. You may expect to hear of some handsome performances of his.* The nature of the war there requires all his abilities, spirit, and address. The harbour of Halifax is a most excellent port, and of infinite consequence to us, both from its situation and goodness. If you saw in what manner it is fortified, you would hardly think that we judge it worth our care. There are guns indeed in different spots, but so exposed from behind, that the batteries would soon be abandoned. I wish you and my mother a great deal of health, and am, dear Sir,

Your most affectionate Son,

JAM. WOLFE.

* Brigadier-General George Augustus, third Viscount Howe, in the peerage of Ireland, elder brother to the Captain of the 'Magnanime.' "He was," wrote Mr. Pitt, "by the universal voice of army and people, a character of ancient times; a complete model of military virtue in all its branches." (See 'Grenville Correspondence,' vol. i. p. 262.)

CHAPTER XIX.

THE CONQUEST OF CAPE BRETON.

JUNE—OCTOBER, 1758.

MAJOR-GENERAL AMHERST, being detained in England for some time after the departure of the squadron, did not embark until the middle of March, when he sailed from Spithead in Captain Rodney's ship, 'Dublin,' which supplied the place of the lost 'Invincible.' On the 28th of May, as the 'Dublin' approached Halifax, the grand fleet, numbering in all 157 sail, was descried coming out of the harbour; when Amherst went on board the 'Namur,' and Admiral Boscawen, who, until then, held supreme control over the land as well as the sea forces, transferred to him the command of the expeditionary army, and the armament steered towards Cape Breton. For two days, the weather being fine and wind favourable, the vessels kept well together; but, on the afternoon of the 30th, a gale springing up, they were dispersed. On the 1st of June the 'Namur' spoke the 'Sutherland,' which had been cruising off Louisbourg, when Captain Rous informed the Admiral that two more French men-of-war had got into that harbour, in which there were now thirteen ships.

A dense fog, which obscured every object the following morning, having cleared away at noon, the fated fortress became visible; and soon afterwards the British fleet, with some of the transports, anchored in the bay of Gabarouse. The same evening, in spite of a tremendous swell which rolled from the Atlantic, and broke in foaming surf against the rocky shore, the General, with Brigadiers Lawrence and Wolfe, got into a sloop, and having reconnoitred the land, planned dispositions for the descent of the troops at daybreak next morning; but when the time came the elements forbade the attempt, and daylight only rendered "darkness visible." Day after day, for nearly a week, fogs and storms frustrated several endeavours to land; and the willing soldiers, after being for hours tossed about in boats, were obliged to return to their transports. In the meantime the French, who had long been prepared for an invasion, lost not a moment in strengthening their outworks, and adding every means that art could suggest to the natural difficulty of the coast. They likewise kept up a constant cannonade against the invading fleet which occupied the bay.

The island of Cape Breton, whose destiny was now about to be determined, was appropriated by France under the Regency of the Duke of Orleans, after the death of Louis XIV., and named Isle Royale. Appreciating the importance of its position at the entrance to the Gulf of St. Lawrence, no expense was spared by the French Government in the erection of Louisbourg, the stronghold and capital of the island, upon which, according to Raynal, no less a sum than £1,250,000 sterling was expended. Large though the amount appears, it is not incredible, for the stone was quarried and the lime prepared in France, whence engineers, masons, and labourers were sent out to construct the town and citadel, and to fortify the harbour. Although deemed almost impregnable, and styled the Dunkirk of America, Louisbourg was reduced by Pepperel and Warren in 1745; from which time it remained in the possession of England until 1748, when, in accordance with the treaty of Aix-la-Chapelle, she was obliged to restore it; for France attached so much importance to the island, as the bulwark of Canada, and as a central point of communication with her West Indian territories, that she would consent to no terms of peace which did not include its restoration.

In England, and in her American colonies, this provision of the treaty was most unpopular, insomuch that the Duke of Bedford, when First Lord of the Admiralty, is said to have declared, that if the French were masters of Portsmouth, he would hang the man who would give up Cape Breton in exchange for it.* The English, however, did not value the island on account of any positive benefit to be derived from it, though they considered it a post of which the enemy should be deprived; for it not only sheltered swarms of privateers that pillaged the colonial trade, but also encouraged the encroachments of the so-called "Neutrals," or Acadians subject to Great Britain, who, in plain prose, were by no means that primitive, harmless race represented in Longfellow's beautiful poem.

* Maty's 'Life of the Earl of Chesterfield,' vol. i. p. 319.

The Bay of Gabarouse, in which the hostile fleet was now anchored, extends from Cape L'Orembeck on the north-east to Cape Cormoran on the south-west, with an inland sweep of about ten miles. Inside this bay, and completely landlocked, was the magnificent natural harbour of Louisbourg, the narrow entrance to which, between the Lighthouse Point on the right hand and the extremity of the tongue of land upon which stood the town, was further defended by a formidable battery on an island in the centre of the channel. In this inner basin, protected by the cannon of the town and a grand battery on the north bank, lay the French fleet; while the fortress to the left, or west of the harbour, presented heavy batteries towards the sea, and three strongly fortified fronts towards the land. In addition to these permanent works, the French had established, for the present occasion, strong breastworks, defended by 3000 men, posted along the shore of the bay for a distance of several miles westward of the town, at every spot where a descent was possible. At intervals were masked batteries of heavy cannon, and swivels of large calibre; and between the lines and the water's edge, wherever there was not an impenetrable barrier of rocks, there were artificial thickets of prostrate trees, with their branches towards the sea.

Until the 7th of June the tempestuous state of the weather prevented every attempt on the part of the invaders; but the wind and swell abating that evening, the Admiral gave hopes that something might be done next morning. Accordingly, at midnight the troops began to enter their boats, and with the first glimpse of dawn on the 8th the covering cannon of the fleet began to play upon the shore. The fire ceasing in about a quarter of an hour, the boats, in three divisions, made for the land. The division on the right, consisting of five battalions commanded by Brigadier Whitmore, rowed eastward, in the direction of Louisbourg, as if intending to land upon White Point; and the central division, of six battalions, under Brigadier Lawrence, proceeded straight forward towards Freshwater Cove, in order to make a show of landing there, but virtually with the object of diverting the attention of the enemy from the real descent by Wolfe's brigade upon the left.

The detachment commanded by Wolfe comprised twelve companies of Grenadiers, Frazer's Highlanders, Major Scott's Light Infantry corps of 550 marksmen selected from the different regiments, and a company of provincial Rangers. The sailors plied their oars vigorously through the heavy sea, while the strictest order and silence were observed by the soldiers, who were assured by the confidence and calmness of their young leader, towards whom, not only the men, but officers double his age, looked up as the rising star of their profession. No sooner had they got within musket-shot of the shore than a deadly volley issued from the batteries behind the green branches of the trees which concealed them. But cannon and musketry were not their worst antagonisms. The sea, which had grown more and more boisterous since they had set out, now lashing the coast, dashed them against the rocks, shattering several of the boats, upsetting others; and many a brave fellow, who hoped ere night to win renown in the field, found an instant watery grave.

Wolfe, perceiving that some of the Light Infantry had got ashore, beckoned to the rest to follow. Without arms of any kind, his cane only in his hand, he sprang from his boat,* and scrambling through the spray, over rocks and steeps, quickly joined them, and formed the men upon the beach as, one way or another, they reached the land. The troops, in nowise discouraged, but exasperated by the masked fire which raked them, had still to climb a height of about twenty feet in order to reach the hostile lines; but following their chief, they soon gained the ascent, and attacking the defenders of the nearest post with their bayonets, speedily routed them. In like manner post after post was taken. Lawrence's division having landed at the same place immediately after Wolfe's, and additional reinforcements arriving from the fleet, the enemy, forsaking their cannon and stores, fled towards Louisbourg; and for four miles were pursued over hills, hollows, and swamps by Wolfe's and Lawrence's brigades. As soon as the fugitives had gained their refuge, a fierce cannonade from the town was opened upon the pursuers, "which," says General Amherst in his Journal, "was so far of use, that it pointed out how near I might encamp to invest it."†. On the ground before the town then taken possession of, the invaders afterwards formed the encamp-

* From a letter written by Major A. Murray, who also says Wolfe was so pleased with the behaviour of two Highland soldiers, that he gave each of them a guinea.

† Mante says that Pitt approved so highly of Amherst's Diary of the siege, that he requested him to transmit the operations of any army he might afterwards command in similar detail, as it was the best method of conveying a true and explicit idea of military proceedings. History of the War,' etc., p. 116.)

ment which the main army continued to occupy until the end of the siege, and in the course of the same day the remainder of the land force got on shore; but owing to the roughness of the sea and the constant fog, neither artillery, tents, provisions, nor ammunition could be landed for three days.

On the 12th, the Commander-in-chief learned that the French had dismantled their Grand Battery on the north side of the harbour, called in their outposts, and concentrated all their power within the walls of Louisbourg,—a proceeding which gave the English an uninterrupted range of the country. He therefore sent Wolfe, with 1200 men, round the harbour to the Lighthouse Point, which at once commanded the sea-wall of the town, the shipping, and the Island Battery, and at the same time he sent the requisite artillery and stores by sea to meet the Brigadier at L'Orembeck. Wolfe's preliminary measures are shown in the following extracts from the paper he sent to his chief after his arrival at the Lighthouse:*—

Brigadier Wolfe proposes to establish a post of 200 regulars and a company of Rangers at L'Orembeck; he intends likewise to establish another post of 200 regulars and a company of Rangers at the end of the North-east Harbour. The regular troops are to fortify their camp, and the irregulars are to keep a constant patrol, to endeavour to intercept any of the inhabitants of the island, Canadians or others; at least, to give notice of their march to the officer commanding the regular troops, who will inform the Brigadier of it, and give the

* The original document, in the possession of the Right Hon. Earl Amherst, is indorsed in the General's handwriting—"Brigadier Wolfe's Intentions at the Lighthouse Point."

earliest notice he can to Brigadier Lawrence upon the left of the army, who will report it to the Commander-in-chief.

. . . .

Another post of fifty regulars and ten Rangers will be established at the nearest L'Orembeck; the two L'Orembeck parties will be supplied with provisions from the sea, and the party at the end of the harbour will be supplied from the camp or from the Lighthouse. . . . The remaining body of the Light Infantry, and the irregulars, must take post upon the Miré Road, about half-way between the camp and the North-east Harbour, and communicate with both the one and the other by posts and patrols.

The severity of the weather retarded the progress of the Brigadier's works until the 18th, on which day he issued the following orders:—

Two batteries are to be constructed this night, for one iron 24-pounder each, with a firm, well-rammed parapet, and the platforms laid with the utmost care. These must be finished before daybreak, and whatever remains to be done at the Great Mortar Battery must be completed this night; every engineer, and every officer of artillery, exerting himself in his proper department. To-morrow, at sunset, it is proposed to begin to bombard and cannonade the French fleet; the Captain of Artillery to dispose his party so that all the ordnance may be equally well served, according to the following distribution:—

The battery at the end of the North-east Harbour one 24- and one 12-pounder.

Hautbitser [*sic*] Battery, under the hill near the careening wharf, to fire a *ricochet*.

Great Bomb Battery, in the bottom before Goreham's camp, of four mortars and six royals.

Two 24-pounders, to fire a *ricochet* at the masts and rigging from the bottom before Goreham's camp and the Lighthouse Hill.

One 24-pounder and two 12 ditto, from the right of the

Lighthouse Hill, to fire likewise a *ricochet* at the masts and rigging.

Two 24-pounders to be placed in battery, to fire at the ships' hulls or lower masts.

The Captain of Artillery may demand as many men as he thinks necessary to assist in serving the artillery, and as many pioneers as are requisite, and they shall be furnished from the army. The troops are all to be under arms time enough to march to their respective posts before the firing begins. Colonel Morris is to take post, with the detachments of the right brigade, upon the hills above the careening wharf, where the Highlanders now are. Lieut.-Colonel Hales (with three companies of Grenadiers) is to post himself behind the little hills and rising grounds where Captain Goreham's company is encamped, in readiness to support the Great Bomb Battery, if the enemy should think fit to attack it. The remaining company of Grenadiers is to be placed in small parties nearer to the Bomb Battery, in the safest situation that can be found. Goreham's company (if it returns in time) is to be concealed in proper places to the right of this company of Grenadiers, as near the sea as they can lie with safety. As the three companies of Grenadiers are placed near the magazine of the Grand Battery, Lieut.-Colonel Hales must take care that no fire be permitted. Colonel Rollo, with the detachments of the left and centre, is to take post upon the Lighthouse Hill, in readiness to march down to the enemy in case they are disposed to land.

All these detachments are to be placed with the greatest possible regard to their security; because the French ships, in their confusion and disorder, may probably fire their guns at random, and if the men are properly concealed we shall suffer very little loss. The two youngest companies are to be left for the guard of the camp, and the rest to guard the magazine. The officers commanding these companies are to make proper detachments, and place a necessary number of sentries for the preservation of the tents, huts, magazines, stores, etc.; and they are not to allow their men to get in numbers upon the tops of the hills, that no accident may happen.

The firing of the mortars, hautbitsers, and *ricochet* shot is to cease a little before daybreak, that all the troops, except a company at each station, may return to their camp to take their rest and refreshment; and the officers will conduct them back with the utmost caution. The battery at the end of the North-east Harbour, and the two iron 24-pounders that are placed in battery upon the upper part of the Lighthouse Hill, are to continue firing all day at the masts and rigging of the ships, that the enemy may have no rest, nor time to repair their damages. Although it seems improbable that the French should presume to land and attack any of our batteries, yet it is right to be prepared to receive them, or to drive them back to their boats; therefore, when two sky-rockets are fired immediately after each other from the Brigadier's station, all the troops are to move down the hills, and forward with quick pace, and charge the enemy with their bayonets, endeavouring to gain their flanks by detachments made on purpose; Colonel Morris to their left, supposing them to land anywhere near the Bomb Battery, and Colonel Rollo to their right, while the Grenadiers attack them in front without firing a shot.

The Brigadier-General will be all night upon the hill where Colonel Morris's detachment is to be posted, unless some particular business should require him in another part; in which case, he will leave word where he is to be found. One hundred Highlanders will be posted along the shore of the North-east Harbour, from Colonel Morris's post to Major Ross's. Part of the left wing and Light Infantry of the army will be in motion during this attack, ready to sustain the detached posts, to alarm the enemy on every side, and to increase their confusion. A sky-rocket will be fired from Colonel Morris's post, which will be answered by Sir Charles Hardy's squadron and the grand army; and when a second sky-rocket is fired from the same hill, the batteries begin, with short intervals at first, as will make their fire regular and constant. The officers of artillery, the engineers, and Major Ross's detachment, are to have copies of these orders.

The next day Wolfe writes as follows to the Commander-in-chief:—

End of North-east Harbour, 19th June, 1758.

Dear Sir,

My posts are now so fortified that I can afford you the two companies of Yankees, and the more as they are better for ranging and scouting than either work or vigilance. My whole affair now is the spade and pickaxe, and one hundred more pioneers would be of great assistance. I shall recall my out parties, and collect within my entrenchments, in order to carry on the work with greater vigour. I mean to take post on your side the harbour, and erect a battery, provided you will give me any countenance by seizing and entrenching the rising ground above the Grand Battery. I'm very sure that the artillery with me can be carried with greater ease to the *Queue de Franchée* than yours from Gabarouse Bay. You call Green Hill, Green Island, but I understand your meaning. The excess of rum is bad, but that liquor delivered out in small quantities—half a gill a man, and mixed with water—is a most salutary drink, and the cheapest pay for work that can be given. Mr. Boscawen is a very judicious man, but in this particular he is much in the wrong; and he proceeds from his confounding the abuse with the use, and sailors with soldiers.

. . . .

There is a fine brew-house, between us and the Grand Battery, for spruce beer; coppers all in good order and very valuable. I see the smoke of L'Orembeck, and therefore conclude that the straggling inhabitants have rashly attacked our people, and are punished for their insolence. I have ordered Sutherland to bring off any good shallops he can find for the use of the army, when you would have fish.

About ten this night you will see my signals. Are you not surprised to find that I have a battery here? The ground upon which I propose to erect a formidable battery against the Island Battery is so much exposed, that I must wait for a dark night or a fog to get it up. In the meanwhile, the same bomb-battery that annoys the shipping can be turned upon the island, and shall be when I see what effects we work upon their men-of-war, who, I believe, are in a confounded scrape; that is, if our bombardiers are worth a farthing. I have the honour to be,

Dear Sir,

Your most obedient and most humble servant,

JAM: WOLFE.

To his Excellency, Major-General Amherst,
Commander-in-chief.

On the 20th, the Brigadier again writes to the Major-General:—

Dear Sir,

The hautbitser carriage broke after firing about ten rounds, so that we were soon *hors de combat* in our strongest quarter. Two pieces of 24 stuck so fast, as they were carrying down to their battery, that human strength could not move them time enough for service; then my two batteries near the Lighthouse Point were not quite in condition of service; to which an extraordinary circumstance may be added, that one of my 24-pounders—iron—was so stuffed in the touch-hole that it could not be employed all night, besides, the distance was rather too great from the end of the North-east Harbour. I enclose you Captain Strachey's letter,* and beg you will be pleased to provide us with what is necessary to repair these hautbitsers, which we are all convinced are a most tremendous ordnance. The injury they received proceeded, I believe, from the want of a platform of wood, and we are in great want of plank, because a good deal has been used to get the cannon through the bogs. We reckon that the ships were struck with about three shells, and one of them appears to be somewhat damaged; and now that we

* Afterwards Sir Henry Strachey, Bart. In 1763 he became private Secretary to Clive, whom he accompanied to India in 1764. Subsequently he was Secretary of the Treasury, Under-Secretary of State, and Master of the Household.

have got their distance better, I hope the firing will be more effectual. I intend to erect a battery of one 24- and two 12-pounders on the other side the water, to fire red-hot shot; but I can't hope to get it done, nor to support it, unless you will be pleased to take post nearer to the Grand Battery.

I send you an account of the behaviour of my party at L'Orembeck,—I mean the subaltern's, which, I believe, will surprise you. They were, as far as I can find, all drunk and asleep,—sentries, guards, and all. The rum was sold to them by the masters of the ships they went in, whose names you shall have, and who should be made an example of.* Our earth and sod are so very bad that I am obliged to have recourse to sand-bags, and our wood for pickets† is extremely unfavourable; notwithstanding which difficulties I shall persevere till we demolish these gentlemen, and then fall to work upon the island. They have thrown away a vast quantity of shot without hurting a man; and indeed, unless by an extraordinary accident, we are not likely to lose many. Mr. Strachey complains also of his fusees, and he complains that he has no relief for his men, and that as the batteries are augmented and extended, he will hardly be able to serve them. We give them all possible assistance. Their confusion last night when we began was inexpressible, and their ships were lumbered; prepared, I suppose, to sail. They cleared and made ready, and are now altering their position, in order to bring all their

* Wolfe had sent Lieutenant Crosbie, with thirty men, to L'Orembeck, in order to protect the sloops ordered to carry fish for the use of the army. At night, the Lieutenant found several of the Rangers drunk, though, it was said, they had only had some cider from the master of one of the New England vessels. Next day he detached a corporal's guard to turn some fish on the east side of the harbour, when the men were fired upon; but being reinforced, the enemy fled. That night the Rangers were again drunk, and the Lieutenant reported the circumstances to his Captain. The original report is indorsed by General Amherst—"N.B. Captain Sutherland says that there was New England rum found about the dead or wounded men, sold by that Stone."

† Pickets,—small, pointed stakes, which serve to drive through fascines, or gazons, to keep them fast when the earth is bad, or the work raised in haste.

broadsides to bear against the hills. I shall work night and day to forward this business. Fascines, sods, etc., must be heaped up in immense quantities. As our fire increases, theirs will perhaps weaken. I found there was no manner of necessity for keeping the men out, so contented myself with small guards to give the men rest.

From the Lighthouse Point, Wolfe kept up an incessant fire upon the Island Battery, until the 25th of the month, on which day it was silenced. Then leaving a detachment of artillery behind him to keep it from being restored, he returned to the camp of the grand army before Louisbourg to superintend the formation of an approach to the West Gate. In order to prevent the English fleet from getting into the harbour, rendered defenceless by the demolition of the Island Battery, the French sank four men-of-war at the entrance; and of their entire fleet there were now left but three line-of-battle ships, and one 36 gun-frigate.

A large party from the town having crept out on the morning of the 1st of July, Wolfe, ever on the alert, heading the Light Infantry corps, drove them back with a brisk fire. The Brigadier, on the same day, took post on the hills northward of the town, and began to erect a powerful battery, which continued to play with the most destructive effect on the fortress, as well as on the shipping that remained in the harbour. It was perhaps on this occasion that he wrote the following characteristic note to General Amherst:—

Dear Sir,

When the French are in a scrape, they are ready to cry out in behalf of the human species; when fortune favours them, none more bloody, more inhuman. Montcalm has changed the very nature of war, and has forced us, in some measure, to a deterring and dreadful vengeance. I shall set about getting things in readiness for this battery, but must be excused for three or four days from other duty.

On the 3rd, the Brigadier was back again with the grand army, forming an approach to the right within 650 yards of the covered way; but the delays arising from the rugged nature of the country, which necessitated the construction of roads and draining of bogs, together with adverse weather, greatly retarded his operations. The making of fascines, of which the *epaulement* consumed a vast quantity, kept 500 men employed; and constant fogs hindering the cannonade for hours at a time, it could only be resumed at intervals whenever there was an occasional glare of light. Besides these impediments, more than a hundred of Colonel Messervey's company of carpenters were, at one time, disabled by the smallpox, of which the Colonel and his son died; the Admiral, however, rendered great assistance, by sending 400 seamen to work at the batteries.

The garrison seizing every opportunity of making sorties, there were frequent skirmishes; but Wolfe having taught the Light Infantry corps a method of attacking and retreating behind the hills, they invariably compelled the enemy to retire.* It is said that after an occurrence

* The Light Infantry corps consisted of the best marksmen and most active volunteers from the regular battalions. They wore green jackets and drawers, or pantaloons, so that they might easily brush through the woods, with moustaches and whiskers, and bear-skin ruffs round their necks. Their arms were a fusil, cartouche-box for balls and flints, and a powder-horn slung on the left shoulder. The Rangers were a body of the irregulars or provincial troops, who, according to Entick, had a more cut-throat, savage appearance, which carried with it some-

of this kind, many of the English officers having expressed surprise at the expertness of his men, and the novelty of the performance, Wolfe asked one more intelligent than the rest what he thought of it. "I think I see something here of the history of the Carduchi, who harassed Xenophon, and hung upon his rear in his retreat over the mountains," was the reply. "You are right," said Wolfe, "I had it thence; but our friends are astonished at what I have shown them because they have read nothing."*

The most fatal sally from the town was on the night of the 9th of July, when a party surprised a small redan near the sea, occupied by a company of Grenadiers, killing their Captain, Lord Dundonald, with a few of his men, and making prisoners of the rest; but Major Murray, with a detachment of Highlanders, coming to the relief, speedily put the assailants to flight. The Brigadier's report on the 13th shows that he was not satisfied with the engineering. In it he says:—"The parapets in general are too thin, and the banquettes everywhere too narrow. The trench of the parallel should be wide, and the parapets more sloping. . . . No accidents in the trenches; very few shots or shells in the night; but this morning they threw several shells very near the lodgments." Notwithstanding heavy rain, the works were not discontinued for a moment; and on the 16th, Wolfe, with a body of Highlanders and Grenadiers, took

thing of the *real* savage; that of the Light Infantry having in it more of the *artificial* savage. The French, in contradistinction to their own Indian allies, termed our Highlanders, Light Infantry, and Rangers, the "English savages."

* 'Military Dictionary,' by Major James, R.A.: Article "Library."

possession of the heights in front of the fortress, and effected a lodgment in the glacis, which exposed the parapet and embrasures to the fire of his musketry. The approaches, in carrying on which the men underwent great fatigue, were considerably advanced, when an accident happened which afforded them great relief, and increased the distress of the enemy. On the 21st, the 'Entrepreneur' exploded in the harbour, setting on fire two other ships, which burned furiously; whilst, in order to prevent boats from the town coming to their assistance, the batteries kept firing upon them until they were completely destroyed. Next day the besiegers' shells set the citadel in flames; but General Amherst humanely ordered his fire to be directed against the defences, so as not to destroy the town. The following night the barracks were burned to the ground. Meanwhile Wolfe was erecting more batteries, and progressing with his approaches. On the 25th he writes to the General from the "Trenches at daybreak:"—

> The five-gun battery is finished, and the cannon in readiness to mount. We want platforms, artillery officers to take the direction, and ammunition. If these are sent early, we may batter in breach this afternoon. Holland has opened a new boyau, has carried on about 140 or 150 yards, and is now within fifty or sixty yards of the glacis. The enemy were apprehensive of a storm, and fired smartly for about half an hour, which drove the workmen in; but when the fire ceased they returned to their business, and did a great deal. You will be pleased to indulge me with six hours' rest, that I may serve in the trenches at night.

Although M. Drucour, the brave Governor of Louisbourg, was by this time convinced that the reduction of the place was inevitable, he determined to hold it as long as he possibly could; for should he not receive the succour he expected from Montcalm, he at least hoped, by prolonging his resistance, to detain the besiegers until it would be too late in the season for them either to reinforce the British army upon the American continent, or to ascend the river St. Lawrence. In this resolution he was ably seconded by his intrepid wife, who was continually on the ramparts, supplying the wants of the soldiers, and encouraging them by occasionally firing the guns with her own hand.* The condition of the garrison was now such, that for eight days neither officers nor men had a moment's rest, nor, indeed, a place to take rest, for there was not even a secure spot in which to lay the wounded. Yet there was not a murmur amongst them, and none deserted but a few German mercenaries.† The cannonade, which they had kept up night and day, grew weaker and weaker; and instead of balls, they were driven to discharge grape-shot, old iron, or whatever missiles they could find.

Admiral Boscawen having at length resolved to take or destroy the two ships which remained of the French fleet, Captains Balfour and Laforey, with 600 sailors in boats, entered the harbour on the night of the 25th, when they gallantly took the 'Bienfaisant,' of 74 guns, and towed her away from the town; but the 'Prudent' being aground, they were obliged to burn her. In consequence of this misfortune, and Wolfe's batteries having

* 'Anecdotes Américaines.' Paris, 1776.

† See Le Chevalier de Drucour's letter, dated "Andover, October 1," in the 'Annual Register,' 1758.

made several breaches in the King's, the Queen's, and the Dauphin's bastions, while his approaches rapidly neared the covered way, the Governor, advised by a council of war, wrote to General Amherst early on the 26th of July, offering to capitulate upon the same terms as those granted to the English at Port Mahon.

The Admiral had just come ashore, and told the General that he purposed sending six ships into the harbour next day, when the messenger arrived with the Chevalier Drucour's letter. The British commanders immediately answered, by informing him of their intention to attack the town by sea as well as by land; but wishing to avoid the effusion of blood, they allowed him one hour to decide, either to surrender at discretion, or incur the consequences of further resistance. Piqued at this, the Governor replied:—"To answer your Excellencies in as few words as possible, I have the honour to repeat to you that my resolution is still the same, and that I will suffer the consequences and sustain the attack you speak of." His mind was made up to abide by his decision, when M. Prévot, the Intendant of the colony, presented him with a petition from the inhabitants, imploring him to spare them the horrors of a general assault. Satisfied that he had done his duty towards his King, and that obstinacy on his part would only lead to unnecessary bloodshed, he at length yielded, and sent back the officer who had carried his previous communications to inform his more fortunate adversaries that, trusting to the honour of a generous foe, he would submit to the law of force. That night the English troops remained in their trenches as usual. At eight o'clock next morning the

Porte Dauphine was given up to them, and Major Farquhar took possession of the West Gate; while Wolfe placed sentinels upon the ramparts to prevent the now idle soldiers, sutlers, and camp-followers from entering the town through the breaches his guns had made in the shattered walls.* Brigadier Whitmore then proceeded to the esplanade, where, at noon, the assembled garrison laid down their arms, implements, colours, and ornaments of war, which were immediately conveyed to the English encampment. Wolfe, who had not written home since he left Halifax, his work now done, seizes the first opportunity to pen the following letter to his mother:—

Camp before Louisbourg, July 27, 1758.

Dear Madam,

I went into Louisbourg this morning to pay my devoirs to the ladies, but found them all so pale and thin with long confinement in a casemate, that I made my visit very short. The poor women have been heartily frightened, as well they might; but no real harm, either during the siege or after it, has befallen any. A day or two more, and they would have been entirely at our disposal. I was determined to save as many lives, and prevent as much violence as I could, because I am sure such a step would be very acceptable to you, and very becoming. We have gone on slow and sure, and at length have brought things to a very good conclusion with little loss. If the rest of the campaign corresponds with the beginning, the people of England will have no reason to be dissatisfied. Kit Mason paid me a visit yesterday, in perfect health; Gusty is very well; little Herbert has never had an opportunity of coming near me. His ship goes home with the French prisoners, which Mrs. Herbert will be pleased to know. I hope

* Drucour's letter as above, and General Amherst's Journal. Of fifty-two cannon opposed to the batteries of the besiegers, forty were dismounted, broken, or otherwise rendered unserviceable.

to be with you by Christmas, though I protest to you that I had much rather besiege a place than pass four weeks at sea. If you are acquainted with Mrs. Bell, of the Hospital, I beg you will signify to her that her son has been of great use to me during the siege, has carried on business with great spirit and dispatch, and is an excellent officer.* He got a slight scratch upon his right arm, but is quite recovered, though I have forbid his writing for fear of any inflammation. If he does write, Mrs. Bell must not take it amiss that it be an unusual scrawl. His next letter will be writ with a fine hand. I wish you all manner of happiness, and am, dear Madam,

Your very affectionate son,

JAM: WOLFE.

On the same evening the Brigadier wrote to his father; but the letter being for the most part merely a cursory outline of events, a short extract from it will suffice:—"We have been rather slow in our proceedings, but still I hope there will be fine weather enough for another blow; and as our troops are improved by the siege, the sooner we strike the better. I see my name among the new colonels.† I hope Fisher will take care of my affairs, as he is intended for my agent. The climate is very healthy, though the air is foggy and disagreeable. I have been always very well since we landed, and have got through this business unhurt."

The Brigadier, as indefatigable with his pen as with his sword, writes another letter ere he lies down, to his uncle, Major Walter Wolfe. Adapting himself to his correspondent, his style is now critical rather than nar-

* Captain Bell was afterwards one of Wolfe's aides-de-camp.

† The second battalions having been formed into distinct corps, that of the 20th was numbered the 67th Regiment (South Hampshire Foot), and on the 21st of April, 1758, Wolfe was appointed Colonel thereof.

rative, and, judging from his words, it appears that he was neither vain of his own exploits, nor satisfied with what had been already accomplished:—

Camp before Louisbourg.

Dear Sir,

It is impossible to go into any detail of our operations; they would neither amuse nor instruct, and we are all hurried about our letters. In general, it may be said that we made a rash and ill-advised attempt to land, and by the greatest of good fortune imaginable we succeeded. If we had known the country, and had acted with more vigour, half the garrison at least (for they were all out) must have fallen into our hands immediately after we landed. Our next operations were exceedingly slow and injudicious, owing partly to the difficulty of landing our stores and artillery, and partly to the ignorance and inexperience of the engineers.

. . . .

The Indians of the island gave us very little trouble. They attacked one of my posts (for I commanded a detached corps) and were repulsed, and since that time they have been very quiet. I take them to be the most contemptible *canaille* upon earth. Those to the southward are much braver and better men; these are a dastardly set of bloody rascals. We cut them to pieces whenever we found them, in return for a thousand acts of cruelty and barbarity. I do not penetrate our General's intentions. If he means to attack Quebec, he must not lose a moment. If we have good pilots to take us up the river St. Lawrence, and can land at any tolerable distance from the place, I have no doubt of the event.

There is a report that Abercromby's army has attacked the enemy's detached posts, and forced them,—that my Lord Howe is killed. If this last circumstance be true, there is an end of the expedition, for he was the spirit of that army, and the very best officer in the King's service. I lament the loss as one of the greatest that could befall the nation; but perhaps it is not so, though I fear it much from the forward, determined nature of the man.* Louisbourg is a little place and has but one casemate in it, hardly big enough to hold the women.† Our artillery made havoc amongst them (the garrison), and soon opened the ramparts. In two days more we should have assaulted the place by land and by sea, and should certainly have carried it. If this force had been properly managed, there was an end of the French colony in North America in one campaign; for we have, exclusive of seamen and marines, near to 40,000 men in arms. I wish you a great deal of health and peace, and am, dear Sir,

Your obedient nephew,

J. WOLFE.‡

27th July, 1758.

A day or two after the surrender the Brigadier wrote to Captain William Amherst, brother of the Commander-in-chief,§ respecting the construction of roads for the removal of the artillery, and the embarkation of the troops, stores, etc.; to which he adds:—

We have been guilty of a blunder in transporting the French arms to the camp; they should have been deposited, under a guard, in the town, and kept there in readiness to embark.

* For an admirable account of this distinguished officer, who was killed at Ticonderoga on the 6th of July, see 'Letters of an American Lady,' vol. ii.

† The town, situated on a rugged promontory south-west of the inner bay or harbour, was about two miles in circumference; the houses were of stone, and the streets wide and regular, with a fine parade near the citadel. On one side stood the church and the Governor's house, and on the other barracks, thought to be bomb-proof, wherein, until their destruction, the women and children were sheltered. At the north-east end of the harbour was a fine careening wharf, and on the opposite side were stages spacious enough for 2000 boats to cure their fish.

‡ From original, in the possession of Mr. Richardson, Greenwich.

§ Captain William Amherst, who was the father of the late Earl Amherst, subsequently became a Lieut.-General, Adjutant-General of the Forces, and Governor of Newfoundland. He died in 1781.

We have given ourselves a deal of unnecessary trouble, and might have employed the waggons much more to the purpose. Put the General in mind of *pilots;* I dare say there are plenty in Louisbourg; their names should be known, in order to their being carried on board the men-of-war a day or two before we sail. Troops that have lost their arms, or have bad arms, may be supplied from those in the garrison. Please to hint to the General that the French flints are very good, and may be useful in his army. I write this by way of memorandum, knowing how many matters the General must have upon his hands in this hour of business. When does our express go off?

As I am pretty much resolved not to stay in America more than this campaign, I hope the General will not put me to the necessity of insisting upon the Field-Marshal's promise that I should return at the end of it. The corps of Light Infantry requires some regulation; they should have a captain to every 100 or 120, and exact equal numbers from every regiment, thirty per battalion. The volunteers should be again joined to that corps, with command of their respective regiments; by this method they will be formidable. Their powder-horns are good things.*

On the 7th of August, Wolfe writes to his father as follows:—

Camp near Louisbourg.

Dear Sir,

We are gathering strawberries and other wild fruits of the country, with a seeming indifference about what is doing in other parts of the world. Our army, however, on the continent wants our help, as they have been repulsed with loss. My Lord Howe, the noblest Englishman that has appeared in my time, and the best soldier in the army, fell by the hands of a couple of miscreants that did not dare to stay long enough to see him fall. Poor Mrs. Page will die of grief; and I

* The original is indorsed in the handwriting of the late Earl Amherst,—"To my Father."

reckon my good friend Sir Gregory will be greatly concerned.* Heavens, what a loss to the country! the bravest, worthiest, and most intelligent man among us! I thought his brother would have been starved. For several days he refused to eat, and could not bear to have anybody near him, even of his most intimate friends. This excess of grief is at length worn off, and I hope he will do well again.†

I am in a kind of doubt whether I go to the continent or not. Abercromby is a heavy man, and Brigadier P—— the most detestable dog upon earth, by everybody's account. These two officers hate one another. Now, to serve in an army so circumstanced is not a very pleasing business. If my Lord Howe had lived, I should have been very happy to have received his orders; or if I thought that I could be useful or serviceable, the ugly face of affairs there wouldn't discourage me from attempting it. If the King had not been pleased to give me a regiment, I should have ruined myself and you; for we are at a vast expense, and you know I never plunder,—except some dried cod which Captain Rodney‡ is so good to take for you and your friends. I much doubt if it will be worth your acceptance; the Madeira, if it gets home, will be a better present. Amongst other good things that are derived from my new honours, that of paying back to Fisher the kindness he has done me is not the least; of course he is my agent. I send the letter of attorney by this conveyance. The account you give of my mother's improved state of health, and the good condition of your own, is the most pleasing part of your letter. If you will send the like intelligence to the

* Mrs. Page was Judith, daughter of the first Viscount Howe, who had married Thomas, son of Sir Gregory Page, Bart. She was therefore aunt to the late gallant Brigadier-General Lord Howe.

† Lieutenant-Colonel, afterwards Sir William, and fifth Viscount Howe, Commander-in-chief in North America. Dying without issue, in 1814, the title became extinct.

‡ George Brydges Rodney became a Vice-Admiral in 1762, and was created a baronet in 1764. In 1782, after his victory over the French fleet commanded by Comte de Grasse, he was raised to the peerage as Baron Rodney, and died in 1792.

continent, I shall help to make war very cheerfully, though my carcase is not of the toughest.

Wolfe, uneasy lest the season should slip away without further operations, inquired of his Commander what were his intentions. On the 6th, the General replied:— "La belle saison will get away indeed; what I most wish to do is to go to Quebec. I have proposed it to the Admiral, who is the best judge whether or no we can get up there, and yesterday he seemed to think it impracticable."* Not yet satisfied, the Brigadier again writes:—

Tuesday Morning, August 8th, 1758.

Dear Sir,

All accounts agree that General Abercromby's army is cut deep, and all the last advices from those parts trace the bloody steps of those scoundrels the Indians. As an Englishman, I cannot see these things without the utmost horror and concern. We all know how little the Americans are to be trusted; by this time, perhaps, our troops are left to defend themselves, after losing the best of our officers. If the Admiral will not carry us to Quebec, reinforcements should certainly be sent to the continent without losing a moment's time. The companies of Rangers, and the Light Infantry, would be extremely useful at this juncture; whereas here they are perfectly idle, and, like the rest, of no manner of service to the public. If Lawrence has any objection to going I am ready to embark with four or five battalions, and will hasten to the assistance of our countrymen. I wish we were allowed to address the Admiral, or I wish you yourself, Sir, would do it in form. This d—d French garrison take up our time and attention, which might be better bestowed upon the interesting affairs of the continent. The transports are ready, and a small convoy would carry a brigade to Boston or New York. With the rest of the troops we might make an offensive and a

* See 'Chatham Correspondence,' vol. i. p. 330.

destructive war in the Bay of Fundy and in the Gulf of St. Lawrence. I beg pardon for this freedom, but I cannot look coolly upon the bloody inroads of those hell-hounds the Canadians; and if nothing further is to be done, I must desire leave to quit the army.*

In his answer the same day, General Amherst repeats that it had been his first intention to proceed to Quebec with the entire army, which he was still convinced was the best thing that could be done, if it were practicable; but that in consequence of the unlucky affair at Ticonderoga, he now considered it advisable to reinforce Abercromby with five or six battalions, sending at the same time two or three regiments to the Bay of Fundy, and the rest of his force into the Gulf of St. Lawrence. Ending his letter, he says:—"My wishes are to hasten everything for the good of the service, and I have not the least doubt but Mr. Boscawen will do the same. Whatever schemes you may have, or information that you can give, to quicken our motions, your communicating them will be very acceptable, and will be of much more service than your thoughts of quitting the army, which I can by no means agree to, as all my thoughts and wishes are confined at present to pursuing our operations for the good of his Majesty's service, and I know nothing that can tend more to it than your assisting in it."†

Returning to Wolfe's domestic correspondence; in his next letter to his mother, dated "Louisbourg, August 11," he predicts the destiny of North America:—

* Original in the possession of the Right Hon. Earl Amherst.
† 'Chatham Correspondence,' vol. i. p. 332.

The early season in this country,—I mean the months of April and May, are intolerably cold and disagreeable; June and July are foggy; August, rainy; September has always a tempest; October is generally a dry, fair month; and the winter sets in early in November. Further to the south, and along the continent of America which we possess, there is a variety of climate, and, for the most part, healthy and pleasant, so that a man may—if he gives himself the trouble, and his circumstances permit—live in perpetual spring or summer by changing his abode with the several changes of the seasons. Such is our extent of territory upon this fine continent, that an inhabitant may enjoy the kind influence of moderate warmth all the year round. These colonies are deeply tinged with the vices and bad qualities of the mother-country; and, indeed, many parts of it are peopled with those that the law or necessity has forced upon it. Notwithstanding these disadvantages, and notwithstanding the treachery of their neighbours the French, and the cruelty of their neighbours the Indians, worked up to the highest pitch by the former, this will, some time hence, be a vast empire, the seat of power and learning.

Nature has refused them nothing, and there will grow a people out of our little spot, England, that will fill this vast space, and divide this great portion of the globe with the Spaniards, who are possessed of the other half. If we had been as lucky this campaign as we had reason to expect, and had not lost that great man, whom I shall ever lament, the corner-stone would probably have been laid of this great fabric. It is my humble opinion that the French name would soon have been unknown in North America, and still may be rooted out, if our Government will follow the blows they have given, and prosecute the war with the vigour it requires. We have been extremely fortunate in this business. If Abercromby had acted with half as much caution and prudence as General Amherst did, this must have been a dear campaign to the French.

By the 15th of August the late garrison of Louisbourg,

numbering 5637 soldiers and seamen, were all dispatched as prisoners of war to England;* and on the 21st the Brigadier informs his father:—

Sir Charles Hardy and I are preparing to rob the fishermen of their nets, and to burn their huts. When that great exploit is at an end (which we reckon will be a month's or five weeks' work), I return to Louisbourg, and from thence to England, if no orders arrive in the meanwhile that oblige me to stay. The fleet do not go up the river St. Lawrence, nor southward to the West Indies, so that of necessity they must get away from hence before the bad weather sets in, leaving, I suppose, a few ships in the harbour of Halifax, where they may winter very commodiously. The army is about to disperse. General Amherst carries six battalions to the continent; Monckton takes two up the Bay of Fundy; and I have the honour to command three in the Gulf of St. Lawrence, to distress the enemy's fishery, and to alarm them. We are very earnest to hear what has been doing in Europe, or whether anything has been done at all.

By a provision of the capitulation agreed upon between the British commanders and M. Drucour, the surrender of Cape Breton included all its appurtenances, the inhabitants of which, as well as of Louisbourg, were to be carried to France, while the several garrisons were to yield as prisoners of war. General Amherst, therefore, sent Lord Rollo and Major Dalling to take possession of Isle St. Jean, now Prince Edward's Island, which, from its convenient position, mildness of climate, and fertility, had been invaluable to Canada, supplying Quebec

* During the siege the French lost more than 1000 men, while the English had 21 officers and 150 privates killed, with 30 officers and 320 men wounded. The spoil consisted of 240 pieces of ordnance and 15,000 stand of arms, besides great stores of ammunition and provisions.

with corn and cattle. It was likewise a source of great annoyance to Nova Scotia, affording shelter to hostile Indians, who made frequent irruptions into that colony.* The removal of the wretched people, many of whom escaped to Canada, was a painful and tedious operation, which delayed the detachment until the end of the season.†

Admiral Boscawen being determined to reap every advantage from the conquest, Sir Charles Hardy, with seven ships of the line and three frigates, and Wolfe with Amherst's, Bragg's, and Anstruther's regiments, sailed on the 28th of August for Gaspé, and other French settlements in the Gulf of St. Lawrence, where they destroyed the magazines of fish, corn, etc., and dispersed the inhabitants. A secondary object of this expedition was to alarm Quebec, so as to prevent assistance being sent from thence to the army employed against Abercromby. After accomplishing this disagreeable, though necessary service, Wolfe wrote as follows to Major-General Amherst, who had repaired to the continent in order to reinforce the Commander-in-chief:—

Louisbourg, 30th September, 1758.

Dear Sir,

Your orders were carried into execution as far as troops, who are limited in their operations by other powers, could carry them. I have made my report to General Abercromby, to which (as it is pretty long) I beg to refer. Our equipment was very improper for the business, and the numbers, unless

* It appears that Lord Rollo found the local Governor's house decorated with the scalps of English colonists, murdered by the savage allies of France. (See 'Annual Register,' 1758.)

† See Lieutenant Leslie's letter to Wolfe, dated "Louisbourg, 30th October," in 'Chatham Correspondence,' vol. i. p. 384.

the squadron had gone up the river, quite unnecessary. We have done a great deal of mischief,—spread the terror of his Majesty's arms through the whole gulf; but have added nothing to the reputation of them. The Bay of Gaspé and the harbour are both excellent, and now well known to our fleet. By the beginning of the month of July, I hope the river of Quebec will be as well known; although the aversion to that navigation, and the apprehensions about it, are inconceivably great. If you do business up the river, you must have small craft and a number of whale-boats, two at least to each transport. Pilots are easily had for sloops and schooners; every fisherman in the river can conduct them up. If you had sent two large empty cats,* I could have loaded them with 30,000 pounds' worth of the finest dried cod you ever saw; but you won't make money when it is in your power, though there are such *examples* before your eyes. The two regiments are gone to Halifax, except fifty or sixty recovering men, who followed the squadron.

Frontenac is a great stroke. An offensive, daring kind of war will awe the Indians and ruin the French. Blockhouses, and a trembling defensive, encourage the meanest scoundrels to attack us. The navy showed their happy disposition for plundering upon this, as upon all former occasions, and I indulged them to the utmost. I wish you success. Cannonade furiously before you attack, and don't let them go on in lines, but rather in columns: —— ▭ ▭ ▭ ▭ *Cela ne vaut rien pour les retranchements. Voilà l'affaire:* ≣ ≣ ≣ ≣ ≣. Mr. Boscawen is in haste to get back. No return to the express of the surrender of Louisbourg. If you will attempt to cut up New France by the

* "Cat," probably an abbreviation of *catamaran*, which Johnson defines as "a kind of shallow boat, or raft." Under the heading "Chat," a French authority says:—"C'est une sorte de vaisseau du Nord, qui ordinairement n'a qu'un pont: il a le cul rond, et porte des mâts de hune, quoiqu'il n'ait ni hunes, ni barres de hune. Il ne peut être regardé ni comme une pinasse, ni comme une flûte, parce qu'il est construit d'une manière qui tient de la flûte et de la pinasse." ('Dictionnaire Militaire Portatif.')

roots, I will come back with pleasure to assist. I wish you health, and am, dear Sir, with great regard,

Your most obedient and most humble servant,
JAM: WOLFE.

Leaving a sufficient garrison with Brigadier Whitmore, the new Governor of Louisbourg, Wolfe accompanied Admiral Boscawen to England in the 'Namur.'*

Thus, by a happy combination of commanders, was Louisbourg won with an armament considerably inferior to that which had retired from before it the previous year. The harmony which subsisted between the land and sea forces,—now, perhaps, for the first time in our history, really an "United Service,"—may safely be assigned as the principal cause of the unwonted success.† Though the warlike characteristics of the *three* leaders, for Whitmore and Lawrence acted no prominent part, were widely dissimilar, all were influenced by the same motive,—their duty to their country; and this was the tie that bound together Boscawen, full of expedients;‡

* The author of 'The Conquest of Canada' erroneously states that Wolfe sailed from Halifax on the 24th of January, 1759, when he accompanied the unhappy Abercromby in the 'Remmington.'

† An officer of the fleet writes to his uncle, Dr. Ducarel:—"I was in the camp with my uncle Hamilton; he was very kind to me, and so was Brigadier Wolfe, whose gallant behaviour you have heard of, and nobody can say too much in his praise, and that of the whole army. The soldiers worked like horses, making the roads and drawing up the cannon, and the sailors went and lent a hand to build the batteries." (Nichols' 'Literary Illustrations,' vol. iv. p. 624.)

‡ "No stronger testimony of the merit of Boscawen can be given," says Sheward, "than that afforded by Lord Chatham when Prime Minister:—'When I apply,' said he, 'to other officers respecting any expedition I may chance to project, they always raise difficulties, *you* always find expedients.'" ('Anecdotes,' vol. ii. p. 350.)

Amherst, careful and prudent;* and Wolfe, prompt, adventurous, and untiring. How far the merit of the achievement is due to Wolfe, and whether he was rightly called by his contemporaries "the Hero of Louisbourg," the reader may judge. The appellation, however, in nowise disparages General Amherst; for it shows that he not only recognized the abilities of a subordinate officer, but was also too high-minded to permit any jealous feeling to pervert his judgment, or impede the cause he had at heart. And, as Southey considered that no higher compliment could be paid to a commander-in-chief than to say he understood the merits of Nelson, and left him to act as he thought fit; we may add, it is equally complimentary to Amherst to say that he supported rather than curbed the zeal and skill of Wolfe.

Of the other expeditions set on foot in America, that against Crown Point and Ticonderoga was frustrated through the rashness of Abercromby; but the failure was somewhat compensated by the "great stroke," as Wolfe called it, at Frontenac, where, on the 27th of August, Colonel Bradstreet seized the supplies laid up for the more remote French posts, and afterwards captured their shipping on Lake Ontario. The success of this dashing exploit greatly facilitated the operations against Fort du Quesne, which was finally abandoned by the French on the 24th of November, when we became masters of that stronghold, the contention for which had kindled the strife between our colonists and those

* "General Amherst goes on carefully, and will not lose any lives he can save by carrying on approaches." (From original letter of a Scotch officer, July 6.)

of France. On the whole, therefore, the former had reason to be satisfied with the results of the campaign; for by the reduction of Isle St. Jean, Frontenac, and Du Quesne, they were delivered from all fear of incursions. The capture of Cape Breton was, however, the most effectual blow that France had received since the beginning of the war; for with Louisbourg she lost the only spot from whence she could carry on her cod-fishery, her main depôt for reinforcements and stores to support her armies in North America, and the bulwark of Canada.

CHAPTER XX.

SALISBURY.—BATH.—LONDON.

NOVEMBER, 1758—FEBRUARY, 1759.

IN England, the people had so long been accustomed to hear nothing from America but of delays and disasters, that the intelligence of the capture of Cape Breton, and the annihilation of the French fleet, was received with as much surprise as joy. On the 18th of August, Captains Edgecomb and Amherst, who were deputed by the Admiral and General, delivered their dispatches to the King, when his Majesty presented each of them with £500; and on the 7th of September the colours taken at Louisbourg were carried in procession from Kensington, and solemnly deposited in St. Paul's. Although our great success was magnified by English, and misrepresented by French writers,* it nevertheless considerably raised the military reputation of England, and increased her influence throughout Europe. Yet Pitt, who had anxiously watched for tidings from America,† foreseeing that it was there the struggle for supremacy between the

* See 'The Idler,' No. 20, August 26th, 1758.

† See his letter to Lady Hester Pitt, dated "July 1st, 1758." ('Chatham Correspondence,' vol. i. p. 321.)

rival nations must eventually be decided, regarded the war upon the Continent as of secondary moment, and devoted all his energies towards the accomplishment of still grander projects for another campaign in the Western hemisphere. In this determination he was further encouraged by the discovery that England had now one or two Generals to whom he could confidently entrust those bold designs, the execution of which demanded military leaders of vigour, discernment, and patriotism akin to his own.

As the 'Namur,' with her consorts, the 'Royal William' and the captured 'Bienfaisant,' arrived off the Land's End, towards the close of day they fell in with a French fleet of seven men-of-war, homeward-bound from Quebec. A few shots were exchanged, but the enemy slipt away during the night, and were almost out of sight next morning. Admiral Boscawen, therefore, thinking it useless to give chase, the English squadron anchored at St. Helen's on the 1st of November, and the same evening Wolfe dispatched a note to his mother by the Admiralty messenger, announcing his arrival at Portsmouth. Next day he repaired to Salisbury, where his regiment was stationed, and on the 6th writes to his father:—

Somebody told me that you were seen in London within these few days, which I was particularly pleased to hear, because at Portsmouth there was a report of your being out of order. You might well expect that I should have been to pay my duty to you before this time; but it seemed right to wait for the Marshal's leave to go to town, and nowhere so properly as at the regiment. His Excellency hath not done me the honour to answer my letter yet, and I cannot stir till he does; so I must content myself with wishing you and my mother all imaginable good.

He soon afterward came to town, and on the 17th writes from Blackheath to his uncle in Ireland:—

Dear Sir,

I wish I could say that my health was such as a soldier should have. Long passages and foggy weather have left their natural effects upon me. The people here say I look well. No care shall be wanting to get ready for the next campaign. They can propose no service to me that I shall refuse to undertake, unless where capacity is short of the task. We met a squadron of homeward-bound French men-of-war, and did our utmost to engage them, though with inferior force. Their destruction would almost have annihilated the French navy. My father looks well, and is well for the time of life; and my mother does not complain. I hope you continue to enjoy a share of health. My father tells me that he has added something to my cousin Goldsmith's little income; his liberality towards such of our relations as need it is most commendable. If fortune smile upon us, I shall endeavour to follow his example.

Admiral Boscawen, on taking his seat in the House of Commons, received the thanks of Parliament, which were also transmitted to General Amherst; but Wolfe being a subordinate officer, his conduct was not noticed. A few days after his arrival in London, however, he wrote the following "modest and manly" letter to the Prime Minister; in consequence of which he was soon afterwards promoted to the rank of Major-General, and entrusted with the command of the most important undertaking for the ensuing campaign :—

St. James Street, Nov. 22, 1758.

Sir,

Since my arrival in town, I have been told that your intentions were to have continued me upon the service in America. The condition of my health, and other circumstances, made me desire to return at the end of the campaign; and by what my Lord Ligonier did me the honour to say, I understood it was to be so. General Amherst saw it in the same light.

I take the freedom to acquaint you that I have no objection to serving in America, and particularly in the river St. Lawrence, if any operations are to be carried on there. The favour I ask is only to be allowed a sufficient time to repair the injury done to my constitution by the long confinement at sea, that I may be the better able to go through the business of the next summer.

I have the honour to be, with the utmost respect,

Sir, your most obedient and most humble servant,

JAM: WOLFE.*

We find him again with his regiment at Salisbury, on the 1st of December, when he writes as follows to Lieutenant-Colonel Rickson :—

My dear Friend,

Your letter, dated in September, as well as the last you did me the favour to write, are both received, and with the greatest satisfaction. I do not reckon that we have been fortunate this year in America. Our force was so superior to the enemy's that we might hope for greater success; but it pleased the Disposer of all things to check our presumption, by permitting Mr. Abercromby to hurry on that precipitate attack of Ticonderoga, in which he failed with loss. By the

* 'Chatham Correspondence,' vol. i. p. 370.

situation of that fort, by the superiority of our naval force there, and by the strength of our army, which could bear to be weakened by detachments, it seems to me to have been no very difficult matter to have obliged the Marquis de Montcalm to have laid down his arms, and, consequently, to have given up all Canada. In another circumstance, too, we may be reckoned unlucky. The squadron of men-of-war, under De Chaffrueil, failed in their attempt to get into the harbour of Louisbourg, where inevitably they would have shared the fate of those that did, which must have given an irretrievable blow to the marine of France, and delivered Quebec into our hands, if we chose to go up and demand it.

Amongst ourselves be it said, that our attempt to land where we did was rash and injudicious, our success unexpected (by me) and undeserved. There was no prodigious exertion of courage in the affair; an officer and thirty men would have made it impossible to get ashore where we did. Our proceedings in other respects were as slow and tedious as this undertaking was ill-advised and desperate; but this for your private information only. We lost time at the siege, still more after the siege, and blundered from the beginning to the end of the campaign. My Lord Howe's death (who was truly a great man) left the army upon the Continent without life or vigour. This defeat at Ticonderoga seemed to stupify us that were at Louisbourg; if we had taken the first hint of that repulse, and sent early and powerful succours, things would have taken, perhaps, a different turn in those parts before the end of October. I expect every day to hear that some fresh attempts have been made at Ticonderoga, and I can't flatter myself that they have succeeded, not from any high idea of the Marquis de Montcalm's abilities, but from the very poor opinion of our own. You have obliged me much with this little sketch of that important spot; till now I have been ill-acquainted with it. Bradstreet's *coup* was masterly. He is a very extraordinary man; and if such an excellent officer as the late Lord Howe had the use of Bradstreet's batoe knowledge, it would turn to a good public account.

When I went from hence, Lord Ligonier told me that I was to return at the end of the campaign; but I have learned since I came home that an order is gone to keep me there; and I have this day* signified to Mr. Pitt that he may dispose of my slight carcass as he pleases, and that I am ready for any undertaking within the reach and compass of my skill and cunning. I am in a very bad condition both with the gravel and rheumatism, but I had much rather die than decline any kind of service that offers. If I followed my own taste, it would lead me into Germany; and if my poor talent was consulted, they would place me in the cavalry, because nature has given me good eyes, and a warmth of temper to follow the first impressions. However, it is not our part to choose, but to obey. My opinion is, that I shall join the army in America, where, if fortune favours our force and best endeavours, we may hope to triumph.

I have said more than enough of myself. It is time to turn a little to your affairs. Nothing more unjust than the great rank lately thrown away upon little men, and the good servants of the state neglected. Not content with frequent solicitations in your behalf, I writ a letter just before I embarked, putting my Lord George Sackville in mind of you, and requesting his protection; his great business, or greater partialities, has made him overlook your just pretensions. If you come to town in January, I shall be there, and will do you all the service I am able, but Lord Ligonier seems particularly determined not to lay the weight of any one obligation on me; so you may hold my good inclination in higher value than my power to assist. You have my best wishes, and I am, truly,

My dear friend,
Your faithful and obedient servant,
JAMES WOLFE.

Salisbury, 1st December, 1758.

* This letter was probably begun on the 22nd of November, the day he wrote to Mr. Pitt, and not finished until the 1st of December, when the date was affixed.

Remember that I am a Brigadier in America, and Colonel in Europe. Barré was in such favour with General Amherst that he took him to the Continent, and he very well deserves his esteem.*

On Wolfe's promotion to the Colonelcy of the 67th regiment, he was succeeded in the Lieutenant-Colonelcy of the Twentieth by Major Beckwith, Captain Maxwell obtaining the Majority. By none of his numerous friends was he was more highly esteemed than by the officers whom he had formerly commanded; and by none of his countrymen was he more respected and beloved than by the men whom he had trained to a state of discipline until then unknown in the British army. The corps was now serving in Germany, under Prince Ferdinand

* The above is the latest letter to Rickson, and probably the last written to him by Wolfe. William, only son of Joseph Rickson, Esq., a gentleman of considerable property in Wales, was born at Pembroke in 1719, and entered the army as an Ensign of Onslow's (8th regiment of Foot) in 1740. He fought at Dettingen, took part in several engagements during that war, and was severely wounded at Fontenoy and Roucoux. In these campaigns he and Wolfe contracted their warm and lasting friendship; and when Wolfe's father succeeded to the colonelcy of the Eighth, Rickson acquired the General's regard also. With his subsequent career, until 1759, the reader is familiar. He afterwards settled in Scotland, where he was highly esteemed. In 1763 he was appointed by Government to superintend the formation of roads through the shires of Dumfries, Galloway, and Wigton, a duty which he performed with remarkable industry and talent. In 1767 he married Euphemia, daughter of Dr. Bremner, of Edinburgh, and was promoted to the office of Quartermaster-General of North Britain, though only with the rank of Lieutenant-Colonel. The Duke of Queensberry was endeavouring to obtain a Colonel's commission for him, and the matter was nearly settled when this active and amiable officer was attacked by paralysis, and died without issue at Broughton, near Edinburgh, on the 19th of July, 1770. His remains were interred in the churchyard of Restalrig, where a handsome tomb was erected by his widow, who survived him many years. (Condensed from a MS. Memoir, compiled from family papers, by Mr. Buchanan.)

of Brunswick, and a few months afterwards, by their bravery and endurance, earned the distinction of "Minden" upon their colours.

One of the captains, of whom our hero was so proud, having congratulated him upon his return from America, he replies as follows:—

Salisbury, 6th December, 1758.

Dear Parr,

Your remembrance and congratulations upon my return to Europe are most acceptable, and I shall always set a value upon your friendship and good opinion. It gives me the utmost satisfaction to hear of the good behaviour of your regiment, and I don't at all doubt but they will be still more distinguished when they are more tried. They are led by the same captains who have assisted in establishing the sound discipline that prevails amongst you; and there is no reason to suppose other than the natural effects whenever it comes to the proof.* My people, I find, are much out of humour with your chief.† I hope you have no such temper amongst you. It is my fortune to be cursed with American service, yours to serve in an army commanded by a great and able Prince, where I would have been if my choice and inclinations had been consulted. Our old comrade, Howe, is at the head of the best-trained battalion in all America; and his conduct in the course of the last campaign corresponded entirely with the opinion we had all entertained of him.‡ His Majesty has

* In consequence of the heavy loss sustained by the regiment at Minden, on the 1st of August, 1759, Prince Ferdinand ordered next day that the survivors should cease from ordinary duty. Their *esprit de corps*, however, not allowing them to avail themselves of the exemption, in the general orders of the 4th, it was stated that "Kingsley's regiment, at its own request, will resume its proportion of duty in the lines." (Cannon's 'Records,' Twentieth Foot, p. 18.)

† Lord George Sackville, who succeeded the Duke of Marlborough as Commander-in-chief of the British forces in Germany.

‡ The Hon. William Howe, who had been a captain of the Twentieth, was now Lieutenant-Colonel of the 58th Foot.

not a better soldier in those parts,—modest, diligent, and valiant. His brother was a great man; this country has produced nothing like him in my time; his death cannot be enough lamented. You must continue to be upon good terms with the Hanoverian Guards; they deserve your esteem. Your quarters are not, I believe, amongst the best, nor, I fear, amongst the cheapest.

The first news that I heard at Portsmouth was the death of M'Dowall; what a loss was there! I have hardly ever known a better Foot officer, or a better man,—clear, firm, resolute, and cool.* My health is mightily impaired by the long confinement at sea. I am going directly to the Bath, to refit for another campaign. We shall look, I imagine, at the famous post at Ticonderoga, where Mr. Abercromby, by a little soldiership and a little patience, might, I think, have put an end to the war in America. General Amherst thought the entrenchments so improved as to require more ceremony in the second attack than the season would allow of. You will always have my best wishes. I asked immediately,—Did Kingsley's come into action? How did they behave? The answer was;—There is no doubt but that they would have done well, but there was no enemy to try them. My compliments to the corps. I hope Grey has his health, and Carleton.† Fare ye well.

I am, dear Parr,
Your faithful and obedient servant,
J. W.

To Captain Parr, of the
20th Regiment, at Münster, Westphalia.

By pursuing the same course which he had so successfully adopted with the Twentieth, Wolfe soon brought his own newly-raised battalion to a condition scarcely

* Alexander M'Dowall, Captain of the Grenadier company of the Twentieth, was gazetted as Major of the Sixty-seventh; but it would appear from the records of the regiment that he died before joining the corps.

† Thomas, younger brother of Lieut.-Colonel Guy Carleton, was now a captain of the Twentieth.

inferior. Nor did the spirit he evoked in the corps, by his high sense of honour, his disinterestedness, fascinating manners, and fatherly concern for the comfort and welfare of his men, die with him. Ten years after they lost their first Colonel, they were stationed in Minorca, under the command of Major Campbell. Russia being then on friendly terms with England, and engaged in hostilities against Turkey, a Russian fleet put into Port Mahon, in order to refit. Soon after the arrival of the armament the garrison had a field day, when Count Butterlin, the Russian General, was astonished at the contrast between the appearance and discipline of the English troops and those he commanded. Having particularly remarked the precision and rapidity with which the 67th Regiment performed their evolutions, and not thinking how different were the constitutions of the two nations, the Count begged of the Major to give him three or four of his men to drill the Russian soldiers. When told that neither their commanding officer, the Governor of the island, nor even the King himself could do so without the men's own consent, he expressed the greatest surprise. However, with the Governor's sanction, two privates of the Sixty-seventh were eventually *lent* to the foreign General for the purpose he desired. "The regiment," says Major Campbell, "was undoubtedly in a high state of discipline; but the only merit, which on that account was due to me, was the attention and strictness with which I followed the system which had been introduced by its former colonel, the hero of Quebec."*

* 'Memoirs of Sir James Campbell of Ardkinglass, written by Himself,' vol. i. p. 192.

On the 7th of December, Wolfe took leave of the corps, and proceeded to Bath. Two days later he wrote as follows to his father:—

If I had not been scrambling over the country, you should, by this time, have known my state and condition. A man can't write well till he gets into his lodgings; nor is one much inclined to write with self only for a subject. I find a few acquaintances, but no friends since George Warde went away. This is my third day at Bath. My continuance here will be no longer than is pleasant, and as long as it is either useful or convenient. I have got in the square, to be more at leisure, more in the air, and nearer the country. The women are not remarkable, nor the men neither; however, a man must be very hard to please if he does not find some that will suit him. Cheerfulness and good humour recommend as strongly to some tempers as qualities of a stronger cast. There are a number of people that inquire after you and my mother, and some that wish you well wherever you are. I hope health and tranquillity will be with you.

Colonel Wolfe had not been many days in Bath when he was summoned to London by Mr. Pitt. On the 18th or 19th of December, the Minister received a letter from the famous William Beckford, of Fonthill, in which the worthy alderman stated that he had been "constantly ruminating" upon a method of putting an end to the war in America in one campaign. He proposed that an expedition should be sent up the St. Lawrence to Quebec; and that, that city being reduced, Montreal should be attacked. "By taking of Quebec and Montreal," he adds, "the two great heads of Canada, and of the French power in North America, are destroyed; and, consequently, the limbs of that body must wither and decay without any further fighting. And thus you will make an end of the war, and for ever establish the good opinion mankind have of your abilities and public spirit."*

There was, however, nothing new in the scheme, as such an enterprise had been designed for the late campaign. Wolfe, too, has as appeared, had been perpetually urging the prosecution of it upon Admiral Boscawen and General Amherst, and was grieved because the prolongation of the siege of Louisbourg necessitated its postponement. Beckford's letter therefore may have furnished the Prime Minister with a timely corroboration of Wolfe's views; but nothing more. Nay, it is evident that the arrangements for the principal enterprise of the ensuing campaign had been settled prior to the date of the Alderman's letter, Wolfe having already accepted the command of the expedition, and been empowered by Mr. Pitt to select his officers. That such was the case is shown by the following letter from Wolfe to his trusty friend—to whom, however, he does not disclose the particulars of the project—Lieutenant-Colonel George Warde:—

Blackheath, 20th December, 1758.

My dear Colonel,

I need not ask you if you desire to serve. I know your inclinations in that respect; but let me know if I may men-

* Chatham Correspondence, vol. i. p. 376. A letter, dated "Bath, December 29, 1758," has more than once been referred to by compilers as having been written by Wolfe. On investigation, however, it proves to be copied from a portion of Beckford's. The fictitious letter came into the possession of an eminent autograph connoisseur (W. F. Watson, Esq., of Edinburgh), who, suspecting that it was spurious, has withdrawn it from his collection. Had the date been altered to some days earlier, the fraud would not be quite so apparent.

tion you for distant, difficult, and disagreeable service, such as requires all your spirit and abilities. 'Tis not the Indies, which is as much as I can say directly; but if the employment of Adjutant-General, or perhaps of Quartermaster-General to a very hazardous enterprise be to your taste, there are people who would be extremely glad of your assistance. There is no immediate advantage arising from it. That of being useful to the public at the expense of your health and constitution, is an argument that cannot be strongly urged. Write to me by return of post, and send your letter to the Bath, where it will find me.

I am ever your
Faithful friend,
J. Wolfe.

The next day Wolfe returned to Bath. It was here, probably, that he renewed his intimacy with one whose name has been, by tradition, so closely linked with his. The lady was Katherine, daughter of Robert Lowther, Esq., who had been for some time Governor of Barbadoes, and who died in 1745; her eldest brother being the Sir James Lowther who was afterwards raised to the peerage as Earl of Lonsdale. Unlike his first love affair,—so tedious and unavailing,—Wolfe's courtship of Miss Lowther was exceedingly rapid and successful. Although, as has already been hinted, there is nothing in any of his letters confirmatory of the tradition as to their betrothment, its truth, as will hereafter be shown, is placed beyond all doubt. It must suffice to say here that he carried her portrait with him to America, and wore it next his heart until the eve of his death. But neither the calls of love, nor the rest which his health required, made him unmindful of his public duty, as appears from the following letter to Mr. Pitt:—

Bath, December 24, 1758.

Sir,

In a packet of letters from North America, there are two which contain some interesting circumstances, as they throw a light upon the state of men's minds in those parts. They are a confirmation to me of the thorough aversion conceived by the marine of this country against navigating in the river St. Lawrence. The letters are from two gentlemen recommended to act as Assistant Quartermasters-General, and do in some measure point out the hardy, active disposition of the men.* I will add, from my own knowledge, that the second naval officer in command there is vastly unequal to the weight of business;† and it is of the first importance to the country that it doth not fall into such hands. Mr. Caldwell in autumn proposed to attempt bringing off the pilots from the Isle aux Coudres, after the French fleet came down, or was supposed to be come down the river. The seeming danger of the enterprise, and other causes, put a stop to so great an undertaking.

What Caldwell observes in regard to the fleet's anchoring at the Isle Bic is certainly very proper. A squadron of eight or ten sail stationed there, in the earliest opening of the river, would effectually prevent all relief; and it would be a very easy thing for the remainder of that squadron to push a frigate or two, and as many sloops, up the river, even as high as the Isle of Orleans, with proper people on board to acquire a certain knowledge of the navigation, in readiness to pilot such men-of-war and transports as the commanders should think fit to send up, after the junction of the whole fleet at Isle Bic. Nor does there appear any great risk in detaching the North American squadron to that station; as it is hardly probable that a force equal to that squadron could

* The enclosures were from Lieutenants Caldwell and Leslie, who wrote to him from Louisbourg on the 27th and 30th of October. Their letters not only show the merit of the men, but also prove how highly they appreciated Wolfe's esteem. (See Chatham Correspondence, vol. i. pp. 381, 384.)

† Rear-Admiral Durell.

be sent from Europe to force their way up to Quebec, because it is a hundred to one if such a fleet keeps together in that early season; and if they were together, it is next to a certainty that they would be in a very poor condition for action. Besides, it would effectually answer our purpose to engage a French squadron in that river, even with the superiority of a ship or two on their side, seeing that they must be shattered in the engagement, and in the end destroyed.

. . . .

If the enemy cannot pass the squadron stationed in the river, and push up to Quebec, a few ships of war and frigates would do to convoy the transports from the Isle Bic to Quebec, and to assist in the operations of the campaign; and, in this case, the gross of the fleet remaining at the Isle Bic is at hand to prevent any attempt upon Louisbourg or Halifax; whereas, if the whole went up to Quebec, intelligence would be long in getting to them, and their return in proportion. You must excuse the freedom I have taken, both in writing and sending the enclosed papers. If you see one useful hint in either, my intent is fully answered; if not, I beg you will burn them without any further notice.*

Colonel Warde having expressed his readiness to serve under his friend, though he feared that official objections would be started, Wolfe writes to him again:†—

Bath, December 26, 1758.

My dear Friend,

I have told the leading men that if they charge a young soldier with weighty matters they must give him the best assistance. I know none better than those I took the freedom

* From Chatham Correspondence.

† On receiving Wolfe's letter of the 20th, Colonel Warde consulted his friend Colonel G. A. Eliott, afterwards Lord Heathfield, who being then at Bath, replied on the 25th:—"The subject is not unexpected by me, as I knew Wolfe's opinion, though he has not opened his lips to me about any particular service. He will certainly command, and by his own account I should imagine him well prepared;

to mention, and if there be any obstacles on the side of Government I shall desire to be excused from taking the first part. Another circumstance might oblige me to decline these dangerous honours, viz. any situation of affairs that might make it disagreeable for you and another friend to engage in this business with me. The readiness you express encourages me to hope that our united efforts may at least be useful. Nothing shall be pressed upon you, although I know of nothing that you need decline. We shall meet in London towards the middle of next week, and talk the matter over; till then I bid you farewell.*

which, of course, will make the campaign agreeable to his friends, and, no doubt, very instructive. At all events, 'tis better than Scotch quarters, or an ill-digested project on the coast of France." (From original, in the possession of Admiral Warde, K.H.)

* Owing to some unknown cause, Lieut.-Colonel Warde did not accompany the expedition to Quebec; but was sent to Germany, where he distinguished himself in various engagements during the remainder of the war. He was an excellent regimental officer, and brought the 4th Dragoons to so high a state of discipline that George III., whenever he reviewed the corps, invariably complimented their Lieut.-Colonel. In 1773, he was promoted to the colonelcy of the 14th Dragoons, subsequently was Colonel of the 4th Dragoon Guards, and passed through the several grades to the rank of General. In 1792, he was appointed Commander of the Forces in Ireland, where he devoted much of his attention to bringing the cavalry into a perfect condition for active service. General Warde was considered the best cavalry officer of his time, and introduced what is known as the Wardonian system of discipline. He disliked slow movements, and when seventy years of age, frequently led his men across the country, over hedges and ditches, to the great astonishment of the people. Mrs. Wolfe, after she lost her husband and her son, found in General Warde a faithful friend and sound adviser; and nominated him her principal executor. He died, unmarried, on the 11th of March, 1803, and was interred in St. Mary's, Abchurch, City. In a contemporary periodical his decease is recorded as follows:—"In his seventy-eighth year, in the literal as well as the titular sense of the words, the *Right Honourable* General Warde, of inviolable, disinterested integrity, public and private, Colonel of the 4th Dragoon Guards, whose benefactions were scarcely less secret than extensive." ('Gentleman's Magazine,' vol. lxxiii. p. 292.)

The reader will recollect how indignant Wolfe had been in consequence of the King's refusing Lieut.-Colonel Guy Carleton permission to serve with him in Cape Breton.* This admirable officer was the other friend to whom he alluded above. It appears that during the interviews between Mr. Pitt and Wolfe, the Minister stated that so large a force as Wolfe required could not be spared for that particular service. Whereupon the young Commander replied, that the deficiency of numbers might be compensated by allowing him to choose his own staff; in which Mr. Pitt, as we have seen, immediately acquiesced. Soon afterwards Wolfe forwarded his list of names to the Minister, and amongst them was that of Colonel Carleton, for the office of Quartermaster-General. Carleton, however, had made himself obnoxious to the King by some slighting remarks upon the Hanoverian troops, an offence than which none could be more heinous in the Elector's eyes.† So, when the Commander-in-chief submitted the list to the Sovereign, his Majesty, as was expected, drew his pen across Carleton's name, and refused to sign his commission. Neither Pitt nor Wolfe were men likely to humour the stubborn monarch's whim. Lord Ligonier was therefore sent a second time into the royal closet, but with no better success. When his Lordship returned to the Prime Minister, he was ordered to make another trial, and told that on again submitting the name, he should represent the peculiar state of affairs. "And tell his Majesty like-

* See pp. 414, 415, and 417.

† Hence, doubtless, Wolfe's advice to the officers of the Twentieth,—that they should keep on good terms with the Hanoverian Guards. See letter to Captain Parr, p. 469.

wise," said Mr. Pitt, "that in order to render any General completely responsible for his conduct, he should be made, as far as possible, inexcusable, if he should fail; and that, consequently, whatever an officer entrusted with a service of confidence requests should be complied with." After some hesitation, Ligonier obtained a third audience, and delivered his message, when, obstinate and unforgiving though the old King was, the sound sense of the observations prevailed over his prejudice, and he signed the commission as requested.*

In those days the pay of the Commander-in-chief in North America, was £10 a day, with an allowance of £1000 for extraordinary expenses; while the ordinary pay of a major-general, to which rank our hero was now promoted, was but £2 a day.† Wolfe, still nominally serving under General Amherst, though appointed Commander-in-chief of a distinct army, was not considered entitled to more than the latter paltry pay.

* The above anecdote, which rests upon the authority of Mr. Wood, then Under-Secretary of State, is partly borne out by the visible facts that the King prevented Carleton from going to Louisbourg, and afterwards allowed him to join the expedition to Quebec.

† The original of Wolfe's commission as Major-General, etc., dated "January 12, 1759," does not accompany his earlier commissions in Admiral Warde's possession. Probably it was sent to the War Office by Mrs. Wolfe, and never returned to her. It appears that in making out the warrant for the payment of the staff employed in the expedition to Quebec, which, by the way, was not till February, 1761, no record of Wolfe's appointments could be traced in either the Secretary of State's or the War Office. The informality is stated to have arisen from Mr. Pitt's having delivered the commission to Wolfe before registering it in his own department, and to Wolfe's having omitted to enter it at the War Office. (Letter to Mrs. Wolfe from her agent, Mr. Thomas Fisher, dated "Axe Yard, Westminster, 19th February, 1761.")

But usually a special sum for contingencies was granted to officers on their appointment to the leadership of expeditions. Wolfe accordingly waited upon Lord Barrington, then Secretary for War, and represented that while at the head of so large a body of troops, he should be obliged to live at a much greater expense than that pay would afford. "He said, however," wrote Lord Barrington two years afterwards, "he asked nothing; that he had no money himself, but he could borrow some of his father, so he should not be distressed; that perhaps I should not think it unreasonable, however, to allow him some public money to defray a necessary public expense. His modesty touched me; I acknowledged the equity of what he said, and procured a warrant signed by the late King for £500.* . . . With this sum Mr. Wolfe declared himself perfectly satisfied. However, I told him that if he should be obliged to expend a still larger sum, over and above his pay, I would move the King to allow it."†

* The preamble of the Royal warrant is as follows:—"Whereas we have appointed our trusty and well-beloved James Wolfe, Colonel of our 67th regiment of Foot, to command as a Major-General in North America; and whereas the pay of Major-General, which we have been pleased to allow him, will not be sufficient to defray the expense incident to the chief command of so considerable a body of troops as we have thought fit to entrust to his care, upon consideration whereof we, being desirous that the private fortune of the said Colonel Wolfe should not suffer in the performance of those services to us which we have reason to expect from his loyalty, courage, and activity, are graciously pleased, out of mere favour and royal bounty, to bestow on him the sum of £500."

† Letter dated, "Cavendish Square, 7th May, 1761," addressed to the Right Hon. Charles Townshend, his Majesty's Secretary at War. (From MS. volume of 'Wolfiana,' collected by the late Dawson Turner, Esq.)

Mr. Pitt with truth asserted that he sought for merit wherever it was to be found; and the fact was something to be honestly proud of in those times. In the discovery of meritorious officers he was admirably seconded by Wolfe, who, asking nothing for himself, and refusing, as we have seen, to use his interest on behalf of a relation whom he considered unworthy, was never tired of bringing forward those who were deserving. "Nothing pleases me so much," he wrote to an officer who had served under him at Louisbourg, "as to do justice to those gentlemen who have distinguished themselves under my command; and if it were as easy to reward as to praise, they should have no reason to complain."* Notwithstanding Wolfe's influence, and in spite of Pitt's power, it was not possible to break through the old system of political patronage still upheld by the Duke of Newcastle. Even the great War Minister durst not give offence by raising those young and useful officers who were to bear the heat and burden of battle over the heads of their seniors, who reposed upon their laurels at home. Mr. Pitt therefore compromised the matter, by conferring upon the new men whom it was necessary to encourage, only local rank. Thus Wolfe himself, while a Brigadier-General in America, was but plain Colonel Wolfe in England. The niggardly manner in which promotion was dealt out to serviceable officers is clearly exemplified in the following letter to Major Alexander Murray, who had not only greatly distinguished himself at Louisbourg, but had

* Letter to Captain Martin, of the Royal Artillery, printed in the 'Gentleman's Magazine,' vol. lv. p. 759.

been actively engaged for three or four years previously in America, where he still remained:—

London, January 28, 1759.

Dear Murray,

I wish it was as much in my power to assist you as I am inclined to do, and as I know you deserve. In speaking of the transactions of our short campaign, it has fallen in my way sometimes to do you justice; the consequence of which is, that you are to command a little battalion of Grenadiers, with the rank of Lieutenant-Colonel in America. This is an honour and a distinction leading to more solid advantages, for which the best foundation is laid; and if fortune favours our good inclinations and our united efforts, it shall be confirmed to you as you would wish. Boscawen has been pushing for Mr. Hussey, and has such immoderate weight that I consider he will succeed. I have spoke to the Marshal upon it, and begged he would reflect and consider how mortifying a circumstance this must be to a man of honour and service, older in rank and experience than the gentleman in question. Such a torrent of family interest, and the merits of Mr. Boscawen's services, bears down justice itself before it. My poor endeavours to serve you may be useful in some respects, though I am afraid they will be very ineffectual in this.

We shall have, if we can get together, a powerful fleet, and an active, vigorous army, formidable from their spirit and experience more than from their numbers. With this force we shall assist General Amherst's operations in the river St. Lawrence. The French are arming in all their ports with a view to the preservation of their colonies, and will endeavour to throw in succours and provisions early in the year. I hope to be with you in May, and find you in health, with resolutions equal to the task that has fallen to our share.

The original of the above letter is treasured as an heirloom by the grandson of the brave officer to whom Wolfe addressed it. In the same gentleman's possession is a letter from the gallant Colonel Frazer, who, writing to Lieut.-Colonel Murray about his promotion, tells him how much he is indebted to both the Generals, "particularly to honest Wolfe, whose warmth of heart makes him as amiable as his bravery does respectable." The number of meritorious men whom Wolfe brought into notice was very considerable. Not the least remarkable of them was the famous Colonel Isaac Barré, who subsequently acknowledged,—"For want of friends I had lingered a subaltern officer eleven years, when Mr. Wolfe's opinion of me rescued me from that obscurity." There is something very pathetic in the expression of this political gladiator's grateful remembrance of his "only protector and friend," his "zealous and sole advocate," his late General.* It would be tedious to cite more of the many instances which go to prove that "all were swift to follow whom all loved." Nothing, indeed, more forcibly evinces how indisputably established is the high estimation in which Wolfe's name is universally held than the fact, that whenever a writer has occasion to relate some trifling incident apparently adverse to the purity of the hero's fame, he finds it necessary to offer an apology, or to propitiate his readers by pointing a moral. Thus, an elegant and impartial historian introduces the following traditional ancedote, by observing that it "affords a striking proof how much a fault of manner may obscure and disparage high excellence of mind." In the noble author's own words:—"After Wolfe's appointment, and on the day preceding his em-

* See Barré's letter to Mr. Pitt, dated "New York, April 28, 1760," in the 'Chatham Correspondence.' (Vol. ii. p. 41.)

barkation for America, Pitt, desirous of giving his last verbal instructions, invited him to dinner, Lord Temple being the only other guest. As the evening advanced, Wolfe, heated perhaps by his own aspiring thoughts, and the unwonted society of statesmen, broke forth into a strain of gasconade and bravado. He drew his sword, he rapped the table with it, he flourished it round the room, he talked of the mighty things which that sword was to achieve. The two Ministers sat aghast at an exhibition so unusual from any man of real sense and real spirit. And when at last Wolfe had taken his leave, and his carriage was heard to roll from the door, Pitt seemed for the moment shaken in the high opinion which his deliberate judgment had formed of Wolfe; he lifted up his eyes and arms, and exclaimed to Lord Temple, 'Good God! that I should have entrusted the fate of the country and of the Administration to such hands!'"*

Such is the story related of Wolfe in a standard history of England. With the highest respect, however, for the noble author, and the most unshaken confidence in the general integrity of his work, the writer of this memoir considers the above representation so repugnant to the character of the hero as to demand refutation. Is it probable that the man whose modesty touched Lord Barrington,† should have broken forth into a strain of gasconade and bravado in the presence of Mr. Pitt? Is it possible that he who led his soldiers over the rocks

* 'History of England,' by Lord Mahon, vol. iv. p. 228.

† When Lord Barrington wrote thus favourably of Wolfe to his successor as Secretary at War, he was doing everything in his power to prevent Mrs. Wolfe receiving the pay she was advised to claim for her

of Cape Breton with nothing but his cane in his hand, "exposing himself like any grenadier"* to the deadly fire of the enemy, should have drawn his sword and flourished it in a gentleman's dining-room? Is it likely that the man, whose private letters, written on the impulse of the moment, never breathe a boastful syllable, nor aught savouring of personal vanity, should have acted the part of a hireling braggart† in the society of statesmen? And can one imagine the great Minister himself to have entertained a fear for the fate of the expedition under the leadership of him who, in the words of a contemporary historian, "was formed to execute the designs of such a master as Pitt?"‡

The story, we are told, was related to Earl Stanhope by his friend Mr. Grenville, who had it from the lips of Lord Temple. It is needless to remark upon the changes which traditions necessarily undergo in transmission, and the illustrative anecdote of Sir Walter Ra-

late son as a Commander-in-chief. His Lordship afterwards went so far as to tell Colonel Carleton that if the subject were brought before Parliament, he would oppose the grant! (Letter from Thomas Fisher, "March 8, 1762," to Mrs. Wolfe, in 'Wolfiana.')

* Major Murray's letter, as before.

† "On the 19th of November [1805] a number of sails were seen nearing the bay, and 11,000 Russians, 2000 Montenegrins, and a small body of 6000 English landed in Naples. The King, after bidding these troops welcome, placed his own army under the command of the Russian General Lascey, who, inexperienced in war, yet full of arrogance, boasted that victory was certain; and, in the presence of the Court, when receiving a rich sword from the hand of the King in token of supreme command, he brandished it aloft, declaring that he would not lay it down until he had hurled the base Corsican from his usurped throne; for which boast he was secretly ridiculed by those around, including the King." ('History of the Kingdom of Naples,' by General Pietro Colletta; translated by S. Horner; vol. i. p. 453.)

‡ Walpole, 'Memoirs of the Reign of George II.'

leigh is too familiar for repetition. But, tracing the matter backwards to its source, may not the historian have been unconsciously tempted, by desire for effect, to heighten the colouring of Mr. Grenville's version? It may be asked whether that gentleman's antitheses were so striking, or his periods so artistically rounded. As regards Mr. Grenville, without impugning his veracity, we may question the accuracy of his memory; for many years must have intervened between the time when Lord Temple told him the story and the period when it first appeared in print. We now come to Mr. Pitt's "loving brother" and colleague, who, previous to his resignation, was looked upon as an inoffensive, good-natured nobleman, with a magnificent seat; and who, had he not acquired temporary importance by his association with Pitt, "might have crept out of life with as little notice as he crept in, and gone off with no other degree of credit than that of adding a single unit to the bills of mortality."* After their quarrel, Lord Temple was accused by Mr. Pitt of divulging confidential secrets, and torturing private conversations into a thousand time-serving forms. So it appears that his Lordship had a talent for misrepresentation! The fact of the matter, when stripped of all accumulations, would therefore seem to be that the sedate, apathetic, selfish peer, whose highest aspiration was the Garter,† may have been shocked

* See 'Lord Chesterfield's Letters to his Son,' Letter 401, "August 14th, 1766." (Eleventh edition, vol. iv. pp. 281, 282.) The above extract is from the 'Reply' to a "scurrilous and scandalous" pamphlet published by Earl Temple. Speaking of which 'Reply,' Chesterfield says,—"It expresses such supreme contempt, and in so pretty a manner, that I suspect it to be Mr. Pitt's own."

† See Earl Stanhope's 'History of England,' vol. iv. p. 280.

by some hearty outburst of Wolfe's indignation,—probably against the cruel practices of the French and their savage allies in America; and upon some such nucleus of truth the imaginative Minister,—who was utterly incapable of appreciating a man of Wolfe's openness of mind and self-devotion to his country,—founded an *extravaganza*. Lord Temple, it may be added, told Mr. Grenville that Wolfe's ebullition could not have arisen from any excess, as he had partaken most sparingly of wine.

Earl Stanhope comments upon the story thus:—"It confirms Wolfe's own avowal that he was not seen to advantage in the common occurrences of life, and shows how shyness may at intervals rush, as it were, for refuge into the opposite extreme; but it should also lead us to view such defects of manner with indulgence, as proving that they may co-exist with the highest ability and the purest virtue." It could only have been from an extract that the noble historian copied Wolfe's avowal. Had his Lordship had the whole letter before him, he would have seen that the hero's words are inapplicable to so exceptional an event as dining in company with two Ministers of State.* As to the hypothetical shyness and defects of manner, it is hard to conceive how qualities so repelling could have existed in a man whose society was courted by the Duke of Richmond, the Marquis of Blandford, the Earl of Shelburne, and many others, not only of the highest rank, but also of the highest character. These, moreover, were all men of taste and discri-

* See letter dated "Southampton, 28th September, 1755," *ante*, p. 325. In another letter Wolfe writes after the same fashion in reference likewise to housekeeping and domestic affairs.

mination, who, years before he came under public notice, eagerly sought commissions in the regiment commanded by him. Surely, then, instead of a forbidding bearing, there must have been something very attractive in him, who, though he could boast of neither fortune nor family, nor station save what his own right arm had won, could gain the undying love and friendship of men in every condition of life.

It matters little that Lord Temple should have misrepresented Wolfe; but it matters much that so authoritative an historian as Earl Stanhope should perpetuate a story which, but for the stamp of his high name, were unworthy of notice. Minds like Wolfe's are so elevated above the understandings of such men as Lord Temple and the dotard Duke of Newcastle, that honesty of purpose is viewed as rashness, unselfish zeal as madness. It is not surprising, therefore, to find the Duke, who ran to inform the King that Cape Breton was an island, endeavouring to persuade his Majesty that Wolfe was mad. "Mad, is he?" replied the more sagacious monarch; "then I hope he will bite some others of my Generals!" * Neither symptoms of insanity nor signs of gasconade, however, are exhibited by the Major-General on the 29th of January, when he wrote his uncle Walter a letter, containing the following paragraph:—

If the Marquis de Montcalm finds means to baffle our efforts another summer, he may be deemed an able officer; or the colony has resources that we know nothing of; or our Generals are worse than usual. We had Canada in our hands last year; with common prudence on one side, and a little spirit of enterprise on the other, it appears to me that Abercromby might

* Thackeray's 'Life of the Earl of Chatham,' vol. i. p. 425.

have cut off the enemy's retreat from Ticonderoga, and in the end forced them to lay down their arms. If the siege of Louisbourg had been pushed with vigour, Quebec would have fallen. The French are arming in all their ports; their object, no doubt, is the defence of Canada; ours to attack it, and the fleet for that service is formidable. I am to act a greater part in this business than I wished or desired. The backwardness of some of the older officers has in some measure forced the Government to come down so low. I shall do my best, and leave the rest to fortune, as perforce we must when there are not the most commanding abilities. We expect to sail in about three weeks. A London life and little exercise disagrees entirely with me, but the sea still more. If I have health and constitution enough for the campaign, I shall think myself a lucky man; what happens afterwards is of no great consequence.*

It is a remarkable fact, that the truest estimates of Wolfe's character are presented in novels. In 'The Virginians,' notwithstanding some confusion of time and place, we see much of the man as he lived and moved. But Mr. Thackeray had most probably consulted the pages of 'Chrysal.'† Charles Johnstone, the author of this curious work, may have known Wolfe; if not, being a Limerick man, he probably gained an insight into his disposition through the hero's cousin, Captain Edward Goldsmith, a few of whose letters, still preserved, show how highly he appreciated his celebrated relation. Johnstone gives an imaginary account of Wolfe's last interview with

* From original, in the possession of J. H. Anderdon, Esq.

† Sir Walter Scott, in allusion to the exposure of prevalent abuses, says:—"When all exaggeration has been deducted from this singular work, enough of truth will still remain in 'Chrysal' to incline the reader to congratulate himself that these scenes passed more than half a century before his time." (Preface to 'Chrysal,' Novelist's Library, vol. iv.)

Mr. Pitt, which, though fiction, is worthy of notice, as representing no small degree of fundamental truth. The Minister is made to address the Soldier thus:—"I need not put myself, nor you, to the pain of repeating the causes of the shameful inactivity, to give it no severer name, by which this war has been drawn into such length; you know and will avoid them. You will not wear out opportunity in making unnecessary preparations for improbable occasions; you will not damp the ardour of your soldiers by delay, nor prolong a burthensome war to enrich yourself with the spoils of your country. You are young, active, and brave; such a commander only do British soldiers want to lead them to victory. You have no senior, no superior here, to restrain the efforts of your spirit by timid caution. At the same time, your judgment will supply the place of experience, and prevent your falling into the misfortunes which self-sufficient, brutal rashness has made so fatal to others. Your instructions are comprised in a few words:—Make the best use your judgment shall direct you of the forces entrusted to your command, to defend the property and avenge the wrongs of your fellow-subjects, and to vindicate the honour of this abused nation. I know whom I speak to, and therefore I say no more. Proceed, my friend, my soldier; answer my expectations, and you will fulfil the wishes of your country."*

Pitt is then represented as giving the young Commander money to distribute among old and disabled soldiers. Having in this way come into the custody of Wolfe, Chrysal witnesses the parting interview between

* 'Chrysal; or, the Adventures of a Guinea,' chap. xxxviii.

him and Miss Lowther, whose rank and large fortune were, he says, her least recommendations.* Whatever reality may underlie this tender scene, fact is against a somewhat similar one, wherein the hero receives his mother's blessing, and takes his leave of her. That nothing of the kind took place is evident from his farewell letter :—

Dear Madam,

The formality of taking leave should be as much as possible avoided; therefore I prefer this method of offering my good wishes and duty to my father and to you. I shall carry this business through with my best abilities. The rest, you know, is in the hands of Providence, to whose care I hope your good life and conduct will recommend your son.

Saunders talks of sailing on Thursday, if the wind come fair. The 'Arc-en-ciel' is either arrived or expected at Spithead. Brett has been directed to negotiate our affairs there. I heartily wish you health and easy enjoyment of the many good things that have fallen to your share. My best duty to the General.

I am, dear Madam,
Your obedient and affectionate Son,
JAM: WOLFE.

London, Monday Morn.

* Some not very original stanzas, entitled "Lines written at Portsmouth by General Wolfe, and presented to his lady the evening before his embarkation for the Siege of Quebec," were, about twelve years ago, contributed to 'Notes and Queries.' The correspondent said they had been given to him by an old lady, who stated that they came into her possession through some relative of the lady to whom they were addressed, but whose name he had forgotten. The lines are too like the sentimental stuff of an English opera ballad to be the production of Wolfe, if, fond though he was of the works of our best poets, he ever wrote a couplet. (See 'Notes and Queries,' 1st series, vol. iv. p. 322.)

CHAPTER XXI.

EXPEDITION TO THE RIVER ST. LAWRENCE.

FEBRUARY—JUNE, 1759.

MR. PITT, assured by the issue of the late campaign that the French dominions in North America were now within his grasp, devoted all the energies of his mind to the grand object of securing the prize in the campaign of 1759. Parliament unhesitatingly voted the necessary supplies, together with a sum of £200,000 as compensation for the expenses and losses incurred by the colonists. A spirit of confidence in the triumph of the British arms, and the humiliation of France, pervaded every rank and condition of the English people. The unanimous desire and single purpose of the nation was the conquest of Canada. The great Minister's scheme of operations was a modification of that of the preceding year. Having again decided on a triple assault upon New France, his most important designs were simultaneous attacks upon her three principal strongholds—Quebec, Montreal, and Niagara.

The fort at Niagara being, since the reduction of Fort du Quesne, the chief western defence of the French territory, Brigadier Prideaux, with a few regiments of regulars, supported by a large body of provincials, and a number of friendly Indians under Sir William Johnston, were to reduce it. This force was then to embark upon Lake Ontario, descend the St. Lawrence, take Montreal, and join the main army under General Amherst. In the meantime the Commander-in-chief, at the head of 12,000 men, was to invest and destroy the central forts of Ticonderoga and Crown Point, cross Lake Champlain, and proceed by way of the Richelieu river to its confluence with the St. Lawrence, when, being joined by Prideaux's detachment, the combined army was to reinforce the naval and military armaments under Saunders and Wolfe. Upon the junction of all these forces, and not until then, was it hoped that Quebec might be subdued.

On the 14th of February sixty transports, convoyed by six sail of the line and nine frigates, under the command of Rear-Admiral Holmes, left Portsmouth for New York. Another squadron of the great fleet destined for the St. Lawrence departed from Spithead on Saturday the 17th, when Major-General Wolfe embarked with Admiral Saunders, the naval Commander-in-chief, on board the 'Neptune,' of ninety guns. The immediate destination of the latter squadron was Louisbourg, where the several imperial and colonial contingents were to rendezvous. But after entering the Bay of Gabarouse, the harbour was found to be so blocked up with ice that the Admiral steered for Halifax. The 'Neptune' at length came to an anchor in that port on the 30th of April, and next day Wolfe wrote as follows to Mr. Pitt:—

'Neptune,' Halifax Harbour, 1st May, 1759.

Sir,

An officer of Artillery who is recalled to his corps gives me an opportunity of doing myself the honour to inform you of what I have learnt or seen since yesterday, that the squadron came to an anchor. Mr. Amherst has used the utmost diligence in forwarding all things that depended upon him; and I hope that the two battalions from the Bay of Fundy will get round in good time. Schooners, sloops, whaleboats, molasses, and rum are provided, and hourly expected. Governor Lawrence and the Brigadier-Generals have omitted nothing that could possibly forward the service, and our engineers have been employed in some useful preparations. By the 'Ruby,' ordnance ship (the only one of Mr. Holmes's convoy yet arrived in this port), we have learnt that the transports were scattered in a hard gale of wind; but as the 'Ruby' observed only one ship without masts, we conclude that the greater part are safe at New York.

Mr. Durell applied for troops to strengthen his squadron, which were readily granted by the commanding officer here, that there might be no impediment to his sailing. I have added 250 men to the first detachment, and have put the whole under the command of the Quartermaster-General, Colonel Carleton, to assist Mr. Durell's operations in the river St. Lawrence, where perhaps it may be necessary to land upon some of the islands, and push a detachment of his fleet up the basin of Quebec, that the navigation may be perfectly free from transports. By this early attempt it is more than probable that the Canadians will not have time to prepare a defence at the Isle aux Coudres and at the Traverse,—the two most difficult and rapid parts of the river, and where the pilots seem to think they might and would (if not prevented in time) give us a great deal of trouble.* If Mr. Durell had been at sea, as we

* Isle aux Coudres, about sixty-five miles from Quebec, lies at the entrance of St. Paul's Bay, near the north shore of the St. Lawrence. The name was given it by Jacques Cartier, on account of the profusion of filberts he found on landing there. The Traverse, some twenty

imagined, I did intend to have sent Colonel Carleton with this additional force, some artillery and tools, with the first ship that Mr. Saunders might have ordered to reinforce the Rear-Admiral's squadron. The battalions in garrison here were (till very lately that the measles had got amongst them) in very good order, and in health recovered by the more than common care of the officers that command them. They have managed so as to exchange the salt provisions for fresh beef, and have had constant supplies of frozen meat and spruce-beer all the winter. This excellent precaution, their great and generous expense in the regimental hospitals, and the order that has been observed amongst them, have preserved these battalions from utter ruin.

But I believe, Sir, you will be surprised to find that, when the 500 men for the defence of Nova Scotia are deducted from the two American battalions, these four regiments have no more than 2000 men in a condition to serve, including the detachment with Mr. Durell. The levies upon the Continent have prevented their recruiting. Otway's and Bragg's, who cannot have fared so well as these, and have lost in proportion since the siege of Louisbourg, are, by all accounts, in a worse condition; so that, if those from General Amherst should not be very complete, our number of regular forces can hardly exceed the half of my Lord Ligonier's calculation, and yet the Marshal must know that every man in Canada is a soldier. Our troops, indeed, are good and very well disposed. If valour can make amends for the want of numbers, we shall probably succeed. Any accidents on the river, or sickness among the men, might put us to some difficulties. The six companies of Rangers will be pretty near complete. They are in general recruits, without service or experience, and not to be depended upon; and the company of Light Infantry from the three battalions in garrison at Louisbourg has, I believe, been omitted in the directions sent to General Amherst.*

miles higher up the river, is an intricate channel, rendered dangerous by a group of rocky isles, called "The Pillars."

* 'Chatham Correspondence,' vol. i. p. 403.

During his detention in Halifax, Wolfe issued several general orders, which exemplify his great anxiety for the unanimity of the land and sea forces, and his fatherly concern for the men under his charge, as well as his great foresight. In his Order on the 7th of May, he says:—"As the navigation of the river St. Lawrence may in some places be difficult, the troops are to be careful as possible in working the ships, obedient to the Admiral's commands, and attentive to all his signals. No boats are to be hoisted out to sea but on the most urgent occasions." On the 9th, he enjoins:—"After the troops are embarked, the commanding officers will give all necessary directions for the preservation of the health of their men. Guards must mount in every ship, to keep strict order and prevent fire. When the weather permits, the men are to be as much in the open air as possible, and to eat upon deck. Cleanliness in the berths and bedding, and as much exercise as the situation permits, are the best preservatives of health. . . . If any ship by accident should run on shore in the river, small vessels and boats will be sent to their assistance. They have nothing to apprehend from the inhabitants of the north side, and as little from the Canadians on the south. Fifty men with arms may easily defend themselves until succour arrives. If a ship should happen to be lost, the men on shore are to make three distinct fires by night, and three distinct smokes by day, to mark their situation."

Towards the middle of May, as soon as the harbour of Louisbourg was cleared of the winter's ice, the fleet sailed thither. Wolfe had not been many days in Louisbourg when he heard of the death of his father, whose age and infirmity gave his son, on leaving home, little hope of ever seeing him again. The brave and benevolent Lieut.-General Edward Wolfe died, at his house on Blackheath, on the 26th of March, in the 75th year of his age, and was buried in the family vault under the parish church of Greenwich.* A very pathetic letter of condolence was written to Mrs. Wolfe upon the occasion by her nephew, Captain Edward Goldsmith, of Limerick, who, having used several arguments calculated to dissuade her from her overwhelming grief, adds:—"My dear cousin is, I hope, by this time arrived safe at New York. I have been watching the winds and counting the days since his departure, so have good reason to conclude him safe in America, as the winds have been favourable. Then, madam, let the consideration of the figure your most deservedly loved son makes in the world be your consolation in your present affliction. Let the exalted character so universally given him support your spirits; for who can boast a blessing so great as yours? You can say, and say with justice, you have a son who of his age has no equal, either in accomplishments of his profession or in all the social virtues." The Major-General, in the following valuable letter to his uncle Walter, after noticing his father's decease, furnishes details of the preliminary operations of the expedition:—

* From the obituary of the 'Gentleman's Magazine,' it would appear that he died on the 27th; but the inscription on a rubbing from the plate of his coffin is as follows:—"The Honble. Lieutenant-Genl. EDWARD WOLFE, died March 26th, 1759, aged 74 years."

Louisbourg, 19th May, 1759.

Dear Sir,

Since our arrival in this country the news of my father's death has reached me. I left him in so weak a condition that it was not probable we should ever meet again. The general tenor of his conduct through life has been extremely upright and benevolent, from whence one may hope that little failings and imperfections were overbalanced by his many good qualities. I am exceedingly sorry it so fell out that I had it not in my power to assist him in his illness, and to relieve my mother in her distress; and the more as her relations are not affectionate, and you are too far off to give her help. I have writ to Mr. Fisher to continue the pensions which my father had assigned to his kindred; my easy circumstances enabling me to fulfil all his intentions.

We are ordered to attack Quebec,—a very nice operation. The fleet consists of twenty-two sail of the line and many frigates; the army of 9000 men;—in England it is called 12,000. We have ten battalions, three companies of Grenadiers, some Marines (if the Admiral can spare them), and six new-raised companies of North American Rangers—not complete, and the worst soldiers in the universe; a great train of artillery, plenty of provisions, tools, and implements of all sorts; three Brigadiers under me,—all men of great spirit; some Colonels of reputation, Carleton for Quartermaster-General, and upon whom I chiefly rely for the engineering part. Engineers very indifferent, and of little experience; but we have none better. The regular troops in Canada consist of eight battalions of old Foot—about 400 a battalion—and forty companies of Marines (or colony troops)—forty men a company. They can gather together 8000 or 10,000 Canadians, and perhaps 1000 Indians. As they are attacked by the side of Montreal by an enemy of 12,000 fighting men, they must necessarily divide their force; but, as the loss of the capital implies the loss of the colony, their chief attention will naturally be there, and therefore I reckon we may find at Quebec six battalions, some companies of Marines, four or five thousand

Canadians, and some Indians; altogether, not much inferior to their enemy.

Rear-Admiral Durell, with ten sail, is gone up the river, and has orders to take such a station as will effectually cut off all succours; but as he sailed late from Halifax (4th May), there is reason to think that some store-ships have already got up.* If so, our difficulties are like to increase. I have sent a detachment with Mr. Durell to assist his first operations, and to seize the islands in those parts of the river where the navigation is most dangerous. The Admiral has positive instructions to watch the first opening of the river St. Lawrence, so as to push with his squadron as high as the Isle de Bic,† and from thence to detach some small ships to the Bason of Quebec, that all might be free and open behind. The Admiral Commander-in-chief of the fleet is a zealous, brave officer. I don't exactly know what disposition he intends to make in the river after the junction of the two squadrons; but I conclude he will send four or five of his smallest ships of the line to assist us at Quebec, and remain with the rest at an anchor below the Isle aux Coudres, ready to fight whatever fleet the enemy may send to disturb us.

The town of Quebec is poorly fortified, but the ground round about it is rocky. To invest the place, and cut off all communication with the colony, it will be necessary to encamp with our right to the river St. Lawrence, and our left to the river St. Charles. From the river St. Charles to Beauport the communication must be kept open by strong entrenched posts and redoubts. The enemy can pass that river at low water; and it will be proper to establish ourselves

* Durell intercepted two store-ships, but seventeen vessels with recruits, provisions, etc., convoyed by three frigates, got up the river before him. (Mante's 'History of the War,' p. 237.) Excellent charts of the St. Lawrence, which greatly facilitated the progress of the English fleet, were found in the prizes. (Lord Mahon's 'History of England,' vol. iv. p. 233.)

† Bic Island, a pilot station, lying off Cape l'Orignal, on the south shore, below the embouchure of the Saguenay, is about 170 miles from Quebec.

with small entrenched posts from the Point of Levi to La Chaudière. It is the business of our naval force to be masters of the river, both above and below the town. If I find that the enemy is strong, audacious, and well commanded, I shall proceed with the utmost caution and circumspection, giving Mr. Amherst time to use his superiority. If they are timid, weak, and ignorant, we shall push them with more vivacity, that we may be able before the summer is gone to assist the Commander-in-chief. I reckon we shall have a smart action at the passage of the river St. Charles, unless we can steal a detachment up the river St. Lawrence, and land them three, four, five miles, or more, above the town, and get time to entrench so strongly that they won't care to attack.

If General Amherst can manage to have a superiority of naval force upon the Lake Champlain (as he proposes), all the troops within the entrenchments and fort of Ticonderoga will probably be soon obliged to lay down their arms. The least conduct there, or the least spirit of enterprise on our side, would have finished the war last year. It is impossible to conceive how poorly the engineering business was carried on here. This place could not have held out ten days if it had been attacked with common sense. The army under my command is rather too small for the undertaking, but it is well composed. The troops are firm, and were brought into fire at this siege. Those that were with me are most excellent pioneers. If the French had had twenty sail of men-of-war in the harbour (as they intended), and had not gone out early to fight Mr. Boscawen, they must have been all destroyed. If they can collect a sufficient force, they are sure to find us in the river St. Lawrence any time between this and the month of October, and may fight if they chuse. The prize seems to be worth the risk of a battle. If their Mediterranean squadron gets out, I conclude we shall see them.

You may be assured that I shall take all proper care of my own person, unless in case of the last importance, where it becomes a duty to do otherwise. I never put myself unnecessarily into the way of danger. Young troops must be encouraged at first. What appears hazardous sometimes is really not so to people who know the country. The separate corps which I commanded last year, divided as they were into a number of posts—encamped within cannon-shot of the ships or town, and often within the reach of grape-shot—suffered hardly any loss at all, because the ground is so uneven that we could place them everywhere in security. We are every hour in expectation of seeing the regiments arrive which are to compose the army. Most of them are actually at sea, and upon this coast; but the fogs are so frequent and lasting, that ships are obliged to stand out to sea waiting for fair weather. I hope we shall be able to sail in about ten days, and if no accident happens in the river, I hope we shall succeed. I wish you your health—mine is but indifferent; and am, dear sir,

Your obedient Nephew,

J. W.*

Notwithstanding the impediments of floating ice and of constant fogs, which rendered it necessary to fire signal-guns every quarter of an hour for the guidance of vessels in the Bay of Gabarouse, day by day transports with troops from various quarters entered the harbour of Louisbourg. Until the 1st of June, the men landed daily for exercise, and the Commander-in-chief alternately reviewed each battalion. An officer of the 43rd regiment, who arrived on the 25th of May, relates the following characteristic anecdote:—"I flattered myself that I should have seen the Grenadier companies of this garrison reviewed by General Wolfe, but it was over before I could get there. I was told they went

* From original, now in the possession of Mr. Waller, bookseller, Fleet Street. At the sale of Mr. Meigh's collection of autographs by Messrs. Sotheby and Wilkinson, in February, 1856, this letter was sold for £6. 17*s*. 6*d*. Less important letters of Wolfe's to his uncle Walter brought £4. 6*s*. and £4. 4*s*.

through all their manœuvres and evolutions with great exactness and spirit, according to a new system of discipline; and his Excellency was highly pleased with their performance. Some commanding-officers of corps, who expected to be also reviewed in their turn, told the General, by way of apology, that by their regiments having been long cantoned, they had it not in their power to learn or practise this new exercise; to which he answered, 'Poh! poh! new exercise—new fiddlestick! if they are otherwise well disciplined, and will fight, that's all I require of them.'"*

The Army was divided into three brigades:—The 1st commanded by the Hon. ROBERT MONCKTON; the 2nd, by the Hon. GEORGE TOWNSHEND; and the 3rd, by the Hon. JAMES MURRAY. The Staff-officers were:—Lieut.-Colonel Carleton, Quartermaster-General; Major Barré, Adjutant-General; Major Mackeller, Chief Engineer; Captains Hervey Smith and Thomas Bell, Aides-de-camp; Captains Caldwell and Leslie, Deputy-Quartermasters-General; and Captains Guillem, Spittall, and Maitland, Majors of Brigade. In addition to the brigades, there were also a corps consisting of the Grenadiers of the several regiments, under the command of Lieut.-Colonel Carleton; the Louisbourg Grenadiers, commanded by Lieut.-Colonel Alexander Murray;† one Light Infantry corps, under the Hon. Lieut.-Colonel

* 'Journal of Campaign in North America,' by Captain John Knox, i. p. 270.

† The Grenadier companies of the 22nd, 40th, and 45th regiments, had greatly distinguished themselves at the siege of Louisbourg. was the little battalion the command of which Wolfe had obtained for Major Murray, with the local rank of Lieut.-Colonel.

Howe, and another under Major Dalling; wi ınd, when vincial Rangers, headed by Major Scott. ırg. The

"I had the inexpressible pleasure to observe at Louisbourg," wri s the chronicler of the campaign, "that our whole arma aval and military, were in gh spirits; and though all accounts, we shall have a numerous army and iety of difficulties to cope with, yet under such Admi s and Generals, among whom we have the happiness to behold the most cordial unanimity, together with so respectable a fleet, and a body of well-appointed regular troops, we have reason to hope for the greatest success."*

On the 1st of June the grand fleet began to move out of Louisbourg harbour; but all the vessels had not cleared the land before the 6th. As each transport sailed out of the bay, the soldiers who crowded the decks rent the air with shouts of joy; while the prevailing toast of the officers was,—"British colours on every French fort, port, and garrison in America." Having got out to sea, the Admiral sent a ship home with the intelligence; and Wolfe seized the opportunity to write to Mr. Pitt. But ere laying his dispatch before the reader, it is advisable to insert a letter addressed by him to Brigadier Whitmore, the Governor of Louisbourg, on the 19th of May:—

Sir,

In the distribution of forces for the invasion of Canada, my Lord Ligonier had regulated that Bragg's regiment, thr... companies of Grenadiers, and one company of light inf... by besides the Rangers, should be taken from Louisbourg, was ...mcle

* 'Knox's Journal,' vol. i. p. 279.

that eve 1000 of the Boston Militia. By some accident, three re of light infantry has been omitted in the orders sent from ngland; nevertheless, as I know it was designed, his Majest's service requires that I should apply to you for that company; and I do it the more readily, vour garrison will be r r more numerous after the f the Boston Militia than before. We are disappoint the recruits which were intended to be sent from the W ndies to join us;* and as several regiments are much w r than they were thought, in England, to be, I must furth represent to you that good troops only can make amends the want of numbers in an undertaking of this sort. It is therefore my duty to signify to you that it would be much for the public service to let the other two companies of light infantry embark with the army under my command, upon condition of being replaced, man for man, by some of the Rangers and some of Frazer's additional companies, who are not so proper for the field, though very sufficient for the defence of a fortified place. If there was any reason to apprehend that this change might have the least ill consequence, I should not venture to propose it. Mr. Lawrence, who has a very bad fortress and a very weak garrison, accepted of the sick and recovering men of the two American battalions as part of the 500 regulars intended for the defence of Nova Scotia, knowing very well that upon the success of our attacks in Canada, the security of the whole continent of America in a great measure depends.†

The Major-General's dispatch to Mr. Pitt is as follows:—

On board the 'Neptune,' June 6, 1759.

Sir,

By the report which I have the honour to enclose, you

* Two thousand infantry, who were to have been detached from General Hopson's expedition to the West Indies, in order to reinforce Wolfe's army, were subsequently countermanded.

† From 'A History of the Right Honourable William Pitt,' etc., by the Rev. Francis Thackeray, vol. ii. p. 466.

will see the strength of the army under my command, when they embarked, and when they came to Louisbourg. The fogs on this coast are so frequent and lasting, and the climate in every respect so unfavourable to military operations, that if we had been collected a week sooner, I doubt if it would have been possible to sail before we did. One company of Rangers (the best of the six) is not yet arrived, and a very good engineer, by some mistake, has had no orders to join us. General Amherst forwarded everything to the utmost of his power, and the officers employed by him were indefatigable. Finding that several regiments were weak, and that no recruits were likely to come from the West Indies, I applied to Mr. Whitmore for three companies of light infantry of his garrison:—my letter and the Governor's answer are enclosed. If Brigadier Whitmore did not consent to my proposal, it has proceeded from the most scrupulous obedience to orders, believing himself not at liberty to judge and act according to circumstances.* The four new companies of Rangers are so very bad that I expect no service from them, unless mixed with the light infantry; and it was with that view that I applied to the Marshal for a company of volunteers from Louisbourg. Five field-officers of these regiments and several captains are either sick or employed upon the continent; forty men of Bragg's regiment upon duty at St. John's. We leave eighty sick at Louisbourg, and an hundred invalids. Several transports have not yet joined us; their provisions and their boats are very much wanted. However, I have taken 3000 barrels of flour and biscuit from the contractor's store at Louisbourg. I writ to General Amherst for money, but he could send me none; this is one of the first sieges, perhaps,

* Notwithstanding the above vindication, the Governor's conduct upon this occasion proves that the opinion which Wolfe had previously expressed of him was not rashly formed. (See Letter to Lord G. Sackville, *ante*, p. 420.) Major-General Whitmore was drowned, on a voyage from Louisbourg to Boston, in January, 1762. The ship being compelled by stress of weather to put into Plymouth, New England, going upon deck at night, he accidentally fell overboard. ('Gentleman's Magazine.')

that ever was undertaken without it. The camp equipage of three regiments is supposed to be either lost or taken upon the passage from Philadelphia. We have supplied them with tents from the ordnance stores, and must make the old kettles, etc., serve the campaign. There are 1000 of the Boston Militia at Louisbourg. I desired Brigadier Whitmore to complete our companies of Rangers from them, and to give me 100 labourers, solely as pioneers. The men were asked if they chose to go, and as it seldom happens that a New England man prefers service to a lazy life, none of them seemed to approve of the proposal; they did not ask it, and the General would not order them.

If the Admiral had, as I wished, deferred sending his letters till the fleet got up to the Isle of Bic, and till we knew what progress Mr. Durell had made, (of which we are at present entirely ignorant,) you, Sir, would have been able to form some judgment of the state of affairs. There we might learn what succours (if any) got up before the Rear-Admiral, and other circumstances of moment. Since the fleet came out, I have received a letter from the Lieut.-Governor of the Massachusetts Bay, acquainting me that he is preparing to embark 300 of the militia of his province to serve with us. These are the pioneers which I desired Gen. Amherst to send. Colonel Burton and Major Barré, who were employed by the General at Boston, have spoke of Mr. Hutchinson's zeal for the public service, and very great knowledge of the affairs of his province, in a manner much to his advantage.* We ex-

* "The Massachusetts forces this year were of great service. 2500 served in garrison at Louisbourg and Nova Scotia, in room of the regular troops taken from thence to serve under General Wolfe. Several hundreds served on board the King's ships, as seamen, and the remainder of the 6500 men voted in the spring served under General Amherst. Besides this force, upon application from General Wolfe, 300 more were raised and sent to Quebec, by the Lieut.-Governor, in the absence of the Governor at Penobscot. These served as pioneers, and in other capacities in which the regulars must otherwise have been employed." ('History of the Province of Massachusetts Bay,' by Thomas Hutchinson.)

pect to find a good part of the force of Canada at Quebec, and we are prepared to meet them. Whatever the end is, I flatter myself that his Majesty will not be dissatisfied with the behaviour of the troops.

I have the honour to be, etc.,

J. WOLFE.*

The advanced squadron, under Rear-Admiral Durell, on reaching St. Paul's Bay, took possession of Isle aux Coudres, and proceeded towards the Isle of Orleans. On entering the river, the van of the squadron, in order to induce pilots to board the ships, showed the white flag of France; whereupon expresses were immediately sent to Quebec, informing the Governor that a French fleet was approaching, and the tidings caused indescribable delight throughout the country. But a number of canoes having put off with pilots, inconceivable was the dismay of the Canadians who watched on shore, when, instead of the returning boats, they perceived the French flag replaced by British colours. So sudden was the transition from joy to despair, that a priest who stood gazing upon the fleet through a telescope, on discovering the ruse, dropped down and instantly died. Durell also intercepted a French ship, on board of which were some ladies of distinction, including a relation of the Marquis de Vandreuil, Governor-General of Canada, besides several nuns, all of whom were treated with courtesy, and sent back to Quebec under a flag of truce.

The main fleet, under Admiral Saunders, on the 7th

* From copy in 'Wolfiana,' taken by the late Dawson Turner from original in the State Paper Office. With the exception of the concluding passage, the letter has been printed in Thackeray's 'Life of Pitt.'

of June made the coast of Newfoundland, still white with the winter's snow; and on the 9th, in a stiff breeze, passed the Bird Islands. Two days later the high headland of Gaspé was seen, and on the 12th the dangerous and desolate island of Anticosti was passed. The ships having kept well together, on the 18th anchored off the isles of Bic and Barnaby, where they met the 'Richmond' frigate, having Wolfe on board. They weighed early next morning, with thick weather and a violent storm; and in the evening, as the 'Richmond' passed them by, "General Wolfe," says one of the land officers, "politely saluted us, hoping we were all well." As considerate as he was courteous, the young commander had provided for the recreation and health of the soldiers, by ordering that each regiment should be supplied with fishing-hooks and lines, and that a certain quantity of ginger should be given to every man daily for the purpose of mixing with the water they drank. By the 20th most of the ships had doubled the Point of Tadousac, where the powerful current from the dark and deep tributary Saguenay drove back several of the transports, and forced others from their anchors. A favourable wind arising in the night freed them from this perilous situation, and at noon next day the first Canadian settlement upon the banks of the St. Lawrence was in sight.

Until the 23rd, when they made Isle aux Coudres, the sailors were constantly employed in anchoring, weighing, and tacking, while the soldiers on deck beheld with wonder the quaint Canadian villages on both sides of the river, with their numerous churches, crosses, and images of patron saints. Everywhere in advance of the fleet signal fires were lighted upon the shore, to give warning of its approach. The first act of hostility took place near the settlement of St. Joseph's, where one of the sounding boats having been fired upon by the *habitans*, a party of Amherst's regiment was sent to protect the sounders. Although no lives were lost, in order to avenge the assault, the village was subsequently burned, and the fields laid waste, by a detachment of troops from before Quebec. A high wind on the 24th drove many vessels from their moorings; yet some progress was made by working up with the tide.

Although most of the native pilots made a virtue of necessity, some few gave their captors plainly enough to understand that they were not willing guides. The man who fell to the lot of the 'Goodwill' transport, we are told, talked so extravagantly, that the sailors would certainly have pitched him overboard but for the Admiral's injunctions that none of these men should suffer the least ill-usage. "Some of your ships," said he, "may return to England, but they will have a dismal tale to carry, for Canada will be the grave of the whole army; and I hope, ere long, to see the walls of Quebec decorated with English scalps." The master of the 'Goodwill,' who was an old Trinity-house man, refused to entrust his ship to the guidance of this irate official, notwithstanding his asseveration that no French navigator ever presumed to pass through the Traverse without a local pilot. "Ay, ay, my dear," retorted the bluff master, "but I'll convince you that an Englishman shall go where no Frenchman dare show his nose." Placing his mate at the helm, old Killick, as he called himself, went forward, and gave his orders with great coolness, at the same time bantering the men in the sounding-boats, which lay off on either side the channel with various coloured flags. And when any of the sounders would call to him, or point out the course, his reply was, "Ay, ay, my dears, chalk it down a d—d dangerous navigation. If you don't make a sputter about it, you'll get no credit in England." Having successfully cleared the perilous passage, "D—n me," cried Killick, "if there are not a thousand places in the Thames fifty times more dangerous! I'm ashamed that Englishmen should make such a rout about it." When the Canadian pilot was informed that this fearless mariner had not previously navigated the St. Lawrence, he expressed the greatest admiration, raising his eyes and arms to heaven with astonishment.

All the transports having safely arrived off the east end of Orleans by the afternoon of the 25th, were next morning signalled to work up further under the Commodore's stern, and, after a few hours, they cast anchor near the island village of St. Laurent. "Here," writes an officer, who had an eye for the picturesque, "we are entertained with a most agreeable prospect of a delightful country on every side,—windmills, watermills, churches, chapels, and compact farmhouses, all built with stone, and covered, some with wood and others with straw. The land appears to be everywhere well cultivated, sowed with flax, wheat, barley, pease, etc., and the grounds enclosed with wooden pales. The weather to-day agreeably warm. A light fog sometimes hangs over the highlands, but in the river a fine clear air." *

* Captain Knox's Journal.

On the afternoon of the 26th, Wolfe, from on board the 'Richmond,' issued his orders for the landing of the army upon the Isle of Orleans at six o'clock the following morning. Meanwhile, at midnight, he sent Lieutenant Meech, with forty Rangers, ashore. Landing without opposition, the party pushed on for a considerable way through the darkness until they suddenly came upon a large body of armed peasantry, who were burying their effects in a wood. The Rangers, finding themselves outnumbered, wished to avoid an encounter; but, being presently surrounded, Lieutenant Meech ordered his men to fire, whereupon the enemy retired. Suspecting a snare, the party, instead of pursuing, took possession of a farmhouse, where they remained until daylight. Missing one of their comrades, they went in search of him, and were shocked at finding that he had been scalped and brutally butchered. They then followed the fugitives, and traced them to the north coast, where they had embarked for the opposite shore; and not a native now remained upon the island.

Early on the morning of the 27th the army landed in a cove under the church of St. Laurent, and while the light troops were sent to scour the country, the main body, after marching about a mile from the landing-place, encamped in one line, with their front to the north. An interesting little episode of the landing claims notice here. One of the ensigns of Bragg's regiment was William Henry Fairfax, of the noble Virginian family, the friends of Washington in early life,—a youth of much promise, who had been educated in England. It is related, says Sparks, that Wolfe saw him, as the army landed, seated near the bank of the river, and that, touching him on the shoulder, he said, "Young man, when you come into action remember your name!" * The injunction was not forgotten. The worthy inheritor of his noble name, young Fairfax of the Twenty-eighth, ere long fell on the same glorious field, about the same time, and close by his Commander.

They had been so long cooped up on shipboard, that officers and privates alike were well pleased to be once more on land; and, stringent though were the Commander-in-chief's orders that none should go beyond the outposts, it was difficult to keep the men within the prescribed bounds. The neighbouring village of St. Laurent was completely deserted by the inhabitants. The curé of the parish having stripped the church of its ornaments and movables, left behind him a letter, addressed to "The Worthy Officers of the British Army," praying that, from their well-known humanity and generosity, they would protect the sacred building, as well as his house and tenements adjoining; adding, with French politeness, that he regretted they had not arrived earlier in the season, when they might have enjoyed his asparagus and other products of his garden, now gone to seed, and ending with frothy compliments and good wishes.

The beautiful and fertile Isle of Orleans,—twenty miles in length, and five miles and a half across its greatest breadth,—shelters the splendid basin of Quebec on the east, where it divides the St. Lawrence into two

* "Address on the Death of General Wolfe," delivered before the Massachusetts Historical Society, by Lorenzo Sabine. (Boston, 1859.)

branches; the western extremity of the island being rather more than a league from the end of Cape Diamond, on which the city stands, and about half that distance from the opposite promontory of Point Levi.* A large portion of the land was even then cleared and laid out in small farms, the carefully cultivated fields, which sloped down to the water's edge, contrasting agreeably with the dark pines of the primæval forest that covered the higher ground of the interior.

No sooner had Wolfe seen his army encamped, than, accompanied by Major Mackeller, the Engineer-in-chief, and an escort of light troops, he proceeded to the west point of the island, in order to reconnoitre the surrounding country, and the position of the enemy. The sight he then beheld, naturally magnificent as it was, was rendered still more imposing by the warlike adjuncts of the occasion. On the summit of Cape Diamond, high above the narrowed strait of the great river from whence opened the basin before him, stood the citadel, over which the French flag waved; and on the elevated bank opposite to him an army of 12,000 men presented its formidable front, which extended from Quebec to the river Montmorenci,—a distance of eight miles. In the centre, amidst the battalions of Old France, rose the picturesque village of Beauport; the right rested upon

* Cape Diamond is composed of dark-coloured slate, in which are found quartz crystals, in veins, along with crystallized carbonate of lime. From these beautiful crystals, which sparkle like diamonds, the lofty Cape derives its name. Professor Silliman considers the prevailing rock to be of the transition formation, Point Levi and the district on the south side of the St. Lawrence being decidedly of that class. ('Guide to Quebec,' by Alfred Hawkins.)

the river St. Charles, with Charlesbourg in the rear; and the left was bounded by the rocky chasm of the cataract. The whole border of the acclivity was entrenched; every assailable spot along the shore of the St. Lawrence was defended by a redoubt; and, to communicate with the city and garrison, a bridge, protected by *têtes-de-pont*, with strong works at each end, was thrown across the St. Charles, while two heavy batteries were mounted upon hulks sunk in the channel.

The forces, under the chief command of the Marquis de Montcalm, consisted of six battalions of regulars—the flower of the French line—with as many well-disciplined Canadian Militia, and some light cavalry, besides a large body of Indians. The right was headed by Brigadier-General the Baron de St. Ours; the centre by Brigadier-General de Senezergues; and the left by M. Herbin; the garrison being commanded by M. de Ramezay. A single glance of Wolfe's quick eye was sufficient to make him comprehend the unparalleled strength of the enemy's position, but as promptly his ardent spirit was aroused by the glory of surmounting every difficulty. Nor was his poetic mind insensible to the natural beauties of the scene, the tranquillity of which was so soon to be disturbed by the turmoils of war.

Before the Commander-in-chief had returned to his encampment, one of those terrific storms of wind and rain frequent in the St. Lawrence burst forth with sudden violence. It was fortunate that the troops had disembarked, for the hurricane which swept over the river drove the transports from their moorings, and cast several of them ashore; while the smaller vessels were dashed against each other, and it was with difficulty the men-of-war held by their cables. But, happily, no lives were lost through the tempest that marked the day on which Great Britain first permanently fixed her flag upon Canadian soil.

The storm passed away almost as suddenly as it came, and during the next day nothing happened to disturb the invaders. Wolfe was occupied establishing various posts throughout the island, and in drawing up regulations for the conduct of his forces. In his orders of the day, he directs, "once for all," that the soldiers must not wander about in a disorderly manner; and adds, "The army must hold themselves in readiness always to get under arms, either to march or fight, at the shortest notice." The evening of the 28th was perfectly calm. Without the intervening twilight, to which Europeans are accustomed, night fell apace, enshrouding citadel, cape, and camp. The river only was discernible by the reflection from its surface of the few stars which studded the otherwise intensely dark sky. All around was still; not a sound disturbed the air, save the subdued murmur from the distant falls of Montmorenci, the ripple of the receding tide, and the oft-recurring "All's well!" of the watch aboard some man-of-war.

It was near midnight when the sentinel on the western point of Orleans noticed a number of black objects upon the water. Perceiving that they neared the island he aroused his companions, when instantly a flash and a terrific discharge of artillery so disconcerted them, that, without waiting to discover the cause, the whole picquet retreated, communicating their fear to the next detachment, and so on, one party fell back upon another until they reached the camp, where they caused the greatest alarm and confusion by their report that the French were upon them. The whole army immediately turned out, and hastily prepared for action; and it was not till daylight showed there was no enemy at hand that order and confidence were restored. Meanwhile, upon the river, the real danger, which threatened the fleet, was averted by the cool courage of the sailors.

The French had laboriously prepared eight large fire-ships and rafts, freighted with the most destructive combustibles, by means of which they hoped to destroy the British shipping. Under the darkness of the night, these infernal machines were launched from Quebec; but the officers in charge of them, fearing an explosion while they remained on board, prematurely lighted the matches, and, hastening to their boats, rowed rapidly ashore, leaving the deadly messengers to the direction of the ebbing tide.* Fortunately, the precipitation of these timid Frenchmen gave Admiral Saunders timely notice of the impending danger; and before any of the fire-ships reached his fleet, their tremendous discharges of shells and shot, which rattled against the rocky shores, and reverberated through the woods, showed that their destructive power was almost spent. Two burning rafts drifted down the north channel, and ran harmlessly aground. As the rest of the floating-fires approached, in spite of the flames that issued from them on all sides, and ran like lightning up the masts and through the rigging, the suffocating clouds of smoke, the occasional

* 'Vie Privée de Louis XV.,' vol. iii. p. 200.

discharge of an unspent grenade or gun, and the crackling of every variety of explosive matter, the fearless English tars, grappling the *brûlots*, towed them away from the fleet, and then ran them ashore, where they continued to burn until five o'clock next morning. By their lurid light, not only were the crowded river and island brightly illuminated, but likewise, for two or three hours of the night, the far-off mountains, the city-covered cape, and the French encampment were clearly revealed. "They were certainly," says an eye-witness, "the grandest fireworks (if I may be allowed to call them so) that can possibly be conceived, every circumstance having contributed to their awful, yet beautiful appearance, and afforded a scene infinitely superior to any adequate description."*

In his "orders" of the 29th, the Commander-in-chief severely rebuked the conduct of the men who had abandoned their posts and spread groundless alarm to the camp. "Next to valour," he added, "the best qualities in a military man are vigilance and caution." The officer who commanded the advanced parties was put under arrest, for trial by court-martial; but, on account of his excellent character, at the intercession of Brigadier Monckton, Wolfe subsequently pardoned him.

The storm of the 27th having taught Admiral Saunders that the channel between the Isle of Orleans and the south shore did not afford secure anchorage, he determined upon carrying the shipping under his command into the basin of Quebec. It being believed, however, that the French had constructed redoubts upon Point

* Captain Knox's Journal, vol. i. p. 298.

Levi, from whence they might annoy the fleet, the Admiral requested of Wolfe to drive the enemy from this commanding position, and occupy it himself. Accordingly, on the 30th, Monckton's brigade crossed over to the village of Beaumont, and after a slight skirmish with a detachment of Canadian Militia, took possession of the church, on the doors of which the Brigadier posted a translation, in French, of the following manifesto:—

By his Excellency James Wolfe, Esq., Colonel of a Regiment of Infantry, Major-General, and Commander-in-chief of his Britannic Majesty's Forces in the River St. Lawrence, etc.

The formidable sea and land armament which the people of Canada now behold in the heart of their country, is intended by the King, my master, to check the insolence of France, to revenge the insults offered to the British colonies, and totally to deprive the French of their most valuable settlement in North America. For these purposes is the formidable army under my command intended. The King of Great Britain wages no war with the industrious peasant, the sacred orders of religion, or the defenceless women and children; to these, in their distressful circumstances, his royal clemency offers protection. The people may remain unmolested on their lands, inhabit their houses, and enjoy their religion in security. For these inestimable blessings I expect the Canadians will take no part in the great contest between the two crowns. But if, by a vain obstinacy and misguided valour, they presume to appear in arms, they must expect the most fatal consequences,—their habitations destroyed, their sacred temples exposed to an exasperated soldiery, their harvest utterly ruined, and the only passage for relief stopped up by a most formidable fleet. In this unhappy situation, and closely attacked by another great army, what can the wretched natives expect from opposition?

The unparalleled barbarities exerted by the French against

our settlements in America might justify the bitterest revenge in the army under my command; but Britons breathe higher sentiments of humanity, and listen to the merciful dictates of the Christian religion. Yet, should you suffer yourselves to be deluded by an imaginary prospect of our want of success; should you refuse these terms, and persist in opposition, then surely will the law of nations justify the waste of war, so necessary to crush an ungenerous enemy; and then the miserable Canadians must in the winter have the mortification of seeing their very families, for whom they have been exerting but a fruitless and indiscreet bravery, perish by the most dismal want and famine. In this great dilemma, let the wisdom of the people of Canada show itself. Britain stretches out a powerful, yet merciful hand; faithful to her engagements, and ready to secure her in her most valuable rights and possessions. France, unable to support Canada, deserts her cause at this important crisis, and during the whole war has assisted her with troops, who have been maintained only by making the natives feel all the weight of grievous and lawless oppression.

Given at Laurent, in the Island of Orleans, this 28th day of June, 1759.

CHAPTER XXII.

BANKS OF THE ST. LAWRENCE.

JULY—AUGUST, 1759.

CANADA, dating from the foundation by Champlain of the fort and city of Quebec, had now been about one hundred and fifty years in the possession of France. But it was not until 1663, when M. de Mezy was appointed Governor, with a council of seven officials to assist him in the administration, that New France attained the distinction of a royal government; the control of the colony having hitherto been vested in adventurers, who assumed the management of its affairs solely with a view to trading speculations. At a later period an Intendant of Police, Finance, and Marine was sent from France, an appointment which excited great jealousy on the part of the Governors, with whose authority the power of the Intendants frequently came into collision, and gave rise to endless disputes about the relative rank and province of the two functionaries. Quebec became a bishopric in 1670, when, at the desire of the Jesuit missionaries, who had gained great influence in the colony, and wished to have a person of distinction at the head of their Church, François de Laval, Abbot of Montigny, was sent out as the first colonial bishop.

The population of Canada, in 1759, did not number more than 65,000 souls, of whom nearly 7000 dwelt in Quebec, 4000 in Montreal, and 1500 in the village of Trois Rivières.* The remainder occupied little settlements and farms on the fertile banks of the St. Lawrence and its tributaries; a few of the more adventurous being trappers and *voyageurs*, who wandered through the northern forests and the western prairies, or upon the shores of the Great Lakes, intermixing with the aborigines, than whom they were hardly more civilized. The *élite* of the Canadian aristocracy were the descendants of those officers, civil and military, who had from time to time settled in the country, and to whom extensive grants of land were assigned. These were the seigneurs, who enjoyed various immunities, and exercised feudal rights. They were, for the most part, vain and ostentatious men, who disdained business of every kind, and prided themselves upon their high descent and dignity. Having, as they thought, much to fear and nothing to hope for from a change of sovereigns, they were essentially loyal to the French crown. Neither did the ecclesiastical dignitaries, who ranked next after the seigneurs, and were generally of French birth, desire a heretic government. But it was not altogether so with the parochial priests and curés born and educated in the colony, who, jealous of the foreign hierarchy, to none of whose offices they might aspire, were at the same time impoverished through the government monopolies and extortions which oppressed the small traders, farmers, and peasantry, from whom they derived their fluctuating incomes.

* Bouchette.

In Buade Street, near Prescott Gate, in the Upper Town of Quebec, there existed a few years ago, and probably still remains, a remarkable memorial of the old French *régime*. It is a small tablet, representing a dog gnawing a bone, with a rhyming inscription, the covert language of which was designed as a satire upon an Intendant even more notorious than his fellows for his iniquitous management of the fiscal affairs of the colony. The romantic story of murder and revenge may be found in local guide-books; it sufficiently meets our purpose to point to "Le Chien d'Or." Indeed, Canada would seem to have been to French fortune-seekers what India has been to English nabobs, inasmuch as it is said that a King of France was once asked by his Queen whether the walls of Quebec were made of gold. The government suffered as well as the people from the peculations of its administrators, of whom M. Bigot, the last of the Intendants, was not the least distinguished for his rapacity. Adjacent to his splendid palace was a large storehouse, used as a repository for goods laid up for the service of the State, and a monopoly, at extravagant prices, was secured to the persons who erected the building under M. Bigot's patronage.* By the oppressed *habitans*, the edifice, on account of the purpose to which it was applied, was familiarly known as "La Friponne." The monopoly in corn, however, which exorbitantly raised the price of bread, entailed the deepest misery upon the poorer classes; wheat, arbitrarily purchased at twelve sous the bushel, was never sold without leaving an enormous profit.

* M. Bigot, as the chief instigator of the fraudulent system which had prevailed in the colony, was banished from France in 1763.

To superficial readers, Wolfe's manifesto, calling upon colonists to transfer their allegiance from their parent crown to a strange and heretic king, may indeed seem romantic, if not absurd; but it must be regarded very differently by those who are familiar, as Wolfe evidently was, with the enslaved condition of the Canadians. The *habitans* were generally a simple, hardy, and virtuous race; brave and adventurous, they were at the same time inconstant, credulous, and superstitious. That but few of them could read or write is not surprising, from the well-known fact that the instinct of their Church, as well as the jealousy of their government, prevented the introduction of a printing-press into the colony while in the possession of France. Previous to their long-continued warfare with the neighbouring British colonists, and the internal corruption which exhausted the resources of the country, no people perhaps ever enjoyed a happier lot than the primitive inhabitants of Canada, blessed as they were with a fertile soil, an unlimited territory, and a healthy climate. And, though aversion to steady application, impatience of control, and love of variety, urged many of the more robust and energetic to prefer the allurements of the lake, the prairie, and the forest to the laborious routine of agricultural life, along the populous banks of the St. Lawrence, where the ground was cleared and rudely cultivated, little effort on the part of man was required to ensure rich and abundant harvests.

But in the year 1759 the *habitans* were no longer a light-hearted and contented people. The farmers cared not to store the harvest, which was exposed to the licensed plunder of avaricious officials, and served only to show where the soldiers of France might find free quarters. "Often," says Major Warburton, "when the golden fields were almost ripe for the sickle, the war-summons sounded in the Canadian hamlets, and the whole male population were hurried away to stem some distant Indian onslaught, or to inflict on some British settlement a ruin scarcely more complete than their own. As year after year the vain strife continued, and, despite their valour and even success, the British power hemmed them more closely in, their hearts sickened at the hopeless quarrel, and they longed for peace even under a stranger's sway. Their fields desolate, their villages deserted, their ships driven from the seas, what cared they for the pride of France, when its fruit to them was ruin, oppression, and contempt? What cared they for the Bourbon lily, when known but as the symbol of avarice and wrong?"*

Towards the end of the year 1758 the Governor-General issued a proclamation, ordering the enrolment of every male in the province from sixteen to sixty years of age, to serve in the Militia, and be ready to march at a moment's notice. "The state of the colony is perilous," he declared; "the enemy are making great efforts, both by sea and land; we must prepare therefore to meet them." But nevertheless the *habitans* showed the greatest reluctance to obey the summons; and those who were compelled to serve against the English would gladly have laid down their arms, were it not for fear of the savages, whom, on the least murmur of discontent, De Vandreuil threatened to let loose upon them. In ad-

* 'The Conquest of Canada,' ch. xxi.

dition to the Militia, there were in Canada eight or ten veteran battalions of French infantry,—soldiers who had served under Saxe, and whose imperious and domineering conduct made them hateful to the people. M. Cadet, a heartless man, and a creature of the Intendant's, who filled the office of Commissary-General solely with a view to self-aggrandisement, under the pretence that he could not obtain the necessary supplies, freely quartered these haughty troops upon the unhappy villagers, whose popular songs were,—"Les habitans mangent maigre; les soldats mangent gros;" and "Adieu mes amis en le pauvre Canada." *

The Governor-General, on receiving intelligence of the English designs, again endeavoured to excite the dormant patriotism of the people by a stirring appeal to their valour and loyalty. A council of war was then held at Montreal, when it was arranged that M. de Boulemarque, with an adequate force, should proceed to Ticonderoga, and encounter the army under General Amherst; while the Chevalier de la Corne, with 800 Regulars and a body of Militia, held the rapids above the island of Montreal. To Montcalm, as Commander-in-chief, was assigned the most important duty—the preservation of

* From a private letter written by Lieut.-Colonel Murray, who was for some time cantoned with his battalion in the village of L'Ange Gardien, four leagues below Quebec, covering a body of Highlanders and Rangers employed in destroying a country which he describes as the finest, most fruitful, and best inhabited he had seen in America. "I am," he adds, "quartered in a fine church, which I have fortified, and, as it is all stone, is a very strong castle, and am lodged in the vestry. The church and village take their name from two angels, under whose wings my hammock hangs. We have not hurt any of their ornaments, as the General has excepted everything sacred in his orders for destroying the country."

the capital. He consequently hastened to Quebec, and, with the assistance of the Marquis de Levi, pushed on the defences of the city and its outposts, had the buoys and other aids to the navigation of the river removed, in order to embarrass the invading fleet, prepared fire-ships for its destruction, and strove, above all, to cheer the drooping spirit of the citizens.

Wolfe's competitor, Louis Joseph de St. Véran, Marquis de Montcalm, was his senior by fifteen years. Born at the château of Candiac, in 1712, and carefully educated, he entered the army at an early age, and, after serving seventeen years, was appointed Colonel of the regiment of Auxerrais. The campaigns in Germany and Italy afforded him many opportunities to display the activity, courage, endurance, and military ability which rendered him remarkable, and, in consequence of which, in 1749, he was promoted to the rank of Brigadier-General. In 1756 he was created Maréchal-de-camp, and entrusted with the chief command of the French forces in Canada, where, by the successful resistance he for three years opposed to the attacks of the English, he fully sustained his high reputation. The purity of Montcalm's fame was for awhile dimmed, on account of his imputed sanction of the massacre near Fort William-Henry in 1757; but it is now generally acknowledged that he did everything in his power to restrain his savage allies.* The following year his services were rewarded by the rank of Lieutenant-General; and in his last campaign, by the skilful disposition of his army, he retarded the fall of Quebec. Montcalm, who seems to have been the

* See 'The Conquest of Canada,' ch. xviii.

only truly disinterested and patriotic official then in Canada, like Wolfe, retained amid the tumults of war a love for science and literature. A French writer, somewhat grandiloquously, says of him:—"Il apprit la langue d'Homère avant de prendre la lance d'Achille. Son esprit se développait comme son courage; et également propre aux batailles et aux académies, son désir était d'unir aux lauriers de Mars les palmes de Minerve."* Being a man of low stature, an Indian chief, on seeing Montcalm for the first time, is said to have exclaimed, "Ah! que tu es petit! mais je vois dans tes yeux la hauteur du chêne et la vivacité des aigles." There existed little sympathy between Montcalm and the Marquis de Vandreuil. It is even stated that the Commander-in-chief was heard to tell the Governor-General, "You have sold your country; but while I live I will not deliver it up."† De Vandreuil, to whom the Canadians had hopefully looked for protection and redress against the nefarious extortions of the Intendant, the commissaries, and other official oppressors, by sanctioning the abuses under which they groaned, soon lost the confidence and respect of the people.

Montcalm, foreseeing the great advantage which the possession of Point Levi would give the invaders, before the English fleet had ascended the river, proposed that 4000 men should be entrenched and batteries erected upon this commanding position. But in a council of war he was over-ruled by the Governor, who insisted that, though the enemy might injure some houses of the

* 'L'Année Française,' par Manuel.

† 'Knox's Journal,' vol. i. p. 346.

Lower Town, they could not bring artillery to bear across the river upon Quebec. Discovering their error, the French, on the morning of the 1st of July, sent three floating-batteries to dislodge the brigade which held possession of the Point; but, after a harmless cannonade for an hour and a half, Admiral Saunders sent a frigate to check the assault, and a single broadside compelled the assailants to withdraw. Wolfe also quickly came to the assistance of the detachment, and immediately ordered workmen from each battalion to erect a barbet-battery close by the shore, in order to prevent further annoyance from the water. Next day, accompanied by the 48th regiment, he marched up the right bank of the river, and marked out ground on which to erect batteries for the bombardment of the city, and for several days he was incessantly occupied in superintending the works here as well as on the western point of Orleans; for until these two positions were secured, the safety of the fleet in the basin was not complete. On the 5th, he issued the following general orders:—

Camp at the Island of Orleans.

The object of the campaign is to complete the conquest of Canada, and to finish the war in America. The army under the Commander-in-chief will enter the colony on the side of Montreal, while the fleet and army here attack the Governor-General and his forces. Great sufficiency of provisions and a numerous artillery are provided; and from the known valour of the troops, the nation expects success. These battalions have acquired reputation in the last campaign, and it is not to be doubted but they will be careful to preserve it. From this confidence the General has assured the Secretary of State, in his letters, that, whatever may be the event of the campaign, his Majesty and the country will have reason to be satisfied with the behaviour of the army under his command. The General means to carry the business through with as little loss as possible, and with the highest regard to the preservation of the troops. To that end he expects that the men work cheerfully and without the least unsoldierlike murmur or complaint, and that his few but necessary orders be strictly obeyed. . . .

As the safety of the army depends in a great measure upon the vigilance of the outguards, any officer or non-commissioned officer who shall suffer himself to be surprised by the enemy, must not expect to be forgiven. False alarms are hurtful in an army, and dishonourable to those who occasion them. The outposts are to be sure that the enemy are in motion before they send their intelligence. . . . In most attacks by night, it must be remembered that bayonets are preferable to fire. . . . No churches, houses, or buildings of any kind are to be burned or destroyed without orders. The persons that remain in their habitations, their women and children, are to be treated with humanity. If any violence is offered to a woman, the offender shall be punished with death. If any persons are detected robbing the tents of officers or soldiers, they will be, if condemned, certainly executed. The commanders of regiments are to be answerable that no rum, or spirits of any kind, be sold in or near the camp. When the soldiers are fatigued with work, or wet upon duty, the General will order such refreshment as he knows will be of service to them, but is determined to allow no drunkenness nor licentiousness in the army. If any sutler has the presumption to bring rum on shore, in contempt of the General's regulations, such sutler shall be sent to the Provost in irons, and his goods confiscated. The General will make it his business, as far as he is able, to reward such as shall particularly distinguish themselves, and, on the other hand, will punish any misbehaviour in an exemplary manner.*

* The following extract from 'The Register' (1813) appears in 'Notes and Queries:'—" When the immortal General Wolfe was on his

By the 7th, the 48th Regiment had secured themselves at their new post within a strong redoubt, henceforth known as "Burton's Redoubt," upon an eminence projecting into the river. Next day they were vigorously, though unsuccessfully, bombarded from the town; but Wolfe being then in the redoubt, by ordering the men to lie down or get under cover as soon as a flash was perceived, not one of them was wounded. The works on the south bank of the St. Lawrence and on the west point of Orleans being now sufficiently advanced to render these positions tenable by detachments, Wolfe, having observed that the ground eastward of the Montmorenci commanded the French camp, determined to take possession of it, and hold it as his head-quarters. To conceal his design from the enemy, on the morning of the 9th, Monckton's brigade having formed on the heights in view of Quebec, marched from Point Levi up the right bank of the river for some miles above the town; and at the same time the lighter vessels of the fleet, coming as close in shore as the depth of water permitted, opened fire upon the French lines between the rivers St. Charles and Montmorenci. While Montcalm's attention was thus distracted, Wolfe, with the greater part of his army, crossed over from the island, and, with little opposition and inconsiderable loss, encamped on

passage to Canada, he showed to Admiral Saunders the Ministerial list of officers in his army he was expected to promote, when, after observing that such was not the way to conquer countries, he tore the list to atoms and indignantly threw it into the sea." (2nd Series, vol. v. p. 346.) Captain Knox, also, states that Mr. Cameron, a Light Infantry volunteer, having bravely defended a house, with only eighteen men, against a large body of Canadian Militia and Indians, Wolfe ordered that the first vacant commission should be given to him. (Journal, vol. ii. p. 23.)

the north bank of the St. Lawrence, where, being separated from the enemy's entrenchments only by the rocky chasm of the turbulent tributary, he immediately placed his artillery in position, and began to entrench himself.

The Montmorenci is one continuous torrent from its source in the *Lac des Neiges* until it disgorges itself into the St. Lawrence at the grand Falls which bear its name. The dense volume of water—about twenty yards in width—which here bounds with incredible velocity from a height of 250 feet and acquires in its descent the whiteness of snow, with its frame of dark, almost black, rugged cliffs, whose nakedness is only relieved by a few dwarf firs, forms a picture as sublime as it is beautiful. After emerging from the rocky chasm, which spreads into a wide gap in the north bank of the great river, the affluent passes in a broad shallow stream into the St. Lawrence. Two or three miles above the Falls, the sudden declination of the bed of the torrent, the narrowness of the channel, and the obstructions presented by projecting rocks, cause a series of rapids which descend with tumultuous force where the action of the water, when swollen in Spring, has produced the singular formation which, from its appearance, is called the Natural Steps. Not far from here, and also a few miles higher up, as well as on the St. Lawrence shore below the Falls, the Montmorenci, in dry weather, is fordable; and by some one or other of these passages Wolfe hoped to penetrate the enemy's entrenchments, and bring on what he eagerly desired—a general engagement.

The French camp soon beginning to suffer from the proximity of the English, Montcalm attempted to erect new batteries, but Wolfe's incessant fire of cannon and howitzers compelled him to desist. At first, indeed, Montcalm pretended indifference as to the situation of his assailants, and when M. de Levi urged him to dislodge them, he replied, "Drive them thence, and they will give us more trouble; while they are there they cannot hurt us. Let them amuse themselves." Wolfe strenuously endeavoured, by frequently countermarching in view of their camp, and making feints to cross the stream as if intending to attack them, to draw the French out of their trenches; but Montcalm, too wary to be tempted, satisfied himself by annoying his foe with bands of savages and Canadians disguised as such, who, concealing themselves in the woods, surprised the sentinels, and scalped them. After many fruitless protests against this barbarous kind of warfare, Wolfe was at length obliged to retaliate; hence, in his orders of the 24th of July, he says,—"The General strictly forbids the inhuman practice of scalping, *except when the enemy are Indians, or Canadians dressed like Indians.*" But he preferred rewarding his men for vigilance. On one occasion he ordered two sheep and some rum to a company of Grenadiers for routing a large body of savages, and another time he gave a sentry five guineas for taking an Indian prisoner.

The northern camp being in a state of complete defence, on the evening of the 12th a sky-rocket was fired as a signal for the batteries on the south shore and the bomb-ketches to play upon Quebec. The first shells falling short of the mark, the enemy cheered derisively, but nevertheless the bombardment, which was kept up during the night, seriously injured the Lower Town; and a day or two afterwards shells from Point Levi caused a fire in the Upper Town, by which the cathedral was burned. Galled by their sufferings, some 500 of the principal citizens, headed by the Town-Major and the Seigneur of Point Levi, with 300 students, 700 Militia, and a number of Indians, crossed the river and reconnoitred the English works; but, finding them stronger than was expected, they deferred their attack until reinforced by 300 colony troops. The project, however, was eventually frustrated, owing to one of their columns mistaking the other for the enemy, and firing upon their companions in the night. In consequence of this mishap, after losing seventy of their men, they retreated in confusion, and never renewed the attempt. Wolfe, having been forewarned by deserters, had passed over to Point Levi with the Grenadiers, Light Infantry, and a company of Marines, and was greatly disappointed that the enemy did not allow him an opportunity of encountering them. After this affair, the bearer of a flag of truce from Montcalm having said to the English Commander,—"We do not doubt but you will demolish the town; yet we are determined that your army shall never get footing within its walls;" Wolfe replied,—"I will be master of Quebec, if I stay here until the end of November." Another French officer, on a like errand, having remarked that he wondered the English were such fools as to undertake the siege of Quebec with a mere handful of troops, he was answered,—"Though few the English are, and subdivided, your army, notwithstanding their superior numbers, are afraid of us, as is evident from your not daring to leave your strong entrenchments to attack any of our camps or batteries."

Taking advantage of the flood-tide and a favourable wind, on the night of the 18th the 'Sutherland' and 'Squirrel' frigates, with several sloops, succeeded in passing the town uninjured by the enemy's guns. This was an event of great interest to Wolfe, who anxiously watched the progress of the squadron, and a heavy blow to the garrison, as their water-communication with Montreal was thereby cut off. From intercepted letters it appeared that their situation was very wretched. A priest, writing from Quebec, said,—"The English are too many for us; and who could have suspected it? Part of their fleet passed all our batteries, and are riding in safety above the capital. They have made this town so hot, that there is but one place left where we can with safety pay adoration to our most gracious, but now wrathful and displeased God, who, we fear, has forsaken us." On the 21st, the weather being exceedingly wet and uncomfortable, Wolfe again visited the batteries on Point Levi, and with an escort from thence proceeded up the south shore to Goreham's advanced post, where, entering a barge, he reconnoitred the upper river, and then went on board the 'Sutherland.' His exertions were untiring. "No man," says Captain Knox, "can display greater activity than he does between the different camps of his army."

While the General was thus personally engaged, the country was scoured by detachments of Rangers and Light Infantry, who usually acted with as much leniency as the state of affairs permitted, unless they were resisted by the unhappy inhabitants.* One of these out-parties having brought in a number of prisoners, amongst whom were several females, the Marquis of Beauport, and a Jesuit, Wolfe's aide-de-camp Captain Smith conducted the women, under a flag of truce, to Quebec. The captain being rather uncourteously treated by the civic authorities, Wolfe immediately wrote to Montcalm complaining of the incivility. Some days after, Major Dalling's corps carried 250 male and female captives, one of whom was a priest, to Brigadier Monckton's camp, where the priest and a few more were entertained by the Brigadier in his tent, while the others were kindly treated by the soldiers, who shared their provisions, tobacco, and rum with the unfortunate peasants. Those able to carry arms were then sent on board the transports in the river, and the rest escorted to the city. Next day the Town-Major came to the British camp, to complain of the conduct of the English in seizing old men, women, and children, and sneeringly insinuated that such prisoners were returned only because their captors could not otherwise dispose of them. In reply, he was told to inform his superiors that since they viewed the English commander's leniency and generosity in an unfavourable light, he would not trouble himself to restore any more prisoners, but, having plenty of provisions, would accommodate them in the transports.

On the night of the 28th, the French made a second attempt to burn the English fleet, by sending down a

* Although the light troops from time to time brought in a great deal of cattle, the officers, as well as the men, were frequently obliged to eat horse-flesh; Wolfe having ordered that the hospitals should be supplied with beef and mutton before any was distributed to the army. (Knox, vol. ii. p. 28.)

formidable fire-raft, composed of several schooners, shallops, etc., chained together, measuring 100 fathoms in length, and laden with grenades, shells, swivels, and guns loaded to their muzzles, with every description of combustible matter. As before, the design of this malicious contrivance was obviated by the intrepidity of the sailors, who, grappling the raft ere it entered the Basin, towed it ashore. As they laboriously plied their oars, one of these fearless tars was heard calling out to a comrade, "D—n me, Jack, didst thee ever take hell in tow before?"* Next morning, Wolfe sent a flag of truce with the following message to the commander of the garrison:—"If you presume to send down any more fire-rafts, they shall be made fast to the two transports in which the Canadian prisoners are confined, in order that they may perish by your own base inventions." The threat had the desired effect.

All Wolfe's previous efforts to decoy Montcalm to a general engagement having proved unsuccessful, finding that the ford at the foot of Montmorenci Falls was passable for some hours during the latter part of the ebb and the beginning of the flood-tide, he made dispositions accordingly for a formidable attack upon the French camp, on the 31st of July. No pen can describe the events of that unlucky day so well as Wolfe's own; we shall therefore transcribe—with the exception of a few paragraphs, the substance of which has been anticipated—that portion of his celebrated dispatch to Mr. Pitt which brings the story of the campaign down to the beginning of August:—

* Knox's Journal, vol. i. p. 351.

Head Quarters of Montmorenci,
in the River St. Lawrence.

Sir,

I wish I could, upon this occasion, have the honour of transmitting to you a more favourable account of the progress of his Majesty's arms, but the obstacles we have met with in the operations of the campaign are much greater than we had reason to expect, or could foresee; not so much from the number of the enemy (though superior to ours) as from the natural strength of the country, which the Marquis de Montcalm seems wisely to depend upon. When I learned that succours of all kinds had been thrown into Quebec, that five battalions of regular troops, completed from the best inhabitants of the country, some of the troops of the colony, and every Canadian that was able to carry arms, besides several nations of savages, had taken the field in a very advantageous situation, I could not flatter myself that I should be able to reduce the place. I sought, however, an occasion to attack their army, knowing well that with those troops I was able to fight, and hoping that a victory might disperse them. . . .

The 18th July, two men-of-war, two armed sloops, and two transports, with some troops on board, passed by the town without any loss, and got into the upper river. This enabled me to reconnoitre the country above, where I found the same attention on the enemy's side, and great difficulties on ours, arising from the nature of the ground and the obstacles to our communication with the fleet. But what I feared most was, that if we should have landed between the town and the river of Cap Rouge, the body first landed could not be reinforced before they were attacked by the enemy's whole army. Notwithstanding these difficulties, I thought once of attempting it at St. Michael's, about three miles above the town; but perceiving that the enemy were jealous of the design, were preparing against it, and had actually brought artillery and a mortar (which, being so near to Quebec, they could increase as they pleased) to play upon the shipping, and as it must have been many hours before we could attack them,—even supposing a favourable night for the boats to pass by the town unhurt,—it seemed to me so hazardous that I thought it best to desist.

However, to divide the enemy's force, and to draw their attention as high up the river as possible, and to procure some intelligence, I sent a detachment, under the command of Colonel Carleton, to land at the *Point au Tremble,* to attack whatever he might find there, bring off some prisoners, and all the useful papers he could get. I had been informed that a number of the inhabitants of Quebec had retired to that place, and that probably we should find a magazine of provisions there. The Colonel was fired upon by a body of Indians the moment he landed, but they were soon dispersed and driven into the woods; he searched for magazines, but to no purpose, brought off some prisoners, and returned with little loss. After this business I came back to Montmorenci, where I found that Brigadier Townshend had, by a superior fire, prevented the French from erecting a battery on the bank of the river, from whence they intended to cannonade our camp.

I now resolved to take the first opportunity which presented itself of attacking the enemy, though posted to great advantage, and everywhere prepared to receive us. As the men-of-war cannot (for want of sufficient depth of water) come near enough to the enemy's entrenchments to annoy them in the least, the Admiral had prepared two transports,—drawing but little water,—which, upon occasions, could be run aground, to favour a descent. With the help of these vessels, which I understood would be carried by the tide close in shore, I proposed to make myself master of a detached redoubt near to the water's edge, and whose situation appeared to be out of musket-shot of the entrenchment upon the hill. If the enemy supported this detached post, it would necessarily bring on an engagement, which we most wished for; and if not, I should have it in my power to examine their situation, so as to be able to determine where we could best attack them. Preparations were accordingly made for an engagement.

The 31st of July, in the forenoon, the boats of the fleet

were filled with Grenadiers, and a part of Brigadier Monckton's brigade from Point Levi. The two brigades, under the Brigadiers Townshend and Murray, were ordered to be in readiness to pass the ford, when it should be thought necessary. To facilitate the passage of this corps, the Admiral had placed the 'Centurion' in the channel, so that she might check the fire of the lower battery which commanded the ford. This ship was of great use, as her fire was very judiciously directed. A great quantity of artillery was placed upon the eminence, so as to batter and enfilade the left of their entrenchments. From the vessel which ran aground nearest in, I observed that the redoubt was too much commanded to be kept without very great loss; and the more, as the two armed ships could not be brought near enough to cover both with their artillery and musketry, which I at first conceived they might. But as the enemy seemed in some confusion, and we were prepared for an action, I thought it a proper time to make an attempt upon their entrenchment. Orders were sent to the Brigadiers-General to be ready with the corps under their command,—Brigadier Monckton to lead, and the Brigadiers Townshend and Murray to pass the ford.

At a proper time of the tide, the signal was made, but in rowing towards the shore many of the boats grounded upon a ledge that runs off a considerable distance. This accident put us into some disorder, lost a great deal of time, and obliged me to send an officer to stop Brigadier Townshend's march, whom I then observed to be in motion. While the seamen were getting their boats off, the enemy fired a number of shells and shot, but did no considerable damage. As soon as the disorder could be set a little to rights, and the boats were ranged in a proper manner, some of the officers of the navy went in with me to find a better place to land. We took one flat-bottomed boat with us to make the experiment, and as soon as we had found a fit part of the shore, the troops were ordered to disembark, thinking it not yet too late for the attempt. The thirteen companies of Grenadiers, and 200 of the Royal American battalion, got on shore. The Grenadiers were ordered to form themselves into four distinct bodies, and to begin the attack, supported by Brigadier Monckton's corps, as soon as the troops had passed the ford, and we were at hand to assist.

But whether from the noise and hurry at landing, or from some other cause, the Grenadiers, instead of forming themselves as they were directed, ran on impetuously towards the enemy's entrenchments in the utmost disorder and confusion, without waiting for the corps which were to sustain them, and join in the attack.* Brigadier Monckton was not landed, and Brigadier Townshend was still at a considerable distance, though upon his march to join us, in very great order. The Grenadiers were checked by the enemy's first fire, and obliged to shelter themselves in or about the redoubt, which the French had abandoned upon their approach. In this situation they continued for some time, unable to form under so hot a

* The day after the repulse, Wolfe rebuked the Grenadiers in these terms :—" The check which the Grenadiers met with yesterday will, it is hoped, be a lesson to them for the time to come. Such impetuous, irregular, and unsoldierlike proceedings destroy all order, make it impossible for the commanders to form any disposition for an attack, and put it out of the General's power to execute his plans. . . . The very first fire of the enemy was sufficient to repulse men who had lost all sense of order and military discipline. . . . The loss, however, is inconsiderable, and may be easily repaired when a favourable opportunity offers, if the men will show a proper attention to their officers."

An officer of Frazer's regiment says :—" Some impute this to be the reason of the Grenadiers' mistake: that the sailors who landed with them huzzaed that the Grenadiers from Orleans and Montmorenci had joined; and that a certain captain ordered his drummer to beat the march without the desire of the commanding officer; which occasioned the miscarriage of the day." ('Journal of the Particular Transactions during the Siege of Quebec.' See 'Notes and Queries,' 2nd series, vol. viii. p. 165.)

From private letters it appears that Wolfe showed the kindest feeling for the wounded officers. Before taking any rest himself, he visited every one of them; and, that they might not consider themselves under any slur, such of them as were able he invited to sup with him that night.

fire, and having many gallant officers wounded who (careless of their persons) had been solely intent upon their duty. I saw the absolute necessity of calling them off, that they might form themselves behind Brigadier Monckton's corps, which was now landed, and drawn up on the beach, in extreme good order.

By this new accident, and this second delay, it was near night, a sudden storm came on, and the tide began to make; so that I thought it most advisable not to persevere in so difficult an attack, lest (in case of a repulse) the retreat of Brigadier Townshend's corps might be hazardous and uncertain. Our artillery had a great effect upon the enemy's left, where Brigadiers Townshend and Murray were to have attacked; and it is probable that if those accidents I have spoken of had not happened, we should have penetrated there, whilst our left and centre—more remote from our artillery—must have borne all the violence of their musketry. The French did not attempt to interrupt our march. Some of the savages came down to murder such wounded as could not be brought off, and to scalp the dead, as their custom is.*

The place where the attack was intended has these advantages over all others hereabout. Our artillery may be brought into use. The greatest part, or even the whole, of the troops might act at once; and the retreat, in case of a repulse, was secure, at least for a certain time of the tide. Neither one or

* It was on this occasion that Peyton and Ochterlony, the touching story of whose friendship has been often told, were wounded. Peyton was rescued, and Ochterlony, having been protected from the tomahawks of the Indians by a French soldier, was carried by him as a prisoner to Quebec. Subsequently, whenever Wolfe sent a flag of truce to the city, he contributed to the comfort of the captive officer, and also sent a reward of twenty guineas to the soldier who had saved his life. But Montcalm returned the money, saying that the man had not particularly merited such a gratuity, having only done his duty, and what he hoped every Frenchman in his army would do under the like circumstances. "An absurd piece of ostentation," comments Captain Knox, "which the enemy greatly affect on particular occasions."

It is likewise stated ('British Magazine,' 1761) that Wolfe wrote a polite note to Madame de Ramezay, Directress of the General Hospital other of these advantages can anywhere else be found. The enemy were, indeed, posted upon a commanding eminence. The beach, upon which the troops were drawn up, was of deep mud, with holes, and cut by several gullies. The hill to be ascended, very steep and not everywhere practicable. The enemy numerous in their entrenchments, and their fire hot. If the attack had succeeded, our loss must certainly have been great and theirs inconsiderable, from the shelter which the neighbouring woods afforded them. The river of St. Charles still remained to be passed before the town was invested. All these circumstances I considered, but the desire to act in conformity with the King's instructions induced me to make this trial, persuaded that a victorious army finds no difficulties.

In order to preserve the continuity of our narrative, it may not be amiss to notice some incidents which occurred during the month of August, before the reader peruses the sequel of Wolfe's dispatch. The bombardment of Quebec being almost unintermittingly kept up, on the 9th, the church of Notre Dame des Victoires, in the Lower Town, was destroyed, and the fire having spread to one of the batteries, a magazine exploded; while in the English batteries, such was the General's precaution, no accident from either shot or shell happened until the 17th, when one man was killed and three men were wounded by the enemy's fire. The Rangers scoured the country as heretofore, and at the same time circulated copies of Wolfe's placard, wherein he limited

in Quebec, begging of her as a favour to take particular care of Captain Ochterlony, for whom he had a great regard; assuring her at the same time that, should fortune crown his Britannic Majesty's arms with success, she might depend upon the General's best offices and protection. The good lady accordingly nursed the gallant officer with all the tenderness of a mother; but notwithstanding, he died of his wounds on the 24th of August, when the commander of the garrison sent a flag of truce with the report of his death, and returned his baggage.

the time to a certain day for the *habitans* to disperse and observe neutrality. In this dilemma they deputed some of their leaders to inquire of the Governor-General what they were to do when the time should expire. The answer they got was:—"This is a piece of policy in the British General. Continue to defend your country as ye have hitherto nobly done, for I have certain intelligence that their fleet is only victualled, at full allowance, to the end of this month." The Indians, too, began to lose their confidence in the French power. Montcalm having boasted to some of their chiefs, after the affair at Montmorenci, "You see we have beaten the English; we drove them away; we defeated them; we conquered them!" the savages replied, "Conquered them? we will never believe that until you drive them back to their ships. Are they not still firing against Quebec? Are they not as unconcerned in their camps as if nothing had happened?"

Wolfe's delicate constitution at length succumbed under the disappointments and anxiety he had suffered. These, together with bodily fatigue, brought on a severe attack of his chronic malady and a fever, which totally disabled him for several days. "It is with the greatest concern to the whole army," writes Captain Knox on the 22nd of August, "that we are now informed of our amiable General being very ill of a slow fever. The soldiers lament him exceedingly, and seemed apprehensive of this event, before we were ascertained of it, by his not visiting the camp for several days." During his illness, Wolfe was heard to assert that he would cheerfully sacrifice a leg or an arm to be in possession of Quebec; and to his medical attendant he said, "I know perfectly well you cannot cure my complaint; but pray make me up so that I may be without pain for a few days, and able to do my duty; that is all I want."* On the 24th, Captain Knox writes:—"I crossed the river this morning [from Point Levi to Montmorenci], to wait on the General and receive his orders for this brigade. A tolerable house stood convenient here for his quarters; but he was so ill above-stairs as not to be able to come down to dinner."† Next day the Captain notes in his diary:—"General Wolfe is on the recovery, to the inconceivable joy of the whole army." His strength, however, was not sufficiently restored to enable him to visit the distant camps and posts upon the Isle of Orleans and the right bank of the St. Lawrence until the last day of the month, when his reappearance amongst them was hailed with the warmest expressions of delight by officers and men. A few days previously, while labouring under mental and bodily anguish, he sent the following communication, together with his Majesty's "Secret Instructions for our trusty and well-beloved James Wolfe, etc.," to the Brigadier-Generals Monckton, Townshend, and Murray:—

* 'European Magazine,' 1798, p. 170.

† Wolfe, while he was in health, daily entertained officers of the several corps. It is said that a Scotch captain, who was engaged to dine with him one day, was also invited by some brother officers. "You must excuse me," said he, "as I am already engaged to Wolfe." A smart subaltern having observed that he ought to have expressed himself more respectfully, and said *General* Wolfe, "Sir," promptly replied the Scotchman, "we never say General Alexander or General Cæsar." Wolfe, who was within hearing—as the story goes—by a low bow tacitly acknowledged the compliment. ('The Soldier's Companion, or Martial Recorder.')

That the public service may not suffer by the General's indisposition, he begs the Brigadiers will meet and consult for the public utility and advantage, and consider of the best method to attack the enemy. If the French army be attacked and defeated, the General concludes that the town would immediately surrender, because he does not find they have any provisions in that place. The General is of opinion that the army should be attacked in preference to the place, because of the difficulties of penetrating from the Lower to the Upper Town; in which attempt, neither the guns of the shipping nor our own batteries could be of much use.

There appear to be three methods of attacking the army:—

First. In dry weather, a large detachment may march in a day and night, so as to arrive at Beauport,—fording the Montmorenci eight or nine miles up,—before day in the morning. It is likely they would be discovered upon this march on both sides of the river. If such detachment penetrates to the intrenchments, and the rest of the troops are ready, the consequence is plain.

Second. If the troops encamped here [on the north shore] pass the ford with the falling water, and in the night march on directly towards the point of Beauport, the light infantry have a good chance to get up the Woody-hill; trying different places and moving quick to the right, would soon discover a proper place for the rest. The upper redoubt must be attacked, and kept by a company of Grenadiers. Brigadier Monckton must be ready, off the point of Beauport, to land where our people get up the hill; for which signals may be appointed.

Third. All the chosen troops of the army may attack at Beauport at low water. A diversion must be made across the ford an hour before the second attack.

N.B.—For the first attack, it is sufficient if the water begins to fall a little before daylight, or about it. For the other two, it will be best to have the low water half an hour before day. The General thinks the country should be ruined and destroyed, as much as can be done consistent with a more capital operation. There are guides in the army, for the detachments in question.*

The Brigadier-Generals replied as follows :—

Point Levi, August 29, 1759.

Having met this day in consequence of General Wolfe's desire, to consult together for the public utility and advantage, and to consider of the best method of attacking the enemy; and having read His Majesty's private instructions, which the General was pleased to communicate to us; and having considered some propositions of his with respect to our future operations, we think it our duty to offer our opinion as follows :—

The natural strength of the enemy's situation between the rivers St. Charles and Montmorenci, now improved by all the art of their engineers, makes the defeat of their army, if attacked there, very doubtful. The advantage which their easy communication along the shore gives over our attack from boats, and by the ford of the river Montmorenci, is evident from late experience; and it appears to us that that part of the army which is proposed to march through the woods, nine miles up the Montmorenci, to surprise their camp, is exposed to certain discovery, and, consequently, to the disadvantage of a constant wood fight. But allowing that we could get footing on the Beauport side, the Marquis de Montcalm will still have it in his power to dispute the passage of the river St. Charles, till the place is supplied with provisions from the ships and magazines above, from which it appears they draw their subsistence.

We are therefore of opinion that the most probable method of striking an effectual blow is to bring the troops to the south shore, and to carry the operations above the town. If we can establish ourselves on the north shore, the Marquis de Montcalm must fight us on our own terms; we are between him and his provisions, and between him and the army opposing General Amherst. If he gives us battle and we defeat him, Quebec, and probably all Canada, will be our own, which is beyond any advantage we can expect by the Beauport side; and

* From Mante's 'History of the War.'

should the enemy pass over the river St. Charles with force sufficient to oppose this operation, we may still, with more ease and probability of success, execute the General's third proposition (which is, in our opinion, the most eligible), or undertake anything else on the Beauport shore, necessarily weakened by the detachments made to oppose us above the town.

(Signed)

Brigadiers { MONCKTON, TOWNSHEND, MURRAY.*

The circumstances which inclined Wolfe to act conformably to the opinion of his Brigadiers are detailed in the continuation of his dispatch to the Prime Minister.

Immediately after the check [at Montmorenci], I sent Brigadier Murray above the town with 1200 men, directing him to assist Rear-Admiral Holmes in the destruction of the French ships, if they could be got at, in order to open a communication with General Amherst. The Brigadier was to seek every favourable opportunity of fighting some of the enemy's detachments, provided he could do it upon tolerable terms, and to use all the means in his power to provoke them to attack him. He made two different attempts to land upon the north shore, without success; but in a third was more fortunate. He landed unexpectedly at *De Chambaud*, and burnt a magazine there, in which were some provisions, some ammunition, and all the spare stores, clothing, arms, and baggage of their army. The prisoners he took informed him of the surrender of the Fort of Niagara; and we discovered, by intercepted letters, that the enemy had abandoned Carillon † and Crown Point, were retired to the Isle aux Noix, and that General Amherst was making preparations to pass the Lake Champlain, to fall upon M. Bourlemaque's corps, which consists of three battalions of Foot, and as many Canadians as make the whole amount to 3000.

The Admiral's dispatches and mine would have gone eight or

* Mante, p. 252.

† Carillon was the name given by the French to the place more commonly known by the Indian term Ticonderoga.

ten days sooner, if I had not been prevented from writing by a fever. I found myself so ill, and am still so weak, that I begged the General Officers to consult together for the general utility. They are all of opinion that, as more ships and provisions have now got above the town, they should try, by conveying up a corps of 4000 or 5000 men (which is nearly the whole strength of the army, after the Points of Levi and Orleans are left in a proper state of defence), to draw the enemy from their present situation, and bring them to an action. I have acquiesced in the proposal, and we are preparing to put it into execution.

The Admiral and I have examined the town, with a view to a general assault; but, after consulting with the chief engineer, who is well acquainted with the interior parts of it, and after viewing it with the utmost attention, we found that though the batteries of the Lower Town might be easily silenced by the men-of-war, yet the business of an assault would be little advanced by that, since the few passages that lead from the Lower to the Upper Town are carefully entrenched; and the upper batteries cannot be affected by the ships, which must receive considerable damage from them, and from the mortars. The Admiral would readily join in this, or in any other measure for the public service; but I could not propose to him an undertaking of so dangerous a nature, and promising so little success.

To the uncommon strength of the country, the enemy have added, for the defence of the river, a great number of floating batteries and boats. By the vigilance of these, and the Indians round our different posts, it has been impossible to execute anything by surprise. We have had almost daily skirmishes with these savages, in which they are generally defeated, but not without loss on our side. By the list of disabled officers,* many of whom are of rank, you may perceive, Sir, that the

* Return of killed, wounded, and missing:—

	killed	wounded	missing
Officers	11	46	0
Sergeants	9	26	0
Drummers	0	7	0
Rank and file	162	572	17
Total	182	651	17

army is much weakened. By the nature of the river, the most formidable part of this armament is deprived of the power of acting, yet we have almost the whole force of Canada to oppose.

In this situation there is such a choice of difficulties, that I own myself at a loss how to determine. The affairs of Great Britain, I know, require the most vigorous measures; but, then, the courage of a handful of brave men should be exerted only where there is some hope of a favourable event. However, you may be assured, Sir, that the small part of the campaign which remains shall be employed, as far as I am able, for the honour of His Majesty and the interest of the nation, in which I am sure of being well seconded by the Admiral and by the Generals. Happy if our efforts here can contribute to the success of His Majesty's arms in any other part of America,

I have the honour to be, etc.,

JAM: WOLFE.

September 2, 1759.

The General having submitted to Admiral Saunders his first draft of the foregoing dispatch, the Admiral considered that an undue share of the misadventure at Montmorenci was attributed to his department, and wrote to that effect. Wolfe being then dangerously ill, his attached friend the Adjutant-General did not show him the letter immediately; but as soon as he was able to use his pen, the momentarily desponding hero replied thus:

Dear Sir,

I did not see the letter you did me the honour to write till just now, nor indeed could I have answered it before if Major Barré had shown it to me. I shall leave out that part of my letter to Mr. Pitt which you object to, although the matter of fact, to the best of my recollection, is strictly as I have stated it. I am sensible of my own errors in the course of the campaign; see clearly wherein I have been deficient; and think a little more or less blame, to a man that must necessarily be ruined, of little or no consequence.

If you had recollected the purport of my letter, you would not have found "that it throws any difficulties I met with in landing on the two cats not being placed so as to annoy the two small batteries with their great guns." On the contrary, the cats did annoy the upper battery with their great guns, and performed that part of the service as well as could be expected, and yet that upper battery was not abandoned by the enemy, but continued firing till the Grenadiers ran, like blockheads, up to it. However, its fire was of no consequence, and not worth mentioning, nor the least impediment to landing. Mr. Cook* said he believed the cats could be carried within forty or fifty yards of the redoubts. I told him at the time that I would readily compound for 150 or 200 yards, which would have been near enough had the upper redoubt been as far from the enemy's entrenchments as it appeared from our camp to be, and had I judged it advisable to attack it with a view to lodge in it, which I did not upon seeing it was too much commanded. You will please to consider the difference between landing at high water, with four companies of Grenadiers, to attack a redoubt under the protection of the artillery of a vessel, and landing part of an army to attack the enemy's entrenchments. For the last business a junction of our corps was necessary; and to join, the water must fall a certain degree. I gave up the first point (that of the redoubt) upon finding my mistake as to the distance from the entrenchment, and determined upon the latter, which I always had in view, upon observing the enemy's disorder, and remarking their situation much better than I ever could do before. The fire of the lower redoubt was so smart during the

* The future famous navigator, Captain James Cook, then master of the 'Mercury.' It was he who took the soundings of the channel between the Isle of Orleans and the north shore, in front of the French camp, in order to enable the Admiral to place his ships so as to cover the landing. In this work he had been engaged for several nights, and once narrowly escaped capture by the Indians. (Kippis, 'Biographia Britannica.')

time that we were on board the 'Russell' (I think it was), that, as neither her guns nor the guns of the other cat could be brought to bear against it, I thought fit to order the Grenadiers out of her, by which I saved many lives. I was no less than three times struck with the splinters in that ship, and had my stick knocked out of my hand with a cannon-ball while I was on board reconnoitring the position and movements of the enemy; and yet you say in your letter, they did (the cats) great execution against the two small batteries, and on your first landing you did not lose a man.

With regard to the 'Centurion,' I am ready to do justice to Captain Mantle; but I am very sure, whatever his merits may be, the approbation would be more to the purpose coming from you than from me. In reality, the position of the ship was in consequence of your orders; and I am sure that if you could have placed the whole fleet so as to have been useful to us, you would have done it.* The 'Centurion' had no enemy to encounter; her position was assigned, and her guns were fired judiciously. The fire of that ship, and of the four-gun battery near the water-side, together with the want of ammunition, kept the lower battery silent for a time, but yet we received many shot from that battery at landing; and Brigadier Townshend's corps was fired upon, particularly in returning over the ford, though with little damage.

When I resolved to attack the French army, I sent Mr. Leslie in to see how the water fell, that I might land at a proper time to join with Townshend; and when he made me his report I made the signal to Colonel Burton. Many of the boats ran upon the ledge, and the delay occasioned by

* Sir Charles Saunders, who had been Lieutenant of the 'Centurion' and Commander of the 'Tryal' in Anson's expedition, became Rear-Admiral of the White in 1758. He was recalled from the Mediterranean to take the chief command of the American fleet in February, 1759, and hoisted his flag on board the 'Neptune' as Vice-Admiral of the Blue. In 1761 he received the insignia of the Bath, and died in 1775. His remains were privately interred in Westminster Abbey, near Wolfe's monument. Interesting anecdotes of this gallant, skilful, and amiable sailor will be found in 'The Annual Register,' 1759, and 1755; also in 'The European Magazine,' 1796.

the accident was such that I sent Captain Smith, my aide-de-camp, to stop Townshend, who was then crossing the ford; and yet, Sir, you assert that there was no delay by this accident;—none, indeed, that could have had any consequence if the strange behaviour of the Grenadiers had not lost us more time, and brought on the night, and, perhaps, very luckily for the army, considering the disadvantageous nature of the attack. I remember you did me the honour to call to me from your boat to go in and see for a landing-place, and I remember some gentleman's calling out at the same time from the boat that it was a proper time to land; and you may remember I went in, and made the experiment with a flat-bottomed boat and one of the captains (I believe Captain Shade); and when we had found what we sought for, I desired him to bring the boats forward.

The rest makes up the remaining part of the story of that unlucky day, the blame of which I take entirely upon my own shoulders, and I expect to suffer for it. Accidents cannot be helped. As much as the plan was defective falls justly upon me; and it is, I think, a matter of no vast consequence whether the cats fired well or ill, were well or ill placed; of no great consequence whether an hour or two were or were not lost by the boats grounding; and of as little consequence whether the 'Centurion's' gunner directed his shot well or ill. In none of these circumstances the essential matter resides. The great fault of that day consists in putting too many men into boats, who might have been landed the day before, and might have crossed the ford with certainty, while a small body remained afloat, and the superfluous boats of the fleet employed in a feint that might divide the enemy's force. A man sees his errors often too late to remedy.

My ill state of health hinders me from executing my own plan; it is of too desperate a nature to order others to execute. The Generals seem to think alike as to the operations; I therefore join with them, and perhaps we may find some opportunity to strike a blow. We shall need your immediate assistance to convey away this artillery, which I believe may be done in one, or at most two nights. The light six-pounders, a few light howitzers, and some tools will be wanted above, as well as provisions and rum. My letters, I hope, will be ready to-morrow, and I hope I shall have strength to lead these men to wherever we can find the enemy. Beyond the month of September I conclude our operations cannot go. We can embark the superfluous artillery, and Barré has a list ready for you of quarters for the troops, supposing (as I have very little hope of) they do not quarter here.* We shall want a pull of seamen to get Major Douglas's guns from off the low battery; as their wheels are small, they pull heavy. I am always, with great esteem, dear Sir,

Your most obedient and most humble servant,

JAM: WOLFE.

August 30th, 1759.

P.S.—It will be necessary to run as many small craft as possible by the town, with provisions and rum for six weeks for about 5000, which is all I intend to take. The small vessels can take us in occasionally, if it be necessary, and run us back again in a tide. The Marines here, and Captain Leward's detachment, shall go to-morrow to Orleans. The volunteers shall go off this night, if you be pleased to send the boats; and they may remain up and down that country till it is totally destroyed. It will be necessary to keep two or three armed vessels in this channel, and it will be right every three or four days to send a detachment of 100 soldiers and 100 seamen down along this shore of the Isle of Orleans,

* Barré, there is reason to believe, was introduced to Wolfe by their common friend Lord Fitzmaurice, afterwards Earl of Shelburne. "You may be sure," wrote Wolfe to Rickson, "that my information came from the best hands." (See *ante*, p. 421.) And, from a letter written in 1762, cited in 'The Chatham Correspondence,' it appears that Barré was "found out, pushed, and brought into Parliament by Lord Shelburne." His conduct as Adjutant-General of the expedition was so highly appreciated by his commander, that, when the success of the campaign seemed hopeless, Wolfe regretted his want of power to serve him, and only wished for an opportunity to make him the messenger of good news,—an honour of which the battle of Quebec deprived him. In the following year, however, Barré was the bearer of General Amherst's dispatches announcing the surrender of Montreal.

and up the other, to scour it, and to keep them from thinking of landing upon it.*

Reticent though he is of his ill health, the dejection of the hero at this time is apparent in the last letter he ever wrote to his widowed mother:—

Banks of the St. Lawrence, 31st August, 1759.

Dear Madam,

My writing to you will convince you that no personal evils, worse than defeats and disappointments, have fallen upon me. The enemy puts nothing to risk, and I can't, in conscience, put the whole army to risk. My antagonist has wisely shut himself up in inaccessible entrenchments, so that I can't get at him without spilling a torrent of blood, and that perhaps to little purpose. The Marquis de Montcalm is at the head of a great number of bad soldiers, and I am at the head of a small number of good ones, that wish for nothing so much as to fight him; but the wary old fellow avoids an action, doubtful of the behaviour of his army. People must be of the profession to understand the disadvantages and difficulties we labour under, arising from the uncommon natural strength of the country.

I approve entirely of my father's disposition of his affairs, though perhaps it may interfere a little matter with my plan of quitting the service, which I am determined to do the first opportunity,—I mean so as not to be absolutely distressed in circumstances, nor burdensome to you or anybody else. I wish you much health, and am, dear Madam,

Your obedient and affectionate Son,

JAM: WOLFE.

If any sums of money are paid to you of what is due to my Father from Government, let me recommend you not to meddle with the funds, but keep it for your support until better times.

* From 'The Gentleman's Magazine,' June, 1801.

CHAPTER XXIII.

ABOVE QUEBEC.—HEIGHTS OF ABRAHAM.

SEPTEMBER 1-13, 1759.

SIR EDWARD HAWKE told the military commanders of the expedition against Rochefort that he would put them ashore "without wetting their shoes;" yet, with an overwhelming force, Mordaunt and Conway summoned a council of war to consider whether it was expedient to land upon an unprotected coast. Wolfe, by forcing his way to Louisbourg, in spite of storm, fog, entrenchments, and masked batteries, and by his conduct during the siege, raised a new standard whereby English generals were in future to be judged. The conquest of Cape Breton, however, did not present the "choice of difficulties" that confronted the hero at Quebec.* Al-

* Upon the publication of Wolfe's dispatch of the 2nd of September, Charles Townshend is said to have declared that it was written by his brother; "for," said he, "Wolfe is a fiery-headed fellow, only fit for fighting;" and the falsehood was credited by those who knew nothing of Wolfe's abilities. But when the Honourable Brigadier had occasion to write to the Secretary of State, giving an account of events subsequent to Wolfe's death, the inferiority of his dispatch was generally remarked. And George Selwyn, meeting Townshend one day at the Treasury, facetiously inquired, "Charles, if your brother wrote Wolfe's dispatch, who the devil wrote your brother George's?" ('The Soldier's Companion.') The composition has likewise been absurdly attributed to Colonel Barré. (See Britton's 'Junius Elucidated.') Every

though previously informed of the natural obstacles to the capture of the Canadian capital, until his own eyes had beheld them he could not comprehend all their bearings. Yet, strange to say, before he had acquired a knowledge of his opponent's plans, different though they proved from any mode of defence he could have anticipated when forecasting how he should invest the city, he selected for the site of his camp the very ground whereon his crowning victory was achieved.*

But when Wolfe became practically aware of all the obstructions to be overcome before the stronghold could be besieged; when he saw that he must first defeat an army

reader of this volume will at once perceive that the letter in question was written by none other than Wolfe; and, although at the time it was considered a *chef d'œuvre* of military description, it is, considering the difference of years, by no means a more remarkable production than his boyish account of the battle of Dettingen, now first given to the world. Wolfe, moreover, was wont to repeat certain phrases, which he usually varied in the repetition. Thus, we find that the phrase, "a choice of difficulties,"—rendered remarkable by Dr. Johnson's citation,—is a variation of "an option of difficulties," which he had used on a previous occasion. (See *ante*, p. 397, line 1.)

* See his last letter to his uncle (*ante*, p. 498). In Smith's 'Topographical and Historical Account of Mary-le-bone' (p. 272, note), there is a notice of Lieutenant John M'Culloch, a native of the north of Ireland, who, in 1793, died in the parish poorhouse. On the surrender of Oswego, in 1756, he had been taken prisoner by the French and carried to Quebec, where he had an opportunity of observing the situation and defences of the place. Being exchanged, he returned to England, and, as a proper person to assist in the expedition of 1759, was introduced to Wolfe, who, it is said, took memoranda of his information. On the strength of this, it has been foolishly asserted that M'Culloch devised the scheme whereby Quebec was eventually captured. It is evident, however, that Wolfe's accurate preconception of the nature of the country, the number of the enemy, etc., could only have been arrived at through the communication of some one who had been in Canada. It is not improbable, therefore, that Lieutenant M'Culloch was the man from whom Wolfe learned the details of which he informed his uncle.

much larger than his own, commanded by the most skilful French captain of the time; and when he found that his prudent adversary was surrounded by impregnable defences, it is no wonder that even to his ardent mind the reduction of Quebec should seem hopeless, and that his strong soul should have despaired. Nevertheless, although other commanders might consider that such hindrances would justify them in at once giving up so unpromising a labour, he resolved to leave nothing unattempted, and day after day he made every effort towards the accomplishment of his object. Yet after nine weeks of anxiety and watching; after fatigues "too great to be supported by a delicate constitution, and a body unequal to the vigorous and enterprising soul that it lodged,"* all his endeavours were apparently to no purpose. The season was wellnigh spent, his little army was dwindling away, and there remained scarcely a probability of timely reinforcement.

"Among those who shared his confidence," says Smollett, "he was often seen to sigh, and he was often heard to complain; and even in the transports of his chagrin declare that he would never return without success, to be exposed, as other unfortunate commanders had been, to the censure and reproach of an ignorant populace."† On the other hand, Mauduit says:—"From a letter of Mr. Wolfe's, writ at the time, I could show that he had once actually resolved to return. Suppose he had returned; no one could have said but that he had executed Mr. Pitt's counsels, and much more;—all, I mean, which related to his part of the scheme. Every

* Burke, Annual Register, 1759, p. 39. † History of England.

one must remember the universal concern which his public letter occasioned. They who best knew the country had declared their opinion before; but all men then wished that the forces had gone together, and the success of the expedition not been left to the uncertainty of an after conjunction."*

Contradictory though Smollett's and Mauduit's assertions appear, they are doubtless both perfectly true; nor are they irreconcileable. They only show the conflicting phases of a sensitive mind. However, any idea Wolfe may have had of returning before his work was accomplished must have been but a mere passing thought. That he never seriously contemplated doing so is certain, from the fact that he had plans drawn for a fort on Isle aux Coudres, wherein to establish himself in case he could not become master of Quebec before the winter should put an end to the campaign.† Wolfe knew that every eye in England was fixed upon him; he knew what his King, what the great Minister who had entrusted him with the command, and, in short, what every one of his countrymen expected of him; he knew what implicit

* From 'An Apology for the Life and Actions of General Wolfe, against the Misrepresentations in a pamphlet called A Counter-Address to the Public,' by Israel Mauduit. (London, 1765.) The title is calculated to mislead those who have not read this rare party pamphlet, which, after a few copies had been printed, was suppressed by desire of Mr. Grenville. (See the author's autograph letter in copy belonging to the Grenville Library, British Museum.) The 'Counter-Address' was written by General Conway, or one of his partisans; and the "misrepresentations" complained of consist in Conway's having slighted Wolfe's services, by stating that "he achieved his glorious career in *one* important action." The argument of the 'Apology' is a comparison between Mordaunt's and Conway's conduct at Rochefort, and Wolfe's at Rochefort, Louisbourg, and Quebec.

† Knox's Journal, vol. ii. p. 14.

confidence his own soldiery placed, not only in his courage and ability, but likewise in his fortitude and perseverance; and, conscious that a magnificent empire trembled in the scale, he determined not to fall short of the standard which he himself had set up.

When bowed down by the illness which followed his repulse at Montmorenci, he never thought of lightening his responsibility by calling a council of war to consider whether further efforts should be made; but, that valuable time might not be lost through his indisposition, he submitted three schemes of attack to the judgment of his Brigadiers. The Brigadiers, not pleased with any of them, proposed another scheme. It was not a new one, however, for it had been already conceived and discarded by Wolfe himself. This is evident from the dispatch to Mr. Pitt, wherein Wolfe represents that he had once thought of attempting a landing at St. Michael's about three miles above Quebec, but it seemed so hazardous that he judged it better to desist. Major Warburton's assertion, therefore, that "the merit of this daring and skilful proposition belongs to Colonel George Townshend, although long disputed, or withheld by jealousy, or political hostility," is erroneous.* Earl Stanhope more accurately remarks: "The honour of the first thought belongs to Wolfe alone; and once conceived, it was no less ably and nobly pursued."† But, seeing that the Brigadiers revived the scheme which allured Montcalm from his entrenchments, we cannot completely agree with the writer of the "Character of

* Conquest of Canada, chap. xxvi.

† 'History of England,' vol. iv. p. 243.

General Wolfe," in the 'Annual Register,' who says, "*Singly, and alone in opinion,* he formed and executed that great, that dangerous, yet necessary plan which drew out the French to their defeat." Concerning the skilfulness of the plan in a strictly military point of view, military men differ in opinion. The boldness, or perhaps rashness, and consequently the fitness of it for the emergency of the occasion, is possibly its best recommendation. Wolfe's merit, so far as relates to it, consists in his re-adopting it in deference to the unanimous judgment of his subordinates, and in carrying it out with all his mind, with all his heart, with all his might. What cared he about the honour of the plan? His object was neither present glory nor future fame, but to fulfil the expectations of his country.

Although Wolfe had had the nomination of his principal officers, the Hon. George Townshend was not the man he would have preferred for his second Brigadier. Walpole, who describes Townshend as being, so far as wrong-headedness went, very proper for a hero, says that he had thrust himself into the service;* and a letter of Townshend's to Mr. Pitt shows that he had been very desirous of military employment.† It is therefore probable that he was accepted by Wolfe on the recommendation of the Prime Minister, and not, like Monckton, Murray, Barré, Carleton, chosen from the General's personal experience of his worth. Indeed, Townshend's appointment was not confirmed until within a few days of sailing; and in the original draft of "Proposals for the Expedition of Quebec," the space for the name of the

* Letter to Mann, February 9, 1759.

† See Chatham Correspondence, vol. i. p. 345.

second Brigadier remains blank.* Walpole asserts that Townshend "did his utmost to traverse Wolfe's plans."† But in numerous instances Walpole's charges are too sweeping to be trustworthy, at least without considerable modification. Still, private letters from a very intelligent colonel in Wolfe's army prove that the Brigadier did cause some disquiet in the camp. In one written on the 8th of August, we read: "Townshend is well, but a *malcontent*. I meddle with no politics or party."

The Hon. George, eldest son of Viscount Townshend, and afterwards first Marquis of the name, was three years older than his commander. Though brave, talented, and not altogether devoid of good feeling, he was impatient of authority, and possessed in a remarkable degree the faculty of exaggerating the peculiarities of his superiors. In early life he had attached himself to the Duke of Cumberland, whose party he quitted for that of the Prince of Wales; and, retiring from the army, he gratified his spleen and amused his friends by ridiculing the Duke in caricatures, which, though gross, were exceedingly clever.‡ He had thus drawn on himself

* In the original document, amongst Lord Amherst's papers, twelve battalions, besides artillery, comprising altogether 12,005 men, are marked off for the expedition; and Colonel Burton's name appears as that of a fourth Brigadier's. The number of men having been reduced, but three Brigadier-Generals were appointed.

† Memoirs of the Reign of George III., vol i. p. 20.

‡ It appears that Townshend exercised his mischievous talent even in the camp; for it is related, in a compilation of military anecdotes, that, in ridicule of Wolfe's measures, he once made a sketch of the hero drawing lines of circumvallation round a disreputable building. The officers being assembled at mess, Townshend handed round the caricature, which, having at length reached Wolfe himself, he quietly put it into his pocket, saying, "If we live, this shall be inquired into; but we must first beat the enemy." (The Soldier's Companion.)

the resentment of his Royal Highness, to whom he was under many obligations, and had fallen into difficulties, from which he was extricated by the all-powerful patronage of Mr. Pitt.*

The Hon. Robert Monckton, second son of the first Viscount Galway, was a very different man. Liberal, straightforward, and modest, he was a perfect gentleman as well as a thorough soldier, and by his subsequent services proved himself no mean General. He had previously distinguished himself in America, and on account of his high character and his knowledge of the warfare, was selected by Wolfe himself for the post of senior Brigadier-General. The third Brigadier, the Hon. James Murray, son of the fourth Lord Elibank, whose intrepidity and zeal for the service Wolfe had discerned at Louisbourg, was likewise chosen by the General himself; and the high opinion which Wolfe entertained of Murray's courage and ability is evident from the fact that he singled him out for the most hazardous experiments of the campaign.

Rear-Admiral Holmes's squadron lying above Quebec, and every preparation having been made, on the morning of the 3rd of September Townshend's and Murray's brigades decamped from Montmorenci. Montcalm, anticipating such a movement from the stir in the British lines, marched two of his battalions towards the upper ford of the tributary, with the design of attacking Wolfe's

* Note, by Sir Denis Le Marchant, to Walpole's 'George III., vol. i. p. 20.

rear during the embarkation. But in consequence of a feint upon the Beauport shore by Monckton's brigade, the French detachment was recalled, and their adversaries were permitted to depart without molestation. While the boats were passing the Point of Orleans a smart fire of shells and shot was opened upon them from the enemy's camp; yet, without a single accident, they reached Point Levi, where the men landed. On the 4th, messengers arrived from General Amherst, whom they had left at Crown Point on the 8th of August. The intelligence gave Wolfe but faint hope of timely reinforcement. That night he was alarmingly ill, and his soldiers regretted lest he might not be able to lead the expected grand enterprise in person; but his re-appearance amongst them next day gladdened every eye and cheered every heart. On the following morning he ordered a corps of 600 men to proceed from Point Levi along the south shore, while sloops with a month's provisions sailed up the river; and on the 6th the main body received orders to march some distance above Quebec. After fording the Etchemin they made for a cove, where they embarked on board the men-of-war and transports under Rear-Admiral Holmes, who conveyed them to the anchorage off Cape Rouge. At night they were joined by the General, who next day, in the 'Hunter' sloop-of-war, reconnoitred so far westward as Point au Tremble. Returning on the 8th, he ordered 1500 men, commanded by Brigadiers Monckton and Murray, to be in readiness by the night tide for a feigned attack upon the north shore; but the weather continued so very wet for two days that the attempt was countermanded.

Such was the position when Wolfe wrote as follows to the Earl of Holderness, one of the principal Secretaries of State :—

On board the 'Sutherland,' at anchor off Cape Rouge,
September 9, 1759.

My Lord,

If the Marquis de Montcalm had shut himself up in the town of Quebec, it would have been long since in our possession, because the defences are inconsiderable, and our artillery very formidable; but he has a numerous body of armed men (I cannot call it an army), and the strongest country, perhaps, in the world, to rest the defence of the town and colony upon. The ten battalions and the Grenadiers of Louisbourg are a chosen body of troops, and able to fight the united force of Canada upon even terms. Our field artillery brought into use would terrify the Militia and the savages, and our battalions are in every respect superior to those commanded by the Marquis, who acts a circumspect, prudent part, and entirely defensive, except in one extraordinary instance,—he sent 1600 men over the river to attack our batteries upon the Point Levi, defended by four battalions. Bad intelligence, no doubt, of our strength induced him to this measure; however, the detachment judged better than their General, and retired. They dispute the water with the boats of the fleet by the means of floating batteries, suited to the nature of the river, and innumerable battoes. They have a great artillery upon the ramparts towards the sea, and so placed that shipping cannot affect it. I meant to attack the left of their entrenchments, favoured by our artillery, the 31st July. A multitude of traverses prevented, in some measure, its effect, which was nevertheless very considerable. Accidents hindered the attack, and the enemy's care to strengthen that post has made it since too hazardous. The town is totally demolished, and the country in a great measure ruined, particularly the Lower Canada. Our fleet blocks up the river, both above and below the town, but can give no manner of assistance in an attack upon the Canadian army. We have continual skirmishes; old people seventy years of age, and boys of fifteen fire on our detachments, and kill or wound our men from the edges of the woods. Every man able to bear arms, both above and below Quebec, is in the camp at Beauport. The old men, women, and children are retired into the woods. The Canadians are extremely dissatisfied; but, curbed by the force of the Government, and terrified by the savages that are posted round about them, they are obliged to keep together to work and man the entrenchments.

Upwards of twenty sail of ships got in before our squadron, and brought succours of all sorts, which were exceedingly wanted in the colony. The sailors of these ships help to work the guns, and others conduct the floating batteries. Their ships are lightened, and carried up the river out of our reach—at least out of the reach of the men-of-war. These ships serve a double purpose; they are magazines for their provisions, and at the same time cut off all communication between General Amherst's army and the corps under my command, so that we are not able to make any detachment to attack Montreal, or favour the junction, or, by attacking the fort of Chambly or Boulemarque's corps behind, open the General's way into Canada,—all which might have been easily done with ten floating batteries, carrying each a gun, and twenty flat-bottomed boats, if there had been no ships in the river. Our poor soldiery have worked without ceasing, and without murmuring; and as often as the enemy have attempted upon us, they have been repulsed by the valour of the men. A woody country, so well known to the enemy, and an enemy so vigilant and hardy as the Indians and Canadians are, make entrenchments everywhere necessary, and by this precaution we have saved a number of lives; for scarce a night passes that they are not close in upon our posts, watching an opportunity to surprise and murder. There is very little quarter given on either side.

We have seven hours, and sometimes,—above the town after rain,—near eight hours of the most violent ebb tide that can be imagined, which loses us an infinite deal of time in every operation on the water; and the stream is so strong, particularly here, that the ships often drag their anchors by the mere force of the current. The bottom is a bed of rock, so that a ship, unless it hooks a ragged rock, holds by the weight only of the anchor. Doubtless, if the equinoctial gale has any force, a number of ships must necessarily run ashore and be lost. The day after the troops landed upon the Isle of Orleans, a violent storm had nigh ruined the expedition altogether. Numbers of boats were lost; all the whaleboats and most of the cutters were stove; some flat-bottomed boats destroyed, and others damaged. We never had half as many of the latter as are necessary for this extraordinary and very important service. The enemy is able to fight us upon the water whenever we are out of the reach of the cannon of the fleet.

The extreme heat of the weather in August, and a good deal of fatigue, threw me into a fever; but that the business might go on, I begged the Generals to consider amongst themselves what was fittest to be done. Their sentiments were unanimous, that, as the easterly winds begin to blow, and ships can pass the town in the night with provisions, artillery, etc., we should endeavour, by conveying a considerable corps into the upper river, to draw them from their inaccessible situation, and bring them to an action. I agreed to the proposal, and we are now here, with about 3600 men, waiting an opportunity to attack them when and wherever they can best be got at. The weather has been extremely unfavourable for a day or two, so that we have been inactive. I am so far recovered as to do business, but my constitution is entirely ruined, without the consolation of having done any considerable service to the State, or without any prospect of it.

I have the honour to be, etc.,

JAM: WOLFE.*

Cape Rouge, off which the 'Sutherland' now lay,

* From Chatham Correspondence.

about eight miles above Quebec, is the western point of an oblong tongue of high land, bounded on the east by the river St. Charles, on the west by the valley of Carouge, and on the south by the St. Lawrence. After attaining a sudden rise of about 100 feet at the Coteau St. Geneviève to the north, the elevation gradually increases, until, at the summit of Cape Diamond, it attains an altitude of 345 feet,—"rising above the general level like an island above the surface of the ocean."* On the eastern point of this promontory stands the city of Quebec, below which is the magnificent basin, that, at a distance of 360 miles from the sea, is capable of sheltering several fleets; while above the town and the opposite Point of Levi, the St. Lawrence, after flowing for some miles between lofty and almost perpendicular cliffs, is contracted to a width of 1300 yards. Towards the water-side the approach to the city was then defended by a port, flanked by bastions which at high tide were washed by the river. Above these was another bastion, cut in the rock; still higher, a battery of twenty-five guns; and over all, the citadel from which waved the Bourbon banner. To the left of the port, along the road bordering the *embouchure* of the St. Charles, were several cannon and mortar batteries, and similar works defended the western shore of the Lower Town.† The avenue of communication between the Lower and the Upper Town, by the steep and winding way now known as Mountain Street, was also strongly protected.

After the fur trade had proved profitable enough to

* Bouchette, 'British Dominions in North America.'

† Charlevoix, 'Histoire de la Nouvelle France.'

induce the merchants of France to maintain their property in the country, the prime object of the French settlement in Canada was, by means of the priesthood, to acquire predominance in the American continent. The missionaries, by their attention to the temporal as well as the spiritual wants of the aborigines, in time gained ascendency over them. But while the savages became nominally christianized, many of the *habitans*, through intercourse with them, became much more effectually brutalized; hence those border raids upon the British provinces which made Canada the great field of battle between France and England, and Quebec the place whose fall was to dissolve the whole system of French colonial empire. The French policy so influenced even the character of the buildings, that the only permanent structures were those for either religious or warlike purposes. To this cause, no less than to the inequality of the surface, is attributable the irregularity of the city. The extensive space within the walls was chiefly occupied by convents, hospitals, and palaces, each of which had a large garden; so that the humbler residents, who were drawn thither by the protection of the fort and the vicinity of the churches, were obliged to erect their small and fragile houses in the intervals between the religious buildings. The old fortress, or castle of St. Louis, reached from where Prescott Gate now stands to the edge of the declivity, and the various magazines and Government edifices, together with the ground reserved for military use, filled up the remaining space within the ramparts.*

* Hawkins's 'Picture of Quebec.'

Westward of the city lies the elevated table-land called the Plains or Heights of Abraham,—the only place where the nature of the country, and the interposition of Montcalm's entrenched army, had left the stronghold vulnerable. These heights are from 200 to 250 feet above the level of the St. Lawrence; and as the cliffs, which must be ascended in order to reach them, were considered inaccessible, they were only lined by a few posts for the purpose of watching the movements of the invaders. After Wolfe had decamped from Montmorenci, Montcalm sent Bougainville, with a detachment of 1500 men, up the left bank of the river; but, deceived by Rear-Admiral Holmes's manœuvres, and fearing he would attack the French ships in the Batiscan, to which tributary they had retired, Bougainville marched thither. Meanwhile Wolfe, having reconnoitred every inch of the rocky barrier he had resolved to climb, at length pitched upon a spot for the ascent, about a mile nearer to Quebec than St. Michael's, and now known as Wolfe's Cove, but then bearing the name of *L'Anse du Foulon*.

The 48th, or Webb's Regiment, still remaining at Point Levi, the General wrote the following letter to the commander of the corps—Colonel Burton:—

Dear Colonel,

You perfectly understood my meaning in every particular. Goreham's first post is under the point of a hill, where there is a little road running from Dalling's old quarter up to the river; the way down is very steep, but I believe the troops can march at low water all along the beach from the Point of Levi. I think it is not above a mile and a half, or two miles, from our batteries. The deserter's intelligence in respect to Mons. de Vaudreuil's movements agrees in part with our observations; but it is absolutely impossible that the Marquis can have so large a corps; I don't believe their whole army amounts to that number. That De Levi may be gone towards Montreal is likely enough, and seems to mark our General's progress: the more necessity for vigour on our side to second his endeavours.

Sixteen hundred of our men are upon the south shore, to clean and refresh themselves and their transports; and, indeed, to save the whole army, which must have perished if they had continued forty-eight hours longer on board. To-morrow the troops re-embark, the fleet sails up the river a little higher, as if intending to land above upon the north shore, keeping a convenient distance for the boats and armed vessels to fall down to the *Foulon;* and we count (if no accident of weather or other prevents) to make a powerful effort at that spot about *four* in the morning of the 13th. At ten or eleven, or twelve at night, sooner or later, as it may be necessary, of Wednesday, the 12th, we get into our boats. If we are forced to alter these measures, you shall know it; if not, it stands fixed: be you careful not to drop it to any, for fear of desertion; and it would not be amiss for Carleton to pass his troops [from Orleans] in the beginning of Wednesday night. Crofton can file along the shore to his right, and meet you at the post you take; let the men have their blankets, and let the tents be struck, bundled up, and ready to bring over. If we succeed in the first business, it may produce an action, which may produce the total conquest of Canada; in all cases it is our duty to try the most likely way, whatever may be the event.

What the deserter says of the bread made of new wheat is exactly what has been told me by other deserters, and I believe the scarcity in the colony to be excessive. Their army is kept together by the violent strong hand of the Government and by the terror of savages, joined to a situation which makes it difficult to evade. The Canadians have no affection for their Government, nor no tie so strong as their wives and children; they are a disjointed, discontented, dispirited peasantry, beat into cowardice by Cadet, Bigot, Montcalm, and the savages.

Yours affectionately,
J. Wolfe.*

'Sutherland,' above Carouge.
Monday, Sept. 10, 1759.

The General's plans were all by this time formed, yet he took no rest. He reconnoitred on the river and on the land. He also inspected every one of the ships and transports, looking after the health and comfort of his soldiers. Nor did he consider that the officers needed not his attention. Finding that two subalterns of the 43rd were indisposed, he expressed the greatest tenderness and good-nature towards them; and, desiring they would not remain on board, offered to lend them his own barge, in which they might go to Goreham's post, and thence have an escort to Point Levi. But, gratefully acknowledging his condescension and kindness, they assured their chief that no consideration whatever would induce them to quit their posts until they had seen the end of the enterprise. A captain of the regiment happening subsequently to inquire of another after the health of one of these gentlemen, was informed that he was very poorly, and had but a puny, delicate constitution. Wolfe, who was nigh, reminded probably of his own condition, interrupted them by saying, "Don't tell me of constitution; that gentleman has a good spirit, and spirit will carry a man through everything."† On the 11th, the General issued the following orders:—

The troops on shore, except the Light Infantry and Ame-

* European Magazine, vol. xiii. 1788.

† Knox's Journal, vol. ii. p. 61.

ricans, are to be upon the beach to-morrow morning at five o'clock, in readiness to embark; the Light Infantry and Americans will re-embark at or about eight o'clock. The army to hold themselves in readiness to land and attack the enemy. . . . The troops must go into the boats about nine to-morrow night, or when it is pretty near high-water. . . . As there will be a necessity for remaining some part of the night in the boats, the officers will provide accordingly. When the boats are to drop away from the 'Sutherland,' she will show two lights in the maintopmast shrouds, one over the other. The men are to be quite silent, and when they are about to land must not upon any account fire out of the boats. The officers of the Navy are not to be interrupted in their part of the duty; they will receive their orders from the proper officer appointed to superintend the whole, to whom they are answerable. The frigates are not to fire till broad daylight; so that no mistake can be made.

Although thus informed that the decisive blow was at hand, the men were kept in ignorance of the particulars, which were disclosed to the commanding officers only. The precaution was fortunate, for one of the Royal Americans, who deserted on the morning of the 12th, had it not in his power to tell the enemy where their danger lay; while a French deserter had informed Wolfe that Montcalm still remained within his entrenchments, that De Levi had marched with a large detachment towards Montreal, and that Bougainville was watching the movements of the fleet in the Upper River. The same afternoon Wolfe issued his last "general orders:"—

On board His Majesty's ship 'Sutherland,'
September 12, 1759.

The enemy's force is now divided; great scarcity of provisions is in their camp, and universal discontent among the

Canadians. The second officer in command is gone to Montreal, or St. John's, which gives reason to think that General Amherst is advancing into the colony. A vigorous blow struck by the army at this juncture may determine the fate of Canada. Our troops below are in readiness to join us; all the light artillery and tools are embarked at Point Levi, and the troops will land where the French seem least to expect it.

The first body that gets on shore is to march directly to the enemy, and drive them from any little post they may occupy. The officers must be careful that the succeeding bodies do not by any mistake fire upon those who go before them. The battalions must form on the upper ground with expedition, and be ready to charge whatever presents itself. When the artillery and troops are landed, a corps will be left to secure the landing-place, while the rest march on, and endeavour to bring the French and Canadians to a battle. The officers and men will remember what their country expects from them, and what a determined body of soldiers, inured to war, is capable of doing against five weak French battalions mingled with disorderly peasantry. The soldiers must be attentive and obedient to their officers, and the officers resolute in the execution of their duty.

An old bacchanalian ditty,—"How stands the glass around?"—commonly known as "General Wolfe's song," is said to have been written and sung by the hero on the night preceding the battle of Quebec. Unfortunately for the truth of the tradition, not only the music but the words are of older date.* Neither does there

* The words were printed in 1710, and the melody, according to Sir Henry Bishop, "bears so strong a resemblance to the tune of 'Why, Soldiers, why,' a song popular in the earlier part of the last century, as to render it very probable that the few alterations which it contains were chiefly made to suit the metre and sentiment of the words beginning 'How stands the glass around?'" (See 'Illustrated London News,' January 24, 1852.) Most probably the re-arrangement was a speculation of some enterprising musicseller, who, to suit the times, published it as "General Wolfe's Song," just as one Vaughan advertised

exist a particle of evidence—at least, that we are aware of—to prove that Wolfe so much as sang the song at a farewell carouse with his officers; on the contrary, it appears that he was otherwise occupied on the eve of his last day upon earth. In the fleet was a young officer, who, though then of little note, afterwards became the renowned Admiral, Earl St. Vincent. John Jervis, as Commander of the 'Porcupine' sloop-of-war, had, a few weeks previously, saved the General from either captivity or death. In one of his passages up the river, Wolfe happened to sail in the 'Porcupine.' While passing the batteries of the Lower Town, the wind dying away, the sloop was carried by the current towards the hostile shore. The French gunners, perceiving her helplessness, cannonaded her; but Jervis, instantly seeing what he ought to do, hoisted out his boats, and cheered his sailors, who, in the midst of the fire, towed the vessel out of the reach of danger. This circumstance naturally confirmed Wolfe's confidence in his old schoolfellow, and may have induced him to repose in Jervis his last sacred trust. On the evening of the 12th he invited the young Commander to spend an hour or two with him in his private cabin aboard the 'Sutherland.' Wolfe, in the course of their conversation, said that he knew by presentiment he should not survive the morrow; and when they were about to separate, he took from his bosom the picture of Miss Lowther, and deli-

"Map-fans of America, showing the exact situation of Crown Point, Niagara, and Quebec, lately conquered. . . . Very useful and entertaining, especially during the time of war." ('Public Advertiser,' Thursday, October 18, 1759.)

vered it into the hands of his friend, whom he requested, should the foreboding be fulfilled, to restore the pledge to the lady, on his arrival in England. Jervis accepted the charge, so they bade one another farewell.* Wolfe had already made his will, to which he now added a codicil, disposing of his effects in America. His regard for his naval colleague is shown by the bequest of his plate to Admiral Saunders; while to Brigadier Monckton he bequeathed his camp equipage; and to Colonel Carleton, his books and papers.

In pursuance of an arrangement between the Admiral and the General, a little before sunset the ships of the line, which still remained in the basin, moved as close as the depth of water allowed to the Beauport shore. Their boats were then lowered, manned with sailors and Marines, and ranged in order as if about to make a descent; while the lighter ships set sail, and, sweeping past the batteries of Quebec, joined the squadron off Cape Rouge. Immediately after nightfall detachments from the Isle of Orleans and Point Levi marched rapidly up the right bank of the St. Lawrence, and, unperceived by the

* Tucker's 'Memoirs of John Jervis, Earl St. Vincent.' Mr. Tucker erroneously adds,—"Commander Jervis had the most painful duty of delivering the pledge to Miss Lowther." But the following passage in a note written by one of the General's aides-de-camp to Mrs. Wolfe on the 24th of November, 1759, proves otherwise:—"Captain Bell hopes the will, codicil, little notes, *and the picture*, got safe into Mrs. Wolfe's hands." It will presently appear that the picture was that of Miss Lowther. Wolfe may have entrusted it to Jervis in preference to Colonel Carleton, because Carleton ran the same risk as himself, whereas Jervis was not engaged in the battle. And when the General's undisposed-of effects were about to be carried to England, Jervis, by desire of Colonel Carleton, one of Wolfe's executors, delivered the miniature to Captain Bell.

enemy, arrived opposite to Cape Rouge, where, taking boat, they joined the assembled army.

At midnight, a light being shown by the 'Sutherland,' the first division entered flat-bottomed boats, which, as they were filled, repaired to the rendezvous. They were then ranged in a line, the Light Infantry in the van, the other corps by seniority, and at two o'clock the signal for proceeding being given, the General's barge took the lead, and the rest followed in order. The oarsmen, assisted by the ebbing tide, rowed as gently as possible close by the north bank; and while the soldiers sat silent and motionless, the flotilla dropped swiftly down the river. The night was calm, but dark. As in death-like stillness they were borne along, Wolfe, in whispers only audible to the officers who accompanied him, repeated Gray's 'Elegy.' With thoughts of his betrothed and of his mother, and impressed by the foreboding of which he told Jervis, his feelings may be imagined as he recited the lines:—

"The boast of heraldry, the pomp of power,
And all that beauty, all that wealth e'er gave,
Await alike th' inevitable hour.
The paths of glory lead but to the grave."

When, in the poet's words, he had spoken of his merits and his frailties alike in trembling hope, reposing in the bosom of his Father and his God, "Now, gentlemen," he added, in a low, but earnestly emphatic tone, "I would rather be the author of that piece than take Quebec."* But Wolfe was not the man to let his feel-

* This anecdote, which is recorded in the Transactions of the Royal Society of Edinburgh, rests upon the indisputable authority of Professor Robinson, who had been a midshipman in Admiral Saunders's

ings prevail over his sense of duty. As he was carried along the base of the dark precipice, guided only by the glimmering of a few stars, he watched for the landmarks which in his reconnoitres he had mapped in his mind; for, as he told Rickson, nature had given him good eyes and a warmth of temper to follow first impressions.

Four-and-twenty officers and men of the Light Infantry corps, under Captain Delaune, volunteered to precede the first division. The enemy had a line of posts extending from the Lower Town for some distance along the beach. The volunteers passed two of them unnoticed, but as they were about to land, they were challenged. An English Captain, who spoke French, instantly replied in a low voice, "La France." The sentinel inquiring "A quel régiment?" the Captain, who fortunately knew that the Queen's battalion formed part of Bougainville's detachment, answered, "De la Reine," when they were allowed to pass. But presently another soldier of the guard, whose suspicion was excited by the subdued tone in which the English officer spoke, asked him why he did not speak louder. "Hush!" said the Captain, "we may be heard by the enemy in the river:" the 'Hunter' lying not far off.* Meanwhile, the main body of Light Infantry

fleet. (The circumstances under which he served in the Royal Navy may be found in Chambers's 'Eminent Scotchmen.') It was related by the Professor, in the year 1804, to Mr. William Wallace Currie, who published it in his Life of his father, Dr. James Currie; and was also communicated by the Professor's son to Dr. Grahame, who has printed it in his 'History of the United States of North America.' The two narrations do not completely accord; Dr. Grahame's, being the clearest, is the one more approximately followed above.

* It is difficult to reconcile the various statements of officers. Cap-

who were carried by the current a little below the cove, landed, and, following the volunteers, began to climb the cliff, when the commander of the post, who had been called out, ordered his men to fire upon them. But by this time the whole corps, grasping crags and the stumps and boughs of the stunted trees that found root in the crevices of the rock, were halfway up.

L'Anse du Foulon, the spot Wolfe had pitched upon for the general landing, is a little basin, formed by two projections, with a narrow margin of dry ground from which the curved precipice rises almost vertically 250 feet. There was a winding path leading to the heights, but so strait that two men could barely ascend it abreast.* This track, moreover, was entrenched, and

tain Knox, who is generally accurate, represents the *ruse* to have been played on the guard above, and says that Captain M'Donald, of "Frazer's," told the sentinel he was sent there with a large command to take post, ordering him, at the same time, to go and call off all the other men of his party, for he would engage to give a good account of the English, should they persist. "This *finesse*," continues Knox, "had the desired effect, and saved many lives." On the other hand, the writer of 'Particular Transactions' describes the scene as on the beach, and makes Captain *Frazer* add,—"We are the provision boats from Montreal, etc." (See 'Notes and Queries,' 2nd series, vol. viii.) It is hard to conceive, however, that the garrison should expect provisions by water, when the river was blocked up by Holmes's squadron. This writer likewise states that the captain of the 'Hunter,' not having been apprised of their coming down, mistook the boats for the enemy's.' But the assertion, and an anecdote founded upon it, are refuted by Wolfe's general orders of the 11th.

* Admiral Saunders's dispatch, "September 20th." The Admiral adds,—"Considering the darkness of the night and the rapidity of the current, this was a very critical operation, and very properly and successfully executed. When General Wolfe and the troops with him had landed, the difficulty of gaining the top of the hill is scarce credible."

at top defended by a captain's guard. The first division having landed, some of the men ascended by this way, the rest as best they could. Wolfe, who was one of the foremost on shore, when he stood at the foot of the acclivity, is said to have remarked to Captain M'Donald, of Frazer's Highlanders, "There seems scarcely a possibility of getting up, but you must do your endeavours." Before the van had reached the top, the rustling they made amongst the rocks warned the French guard of their approach, and the officer in command of the post ordered his men to fire down the precipice. But the British troops, whom neither darkness nor danger could daunt, having surmounted every obstacle, discharged their pieces as they gained the heights, and put the picquet to flight. Captain de Vergor, who alone stood his ground, after firing at the officer who led on the assailants, was taken prisoner; and the men who captured him, as a punishment for what they thought an unfair act, cut off his cross of St. Louis. When the brigades under Wolfe, Monckton, and Murray had landed, the boats rowed back until they met the squadron commanded by Rear-Admiral Holmes, who, in order to cover the debarkation, sailed down the river about an hour after the starting of the first division. The second division, under Brigadier Townshend, then entering the boats, soon reached the cove, and, after forming on the beach, ascended the path, from which every obstruction had been removed.

Wolfe's joy when, as day dawned on the 13th of September, he found himself upon the Heights of Abraham, may easily be conceived. He had run a frightful risk;

for, had the precipice been properly defended, his whole army must have been sacrificed. But he had the courage to dare as well as the genius to contrive; and he well knew that to achieve a great action he must transgress ordinary rules. After nearly three weary months, the object of his solicitude lay before him. The hazard surmounted with little loss, but one wish remained to be fulfilled—that Montcalm would meet him in the field. Of the result he had no doubt. The triumph he had so long sought for was now at hand. Before the walls of her great American stronghold he hoped that day to wrest Canada from the grasp of France, and establish the supremacy of the Saxon race in the Western World. Yet, with thoughts like these, and notwithstanding the cares and duties of his commandership, he could act the part of the Good Samaritan; for his was a noble nature: his feelings were as tender as his spirit was ardent. Sir Denis Le Marchant relates the following anecdote:—"We recollect a respectable veteran, who, after having served under him at Louisbourg, commanded one of the first detachments that scaled the Heights of Abraham. In that exploit Captain —— was shot through the lungs. On recovering his senses, he saw Wolfe standing by his side. Amidst the anxieties of such a critical hour the General stopped to press the hand of the wounded man; praised his services; encouraged him not to abandon the hope of life; assured him of leave of absence and early promotion; nay more, he desired an aide-de-camp to give a message to that effect to General Monckton should he himself fall in the action; and, to the credit of General Monckton, the promise was kept. No wonder that these qualities, coupled with his brilliant success, won the hearts of the soldiery."*

The Light Infantry, under Lieut.-Colonel Howe, had routed every picquet and taken possession of a four-gun redoubt; all was quiet; not a shot was heard when Townshend's brigade joined their companions on the heights. Wolfe's little army, which, excluding the small detachments that kept possession of the Isle of Orleans and Point Levi, numbered but 4826 of all ranks, was then formed by the Brigadiers, with their right towards Quebec, the left to Sillery, and the rear to the river. Each man had seventy rounds of ammunition; but, one gun only could, with great labour, be trailed up the cliff. In this position they remained for a short time, while the General surveyed the ground. They then faced to the right, and marched in files towards the city, until they came to the Plains of Abraham, where they were ordered to halt. It was now clear daylight; the weather showery.

Montcalm, who fancied that the demonstrations by the great ships in the basin were preparatory to a general descent upon Beauport, little imagined that a grand struggle awaited him in a different quarter. During the night he had taken every precaution against the attack which he expected upon his entrenched line between the rivers St. Charles and Montmorenci. When, therefore, soon after daybreak, the disconcerted picquets fled to his camp with intelligence that the whole English army was established on the heights westward of Quebec, he was

* Walpole's 'Memoirs of the Reign of George III.,' edited by Sir D. Le Marchant, Bart., vol. i. p. 22, note.

utterly incredulous. "It is but a small party come to burn a few houses and retire," said he. But when other fugitives confirmed the alarming report, he ascended an eminence, and beholding the enemy, admitted,—"Yes, I see them where they ought not to be." Conscious that the English fleet and army were now so situated that the Lower and Upper Towns might be simultaneously assaulted, and that nothing but a battle could save Quebec, he immediately dispatched bodies of Indians and Canadians to keep the adversary in play until he should have made his dispositions. He then summoned Bougainville to his assistance, and, leaving the Governor-General with 1500 men to defend the camp, assembled the flower of his army, saying, "Since they have got to the weak side of this miserable garrison, we must give battle, and crush them before midday."

When, about six o'clock, the first detachments of irregulars began to make their appearance, Wolfe formed his army in order of battle. The right of his first line, which extended to the brow of the declivity, consisted of the 35th (Otway's), the Louisbourg Grenadiers, and the 28th (Bragg's); the 43rd (Kennedy's), with the 47th (Lascelles') formed the centre; while on the left the 78th (Frazer's) and 58th (Anstruther's) prolonged the line to the ridge overlooking the valley of the St. Charles. Wolfe in person commanded the right, Monckton the centre, and Murray the left. The second line, comprising the 15th (Amherst's) and two battalions of the 60th (Monckton's), was under the command of Townshend; Colonel Burton with the 48th (Webb's), in eight subdivisions with large intervals, formed the reserve; and the Light Infantry, under Colonel Howe, covered the rear. The battle-field presented nearly a level surface, without fence or enclosure, but was dotted with bushes and shrubs, and flanked by woods and coppices, which afforded shelter to the Indian and Canadian marksmen. The *Grande Allée*, or road to Cape Rouge, ran through the centre of the plain; and perhaps, on the whole, no site could have been better adapted for the display of military discipline and skill, or for the exercise of resolute valour.*

Montcalm, as fast as he could muster his battalions, hurried them over the bridge across the St. Charles. They marched in one line up the hill and by the northern ramparts of the city, until they came within reconnoitring distance, when they halted, while a body of irregulars advanced under the western wall, and three field-pieces were got into position. Then, wheeling back from the centre, under cover of their cannon, they formed into three powerful columns. That to the right consisted of one-half the colony troops, supported by the battalions of La Saare and Languedoc; the centre comprised the battalions of Béarn and Guienne; and the left was composed of the remainder of the colony troops and the Royal Roussillon Regiment. Altogether 7520 men, besides Indians. About eight o'clock their guns opened upon the English, who, however, suffered much more from the fire of a band of savages concealed in a cornfield opposite the right wing, until Colonel Hale, by Monckton's order, sent some platoons to drive them away. To counteract an attempt of the French to out-

* Hawkins, 'Picture of Quebec.'

flank the left of the British line, Wolfe ordered Townshend to form the 15th *en potence*, so as to present a double front to the enemy, when Montcalm, frustrated in his design, occupied the ground between the ramparts of the city and the hostile army. Wolfe then desired his men to lie down. In this position they remained until nine o'clock, when Montcalm moved his columns a little forward. About an hour later, the French, with loud shouts, advanced rapidly while they fired obliquely towards the extremities of the English line. Not a shot was returned by Wolfe's men until their assailants had come within a distance of forty yards, when they levelled and fired a volley with such precision and deadly effect that the Canadians, unaccustomed to fire in the field, became thoroughly disordered.*

Before the smoke cleared away the English had reloaded, when Wolfe, placing himself at the head of the Louisbourg Grenadiers and the 28th, led them on so far as to make the enemy feel bullets and bayonets almost at the same moment.† He had already been shot in the wrist, but, wrapping his handkerchief round the wound, continued to lead on and cheer his followers. His bright uniform rendering him the more conspicuous while he exposed himself in the front of his Grenadiers, some Canadian marksmen on the enemy's left singled him out for destruction.‡ He had just given his order for the

* "Well might the French officers say," writes Knox, "they never opposed such a shock as they received from the centre of our line, for they believed that every ball took effect, and such regularity and discipline they had never before experienced, our troops having levelled and fired *comme un coup de canon*." (Journal, vol. ii. p. 70.)

† Letter from an English officer, 'Scots Magazine,' 1759, p. 552.

‡ It is related that Wolfe was shot by one of his own men, a sergeant,

whole British line to charge, when he was again dangerously wounded; but, acting up to his own words,—"while a man is able to do his duty, and can stand and hold his arms, it is infamous to retire,"*—in spite of pain and weakness, he still persevered. Although not more than fifteen minutes had elapsed since the first charge of the French, the battle was now virtually decided. De Senezergues, the second in command, had fallen mortally maimed, and the officer next in rank, the Baron de St. Ours, had been killed. Such of the terrified Canadians as survived the slaughter, and were able to run, fled from the field; while all that remained of the veteran battalions of France could hardly be induced to prolong the struggle, although Montcalm rode through their broken ranks, and made every effort to re-encou-

whom he had reduced to the ranks for striking a soldier. The man, it is said, in consequence of the punishment, deserted to the enemy, and was one of those who made the English General their aim. It further appears, that after the battle the deserter was sent to Crown Point, which fort being soon afterwards captured by the British army, he was condemned to die for desertion; and shortly before he was hanged, he confessed that he was one of those who fired at Wolfe. "This account," adds Sir William Musgrave, "was had from a gentleman who heard the confession." (Additional MSS. 5723, British Museum; see also Hone's 'Table Book,' vol. iii., and 'Notes and Queries,' vol. vii. 1853.) The story is not impossible, nor indeed altogether improbable, for Wolfe was the very man to degrade a sergeant for maltreating a soldier. Yet it is equally probable that a culprit already doomed might think to make himself famous, though as the murderer of Wolfe; just as one man sought fame by burning a library, and another by smashing the Portland Vase. Captain Knox, the most trustworthy chronicler of the campaign, who was himself upon the spot, says nothing in relation to the subject, beyond noting that on the 1st of August a sergeant of one of the regiments in the north camp deserted, and took his company's orderly book with him. (Journal, vol. ii. p. 3.)

* "Instructions for the 20th Regiment in case the French land." (1755.)

rage them. But in vain. They could not withstand the bayonets and musketry of the English infantry; and when Montcalm himself fell, they gave way in every direction.

Not long ere this Wolfe had received a third and mortal wound in the breast. When no longer able to stand, his only concern was lest his men should be disheartened by his fall. "Support me," he whispered to an officer near him; "let not my brave soldiers see me drop. The day is ours—keep it!"* He was then carried to the rear. When an aide-de-camp came to inform Monckton that he commanded, the gallant Brigadier was found incapacitated by a severe wound, which he had received while leading on Lascelles', whereupon the command devolved upon Townshend. Meanwhile, the Highlanders chased some of the fugitives to the verge of the St. Charles, and the 58th followed others to St. John's gate. A gun, which a few of the enemy who still stood their ground brought to bear, checked the progress of the regiments on the right, who were pursuing with like ardour. Another body of the enemy made a stand in a coppice, as if willing to renew the action, but a few platoons from Bragg's and Kennedy's completed the victory. Townshend, then assuming the command, recalled the pursuers, and ordered the whole line to dress and resume their former ground. By this time the weather, which had been lowering, cleared up with warm sunshine. No sooner had the English reassembled than Bougainville's detachment was seen advancing. Two battalions, however, sufficed to make him retrace

* 'Gentleman's Magazine,' 1759, p. 496.

his steps to Cape Rouge. De Vandreuil, with his 1500 Canadians, immediately deserted the entrenched camp. Leaving artillery, ammunition, and stores behind, he made for Montreal; and Quebec was without defence, beyond what the small garrison and the walls afforded.

After Wolfe was borne from the field, when those who attended him had reached a small redoubt that had been captured early in the morning, he desired them to lay him down. An officer having proposed to send for a surgeon, he replied, "It is needless; it is all over with me." The mourning group thought their beloved commander was already lifeless, when the cry was heard, "They run—they run!" Like one suddenly aroused from heavy sleep, Wolfe demanded, with great earnestness, "Who—who run?" "The enemy, Sir," he was answered; "they give way everywhere." Thereupon the expiring hero, summoning all his fleeting strength, rejoined, "Go, one of you, my lads, to Colonel Burton; tell him to march Webb's regiment with all speed down to Charles river, to cut off the retreat of the fugitives from the bridge." He then turned upon his side, and his last words were—"Now God be praised; I die in peace!"* Thus, in his three-and-thirtieth year, died—

> "Wolfe, upon the lap
> Of smiling Victory that moment won."

* Knox, 'Journal of Campaigns,' etc. London, 1769. Captain Knox appends the following note:—"Various accounts have been circulated of General Wolfe's manner of dying, his last words, and the officers into whose hands he fell; and many, from a vanity of talking, claimed the honour of being his supporters after he was wounded. But the foregoing circumstances were ascertained to me by Lieutenant Brown, of the Grenadiers of Louisbourg and the 22nd regiment, who, with Mr.

Henderson, a volunteer in the same company, and a private man, were the three persons who carried his Excellency to the rear, which an artillery officer seeing, immediately flew to his assistance; and these were all that attended him in his dying moments. I do not recollect the artillery officer's name, or it should be recorded here." Captain Knox's text may be accepted without hesitation, since he could not have invented the command for a particular corps to follow the fugitives, and since also his statement was made on the authority of an eye-witness, with the intention of correcting previous mis-statements. On the other hand, I have been favoured with a copy of a letter, written in 1803 by the centenarian Thomas Wilkins, who states that he was the only surgeon on the field of battle; that he was speaking to Wolfe about ten minutes before he received his mortal wound; and that the hero's "last and dying words were, 'Lay me down, I am suffocating.'" It is needless to particularize the various other persons who, either from the "vanity of talking," or the more pardonable desire of being associated with Wolfe, have asserted that they carried him from the field, or were present at his death.

CONCLUSION.

The Battle of Quebec is one of the most remarkable on record. Whether we consider the value of the stake, the consequences to which the victory led, the loss of the two first Generals of their time, the almost insuperable obstacles overcome by Wolfe, or the grandeur of the site high over the great river, we cannot but wonder and admire. Nor does the smallness of the opposing powers lessen the interest of the story. When we read of the unwieldy masses now contending in America without any telling result, of cannon, shells, rifles, such as were undreamt of by Marlborough, Wolfe, or Wellington, yet perfectly indecisive in effect, we lose all sympathy with the combatants, and regard them as mere machines; while a man-to-man conflict, like that of the Plains of Abraham, inspires us with personal feelings akin to those we should have for duellists.

In a military aspect, the Battle of Quebec was one of the most regular battles ever fought. The issue was determined by the superiority of the English to their more numerous enemy in unity, discipline, and prowess. This was acknowledged by Montcalm himself, who, at the point of death, declared,—"Since it is my misfortune to be discomfited and mortally wounded, it is a great consolation to me to be vanquished by so brave an enemy. If I could survive, I would engage to beat three times the number of such forces as I commanded with a third of British troops." Whether the defeated hero meant it so or not, he could not have paid a higher compliment to the General who had brought his little army to such perfection. The English, led by one whom they obeyed with confidence and love, and elated by the success of their morning's enterprise, were full of fearless ardour. The death of their chief, whose spirit still survived, instead of enervating them, only added to their enthusiasm. Amongst the Highlanders especially it was so. An officer wrote home on the 20th of September:—"Our loss has been inconsiderable, separate from our dear, courageous, yet mild Wolfe, whose fall added revenge to intrepidity. The regiment of Lascelles, Kennedy's, and Wolfe's Grenadiers did wonders; the Highlanders, if anything, exceeded them. When they betook to their broad-swords, what havoc they made! drove everything before them that came in their way, and walls could not resist their fury!"*

* 'Public Advertiser,' Tuesday, October 23, 1759. Mr. Pitt, following the liberal policy he had determined to pursue in relation to Scotland, in 1757 prevailed upon George II. to appoint the Hon. Simon Frazer, son of Lord Lovat, colonel of a regiment to be raised amongst his clan. Such was the influence of clanship, that Frazer, though not possessed of an inch of land, in a few weeks raised a corps of 800 men (78th Highlanders), to whom as many more were soon afterwards added. The Highland costume being thought ill-adapted for the climate of America, the authorities proposed to alter it; but officers and men protested strongly against any change. "Thanks to our gracious chief," said a veteran of the corps, "we were allowed to wear the garb of our fathers, and, in the course of six winters, showed the doctors that they

While the fall of Wolfe infused such an invincible spirit into his soldiers, the loss of Montcalm produced a most depressing effect upon the enemy. If any chance remained of reinvigorating his regular troops after the discomfiture of their Canadian allies, it was lost when the French General was borne from the field. Even the veterans who had served under Saxe fled before their conquerors; while their officers, apprehensive of rigorous treatment, with their hats off, sued piteously for quarter, declaring that they took no part in the massacre at Fort William-Henry in 1757. Five hundred French and Canadians were killed in the battle, and about one thousand surrendered or were made prisoners.* The French soldiers were treated by their victors with the greatest clemency, though the Canadians were at first hardly dealt with; but after the heat of the action, owing to the perseverance of the officers in restraining their men, there was no slaughter or cruelty. Montcalm, who had previously been struck by a musket-shot, received his death-wound from the single gun which the English had in

did not understand our constitutions; for in the coldest winters our men were more healthy than those who wore breeches and warm clothing." (Browne's 'History of the Highlands.') The Canadians, who formed the most absurd notions of the *sauvages d'Écosse*, as they called them, believed that they were so swift of foot that no one could catch them, that they neither gave nor took quarter, and spared neither sex nor age.

* The English had one general, one captain, six lieutenants, one ensign, three sergeants, and forty-five rank and file killed; one brigadier, four staff-officers, twelve captains, twenty-six lieutenants, ten ensigns, twenty-five sergeants, four drummers, and five hundred and six rank and file wounded. Of the artillery company, one gunner was killed, and seven were wounded. Amongst the wounded officers were Carleton and Barré. Barré lost an eye, and the other was so severely injured that he subsequently became totally blind.

the field. When carried to the General Hospital, he desired the surgeons in attendance to tell him at once if his wounds were mortal. When told that they were, he inquired how long he might survive; and on being answered, "Ten or twelve hours, or perhaps less," he rejoined, "So much the better, I shall not live to see the surrender of Quebec." Then, addressing M. de Ramezay and the Commandant de Roussillon, he said:—"Gentlemen, I commend to your keeping the honour of France. Endeavour to secure the retreat of my army to-night beyond Cape Rouge; I shall myself pass the night with God, and prepare for death." When the commander of the garrison pressed for his orders respecting the defence of Quebec, Montcalm, with much emotion, exclaimed, "I will neither give orders, nor interfere any further. I have business to attend to of greater moment than your ruined garrison and this wretched country. My time is very short, so pray leave me. I wish you all comfort, and to be speedily extricated from your present perplexity."* He died early on the morning of the 14th. Five days after the battle Quebec surrendered, and in the following year Canada became a British province.

In England, where the difficulties of the expedition were little understood, even by the Great Minister who devised it, the highest hopes were at first entertained of its success. But, as time wore on, people began to doubt, and the prudence of Pitt's plan of the cam-

* Knox, vol. ii. p. 77. The General Hospital, nearly a mile beyond the city wall, was taken possession of by Townshend just as Montcalm, attended by the Bishop of Quebec and his chaplains, was on the point of death.

paign was openly questioned. During the summer, something like the old dread of invasion spread amongst the populace. On the 9th of July, indeed, it was reported in London that the French had actually landed.* The victory at Minden, where Wolfe's old regiment, the 20th, was so highly distinguished, restored the common confidence. But when the as yet unsuccessful hero's dispatches were gazetted, the most sanguine ceased to hope; for, "when the General doubted, the public thought they had reason to despair." Three days later came Townshend's letter, announcing the surrender of Quebec and the death of Wolfe. "The effect of so joyful news," says Burke, "immediately on such a dejection, and then the mixture of grief and pity which attended the public congratulations and applauses, was very singular and affecting. The sort of mourning triumph that manifested itself on that occasion did equal honour to the memory of the General and to the humanity of the nation."† Walpole's account is still more graphic:—"The incidents of dramatic fiction could not be conducted with more address to lead an audience from despondency to sudden exultation, than accident prepared to excite the

* 'Annual Register,' p. 101.

† 'Annual Register,' 1759, p. 43. Burke likewise says:—"However glorious this victory was, and however important in its consequences, it must be admitted that it was very dearly bought. Soldiers may be raised; officers will be formed by experience; but the loss of a genius in war is a loss that we know not how to repair. The death of Wolfe was indeed grievous to his country, but to himself the most happy that can be imagined, and the most to be envied by all those who have a true relish for military glory. Unindebted to family or connections, unsupported by intrigue or faction, he had accomplished the whole business of life at a time when others are only beginning to appear" (p. 41).

passions of a whole people. They despaired, they triumphed, and they wept; for Wolfe had fallen in the hour of victory! Joy, curiosity, astonishment, were painted on every countenance; the more they inquired, the higher their admiration rose. Not an incident but was heroic and affecting."*

After the old fashion, on the night of the 17th of October, the streets of London were noisy with marrow-bones and cleavers. Yet, according to newspaper reports, even the London mob showed by their behaviour that the lowest felt for the fall of the hero. Not only London, but, as the tidings spread, every town and village in Great Britain blazed with bonfires and illuminations. One spot alone—Blackheath—was dark, for there the mourning mother wept for the loss of the best of sons; and her neighbours, in sympathy with her sorrow, refrained from the display of their participation in the national joy.† While such were the mixed sentiments of those who knew nothing of the late General beyond what related to his official capacity, the grief of those who were personally acquainted with him was, as may be imagined, heartfelt. Numerous private letters still forcibly attest the sorrow of his friends. One example may suffice. John Warde, Esq., of Squerries, writing to his brother George, then Lieutenant-Colonel of the 4th Dragoons, says:—" Amidst the public great

* 'Memoirs of the Reign of George II.,' vol. ii. p. 385.

† The incident has been preserved by Burke, but he does not name the place. Mrs. Wolfe, however, was then at Blackheath. Doubtless, Mr. Swinden, the Bretts, and many others of Wolfe's personal friends who lived in that neighbourhood, gratified their own feelings, as well as the chief mourner's, in not illuminating their houses.

events, you know I have lost too much in your friend to partake of the fulness of its joy. I sincerely condole with you on the loss of poor Wolfe; but, as I know you always foresaw some such calamity from his too great intrepidity, conclude you received the fatal event with less surprise. You will not, I believe, subscribe to my opinion; but, honourable as the expedition proves, I rejoice you was not there. To have seen your friend fall would have been bitter to yourself, and to have shared his fate how grievous to us all! His poor mother bears it heavily; how should she do otherwise? And the public funeral which is talked of for his remains will (if true) possibly overset her quite."

Wolfe's body was conveyed to England by the 'Royal William,' man-of-war. On the 17th of November, at seven o'clock A.M., two signal guns announced the removal of the remains. The coffin was then lowered into a twelve-oared barge, which was towed by two twelve-oared barges, and followed by twelve more of the same, in a train of sombre, silent pomp. Minute guns were fired by the ships at Spithead from the time the body was removed from the 'Royal William' until it was landed at the Point of Portsmouth, where it was received by the regiment of Invalides and the company of Artillery in the garrison. At nine o'clock the coffin was put into a travelling hearse, followed by attendants in a mourning-coach. Captains Hervey Smith and Thomas Bell, the General's aides-de-camp, entered a carriage which stood ready for them at the Fountain Inn, and the solemn procession passed through the town, the company of the train in the van, and the Invalides, with arms reversed, in the rear. The colours of the fort were struck half-flagstaff, the bells tolled muffled peals, and minute guns were fired on the platform until the Landport Gate was reached, when the train opened to the right and left, and the hearse and coaches passed through on the way to London. Although thousands of people were assembled to witness the ceremony, there was not the least indecorum, and not a voice was to be heard but in whispers of praise and regret for the dead hero.* On the 20th, Wolfe's body was deposited, beside his father's, in the family vault under the parish church of Greenwich.

Many persons felt even more for Miss Lowther than for Mrs. Wolfe. Thus, Lady Mary Wortley Montagu wrote to the Countess of Bute:—"General Wolfe is to be lamented, but not pitied. I am of your opinion, that compassion is only owing to his mother and his intended bride, who I think the greater sufferer, however sensible I am of a parent's tenderness. Disappointments in youth are those which are felt with the greatest anguish, when we are all in expectation of happiness perhaps not to be found in life."† Major Warburton notices a tradition, according to which Miss Lowther wore henceforth a pearl necklace that Wolfe had given her, covered with black velvet, in memory of the departed;‡ and a correspondent of 'Notes and Queries' states, that after Wolfe's death, his family, desiring to give her some memorial of him, consulted her as to what it should be. Her answer, it is said, was, "A diamond necklace;"

* 'Annual Register,' and Allen's 'History of Portsmouth.'
† Lady M. W. Montagu's Letters, etc., vol. iii. p. 191.
‡ 'Conquest of Canada,' vol. ii. p. 497.

and the reason she assigned is represented to have been, because she was going to be married to another, and would have occasion for such an ornament: "My informant," adds the contributor, "had, in her earlier days, often met the lady, and described her as showing remains of beauty, but as no wiser than this anecdote would lead us to suppose."* The first story is merely a perversion of truth; but the imputation of the last, as the reader will find, does great injustice to the lady of Wolfe's choice. After Captain Bell delivered to Mrs. Wolfe the picture which her son had carried with him to Quebec, she had it set with diamonds, and then restored it to Miss Lowther, who wore it in remembrance of her lover. But, as it was the portrait of herself, she very naturally concealed it; hence the black-velvet cover.† Whether Miss Lowther was the frivolous, heartless woman portrayed above, the reader of the subjoined letter may judge. It is printed *verbatim et literatim* after the original, which, it may be added, is written in a fine, bold, yet most ladylike hand. Owing possibly to the letter having been enclosed in a franked cover, there is nothing to show to whom it was addressed; but there is reason to believe that the lady to whom Miss Lowther

* 'Notes and Queries' (1851), vol. iv. p. 489.

† The following is a copy of the jeweller's bill amongst the Wolfe papers at Squerries:—

"Mrs. Wolfe Debtr. to Philip Hardel.

"For a large picture containing 8 large and 163 small brilliands [*sic*], and a case with 23 brilliands, and a gold joint and hooks studded with gold, £525.

"Received the 5th June, 1760, of Mrs. Henrietta Wolfe, by the hands of the Rev. Mr. Samuel Francis Swinden, Five hundred and twenty-five pounds in full, by me, PHILIP HARDEL.'

wrote was Mrs. Wolfe's most confidential female friend, Mrs. Scott :—

Mad[m].

Miss Aylmer's having once answer[d] a letter I wrote M[rs] Wolfe, drew me into the error of addressing her again; but I now desire you to accept my sincere thanks for your obliging (tho') melancholy epistle. I'm not surpriz'd to hear y[e] patient sufferer submits with calmness and resignation to this severe trial, because I could never doubt the magnanimity of General Wolfe's mother;—but I wish, if her health wou'd permit, she c[d] by degrees be brought to bear new objects; perhaps they might call her attention one moment from y[e] melancholy subject which engrosses it, and in time dissipate, tho' not efface or drive away from y[e] memory so just and deep a sorrow :—not that I shall ever attempt intruding my company, since (tho' I feel for her more than words can express, and should, if it was given me to alleviate her grief, gladly exert every power which nature or compassion has bestowed)—yet I feel we are y[e] last people in the world who ought to meet.

I knew not my picture was to be set; but I beg Mad[m] y[u] will tell M[rs] Wolfe I entreat her to take her own time about giving y[e] necessary directions. I can't, as a mark of His affection, refuse it; otherwise wou'd willingly spare myself y[e] pain of seeing a picture given under far different hopes and expectations. M[rs] Wolfe will, I hope, accept my acknowledgments for her good wishes, and that Almighty God may comfort and support her is y[e] earnest prayer of,

Madam,
Your obliged, humble
Servant
K. LOWTHER.

Raby Castle, 18th Dec[r], 1759.*

* The original is in the possession of Admiral Warde. Miss Lowther remained unmarried until the 8th of April, 1765, when she became the second wife of Harry, sixth and last Duke of Bolton. Her Grace died

Parliament met on the 14th of November, and on the 21st the House of Commons resolved to address the King, praying that his Majesty would order a monument to be erected in Westminster Abbey to the memory of Wolfe. At the same time, the thanks of the House were given to the Admirals and Generals employed in "the glorious and successful expedition against Quebec." The address was proposed by Mr. Pitt, who, in a low and plaintive voice, pronounced an elaborate panegyric on the dead warrior. "It was perhaps," says Walpole, "the worst harangue he ever uttered. His eloquence was too native not to suffer by being crowded into a ready mould. The parallels which he drew from Greek and Roman story did but flatten the pathetic of the topic. . . . The horror of the night, the precipice scaled by Wolfe, the empire he with a handful of men added to England, and the glorious catastrophe of contentedly terminating his life when his fame began,—ancient story may be ransacked, and ostentatious philosophy thrown into the account, before an episode can be found to rank with Wolfe's."* The Prime Minister's motion was seconded by Alderman Beckford, who remarked, that in the appointment of Wolfe neither parliamentary interest, family influence, nor aristocratic views had been consulted, and that the General and the Minister seemed to

at Grosvenor Square, in the year 1809, aged 75, leaving two daughters. I regret that, notwithstanding the courteous assistance of the Marquis of Winchester, my endeavours to discover whether the fore-mentioned portrait of the Duchess is still preserved, have proved ineffectual. Inquiries of her Grace's lineal representatives remain unanswered, owing probably to the recent death of the late Duke of Cleveland.

* 'Memoirs of the Reign of George II.,' vol. ii. p. 393.

have been made for each other. There were some circumstances, he also said, almost similar between them,—Wolfe lost his life, and Pitt had hazarded his head, for his country.*

The King nominated a monument committee, over which the Duke of Devonshire presided. Wilton, Adam, Chambers and others, sent in drawings. Wilton's design was chosen. The sculpture was not finished until 1772. On the 4th of October, 1773, the national monument was uncovered. It stands near the north transept of the Abbey church, and occupies a large space in St. John the Evangelist's Chapel, facing the ambulatory. It is chiefly composed of white marble, and consists of an elevated base and sarcophagus, upon which, on a couch within an open tent, is the naked figure of the dying warrior, supported by a Grenadier, who points with his right hand to Victory descending with a palm-branch and laurel crown. In the background stands a mourning Highland sergeant; and the branches of an oak, on which tomahawks, scalping-knives, and suchlike emblems of American warfare are hung, project from behind the tent. The General's clothes and arms are scattered around, and the French flag lies under his feet. Two lions couchant rest upon the basement, on each flank of which, in low relief, is the family crest—a wolf's head erased. The convex front of the base is ornamented with a remarkable representation in bronzed lead of the troops landing beneath the Heights of Abraham, and a large oval tablet in the middle of the sarcophagus contains the inscription:—

* Entick's 'History of the War,' vol. iv. p. 91.

TO THE MEMORY OF
JAMES WOLFE,
MAJOR-GENERAL AND COMMANDER-IN-CHIEF
OF THE BRITISH LAND FORCES
ON AN EXPEDITON AGAINST QUEBEC,
WHO, AFTER SURMOUNTING BY ABILITY AND VALOUR
ALL OBSTACLES OF ART AND NATURE,
WAS SLAIN, IN THE MOMENT OF VICTORY,
ON THE XIII. OF SEPTEMBER, MDCCLIX.,
THE KING AND PARLIAMENT OF GREAT BRITAIN
DEDICATE THIS MONUMENT.

In 1760, a few gentlemen of Westerham placed a tablet of white marble to their fellow-townsman's memory over the door of their parish church. Besides the dedicatory inscription, the tablet bears these lines:—

"While George in sorrow bows his laurell'd head,
And bids the artist grace the soldier dead;
We raise no sculptur'd trophy to thy name,
Brave youth! the fairest in the list of fame.
Proud of thy birth, we boast th' auspicious year,
Struck with thy fall, we shed a general tear;
With humble grief inscribe one artless stone,
And from thy matchless honours date our own.
I. Decus I. Nostrum."

About the same time the Warde family raised a cenotaph in Squerries Park upon the spot where Wolfe received his first commission. And, in 1762, Earl Temple erected upon a hill at Stowe an obelisk one hundred feet high, inscribed,—

TO
TO MAJOR-GENERAL WOLFE.
OSTENDUNT TERRIS HUNC TANTUM FATA.*

* Annual Register, 1762.

The people of the then British provinces in North America, who were much benefited through the subjugation of their old enemies by Wolfe, were not less elated on account of his victory than were the populace at home and the army in Germany. But, while they lauded the hero, they took to themselves no small share of merit; because, forsooth, they furnished a few companies of Rangers, for whose services they made sure to be doubly compensated. The State of Massachusetts Bay, however, not only voted a marble statue of Wolfe, but went so far as to fix upon a site for it in Boston.* The statue, nevertheless, has not yet been erected. At the same time, Bancroft's, Grahame's, and other histories prove the interest with which Americans still regard Wolfe's name. And, in further proof, one of their literary associations celebrated the centenary of the Battle of Quebec by the delivery of an appropriate address.†

The earliest Canadian testimonial was a large stone, on which was drawn a meridional line to mark the spot where the General expired.‡ In 1832, Lord Aylmer, Governor of the colony, erected a small pillar, inscribed—

HERE DIED WOLFE VICTORIOUS.

But, as it was unfenced, it was ere long defaced. In

* 'Annual Register,' 1760. Almon relates that assurances were made to Mr. Grenville that the Americans entertained thoughts of independence so early as 1757. Letters written, it was asserted, by Montcalm were put into his hands, and Mr. Grenville considered them genuine. Americans, however, repudiated the papers, insisting that they had been fabricated to provoke the English government against America. ('Anecdotes, Biographical, Political,' etc., vol. ii. p. 99.)

† The address before the New England Historic-Genealogical Society, "On the Death of Wolfe," with illustrative notes, by Lorenzo Sabine, was subsequently published.

‡ Weld's 'Travels in North America.' London, 1799.

1849, under the governorship of Sir B. D'Urban, it gave place to a more pretentious column, protected by an iron railing, the expense of which was contributed by the British troops serving in Canada. A monument, in memory of Wolfe and Montcalm, was erected in the Public Garden of Quebec, in 1828, by Canadians of French and English descent. It consists of a tapering column or obelisk, rising from a sarcophagus and basement to a height of sixty-five feet above the ground. The site was judiciously chosen, the monument being conspicuous from the river. The north side of the column bears the name "Montcalm;" the south, "Wolfe." On the front is the inscription,—

MORTEM . VIRTUS . COMMUNEM .
FAMAM . HISTORIA .
MONUMENTUM. POSTERITAS .
DEDIT.*

Romney was the painter who first made Wolfe's death the subject of an historical picture. In 1763 the Society of Arts awarded him their prize of fifty guineas. But the decision was revoked, and the young artist, instead of the prize, was presented with half the amount. The

* Another Latin inscription states that the joint tribute to the rival heroes was promoted by Lord Dalhousie. The French, it appears, subscribed as readily to the monument of Wolfe as the English to Montcalm's. "The latter," says a Canadian historian, "is easily intelligible, for Montcalm was a brave and esteemed man, though unfortunate as a general; and it is easy for the victorious to show generosity to the memory of a respected though vanquished foe. But that the Canadian French should have contributed to a monument to their conqueror, Wolfe, and even regarded it as a duty to do so, this I saw explained in a Canadian journal:—' Wolfe did not by his victory so much bring the French under a foreign yoke as free them from an antiquated one, extremely unfavourable to progress. He and his Britons founded a

popularity of the subject, and the merit of the work, however, were the means of his procuring considerable employment. Romney's picture of "The Death of Wolfe" was afterwards bought by his friend Stephenson, the banker, and by him presented to Governor Varelst, who placed it in the council-chamber of Calcutta.* A few years later, West painted the well-known picture by which he acquired fame, and the engraver Woollett acquired fortune. What Kemble did for the stage, it has been remarked, West did for art. He discarded classic costume, and painted British soldiers in British soldiers' uniform. "The same truth which gives law to the historian," said West himself to Reynolds, "should rule the painter."† West's picture, withal, does not represent the truth, and nothing can be more absurd than to call it historical. "The Indian warrior," says a critic, "watching the dying hero to see if he equalled in fortitude the children of the deserts, is a fine stroke of nature and poetry."‡ But, what if no Indian warrior was there? Monckton, Barré, and other persons portrayed

new era for Canada, and the 60,000 poor colonists who have been raised by his means to a million of prosperous artisans have much to thank him for.'" (Professor Garneau; quoted by Kohl.) In 1762, M. de Bougainville applied to Mr. Pitt for permission to forward to Quebec an epitaph engraved on marble to be placed over Montcalm's tomb in the Ursuline Convent. The request was cordially responded to; but, from some unknown cause, the memorial never reached Canada. (See 'Annual Register,' 1762, p. 266.) Lord Aylmer, however, erected a plain marble slab in the Ursuline Chapel, inscribed:— "Honneur à Montcalm! Le destin, en lui dérobant la victoire, l'a récompensé par une mort glorieuse!"

* Life of George Romney, by his Son.

† Galt's Life of West.

‡ Allan Cunningham, Lives of Painters, etc.

in the group around Wolfe were not on the spot. Monckton had been shot through the lung; Barré had been blinded; and Surgeon Adair, who is represented in attendance, was then at Crown Point. West wished General Murray to figure in the picture; but the honest Scot refused, saying, "No, no! I was not by; I was leading the left."* As further evidence that West's notions of artistic truth did not go beyond dress, we may add that, as every one who has stood upon the ground has discovered, the painter drew upon his fancy, and not upon his knowledge, for his scenery.†

Numerous so-called portraits of Wolfe were painted and engraved after his death. One published in Paris, as a pendant to Montcalm's, is marked "J. Reynolds *pinxt.*" But surely, if Sir Joshua painted a picture of Wolfe, we should have heard of it in England. Fulcher, in his catalogue of Gainsborough's portraits, includes "General Wolfe (head and bust). He is in uniform, and wears his hat; the silver lace on which, and on his coat, is touched with great brilliancy." But, for reasons elsewhere assigned, it is highly improbable that Wolfe ever sat for Gainsborough.‡ We know of but two undoubted portraits; one, painted by Highmore, which has been presented by the King of the Belgians to the National Portrait Gallery, and that from which the frontispiece to this volume has been taken. The latter is the property of Admiral Warde, who inherited

* Communicated by Lady O'Donnell, grand-daughter of General Murray.

† See Kohl's 'Travels in America.'

‡ See 'Notes and Queries,' 3rd series, vol. v. p. 36.

it from his grand-uncle, the Right Hon. General George Warde. It was painted by some artist of no repute, whose name is unknown, not long after Wolfe entered the army, and was considered by those who knew him then to be an excellent likeness. Besides these, there is an outline of Wolfe's profile, which was sketched a short time before his death, by his aide-de-camp, Captain Smith.* Some of the fictitious portraits were taken from a plaster bust, which represents the General in armour; and all, except one or two that bear no resemblance whatever to him, present side views of his face.

About the year 1775, West painted another picture of Wolfe, in which the hero is represented as a boy studying a map of the battle of Blenheim. It appears that General Warde, desiring a companion to a small portrait of his nephew, sent West his original picture of Wolfe to serve as a model. When the painter had finished his work, the General was dissatisfied with it, and required some alterations to be made in the face. Whereupon West replied that he wished he had known of the original before he painted his great picture; but that as he had already given to the world his impression of Wolfe, a portrait at variance with it ought not to come from his pencil.†

A medal, commemorative of the siege of Louisbourg, was devised by Hollis, and executed by Kirk, after

* The face of the plaster bust of Wolfe was modelled after this sketch. The original drawing belonged to Colonel Guillem, and passed into the possession of the late Duke of Northumberland, who presented it to the United Service Museum.

† Letter written by the late General Warde to the Rev. Thomas Streatfeild, "December 6, 1822."

the design of Cipriani. On one face was the head of Britannia, encircled by the words "O fair Britannia, hail!" and on the other a trophy, with the same legend.* Another medal, of which there are specimens in various metals in the British Museum, is somewhat similar, with the addition of "Louisbourg, taken 1758." There are also in the national collection specimens, in silver and in bronze, of a medal bearing a head of Wolfe, with the inscription:—"Jacobus Wolfe Anglus. Victoria Cæsus. Quebecæ, Sept. 13, 1759," and the motto "Pro Patria." Several relics of Wolfe are still preserved. The sword he wore at Quebec—a short, straight weapon, of Flemish manufacture—was presented by the late George Warde, Esq., to the United Service Museum; and a book, 'The Treasury of Fortification,' by John Barker, Engineer, which was found in his pocket after his death, was presented by the Board of Ordnance to the Officers' Library, Woolwich. On the fly-leaf is written,—"This is an exceeding book of fortification. —WOLFE." The handwriting, however, is not James Wolfe's, but is very like his brother's. His cloak is in the Tower of London; his writing-case, gloves, and spurs, in private hands; and his sash is said to be in America. Wolfe's autographs are much sought after by collectors, and fetch high prices; but his letters—the greater number of them being family heir-looms—are seldom on sale.

Mrs. Wolfe survived her son more than five years. On the 6th of November, 1759, she addressed a short letter to Mr. Pitt, in which she wrote:—"As you did my dear son the honour to entrust him with so great and

* 'Memoirs of Thomas Hollis,' vol. i. p. 80.

important an office as the taking of Quebec, which you, Sir, planned, and he executed, I hope to his Majesty's, your, and his country's satisfaction, though to my irreparable loss, it occurs to me that there may be some papers or orders of yours relating to the Government service which will come to me. If you will honour me with your commands, I shall send them by a faithful and trusty gentleman, who carries this, Lieutenant Scott; and no eye shall see them but your own." Mr. Pitt immediately replied, saying that Mrs. Wolfe's proposal was worthy of the mother of such a son. "Your affliction," he added, "is too just to receive any degree of consolation from one who feels the cause of your sorrow too sincerely and sensibly to be able to offer any topics of relief to you. May Heaven, who assists the virtuous, grant you every possible comfort under a loss which nothing can repair to you or to England." Mrs. Wolfe did not receive her son's papers till the end of the month, when Captain Bell delivered them to her, after having examined and sorted them. A proceeding which aggrieved her much, and defeated her intention that Mr. Pitt should be the first to inspect them.

Wolfe, under the expectation of immediately inheriting part of his father's property, made a will, by which he bequeathed £1000 each to Colonels Warde, Carleton, Oughton, and Harvey, his uncle Major Wolfe, and his cousin Goldsmith; and to Major Barré and Captains Delaune, Smith, Bell, Caldwell, and Leslie, one hundred guineas each. This circumstance caused Mrs. Wolfe to write again to Mr. Pitt. In her letter, dated "Blackheath, November 30, 1759," she says:—"My dear son, not knowing the disposition his father had made of his fortune—which was wholly settled on me for life, and magnified by fame greatly beyond what it really is—has left to his friends more than a third part of it; and though I should have the greatest pleasure imaginable in discharging these legacies in my lifetime, I cannot do it without distressing myself to the highest degree. My request to you, good and great Sir, is that you will honour me with your instructions how I may, in the properest manner, address His Majesty for a pension to enable me to fulfil the generous and kind intentions of my most dear lost son to his friends, and to live like the relict of General Wolfe, and General Wolfe's mother." Mr. Pitt replied as follows:—

St. James's Square, January 17, 1760.

Madam,

I think myself much honoured by your letter wherein you are pleased to desire my advice in a matter that concerns your ease. Had I more than information in my power to offer on a subject so interesting, I beg you will be assured, Madam, that your trouble would be rendered very short, as well as my own satisfaction become very sensible. But the thing you are pleased to mention being totally in the Duke of Newcastle's department, I can only desire leave to apprise you that it is to his Grace that all applications of such a nature are to be addressed. If you shall judge proper to take that step (with regard to which I cannot venture to advise), you will command, on that, as well as every other occasion, all good offices and sincerest endeavours for your service from him who has the honour ever to remain, with the truest respect, Madam,

Your most obedient and most humble servant,

Wm. Pitt.*

* From original in 'Wolfiana.' The previous extracts are from letters in the 'Chatham Correspondence.'

Mrs. Wolfe received neither pension nor reward from the Government, and consequently was not in a position to pay the legacies bequeathed by her son. But she confirmed them by her own will, and they were paid after her death. When, in February, 1761, warrants for the payment of the staff of the Quebec expedition were ordered to be made out, Mr. Fisher, on the part of Mrs. Wolfe, demanded the pay of a Commander-in-chief for her late son from the date of his last commission until his death. But the War Office authorities, considering that Wolfe was entitled to no more than a Major-General's ordinary pay, rejected the claim. Mrs. Wolfe was then advised by her friends to memorialize the King. She did so; but, notwithstanding the hearty support of the Earl of Shelburne, Sir Robert Rich,* and other influential persons, was unsuccessful, owing principally to the opposition of Lord Barrington and the Right Hon. Charles Townshend. Her correspondence on the subject was not finally closed until the 14th of September, 1764, on which day she had a letter from the Right Hon. Welbore Ellis, Secretary at War, saying,—"I am to inform you that his Majesty commanded me to acquaint you that when Mr. Townshend was Secretary at War a full state of this demand was laid before him, and his

* Rich, in a letter on the subject, writes:—"I mean to consult Mr. Wood, and to know from him the best method for me to proceed in this affair, for it must not drop so. You may recollect the justice done to my honoured friend, and a national monument raising as a *præmium virtutis militaris*. How will this appear if he should be refused his pay equal to others whose services, though good, have not been deemed of that importance as to render them the object of national thanks and national loss? . . . I loved Wolfe; no wonder I should grow warm on the subject."

decision thereon taken, which was that his Majesty did not think the General entitled to £10 a day during the expedition, and his Majesty sees no reason to alter that determination."*

Soon after her son's death, Mrs. Wolfe was visited by her nephew Captain Edward Goldsmith, who for awhile acted as her secretary, and assisted in the arrangement of her affairs. On his return to Limerick she gave him a large sum of money,—so much as to enable him to invest £600 in the funds and buy household furniture, a hogshead of very good wine, etc.† In March, 1760, Mrs. Wolfe took a house in Bath, where she afterwards chiefly resided, but still retained her mansion on Blackheath, her occasional visits to which were cheered by the society of Mrs. Mason, Mrs. Scott, and other female neighbours. In the transactions relating to her husband's and son's military affairs she was aided and guided by Colonels Lafausille, Carleton, and Warde; while her old friend the Rev. Samuel Francis Swinden, F.R.S., Rector of Stifford, Essex, and master of an academy at Greenwich, acted as

* From original in 'Wolfiana.'

† Goldsmith's first letter after his return to Ireland was from Dublin, where he spent some time endeavouring to obtain half-pay, but was unsuccessful. He suffered much from the ague, on which account he left Limerick in 1761, and settled at Finglass, near Dublin, where he died in 1764. His letters, which amused his aunt, exhibit a degree of humour not unlike that of his cousin Oliver. They were sealed with Wolfe's seals, one of which bears the family arms,—three wolves' heads erased, with chevron, etc.,—the other a female head. The last of the male branch of the Wolfes was the old General's brother, Major Walter Wolfe ("Uncle Wat"), who died in 1771, and to whose early and judicious instructions, according to an Irish obituary, his celebrated nephew was indebted for much of his knowledge of the art of war.

her almoner and confidential adviser until his death on the 4th of July, 1764. The good lady herself died on the 26th of September in the same year, and, according to her wish, her remains were privately and unostentatiously placed between the bodies of her husband and her son in the family vault.*

Mrs. Wolfe's property, at the time of her death, was valued at about £17,000, and her last will, dated February 25th, 1763, was proved by her surviving executors, Colonels Carleton and Warde.† In addition to the bequests of her son, she left £3000 to her nephew Wm. Burcher, and £2000 to the children of another sister of the old General's named Langley, besides various legacies to some of her own relations, her friends, and domestics.‡ She also devised £1000 to the Incorporated Society for promoting Protestant Schools in Ireland,

* The plate on Wolfe's coffin was simply inscribed, "Major-Genl. James Wolfe, aged 32 years. 1759." His mother's—"Mrs. Henrietta Wolfe, died 26th Septr., 1764, aged 60 years." A marble slab over the door of the vault was lettered—"The family vault of Major-Gen. James Wolfe. 1759." In 1859, by order of the Privy Council, the vault was filled with earth and charcoal, and the entrance built up. The gentleman who was then churchwarden and superintended the works, states that the coffins showed no signs of decay, the black cloth with which they were covered being but slightly damaged by moths. About the same time, some persons who represented themselves to be members of the family, attempted to raise a subscription for the purpose of removing Wolfe's remains to Westminster Abbey.

† Colonels Carleton and Warde being her son's administrators, Mrs. Wolfe appointed them, together with Mr. Swinden, her executors.

‡ Mrs. Wolfe bequeathed a considerable share of her plate to her niece and goddaughter, Henrietta Sotheron. The late Admiral Sotheron, who inherited it, sent various articles to a silversmith to be melted down and manufactured into a large salver, ornamented with appropriate devices. The plate is now the property of the Right Hon. Thomas Sotheron-Estcourt, M.P.

£500 to Bath Hospital, £500 to Bromley College, and smaller amounts to other charities. The residue of her estate she ordered to be disposed of amongst the widows or families of poor officers who had served under her son; but no such application having been made, in 1774 the executors, governed by the opinion of counsel, and believing that no disposition could better accord with the tenor of the will, bestowed the amount—£3000—upon the Hibernian School for Soldiers' Sons.

In 1760 an anonymous pamphlet was published, under the title of 'A Letter to an Hon. Brigadier-General, Commander-in-chief of his Majesty's forces in Canada.' It is written in a pointed and vigorous style, not unlike that of Junius, to whom, indeed, it has been ascribed, and virulently attacks the Hon. George Townshend for his vanity in arrogating the glory of the conquest of Quebec, although the honour of signing the capitulation had only fallen to him through Wolfe's death and Monckton's wounds. The pamphleteer pleads the justice of animadverting upon the conduct of a man who seized every opportunity of ridiculing those whom he disliked by exhibiting their personal defects in caricatures. "You should be apprehensive," he says, "of the usual fate of imitators, who generally copy rather errors than excellences, as indeed it is easier to bend the head like Alexander or Boscawen than to imitate their courage and intrepidity." The leading charges, so far as relates to our particular subject, are, that Townshend thwarted Wolfe's plans; that he neglected to order the officers to wear mourning for their late commander; and ungrateful disrespect to the memory of the man who had led him to victory, by the passive and callous manner in which he spoke of Wolfe's death in his official dispatch.* The 'Letter' was followed by 'A Refutation,' very inferior in style and ability. The first charge, however, is decisively disproved. The others are met by an excuse, and because of the impropriety of writing a panegyric to a Minister when nothing but the exigence and situation of affairs ought to be noticed. But Townshend soon found that the last-mentioned accusation had not been answered in the 'Refutation' so as to satisfy the public sentiment; that the gratitude of the nation towards Wolfe's memory overbore all attempts to lessen his fame and that it was not by surviving him he was to be eclipsed.† The Honourable Brigadier-General, therefore, in order to show his esteem for his late Commander, immediately published a letter which he had written, soon after the battle, to a friend in England. In this letter, he said:—"I am not ashamed to own to you, that my heart does not exult in the midst of this success. I have lost but a friend in General Wolfe. Our country has lost a sure support, and a perpetual honour. If the world were sensible at how high a price we have purchased Quebec in his death, it would damp the public joy. Our best consolation is, that Providence seemed not to promise that he should

* Walpole says that the pamphlet was written under the direction of Mr. Fox. Townshend, in the blindness of his rage, concluded that it came from the Duke of Cumberland, and his Royal Highness being beyond the reach of his resentment, he challenged the Duke's chief favourite, the Earl of Albemarle. "Though no man," says the historian, "was less of an author than the Earl." ('Memoirs of the Reign of George III.')

† Walpole's 'George II.,' vol. ii. p. 387.

remain long among us. He was himself sensible of the weakness of his constitution, and determined to crowd into a few years, actions that would have adorned length of life."*

Notwithstanding this eulogy, we cannot but think, that Townshend was jealous of Wolfe's genius and knowledge as well as of his posthumous fame. Walpole says that Mr. Pitt sent him with the expedition in order to get rid of him; and the assertion is supported by Townshend's letter of application for employment, which shows that he would have preferred service nearer home and under an older General. It must have galled a man so impatient of authority, to be commanded by one who, however superior to him in every other respect, was his inferior by birth, and his junior in years. Although Townshend afterwards rose to the highest nominal military rank, he never—in any sense above animal courage—was a soldier. His leading passion was ambition, and so that he arrived at power and station, he cared little for the means by which they were acquired. Proud, sullen, and sarcastic, he was but a politician in the lowest sense of the term. There was in him as little of the statesman as of the General. The future Marquis was more at home in Dublin Castle than in the senate or the camp. Of Townshend's abilities as an officer, it is obvious that Wolfe entertained a lower opinion than of Monckton's, Murray's, or Carleton's. How, otherwise, can we account for the facts, that he kept the second

* The letter itself, as well as the publication of it, was considered by many to be an afterthought of Townshend's. Sir Denis Le Marchant attributes the composition to Charles Townshend, whose Parliamentary speeches it resembles in style.

Brigadier under his eye in the camp with himself, that he never entrusted him with a detached command, and that he placed him in the background in the ascent and in the battle? It surely was not owing to any personal pique on Wolfe's part, for as Walpole truly says:—"Wolfe was not a man to waive his pre-eminence from fear of caricatures. He felt his superior knowledge and power, and had spirit enough to make Townshend sensible at least of the latter,—a confidence in himself that was fortunate for his country."*

Walpole, notwithstanding his friendship for Conway, against whose conduct at Rochefort Wolfe's evidence told unfavourably, has on the whole done justice to the memory of the hero. Yet his estimate of Wolfe's character is not altogether correct. The same indeed may be said of other contemporary historians. Situated as these great writers were, they could only judge of the inner man through inferences drawn from his achievements, and these achievements together with the circumstances of his death, were such as to lead them to imagine, that Wolfe's leading passion was the desire of military renown. Thus Walpole says:—"He seemed to breathe for nothing but fame, and lost no moments in qualifying himself to compass his object."† But was that object empty fame? Every one who has carefully read his letters will probably agree that it was not, and will coincide in the conviction, that—as Lord Macaulay says of Hampden—Wolfe "found glory only because glory lay in the plain path of duty." It is also erroneous, we believe, to

* 'Memoirs of the Reign of George II.,' vol. ii. p. 346.

† Ibid. p. 345.

conclude that Wolfe's was exclusively a military genius. On the contrary, his mental ability coupled with his intensity of purpose, must have raised him to distinction in any other profession he might have adopted. Circumstances, and no doubt a boyish love of glory led him into the army, and that profession was as well suited for him as he was suited for it. But his mind soon began to penetrate through the surface of things; he saw that the army was not the mere stepping-stone to glory, and that glory was not the highest object of aspiration for an intellectual being. His experience taught him, long before the Government was aware of the fact, that education was as necessary for an officer as for a barrister or a physician, and in spite of every impediment, he educated himself. Nor did this self-instruction consist in book-learning alone. He acquired a knowledge of himself, and once conscious of his strong natural passions, he struggled with them long and, as much as in him lay, brought them under the mastery of his reason.

Although the short duration of his life hinders Wolfe from being classed with the greatest Generals, the genius which he exhibited during his brief career as the commander of an army, proves that had his years been more he would not have fallen short of the most distinguished in ability. It is not because of his success,—great though it was,—that he deserves our applause; but because of the causes of that success. Passing over his instinctive perception of the course that ought to have been adopted at Rochefort, and his preconception of the vigorous means whereby Louisbourg was taken, if we review his dispositions before Quebec we cannot but conclude that no enterprise of equal difficulty was ever more judiciously accomplished. It is impossible to convey to those who have not seen Quebec any adequate idea of its warlike strength. Before the city—more strongly fortified by nature than by art—could be attacked, a vast theatre, exceeding thirty miles in extent, and embracing both sides of a prodigious river, had to be occupied by an army numbering not quite 7000 men. Within view of a much superior force, in a hostile country, and surrounded by prowling savages, it was necessary that distinct operations should be carried on by several detachments; but, distant though these detachments were, Wolfe, by his constant presence, as well as by his master-mind, so directed them that they acted with all the unity and precision of a single battalion. Between the invaders and the only weak side of the city lay a defensive army, surrounded by impregnable entrenchments, and commanded by a cautious and hitherto successful General. But Wolfe, by his unwearied vigilance and his untiring perseverance, at length beguiled his unwilling adversary to meet him in the open field. With truth says Burke:—"In this contest with so many difficulties, one may say, with nature itself, the genius of the Commander showed itself superior to everything. All the dispositions to that daring but judicious attempt near Sillery, which at last drew Montcalm from his entrenchments, were so many masterpieces in the art of war."*

If, however, from lack of opportunity, Wolfe as a General is not to be ranked with Marlborough and

* Annual Register, 1759, p. 42.

Wellington, in other respects his fame is more enviable. While we must admire the military genius of Marlborough, we cannot respect the man. While Wellington commands both admiration and respect, yet the "iron Duke" was not one to be generally loved. Wolfe alone—"the pattern of the officer, the darling of the soldier"—wins at once our admiration, our respect, and our love. Although by nature passionate, he was void of uncalled-for offence. He was impulsive, but not rash; persistent, but not obstinate; self-confident, yet modest; aspiring, but not vainglorious; generous, hospitable, and charitable, but not extravagant; stern, yet gentle; ingenuous, but not egotistic; free-spoken, yet courteous. If ever high honour, strict integrity, and all the qualities which constitute a dutiful and affectionate son, a true and constant lover, a sincere friend, a loyal subject, and a pure patriot, were combined with fearless valour, untiring industry, and great mental capacity, they were combined in JAMES WOLFE.

INDEX.

THE END.

CPSIA information can be obtained
at www.ICGtesting.com
Printed in the USA
LVHW022023120422
716028LV00006B/145

9 783752 591545